D1520634

THE CLASSIC GHOST STORIES COLLECTION

THE CLASSIC GHOST STORIES COLLECTION

CHILLING TALES FROM

GUY DE MAUPASSANT • M. R. JAMES • EDITH WHARTON
E. F. BENSON • SHERIDAN LE FANU • HENRY JAMES

ARCTURUS

Disclaimer
Throughout the text readers may find that some of the language used and sentiments expressed are offensive and unacceptable by today's standards. These reflect the attitudes and usage common at the time the book was written. In no way do they reflect the attitude of the publishers.

ARCTURUS
This edition published in 2020 by Arcturus Publishing Limited
26/27 Bickels Yard, 151–153 Bermondsey Street,
London SE1 3HA

Copyright © Arcturus Holdings Limited

All rights reserved. No part of this publication may be reproduced, stored in a retrieval system, or transmitted, in any form or by any means, electronic, mechanical, photocopying, recording or otherwise, without prior written permission in accordance with the provisions of the Copyright Act 1956 (as amended). Any person or persons who do any unauthorised act in relation to this publication may be liable to criminal prosecution and civil claims for damages.

Cover design: Peter Ridley

ISBN: 978-1-83857-401-7
AD007843UK

Printed in China

Contents

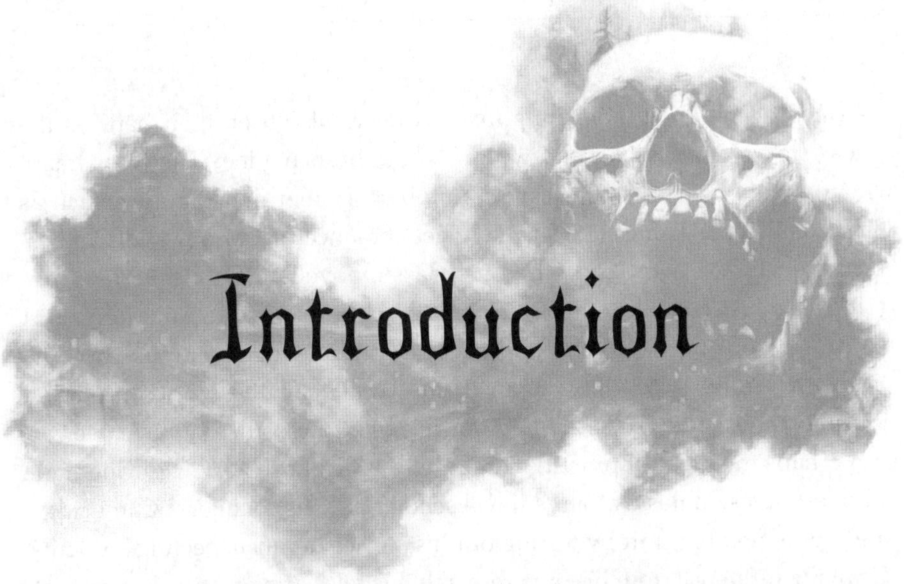

Introduction

Ghosts have haunted the human imagination for centuries. They have long been a subject of folklore and religion as men and women wonder what happens after we die. In more recent times, superstition has been joined by semi-scientific approaches to discover the true nature of ghosts – though no real evidence of their existence has ever been uncovered. Nonetheless, these supernatural beings have remained a favourite subject of fiction writers, even as fewer and fewer people believe in ghosts.

These phantoms come in a range of shapes and sizes – some remain in the shadows, little more than a flicker of light in the corner of the eye, while others announce their presence through violent action and promise terrible vengeance. Not all were considered evil, however. Some are souls searching for final peace, some seek to finish their unfinished business in life, while others on rare occasions could even provide a helping hand to the living.

While ghost stories have existed since the Roman Empire or even earlier, the modern form of the story truly arrived in the nineteenth century. Many began their lives in serial form in the newspapers of the day. Widely accessible and deeply entertaining, the ghost story proliferated during this period. These stories were equally popular on both sides of the Atlantic, as American writers like Vincent O'Sullivan, William Fryer Harvey, and Ralph Adams Cram added their own twists to the genre. The Irish Gothic writer Sheridan Le Fanu went against the grain in 'An Account of Some Strange Disturbances in Aungier Street' (1851) at a time when providing a moral message was the norm for contemporary ghost stories.

Many of the great literary figures of the era also tried their hand at the ghost story. Charles Dickens wrote 'No. 1 Branch Line: The Signalman' (1866), while Henry James wrote a number of other ghost stories, such as 'The Real Right Thing' (1899) and 'The Romance of Certain Old Clothes' (1868), included here, as well as his classic novella *The Turn of the Screw* (1898). Ambrose Bierce, one of the great practitioners of the American short story, was not averse to the ghost story either, as demonstrated by 'The Damned Thing' (1893). A veteran of the Civil War and an accomplished journalist, he wrote more than 200 stories over the course of his career.

Perhaps the greatest practitioner of the classic ghost story was Montague Rhodes James. James was a medieval scholar at King's College, Cambridge, and he refined his craft by testing out his stories on unsuspecting students. Drawing influence from his own research, his tales often feature antiquarian manuscripts and ancient objects which hold terrible secrets, and build a sense of dread through atmosphere and suggestion rather than direct description. This collection includes two of his most famous stories – 'The Stalls of Barchester Cathedral' and 'O, Whistle and I'll Come to You My Lad'. The former, first published in 1910, features a mysterious death, ancient architecture, and a dangerously inquisitive academic – all hallmarks of the traditional Jamesian story. The latter, first published in 1904, is perhaps his most famous tale. In it, a Cambridge professor discovers two curious Latin inscriptions. These lead to a series of eerie events which force the protagonist to question the truth about the world he lived in.

William Hope Hodgson took a very different approach. His Carnacki stories merged the fledgling detective genre with the established traditions of the classic ghost story. Initially published as a series of six stories in *The Idler* and *The New Magazine* between 1910 and 1912, they were collected together in *Carnacki, the Ghost Finder* (1913). As Thomas Carnacki seeks to unravel these occult mysteries, he actively confronts the supernatural forces that arise using his wits, his gun, and occasionally, paranormal rituals of his own.

Many of the greatest ghost stories of the period were written by women. Works like 'The Phantom Coach' (1864) by Amelia Edwards, 'The Striding Place' (1896) by Gertrude Atherton and 'The Red Bungalow' (1919) by Bithia Mary Croker were some of the most compelling and innovative tales of the era, as they pushed the bounds of their imagination and provided an empowering opportunity to present their own voice, unconstrained by the conventions of the time.

Meanwhile, Edith Nesbit wrote her own tales of terror. Best known for children's novels such as *Five Children and It* (1902) and *The Railway Children* (1906), she was also an accomplished writer of ghost stories. These dark tales, such as 'Man-size in Marble' and 'John Charrington's Weddings', have a sinister and disturbing core. Emotional and powerful, Nesbit does not shy away from the darker sides of life, where jealousy, guilt and hate are as dangerous as the predatory spirits that roam these stories.

These are just a few of the compelling tales that await you in the pages to come. Prepare yourself for the terrors ahead…

A Ghost

Guy de Maupassant

We were talking of Processes of Sequestration, apropos of a recent law-case. It was towards the end of a friendly evening, in an ancient mansion in the Rue de Grenelle, and each one had his story, his story which he affirmed to be true.

Then the old Marquis de la Tour-Samuel, who was eighty-two years old, rose, and went and leaned upon the mantle-piece. He said, with a voice which shook a little:

'I too, I know a strange story, so strange that it has simply possessed my life. It is fifty-six years since that adventure happened, yet not a month passes without me seeing it all again in dreams. That day has left a mark, and imprint of fear, stamped on me, do you understand? Yes, for ten minutes I suffered such horrible terror that from that hour to this a sort of constant dread has rested on my soul. Unexpected noises make me tremble all over; objects which in the shades of evening I do not well distinguish cause me a mad desire to escape. The fact is, I am afraid of the night.

'No! I admit I should never have confessed this before arriving at my present age. But I can say what I like now. When a man is eighty-two years old it is permitted him to be afraid of imaginary dangers. And in the face of real ones I have never drawn back, mesdames.

'The affair so disturbed my spirit, and produced in me so profound, so mysterious, so dreadful a sense of trouble, that I have never even told it. I have kept it in the intimate recesses of my heart, in that corner where we hide our bitter and our shameful secrets, and all those unspeakable stories of weaknesses which we have committed but which we cannot confess.

'I shall tell you the tale exactly as it happened, without trying to explain it. Certainly it can be explained – unless we assume that for an hour I was mad. But no, I was not mad, and I will give you the proof of it. Imagine what you like. Here are the plain facts:

'It was in the month of July, 1827. I found myself in garrison at Rouen.

'One day, as I was taking a walk upon the quay, I met a man whom I thought I recognized, although I did not remember exactly who he might be. I instinctively made a motion to stop. The stranger noticed the gesture, looked at me, and fell into my arms.

'It was a friend of my youth whom I had once loved dearly. The five years since I had seen him seemed to have aged him fifty. His hair was quite white; and when he walked he stooped as if exhausted. He understood my surprise, and told me about his life. He had been broken by a terrible sorrow.

'He had fallen madly in love with a very young girl, and he had married her with a kind of joyful ecstasy. But after one single year of superhuman happiness, she had suddenly died of a trouble at the heart, slain, no doubt, by love itself.

'He had left his château the very day of the funeral, and had come to reside in his hotel at Rouen. He was now living there, solitary and desperate, preyed on by anguish, and so miserable that his only thought was suicide.

'"Now that I've found you again," said he, "I shall ask you to do me a great service. It is to go out to the château and bring me some papers of which I stand in urgent need. They are in the secretary in my room, in our room. I cannot intrust this commission to an inferior, or to a man of business, because I desire impenetrable discretion and absolute silence. And as to myself, I would not go back to that house for anything in the world.

'"I will give you the key of that chamber, which I closed myself when I went away. And I will give you the key of the secretary. Besides that, you shall have a line from me to my gardener, which will make you free of the château. But come and breakfast with me tomorrow, and we can talk about all that."

'I promised to do him this service. It was indeed a mere excursion for me, since his estate lay only about five leagues from Rouen, and I could get there on horseback in an hour.

'I was with him at ten o'clock the next morning. We breakfasted alone together; yet he did not say twenty words. He begged me to forgive him for his silence. The thought of the visit which I was about to make to that chamber where his happiness lay dead, overwhelmed him completely, said he to me. And for a fact, he did seem strangely agitated and preoccupied, as if a mysterious struggle were passing in his soul.

'Finally, however, he explained to me exactly what I must do. It was quite simple. I must secure two packages of letters and a bundle of papers which were shut up in the first drawer on the right of the desk of which I had the key. He added:

'"I don't need to ask you not to look at them."

'I was almost wounded by this, and I told him so a little hotly. He stammered:

'"Forgive me, I suffer so much."

'And he fell to weeping.

'I left him about one o'clock, to accomplish my mission.

'It was brilliant weather, and I trotted fast across the fields, listening to the songs of the larks and the regular ring of my sabre on my boot.

'Next I entered the forest and walked my horse. Branches of trees caressed my face; and sometimes I would catch a leaf in my teeth, and chew it eagerly, in one of those ecstasies at being alive which fill you, one knows not why, with a tumultuous and almost elusive happiness, with a kind of intoxication of strength.

'On approaching the château, I looked in my pocket for the note which I had for the gardener, and I found to my astonishment that it was sealed. I was so surprised and irritated that I came near returning at once, without acquitting myself of my errand. But I reflected that I should in that case display a susceptibility which would be in bad taste. And, moreover, in his trouble, my friend might have sealed the note unconsciously.

'The manor looked as though it had been deserted these twenty years. How the gate, which was open and rotten, held up, was hard to tell. Grass covered the walks. You no longer made out the borders of the lawn.

'At the noise which I made by kicking a shutter with my foot, an old man came out of a side door and seemed stupefied at the sight. I leaped to the ground and delivered my letter. He read it, read it again, turned it round, looked at me askance, put the paper in his pocket, and remarked:

'"Well! What do you want?" I answered sharply:

'"You ought to know, since you have received the orders of your master in that letter. I want to enter the château."

'He seemed overwhelmed. He said:

'"So, you are going into... into his room?" I began to grow impatient.

'"Parbleu! But do you mean to put me through an examination, my good man?"

'He stammered:

'"No... monsier... only ... it has not been opened since... since the... death. If you will wait five minutes, I will go... go and see whether..."

'I interrupted him, angrily:

'"Come, come! Are you playing with me? You know you can't get in. I have the key."

'He had nothing more to say.

'"Well, monsieur, I will show you the way."

'"Show me the staircase, and leave me alone. I shall find the room well enough without you."

'"But... monsieur... but..."

'This time I went fairly into a rage:

'"Be quiet! do you hear? Or you will have to reckon with me." I pushed him violently aside, and I penetrated into the house.

'First I crossed the kitchen, then two little rooms inhabited by the fellow and his wife. I next passed into the great hall, I climbed the stairs, and I recognized the door as indicated by my friend.

'I opened it without trouble, and entered.

'The room was so dark that at first I hardly made out anything. I paused, struck by that mouldy and lifeless odor so peculiar to apartments which are uninhabited and condemned, and, as you might say, dead. Then, little by little, my eyes became accustomed to the gloom, and I saw, clearly enough, a great apartment all in disorder; the bed without sheets, yet with its mattress and its pillows, one of which bore the deep impress of an elbow or a head, as if someone had just lain on it.

'The chairs seemed all in confusion. I noticed that a door (into a closet, no doubt) had remained half open.

'I went to the window to let in some light, and I opened it; but the iron fastenings of the outside shutter were so rusty that I could not make them yield.

'I even tried to break them with my sabre, but without success. And as I was growing angry at these useless efforts, and as my eyes had at last perfectly accustomed themselves to the darkness, I gave up the hope of seeing more clearly, and I went to the desk.

'I seated myself in an armchair, lowered the shelf, and opened the indicated drawer. It was full to the top. I needed only three packets, which I knew how to tell. And I set myself to looking.

'I was straining my eyes to decipher the inscriptions, when behind me I thought I heard a slight rustle. I paid no heed to it, thinking that a current of air had made some of the hangings stir. But, in a minute, another almost imperceptible movement caused a singular, unpleasant little shiver to pass over my skin. It was so stupid to be even in the least degree nervous that I would not turn round, being ashamed for myself in my own presence. I had then just discovered the second of the bundles which I wanted. And now, just as I lit upon the third, the breath of a great and painful sigh against my shoulder caused me to give one mad leap two yards away. In my start I had turned quite round, with my hand upon my sabre, and if I had not felt it by my side I should certainly have run like a coward.

'A tall woman dressed in white stood looking at me from behind the armchair in which, a second before, I had been sitting.

'Such a shudder ran through my limbs that I almost fell backward! Oh, no one who has not felt it can understand a dreadful yet foolish fear like that. The soul fairly melts away; you are conscious of a heart no longer; the whole body becomes as lax as a sponge; and you would say that everything within you was falling to pieces.

'I do not believe in ghosts at all. – Well, I tell you that at that moment I grew faint under the hideous fear of the dead. And from the irresistible anguish caused by supernatural terrors I suffered, oh, I suffered in a few seconds more than I have done all the rest of my life.

'If she had not spoken I should perhaps have died! But she did speak; she spoke in a sweet dolorous voice which made my nerves quiver. I should not venture to say that I became master of myself and that I recovered my reason. No. I was so frightened that I no longer knew what I was doing; but a kind of personal dignity which I have in me, and also a little professional pride, enabled me to keep up an honourable countenance almost in spite of myself. I posed for my own benefit, and for hers, no doubt – for hers, woman or spectre, whatever she might be. I analyzed all this later, because, I assure you, that at the instant of the apparition I did not do much thinking. I was afraid.

'She said:

'"Oh, monsieur, you can do me a great service!"

'I tried to answer, but it was simply impossible for me to utter a word. A vague sound issued from my throat.

'She continued:

'"Will you do it? You can save me, cure me. I suffer dreadfully. I suffer, oh, I suffer!"

'And she sat down gently in my armchair. She looked at me:

'"Will you do it?"

'I made the sign "yes" with my head, for my voice was gone.

'Then she held out to me a tortoise-shell comb and she murmured:

'"Comb my hair; oh, comb my hair. That will cure me. You must comb my hair. Look at my head. How I suffer! And my hair, how it hurts me!"

'Her hair, which was loose and long and very black (as it seemed to me), hung down over the armchair's back and touched the ground.

'Why did I do that? Why, all shivering, did I receive the comb? And why did I take into my hands that long hair, which gave my skin a feeling of atrocious cold, as if I were touching serpents? I do not know.

'That feeling still clings about my fingers. And when I think of it I tremble.

'I combed her. I handled, I know not how, that icy hair. I twisted it. I bound it and unbound it. I plaited it as we plait a horse's mane. She sighed, bent her head, seemed happy.

'Suddenly she said to me, "I thank you!" caught the comb out of my hands, and fled through the half-open door which I had noticed.

'For several seconds after I was left alone, I experienced that wild trouble of the soul which one feels after a nightmare from which one has just awakened. Then at last I recovered my senses; I ran to the window, and I broke the shutters open with violent blows.

'A flood of daylight entered. I rushed upon the door by which she had disappeared. I found it shut and immovable.

'Then a fever of flight seized on me, a panic, a real panic such as overcomes an army. I caught up roughly the three packets of letters from the open desk; I crossed the room at a run; I took the steps of the staircase four at a time; I found myself outside, I don't know how; and, perceiving my horse ten paces off, I mounted him with one leap and went off at full gallop.

'I did not pause till I was before the door of my lodgings in Rouen. Throwing the reigns to my orderly, I escaped to my room, where I locked myself in to think.

'And then for an hour I kept anxiously asking whether I had not been the sport of some hallucination. I had certainly had one of those incomprehensible nervous shocks, one of those affections of the brain which dwarf the miracles to which the supernatural owes its power.

'And I had almost come to believe it as a delusion, an error of my senses, when I drew near the window, and my eyes lit by chance upon my breast. My dolman was covered with long woman's hairs which had rolled themselves around the buttons!

'I took them one by one and I threw them out of the window, with trembling in my fingers.

'Then I called my orderly. I felt too much moved, too much troubled, to go near my friend that day. And I wished also to ponder carefully what I should say to him about all this.

'I had the letters taken to his house. He gave the soldier a receipt. He asked many questions about me, and my soldier told him that I was unwell; that I had had a sun-stroke – something. He seemed uneasy.

'I went to him the next day, early in the morning, having resolved to tell him the truth. He had gone out the evening before, and had not come back.

'I returned in the course of the day. They had seen nothing of him. I waited a week. He did not reappear. Then I informed the police. They searched for him everywhere without discovering a trace of his passing or of his final retreat.

'A minute inspection of the abandoned château was instituted. Nothing suspicious was discovered.

'No sign that a woman had been hidden there revealed itself.

'The inquiry proving fruitless, the search was interrupted.

'And for fifty-six years I have learned nothing. I know nothing more.'

The Stalls of Barchester Cathedral

Montague Rhodes James

This matter began, as far as I am concerned, with the reading of a notice in the obituary section of the *Gentleman's Magazine* for an early year in the nineteenth century:

On February 26th, at his residence in the Cathedral Close of Barchester, the Venerable John Benwell Haynes, D.D., aged 57, Archdeacon of Sowerbridge and Rector of Pickhill and Candley. He was of —— College, Cambridge, and where, by talent and assiduity, he commanded the esteem of his seniors; when, at the usual time, he took his first degree, his name stood high in the list of *wranglers*. These academical honours procured for him within a short time a Fellowship of his College. In the year 1783 he received Holy Orders, and was shortly afterwards presented to the perpetual Curacy of Ranxton-sub-Ashe by his friend and patron the late truly venerable Bishop of Lichfield.... His speedy preferments, first to a Prebend, and subsequently to the dignity of Precentor in the Cathedral of Barchester, form an eloquent testimony to the respect in which he was held and to his eminent qualifications. He succeeded to the Archdeaconry upon the sudden decease of Archdeacon Pulteney in 1810. His sermons, ever conformable to the principles of the religion and Church which he adorned, displayed in no ordinary degree, without the least trace of enthusiasm, the refinement of the scholar united with the graces of the Christian. Free from sectarian violence,

> and informed by the spirit of the truest charity, they will long dwell in the memories of his hearers. [Here a further omission.] The productions of his pen include an able defence of Episcopacy, which, though often perused by the author of this tribute to his memory, affords but one additional instance of the want of liberality and enterprise which is a too common characteristic of the publishers of our generation. His published works are, indeed, confined to a spirited and elegant version of the *Argonautica* of Valerius Flacus, a volume of *Discourses upon the Several Events in the Life of Joshua*, delivered in his Cathedral, and a number of the charges which he pronounced at various visitations to the clergy of his Archdeaconry. These are distinguished by etc., etc. The urbanity and hospitality of the subject of these lines will not readily be forgotten by those who enjoyed his acquaintance. His interest in the venerable and awful pile under whose hoary vault he was so punctual an attendant, and particularly in the musical portion of its rites, might be termed filial, and formed a strong and delightful contrast to the polite indifference displayed by too many of our Cathedral dignitaries at the present time.

The final paragraph, after informing us that Dr Haynes died a bachelor, says:

> It might have been augured that an existence so placid and benevolent would have been terminated in a ripe old age by a dissolution equally gradual and calm. But how unsearchable are the workings of Providence! The peaceful and retired seclusion amid which the honoured evening of Dr Haynes' life was mellowing to its close was destined to be disturbed, nay, shattered, by a tragedy as appalling as it was unexpected. The morning of the 26th of February—

But perhaps I shall do better to keep back the remainder of the narrative until I have told the circumstances which led up to it. These, as far as they are now accessible, I have derived from another source.

I had read the obituary notice which I have been quoting, quite by chance, along with a great many others of the same period. It had excited some little speculation in my mind, but, beyond thinking that, if I ever had an opportunity of examining the local records of the period indicated, I would try to remember Dr Haynes, I made no effort to pursue his case.

Quite lately I was cataloguing the manuscripts in the library of the college to which he belonged. I had reached the end of the numbered volumes on the shelves, and I proceeded to ask the librarian whether there were any more books which he thought I ought to include in my description. 'I don't think there are,' he said, 'but we had better come and look at the manuscript class and make sure. Have you time to do that now?' I had time. We went to the library, checked off the manuscripts, and, at the end of our survey, arrived at a shelf of which I had seen nothing. Its contents consisted for the most part of sermons, bundles of fragmentary papers, college exercises, *Cyrus*, an epic poem in several cantos, the product of a country clergyman's leisure, mathematical tracts by a deceased professor, and other similar material of a kind with which I am only too familiar. I took brief notes of these. Lastly, there was a tin box, which was pulled out and dusted. Its label, much faded, was thus inscribed: 'Papers of the Ven. Archdeacon Haynes. Bequeathed in 1834 by his sister, Miss Letitia Haynes.'

I knew at once that the name was one which I had somewhere encountered, and could very soon locate it. 'That must be the Archdeacon Haynes who came to a very odd end at Barchester. I've read his obituary in the *Gentleman's Magazine*. May I take the box home? Do you know if there is anything interesting in it?'

The librarian was very willing that I should take the box and examine it at leisure. 'I never looked inside it myself,' he said, 'but I've always been meaning to. I am pretty sure that is the box which our old Master once said ought never to have been accepted by the college. He said that to Martin years ago; and he said also that as long as he had control over the library it should never be opened. Martin told me about it, and said that he wanted terribly to know what was in it; but the Master was librarian, and always kept the box in the lodge, so there was no getting at it in his time, and when he died it was taken away by mistake by his heirs, and only returned a few years ago. I can't think why I haven't opened it; but, as I have to go away from Cambridge this afternoon, you had better have first go at it. I think I can trust you not to publish anything undesirable in our catalogue.'

I took the box home and examined its contents, and thereafter consulted the librarian as to what should be done about publication, and, since I have his leave to make a story out of it, provided I disguised the identity of the people concerned, I will try what can be done.

The materials are, of course, mainly journals and letters. How much I shall quote and how much epitomize must be determined by considerations of space. The proper understanding of the situation has necessitated a little – not very arduous – research, which has been greatly facilitated by the excellent illustrations and text of the Barchester volume in Bell's *Cathedral Series*.

When you enter the choir of Barchester Cathedral now, you pass through a screen of metal and coloured marbles, designed by Sir Gilbert Scott, and find yourself in what I must call a very bare and odiously furnished place. The stalls are modern, without canopies. The places of the dignitaries and the names of the prebends have fortunately been allowed to survive, and are inscribed on small brass plates affixed to the stalls. The organ is in the triforium, and what is seen of the case is Gothic. The reredos and its surroundings are like every other.

Careful engravings of a hundred years ago show a very different state of things. The organ is on a massive classical screen. The stalls are also classical and very massive. There is a baldacchino of wood over the altar, with urns upon its corners. Farther east is a solid altar screen, classical in design, of wood, with a pediment, in which is a triangle surrounded by rays, enclosing certain Hebrew letters in gold. Cherubs contemplate these. There is a pulpit with a great sounding-board at the eastern end of the stalls on the north side, and there is a black and white marble pavement. Two ladies and a gentleman are admiring the general effect. From other sources I gather that the archdeacon's stall then, as now, was next to the bishop's throne at the south-eastern end of the stalls. His house almost faces the west front of the church, and is a fine red-brick building of William the Third's time.

Here Dr Haynes, already a mature man, took up his abode with his sister in the year 1810. The dignity had long been the object of his wishes, but his predecessor refused to depart until he had attained the age of ninety-two. About a week after he had held a modest festival in celebration of that ninety-second birthday, there came a morning, late in the year, when Dr Haynes, hurrying cheerfully into his breakfast-room, rubbing his hands and humming a tune, was greeted, and checked in his genial flow of spirits, by the sight of his sister, seated, indeed, in her usual place behind the tea-urn, but bowed forward and sobbing unrestrainedly into her handkerchief. 'What—what is the matter? What bad news?' he began. 'Oh, Johnny, you've not heard? The poor dear archdeacon!' 'The archdeacon, yes? What is it—ill, is he?' 'No, no; they found him on the staircase this morning; it is so shocking.' 'Is it possible! Dear, dear, poor Pulteney! Had there been any seizure?' 'They don't think so, and that is almost the worst thing about it. It seems to have been all the fault of that stupid maid of theirs, Jane.' Dr Haynes paused. 'I don't quite understand, Letitia. How was the maid at fault?' 'Why, as far as I can make out, there was a stair-rod missing, and she never mentioned it, and the poor archdeacon set his foot quite on the edge of the step—you know how slippery that oak is—and it seems he must have fallen almost the whole flight and broken his neck. It *is* so sad for poor Miss Pulteney. Of course, they will get rid of the girl at once. I never liked her.' Miss Haynes's grief resumed its sway, but eventually relaxed so far as to permit of her taking some breakfast. Not so her brother, who, after standing in silence before the window for some minutes, left the room, and did not appear again that morning.

I need only add that the careless maid-servant was dismissed forthwith, but that the missing stair-rod was very shortly afterwards found *under* the stair-carpet – an additional proof, if any were needed, of extreme stupidity and carelessness on her part.

For a good many years Dr Haynes had been marked out by his ability, which seems to have been really considerable, as the likely successor of Archdeacon Pulteney, and no disappointment was in store for him. He was duly installed, and entered with zeal upon the discharge of those functions which are appropriate to one in his position. A considerable space in his journals is occupied with exclamations upon the confusion in which Archdeacon Pulteney had left the business of his office and the documents appertaining to it. Dues upon Wringham and Barnswood have been uncollected for something like twelve years, and are largely irrecoverable; no visitation has been held for seven years; four chancels are almost past mending. The persons deputized by the archdeacon have been nearly as incapable as himself. It was almost a matter for thankfulness that this state of things had not been permitted to continue, and a letter from a friend confirms this view. '[Greek: ho katechôn],' it says (in rather cruel allusion to the Second Epistle to the Thessalonians), 'is removed at last. My poor friend! Upon what a scene of confusion will you be entering! I give you my word that, on the last occasion of my crossing his threshold, there was no single paper that he could lay hands upon, no syllable of mine that he could hear, and no fact in connexion with my business that he could remember. But now, thanks to a negligent maid and a loose stair-carpet, there is some prospect that necessary business will be transacted without a complete loss alike of voice and temper.' This letter was tucked into a pocket in the cover of one of the diaries.

There can be no doubt of the new archdeacon's zeal and enthusiasm. 'Give me but time to reduce to some semblance of order the innumerable errors and complications with which I am confronted, and I shall gladly and sincerely join with the aged Israelite in the canticle which too many, I fear, pronounce but with their lips.' This reflection I find, not in a diary, but a letter; the doctor's friends seem to have returned his correspondence to his surviving sister. He does not confine himself, however, to reflections. His investigation of the rights and duties of his office are very searching and business-like, and there is a calculation in one place that a period of three years will just suffice to set the business of the Archdeaconry upon a proper footing. The estimate appears to have been an exact one. For just three years he is occupied in reforms; but I look in vain at the end of that time for the promised *Nunc dimittis*. He has now found a new sphere of activity. Hitherto his duties have precluded him from more than an occasional attendance at the Cathedral services. Now he begins to take an interest in the fabric and the music. Upon his struggles with the organist, an old gentleman who had been in office since 1786, I have no time to dwell; they were not attended with any marked success. More to the purpose is his sudden growth of enthusiasm for the Cathedral itself and its furniture. There is a draft of a letter to Sylvanus Urban (which I do not think was ever sent) describing the stalls in the choir. As I have said, these were of fairly late date – of about the year 1700, in fact.

'The archdeacon's stall, situated at the south-east end, west of the episcopal throne (now so worthily occupied by the truly excellent prelate who adorns the See of Barchester), is distinguished by some curious ornamentation. In addition to the arms of Dean West, by whose efforts the whole of the internal furniture of the choir was completed, the prayer-desk is terminated at the eastern extremity by three small but remarkable statuettes in the grotesque manner. One is an exquisitely modelled figure of a cat, whose crouching posture suggests with admirable spirit the suppleness, vigilance, and craft of the redoubted adversary of the genus *Mus*. Opposite to this is a figure seated upon a throne and invested with the attributes of royalty; but it is no earthly monarch whom the carver has sought to portray. His feet are studiously concealed by the long robe in which he is draped: but neither the crown nor the cap which he wears suffice to hide the prick-ears and curving horns which betray his Tartarean origin; and the hand which rests upon his knee, is armed with talons of horrifying length and sharpness. Between these two figures stands a shape muffled in a long mantle. This might at first sight be mistaken for a monk or "friar of orders gray", for the head is cowled and a knotted cord depends from somewhere about the waist. A slight inspection, however, will lead to a very different conclusion. The knotted cord is quickly seen to be a halter, held by a hand all but concealed within the draperies; while the sunken features and, horrid to relate, the rent flesh upon the cheek-bones, proclaim the King of Terrors. These figures are evidently the production of no unskilled chisel; and should it chance that any of your correspondents are able to throw light upon their origin and significance, my obligations to your valuable miscellany will be largely increased.'

There is more description in the paper, and, seeing that the woodwork in question has now disappeared, it has a considerable interest. A paragraph at the end is worth quoting:

> Some late researches among the Chapter accounts have shown me that the carving of the stalls was not as was very usually reported, the work of Dutch artists, but was executed by a native of this city or district named Austin. The timber was procured from an oak copse in the vicinity, the property of the Dean and Chapter, known as Holywood. Upon a recent visit to the parish within whose boundaries it is situated, I learned from the aged and truly respectable

> incumbent that traditions still lingered amongst the inhabitants of the great size and age of the oaks employed to furnish the materials of the stately structure which has been, however imperfectly, described in the above lines. Of one in particular, which stood near the centre of the grove, it is remembered that it was known as the Hanging Oak. The propriety of that title is confirmed by the fact that a quantity of human bones was found in the soil about its roots, and that at certain times of the year it was the custom for those who wished to secure a successful issue to their affairs, whether of love or the ordinary business of life, to suspend from its boughs small images or puppets rudely fashioned of straw, twigs, or the like rustic materials.

So much for the archdeacon's archaeological investigations. To return to his career as it is to be gathered from his diaries. Those of his first three years of hard and careful work show him throughout in high spirits, and, doubtless, during this time, that reputation for hospitality and urbanity which is mentioned in his obituary notice was well deserved. After that, as time goes on, I see a shadow coming over him – destined to develop into utter blackness – which I cannot but think must have been reflected in his outward demeanour. He commits a good deal of his fears and troubles to his diary; there was no other outlet for them. He was unmarried and his sister was not always with him. But I am much mistaken if he has told all that he might have told. A series of extracts shall be given:

> *Aug. 30th 1816*—The days begin to draw in more perceptibly than ever. Now that the Archdeaconry papers are reduced to order, I must find some further employment for the evening hours of autumn and winter. It is a great blow that Letitia's health will not allow her to stay through these months. Why not go on with my *Defence of Episcopacy*? It may be useful.
>
> *Sept. 15*—Letitia has left me for Brighton.
>
> *Oct. 11*—Candles lit in the choir for the first time at evening prayers. It came as a shock: I find that I absolutely shrink from the dark season.

Nov. 17—Much struck by the character of the carving on my desk: I do not know that I had ever carefully noticed it before. My attention was called to it by an accident. During the *Magnificat* I was, I regret to say, almost overcome with sleep. My hand was resting on the back of the carved figure of a cat which is the nearest to me of the three figures on the end of my stall. I was not aware of this, for I was not looking in that direction, until I was startled by what seemed a softness, a feeling as of rather rough and coarse fur, and a sudden movement, as if the creature were twisting round its head to bite me. I regained complete consciousness in an instant, and I have some idea that I must have uttered a suppressed exclamation, for I noticed that Mr Treasurer turned his head quickly in my direction. The impression of the unpleasant feeling was so strong that I found myself rubbing my hand upon my surplice. This accident led me to examine the figures after prayers more carefully than I had done before, and I realized for the first time with what skill they are executed.

Dec. 6—I do indeed miss Letitia's company. The evenings, after I have worked as long as I can at my *Defence*, are very trying. The house is too large for a lonely man, and visitors of any kind are too rare. I get an uncomfortable impression when going to my room that there *is* company of some kind. The fact is (I may as well formulate it to myself) that I hear voices. This, I am well aware, is a common symptom of incipient decay of the brain – and I believe that I should be less disquieted than I am if I had any suspicion that this was the cause. I have none – none whatever, nor is there anything in my family history to give colour to such an idea. Work, diligent work, and a punctual attention to the duties which fall to me is my best remedy, and I have little doubt that it will prove efficacious.

Jan. 1—My trouble is, I must confess it, increasing upon me. Last night, upon my return after midnight from the Deanery, I lit my candle to go upstairs. I was nearly at the top when something whispered to me, 'Let me wish you a happy New Year.' I could not be mistaken: it spoke distinctly and with a peculiar emphasis. Had I dropped my candle, as I all but did, I tremble to think what the consequences must have been. As it was, I managed to get up the last flight, and was quickly in my room with the door locked, and experienced no other disturbance.

Jan. 15—I had occasion to come downstairs last night to my workroom for my watch, which I had inadvertently left on my table when I went up to bed. I think I was at the top of the last flight when I had a sudden impression of a sharp whisper in my ear '*Take care*.' I clutched the balusters and naturally looked round at once. Of course, there was nothing. After a moment I went on – it was no good turning back – but I had as nearly as possible fallen: a cat – a large one by the feel of it – slipped between my feet, but again, of course, I saw nothing. It *may* have been the kitchen cat, but I do not think it was.

Feb. 27—A curious thing last night, which I should like to forget. Perhaps if I put it down here I may see it in its true proportion. I worked in the library from about 9 to 10. The hall and staircase seemed to be unusually full of what I can only call movement without sound: by this I mean that there seemed to be continuous going and coming, and that whenever I ceased writing to listen, or looked out into the hall, the stillness was absolutely unbroken. Nor, in going to my room at an earlier hour than usual – about half-past ten – was I conscious of anything that I could call a noise. It so happened that I had told John to come to my room for the letter to the bishop which I wished to have delivered early in the morning at the Palace. He was to sit up, therefore, and come for it when he heard me retire. This I had for the moment forgotten, though I had remembered to carry the letter with me to my room. But when, as I was winding up my watch, I heard a light tap at the door, and a low voice saying, 'May I come in?' (which I most undoubtedly did hear), I recollected the fact, and took up the letter from my dressing-table, saying 'Certainly: come in.' No one, however, answered my summons, and it was now that, as I strongly suspect, I committed an error: for I opened the door and held the letter out. There was certainly no one at that moment in the passage, but, in the instant of my standing there, the door at the end opened and John appeared carrying a candle. I asked him whether he had come to the door earlier; but am satisfied that he had not. I do not like the situation; but although my senses were very much on the alert, and though it was some time before I could sleep, I must allow that I perceived nothing further of an untoward character.

With the return of spring, when his sister came to live with him for some months, Dr Haynes's entries become more cheerful, and, indeed, no symptom of depression is discernible until the early part of September when he was again left alone. And now, indeed, there is evidence that he was incommoded again, and that more pressingly. To this matter I will return in a moment, but I digress to put in a document which, rightly or wrongly, I believe to have a bearing on the thread of the story.

The account-books of Dr Haynes, preserved along with his other papers, show, from a date but little later than that of his institution as archdeacon, a quarterly payment of £25 to J.L. Nothing could have been made of this, had it stood by itself. But I connect with it a very dirty and ill-written letter, which, like another that I have quoted, was in a pocket in the cover of a diary. Of date or postmark there is no vestige, and the decipherment was not easy. It appears to run:

Dr Sr.
I have bin expctin to her off you theis last wicks, and not Haveing done so must supose you have not got mine witch was saying how me and my man had met in with bad times this season all seems to go cross with us on the farm and which way to look for the rent we have no knowledge of it this been the sad case with us if you would have the great [liberality *probably, but the exact spelling defies reproduction*] to send fourty pounds otherwise steps will have to be took which I should not wish. Has you was the Means of me losing my place with Dr Pulteney I think it is only just what I am asking and you know best what I could say if I was Put to it but I do not wish anything of that unpleasant Nature being one that always wish to have everything Pleasant about me.

Your obedt Servt,
Jane Lee.

About the time at which I suppose this letter to have been written there is, in fact, a payment of £40 to J.L.

We return to the diary:

Oct. 22—At evening prayers, during the Psalms, I had that same experience which I recollect from last year. I was resting my hand on one of the carved figures, as before (I usually avoid that of the cat now), and – I was going to have said – a change came over it, but that seems attributing too much importance to what must, after all, be due to some physical affection in myself: at any rate, the wood seemed to become chilly and soft as if made of wet linen. I can assign the moment at which I became sensible of this. The choir were singing the words (*Set thou an ungodly man to be ruler over him and let Satan stand at his right hand.*)

The whispering in my house was more persistent tonight. I seemed not to be rid of it in my room. I have not noticed this before. A nervous man, which I am not, and hope I am not becoming, would have been much annoyed, if not alarmed, by it. The cat was on the stairs tonight. I think it sits there always. There *is* no kitchen cat.

Nov. 15—Here again I must note a matter I do not understand. I am much troubled in sleep. No definite image presented itself, but I was pursued by the very vivid impression that wet lips were whispering into my ear with great rapidity and emphasis for some time together. After this, I suppose, I fell asleep, but was awakened with a start by a feeling as if a hand were laid on my shoulder. To my intense alarm I found myself standing at the top of the lowest flight of the first staircase. The moon was shining brightly enough through the large window to let me see that there was a large cat on the second or third step. I can make no comment. I crept up to bed again, I do not know how. Yes, mine is a heavy burden. [Then follows a line or two which has been scratched out. I fancy I read something like 'acted for the best'.]

Not long after this it is evident to me that the archdeacon's firmness began to give way under the pressure of these phenomena. I omit as unnecessarily painful and distressing the ejaculations and prayers which, in the months of December and January, appear for the first time and become increasingly frequent. Throughout this time, however, he is obstinate in clinging to his post. Why he did not plead ill-health and take refuge at Bath or Brighton I cannot tell; my impression is that it would have done him no good; that he was a man who, if he had confessed himself beaten by the annoyances, would have succumbed at once, and that he was conscious of this. He did seek to palliate them by inviting visitors to his house. The result he has noted in this fashion:

Jan. 7—I have prevailed on my cousin Allen to give me a few days, and he is to occupy the chamber next to mine.

Jan. 8—A still night. Allen slept well, but complained of the wind. My own experiences were as before: still whispering and whispering: what is it that he wants to say?

Jan. 9—Allen thinks this a very noisy house. He thinks, too, that my cat is an unusually large and fine specimen, but very wild.

Jan. 10—Allen and I in the library until 11. He left me twice to see what the maids were doing in the hall: returning the second time he told me he had seen one of them passing through the door at the end of the passage, and said if his wife were here she would soon get them into better order. I asked him what coloured dress the maid wore; he said grey or white. I supposed it would be so.

Jan. 11—Allen left me today. I must be firm.

These words, *I must be firm*, occur again and again on subsequent days; sometimes they are the only entry. In these cases they are in an unusually large hand, and dug into the paper in a way which must have broken the pen that wrote them.

Apparently the archdeacon's friends did not remark any change in his behaviour, and this gives me a high idea of his courage and determination. The diary tells us nothing more than I have indicated of the last days of his life. The end of it all must be told in the polished language of the obituary notice:

> The morning of the 26th of February was cold and tempestuous. At an early hour the servants had occasion to go into the front hall of the residence occupied by the lamented subject of these lines. What was their horror upon observing the form of their beloved and respected master lying upon the landing of the principal staircase in an attitude which inspired the gravest fears. Assistance was procured, and an universal consternation was experienced upon the discovery that he had been the object of a brutal and a murderous attack. The vertebral column was fractured in more than one place. This might have been the result of a fall: it appeared that the stair-carpet was loosened at one point. But, in addition to this, there were injuries inflicted upon the eyes, nose and mouth, as if by the agency of some savage animal, which, dreadful to relate, rendered those features unrecognizable. The vital spark was, it is needless to add, completely extinct, and had been so, upon the testimony of respectable medical authorities, for several hours. The author or authors of this mysterious outrage are alike buried in mystery, and the most active conjecture has hitherto failed to suggest a solution of the melancholy problem afforded by this appalling occurrence.

The writer goes on to reflect upon the probability that the writings of Mr Shelley, Lord Byron, and M. Voltaire may have been instrumental in bringing about the disaster, and concludes by hoping, somewhat vaguely, that this event may 'operate as an example to the rising generation'; but this portion of his remarks need not be quoted in full.

I had already formed the conclusion that Dr Haynes was responsible for the death of Dr Pulteney. But the incident connected with the carved figure of death upon the archdeacon's stall was a very perplexing feature. The conjecture that it had been cut out of the wood of the Hanging Oak was not difficult, but seemed impossible to substantiate. However, I paid a visit to Barchester, partly with the view of finding out whether there were any relics of the woodwork to be heard of. I was introduced by one of the canons to the curator of the local museum, who was, my friend said, more likely to be able to give me information on the point than anyone else. I told this gentleman of the description of certain carved figures and arms formerly on the stalls, and asked whether any had survived. He was able to show me the arms of Dean West and some other fragments. These, he said, had been got from an old resident, who had also once owned a figure – perhaps one of those which I was inquiring for. There was a very odd thing about that figure, he said. 'The old man who had it told me that he picked it up in a woodyard, whence he had obtained the still extant pieces, and had taken it home for his children. On the way home he was fiddling about with it and it came in two in his hands, and a bit of paper dropped out. This he picked up and, just noticing that there was writing on it, put it into his pocket, and subsequently into a vase on his mantelpiece. I was at his house not very long ago, and happened to pick up the vase and turn it over to see whether there were any marks on it, and the paper fell into my hand. The old man, on my handing it to him, told me the story I have told you, and said I might keep the paper. It was crumpled and rather torn, so I have mounted it on a card, which I have here. If you can tell me what it means I shall be very glad, and also, I may say, a good deal surprised.'

He gave me the card. The paper was quite legibly inscribed in an old hand, and this is what was on it:

When I grew in the Wood
I was water'd w'th Blood
Now in the Church I stand
Who that touches me with his Hand
If a Bloody hand he bear
I councell him to be ware
Lest he be fetcht away
Whether by night or day,
But chiefly when the wind blows high
In a night of February.
This I drempt, 26 Febr. Anno 1699.

JOHN AUSTIN.

'I suppose it is a charm or a spell: wouldn't you call it something of that kind?' said the curator.

'Yes,' I said, 'I suppose one might. What became of the figure in which it was concealed?'

'Oh, I forgot,' said he. 'The old man told me it was so ugly and frightened his children so much that he burnt it.'

O, Whistle and I'll Come to You My Lad

Montague Rhodes James

'I suppose you will be getting away pretty soon, now Full term is over, Professor,' said a person not in the story to the Professor of Ontography, soon after they had sat down next to each other at a feast in the hospitable hall of St James's College.

The Professor was young, neat, and precise in speech.

'Yes,' he said; 'my friends have been making me take up golf this term, and I mean to go to the East Coast – in point of fact to Burnstow – (I dare say you know it) for a week or ten days, to improve my game. I hope to get off tomorrow.'

'Oh, Parkins,' said his neighbour on the other side, 'if you are going to Burnstow, I wish you would look at the site of the Templars' preceptory, and let me know if you think it would be any good to have a dig there in the summer.'

It was, as you might suppose, a person of antiquarian pursuits who said this, but, since he merely appears in this prologue, there is no need to give his entitlements.

'Certainly,' said Parkins, the Professor: 'if you will describe to me whereabouts the site is, I will do my best to give you an idea of the lie of the land when I get back; or I could write to you about it, if you would tell me where you are likely to be.'

'Don't trouble to do that, thanks. It's only that I'm thinking of taking my family in that direction in the Long, and it occurred to me that, as very few of the English preceptories have ever been properly planned, I might have an opportunity of doing something useful on off-days.'

The Professor rather sniffed at the idea that planning out a preceptory could be described as useful. His neighbour continued:

'The site – I doubt if there is anything showing above ground – must be down quite close to the beach now. The sea has encroached tremendously, as you know, all along that bit of coast. I should think, from the map, that it must be about three-quarters of a mile from the Globe Inn, at the north end of the town. Where are you going to stay?'

'Well, *at* the Globe Inn, as a matter of fact,' said Parkins; 'I have engaged a room there. I couldn't get in anywhere else; most of the lodging-houses are shut up in winter, it seems; and, as it is, they tell me that the only room of any size I can have is really a double-bedded one, and that they haven't a corner in which to store the other bed, and so on. But I must have a fairly large room, for I am taking some books down, and mean to do a bit of work; and though I don't quite fancy having an empty bed – not to speak of two – in what I may call for the time being my study, I suppose I can manage to rough it for the short time I shall be there.'

'Do you call having an extra bed in your room roughing it, Parkins?' said a bluff person opposite. 'Look here, I shall come down and occupy it for a bit; it'll be company for you.'

The Professor quivered, but managed to laugh in a courteous manner.

'By all means, Rogers; there's nothing I should like better. But I'm afraid you would find it rather dull; you don't play golf, do you?'

'No, thank Heaven!' said rude Mr Rogers.

'Well, you see, when I'm not writing I shall most likely be out on the links, and that, as I say, would be rather dull for you, I'm afraid.'

'Oh, I don't know! There's certain to be somebody I know in the place; but, of course, if you don't want me, speak the word, Parkins; I shan't be offended. Truth, as you always tell us, is never offensive.'

Parkins was, indeed, scrupulously polite and strictly truthful. It is to be feared that Mr Rogers sometimes practised upon his knowledge of these characteristics. In Parkins's breast there was a conflict now raging, which for a moment or two did not allow him to answer. That interval being over, he said:

'Well, if you want the exact truth, Rogers, I was considering whether the room I speak of would really be large enough to accommodate us both comfortably; and also whether (mind, I shouldn't have said this if you hadn't pressed me) you would not constitute something in the nature of a hindrance to my work.'

Rogers laughed loudly.

'Well done, Parkins!' he said. 'It's all right. I promise not to interrupt your work; don't you disturb yourself about that. No, I won't come if you don't want me; but I thought I should do so nicely to keep the ghosts off.' Here he might have been seen to wink and to nudge his next neighbour. Parkins might also have been seen to become pink. 'I beg pardon, Parkins,' Rogers continued; 'I oughtn't to have said that. I forgot you didn't like levity on these topics.'

'Well,' Parkins said, 'as you have mentioned the matter, I freely own that I do *not* like careless talk about what you call ghosts. A man in my position,' he went on, raising his voice a little, 'cannot, I find, be too careful about appearing to sanction the current beliefs on such subjects. As you know, Rogers, or as you ought to know; for I think I have never concealed my views—'

'No, you certainly have not, old man,' put in Rogers *sotto voce*.

'—I hold that any semblance, any appearance of concession to the view that such things might exist is to me a renunciation of all that I hold most sacred. But I'm afraid I have not succeeded in securing your attention.'

'Your *undivided* attention, was what Dr Blimber actually *said,*' Rogers interrupted, with every appearance of an earnest desire for accuracy. 'But I beg your pardon, Parkins: I'm stopping you.'

'No, not at all,' said Parkins. 'I don't remember Blimber; perhaps he was before my time. But I needn't go on. I'm sure you know what I mean.'

'Yes, yes,' said Rogers, rather hastily – 'just so. We'll go into it fully at Burnstow, or somewhere.'

In repeating the above dialogue I have tried to give the impression which it made on me, that Parkins was something of an old woman – rather henlike, perhaps, in his little ways; totally destitute, alas! of the sense of humour, but at the same time dauntless and sincere in his convictions, and a man deserving of the greatest respect. Whether or not the reader has gathered so much, that was the character which Parkins had.

On the following day Parkins did, as he had hoped, succeed in getting away from his college, and in arriving at Burnstow. He was made welcome at the Globe Inn, was safely installed in the large double-bedded room of which we have heard, and was able before retiring to rest to arrange his materials for work in apple-pie order upon a commodious table which occupied the outer end of the room, and was surrounded on three sides by windows looking out seaward; that is to say the central window looked straight out to sea, and those on the left and right commanding prospects along the shore to the north and south respectively. On the south you saw the village of Burnstow. On the north no houses were to be seen, but only the beach and the low cliff backing it. Immediately in front was a strip – not considerable – of rough grass, dotted with old anchors, capstans, and so forth; then a broad path; then the beach. Whatever may have been the original distance between the Globe Inn and the sea, not more than sixty yards now separated them.

The rest of the population of the inn was, of course, a golfing one, and included few elements that call for a special description. The most conspicuous figure was, perhaps, that of an *ancien militaire*, secretary of a London club, and possessed of a voice of incredible strength, and of views of a pronouncedly Protestant type. These were apt to find utterance after his attendance upon the ministrations of the Vicar, an estimable man with inclinations towards a picturesque ritual, which he gallantly kept down as far as he could out of deference to East Anglian tradition.

Professor Parkins, one of whose principal characteristics was pluck, spent the greater part of the day following his arrival at Burnstow in what he had called improving his game, in company with this Colonel Wilson: and during the afternoon – whether the process of improvement were to blame or not, I am not sure – the Colonel's demeanour assumed a colouring so lurid that even Parkins jibbed at the thought of walking home with him from the links. He determined, after a short and furtive look at that bristling moustache and those incarnadined features, that it would be wiser to allow the influences of tea and tobacco to do what they could with the Colonel before the dinner-hour should render a meeting inevitable.

'I might walk home tonight along the beach,' he reflected – 'yes, and take a look – there will be light enough for that – at the ruins of which Disney was talking. I don't exactly know where they are, by the way; but I expect I can hardly help stumbling on them.'

This he accomplished, I may say, in the most literal sense, for in picking his way from the links to the shingle beach his foot caught, partly in a gorse-root and partly in a biggish stone, and over he went. When he got up and surveyed his surroundings, he found himself in a patch of somewhat broken ground covered with small depressions and mounds. These latter, when he came to examine them, proved to be simply masses of flints embedded in mortar and grown over with turf. He must, he quite rightly concluded, be on the site of the preceptory he had promised to look at. It seemed not unlikely to reward the spade of the explorer; enough of the foundations was probably left at no great depth to throw a good deal of light on the general plan. He remembered vaguely that the Templars, to whom this site had belonged, were in the habit of building round churches, and he thought a particular series of the humps or mounds near him did appear to be arranged in something of a circular form. Few people can resist the temptation to try a little amateur research in a department quite outside their own, if only for the satisfaction of showing how successful they would have been had they only taken it up seriously. Our Professor, however, if he felt something of this mean desire, was also truly anxious to oblige Mr Disney. So he paced with care the circular area he had noticed, and wrote down its rough dimensions in his pocket-book. Then he proceeded to examine an oblong eminence which lay east of the centre of the circle, and seemed to his thinking likely to be the base of a platform or altar. At one end of it, the northern, a patch of the turf was gone – removed by some boy or other creature *feræ naturæ*. It might, he thought, be as well to probe the soil here for evidences of masonry, and he took out his knife and began scraping away the earth. And now followed another little discovery: a portion of soil fell inward as he scraped, and disclosed a small cavity. He lighted one match after another to help him to see of what nature the hole was, but the wind was too strong for them all. By tapping and scratching the sides with his knife, however, he was able to make out that it must be an artificial hole in masonry. It was rectangular, and the sides, top, and bottom, if not actually plastered, were smooth and regular. Of course it was empty. No! As he withdrew the knife he heard a metallic clink, and when he introduced his hand it met with a cylindrical object lying on the floor of the hole. Naturally enough, he picked it up, and when he brought it into the light, now fast fading, he could see that it, too, was of man's making – a metal tube about four inches long, and evidently of some considerable age.

By the time Parkins had made sure that there was nothing else in this odd receptacle, it was too late and too dark for him to think of undertaking any further search. What he had done had proved so unexpectedly interesting that he determined to sacrifice a little more of the daylight on the morrow to archæology. The object which he now had safe in his pocket was bound to be of some slight value at least, he felt sure.

Bleak and solemn was the view on which he took a last look before starting homeward. A faint yellow light in the west showed the links, on which a few figures moving towards the club-house were still visible, the squat martello tower, the lights of Aldsey village, the pale ribbon of sands intersected at intervals by black wooden groynings, the dim and murmuring sea. The wind was bitter from the north, but was at his back when he set out for the Globe. He quickly rattled and clashed through the shingle and gained the sand, upon which, but for the groynings which had to be got over every few yards, the going was both good and quiet. One last look behind, to measure the distance he had made since leaving the ruined Templars' church, showed him a prospect of company on his walk, in the shape of a rather indistinct personage in the distance, who seemed to be making great efforts to catch up with him, but made little, if any, progress. I mean that there was an appearance of running about his movements, but that the distance between him and Parkins did not seem materially to lessen. So, at least, Parkins thought, and decided that he almost certainly did not know him, and that it would be absurd to wait until he came up. For all that, company, he began to think, would really be very welcome on that lonely shore, if only you could choose your companion. In his unenlightened days he had read of meetings in such places which even now would hardly bear thinking of. He went on thinking of them, however, until he reached home, and particularly of one which catches most people's fancy at some time of their childhood. 'Now I saw in my dream that Christian had gone but a very little way when he saw a foul fiend coming over the field to meet him.' 'What should I do now,' he thought, 'if I looked back and caught sight of a black figure sharply defined against the yellow sky, and saw that it had horns and wings? I wonder whether I should stand or run for it. Luckily, the gentleman behind is not of that kind, and he seems to be about as far off now as when I saw him first. Well, at this rate he won't get his dinner as soon as I shall; and, dear me! it's within a quarter of an hour of the time now. I must run!'

Parkins had, in fact, very little time for dressing. When he met the Colonel at dinner, Peace – or as much of her as that gentleman could manage – reigned once more in the military bosom; nor was she put to flight in the hours of bridge that followed dinner, for Parkins was a more than respectable player. When, therefore, he retired towards twelve o'clock, he felt that he had spent his evening in quite a satisfactory way, and that, even for so long as a fortnight or three weeks, life at the Globe would be supportable under similar conditions – 'especially,' thought he, 'if I go on improving my game.'

As he went along the passages he met the boots of the Globe, who stopped and said:

'Beg your pardon, sir, but as I was a-brushing your coat just now there was somethink fell out of the pocket. I put it on your chest of drawers, sir, in your room, sir – a piece of a pipe or somethink of that, sir. Thank you, sir. You'll find it on your chest of drawers, sir – yes, sir. Good-night, sir.'

The speech served to remind Parkins of his little discovery of that afternoon. It was with some considerable curiosity that he turned it over by the light of his candles. It was of bronze, he now saw, and was shaped very much after the manner of the modern dog-whistle; in fact it was – yes, certainly it was – actually no more nor less than a whistle. He put it to his lips, but it was quite full of a fine, caked-up sand or earth, which would not yield to knocking, but must be loosened with a knife. Tidy as ever in his habits, Parkins cleared out the earth on to a piece of paper, and took the latter to the window to empty it out. The night was clear and bright, as he saw when he had opened the casement, and he stopped for an instant to look at the sea and note a belated wanderer stationed on the shore in front of the inn. Then he shut the window, a little surprised at the late hours people kept at Burnstow, and took his whistle to the light again. Why, surely there were marks on it, and not merely marks, but letters! A very little rubbing rendered the deeply-cut inscription quite legible, but the Professor had to confess, after some earnest thought, that the meaning of it was as obscure to him as the writing on the wall to Belshazzar. There were legends both on the front and on the back of the whistle. The one read thus:

FLA
FUR BIS
FLE

The other:

✠ QUIS EST ISTE QUI UENIT ✠

'I ought to be able to make it out,' he thought; 'but I suppose I am a little rusty in my Latin. When I come to think of it, I don't believe I even know the word for a whistle. The long one does seem simple enough. It ought to mean, "Who is this who is coming?" Well, the best way to find out is evidently to whistle for him.'

He blew tentatively and stopped suddenly, startled and yet pleased at the note he had elicited. It had a quality of infinite distance in it, and, soft as it was, he somehow felt it must be audible for miles round. It was a sound, too, that seemed to have the power (which many scents possess) of forming pictures in the brain. He saw quite clearly for a moment a vision of a wide, dark expanse at night, with a fresh wind blowing, and in the midst a lonely figure – how employed, he could not tell. Perhaps he would have seen more had not the picture been broken by the sudden surge of a gust of wind against his casement, so sudden that it made him look up, just in time to see the white glint of a sea-bird's wing somewhere outside the dark panes.

The sound of the whistle had so fascinated him that he could not help trying it once more, this time more boldly. The note was little, if at all, louder than before, and repetition broke the illusion – no picture followed, as he had half hoped it might. 'But what is this? Goodness! what force the wind can get up in a few minutes! What a tremendous gust! There! I knew that window-fastening was no use! Ah! I thought so – both candles out. It is enough to tear the room to pieces.'

The first thing was to get the window shut. While you might count twenty Parkins was struggling with the small casement, and felt almost as if he were pushing back a sturdy burglar, so strong was the pressure. It slackened all at once, and the window banged to and latched itself. Now to relight the candles and see what damage, if any, had been done. No, nothing seemed amiss; no glass even was broken in the casement. But the noise had evidently roused at least one member of the household: the Colonel was to be heard stumping in his stockinged feet on the floor above, and growling.

Quickly as it had risen, the wind did not fall at once. On it went, moaning and rushing past the house, at times rising to a cry so desolate that, as Parkins disinterestedly said, it might have made fanciful people feel quite uncomfortable; even the unimaginative, he thought after a quarter of an hour, might be happier without it.

Whether it was the wind, or the excitement of golf, or of the researches in the preceptory that kept Parkins awake, he was not sure. Awake he remained, in any case, long enough to fancy (as I am afraid I often do myself under such conditions) that he was the victim of all manner of fatal disorders: he would lie counting the beats of his heart, convinced that it was going to stop work every moment, and would entertain grave suspicions of his lungs, brain, liver, etc. – suspicions which he was sure would be dispelled by the return of daylight, but which until then refused to be put aside. He found a little vicarious comfort in the idea that someone else was in the same boat. A near neighbour (in the darkness it was not easy to tell his direction) was tossing and rustling in his bed, too.

The next stage was that Parkins shut his eyes and determined to give sleep every chance. Here again over-excitement asserted itself in another form – that of making pictures. *Experto crede,* pictures do come to the closed eyes of one trying to sleep, and often his pictures are so little to his taste that he must open his eyes and disperse the images.

Parkins's experience on this occasion was a very distressing one. He found that the picture which presented itself to him was continuous. When he opened his eyes, of course, it went; but when he shut them once more it framed itself afresh, and acted itself out again, neither quicker nor slower than before. What he saw was this:

A long stretch of shore – shingle edged by sand, and intersected at short intervals with black groynes running down to the water – a scene, in fact, so like that of his afternoon's walk that, in the absence of any landmark, it could not be distinguished therefrom. The light was obscure, conveying an impression of gathering storm, late winter evening, and slight cold rain. On this bleak stage at first no actor was visible. Then, in the distance, a bobbing black object appeared; a moment more, and it was a man running, jumping, clambering over the groynes, and every few seconds looking eagerly back. The nearer he came the more obvious it was that he was not only anxious, but even terribly frightened, though his face was not to be distinguished. He was, moreover, almost at the end of his strength. On he came; each successive obstacle seemed to cause him more difficulty than the last. 'Will he get over this next one?' thought Parkins; 'it seems a little higher than the others.' Yes; half climbing, half throwing himself, he did get over, and fell all in a heap on the other side (the side nearest to the spectator). There, as if really unable to get up again, he remained crouching under the groyne, looking up in an attitude of painful anxiety.

So far no cause whatever for the fear of the runner had been shown; but now there began to be seen, far up the shore, a little flicker of something light-coloured moving to and fro with great swiftness and irregularity. Rapidly growing larger, it, too, declared itself as a figure in pale, fluttering draperies, ill-defined. There was something about its motion which made Parkins very unwilling to see it at close quarters. It would stop, raise arms, bow itself toward the sand, then run stooping across the beach to the water-edge and back again; and then, rising upright, once more continue its course forward at a speed that was startling and terrifying. The moment came when the pursuer was hovering about from left to right only a few yards beyond the groyne where the runner lay in hiding. After two or three ineffectual castings hither and thither it came to a stop, stood upright, with arms raised high, and then darted straight forward towards the groyne.

It was at this point that Parkins always failed in his resolution to keep his eyes shut. With many misgivings as to incipient failure of eyesight, overworked brain, excessive smoking, and so on, he finally resigned himself to light his candle, get out a book, and pass the night waking, rather than be tormented by this persistent panorama, which he saw clearly enough could only be a morbid reflection of his walk and his thoughts on that very day.

The scraping of match on box and the glare of light must have startled some creatures of the night – rats or what not – which he heard scurry across the floor from the side of his bed with much rustling. Dear, dear! the match is out! Fool that it is! But the second one burnt better, and a candle and book were duly procured, over which Parkins pored till sleep of a wholesome kind came upon him, and that in no long space. For about the first time in his orderly and prudent life he forgot to blow out the candle, and when he was called next morning at eight there was still a flicker in the socket and a sad mess of guttered grease on the top of the little table.

After breakfast he was in his room, putting the finishing touches to his golfing costume – fortune had again allotted the Colonel to him for a partner – when one of the maids came in.

'Oh, if you please,' she said, 'would you like any extra blankets on your bed, sir?'

'Ah! thank you,' said Parkins. 'Yes, I think I should like one. It seems likely to turn rather colder.'

In a very short time the maid was back with the blanket.

'Which bed should I put it on, sir?' she asked.

'What? Why, that one – the one I slept in last night,' he said, pointing to it.

'Oh yes! I beg your pardon, sir, but you seemed to have tried both of 'em; leastways, we had to make 'em both up this morning.'

'Really? How very absurd!' said Parkins. 'I certainly never touched the other, except to lay some things on it. Did it actually seem to have been slept in?'

'Oh yes, sir!' said the maid. 'Why, all the things was crumpled and throwed about all ways, if you'll excuse me, sir – quite as if anyone 'adn't passed but a very poor night, sir.'

'Dear me,' said Parkins. 'Well, I may have disordered it more than I thought when I unpacked my things. I'm very sorry to have given you the extra trouble, I'm sure. I expect a friend of mine soon, by the way – a gentleman from Cambridge – to come and occupy it for a night or two. That will be all right, I suppose, won't it?'

'Oh yes, to be sure, sir. Thank you, sir. It's no trouble, I'm sure,' said the maid, and departed to giggle with her colleagues.

Parkins set forth, with a stern determination to improve his game.

I am glad to be able to report that he succeeded so far in this enterprise that the Colonel, who had been rather repining at the prospect of a second day's play in his company, became quite chatty as the morning advanced;

and his voice boomed out over the flats, as certain also of our own minor poets have said, 'like some great bourdon in a minster tower'.

'Extraordinary wind, that, we had last night,' he said. 'In my old home we should have said someone had been whistling for it.'

'Should you, indeed!' said Parkins. 'Is there a superstition of that kind still current in your part of the country?'

'I don't know about superstition,' said the Colonel. 'They believe in it all over Denmark and Norway, as well as on the Yorkshire coast; and my experience is, mind you, that there's generally something at the bottom of what these country-folk hold to, and have held to for generations. But it's your drive' (or whatever it might have been: the golfing reader will have to imagine appropriate digressions at the proper intervals).

When conversation was resumed, Parkins said, with a slight hesitancy:

'Apropos of what you were saying just now, Colonel, I think I ought to tell you that my own views on such subjects are very strong. I am, in fact, a convinced disbeliever in what is called the "supernatural".'

'What!' said the Colonel, 'do you mean to tell me you don't believe in second-sight, or ghosts, or anything of that kind?'

'In nothing whatever of that kind,' returned Parkins firmly.

'Well,' said the Colonel, 'but it appears to me at that rate, sir, that you must be little better than a Sadducee.'

Parkins was on the point of answering that, in his opinion, the Sadducees were the most sensible persons he had ever read of in the Old Testament; but, feeling some doubt as to whether much mention of them was to be found in that work, he preferred to laugh the accusation off.

'Perhaps I am,' he said; 'but – Here, give me my cleek, boy! – Excuse me one moment, Colonel.' A short interval. 'Now, as to whistling for the wind, let me give you my theory about it. The laws which govern winds are really not at all perfectly known – to fisher-folk and such, of course, not known at all. A man or woman of eccentric habits, perhaps, or a stranger, is seen repeatedly on the beach at some unusual hour, and is heard whistling. Soon afterwards a violent wind rises; a man who could read the sky perfectly or who possessed a barometer could have foretold that it would. The simple people of a fishing-village have no barometers, and only a few rough rules for prophesying weather. What more natural than that the eccentric personage I postulated should be regarded as having raised the wind, or that he or she should clutch eagerly at the reputation of being able to do so? Now, take last night's wind: as it happens, I myself was whistling. I blew a whistle twice, and the wind seemed to come absolutely in answer to my call. If anyone had seen me—'

The audience had been a little restive under this harangue, and Parkins had, I fear, fallen somewhat into the tone of a lecturer; but at the last sentence the Colonel stopped.

'Whistling, were you?' he said. 'And what sort of whistle did you use? Play this stroke first.' Interval.

'About that whistle you were asking, Colonel. It's rather a curious one. I have it in my – No; I see I've left it in my room. As a matter of fact, I found it yesterday.'

And then Parkins narrated the manner of his discovery of the whistle, upon hearing which the Colonel grunted, and opined that, in Parkins's place, he should himself be careful about using a thing that had belonged to a set of Papists, of whom, speaking generally, it might be affirmed that you never knew what they might not have been up to. From this topic he diverged to the enormities of the Vicar, who had given notice on the previous Sunday that Friday would be the Feast of St Thomas the Apostle, and that there would be service at eleven o'clock in the church. This and other similar proceedings constituted in the Colonel's view a strong presumption that the Vicar was a concealed Papist, if not a Jesuit; and Parkins, who could not very readily follow the Colonel in this region, did not disagree with him. In fact, they got on so well together in the morning that there was no talk on either side of their separating after lunch.

Both continued to play well during the afternoon, or, at least, well enough to make them forget everything else until the light began to fail them. Not until then did Parkins remember that he had meant to do some more investigating at the preceptory; but it was of no great importance, he reflected. One day was as good as another; he might as well go home with the Colonel.

As they turned the corner of the house, the Colonel was almost knocked down by a boy who rushed into him at the very top of his speed, and then, instead of running away, remained hanging on to him and panting. The first words of the warrior were naturally those of reproof and objurgation, but he very quickly discerned that the boy was almost speechless with fright. Inquiries were useless at first. When the boy got his breath he began to howl, and still clung to the Colonel's legs. He was at last detached, but continued to howl.

'What in the world is the matter with you? What have you been up to? What have you seen?' said the two men.

'Ow, I seen it wive at me out of the winder,' wailed the boy, 'and I don't like it.'

'What window?' said the irritated Colonel. 'Come, pull yourself together, my boy.'

'The front winder it was, at the 'otel,' said the boy.

At this point Parkins was in favour of sending the boy home, but the Colonel refused; he wanted to get to the bottom of it, he said; it was most dangerous to give a boy such a fright as this one had had, and if it turned out that people had been playing jokes, they should suffer for it in some way. And by a series of questions he made out this story: The boy had been playing about on the grass in front of the Globe with some others; then they had gone home to their teas, and he was just going, when he happened to look up at the front winder and see it a-wiving at him. *It* seemed to be a figure of some sort, in white as far as he knew – couldn't see its face; but it wived at him, and it warn't a right thing – not to say not a right person. Was there a light in the room? No, he didn't think to look if there was a light. Which was the window? Was it the top one or the second one? The seckind one it was – the big winder what got two little uns at the sides.

'Very well, my boy,' said the Colonel, after a few more questions. 'You run away home now. I expect it was some person trying to give you a start. Another time, like a brave English boy, you just throw a stone – well, no, not that exactly, but you go and speak to the waiter, or to Mr Simpson, the landlord, and – yes – and say that I advised you to do so.'

The boy's face expressed some of the doubt he felt as to the likelihood of Mr Simpson's lending a favourable ear to his complaint, but the Colonel did not appear to perceive this, and went on:

'And here's a sixpence – no, I see it's a shilling – and you be off home, and don't think any more about it.'

The youth hurried off with agitated thanks, and the Colonel and Parkins went round to the front of the Globe and reconnoitred. There was only one window answering to the description they had been hearing.

'Well, that's curious,' said Parkins; 'it's evidently my window the lad was talking about. Will you come up for a moment, Colonel Wilson? We ought to be able to see if anyone has been taking liberties in my room.'

They were soon in the passage and made as if to open the door. Then he stopped and felt in his pockets.

'This is more serious than I thought,' was his next remark. 'I remember now that before I started this morning I locked the door. It is locked now, and, what is more, here is the key.' And he held it up. 'Now,' he went on, 'if the servants are in the habit of going into one's room during the day when one is away, I can only say that – well, that I don't approve of it at all.' Conscious of a somewhat weak climax, he busied himself in opening the door (which was indeed locked) and in lighting candles. 'No,' he said, 'nothing seems disturbed.'

'Except your bed,' put in the Colonel.

'Excuse me, that isn't my bed,' said Parkins. 'I don't use that one. But it does look as if someone had been playing tricks with it.'

It certainly did: the clothes were bundled up and twisted together in a most tortuous confusion. Parkins pondered.

'That must be it,' he said at last: 'I disordered the clothes last night in unpacking, and they haven't made it since. Perhaps they came in to make it, and that boy saw them through the window and then they were called away and locked the door after them. Yes, I think that must be it.'

'Well, ring and ask,' said the Colonel, and this appealed to Parkins as practical.

The maid appeared, and, to make a long story short, deposed that she had made the bed in the morning when the gentleman was in the room, and hadn't been there since. No, she hadn't no other key. Mr Simpson he kep' the keys; he'd be able to tell the gentleman if anyone had been up.

This was a puzzle. Investigation showed that nothing of value had been taken, and Parkins remembered the disposition of the small objects on tables and so forth well enough to be pretty sure that no pranks had been played with them. Mr and Mrs Simpson furthermore agreed that neither of them had given the duplicate key of the room to any person whatever during the day. Nor could Parkins, fair-minded man as he was, detect anything in the demeanour of master, mistress, or maid that indicated guilt. He was much more inclined to think that the boy had been imposing on the Colonel.

The latter was unwontedly silent and pensive at dinner and throughout the evening. When he bade good-night to Parkins, he murmured in a gruff undertone:

'You know where I am if you want me during the night.'

'Why, yes, thank you, Colonel Wilson, I think I do; but there isn't much prospect of my disturbing you, I hope. By the way,' he added, 'did I show you that old whistle I spoke of? I think not. Well, here it is.'

The Colonel turned it over gingerly in the light of the candle.

'Can you make anything of the inscription?' asked Parkins, as he took it back.

'No, not in this light. What do you mean to do with it?'

'Oh, well, when I get back to Cambridge I shall submit it to some of the archaeologists there, and see what they think of it; and very likely, if they consider it worth having, I may present it to one of the museums.'

''M!' said the Colonel 'Well, you may be right. All I know is that, if it were mine, I should chuck it straight into the sea. It's no use talking, I'm well aware, but I expect that with you it's a case of live and learn. I hope so, I'm sure, and I wish you a good night.'

He turned away, leaving Parkins in act to speak at the bottom of the stair, and soon each was in his own bedroom.

By some unfortunate accident, there were neither blinds nor curtains to the windows of the Professor's room. The previous night he had thought little of this, but tonight there seemed every prospect of a bright moon rising to shine directly on his bed, and probably wake him later on. When he noticed this he was a good deal annoyed, but, with an ingenuity which I can only envy, he succeeded in rigging up, with the help of a railway-rug, some safety-pins, and a stick and umbrella, a screen which, if it only held together, would completely keep the moonlight off his bed. And shortly afterwards he was comfortably in that bed. When he had read a somewhat solid work long enough to produce a decided wish for sleep, he cast a drowsy glance round the room, blew out the candle, and fell back upon the pillow.

He must have slept soundly for an hour or more, when a sudden clatter shook him up in a most unwelcome manner. In a moment he realized what had happened: his carefully constructed screen had given way, and a very bright frosty moon was shining directly on his face. This was highly annoying. Could he possibly get up and reconstruct the screen? or could he manage to sleep if he did not?

For some minutes he lay and pondered over the possibilities; then he turned over sharply, and with all his eyes open lay breathlessly listening. There had been a movement, he was sure, in the empty bed on the opposite side of the room. Tomorrow he would have it moved, for there must be rats or something playing about in it. It was quiet now. No! the commotion began again. There was a rustling and shaking: surely more than any rat could cause

I can figure to myself something of the Professor's bewilderment and horror, for I have in a dream thirty years back seen the same thing happen; but the reader will hardly, perhaps, imagine how dreadful it was to him to see a figure suddenly sit up in what he had known was an empty bed. He was out of his own bed in one bound, and made a dash towards the window, where lay his only weapon, the stick with which he had propped his screen. This was, as it turned out, the worst thing he could have done, because the personage in the empty bed, with a sudden smooth motion, slipped from the bed and took up a position, with outspread arms, between the two beds, and in front of the door. Parkins watched it in a horrid perplexity. Somehow, the idea of getting past it and escaping through the door was intolerable to him; he could not have borne – he didn't know why – to touch it; and as for its touching him, he would sooner dash himself through the window than have that happen. It stood for the moment in a band of dark shadow, and he had not seen what its face was like. Now it began to move, in a stooping posture, and all at once the spectator realized, with some horror and some relief, that it must be blind, for it seemed to feel about it with its muffled arms in a groping and random fashion. Turning half away from him, it became suddenly conscious of the bed he had just left, and darted towards it, and bent and felt over the pillows in a way which made Parkins shudder as he had never in his life thought it possible. In a very few moments it seemed to know that the bed was empty, and then, moving forward into the area of light and facing the window, it showed for the first time what manner of thing it was.

Parkins, who very much dislikes being questioned about it, did once describe something of it in my hearing, and I gathered that what he chiefly remembers about it is a horrible, an intensely horrible, face *of crumpled linen*.

What expression he read upon it he could not or would not tell, but that the fear of it went nigh to maddening him is certain.

But he was not at leisure to watch it for long. With formidable quickness it moved into the middle of the room, and, as it groped and waved, one corner of its draperies swept across Parkins's face. He could not, though he knew how perilous a sound was – he could not keep back a cry of disgust, and this gave the searcher an instant clue. It leapt towards him upon the instant, and the next moment he was halfway through the window backwards, uttering cry upon cry at the utmost pitch of his voice, and the linen face was thrust close into his own. At this, almost the last possible second, deliverance came, as you will have guessed: the Colonel burst the door open, and was just in time to see the dreadful group at the window. When he reached the figures only one was left. Parkins sank forward into the room in a faint, and before him on the floor lay a tumbled heap of bedclothes.

Colonel Wilson asked no questions, but busied himself keeping everyone else out of the room and in getting Parkins back to his bed; and himself, wrapped in a rug, occupied the other bed, for the rest of the night. Early on the next day Rogers arrived, more welcome than he would have been a day before, and the three of them held a very long consultation in the Professor's room. At the end of it the Colonel left the hotel door carrying a small object between his finger and thumb, which he cast as far into the sea as a very brawny arm could send it. Later on the smoke of a burning ascended from the back premises of the Globe.

Exactly what explanation was patched up for the staff and visitors at the hotel I must confess I do not recollect. The Professor was somehow cleared of the ready suspicion of delirium tremens, and the hotel of the reputation of a troubled house.

There is not much question as to what would have happened to Parkins if the Colonel had not intervened when he did. He would either have fallen out of the window or else lost his wits. But it is not so evident what more the creature that came in answer to the whistle could have done than frighten. There seemed to be absolutely nothing material about it save the bedclothes of which it had made itself a body. The Colonel, who remembered a not very dissimilar occurrence in India, was of opinion that if Parkins had closed with it it could really have done very little, and that its one power was that of frightening. The whole thing, he said, served to confirm his opinion of the Church of Rome.

There is really nothing more to tell, but, as you may imagine, the Professor's views on certain points are less clear cut than they used to be. His nerves, too, have suffered: he cannot even now see a surplice hanging on a door quite unmoved, and the spectacle of a scarecrow in a field late on a winter afternoon has cost him more than one sleepless night.

The Open Door

Margaret Oliphant

I took the house of Brentwood on my return from India in 18—, for the temporary accommodation of my family, until I could find a permanent home for them. It had many advantages which made it peculiarly appropriate. It was within reach of Edinburgh; and my boy Roland, whose education had been considerably neglected, could ride in and out to school; which was thought to be better for him than either leaving home altogether or staying there always with a tutor. The lad was doubly precious to us, being the only one left to us of many; and he was fragile in body, we believed, and deeply sensitive in mind. The two girls also found at Brentwood everything they wanted. They were near enough to Edinburgh to have masters and lessons as many as they required for completing that never-ending education which the young people seem to require nowadays.

Brentwood stands on that fine and wealthy slope of country – one of the richest in Scotland – which lies between the Pentland Hills and the Firth. In clear weather you could see the blue gleam of the great estuary on one side of you; and on the other the blue heights. Edinburgh – with its two lesser heights, the Castle and the Calton Hill, its spires and towers piercing through the smoke, and Arthur's Seat lying crouched behind, like a guardian no longer very needful, taking his repose beside the well-beloved charge, which is now, so to speak, able to take care of itself without him – lay at our right hand.

The village of Brentwood, with its prosaic houses, lay in a hollow almost under our house. Village architecture does not flourish in Scotland. Still a cluster of houses on different elevations, with scraps of garden coming in between, a hedgerow with clothes laid out to dry, the opening of a street with its rural sociability, the women at their doors, the slow wagon lumbering along, gives a centre to the landscape. In the park which surrounded the house were the ruins of the former mansion of Brentwood, – a much smaller and less important house than the solid Georgian edifice which we inhabited. The ruins were picturesque, however, and gave importance to the place. Even we, who were but temporary tenants, felt a vague pride in them, as if they somehow reflected a certain consequence upon ourselves. The old building had the remains of a tower, – an indistinguishable mass of masonwork, overgrown with ivy; and the shells of the walls attached to this were half filled up with soil. At a little distance were some very commonplace and disjointed fragments of buildings, one of them suggesting a certain pathos by its very commonness and the complete wreck which it showed. This was the end of a low gable, a bit of grey wall, all incrusted with lichens, in which was a common door-way. Probably it had been a servants' entrance, a backdoor, or opening into what are called 'the offices' in Scotland. No offices remained to be entered, – pantry and kitchen had all been swept out of being; but there stood the door-way open and vacant, free to all the winds, to the rabbits, and every wild creature. It struck my eye, the first time I went to Brentwood, like a melancholy comment upon a life that was over. A door that led to nothing, – closed once, perhaps, with anxious care, bolted and guarded, now void of any meaning. It impressed me, I remember, from the first; so perhaps it may be said that my mind was prepared to attach to it an importance which nothing justified.

The summer was a very happy period of repose for us all; and it was when the family had settled down for the winter, when the days were short and dark, and the rigorous reign of frost upon us, that the incidents occurred which alone could justify me in intruding upon the world my private affairs.

I was absent in London when these events began. In London an old Indian plunges back into the interests with which all his previous life has been associated, and meets old friends at every step. I had been circulating among some half-dozen of these and had missed some of my home letters. It is never safe to miss one's letters. In this transitory life, as the Prayer-book says, how can one ever be certain what is going to happen? All was well at home. I knew exactly (I thought) what they would have to say to me: 'The weather has been so fine, that Roland has not once gone by train, and he enjoys the ride beyond anything.' 'Dear papa, be sure that you don't forget anything, but bring us so-and-so, and so-and-so,' – a list as long as my arm. Dear girls and dearer mother! I would not for the world have forgotten their commissions, or lost their little letters!

When I got back to my club, however, three or four letters were lying for me, upon some of which I noticed the 'immediate,' 'urgent,' which old-fashioned people and anxious people still believe will influence the post-office and quicken the speed of the mails. I was about to open one of these, when the club porter brought me two telegrams, one of which, he said, had arrived the night before. I opened, as was to be expected, the last first, and this was what I read: 'Why don't you come or answer? For God's sake, come. He is much worse.' This was a thunderbolt to fall upon a man's head who had one only son, and he the light of his eyes! The other telegram, which I opened with hands trembling so much that I lost time by my haste, was to much the same purpose: 'No better; doctor afraid of brain-fever. Calls for you day and night. Let nothing detain you.' The first thing I did was to look up the timetables to see if there was any way of getting off sooner than by the night-train, though I knew well enough there was not; and then I read the letters, which furnished, alas! too clearly, all the details. They told me that the boy had been pale for some time, with a scared look. His mother had noticed it before I left home, but would not say anything to alarm me. This look had increased day by day; and soon it was observed that Roland came home at a wild gallop through the park, his pony panting and in foam, himself 'as white as a sheet,' but with the perspiration streaming from his forehead. For a long time he had resisted all questioning, but at length had developed such strange changes of mood, showing a reluctance to go to school, a desire to be fetched in the carriage at night, – which was a ridiculous piece of luxury, – an unwillingness to go out into the grounds, and nervous start at every sound, that his mother had insisted upon an explanation. When the boy – our boy Roland, who had never known what fear was – began to talk to her of voices he had heard in the park, and shadows that had appeared to him among the ruins, my wife promptly put him to bed and sent for Dr Simson, which, of course, was the only thing to do.

I hurried off that evening, as may be supposed, with an anxious heart. How I got through the hours before the starting of the train, I cannot tell. We must all be thankful for the quickness of the railway when in anxiety; but to have thrown myself into a post-chaise as soon as horses could be put to, would have been a relief. I got to Edinburgh very early in the blackness of the winter morning, and scarcely dared look the man in the face, at whom I gasped, 'What news?' My wife had sent the brougham for me, which I concluded, before the man spoke, was a bad sign. His answer was that stereotyped answer which leaves the imagination so wildly free, – 'Just the same.' Just the same! What might that mean? The horses seemed to me to creep along the long dark country road. As we dashed through the park, I thought I heard someone moaning among the trees, and clenched my fist at him (whoever he might be) with fury. Why had the fool of a woman at the gate allowed any one to come in to disturb the quiet of the place? If I had not been in such hot haste to get home, I think I should have stopped the carriage and got out to see what tramp it was that had made an entrance, and chosen my grounds, of all places in the world, – when my boy was ill! – to grumble and groan in. But I had no reason to complain of our slow pace here. The horses flew like lightning along the intervening path, and drew up at the door all panting, as if they had run a race. My wife stood waiting to receive me, with a pale face, and a candle in her hand, which made her look paler still as the wind blew the flame about. 'He is sleeping,' she said in a whisper, as if her voice might wake him. And I replied, when I could find my voice, also in a whisper, as though the jingling of the horses' furniture and the sound of their hoofs must not have been more dangerous. I stood on the steps with her a moment, almost afraid to go in, now that I was here; and it seemed to me that I saw without observing, if I may so say, that the horses were unwilling to turn round, though their stables lay that way, or that the men were unwilling. These things occurred to me afterwards, though at the moment I was not capable of anything but to ask questions and to hear of the condition of the boy.

I looked at him from the door of his room, for we were afraid to go near, lest we should disturb that blessed sleep. It looked like actual sleep, not the lethargy into which my wife told me he would sometimes fall. She told me everything in the next room, which communicated with his, rising now and then and going to the door of the communication; and in this there was much that was very startling and confusing to the mind. It appeared that ever since the winter began – since it was early dark, and night had fallen before his return from school – he had been hearing voices among the ruins; at first only a groaning, he said, at which his pony was as much alarmed as he was, but by degrees a voice. The tears ran down my wife's cheeks as she described to me how he would start up in the night and cry out. 'Oh, mother, let me in! oh, mother, let me in!' with a pathos which rent her heart. And she sitting there all the time, only longing to do everything his heart could desire! But though she would try to soothe him, crying, 'You are at home, my darling. I am here. Don't you know me? Your mother is here!' he would only stare at her, and after a while spring up again with the same cry. At other times he would be quite reasonable, she said, asking eagerly when I was coming, but declaring that he must go with me as soon as I did so, 'to let them in.' 'The doctor thinks his nervous system must have received a shock,' my wife said. 'Oh, Henry, can it be that we have pushed him on too much with his work—a delicate boy like Roland? And what is his work in comparison with his health? Even you would think little of honours or prizes if it hurt the boy's health.' Even I! – as if I were an inhuman father sacrificing my child to my ambition. But I would not increase her trouble by taking any notice.

There was just daylight enough to see his face when I went to him; and what a change in a fortnight! He was paler and more worn, I thought, than even in those dreadful days in the plains before we left India. His hair seemed to me to have grown long and lank; his eyes were like blazing lights projecting out of his white face. He got hold of my hand in a cold and tremulous clutch, and waved to everybody to go away. 'Go away—even mother,' he said; 'go away.' This went to her heart; for she did not like that even I should have more of the boy's confidence than herself; but my wife has never been a woman to think of herself, and she left us alone. 'Are they all gone?' he said eagerly. 'They would not let me speak. The doctor treated me as if I were a fool. You know I am not a fool, papa.'

'Yes, yes, my boy, I know. But you are ill, and quiet is so necessary. You are not only not a fool, Roland, but you are reasonable and understand. When you are ill you must deny yourself; you must not do everything that you might do being well.'

He waved his thin hand with a sort of indignation. 'Then, father, I am not ill,' he cried. 'Oh, I thought when you came you would not stop me, – you would see the sense of it! What do you think is the matter with me, all of you? Simson is well enough; but he is only a doctor. What do you think is the matter with me? I am no more ill than you are. A doctor, of course, he thinks you are ill the moment he looks at you – that's what he's there for – and claps you into bed.'

'Which is the best place for you at present, my dear boy.'

'I made up my mind,' cried the little fellow, 'that I would stand it till you came home. I said to myself, I won't frighten mother and the girls. But now, father,' he cried, half jumping out of bed, 'it's not illness: it's a secret.'

His eyes shone so wildly, his face was so swept with strong feeling, that my heart sank within me. It could be nothing but fever that did it, and fever had been so fatal. I got him into my arms to put him back into bed. 'Roland,' I said, humouring the poor child, which I knew was the only way, 'if you are going to tell me this secret to do any good, you know you must be quite quiet, and not excite yourself. If you excite yourself, I must not let you speak.'

'Yes, father,' said the boy. He was quiet directly, like a man, as if he quite understood. When I had laid him back on his pillow, he looked up at me with that grateful, sweet look with which children, when they are ill, break one's heart, the water coming into his eyes in his weakness. 'I was sure as soon as you were here you would know what to do,' he said.

'To be sure, my boy. Now keep quiet, and tell it all out like a man.' To think I was telling lies to my own child! for I did it only to humour him, thinking, poor little fellow, his brain was wrong.

'Yes, father. Father, there is someone in the park, – someone that has been badly used.'

'Hush, my dear; you remember there is to be no excitement. Well, who is this somebody, and who has been ill-using him? We will soon put a stop to that.'

'Ah,' cried Roland, 'but it is not so easy as you think. I don't know who it is. It is just a cry. Oh, if you could hear it! It gets into my head in my sleep. I heard it as clear – as clear; and they think that I am dreaming, or raving perhaps,' the boy said, with a sort of disdainful smile.

This look of his perplexed me; it was less like fever than I thought. 'Are you quite sure you have not dreamed it, Roland?' I said.

'Dreamed? – that!' He was springing up again when he suddenly bethought himself, and lay down flat, with the same sort of smile on his face. 'The pony heard it, too,' he said. 'She jumped as if she had been shot. If I had not grasped at the reins – for I was frightened, father—'

'No shame to you, my boy,' said I, though I scarcely knew why.

'If I hadn't held to her like a leech, she'd have pitched me over her head, and never drew breath till we were at the door. Did the pony dream it?' he said, with a soft disdain, yet indulgence for my foolishness. Then he added slowly, 'It was only a cry the first time, and all the time before you went away. I wouldn't tell you, for it was so wretched to be frightened. I thought it might be a hare or a rabbit snared, and I went in the morning and looked; but there was nothing. It was after you went I heard it really first; and this is what he says.' He raised himself on his elbow close to me, and looked me in the face: 'Oh, mother, let me in! oh, mother, let me in!' As he said the words a mist came over his face, the mouth quivered, the soft features all melted and changed, and when he had ended these pitiful words, dissolved in a shower of heavy tears.

Was it a hallucination? Was it the fever of the brain? Was it the disordered fancy caused by great bodily weakness? How could I tell? I thought it wisest to accept it as if it were all true.

'This is very touching, Roland,' I said.

'Oh, if you had just heard it, father! I said to myself, if father heard it he would do something; but mamma, you know, she's given over to Simson, and that fellow's a doctor, and never thinks of anything but clapping you into bed.'

'We must not blame Simson for being a doctor, Roland.'

'No, no,' said my boy, with delightful toleration and indulgence; 'oh, no: that's the good of him; that's what he's for; I know that. But you – you are different; you are just father; and you'll do something – directly, papa, directly; this very night.'

'Surely,' I said. 'No doubt it is some little lost child.'

He gave me a sudden, swift look, investigating my face as though to see whether, after all, this was everything my eminence as 'father' came to, – no more than that. Then he got hold of my shoulder, clutching it with his thin hand: 'Look here,' he said, with a quiver in his voice: 'suppose it wasn't – living at all!'

'My dear boy, how then could you have heard it?' I said.

He turned away from me with a pettish exclamation, – 'As if you didn't know better than that!'

'Do you want to tell me it is a ghost?' I said.

Roland withdrew his hand; his countenance assumed an aspect of great dignity and gravity; a slight quiver remained about his lips. 'Whatever it was—you always said we were not to call names. It was something – in trouble. Oh, father, in terrible trouble!'

'But, my boy,' I said (I was at my wits' end), 'if it was a child that was lost, or any poor human creature – but, Roland, what do you want me to do?'

'I should know if I was you,' said the child eagerly. 'That is what I always said to myself, – Father will know. Oh, papa, papa, to have to face it night after night, in such terrible, terrible trouble, and never to be able to do it any good! I don't want to cry; it's like a baby, I know; but what can I do else? Out there all by itself in the ruin, and nobody to help it! I can't bear it!' cried my generous boy. And in his weakness he burst out, after many attempts to restrain it, into a great childish fit of sobbing and tears.

I do not know that I was ever in a greater perplexity in my life; and afterwards, when I thought of it, there was something comic in it too. It is bad enough to find your child's mind possessed with the conviction that he had seen, or heard, a ghost; but that he should require you to go instantly and help that ghost was the most bewildering experience that had ever come my way. I did my best to console my boy without giving any promise of this astonishing kind; but he was too sharp for me; he would have none of my caresses. With sobs breaking in at intervals upon his voice, and the rain-drops hanging on his eyelids, he yet returned to the charge.

'It will be there now!—it will be there all the night! Oh, think, papa, – think if it was me! I can't rest for thinking of it. Don't!' he cried, putting away my hand, – 'don't! You go and help it, and mother can take care of me.'

'But, Roland, what can I do?'

My boy opened his eyes, which were large with weakness and fever, and gave me a smile such, I think, as sick children only know the secret of. 'I was sure you would know as soon as you came. I always said, 'Father will know.' And mother,' he cried, with a softening of repose upon his face, his limbs relaxing, his form sinking with a luxurious ease in his bed, – 'mother can come and take care of me.'

I called her, and saw him turn to her with the complete dependence of a child; and then I went away and left them, as perplexed a man as any in Scotland. I must say, however, I had this consolation, that my mind was greatly eased about Roland. He might be under a hallucination; but his head was clear enough, and I did not think him so ill as everybody else did. The girls were astonished even at the ease with which I took it. 'How do you think he is?' they said in a breath, coming round me, laying hold of me. 'Not half so ill as I expected,' I said; 'not very bad at all.' 'Oh, papa, you are a darling!' cried Agatha, kissing me, and crying upon my shoulder; while little Jeanie, who was as pale as Roland, clasped both her arms round mine, and could not speak at all. I knew nothing about it, not half so much as Simson; but they believed in me: they had a feeling that all would go right now. God is very good to you when your children look to you like that. It makes one humble, not proud. I was not worthy of it; and then I recollected that I had to act the part of a father to Roland's ghost, – which made me almost laugh, though I might just as well have cried. It was the strangest mission that ever was intrusted to mortal man.

It was then I remembered suddenly the looks of the men when they turned to take the brougham to the stables in the dark that morning. They had not liked it, and the horses had not liked it. I remembered that even in my anxiety about Roland I had heard them tearing along the avenue back to the stables, and had made a memorandum mentally that I must speak of it. It seemed to me that the best thing I could do was to go to the stables now and make a few inquiries. The coachman was the head of this little colony, and it was to his house I went to pursue my investigations. He was a native of the district, and had taken care of the place in the absence of the family for years; it was impossible but that he must know everything that was going on, and all the traditions of the place. The men, I could see, eyed me anxiously when I thus appeared at such an hour among them, and followed me with their eyes to Jarvis's house, where he lived alone with his old wife, their children being all married and out in the world. Mrs Jarvis met me with anxious questions. How was the poor young gentleman? But the others knew, I could see by their faces, that not even this was the foremost thing in my mind.

After a while I elicited without much difficulty the whole story. In the opinion of the Jarvises, and of everybody about, the certainty that the place was haunted was beyond all doubt. As Sandy and his wife warmed to the tale, one tripping up another in their eagerness to tell everything, it gradually developed as distinct a superstition as I ever heard, and not without poetry and pathos. How long it was since the voice had been heard first, nobody could tell with certainty. Jarvis's opinion was that his father, who had been coachman at Brentwood before him, had never heard anything about it, and that the whole thing had arisen within the last ten years, since the complete dismantling of the old house; which was a wonderfully modern date for a tale so well authenticated. According to these witnesses, and to several whom I questioned afterwards, and who were all in perfect agreement, it was only in the months of November and December that 'the visitation' occurred. During these months, the darkest of the year, scarcely a night passed without the recurrence of these inexplicable cries. Nothing, it was said, had ever been seen, – at least, nothing that could be identified. Some people, bolder or more imaginative than the others, had seen the darkness moving, Mrs Jarvis said, with unconscious poetry. It began when night fell, and continued at intervals till day broke. Very often it was only an inarticulate cry and moaning, but sometimes the words which had taken possession of my poor boy's fancy had been distinctly audible, – 'Oh, mother, let me in!' The Jarvises were not aware that there had ever been any investigation into it. The estate of Brentwood had lapsed into the hands of a distant branch of the family, who had lived but little there; and of the many people who had taken it, as I had done, few had remained through two Decembers. And nobody had taken the trouble to make a very close examination into the facts. 'No, no,' Jarvis said, shaking his head, 'No, no, Cornel. Wha wad set themsels up for a laughin'-stock to a' the country-side, making a wark about a ghost? Naebody believes in ghosts. It bid to be the wind in the trees, the last gentleman said, or some effec' o' the water wrastlin' among the rocks. He said it was a' quite easy explained; but he gave up the hoose. And when you cam, Cornel, we were awfu' anxious you should never hear. What for should I have spoiled the bargain and hairmed the property for no-thing?'

'Do you call my child's life nothing?' I said in the trouble of the moment, unable to restrain myself. 'And instead of telling this all to me, you have told it to him, – to a delicate boy, a child unable to sift evidence or judge for himself, a tender-hearted young creature—'

I was walking about the room with an anger all the hotter that I felt it to be most likely quite unjust. My heart was full of bitterness against the stolid retainers of a family who were content to risk other people's children and comfort rather than let a house lie empty. If I had been warned I might have taken precautions, or left the place, or sent Roland away, a hundred things which now I could not do; and here I was with my boy in a brain-fever, and his life, the most precious life on earth, hanging in the balance, dependent on whether or not I could get to the reason of a commonplace ghost story!

'Cornel,' said Jarvis solemnly, 'and *she'll* bear me witness, – the young gentleman never heard a word from me – no, nor from either groom or gardner; I'll gie ye my word for that. In the first place, he's no a lad that invites ye to talk. There are some that are, and that arena. Some will draw ye on, till ye've tellt them a' the clatter of the toun, and a' ye ken, and whiles mair. But Maister Roland, his mind's fu' of his books. He's aye civil and kind, and a fine lad; but no that sort. And ye see it's for a' our interest, Cornel, that you should stay at Brentwood. I took it upon me mysel to pass the word, – 'No a syllable to Maister Roland, nor to the young leddies – no a syllable.' The women-servants, that have little reason to be out at night, ken little or nothing about it. And some think it grand to have a ghost so long as they're no in the way of coming across it. If you had been tellt the story to begin with, maybe ye would have thought so yourself.'

This was true enough. I should not have been above the idea of a ghost myself! Oh, yes, I claim no exemption. The girls would have been delighted. I could fancy their eagerness, their interest, and excitement. No; if we had been told, it would have done no good, – we should have made the bargain all the more eagerly, the fools that we are.

'Come with me, Jarvis,' I said hastily, 'and we'll make an attempt at least to investigate. Say nothing to the men or to anybody. Be ready for me about ten o'clock.'

'Me, Cornel!' Jarvis said, in a faint voice. I had not been looking at him in my own preoccupation, but when I did so, I found that the greatest change had come over the fat and ruddy coachman. 'Me, Cornel!' he repeated, wiping the perspiration from his brow. 'There's nothin' I wouldna do to pleasure ye, Cornel, but if ye'll reflect that I am no used to my feet. With a horse atween my legs, or the reins in my hand, I'm maybe nae worse than other men; but on fit, Cornel – it's no the – bogles; – but I've been cavalry, ye see,' with a little hoarse laugh, 'a' my life. To face a thing ye dinna understan' – on your feet, Cornel.'

'He believes in it, Cornel, and you dinna believe in it,' the woman said.

'Will you come with me?' I said, turning to her.

She jumped back, upsetting her chair in her bewilderment. 'Me!' with a scream, and then fell into a sort of hysterical laugh. 'I wouldna say but what I would go; but what would the folk say to hear of Cornel Mortimer with an auld silly woman at his heels?'

The suggestion made me laugh too, though I had little inclination for it. 'I'm sorry you have so little spirit, Jarvis,' I said. 'I must find someone else, I suppose.'

Jarvis, touched by this, began to remonstrate, but I cut him short. My butler was a soldier who had been with me in India, and was not supposed to fear anything – man or devil – certainly not the former; and I felt that I was losing time. The Jarvises were too thankful to get rid of me. They attended me to the door with the most anxious courtesies. Outside, the two grooms stood close by, a little confused by my sudden exit. I don't know if perhaps they had been listening – at least standing as near as possible, to catch any scrap of the conversation. I waved my hand to them as I went past, in answer to their salutations, and it was very apparent to me that they also were glad to see me go.

And it will be thought very strange, but it would be weak not to add, that I myself, though bent on the investigation I have spoken of, pledged to Roland to carry it out, and feeling that my boy's health, perhaps his life, depended on the result of my inquiry, – I felt the most unaccountable reluctance, now that it was dark, to pass the ruins on my way home. My curiosity was intense; and yet it was all my mind could do to pull my body along. I dare say the scientific people would describe it the other way, and attribute my cowardice to the state of my stomach. I went on; but if I had followed my impulse, I should have turned and bolted. Everything in me seemed to cry out against it; my heart thumped, my pulses all began, like sledge-hammers, beating against my ears and every sensitive part. It was very dark, as I have said; the old house, with its shapeless tower, loomed a heavy mass through the darkness, which was only not entirely so solid as itself. On the other hand, the great dark cedars of which we were so proud seemed to fill up the night. My foot strayed out of the path in my confusion and the gloom together, and I brought myself up with a cry as I felt myself knocked against something solid. What was it? The contact with hard stone and lime and prickly bramble-bushes restored me a little to myself. 'Oh, it's only the old gable,' I said aloud, with a little laugh to reassure myself. The rough feeling of the stones reconciled me. As I groped about thus, I shook off my visionary folly. What so easily explained as that I should have strayed from the path in the darkness? This brought me back to common existence, as if I had been shaken by a wise hand out of all the silliness of superstition. How silly it was, after all! What did it matter which path I took? I laughed again, this time with better heart, when suddenly, in a moment, the blood was chilled in my veins, a shiver stole along my spine, my faculties seemed to forsake me. Close by me, at my side, at my feet, there was a sigh. No, not a groan, not a moaning, not anything so tangible, – a perfectly soft, faint, inarticulate sigh. I sprang back, and my heart stopped beating. Mistaken! no, mistake was impossible. I heard it as clearly as I hear myself speak; a long, soft, weary sigh, as if drawn to the utmost, and emptying out a load of sadness that filled the breast. To hear this in the solitude, in the dark, in the night (though it was still early), had an effect which I cannot describe. I feel it now, – something cold creeping over me up into my hair, and down to my feet, which refused to move. I cried out, with a trembling voice, 'Who is there?' as I had done before; but there was no reply.

I got home I don't quite know how; but in my mind there was no longer any indifference as to the thing, whatever it was, that haunted these ruins.

My scepticism disappeared like a mist. I was as firmly determined that there was something as Roland was. I did not for a moment pretend to myself that it was possible I could be deceived; there were movements and noises which I understood all about, – cracklings of small branches in the frost, and little rolls of gravel on the path, such as have a very eerie sound sometimes, and perplex you with wonder as to who has done it, *when there is no real mystery*; but I assure you all these little movements of nature don't affect you one bit *when there is something*. I understood *them*. I did not understand the sigh. That was not simple nature; there was meaning in it, feeling, the soul of a creature invisible. This is the thing that human nature trembles at, – a creature invisible, yet with sensations, feelings, a power somehow of expressing itself. Bagley was in the hall as usual when I went in. He was always there in the afternoon, always with the appearance of perfect occupation, yet, so far as I know, never doing anything. The door was open, so that I hurried in without any pause, breathless; but the sight of his calm regard, as he came to help me off with my overcoat, subdued me in a moment. Anything out of the way, anything incomprehensible, faded to nothing in the presence of Bagley. You saw and wondered how *he* was made: the parting of his hair, the tie of his white neckcloth, the fit of his trousers, all perfect as works of art: but you could see how they were done, which makes all the difference. I flung myself upon him, so to speak, without waiting to note the extreme unlikeness of the man to anything of the kind I meant. 'Bagley,' I said, 'I want you to come out with me tonight to watch for—'

'Poachers, Colonel?' he said, a gleam of pleasure running all over him.

'No, Bagley; a great deal worse,' I cried.

'Yes, Colonel; at what hour, sir?' the man said; but then I had not told him what it was.

It was ten o'clock when we set out. All was perfectly quiet indoors. My wife was with Roland, who had been quite calm, she said, and who (though, no doubt, the fever must run its course) had been better ever since I came. I told Bagley to put on a thick greatcoat over his evening coat, and did the same myself, with strong boots; for the soil was like a sponge, or worse. Talking to him, I almost forgot what we were going to do. It was darker even than it had been before, and Bagley kept very close to me as we went along. I had a small lantern in my hand, which gave us a partial guidance. We had come to the corner where the path turns. On one side was the bowling-green, which the girls had taken possession of for their croquet-ground,—a wonderful enclosure surrounded by high hedges of holly, three hundred years old and more; on the other, the ruins. Both were black as night; but before we got so far, there was a little opening in which we could just discern the trees and the lighter line of the road. I thought it best to pause there and take breath. 'Bagley,' I said, 'there is something about these ruins I don't understand. It is there I am going. Keep your eyes open and your wits about you. Be ready to pounce upon any stranger you see, – anything, man or woman. Don't hurt, but seize – anything you see.' 'Colonel,' said Bagley, with a little tremor in his breath, 'they do say there's things there – as is neither man nor woman.' There was no time for words. 'Are you game to follow me, my man? that's the question,' I said. Bagley fell in without a word, and saluted. I knew then I had nothing to fear.

We went, so far as I could guess, exactly as I had come, when I heard that sigh. The darkness, however, was so complete that all marks, as of trees or paths, disappeared. One moment we felt our feet on the gravel, another sinking noiselessly into the slippery grass, that was all. I had shut up my lantern, not wishing to scare any one, whoever it might be. Bagley followed, it seemed to me, exactly in my footsteps as I made my way, as I supposed, towards the mass of the ruined house. We seemed to take a long time groping along seeking this; the squash of the wet soil under our feet was the only thing that marked our progress. After a while I stood still to see, or rather feel, where we were. The darkness was very still, but no stiller than is usual in a winter's night. The sounds I have mentioned – the crackling of twigs, the roll of a pebble, the sound of some rustle in the dead leaves, or creeping creature on the grass – were audible when you listened, all mysterious enough when your mind is disengaged, but to me cheering now as signs of the livingness of nature, even in the death of the frost. As we stood still there came up from the trees in the glen the prolonged hoot of an owl. Bagley started with alarm, being in a state of general nervousness, and not knowing what he was afraid of. But to me the sound was encouraging and pleasant, being so comprehensible. 'An owl,' I said, under my breath. 'Y—es, Colonel,' said Bagley, his teeth chattering. We stood still about five minutes, while it broke into the still brooding of the air, the sound widening out in circles, dying upon the darkness. This sound, which is not a cheerful one, made me almost gay. It was natural, and relieved the tension of the mind. I moved on with new courage, my nervous excitement calming down.

When all at once, quite suddenly, close to us, at our feet, there broke out a cry. I made a spring backwards in the first moment of surprise and horror, and in doing so came sharply against the same rough masonry and brambles that had struck me before. This new sound came upwards from the ground, – a low, moaning, wailing voice, full of suffering and pain. The contrast between it and the hoot of the owl was indescribable, – the one with a wholesome wildness and naturalness that hurt nobody; the other, a sound that made one's blood curdle, full of human misery. With a great deal of fumbling, – for in spite of everything I could do to keep up my courage my hands shook, – I managed to remove the slide of my lantern. The light leaped out like something living, and made the place visible in a moment. We were what would have been inside the ruined building had anything remained but the gable-wall which I have described. It was close to us, the vacant doorway in it going out straight into the blackness outside. The light showed the bit of wall, the ivy glistening upon it in clouds of dark green, the bramble-branches waving, and below, the open door, – a door that led to nothing. It was from this the voice came which died out just as the light flashed upon this strange scene. There was a moment's silence, and then it broke forth again. The sound was so near, so penetrating, so pitiful, that, in the nervous start I gave, the light fell out of my hand. As I groped for it in the dark my hand was clutched by Bagley, who, I think, must have dropped upon his knees; but I was too much perturbed myself to think much of this. He clutched at me in the confusion of his terror, forgetting all his usual decorum. 'For God's sake, what is it, sir?' he gasped. If I yielded, there was evidently an end of both of us. 'I can't tell,' I said, 'any more than you; that's what we've got to find out. Up, man, up!' I pulled him to his feet. 'Will you go round and examine the other side, or will you stay here with the lantern?' Bagley gasped at me with a face of horror. 'Can't we stay together, Colonel?' he said; his knees were trembling under him. I pushed him against the corner of the wall, and put the light into his hands. 'Stand fast till I come back; shake yourself together, man; let nothing pass you,' I said. The voice was within two or three feet of us; of that there could be no doubt.

I went myself to the other side of the wall, keeping close to it. The light shook in Bagley's hand, but, tremulous though it was, shone out through the vacant door, one oblong block of light marking all the crumbling corners and hanging masses of foliage. Was that something dark huddled in a heap by the side of it? I pushed forward across the light in the doorway, and fell upon it with my hands; but it was only a juniper-bush growing close against the wall. Meanwhile, the sight of my figure crossing the doorway had brought Bagley's nervous excitement to a height; he flew at me, gripping my shoulder. 'I've got him, Colonel! I've got him!' he cried, with a voice of sudden exultation. He thought it was a man, and was at once relieved. But at the moment the voice burst forth again between us, at our feet, – more close to us than any separate being could be. He dropped off from me, and fell against the wall, his jaw dropping as if he were dying. I suppose, at the same moment, he saw that it was me whom he had clutched. I for my part, had scarcely more command of myself. I snatched the light out of his hand, and flashed it all about me wildly. Nothing, – the juniper-bush which I thought I had never seen before, the heavy growth of the glistening ivy, the brambles waving. It was close to my ears now, crying, crying, pleading as if for life. Either I heard the same words Roland had heard, or else, in my excitement, his imagination got possession of mine. The voice went on, growing into distinct articulation, but wavering about, now from one point, now from another, as if the owner of it were moving slowly back and forward. 'Mother! mother!' and then an outburst of wailing. As my mind steadied, getting accustomed (as one's mind gets accustomed to anything), it seemed to me as if some uneasy, miserable creature was pacing up and down before a closed door. Sometimes – but that must have been excitement – I thought I heard a sound like knocking, and then another burst, 'Oh, mother! mother!' All this close, close to the space where I was standing with my lantern, now before me, now behind me: a creature restless, unhappy, moaning, crying, before the vacant door-way, which no one could either shut or open more.

'Do you hear it, Bagley? do you hear what it is saying?' I cried, stepping in through the doorway. He was lying against the wall, his eyes glazed, half dead with terror. He made a motion of his lips as if to answer me, but no sounds came; then lifted his hand with a curious imperative movement as if ordering me to be silent and listen. And how long I did so I cannot tell. It began to have an interest, an exciting hold upon me, which I could not describe. It seemed to call up visibly a scene any one could understand, – a something shut out, restlessly wandering to and fro; sometimes the voice dropped, as if throwing itself down, sometimes wandered off a few paces, growing sharp and clear. 'Oh, mother, let me in! oh, mother, mother, let me in! oh, let me in.' Every word was clear to me. No wonder the boy had gone wild with pity. I tried to steady my mind upon Roland, upon his conviction that I could do something, but my head swam with the excitement, even when I partially overcame the terror. At last the words died away, and there was a sound of sobs and moaning. I cried out, 'In the name of God who are you?' with a kind of feeling in my mind that to use the name of God was profane, seeing that I did not believe in ghosts or anything supernatural; but I did it all the same, and waited, my heart giving a leap of terror lest there should be a reply. Why this should have been I cannot tell, but I had a feeling that if there was an answer it would be more than I could bear. But there was no answer, the moaning went on, and then, as if it had been real, the voice rose a little higher again, the words recommenced, 'Oh, mother, let me in! oh, mother, let me in!' with an expression that was heartbreaking to hear.

As if it had been real! What do I mean by that? I suppose I got less alarmed as the thing went on. I began to recover the use of my senses, – I seemed to explain it all to myself by saying that this had once happened, that it was a recollection of a real scene. Why there should have seemed something quite satisfactory and composing in this explanation I cannot tell, but so it was. I began to listen almost as if it had been a play, forgetting Bagley, who, I almost think, had fainted, leaning against the wall. I was started out of this strange spectatorship that had fallen upon me by the sudden rush of something which made my heart jump once more, a large black figure in the doorway waving its arms. 'Come in! come in! come in!' it shouted out hoarsely at the top of a deep bass voice, and then poor Bagley fell down senseless across the threshold. He was less sophisticated than I, – he had not been able to bear it any longer. I took him for something supernatural, as he took me, and it was some time before I awoke to the necessities of the moment. I remembered only after, that from the time I began to give my attention to the man, I heard the other voice no more. It was some time before I brought him to. It must have been a strange scene: the lantern making a luminous spot in the darkness, the man's white face lying on the black earth, I over him, doing what I could for him. Probably I should have been thought to be murdering him had any one seen us. When at last I succeeded in pouring a little brandy down his throat, he sat up and looked about him wildly. 'What's up?' he said; then recognizing me, tried to struggle to his feet with a faint 'Beg your pardon, Colonel.' I got him home as best I could, making him lean upon my arm. The great fellow was as weak as a child. Fortunately he did not for some time remember what had happened. From the time Bagley fell the voice had stopped, and all was still.

'You've got an epidemic in your house, Colonel,' Simson said to me next morning. 'What's the meaning of it all? Here's your butler raving about a voice. This will never do, you know; and so far as I can make out, you are in it too.'

'Yes, I am in it, Doctor. I thought I had better speak to you. Of course you are treating Roland all right, but the boy is not raving, he is as sane as you or me. It's all true.'

'As sane as – I – or you. I never thought the boy insane. He's got cerebral excitement, fever. I don't know what you've got. There's something very queer about the look of your eyes.'

'Come,' said I, 'you can't put us all to bed, you know. You had better listen and hear the symptoms in full.'

The Doctor shrugged his shoulders, but he listened to me patiently. He did not believe a word of the story, that was clear; but he heard it all from beginning to end. 'My dear fellow,' he said, 'the boy told me just the same. It's an epidemic. When one person falls a victim to this sort of thing, it's as safe as can be, – there's always two or three.'

'Then how do you account for it?' I said.

'Oh, account for it! – that's a different matter; there's no accounting for the freaks our brains are subject to. If it's delusion, if it's some trick of the echoes or the winds, – some phonetic disturbance or other—'

'Come with me tonight and judge for yourself,' I said.

Upon this he laughed aloud, then said, 'That's not such a bad idea; but it would ruin me forever if it were known that John Simson was ghost-hunting.'

'There it is,' said I; 'you dart down on us who are unlearned with your phonetic disturbances, but you daren't examine what the thing really is for fear of being laughed at. That's science!'

'It's not science, – it's common-sense,' said the Doctor. 'The thing has delusion on the front of it. It is encouraging an unwholesome tendency even to examine. What good could come of it? Even if I am convinced, I shouldn't believe.'

'I should have said so yesterday; and I don't want you to be convinced or to believe,' said I. 'If you prove it to be a delusion, I shall be very much obliged to you for one. Come; somebody must go with me.'

'You are cool,' said the Doctor. 'You've disabled this poor fellow of yours, and made him – on that point – a lunatic for life; and now you want to disable me. But, for once, I'll do it. To save appearance, if you'll give me a bed, I'll come over after my last rounds.'

It was agreed that I should meet him at the gate, and that we should visit the scene of last night's occurrences before we came to the house, so that nobody might be the wiser. It was scarcely possible to hope that the cause of Bagley's sudden illness should not somehow steal into the knowledge of the servants at least, and it was better that all should be done as quietly as possible. The day seemed to me a very long one. I had to spend a certain part of it with Roland, which was a terrible ordeal for me, for what could I say to the boy? The improvement continued, but he was still in a very precarious state, and the trembling vehemence with which he turned to me when his mother left the room filled me with alarm. 'Father?' he said quietly. 'Yes, my boy, I am giving my best attention to it; all is being done that I can do. I have not come to any conclusion – yet. I am neglecting nothing you said,' I cried. What I could not do was to give his active mind any encouragement to dwell upon the mystery. It was a hard predicament, for some satisfaction had to be given him. He looked at me very wistfully, with the great blue eyes which shone so large and brilliant out of his white and worn face. 'You must trust me,' I said. 'Yes, father. Father understands,' he said to himself, as if to soothe some inward doubt. I left him as soon as I could. He was about the most precious thing I had on earth, and his health my first thought; but yet somehow, in the excitement of this other subject, I put that aside, and preferred not to dwell upon Roland, which was the most curious part of it all.

That night at eleven I met Simson at the gate. He had come by train, and I let him in gently myself. I had been so much absorbed in the coming experiment that I passed the ruins in going to meet him, almost without thought, if you can understand that. I had my lantern; and he showed me a coil of taper which he had ready for use. 'There is nothing like light,' he said in his scoffing tone. It was a very still night, scarcely a sound, but not so dark. We could keep the path without difficulty as we went along. As we approached the spot we could hear a low moaning, broken occasionally by a bitter cry. 'Perhaps that is your voice,' said the Doctor; 'I thought it must be something of the kind. That's a poor brute caught in some of these infernal traps of yours; you'll find it among the bushes somewhere.' I said nothing. I felt no particular fear, but a triumphant satisfaction in what was to follow. I led him to the spot where Bagley and I had stood on the previous night. All was silent as a winter night could be, – so silent that we heard far off the sound of the horses in the stables, the shutting of a window at the house. Simson lighted his taper and went peering about, poking into all the corners. We looked like two conspirators lying in wait for some unfortunate traveller; but not a sound broke the quiet. The moaning had stopped before we came up; a star or two shone over us in the sky, looking down as if surprised at our strange proceedings. Dr Simson did nothing but utter subdued laughs under his breath. 'I thought as much,' he said. 'It is just the same with tables and all other kinds of ghostly apparatus; a sceptic's presence stops everything. When I am present nothing ever comes off. How long do you think it will be necessary to stay here? Oh, I don't complain; only when *you* are satisfied I am – quite.'

I will not deny that I was disappointed beyond measure by this result. It made me look like a credulous fool. It gave the Doctor such a pull over me as nothing else could. I should point all his morals for years to come; and his materialism, his scepticism, would be increased beyond endurance. 'It seems, indeed,' I said, 'that there is to be no—' 'Manifestation,' he said, laughing; 'that is what all the mediums say. No manifestations, in consequence of the presence of an unbeliever.' His laugh sounded very uncomfortable to me in the silence; and it was now near midnight. But that laugh seemed the signal; before it died away the moaning we had heard before was resumed. It started from some distance off, and came towards us, nearer and nearer, like someone walking along and moaning to himself. There could be no idea now that it was a hare caught in a trap. The approach was slow, like that of a weak person, with little halts and pauses. We heard it coming along the grass straight towards the vacant doorway. Simson had been a little startled by the first sound. He said hastily, 'That child has no business to be out so late.' But he felt, as well as I, that this was no child's voice. As it came nearer, he grew silent, and, going to the door-way with his taper, stood looking out towards the sound. The taper being unprotected blew about in the night air, though there was scarcely any wind. I threw the light of my lantern steady and white across the same space. It was in a blaze of light in the midst of the blackness. A little icy thrill had gone over me at the first sound, but as it came close, I confess that my only feeling was satisfaction. The scoffer could scoff no more. The light touched his own face, and showed a very perplexed countenance. If he was afraid, he concealed it with great success, but he was perplexed. And then all that had happened on the previous night was enacted once more. It fell strangely upon me with a sense of repetition. Every cry, every sob seemed the same as before. I listened almost without any emotion at all in my own person, thinking of its effect upon Simson. He maintained a very bold front, on the whole. All that coming and going of the voice was, if our ears could be trusted, exactly in front of the vacant, blank doorway, blazing full of light, which caught and shone in the glistening leaves of the great hollies at a little distance. Not a rabbit could have crossed the turf without being seen; but there was nothing. After a time, Simson, with a certain caution and bodily reluctance, as it seemed to me, went out with his roll of taper into this space. His figure showed against the holly in full outline. Just at this moment the voice sank, as was its custom, and seemed to fling itself down at the door. Simson recoiled violently, as if someone had come up against him, then turned, and held his taper low, as if examining something. 'Do you see anybody?' I cried in a whisper, feeling the chill of nervous panic steal over me at this action. 'It's nothing but a – confounded juniper-bush,' he said. This I knew very well to be nonsense, for the juniper-bush was on the other side. He went about after this, round and round, poking his taper everywhere, then returned to me on the inner side of the wall. He scoffed no longer; his face was contracted and pale. 'How long does this go on?' he whispered to me, like a man who does not wish to interrupt someone who is speaking. I had become too much perturbed myself to remark whether the successions and changes of the voice were the same as last night. It suddenly went out in the air almost as he was speaking, with a soft reiterated sob dying away. If there had been anything to be seen, I should have said that the person was at that moment crouching on the ground close to that door.

We walked home very silent afterwards. It was only when we were in sight of the house that I said, 'What do you think of it?' 'I can't tell what to think of it,' he said quickly. He took – though he was a very temperate man – not the claret I was going to offer him, but some brandy from the tray, and swallowed it almost undiluted. 'Mind you, I don't believe a word of it,' he said, when he had lighted his candle; 'but I can't tell what to think,' he turned round to add, when he was half-way upstairs.

All of this, however, did me no good with the solution of my problem. I was to help this weeping, sobbing thing, which was already to me as distinct a personality as anything I knew; or what should I say to Roland? It was on my heart that my boy would die if I could not find some way of helping this creature. You may be surprised that I should speak of it in this way. I did not know if it was man or woman; but I no more doubted that it was a soul in pain than I doubted my own being; and it was my business to soothe this pain, – to deliver it, if that was possible. Was ever such a task given to an anxious father trembling for his only boy? I felt in my heart, fantastic as it may appear, that I must fulfil this somehow, or part with my child; and you may conceive that rather than do that I was ready to die. But even my dying would not have advanced me, unless by bringing me into the same world with that seeker at the door.

Next morning Simson was out before breakfast, and came in with evident signs of the damp grass on his boots, and a look of worry and weariness, which did not say much for the night he had passed. He improved a little after breakfast, and visited his two patients, – for Bagley was still an invalid. I went out with him on his way to the train, to hear what he had to say about the boy. 'He is going on very well,' he said; 'there are no complications as yet. But mind you, that's not a boy to be trifled with, Mortimer. Not a word to him about last night.' I had to tell him then of my last interview with Roland, and of the impossible demand he had made upon me, by which, though he tried to laugh, he was much discomposed, as I could see.

'We must just perjure ourselves all round,' he said, 'and swear you exorcised it'; but the man was too kind-hearted to be satisfied with that. 'It's frightfully serious for you, Mortimer. I can't laugh as I should like to. I wish I saw a way out of it, for your sake. By the way,' he added shortly, 'didn't you notice that juniper-bush on the left-hand side?' 'There was one on the right hand of the door. I noticed you made that mistake last night.' 'Mistake!' he cried, with a curious low laugh, pulling up the collar of his coat as though he felt the cold, – 'there's no juniper there this morning, left or right. Just go and see.' As he stepped into the train a few minutes after, he looked back upon me and beckoned me for a parting word. 'I'm coming back tonight,' he said.

I don't think I had any feeling about this as I turned away from that common bustle of the railway which made my private preoccupations feel so strangely out of date. There had been a distinct satisfaction in my mind before, that his scepticism had been so entirely defeated. But the more serious part of the matter pressed upon me now. I went straight from the railway to the manse, which stood on a little plateau on the side of the river opposite to the woods of Brentwood. The minister was one of a class which is not so common in Scotland as it used to be. He was a man of good family, well educated in the Scotch way, strong in philosophy, not so strong in Greek, strongest of all in experience, – a man who had 'come across,' in the course of his life, most people of note that had ever been in Scotland, and who was said to be very sound in doctrine, without infringing the toleration with which old men, who are good men, are generally endowed. He was old-fashioned; perhaps he did not think so much about the troublous problems of theology as many of the young men, nor ask himself any hard questions about the Confession of Faith; but he understood human nature, which is perhaps better. He received me with a cordial welcome. 'Come away, Colonel Mortimer,' he said; 'I'm all the more glad to see you, that I feel it's a good sign for the boy. He's doing well? – God be praised, – and the Lord bless him and keep him. He has many a poor body's prayers, and that can do nobody harm.'

'He will need them all, Dr Moncrieff,' I said, 'and your counsel, too.' And I told him the story, – more than I had told Simson. The old clergyman listened to me with many suppressed exclamations, and at the end the water stood in his eyes.

'That's just beautiful,' he said. 'I do not mind to have heard anything like it; it's as fine as Burns when he wished deliverance to one—that is prayed for in no kirk. Ay, ay! so he would have you console the poor lost spirit? God bless the boy! There's something more than common in that, Colonel Mortimer. And also the faith of him in his father!—I would like to put that into a sermon.' Then the old gentleman gave me an alarmed look, and said, 'No, no; I was not meaning a sermon; but I must write it down for the 'Children's Record." I saw the thought that passed through his mind. Either he thought, or he feared I would think, of a funeral sermon. You may believe this did not make me more cheerful.

I can scarcely say that Dr Moncrieff gave me any advice. How could any one advise on such a subject? But he said, 'I think I'll come too. I'm an old man; I'm less liable to be frightened than those that are further off the world unseen. It behooves me to think of my own journey there. I've no cut-and-dry beliefs on the subject. I'll come too; and maybe at the moment the Lord will put into our heads what to do.'

This gave me a little comfort, – more than Simson had given me. To be clear about the cause of it was not my grand desire. It was another thing that was in my mind, – my boy. As for the poor soul at the open door, I had no more doubt, as I have said, of its existence than I had of my own. It was no ghost to me. I knew the creature, and it was in trouble. That was my feeling about it, as it was Roland's. To hear it first was a great shock to my nerves, but not now; a man will get accustomed to anything. But to do something for it was the great problem; how was I to be serviceable to a being that was invisible, that was mortal no longer? 'Maybe at the moment the Lord will put it into our heads.' This is very old-fashioned phraseology, and a week before, most likely, I should have smiled (though always with kindness) at Dr Moncrieff's credulity; but there was a great comfort, whether rational or otherwise I cannot say, in the mere sound of the words.

The road to the station and the village lay through the glen, not by the ruins; but though the sunshine and the fresh air, and the beauty of the trees, and the sound of the water were all very soothing to the spirits, my mind was so full of my own subject that I could not refrain from turning to the right hand as I got to the top of the glen, and going straight to the place which I may call the scene of all my thoughts. It was lying full in the sunshine, like all the rest of the world. The ruined gable looked due east, and in the present aspect of the sun the light streamed down through the doorway as our lantern had done, throwing a flood of light upon the damp grass beyond. There was a strange suggestion in the open door, – so futile, a kind of emblem of vanity: all free around, so that you could go where you pleased, and yet that semblance of an enclosure, – that way of entrance, unnecessary, leading to nothing. And why any creature should pray and weep to get in – to nothing, or be kept out – by nothing! You could not dwell upon it, or it made your brain go round. I remembered, however, what Simson said about the juniper, with a little smile on my own mind as to the inaccuracy of recollection which even a scientific man will be guilty of. I could see now the light of my lantern gleaming upon the wet glistening surface of the spiky leaves at the right hand, – and he ready to go to the stake for it that it was the left! I went round to make sure. And then I saw what he had said. Right or left there was no juniper at all! I was confounded by this, though it was entirely a matter of detail: nothing at all, – a bush of brambles waving, the grass growing up to the very walls. But after all, though it gave me a shock for a moment, what did that matter? There were marks as if a number of footsteps had been up and down in front of the door, but these might have been our steps; and all was bright and peaceful and still. I poked about the other ruin – the larger ruins of the old house – for some time, as I had done before. There were marks upon the grass here and there – I could not call them footsteps – all about; but that told for nothing one way or another. I had examined the ruined rooms closely the first day. They were half-filled up with soil and debris, withered brackens and bramble, – no refuge for any one there. It vexed me that Jarvis should see me coming from that spot when he came up to me for his orders. I don't know whether my nocturnal expeditions had got wind among the servants. But there was a significant look in his face. Something in it I felt was like my own sensation when Simson in the midst of his scepticism was struck dumb. Jarvis felt satisfied that his veracity had been put beyond question. I never spoke to a servant of mine in such a peremptory tone before. I sent him away 'with a flea in his lug,' as the man described it afterwards. Interference of any kind was intolerable to me at such a moment.

But what was strangest of all was, that I could not face Roland. I did not go up to his room, as I would have naturally done, at once. This the girls could not understand. They saw there was some mystery in it. 'Mother has gone to lie down,' Agatha said; 'he has had such a good night.' 'But he wants you so, papa!' cried little Jeanie, always with her two arms embracing mine in a pretty way she had. I was obliged to go at last, but what could I say? I could only kiss him, and tell him to keep still, – that I was doing all I could. There is something mystical about the patience of a child. 'It will come all right, won't it, father?' he said. 'God grant it may! I hope so, Roland.' 'Oh, yes, it will come all right.' Perhaps he understood that in the midst of my anxiety I could not stay with him as I should have done otherwise. But the girls were more surprised than it is possible to describe. They looked at me with wondering eyes. 'If I were ill, papa, and you only stayed with me a moment, I should break my heart,' said Agatha. But the boy had a sympathetic feeling. He knew that of my own will I would not have done it. I shut myself up in the library, where I could not rest, but kept pacing up and down like a caged beast. What could I do? and if I could do nothing, what would become of my boy? These were the questions that, without ceasing, pursued each other through my mind.

Simson came out to dinner, and when the house was all still, and most of the servants in bed, we went out and met Dr Moncrieff, as we had appointed, at the head of the glen. Simson, for his part, was disposed to scoff at the Doctor. 'If there are to be any spells, you know, I'll cut the whole concern,' he said. I did not make him any reply. I had not invited him; he could go or come as he pleased. He was very talkative, far more so than suited my humour, as we went on. 'One thing is certain, you know; there must be some human agency,' he said. 'It is all bosh about apparitions. I never have investigated the laws of sound to any great extent, and there's a great deal in ventriloquism that we don't know much about.' 'If it's the same to you,' I said, 'I wish you'd keep all that to yourself, Simson. It doesn't suit my state of mind.' 'Oh, I hope I know how to respect idiosyncrasy,' he said. The very tone of his voice irritated me beyond measure. These scientific fellows, I wonder people put up with them as they do, when you have no mind for their cold-blooded confidence. Dr Moncrieff met us about eleven o'clock, the same time as on the previous night. He was a large man, with a venerable countenance and white hair, – old, but in full vigour, and thinking less of a cold night walk than many a younger man. He had his lantern, as I had. We were fully provided with means of lighting the place, and we were all of us resolute men. We had a rapid consultation as we went up, and the result was that we divided to different posts. Dr Moncrieff remained inside the wall – if you can call that inside where there was no wall but one. Simson placed himself on the side next the ruins, so as to intercept any communication with the old house, which was what his mind was fixed upon. I was posted on the other side. To say that nothing could come near without being seen was self-evident. It had been so also on the previous night. Now, with our three lights in the midst of the darkness, the whole place seemed illuminated. Dr Moncrieff's lantern, which was a large one, without any means of shutting up, – an old-fashioned lantern with a pierced and ornamental top, – shone steadily, the rays shooting out of it upward into the gloom. He placed it on the grass, where the middle of the room, if this had been a room, would have been. The usual effect of the light streaming out of the doorway was prevented by the illumination which Simson and I on either side supplied. With these differences, everything seemed as on the previous night.

And what occurred was exactly the same, with the same air of repetition, point for point, as I had formerly remarked. I declare that it seemed to me as if I were pushed against, put aside, by the owner of the voice as he paced up and down in his trouble, – though these are perfectly futile words, seeing that the stream of light from my lantern, and that from Simson's taper, lay broad and clear, without a shadow, without the smallest break, across the entire breadth of the grass. But just as it threw itself sobbing at the door (I cannot use other words), there suddenly came something which sent the blood coursing through my veins, and my heart into my mouth. It was a voice inside the wall, – my minister's well-known voice. I would have been prepared for it in any kind of adjuration, but I was not prepared for what I heard. It came out with a sort of stammering, as if too much moved for utterance. 'Willie, Willie! Oh, God preserve us! is it you?'

I made a dash round to the other side of the wall. The old minister was standing where I had left him, his shadow thrown vague and large upon the grass by the lantern which stood at his feet. I lifted my own light to see his face. He was very pale, his eyes wet and glistening, his mouth quivering with parted lips. He neither saw nor heard me. His whole being seemed absorbed in anxiety and tenderness. He held out his hands, which trembled, but it seemed to me with eagerness, not fear. He went on speaking all the time. 'Willie, if it is you, – and it's you, if it is not a delusion of Satan, – Willie, lad! why come ye here frighting them that know you not? Why came ye not to me? Your mother's gone with your name on her lips. Do you think she would ever close her door on her own lad? Do ye think the Lord will close the door, ye faint-hearted creature? No! – I forbid ye! I forbid ye!' cried the old man. The sobbing voice had begun to resume its cries. He made a step forward, calling out the last words in a voice of command. 'I forbid ye! Cry out no more to man. Go home, ye wandering spirit! go home! Do you hear me? – me that christened ye, that have struggled with ye, that have wrestled for ye with the Lord!' Here the loud tones of his voice sank into tenderness. 'And her too, poor woman! poor woman! her you are calling upon. She's no here. You'll find her with the Lord. Go there and seek her, not here. Do you hear me, lad? go after her there. He'll let you in, though it's late. Man, take heart! if you will lie and sob and greet, let it be at heaven's gate, and no your poor mother's ruined door.'

He stopped to get his breath; and the voice had stopped, not as it had done before, when its time was exhausted and all its repetitions said, but with a sobbing catch in the breath as if overruled. Then the minister spoke again, 'Are you hearing me, Will? Oh, laddie, you've liked the beggarly elements all your days. Be done with them now. Go home to the Father – the Father! Are you hearing me?' Here the old man sank down upon his knees, his face raised upwards, his hands held up with a tremble in them, all white in the light in the midst of the darkness. I resisted as long as I could, though I cannot tell why; then I, too, dropped upon my knees. Simson all the time stood in the door-way, with an expression in his face such as words could not tell, his under lip dropped, his eyes wild, staring. It seemed to be to him, that image of blank ignorance and wonder, that we were praying. All the time the voice, with a low arrested sobbing, lay just where he was standing, as I thought.

'Lord,' the minister said, – 'Lord, take him into Thy everlasting habitations. The mother he cries to is with Thee. Who can open to him but Thee? Lord, when is it too late for Thee, or what is too hard for Thee? Lord, let that woman there draw him inower! Let her draw him inower!'

I sprang forward to catch something in my arms that flung itself wildly within the door. The illusion was so strong, that I never paused till I felt my forehead graze against the wall and my hands clutch the ground, – for there was nobody there to save from falling, as in my foolishness I thought. Simson held out his hand to me to help me up. He was trembling and cold, his lower lip hanging, his speech almost inarticulate. 'It's gone,' he said, stammering, – 'it's gone!'

As long as I live I will never forget the shining of the strange lights, the blackness all round, the kneeling figure with all the whiteness of the light concentrated on its white venerable head and uplifted hands. I never knew how long we stood, like sentinels guarding him at his prayers. But at last the old minister rose from his knees, and standing up at his full height, raised his arms, as the Scotch manner is at the end of a religious service, and solemnly gave the apostolical benediction, – to what? to the silent earth, the dark woods, the wide breathing atmosphere; for we were but spectators gasping an Amen!

It seemed to me that it must be the middle of the night, as we all walked back. It was in reality very late. Dr Moncrieff himself was the first to speak. 'I must be going,' he said; 'I will go down the glen, as I came.'

'But not alone. I am going with you, Doctor.'

'Well, I will not oppose it. I am an old man, and agitation wearies more than work. Yes; I'll be thankful of your arm. Tonight, Colonel, you've done me more good turns than one.'

I pressed his hand on my arm, not feeling able to speak. But Simson, who turned with us, and who had gone along all this time with his taper flaring, in entire unconsciousness, became himself, sceptical and cynical. 'I should like to ask you a question,' he said. 'Do you believe in Purgatory, Doctor? It's not in the tenets of the Church, so far as I know.'

'Sir,' said Dr Moncrieff, 'an old man like me is sometimes not very sure what he believes. There is just one thing I am certain of – and that is the loving-kindness of God.'

'But I thought that was in this life. I am no theologian—'

'Sir,' said the old man again, with a tremor in him which I could feel going over all his frame, 'if I saw a friend of mine within the gates of hell, I would not despair but his Father would take him by the hand still, if he cried like *you*.'

'I allow it is very strange, very strange. I cannot see through it. That there must be human agency, I feel sure. Doctor, what made you decide upon the person and the name?'

The minister put out his hand with the impatience which a man might show if he were asked how he recognized his brother. 'Tuts!' he said, in familiar speech; then more solemnly, 'How should I not recognize a person that I know better – far better – than I know you?'

'Then you saw the man?'

Dr Moncrieff made no reply. He moved his hand again with a little impatient movement, and walked on, leaning heavily on my arm. We parted with him at his own door, where his old housekeeper appeared in great perturbation, waiting for him. 'Eh, me, minister! the young gentleman will be worse?' she cried.

'Far from that – better. God bless him!' Dr Moncrieff said.

I think if Simson had begun again to me with his questions, I should have pitched him over the rocks as we returned up the glen; but he was silent, by a good inspiration. And the sky was clearer than it had been for many nights, shining high over the trees, with here and there a star faintly gleaming through the wilderness of dark and bare branches. We went up to the boy's room when we went in. There we found the complete hush of rest. My wife looked up out of a doze, and gave me a smile; 'I think he is a great deal better; but you are very late,' she said in a whisper, shading the light with her hand that the Doctor might see his patient. The boy had got back something like his own colour. He woke as we stood all round his bed. His eyes had the happy, half-awakened look of childhood, glad to shut again, yet pleased with the interruption and glimmer of the light. I stooped over him and kissed his forehead, which was moist and cool. 'All is well, Roland,' I said. He looked up at me with a glance of pleasure, and took my hand and laid his cheek upon it, and so went to sleep.

For some nights after, I watched among the ruins, spending all the dark hours up to midnight patrolling about the bit of wall which was associated with so many emotions; but I heard nothing, and saw nothing beyond the quiet course of nature; nor, so far as I am aware, has anything been heard again. Dr Moncrieff gave me the history of the youth, whom he never hesitated to name. I did not ask, as Simson did, how he recognized him. He had been a prodigal, – weak, foolish, easily imposed upon, and 'led away,' as people say. All that we had heard had passed actually in life, the Doctor said. The young man had come home thus a day or two after his mother died, – who was no more than housekeeper in the old house, – and distracted with the news, had thrown himself down at the door and called upon her to let him in. The old man could scarcely speak of it for tears. He was not terrified, as I had been myself, and all the rest of us. It was no 'ghost,' as I fear we all vulgarly considered it, to him, – but a poor creature whom he knew under these conditions, just as he had known him in the flesh, having no doubt of his identity. And to Roland it was the same. This spirit in pain, – if it was a spirit, – this voice out of the unseen, – was a poor fellow-creature in misery, to be succoured and helped out of his trouble, to my boy. He spoke to me quite frankly about it when he got better. 'I knew father would find out some way,' he said. And this was when he was strong and well, and all idea that he would turn hysterical or become a seer of visions had happily passed away.

I must add one curious fact, which does not seem to me to have any relation to the above, but which Simson made great use of, as the human agency which he was determined to find somehow. One Sunday afternoon Simson found a little hole, – for it was more a hole than a room, – entirely hidden under the ivy and ruins, in which there was a quantity of straw laid in a corner, as if someone had made a bed there, and some remains of crusts about the floor. Someone had lodged there, and not very long before, he made out; and that this unknown being was the author of all the mysterious sounds we heard he is convinced. 'I was puzzled myself, – I could not make it out, – but I always felt convinced human agency was at the bottom of it. And here it is, – and a clever fellow he must have been,' the Doctor says. There is no argument with men of this kind.

Bagley left my service as soon as he got well. He assured me it was no want of respect, but he could not stand 'them kind of things'; and the man was so shaken and ghastly that I was glad to give him a present and let him go. For my own part, I made a point of staying out the time – two years – for which I had taken Brentwood; but I did not renew my tenancy. By that time we had settled, and found for ourselves a pleasant home of our own.

I must add, that when the Doctor defies me, I can always bring back gravity to his countenance, and a pause in his railing, when I remind him of the juniper-bush. To me that was a matter of little importance. I could believe I was mistaken. I did not care about it one way or other; but on his mind the effect was different. The miserable voice, the spirit in pain, he could think of as the result of ventriloquism, or reverberation, or – anything you please: an elaborate prolonged hoax, executed somehow by the tramp that had found a lodging in the old tower; but the juniper-bush staggered him. Things have effects so different on the minds of different men.

The Deserted House

Ernest Theodor Amadeus Hoffmann

You know already that I spent the greater part of last summer in X——, began Theodore. The many old friends and acquaintances I found there, the free, jovial life, the manifold artistic and intellectual interests – all these combined to keep me in that city. I was happy as never before, and found rich nourishment for my old fondness for wandering alone through the streets, stopping to enjoy every picture in the shop windows, every placard on the walls, or watching the passers-by and choosing someone or the other of them to cast his horoscope secretly to myself.

There is one broad avenue leading to the —— Gate and lined with handsome buildings of all descriptions, which is the meeting place of the rich and fashionable world. The shops which occupy the ground floor of the tall palaces are devoted to the trade in articles of luxury, and the apartments above are the dwellings of people of wealth and position. The aristocratic hotels are to be found in this avenue, the palaces of the foreign ambassadors are there, and you can easily imagine that such a street would be the centre of the city's life and gaiety.

I had wandered through the avenue several times, when one day my attention was caught by a house which contrasted strangely with the others surrounding it. Picture to yourselves a low building but four windows broad, crowded in between two tall, handsome structures. Its one upper story was a little higher than the tops of the ground-floor windows of its neighbours, its roof was dilapidated, its windows patched with paper, its discoloured walls spoke of years of neglect. You can imagine how strange such a house must have looked in this street of wealth and fashion. Looking at it more attentively I perceived that the windows of the upper story were tightly closed and curtained, and that a wall had been built to hide the windows of the ground floor. The entrance gate, a little to one side, served also as a door-way for the building, but I could find no sign of latch, lock, or even a bell on this gate. I was convinced that the house must be unoccupied, for at whatever hour of the day I happened to be passing I had never seen the faintest signs of life about it.

You all, the good comrades of my youth, know that I have been prone to consider myself a sort of clairvoyant, claiming to have glimpses of a strange world of wonders, a world which you, with your hard common sense, would attempt to deny or laugh away. I confess that I have often lost myself in mysteries which after all turned out to be no mysteries at all. And it looked at first as if this was to happen to me in the matter of the deserted house, that strange house which drew my steps and my thoughts to itself with a power that surprised me. But the point of my story will prove to you that I am right in asserting that I know more than you do. Listen now to what I am about to tell you.

One day, at the hour in which the fashionable world is accustomed to promenade up and down the avenue, I stood as usual before the deserted house, lost in thought. Suddenly I felt, without looking up, that someone had stopped beside me, fixing his eyes on me. It was Count P——, who told me that the old house contained nothing more mysterious than a cake bakery belonging to the pastry cook whose handsome shop adjoined the old structure. The windows of the ground floor were walled up to give protection to the ovens, and the heavy curtains of the upper story were to keep the sunlight from the wares laid out there. When the Count informed me of this I felt as if a bucket of cold water had been suddenly thrown over me. But I could not believe in this story of the cake and candy factory. Through some strange freak of the imagination I felt as a child feels when some fairy tale has been told it to conceal the truth it suspects. I scolded myself for a silly fool; the house remained unaltered in its appearance, and the visions faded in my brain, until one day a chance incident woke them to life again.

I was wandering through the avenue as usual, and as I passed the deserted house I could not resist a hasty glance at its close-curtained upper windows.

But as I looked at it, the curtain on the last window near the pastry shop began to move. A hand, an arm, came out from between its folds. I took my opera glass from my pocket and saw a beautifully formed woman's hand, on the little finger of which a large diamond sparkled in unusual brilliancy; a rich bracelet glittered on the white, rounded arm. The hand set a tall, oddly formed crystal bottle on the window ledge and disappeared again behind the curtain.

I stopped as if frozen to stone; a weirdly pleasurable sensation, mingled with awe, streamed through my being with the warmth of an electric current. I stared up at the mysterious window and a sigh of longing arose from the very depths of my heart. When I came to myself again, I was angered to find that I was surrounded by a crowd which stood gazing up at the window with curious faces. I stole away inconspicuously, and the demon of all things prosaic whispered to me that what I had just seen was the rich pastry cook's wife, in her Sunday adornment, placing an empty bottle, used for rose-water or the like, on the window sill. Nothing very weird about this.

Suddenly a most sensible thought came to me. I turned and entered the shining, mirror-walled shop of the pastry cook. Blowing the steaming foam from my cup of chocolate, I remarked: 'You have a very useful addition to your establishment next door.' The man leaned over his counter and looked at me with a questioning smile, as if he did not understand me. I repeated that in my opinion he had been very clever to set his bakery in the neighbouring house, although the deserted appearance of the building was a strange sight in its contrasting surroundings. 'Why, sir,' began the pastry cook, 'who told you that the house next door belongs to us? Unfortunately every attempt on our part to acquire it has been in vain, and I fancy it is all the better so, for there is something queer about the place.'

You can imagine, dear friends, how interested I became upon hearing these words, and that I begged the man to tell me more about the house.

'I do not know anything very definite, sir,' he said. 'All that we know for a certainty is that the house belongs to the Countess S——, who lives on her estates and has not been to the city for years. This house, so they tell me, stood in its present shape before any of the handsome buildings were raised which are now the pride of our avenue, and in all these years there has been nothing done to it except to keep it from actual decay. Two living creatures alone dwell there, an aged misanthrope of a steward and his melancholy dog, which occasionally howls at the moon from the back courtyard. According to the general story the deserted house is haunted. In very truth my brother, who is the owner of this shop, and myself have often, when our business kept us awake during the silence of the night, heard strange sounds from the other side of the walls. There was a rumbling and a scraping that frightened us both. And not very long ago we heard one night a strange singing which I could not describe to you. It was evidently the voice of an old woman, but the tones were so sharp and clear, and ran up to the top of the scale in cadences and long trills, the like of which I have never heard before, although I have heard many singers in many lands. It seemed to be a French song, but I am not quite sure of that, for I could not listen long to the mad, ghostly singing, it made the hair stand erect on my head. And at times, after the street noises are quiet, we can hear deep sighs, and sometimes a mad laugh, which seem to come out of the earth. But if you lay your ear to the wall in our back room, you can hear that the noises come from the house next door.' He led me into the back room and pointed through the window. 'And do you see that iron chimney coming out of the wall there? It smokes so heavily sometimes, even in summer when there are no fires used, that my brother has often quarrelled with the old steward about it, fearing danger. But the old man excuses himself by saying that he was cooking his food. Heaven knows what the queer creature may eat, for often, when the pipe is smoking heavily, a strange and queer smell can be smelled all over the house.'

The glass doors of the shop creaked in opening. The pastry cook hurried into the front room, and when he had nodded to the figure now entering he threw a meaning glance at me. I understood him perfectly. Who else could this strange guest be, but the steward who had charge of the mysterious house! Imagine a thin little man with a face the colour of a mummy, with a sharp nose, tight-set lips, green cat's eyes, and a crazy smile; his hair dressed in the old-fashioned style with a high toupet and a bag at the back, and heavily powdered. He wore a faded old brown coat which was carefully brushed, grey stockings, and broad, flat-toed shoes with buckles. And imagine further, that in spite of his meagreness this little person is robustly built, with huge fists and long, strong fingers, and that he walks to the shop counter with a strong, firm step, smiling his imbecile smile, and whining out: 'A couple of candied oranges – a couple of macaroons – a couple of sugared chestnuts—'

The pastry cook smiled at me and then spoke to the old man. 'You do not seem to be quite well. Yes, yes, old age, old age! It takes the strength from our limbs.' The old man's expression did not change, but his voice went up: 'Old age? – Old age? – Lose strength? – Grow weak? – Oho!' And with this he clapped his hands together until the joints cracked, and sprang high up into the air until the entire shop trembled and the glass vessels on the walls and counters rattled and shook. But in the same moment a hideous screaming was heard; the old man had stepped on his black dog, which, creeping in behind him, had laid itself at his feet on the floor. 'Devilish beast – dog of hell!' groaned the old man in his former miserable tone, opening his bag and giving the dog a large macaroon. The dog, which had burst out into a cry of distress that was truly human, was quiet at once, sat down on its haunches, and gnawed at the macaroon like a squirrel. When it had finished its tidbit, the old man had also finished the packing up and putting away of his purchases. 'Good night, honoured neighbour,' he spoke, taking the hand of the pastry cook and pressing it until the latter cried aloud in pain. 'The weak old man wishes you a good night, most honourable Sir Neighbour,' he repeated, and then walked from the shop, followed closely by his black dog. The old man did not seem to have noticed me at all. I was quite dumfoundered in my astonishment.

'There, you see,' began the pastry cook. 'This is the way he acts when he comes in here, two or three times a month, it is. But I can get nothing out of him except the fact that he was a former valet of Count S——, that he is now in charge of this house here, and that every day – for many years now – he expects the arrival of his master's family.' The hour was now come when fashion demanded that the elegant world of the city should assemble in this attractive shop. The doors opened incessantly, the place was thronged, and I could ask no further questions.

This much I knew, that Count P——'s information about the ownership and the use of the house were not correct; also, that the old steward, in spite of his denial, was not living alone there, and that some mystery was hidden behind its discoloured walls. How could I combine the story of the strange and gruesome singing with the appearance of the beautiful arm at the window? That arm could not be part of the wrinkled body of an old woman; the singing, according to the pastry cook's story, could not come from the throat of a blooming and youthful maiden. I decided in favour of the arm, as it was easy to explain to myself that some trick of acoustics had made the voice sound sharp and old, or that it had appeared so only in the pastry cook's fear-distorted imagination. Then I thought of the smoke, the strange odours, the oddly formed crystal bottle that I had seen, and soon the vision of a beautiful creature held enthralled by fatal magic stood as if alive before my mental vision. The old man became a wizard who, perhaps quite independently of the family he served, had set up his devil's kitchen in the deserted house. My imagination had begun to work, and in my dreams that night I saw clearly the hand with the sparkling diamond on its finger, the arm with the shining bracelet. From out thin, grey mists there appeared a sweet face with sadly imploring blue eyes, then the entire exquisite figure of a beautiful girl. And I saw that what I had thought was mist was the fine steam flowing out in circles from a crystal bottle held in the hands of the vision.

'Oh, fairest creature of my dreams,' I cried in rapture, 'reveal to me where thou art, what it is that enthralls thee. Ah, I know it! It is black magic that holds thee captive – thou art the unhappy slave of that malicious devil who wanders about brown-clad and be-wigged in pastry shops, scattering their wares with his unholy springing and feeding his demon dog on macaroons, after they have howled out a Satanic measure in five-eighth time. Oh, I know it all, thou fair and charming vision. The diamond is the reflection of the fire of thy heart. But that bracelet about thine arm is a link of the chain which the brown-clad one says is a magnetic chain. Do not believe it, O glorious one! See how it shines in the blue fire from the retort. One moment more and thou art free. And now, O maiden, open thy rosebud mouth and tell me—' In this moment a gnarled fist leaped over my shoulder and clutched at the crystal bottle, which sprang into a thousand pieces in the air. With a faint, sad moan, the charming vision faded into the blackness of the night.

When morning came to put an end to my dreaming I hurried through the avenue, seeking the deserted house as usual and I saw something glistening in the last window of the upper story. Coming nearer I noticed that the outer blind had been quite drawn up and the inner curtain slightly opened. The sparkle of a diamond met my eye. O kind Heaven! The face of my dream looked at me, gently imploring, from above the rounded arm on which her head was resting. But how was it possible to stand still in the moving crowd without attracting attention? Suddenly I caught sight of the benches placed in the gravel walk in the centre of the avenue, and I saw that one of them was directly opposite the house. I sprang over to it, and leaning over its back, I could stare up at the mysterious window undisturbed. Yes, it was she, the charming maiden of my dream! But her eye did not seem to seek me as I had at first thought; her glance was cold and unfocused, and had it not been for an occasional motion of the hand and arm, I might have thought that I was looking at a cleverly painted picture.

I was so lost in my adoration of the mysterious being in the window, so aroused and excited throughout all my nerve centres, that I did not hear the shrill voice of an Italian street hawker, who had been offering me his wares for some time. Finally he touched me on the arm; I turned hastily and commanded him to let me alone. But he did not cease his entreaties, asserting that he had earned nothing today, and begging me to buy some small trifle from him. Full of impatience to get rid of him I put my hand in my pocket. With the words: 'I have more beautiful things here,' he opened the under drawer of his box and held out to me a little, round pocket mirror. In it, as he held it up before my face, I could see the deserted house behind me, the window, and the sweet face of my vision there.

I bought the little mirror at once, for I saw that it would make it possible for me to sit comfortable and inconspicuously, and yet watch the window. The longer I looked at the reflection in the glass, the more I fell captive to a weird and quite indescribable sensation, which I might almost call a waking dream. It was as if a lethargy had lamed my eyes, holding them fastened on the glass beyond my power to loosen them. And now at last the beautiful eyes of the fair vision looked at me, her glance sought mine and shone deep down into my heart.

'You have a pretty little mirror there,' said a voice beside me. I awoke from my dream, and was not a little confused when I saw smiling faces looking at me from either side. Several persons had sat down upon the bench, and it was quite certain that my staring into the window, and my probably strange expression, had afforded them great cause for amusement.

'You have a pretty little mirror there,' repeated the man, as I did not answer him. His glance said more, and asked without words the reason of my staring so oddly into the little glass. He was an elderly man, neatly dressed, and his voice and eyes were so full of good nature that I could not refuse him my confidence. I told him that I had been looking in the mirror at the picture of a beautiful maiden who was sitting at a window of the deserted house. I went even farther; I asked the old man if he had not seen the fair face himself. 'Over there? In the old house – in the last window?' He repeated my questions in a tone of surprise.

'Yes, yes,' I exclaimed.

The old man smiled and answered: 'Well, well, that was a strange delusion. My old eyes – thank Heaven for my old eyes! Yes, yes, sir. I saw a pretty face in the window there, with my own eyes; but it seemed to me to be an excellently well-painted oil portrait.'

I turned quickly and looked toward the window; there was no one there, and the blind had been pulled down. 'Yes,' continued the old man, 'yes, sir. Now it is too late to make sure of the matter, for just now the servant, who, as I know, lives there alone in the house of the Countess S——, took the picture away from the window after he had dusted it, and let down the blinds.'

'Was it, then, surely a picture?' I asked again, in bewilderment.

'You can trust my eyes,' replied the old man. 'The optical delusion was strengthened by your seeing only the reflection in the mirror. And when I was in your years it was easy enough for my fancy to call up the picture of a beautiful maiden.'

'But the hand and arm moved,' I exclaimed. 'Oh, yes, they moved, indeed they moved,' said the old man smiling, as he patted me on the shoulder. Then he arose to go, and bowing politely, closed his remarks with the words, 'Beware of mirrors which can lie so vividly. Your obedient servant, sir.'

You can imagine how I felt when I saw that he looked upon me as a foolish fantast. I hurried home full of anger and disgust, and promised myself that I would not think of the mysterious house. But I placed the mirror on my dressing-table that I might bind my cravat before it, and thus it happened one day, when I was about to utilize it for this important business, that its glass seemed dull, and that I took it up and breathed on it to rub it bright again. My heart seemed to stand still, every fibre in me trembled in delightful awe. Yes, that is all the name I can find for the feeling that came over me, when, as my breath clouded the little mirror,

I saw the beautiful face of my dreams arise and smile at me through blue mists. You laugh at me? You look upon me as an incorrigible dreamer? Think what you will about it – the fair face looked at me from out of the mirror! But as soon as the clouding vanished, the face vanished in the brightened glass.

I will not weary you with a detailed recital of my sensations the next few days. I will only say that I repeated again the experiments with the mirror, sometimes with success, sometimes without. When I had not been able to call up the vision, I would run to the deserted house and stare up at the windows; but I saw no human being anywhere about the building. I lived only in thoughts of my vision; everything else seemed indifferent to me. I neglected my friends and my studies. The tortures in my soul passed over into, or rather mingled with, physical sensations which frightened me, and which at last made me fear for my reason. One day, after an unusually severe attack, I put my little mirror in my pocket and hurried to the home of Dr K——, who was noted for his treatment of those diseases of the mind out of which physical diseases so often grow. I told him my story; I did not conceal the slightest incident from him, and I implored him to save me from the terrible fate which seemed to threaten me. He listened to me quietly, but I read astonishment in his glance. Then he said: 'The danger is not as near as you believe, and I think that I may say that it can be easily prevented. You are undergoing an unusual psychical disturbance, beyond a doubt. But the fact that you understand that some evil principle seems to be trying to influence you, gives you a weapon by which you can combat it. Leave your little mirror here with me, and force yourself to take up with some work which will afford scope for all your mental energy. Do not go to the avenue; work all day, from early to late, then take a long walk, and spend your evenings in the company of your friends. Eat heartily, and drink heavy, nourishing wines. You see I am endeavouring to combat your fixed idea of the face in the window of the deserted house and in the mirror, by diverting your mind to other things, and by strengthening your body. You yourself must help me in this.'

I was very reluctant to part with my mirror. The physician, who had already taken it, seemed to notice my hesitation. He breathed upon the glass and holding it up to me, he asked: 'Do you see anything?'

'Nothing at all,' I answered, for so it was.

'Now breathe on the glass yourself,' said the physician, laying the mirror in my hands.

I did as he requested. There was the vision even more clearly than ever before.

'There she is!' I cried aloud.

The physician looked into the glass, and then said: 'I cannot see anything. But I will confess to you that when I looked into this glass, a queer shiver overcame me, passing away almost at once. Now do it once more.'

I breathed upon the glass again and the physician laid his hand upon the back of my neck. The face appeared again, and the physician, looking into the mirror over my shoulder, turned pale. Then he took the little glass from my hands, looked at it attentively, and locked it into his desk, returning to me after a few moments' silent thought.

'Follow my instructions strictly,' he said. 'I must confess to you that I do not yet understand those moments of your vision. But I hope to be able to tell you more about it very soon.'

Difficult as it was to me, I forced myself to live absolutely according to the doctor's orders. I soon felt the benefit of the steady work and the nourishing diet, and yet I was not free from those terrible attacks, which would come either at noon, or, more intensely still, at midnight. Even in the midst of a merry company, in the enjoyment of wine and song, glowing daggers seemed to pierce my heart, and all the strength of my intellect was powerless to resist their might over me. I was obliged to retire, and could not return to my friends until I had recovered from my condition of lethargy. It was in one of these attacks, an unusually strong one, that such an irresistible, mad longing for the picture of my dreams came over me, that I hurried out into the street and ran toward the mysterious house. While still at a distance from it, I seemed to see lights shining out through the fast-closed blinds, but when I came nearer I saw that all was dark. Crazy with my desire I rushed to the door; it fell back before the pressure of my hand. I stood in the dimly lighted vestibule, enveloped in a heavy, close atmosphere. My heart beat in strange fear and impatience. Then suddenly a long, sharp tone, as from a woman's throat, shrilled through the house. I know not how it happened that I found myself suddenly in a great hall brilliantly lighted and furnished in old-fashioned magnificence of golden chairs and strange Japanese ornaments. Strongly perfumed incense arose in blue clouds about me. 'Welcome – welcome, sweet bridegroom! the hour has come, our bridal hour!' I heard these words in a woman's voice, and as little as I can tell, how I came into the room, just so little do I know how it happened that suddenly a tall, youthful figure, richly dressed, seemed to arise from the blue mists. With the repeated shrill cry: 'Welcome, sweet bridegroom!' she came toward me with outstretched arms – and a yellow face, distorted with age and madness, stared into mine! I fell back in terror, but the fiery, piercing glance of her eyes, like the eyes of a snake, seemed to hold me spellbound. I did not seem able to turn my eyes from this terrible old woman, I could not move another step. She came still nearer, and it seemed to me suddenly as if her hideous face were only a thin mask, beneath which I saw the features of the beautiful maiden of my vision. Already I felt the touch of her hands, when suddenly she fell at my feet with a loud scream, and a voice behind me cried:

'Oho, is the devil playing his tricks with your grace again? To bed, to bed, your grace. Else there will be blows, mighty blows!'

I turned quickly and saw the old steward in his night clothes, swinging a whip above his head. He was about to strike the screaming figure at my feet when I caught at his arm. But he shook me from him, exclaiming: 'The devil, sir! That old Satan would have murdered you if I had not come to your aid. Get away from here at once!'

I rushed from the hall, and sought in vain in the darkness for the door of the house. Behind me I heard the hissing blows of the whip and the old woman's screams. I drew breath to call aloud for help, when suddenly the ground gave way under my feet; I fell down a short flight of stairs, bringing up with such force against a door at the bottom that it sprang open, and I measured my length on the floor of a small room. From the hastily vacated bed, and from the familiar brown coat hanging over a chair, I saw that I was in the bed-chamber of the old steward. There was a trampling on the stair, and the old man himself entered hastily, throwing himself at my feet. 'By all the saints, sir,' he entreated with folded hands, 'whoever you may be, and however her grace, that old Satan of a witch has managed to entice you to this house, do not speak to any one of what has happened here. It will cost me my position. Her crazy excellency has been punished, and is bound fast in her bed. Sleep well, good sir, sleep softly and sweetly. It is a warm and beautiful July night. There is no moon, but the stars shine brightly.

A quiet good night to you.' While talking, the old man had taken up a lamp, had led me out of the basement, pushed me out of the house door, and locked it behind me. I hurried home quite bewildered, and you can imagine that I was too much confused by the gruesome secret to be able to form any explanation of it in my own mind for the first few days. Only this much was certain, that I was now free from the evil spell that had held me captive so long. All my longing for the magic vision in the mirror had disappeared, and the memory of the scene in the deserted house was like the recollection of an unexpected visit to a madhouse. It was evident beyond a doubt that the steward was the tyrannical guardian of a crazy woman of noble birth, whose condition was to be hidden from the world. But the mirror? and all the other magic? Listen, and I will tell you more about it.

Some few days later I came upon Count P—— at an evening entertainment. He drew me to one side and said, with a smile, 'Do you know that the secrets of our deserted house are beginning to be revealed?' I listened with interest; but before the Count could say more the doors of the dining-room were thrown open, and the company proceeded to the table. Quite lost in thought at the words I had just heard, I had given a young lady my arm, and had taken my place mechanically in the ceremonious procession. I led my companion to the seats arranged for us, and then turned to look at her for the first time. The vision of my mirror stood before me, feature for feature, there was no deception possible! I trembled to my innermost heart, as you can imagine; but I discovered that there was not the slightest echo even, in my heart, of the mad desire which had ruled me so entirely when my breath drew out the magic picture from the glass. My astonishment, or rather my terror, must have been apparent in my eyes. The girl looked at me in such surprise that I endeavoured to control myself sufficiently to remark that I must have met her somewhere before. Her short answer, to the effect that this could hardly be possible, as she had come to the city only yesterday for the first time in her life, bewildered me still more and threw me into an awkward silence. The sweet glance from her gentle eyes brought back my courage, and I began a tentative exploring of this new companion's mind. I found that I had before me a sweet and delicate being, suffering from some psychic trouble. At a particularly merry turn of the conversation, when I would throw in a daring word like a dash of pepper, she would smile, but her smile was pained, as if a wound had been touched. 'You are not very merry tonight, Countess. Was it the visit this morning?' An officer sitting near us had spoken these words to my companion, but before he could finish his remarks his neighbour had grasped him by the arm and whispered something in his ear, while a lady at the other side of the table, with glowing cheeks and angry eyes, began to talk loudly of the opera she had heard last evening. Tears came to the eyes of the girl sitting beside me. 'Am I not foolish?' She turned to me. A few moments before she had complained of headache. 'Merely the usual evidences of a nervous headache,' I answered in an easy tone, 'and there is nothing better for it than the merry spirit which bubbles in the foam of this poet's nectar.' With these words I filled her champagne glass, and she sipped at it as she threw me a look of gratitude. Her mood brightened, and all would have been well had I not touched a glass before me with unexpected strength, arousing from it a shrill, high tone. My companion grew deadly pale, and I myself felt a sudden shiver, for the sound had exactly the tone of the mad woman's voice in the deserted house.

While we were drinking coffee I made an opportunity to get to the side of Count P——. He understood the reason for my movement. 'Do you know that your neighbour is Countess Edwina S——? And do you know also that it is her mother's sister who lives in the deserted house, incurably mad for many years? This morning both mother and daughter went to see the unfortunate woman. The old steward, the only person who is able to control the Countess in her outbreaks, is seriously ill, and they say that the sister has finally revealed the secret to Dr K——.'

Dr K—— was the physician to whom I had turned in my own anxiety, and you can well imagine that I hurried to him as soon as I was free, and told him all that had happened to me in the last days. I asked him to tell me as much as he could about the mad woman, for my own peace of mind; and this is what I learned from him under promise of secrecy.

'Angelica, Countess Z——,' thus the doctor began, 'had already passed her thirtieth year, but was still in full possession of great beauty, when Count S——, although much younger than she, became so fascinated by her charm that he wooed her with ardent devotion and followed her to her father's home to try his luck there. But scarcely had the Count entered the house, scarcely had he caught sight of Angelica's younger sister, Gabrielle, when he awoke as from a dream. The elder sister appeared faded and colourless beside Gabrielle, whose beauty and charm so enthralled the Count that he begged her hand of her father. Count Z—— gave his consent easily, as there was no doubt of Gabrielle's feelings toward her suitor. Angelica did not show the slightest anger at her lover's faithlessness. 'He believes that he has forsaken me, the foolish boy! He does not perceive that he was but my toy, a toy of which I had tired.' Thus she spoke in proud scorn, and not a look or an action on her part belied her words. But after the ceremonious betrothal of Gabrielle to Count S——, Angelica was seldom seen by the members of her family. She did not appear at the dinner table, and it was said that she spent most of her time walking alone in the neighbouring wood.

'A strange occurrence disturbed the monotonous quiet of life in the castle. The hunters of Count Z——, assisted by peasants from the village, had captured a band of gipsies who were accused of several robberies and murders which had happened recently in the neighbourhood. The men were brought to the castle courtyard, fettered together on a long chain, while the women and children were packed on a cart. Noticeable among the last was a tall, haggard old woman of terrifying aspect, wrapped from head to foot in a red shawl. She stood upright in the cart, and in an imperious tone demanded that she should be allowed to descend. The guards were so awed by her manner and appearance that they obeyed her at once.

'Count Z—— came down to the courtyard and commanded that the gang should be placed in the prisons under the castle. Suddenly Countess Angelica rushed out of the door, her hair all loose, fear and anxiety in her pale face. Throwing herself on her knees, she cried in a piercing voice, 'Let these people go! Let these people go! They are innocent! Father, let these people go! If you shed one drop of their blood I will pierce my heart with this knife!' The Countess swung a shining knife in the air and then sank swooning to the ground. 'Yes, my beautiful darling—my golden child—I knew you would not let them hurt us,' shrilled the old woman in red. She cowered beside the Countess and pressed disgusting kisses to her face and breast, murmuring crazy words. She took from out the recesses of her shawl a little vial in which a tiny goldfish seemed to swim in some silver-clear liquid. She held the vial to the Countess's heart. The latter regained consciousness immediately. When her eyes fell on the gipsy woman, she sprang up, clasped the old creature ardently in her arms, and hurried with her into the castle.

'Count Z——, Gabrielle, and her lover, who had come out during this scene, watched it in astonished awe. The gipsies appeared quite indifferent. They were loosed from their chains and taken separately to the prisons. Next morning Count Z—— called the villagers together. The gipsies were led before them and the Count announced that he had found them to be innocent of the crimes of which they were accused, and that he would grant them free passage through his domains. To the astonishment of all present, their fetters were struck off and they were set at liberty. The red-shawled woman was not among them. It was whispered that the gipsy captain, recognizable from the golden chain about his neck and the red feather in his high Spanish hat, had paid a secret visit to the Count's room the night before. But it was discovered, a short time after the release of the gipsies, that they were indeed guiltless of the robberies and murders that had disturbed the district.

'The date set for Gabrielle's wedding approached. One day, to her great astonishment, she saw several large wagons in the courtyard being packed high with furniture, clothing, linen, with everything necessary for a complete household outfit. The wagons were driven away, and the following day Count Z—— explained that, for many reasons, he had thought it best to grant Angelica's odd request that she be allowed to set up her own establishment in his house in X——. He had given the house to her, and had promised her that no member of the family, not even he himself, should enter it without her express permission. He added also, that, at her urgent request, he had permitted his own valet to accompany her, to take charge of her household.

'When the wedding festivities were over, Count S—— and his bride departed for their home, where they spent a year in cloudless happiness. Then the Count's health failed mysteriously. It was as if some secret sorrow gnawed at his vitals, robbing him of joy and strength. All efforts of his young wife to discover the source of his trouble were fruitless. At last, when the constantly recurring fainting spells threatened to endanger his very life, he yielded to the entreaties of his physicians and left his home, ostensibly for Pisa. His young wife was prevented from accompanying him by the delicate condition of her own health.

'And now,' said the doctor, 'the information given me by Countess S—— became, from this point on, so rhapsodical that a keen observer only could guess at the true coherence of the story. Her baby, a daughter, born during her husband's absence, was spirited away from the house, and all search for it was fruitless. Her grief at this loss deepened to despair, when she received a message from her father stating that her husband, whom all believed to be in Pisa, had been found dying of heart trouble in Angelica's home in X——, and that Angelica herself had become a dangerous maniac. The old Count added that all this horror had so shaken his own nerves that he feared he would not long survive it.

'As soon as Gabrielle was able to leave her bed, she hurried to her father's castle. One night, prevented from sleeping by visions of the loved ones she had lost, she seemed to hear a faint crying, like that of an infant, before the door of her chamber. Lighting her candle she opened the door. Great Heaven! there cowered the old gipsy woman, wrapped in her red shawl, staring up at her with eyes that seemed already glazing in death. In her arms she held a little child, whose crying had aroused the Countess. Gabrielle's heart beat high with joy – it was her child – her lost daughter! She snatched the infant from the gipsy's arms, just as the woman fell at her feet lifeless. The Countess's screams awoke the house, but the gipsy was quite dead and no effort to revive her met with success.

'The old Count hurried to X—— to endeavour to discover something that would throw light upon the mysterious disappearance and reappearance of the child. Angelica's madness had frightened away all her female servants; the valet alone remained with her. She appeared at first to have become quite calm and sensible. But when the Count told her the story of Gabrielle's child she clapped her hands and laughed aloud, crying: 'Did the little darling arrive? You buried her, you say? How the feathers of the gold pheasant shine in the sun! Have you seen the green lion with the fiery blue eyes?' Horrified the Count perceived that Angelica's mind was gone beyond a doubt, and he resolved to take her back with him to his estates, in spite of the warnings of his old valet. At the mere suggestion of removing her from the house Angelica's ravings increased to such an extent as to endanger her own life and that of the others.

'When a lucid interval came again Angelica entreated her father, with many tears, to let her live and die in the house she had chosen. Touched by her terrible trouble he granted her request, although he believed the confession which slipped from her lips during this scene to be a fantasy of her madness. She told him that Count S—— had returned to her arms, and that the child which the gipsy had taken to her father's house was the fruit of their love. The rumour went abroad in the city that Count Z—— had taken the unfortunate woman to his home; but the truth was that she remained hidden in the deserted house under the care of the valet. Count Z—— died a short time ago, and Countess Gabrielle came here with her daughter Edwina to arrange some family affairs. It was not possible for her to avoid seeing her unfortunate sister. Strange things must have happened during this visit, but the Countess has not confided anything to me, saying merely that she had found it necessary to take the mad woman away from the old valet. It had been discovered that he had controlled her outbreaks by means of force and physical cruelty; and that also, allured by Angelica's assertions that she could make gold, he had allowed himself to assist her in her weird operations.

'It would be quite unnecessary,' thus the physician ended his story, 'to say anything more to you about the deeper inward relationship of all these strange things. It is clear to my mind that it was you who brought about the catastrophe, a catastrophe which will mean recovery or speedy death for the sick woman. And now I will confess to you that I was not a little alarmed, horrified even, to discover that—when I had set myself in magnetic communication with you by placing my hand on your neck—I could see the picture in the mirror with my own eyes. We both know now that the reflection in the glass was the face of Countess Edwina.'

I repeat Dr K——'s words in saying that, to my mind also, there is no further comment that can be made on all these facts. I consider it equally unnecessary to discuss at any further length with you now the mysterious relationship between Angelica, Edwina, the old valet, and myself – a relationship which seemed the work of a malicious demon who was playing his tricks with us. I will add only that I left the city soon after all these events, driven from the place by an oppression I could not shake off. The uncanny sensation left me suddenly a month or so later, giving way to a feeling of intense relief that flowed through all my veins with the warmth of an electric current. I am convinced that this change within me came about in the moment when the mad woman died.

The Mysterious Sketch

Erckmann-Chatrian

I

Opposite the chapel of Saint Sebalt in Nuremberg, at the corner of Trabaus Street, there stands a little tavern, tall and narrow, with a toothed gable and dusty windows, whose roof is surmounted by a plaster Virgin. It was there that I spent the unhappiest days of my life. I had gone to Nuremberg to study the old German masters; but in default of ready money, I had to paint portraits – and such portraits! Fat old women with their cats on their laps, big-wigged aldermen, burgomasters in three-cornered hats – all horribly bright with ochre and vermilion. From portraits I descended to sketches, and from sketches to silhouettes.

Nothing is more annoying than to have your landlord come to you every day with pinched lips, shrill voice, and impudent manner to say: 'Well, sir, how soon are you going to pay me? Do you know how much your bill is? No; that doesn't worry you! You eat, drink, and sleep calmly enough. God feeds the sparrows. Your bill now amounts to two hundred florins and ten kreutzers – it is not worth talking about.'

Those who have not heard any one talk in this way can form no idea of it; love of art, imagination, and the sacred enthusiasm for the beautiful are blasted by the breath of such an attack. You become awkward and timid; all your energy evaporates, as well as your feeling of personal dignity, and you bow respectfully at a distance to the burgomaster Schneegans.

One night, not having a sou, as usual, and threatened with imprisonment by this worthy Mister Rap, I determined to make him a bankrupt by cutting my throat. Seated on my narrow bed, opposite the window, in this agreeable mood, I gave myself up to a thousand philosophical reflections, more or less comforting.

'What is man?' I asked myself. 'An omnivorous animal; his jaws, provided with canines, incisors, and molars, prove it. The canines are made to tear meat; the incisors to bite fruits; and the molars to masticate, grind, and triturate animal and vegetable substances that are pleasant to smell and to taste. But when he has nothing to masticate, this being is an absurdity in Nature, a superfluity, a fifth wheel to the coach.'

Such were my reflections. I dared not open my razor for fear that the invincible force of my logic would inspire me with the courage to make an end of it all. After having argued so finely, I blew out my candle, postponing the sequel till the morrow.

That abominable Rap had completely stupefied me. I could do nothing but silhouettes, and my sole desire was to have some money to rid myself of his odious presence. But on this night a singular change came over my mind. I awoke about one o'clock – I lit my lamp, and, enveloping myself in my grey gabardine, I drew upon the paper a rapid sketch after the Dutch school – something strange and bizarre, which had not the slightest resemblance to my ordinary conceptions.

Imagine a dreary courtyard enclosed by high dilapidated walls. These walls are furnished with hooks, seven or eight feet from the ground. You see, at a glance, that it is a butchery.

On the left, there extends a lattice structure; you perceive through it a quartered beef suspended from the roof by enormous pulleys. Great pools of blood run over the flagstones and unite in a ditch full of refuse.

The light falls from above, between the chimneys where the weathercocks stand out from a bit of the sky the size of your hand, and the roofs of the neighbouring houses throw bold shadows from story to story.

At the back of this place is a shed, beneath the shed a pile of wood, and upon the pile of wood some ladders, a few bundles of straw, some coils of rope, a chicken-coop, and an old dilapidated rabbit-hutch.

How did these heterogeneous details suggest themselves to my imagination? I don't know; I had no reminiscences, and yet every stroke of the pencil seemed the result of observation, and strange because it was all so true. Nothing was lacking.

But on the right, one corner of the sketch remained a blank. I did not know what to put there…. Something suddenly seemed to writhe there, to move! Then I saw a foot, the sole of a foot. Notwithstanding this improbable position, I followed my inspiration without reference to my own criticism. This foot was joined to a leg – over this leg, stretched out with effort, there soon floated the skirt of a dress. In short, there appeared by degrees an old woman, pale, dishevelled, and wasted, thrown down at the side of a well, and struggling to free herself from a hand that clutched her throat.

It was a murder scene that I was drawing. The pencil fell from my hand.

This woman, in the boldest attitude, with her thighs bent on the curb of the well, her face contracted by terror, and her two hands grasping the murderer's arm, frightened me. I could not look at her. But the man – he, the person to whom that arm belonged – I could not see him. It was impossible for me to finish the sketch.

'I am tired,' I said, my forehead dripping with perspiration; 'there is only this figure to do; I will finish it tomorrow. It will be easy then.'

And again I went to bed, thoroughly frightened by my vision.

The next morning, I got up very early. I was dressing in order to resume my interrupted work, when two little knocks were heard on my door.

'Come in!'

The door opened. An old man, tall, thin, and dressed in black, appeared on the threshold. This man's face, his eyes set close together and his large nose like the beak of an eagle, surmounted by a high bony forehead, had something severe about it. He bowed to me gravely.

'Mister Christian Vénius, the painter?' said he.

'That is my name, sir.'

He bowed again, adding:

'The Baron Frederick Van Spreckdal.'

The appearance of the rich amateur, Van Spreckdal, judge of the criminal court, in my poor lodging, greatly disturbed me. I could not help throwing a stealthy glance at my old worm-eaten furniture, my damp hangings and my dusty floor. I felt humiliated by such dilapidation; but Van Spreckdal did not seem to take any account of these details; and sitting down at my little table:

'Mister Vénius,' he resumed, 'I come—' But at this instant his glance fell upon the unfinished sketch – he did not finish his phrase.

I was sitting on the edge of my little bed; and the sudden attention that this personage bestowed upon one of my productions made my heart beat with an indefinable apprehension.

At the end of a minute, Van Spreckdal lifted his head:

'Are you the author of that sketch?' he asked me with an intent look.

'Yes, sir.'

'What is the price of it?'

'I never sell my sketches. It is the plan for a picture.'

'Ah!' said he, picking up the paper with the tips of his long yellow fingers.

He took a lens from his waistcoat pocket and began to study the design in silence.

The sun was now shining obliquely into the garret. Van Spreckdal never said a word; the hook of his immense nose increased, his heavy eyebrows contracted, and his long pointed chin took a turn upward, making a thousand little wrinkles in his long, thin cheeks. The silence was so profound that I could distinctly hear the plaintive buzzing of a fly that had been caught in a spider's web.

'And the dimensions of this picture, Mister Vénius?' he said without looking at me.

'Three feet by four.'

'The price?'

'Fifty ducats.'

Van Spreckdal laid the sketch on the table, and drew from his pocket a large purse of green silk shaped like a pear; he drew the rings of it—

'Fifty ducats,' said he, 'here they are.'

I was simply dazzled.

The Baron rose and bowed to me, and I heard his big ivory-headed cane resounding on each step until he reached the bottom of the stairs. Then recovering from my stupour, I suddenly remembered that I had not thanked him, and I flew down the five flights like lightning; but when I reached the bottom, I looked to the right and left; the street was deserted.

'Well,' I said, 'this is strange.'

And I went upstairs again all out of breath.

II

The surprising way in which Van Spreckdal had appeared to me threw me into deep wonderment. 'Yesterday,' I said to myself, as I contemplated the pile of ducats glittering in the sun, 'yesterday I formed the wicked intention of cutting my throat, all for the want of a few miserable florins, and now today Fortune has showered them from the clouds. Indeed it was fortunate that I did not open my razor; and, if the same temptation ever comes to me again, I will take care to wait until the morrow.'

After making these judicious reflections, I sat down to finish the sketch; four strokes of the pencil and it would be finished. But here an incomprehensible difficulty awaited me. It was impossible for me to take those four sweeps of the pencil; I had lost the thread of my inspiration, and the mysterious personage no longer stood out in my brain. I tried in vain to evoke him, to sketch him, and to recover him; he no more accorded with the surroundings than with a figure by Raphael in a Teniers inn-kitchen. I broke out into a profuse perspiration.

At this moment, Rap opened the door without knocking, according to his praiseworthy custom. His eyes fell upon my pile of ducats and in a shrill voice he cried:

'Eh! eh! so I catch you. Will you still persist in telling me, Mr Painter, that you have no money?'

And his hooked fingers advanced with that nervous trembling that the sight of gold always produces in a miser.

For a few seconds I was stupefied.

The memory of all the indignities that this individual had inflicted upon me, his covetous look, and his impudent smile exasperated me. With a single bound, I caught hold of him, and pushed him out of the room, slamming the door in his face.

This was done with the crack and rapidity of a spring snuff-box.

But from outside the old usurer screamed like an eagle:

'My money, you thief, my money!'

The lodgers came out of their rooms, asking:

'What is the matter? What has happened?'

I opened the door suddenly and quickly gave Mister Rap a kick in the spine that sent him rolling down more than twenty steps.

'That's what's the matter!' I cried, quite beside myself. Then I shut the door and bolted it, while bursts of laughter from the neighbours greeted Mister Rap in the passage.

I was satisfied with myself; I rubbed my hands together. This adventure had put new life into me; I resumed my work, and was about to finish the sketch when I heard an unusual noise.

Butts of muskets were grounded on the pavement. I looked out of my window and saw three soldiers in full uniform with grounded arms in front of my door.

I said to myself in my terror: 'Can it be that that scoundrel of a Rap has had any bones broken?'

And here is the strange peculiarity of the human mind: I, who the night before had wanted to cut my own throat, shook from head to foot, thinking that I might well be hanged if Rap were dead.

The stairway was filled with confused noises. It was an ascending flood of heavy footsteps, clanking arms, and short syllables.

Suddenly somebody tried to open my door. It was shut.

Then there was a general clamour.

'In the name of the law – open!'

I arose, trembling and weak in the knees.

'Open!' the same voice repeated.

I thought to escape over the roofs; but I had hardly put my head out of the little snuff-box window, when I drew back, seized with vertigo. I saw in a flash all the windows below with their shining panes, their flower-pots, their bird-cages, and their gratings. Lower, the balcony; still lower, the street-lamp; still lower again, the sign of the 'Red Cask' framed in iron-work; and, finally, three glittering bayonets, only awaiting my fall to run me through the body from the sole of my foot to the crown of my head. On the roof of the opposite house a tortoise-shell cat was crouching behind a chimney, watching a band of sparrows fighting and scolding in the gutter.

One cannot imagine to what clearness, intensity, and rapidity the human eye acquires when stimulated by fear.

At the third summons I heard:

'Open, or we shall force it!'

Seeing that flight was impossible, I staggered to the door and drew the bolt.

Two hands immediately fell upon my collar. A dumpy, little man, smelling of wine, said:

'I arrest you!'

He wore a bottle-green redingote, buttoned to the chin, and a stovepipe hat. He had large brown whiskers, rings on every finger, and was named Passauf.

He was the chief of police.

Five bulldogs with flat caps, noses like pistols, and lower jaws turning upward, observed me from outside.

'What do you want?' I asked Passauf.

'Come downstairs,' he cried roughly, as he gave a sign to one of his men to seize me.

This man took hold of me, more dead than alive, while several other men turned my room upside down.

I went downstairs supported by the arms like a person in the last stages of consumption – with hair dishevelled and stumbling at every step.

They thrust me into a cab between two strong fellows, who charitably let me see the ends of their clubs, held to their wrists by a leather string – and then the carriage started off.

I heard behind us the feet of all the urchins of the town.

'What have I done?' I asked one of my keepers.

He looked at the other with a strange smile and said:

'Hans – he asks what he has done!'

That smile froze my blood.

Soon a deep shadow enveloped the carriage; the horses' hoofs resounded under an archway. We were entering the Raspelhaus. Of this place one might say:

'Dans cet antre, Je vois fort bien comme l'on entre, Et ne vois point comme on en sort.'

All is not rose-coloured in this world; from the claws of Rap I fell into a dungeon, from which very few poor devils have a chance to escape.

Large dark courtyards and rows of windows like a hospital, and furnished with gratings; not a sprig of verdure, not a festoon of ivy, not even a weathercock in perspective – such was my new lodging. It was enough to make one tear his hair out by the roots.

The police officers, accompanied by the jailer, took me temporarily to a lock-up.

The jailer, if I remember rightly, was named Kasper Schlüssel; with his grey woollen cap, his pipe between his teeth, and his bunch of keys at his belt, he reminded me of the Owl-God of the Caribs. He had the same golden yellow eyes, that see in the dark, a nose like a comma, and a neck that was sunk between the shoulders.

Schlüssel shut me up as calmly as one locks up his socks in a cupboard, while thinking of something else. As for me, I stood for more than ten minutes with my hands behind my back and my head bowed. At the end of that time I made the following reflection: 'When falling, Rap cried out, 'I am assassinated,' but he did not say by whom. I will say it was my neighbour, the old merchant with the spectacles: he will be hanged in my place.'

This idea comforted my heart, and I drew a long breath. Then I looked about my prison. It seemed to have been newly whitewashed, and the walls were bare of designs, except in one corner, where a gallows had been crudely sketched by my predecessor. The light was admitted through a bull's-eye about nine or ten feet from the floor; the furniture consisted of a bundle of straw and a tub.

I sat down upon the straw with my hands around my knees in deep despondency. It was with great difficulty that I could think clearly; but suddenly imagining that Rap, before dying, had denounced me, my legs began to tingle, and I jumped up coughing, as if the hempen cord were already tightening around my neck.

At the same moment, I heard Schlüssel walking down the corridor; he opened the lock-up, and told me to follow him. He was still accompanied by the two officers, so I fell into step resolutely.

We walked down long galleries, lighted at intervals by small windows from within. Behind a grating I saw the famous Jic-Jack, who was going to be executed on the morrow. He had on a strait-jacket and sang out in a raucous voice:

'Je suis le roi de ces montagnes.'

Seeing me, he called out:

'Eh! comrade! I'll keep a place for you at my right.'

The two police officers and the Owl-God looked at each other and smiled, while I felt the goose-flesh creep down the whole length of my back.

III

Schlüssel shoved me into a large and very dreary hall, with benches arranged in a semicircle. The appearance of this deserted hall, with its two high grated windows, and its Christ carved in old brown oak with His arms extended and His head sorrowfully inclined upon His shoulder, inspired me with I do not know what kind of religious fear that accorded with my actual situation.

All my ideas of false accusation disappeared, and my lips tremblingly murmured a prayer.

I had not prayed for a long time; but misfortune always brings us to thoughts of submission. Man is so little in himself!

Opposite me, on an elevated seat, two men were sitting with their backs to the light, and consequently their faces were in shadow. However, I recognized Van Spreckdal by his aquiline profile, illuminated by an oblique reflection from the window. The other person was fat, he had round, chubby cheeks and short hands, and he wore a robe, like Van Spreckdal.

Below was the clerk of the court, Conrad; he was writing at a low table and was tickling the tip of his ear with the feather-end of his pen. When I entered, he stopped to look at me curiously.

They made me sit down, and Van Spreckdal, raising his voice, said to me:

'Christian Vénius, where did you get this sketch?'

He showed me the nocturnal sketch which was then in his possession. It was handed to me. After having examined it, I replied:

'I am the author of it.'

A long silence followed; the clerk of the court, Conrad, wrote down my reply. I heard his pen scratch over the paper, and I thought: 'Why did they ask me that question? That has nothing to do with the kick I gave Rap in the back.'

'You are the author of it?' asked Van Spreckdal. 'What is the subject?'

'It is a subject of pure fancy.'

'You have not copied the details from some spot?'

'No, sir; I imagined it all.'

'Accused Christian,' said the judge in a severe tone, 'I ask you to reflect. Do not lie.'

'I have spoken the truth.'

'Write that down, clerk,' said Van Spreckdal.

The pen scratched again.

'And this woman,' continued the judge – 'this woman who is being murdered at the side of the well – did you imagine her also?'

'Certainly.'

'You have never seen her?'

'Never.'

Van Spreckdal rose indignantly; then, sitting down again, he seemed to consult his companion in a low voice.

These two dark profiles silhouetted against the brightness of the window, and the three men standing behind me, the silence in the hall – everything made me shiver.

'What do you want with me? What have I done?' I murmured.

Suddenly Van Spreckdal said to my guardians:

'You can take the prisoner back to the carriage; we will go to Metzerstrasse.'

Then, addressing me:

'Christian Vénius,' he cried, 'you are in a deplorable situation. Collect your thoughts and remember that if the law of man is inflexible, there still remains for you the mercy of God. This you can merit by confessing your crime.'

These words stunned me like a blow from a hammer. I fell back with extended arms, crying:

'Ah! what a terrible dream!'

And I fainted.

When I regained consciousness, the carriage was rolling slowly down the street; another one preceded us. The two officers were always with me. One of them on the way offered a pinch of snuff to his companion; mechanically I reached out my hand toward the snuff-box, but he withdrew it quickly.

My cheeks reddened with shame, and I turned away my head to conceal my emotion.

'If you look outside,' said the man with the snuff-box, 'we shall be obliged to put handcuffs on you.'

'May the devil strangle you, you infernal scoundrel!' I said to myself. And as the carriage now stopped, one of them got out, while the other held me by the collar; then, seeing that his comrade was ready to receive me, he pushed me rudely to him.

These infinite precautions to hold possession of my person boded no good; but I was far from predicting the seriousness of the accusation that hung over my head until an alarming circumstance opened my eyes and threw me into despair.

They pushed me along a low alley, the pavement of which was unequal and broken; along the wall there ran a yellowish ooze, exhaling a fetid odour. I walked down this dark place with the two men behind me. A little further there appeared the chiaroscuro of an interior courtyard.

I grew more and more terror-sticken as I advanced. It was no natural feeling: it was a poignant anxiety, outside of nature – like a nightmare. I recoiled instinctively at each step.

'Go on!' cried one of the policemen, laying his hand on my shoulder; 'go on!'

But what was my astonishment when, at the end of the passage, I saw the courtyard that I had drawn the night before, with its walls furnished with hooks, its rubbish-heap of old iron, its chicken-coops, and its rabbit-hutch. Not a dormer window, high or low, not a broken pane, not the slightest detail had been omitted.

I was thunderstruck by this strange revelation.

Near the well were the two judges, Van Spreckdal and Richter. At their feet lay the old woman extended on her back, her long, thin, grey hair, her blue face, her eyes wide open, and her tongue between her teeth.

It was a horrible spectacle!

'Well,' said Van Spreckdal, with solemn accents, 'what have you to say?'

I did not reply.

'Do you remember having thrown this woman, Theresa Becker, into this well, after having strangled her to rob her of her money?'

'No,' I cried, 'no! I do not know this woman; I never saw her before. May God help me!'

'That will do,' he replied in a dry voice. And without saying another word he went out with his companion.

The officers now believed that they had best put handcuffs on me. They took me back to the Raspelhaus, in a state of profound stupidity. I did not know what to think; my conscience itself troubled me; I even asked myself if I really had murdered the old woman!

In the eyes of the officers I was condemned.

I will not tell you of my emotions that night in the Raspelhaus, when, seated on my straw bed with the window opposite me and the gallows in perspective, I heard the watchmen cry in the silence of the night: 'Sleep, people of Nuremberg; the Lord watches over you. One o'clock! Two o'clock! Three o'clock!'

Every one may form his own idea of such a night. There is a fine saying that it is better to be hanged innocent than guilty. For the soul, yes; but for the body, it makes no difference; on the contrary, it kicks, it curses its lot, it tries to escape, knowing well enough that its role ends with the rope. Add to this, that it repents not having sufficiently enjoyed life and at having listened to the soul when it preached abstinence.

'Ah! if I had only known!' it cried, 'you would not have led me around by a string with your big words, your beautiful phrases, and your magnificent sentences! You would not have allured me with your fine promises. I should have had many happy moments that are now lost forever. Everything is over! You said to me: 'Control your passions.' Very well! I did control them. Here I am now. They are going to hang me, and you – later they will speak of you as a sublime soul, a stoical soul, a martyr to the errors of Justice. They will never think about me!'

Such were the sad reflections of my poor body.

Day broke; at first, dull and undecided, it threw an uncertain light on my bull's-eye window with its cross-bars; then it blazed against the wall at the back. Outside the street became lively. This was a market-day; it was Friday. I heard the vegetable wagons pass and also the country people with their baskets. Some chickens cackled in their coops in passing and some butter sellers chattered together. The market opposite opened, and they began to arrange the stalls.

Finally it was broad daylight and the vast murmur of the increasing crowd, housekeepers who assembled with baskets on their arms, coming and going, discussing and marketing, told me that it was eight o'clock.

With the light, my heart gained a little courage. Some of my black thoughts disappeared. I desired to see what was going on outside.

Other prisoners before me had managed to climb up to the bull's-eye; they had dug some holes in the wall to mount more easily. I climbed in my turn, and, when seated in the oval edge of the window, with my legs bent and my head bowed, I could see the crowd, and all the life and movement. Tears ran freely down my cheeks. I thought no longer of suicide – I experienced a need to live and breathe, which was really extraordinary.

'Ah!' I said, 'to live what happiness! Let them harness me to a wheelbarrow – let them put a ball and chain around my leg – nothing matters if I may only live!'

The old market, with its roof shaped like an extinguisher, supported on heavy pillars, made a superb picture: old women seated before their panniers of vegetables, their cages of poultry and their baskets of eggs; behind them the Jews, dealers in old clothes, their faces the colour of old box-wood; butchers with bare arms, cutting up meat on their stalls; countrymen, with large hats on the backs of their heads, calm and grave with their hands behind their backs and resting on their sticks of hollywood, and tranquilly smoking their pipes. Then the tumult and noise of the crowd – those screaming, shrill, grave, high, and short words – those expressive gestures – those sudden attitudes that show from a distance the progress of a discussion and depict so well the character of the individual – in short, all this captivated my mind, and notwithstanding my sad condition, I felt happy to be still of the world.

Now, while I looked about in this manner, a man – a butcher – passed, inclining forward and carrying an enormous quarter of beef on his shoulders; his arms were bare, his elbows were raised upward and his head was bent under them. His long hair, like that of Salvator's Sicambrian, hid his face from me; and yet, at the first glance, I trembled.

'It is he!' I said.

All the blood in my body rushed to my heart. I got down from the window trembling to the ends of my fingers, feeling my cheeks quiver, and the pallor spread over my face, stammering in a choked voice:

'It is he! he is there – there – and I, I have to die to expiate his crime. Oh, God! what shall I do? What shall I do?'

A sudden idea, an inspiration from Heaven, flashed across my mind. I put my hand in the pocket of my coat – my box of crayons was there!

Then rushing to the wall, I began to trace the scene of the murder with superhuman energy. No uncertainty, no hesitation! I knew the man! I had seen him! He was there before me!

At ten o'clock the jailer came to my cell. His owl-like impassibility gave place to admiration.

'Is it possible?' he cried, standing at the threshold.

'Go, bring me my judges,' I said to him, pursuing my work with an increasing exultation.

Schlüssel answered:

'They are waiting for you in the trial-room.'

'I wish to make a revelation,' I cried, as I put the finishing touches to the mysterious personage.

He lived; he was frightful to see. His full-faced figure, foreshortened upon the wall, stood out from the white background with an astonishing vitality.

The jailer went away.

A few minutes afterward the two judges appeared. They were stupefied. I, trembling, with extended hand, said to them:

'There is the murderer!'

After a few minutes of silence, Van Spreckdal asked me:

'What is his name?'

'I don't know; but he is at this moment in the market; he is cutting up meat in the third stall to the left as you enter from Trabaus Street.'

'What do you think?' said he, leaning toward his colleague.

'Send for the man,' he replied in a grave tone.

Several officers retained in the corridor obeyed this order. The judges stood, examining the sketch. As for me, I had dropped on my bed of straw, my head between my knees, perfectly exhausted.

Soon steps were heard echoing under the archway. Those who have never awaited the hour of deliverance and counted the minutes, which seem like centuries – those who have never experienced the sharp emotions of outrage, terror, hope, and doubt – can have no conception of the inward chills that

I experienced at that moment. I should have distinguished the step of the murderer, walking between the guards, among a thousand others. They approached. The judges themselves seemed moved. I raised up my head, my heart feeling as if an iron hand had clutched it, and I fixed my eyes upon the closed door. It opened. The man entered. His cheeks were red and swollen, the muscles in his large contracted jaws twitched as far as his ears, and his little restless eyes, yellow like a wolf's, gleamed beneath his heavy yellowish red eyebrows.

Van Spreckdal showed him the sketch in silence.

Then that murderous man, with the large shoulders, having looked, grew pale – then, giving a roar which thrilled us all with terror, he waved his enormous arms, and jumped backward to overthrow the guards. There was a terrible struggle in the corridor; you could hear nothing but the panting breath of the butcher, his muttered imprecations, and the short words and the shuffling feet of the guard, upon the flagstones.

This lasted only about a minute.

Finally the assassin re-entered, with his head hanging down, his eyes bloodshot, and his hands fastened behind his back. He looked again at the picture of the murderer; he seemed to reflect, and then, in a low voice, as if talking to himself:

'Who could have seen me,' he said, 'at midnight?'

I was saved!

†

Many years have passed since that terrible adventure. Thank Heaven! I make silhouettes no longer, nor portraits of burgomasters. Through hard work and perseverance, I have conquered my place in the world, and I earn my living honourably by painting works of art – the sole end, in my opinion, to which a true artist should aspire. But the memory of that nocturnal sketch has always remained in my mind. Sometimes, in the midst of work, the thought of it recurs. Then I lay down my palette and dream for hours.

How could a crime committed by a man that I did not know – at a place that I had never seen – have been reproduced by my pencil, in all its smallest details?

Was it chance? No! And moreover, what is chance but the effect of a cause of which we are ignorant?

Was Schiller right when he said: 'The immortal soul does not participate in the weaknesses of matter; during the sleep of the body, it spreads its radiant wings and travels, God knows where! What it then does, no one can say, but inspiration sometimes betrays the secret of its nocturnal wanderings.'

Who knows? Nature is more audacious in her realities than man in his most fantastic imagining.

Clarimonde

Théophile Gautier

Brother, you ask me if I have ever loved. Yes. My story is a strange and terrible one; and though I am sixty-six years of age, I scarcely dare even now to disturb the ashes of that memory.

From my earliest childhood I had felt a vocation to the priesthood, so that all my studies were directed with that idea in view. Up to the age of twenty-four my life had been only a prolonged novitiate. Having completed my course of theology I successively received all the minor orders, and my superiors judged me worthy, despite my youth, to pass the last awful degree. My ordination was fixed for Easter week.

I had never gone into the world. My world was confined by the walls of the college and the seminary. I knew in a vague sort of a way that there was something called Woman, but I never permitted my thoughts to dwell on such a subject, and I lived in a state of perfect innocence. Twice a year only I saw my infirm and aged mother, and in those visits were comprised my sole relations with the outer world.

I regretted nothing; I felt not the least hesitation at taking the last irrevocable step; I was filled with joy and impatience. Never did a betrothed lover count the slow hours with more feverish ardour; I slept only to dream that I was saying mass; I believed there could be nothing in the world more delightful than to be a priest; I would have refused to be a king or a poet in preference. My ambition could conceive of no loftier aim.

At last the great day came. I walked to the church with a step so light that I fancied myself sustained in air, or that I had wings upon my shoulders. I believed myself an angel, and wondered at the sombre and thoughtful faces of my companions, for there were several of us. I had passed all the night in prayer, and was in a condition wellnigh bordering on ecstasy. The bishop, a venerable old man, seemed to me God the Father leaning over his Eternity, and I beheld Heaven through the vault of the temple.

You well know the details of that ceremony – the benediction, the communion under both forms, the anointing of the palms of the hands with the Oil of Catechumens, and then the holy sacrifice offered in concert with the bishop.

Ah, truly spake Job when he declared that the imprudent man is one who hath not made a covenant with his eyes! I accidentally lifted my head, which until then I had kept down, and beheld before me, so close that it seemed that I could have touched her – although she was actually a considerable distance from me and on the further side of the sanctuary railing – a young woman of extraordinary beauty, and attired with royal magnificence. It seemed as though scales had suddenly fallen from my eyes. I felt like a blind man who unexpectedly recovers his sight. The bishop, so radiantly glorious but an instant before, suddenly vanished away, the tapers paled upon their golden candlesticks like stars in the dawn, and a vast darkness seemed to fill the whole church. The charming creature appeared in brief relief against the background of that darkness, like some angelic revelation. She seemed herself radiant, and radiating light rather than receiving it.

I lowered my eyelids, firmly resolved not to again open them, that I might not be influenced by external objects, for distraction had gradually taken possession of me until I hardly knew what I was doing.

In another minute, nevertheless, I reopened my eyes, for through my eyelashes I still beheld her, all sparkling with prismatic colours, and surrounded with such a purple penumbra as one beholds in gazing at the sun.

Oh, how beautiful she was! The greatest painters, who followed ideal beauty into heaven itself, and thence brought back to earth the true portrait of the Madonna, never in their delineations even approached that wildly beautiful reality which I saw before me. Neither the verses of the poet nor the palette of the artist could convey any conception of her. She was rather tall, with a form and bearing of a goddess. Her hair, of a soft blonde hue, was parted in the midst and flowed back over her temples in two rivers of rippling gold; she seemed a diademed queen. Her forehead, bluish-white in its transparency, extended its calm breadth above the arches of her eyebrows, which by a strange singularity were almost black, and admirably relieved the effect of sea-green eyes of unsustainable vivacity and brilliancy. What eyes! With a single flash they could have decided a man's destiny. They had a life, a limpidity, an ardour, a humid light which I have never seen in human eyes; they shot forth rays like arrows, which I could distinctly *see* enter my heart. I know not if the fire which illumined them came from heaven or from hell, but assuredly it came from one or the other. That woman was either an angel or a demon, perhaps both. Assuredly she never sprang from the flank of Eve, our common mother. Teeth of the most lustrous pearl gleamed in her ruddy smile, and at every inflection of her lips little dimples appeared in the satiny rose of her adorable cheeks. There was a delicacy and pride in the regal outline of her nostrils bespeaking noble blood. Agate gleams played over the smooth lustrous skin of her half-bare shoulders, and strings of great blonde pearls – almost equal to her neck in beauty of colour – descended upon her bosom. From time to time she elevated her head with the undulating grace of a startled serpent or peacock, thereby imparting a quivering motion to the high lace ruff which surrounded it like a silver trellis-work.

She wore a robe of orange-red velvet, and from her wide ermine-lined sleeves there peeped forth patrician hands of infinite delicacy, and so ideally transparent that, like the fingers of Aurora, they permitted the light to shine through them.

All these details I can recollect at this moment as plainly as though they were of yesterday, for notwithstanding I was greatly troubled at the time, nothing escaped me; the faintest touch of shading, the little dark speck at the point of the chin, the imperceptible down at the corners of the lips, the velvety floss upon the brow, the quivering shadows of the eyelashes upon the cheeks, I could notice everything with astonishing lucidity of perception.

And gazing I felt opening within me gates that had until then remained closed; vents long obstructed became all clear, permitting glimpses of unfamiliar perspectives within; life suddenly made itself visible to me under a totally novel aspect. I felt as though I had just been born into a new world and a new order of things. A frightful anguish commenced to torture my heart as with red-hot pincers. Every successive minute seemed to me at once but a second and yet a century. Meanwhile the ceremony was proceeding, and with an effort of will sufficient to have uprooted a mountain, I strove to cry out that I would not be a priest, but I could not speak; my tongue seemed nailed to my palate, and I found it impossible to express my will by the least syllable of negation. Though fully awake, I felt like one under the influence of a nightmare, who vainly strives to shriek out the one word upon which life depends.

She seemed conscious of the martyrdom I was undergoing, and, as though to encourage me, she gave me a look replete with divinest promise. Her eyes were a poem; their every glance was a song.

She said to me:

'If thou wilt be mine, I shall make thee happier than God Himself in His paradise. The angels themselves will be jealous of thee. Tear off that funeral shroud in which thou art about to wrap thyself. I am Beauty, I am Youth, I am Life. Come to me! Together we shall be Love. Can Jehovah offer thee aught in exchange? Our lives will flow on like a dream, in one eternal kiss.

'Fling forth the wine of that chalice, and thou art free. I will conduct thee to the Unknown Isles. Thou shalt sleep in my bosom upon a bed of massy gold under a silver pavilion, for I love thee and would take thee away from thy God, before whom so many noble hearts pour forth floods of love which never reach even the steps of His throne!'

These words seemed to float to my ears in a rhythm of infinite sweetness, for her look was actually sonorous, and the utterances of her eyes were re-echoed in the depths of my heart as though living lips had breathed them into my life. I felt myself willing to renounce God, and yet my tongue mechanically fulfilled all the formalities of the ceremony. The fair one gave me another look, so beseeching, so despairing that keen blades seemed to pierce my heart, and I felt my bosom transfixed by more swords than those of Our Lady of Sorrows.

All was consummated; I had become a priest.

Never was deeper anguish painted on human face than upon hers. The maiden who beholds her affianced lover suddenly fall dead at her side, the mother bending over the empty cradle of her child, Eve seated at the threshold of the gate of Paradise, the miser who finds a stone substituted for his stolen treasure, the poet who accidentally permits the only manuscript of his finest work to fall into the fire, could not wear a look so despairing, so inconsolable. All the blood had abandoned her charming face, leaving it whiter than marble; her beautiful arms hung lifelessly on either side of her body as though their muscles had suddenly relaxed, and she sought the support of a pillar, for her yielding limbs almost betrayed her. As for myself, I staggered toward the door of the church, livid as death, my forehead bathed with a sweat bloodier than that of Calvary; I felt as though I were being strangled; the vault seemed to have flattened down upon my shoulders, and it seemed to me that my head alone sustained the whole weight of the dome.

As I was about to cross the threshold a hand suddenly caught mine – a woman's hand! I had never till then touched the hand of any woman. It was cold as a serpent's skin, and yet its impress remained upon my wrist, burnt there as though branded by a glowing iron. It was she. 'Unhappy man! Unhappy man! What hast thou done?' she exclaimed in a low voice, and immediately disappeared in the crowd.

The aged bishop passed by. He cast a severe and scrutinizing look upon me. My face presented the wildest aspect imaginable; I blushed and turned pale alternately; dazzling lights flashed before my eyes. A companion took pity on me. He seized my arm and led me out. I could not possibly have found my way back to the seminary unassisted. At the corner of a street, while the young priest's attention was momentarily turned in another direction, a negro page, fantastically garbed, approached me, and without pausing on his way slipped into my hand a little pocket-book with gold-embroidered corners, at the same time giving me a sign to hide it. I concealed it in my sleeve, and there kept it until I found myself alone in my cell. Then I opened the clasp. There were only two leaves within, bearing the words, 'Clarimonde. At the Concini Palace.' So little acquainted was I at that time with the things of this world that I had never heard of Clarimonde, celebrated as she was, and I had no idea as to where the Concini Palace was situated. I hazarded a thousand conjectures, each more extravagant than the last; but, in truth, I cared little whether she were a great lady or a courtesan, so that I could but see her once more.

My love, although the growth of a single hour, had taken imperishable root. I gave myself up to a thousand extravagancies. I kissed the place upon my hand which she had touched, and I repeated her name over and over again for hours in succession. I only needed to close my eyes in order to see her distinctly as though she were actually present; and I reiterated to myself the words she had uttered in my ear at the church porch: 'Unhappy man! Unhappy man! What hast thou done?' I comprehended at last the full horror of my situation, and the funereal and awful restraints of the state into which I had just entered became clearly revealed to me. To be a priest! – that is, to be chaste, to never love, to observe no distinction of sex or age, to turn from the sight of all beauty, to put out one's own eyes, to hide forever crouching in the chill shadows of some church or cloister, to visit none but the dying, to watch by unknown corpses, and ever bear about with one the black soutane as a garb of mourning for one's self, so that your very dress might serve as a pall for your coffin.

What could I do in order to see Clarimonde once more? I had no pretext to offer for desiring to leave the seminary, not knowing any person in the city. I would not even be able to remain there but a short time, and was only waiting my assignment to the curacy which I must thereafter occupy. I tried to remove the bars of the window; but it was at a fearful height from the ground, and I found that as I had no ladder it would be useless to think of escaping thus. And, furthermore, I could descend thence only by night in any event, and afterward how should I be able to find my way through the inextricable labyrinth of streets? All these difficulties, which to many would have appeared altogether insignificant, were gigantic to me, a poor seminarist who had fallen in love only the day before for the first time, without experience, without money, without attire.

'Ah!' cried I to myself in my blindness, 'were I not a priest I could have seen her every day; I might have been her lover, her spouse. Instead of being wrapped in this dismal shroud of mine I would have had garments of silk and velvet, golden chains, a sword, and fair plumes like other handsome young cavaliers. My hair, instead of being dishonoured by the tonsure, would flow down upon my neck in waving curls; I would have a fine waxed moustache; I would be a gallant.' But one hour passed before an altar, a few hastily articulated words, had forever cut me off from the number of the living, and I had myself sealed down the stone of my own tomb; I had with my own hand bolted the gate of my prison!

I went to the window. The sky was beautifully blue; the trees had donned their spring robes; nature seemed to be making parade of an ironical joy. The *Place* was filled with people, some going, others coming; young beaux and young beauties were sauntering in couples toward the groves and gardens; merry youths passed by, cheerily trolling refrains of drinking songs – it was all a picture of vivacity, life, animation, gaiety, which formed a bitter contrast with my mourning and my solitude. On the steps of the gate sat a young mother playing with her child. She kissed its little rosy mouth still impearled with drops of milk, and performed, in order to amuse it, a thousand divine little puerilities such as only mothers know how to invent. The father standing at a little distance smiled gently upon the charming group, and with folded arms seemed to hug his joy to his heart. I could not endure that spectacle. I closed the window with violence, and flung myself on my bed, my heart filled with frightful hate and jealousy, and gnawed my fingers and my bed covers like a tiger that has passed ten days without food.

I know not how long I remained in this condition, but at last, while writhing on the bed in a fit of spasmodic fury, I suddenly perceived the Abbé Sérapion, who was standing erect in the centre of the room, watching me attentively. Filled with shame of myself, I let my head fall upon my breast and covered my face with my hands.

'Romuald, my friend, something very extraordinary is transpiring within you,' observed Sérapion, after a few moments' silence; 'your conduct is altogether inexplicable. You – always so quiet, so pious, so gentle – you to rage in your cell like a wild beast! Take heed, brother – do not listen to the suggestions of the devil. Fear not. Never allow yourself to become discouraged. The most watchful and steadfast souls are at moments liable to such temptation. Pray, fast, meditate, and the Evil Spirit will depart from you.'

The words of the Abbé Sérapion restored me to myself, and I became a little more calm. 'I came,' he continued, 'to tell you that you have been appointed to the curacy of C——. The priest who had charge of it has just died, and Monseigneur the Bishop has ordered me to have you installed there at once. Be ready, therefore, to start tomorrow.'

To leave tomorrow without having been able to see her again, to add yet another barrier to the many already interposed between us, to lose forever all hope of being able to meet her, except, indeed, through a miracle! Even to write her, alas! would be impossible, for by whom could I despatch my letter? With my sacred character of priest, to whom could I dare unbosom myself, in whom could I confide? I became a prey to the bitterest anxiety.

Next morning Sérapion came to take me away. Two mules freighted with our miserable valises awaited us at the gate. He mounted one, and I the other as well as I knew how.

As we passed along the streets of the city, I gazed attentively at all the windows and balconies in the hope of seeing Clarimonde, but it was yet early in the morning, and the city had hardly opened its eyes. Mine sought to penetrate the blinds and window-curtains of all the palaces before which we were passing. Sérapion doubtless attributed this curiosity to my admiration of the architecture, for he slackened the pace of his animal in order to give me time to look around me. At last we passed the city gates and commenced to mount the hill beyond. When we arrived at its summit I turned to take a last look at the place where Clarimonde dwelt. The shadow of a great cloud hung over all the city; the contrasting colours of its blue and red roofs were lost in the uniform half-tint, through which here and there floated upward, like white flakes of foam, the smoke of freshly kindled fires. By a singular optical effect one edifice, which surpassed in height all the neighbouring buildings that were still dimly veiled by the vapours, towered up, fair and lustrous with the gilding of a solitary beam of sunlight – although actually more than a league away it seemed quite near. The smallest details of its architecture were plainly distinguishable – the turrets, the platform, the window-casements and even the swallow-tailed weather vanes.

'What is that place I see over there, all lighted up by the sun?' I asked Sérapion. He shaded his eyes with his hand, and having looked in the direction indicated, replied: 'It is the ancient palace which the Prince Concini has given to the courtesan Clarimonde. Awful things are done there!'

At that instant, I know not yet whether it was a reality or an illusion, I fancied I saw gliding along the terrace a shapely white figure, which gleamed for a moment in passing and as quickly vanished. It was Clarimonde.

Oh, did she know that at that very hour, all feverish and restless – from the height of the rugged road which separated me from her and which, alas! I could never more descend – I was directing my eyes upon the palace where she dwelt, and which a mocking beam of sunlight seemed to bring nigh to me, as though inviting me to enter therein as its lord? Undoubtedly she must have known it, for her soul was too sympathetically united with mine not to have felt its least emotional thrill, and that subtle sympathy it must have been which prompted her to climb – although clad only in her night-dress – to the summit of the terrace, amid the icy dews of the morning.

The shadow gained the palace, and the scene became to the eye only a motionless ocean of roofs and gables, amid which one mountainous undulation was distinctly visible. Sérapion urged his mule forward, my own at once followed at the same gait, and a sharp angle in the road at last hid the city of S—— forever from my eyes, as I was destined never to return thither. At the close of a weary three-days' journey through dismal country fields, we caught sight of the cock upon the steeple of the church which I was to take charge of, peeping above the trees, and after having followed some winding roads fringed with thatched cottages and little gardens, we found ourselves in front of the façade, which certainly possessed few features of magnificence. A porch ornamented with some mouldings, and two or three pillars rudely hewn from sandstone; a tiled roof with counterforts of the same sandstone as the pillars, that was all. To the left lay the cemetery, overgrown with high weeds, and having a great iron cross rising up in its centre; to the right stood the presbytery, under the shadow of the church. It was a house of the most extreme simplicity and frigid cleanliness. We entered the enclosure. A few chickens were picking up some oats scattered upon the ground; accustomed, seemingly, to the black habit of ecclesiastics, they showed no fear of our presence and scarcely troubled themselves to get out of our way. A hoarse, wheezy barking fell upon our ears, and we saw an aged dog running toward us.

It was my predecessor's dog. He had dull bleared eyes, grizzled hair, and every mark of the greatest age to which a dog can possibly attain. I patted him gently, and he proceeded at once to march along beside me with an air of satisfaction unspeakable. A very old woman, who had been the housekeeper of the former curé, also came to meet us, and after having invited me into a little back parlour, asked whether I intended to retain her. I replied that I would take care of her, and the dog, and the chickens, and all the furniture her master had bequeathed her at his death. At this she became fairly transported with joy, and the Abbé Sérapion at once paid her the price which she asked for her little property.

For a whole year I fulfilled all the duties of my calling with the most scrupulous exactitude, praying and fasting, exhorting and lending ghostly aid to the sick, and bestowing alms even to the extent of frequently depriving myself of the very necessaries of life. But I felt a great aridness within me, and the sources of grace seemed closed against me. I never found that happiness which should spring from the fulfilment of a holy mission; my thoughts were far away, and the words of Clarimonde were ever upon my lips like an involuntary refrain. Oh, brother, meditate well on this! Through having but once lifted my eyes to look upon a woman, through one fault apparently so venial, I have for years remained a victim to the most miserable agonies, and the happiness of my life has been destroyed forever.

I will not longer dwell upon those defeats, or on those inward victories invariably followed by yet more terrible falls, but will at once proceed to the facts of my story. One night my door-bell was long and violently rung. The aged housekeeper arose and opened to the stranger, and the figure of a man, whose complexion was deeply bronzed, and who was richly clad in a foreign costume, with a poniard at his girdle, appeared under the rays of Barbara's lantern. Her first impulse was one of terror, but the stranger reassured her, and stated that he desired to see me at once on matters relating to my holy calling. Barbara invited him upstairs, where I was on the point of retiring. The stranger told me that his mistress, a very noble lady, was lying at the point of death, and desired to see a priest. I replied that I was prepared to follow him, took with me the sacred articles necessary for extreme unction, and descended in all haste. Two horses black as the night itself stood without the gate, pawing the ground with impatience, and veiling their chests with long streams of smoky vapour exhaled from their nostrils. He held the stirrup and aided me to mount upon one; then, merely laying his hand upon the pummel of the saddle, he vaulted on the other, pressed the animal's sides with his knees, and loosened rein. The horse bounded forward with the velocity of an arrow. Mine, of which the stranger held the bridle, also started off at a swift gallop, keeping up with his companion. We devoured the road. The ground flowed backward beneath us in a long streaked line of pale grey, and the black silhouettes of the trees seemed fleeing by us on either side like an army in rout. We passed through a forest so profoundly gloomy that I felt my flesh creep in the chill darkness with superstitious fear. The showers of bright sparks which flew from the stony road under the ironshod feet of our horses, remained glowing in our wake like a fiery trail; and had any one at that hour of the night beheld us both – my guide and myself – he must have taken us for two spectres riding upon nightmares. Witch-fires ever and anon flitted across the road before us, and the night-birds shrieked fearsomely in the depth of the woods beyond, where we beheld at intervals glow the phosphorescent eyes of wildcats. The manes of the horses became more and more dishevelled, the sweat streamed over their flanks, and their breath came through their nostrils hard and fast. But when he found them slacking pace, the guide reanimated them by uttering a strange, guttural, unearthly cry, and the gallop recommenced with fury. At last the whirlwind race ceased; a huge black mass pierced through with many bright points of light suddenly rose before us, the hoofs of our horses echoed louder upon a strong wooden drawbridge, and we rode under a great vaulted archway which darkly yawned between two enormous towers. Some great excitement evidently reigned in the castle. Servants with torches were crossing the courtyard in every direction, and above lights were ascending and descending from landing to landing. I obtained a confused glimpse of vast masses of architecture – columns, arcades, flights of steps, stairways – a royal voluptuousness and elfin magnificence of construction worthy of fairyland. A negro page – the same who had before brought me the tablet from Clarimonde, and whom I instantly recognized – approached to aid me in dismounting, and the major-domo, attired in black velvet with a gold chain about his neck, advanced to meet me, supporting himself upon an ivory cane. Large tears were falling from his eyes and streaming over his cheeks and white beard. 'Too late!' he cried, sorrowfully shaking his venerable head. 'Too late, sir priest! But if you have not been able to save the soul, come at least to watch by the poor body.'

He took my arm and conducted me to the death chamber. I wept not less bitterly than he, for I had learned that the dead one was none other than that Clarimonde whom I had so deeply and so wildly loved. A *prie-dieu* stood at the foot of the bed; a bluish flame flickering in a bronze patera filled all the room with a wan, deceptive light, here and there bringing out in the darkness at intervals some projection of furniture or cornice. In a chiselled urn upon the table there was a faded white rose, whose leaves – excepting one that still held – had all fallen, like odorous tears, to the foot of the vase. A broken black mask, a fan, and disguises of every variety, which were lying on the arm-chairs, bore witness that death had entered suddenly and unannounced into that sumptuous dwelling. Without daring to cast my eyes upon the bed, I knelt down and commenced to repeat the Psalms for the Dead, with exceeding fervour, thanking God that He had placed the tomb between me and the memory of this woman, so that I might thereafter be able to utter her name in my prayers as a name forever sanctified by death. But my fervour gradually weakened, and I fell insensibly into a reverie. That chamber bore no semblance to a chamber of death. In lieu of the fœtid and cadaverous odours which I had been accustomed to breathe during such funereal vigils, a languorous vapour of Oriental perfume – I know not what amorous odour of woman – softly floated through the tepid air. That pale light seemed rather a twilight gloom contrived for voluptuous pleasure, than a substitute for the yellow-flickering watch-tapers which shine by the side of corpses. I thought upon the strange destiny which enabled me to meet Clarimonde again at the very moment when she was lost to me forever, and a sigh of regretful anguish escaped from my breast. Then it seemed to me that someone behind me had also sighed, and I turned round to look. It was only an echo. But in that moment my eyes fell upon the bed of death which they had till then avoided. The red damask curtains, decorated with large flowers worked in embroidery, and looped up with gold bullion, permitted me to behold the fair dead, lying at full length, with hands joined upon her bosom. She was covered with a linen wrapping of dazzling whiteness, which formed a strong contrast with the gloomy purple of the hangings, and was of so fine a texture that it concealed nothing of her body's charming form, and allowed the eye to follow those beautiful outlines – undulating like the neck of a swan – which even death had not robbed of their supple grace. She seemed an alabaster statue executed by same skilful sculptor to place upon the tomb of a queen, or rather, perhaps, like a slumbering maiden over whom the silent snow had woven a spotless veil.

I could no longer maintain my constrained attitude of prayer. The air of the alcove intoxicated me, that febrile perfume of half-faded roses penetrated my very brain, and I commenced to pace restlessly up and down the chamber, pausing at each turn before the bier to contemplate the graceful corpse lying beneath the transparency of its shroud. Wild fancies came thronging to my brain. I thought to myself that she might not, perhaps, be really dead; that she might only have feigned death for the purpose of bringing me to her castle, and then declaring her love. At one time I even thought I saw her foot move under the whiteness of the coverings, and slightly disarrange the long, straight folds of the winding sheet.

And then I asked myself: 'Is this indeed Clarimonde? What proof have I that it is she? Might not that black page have passed into the service of some other lady? Surely, I must be going mad to torture and afflict myself thus!' But my heart answered with a fierce throbbing: 'It is she; it is she indeed!' I approached the bed again, and fixed my eyes with redoubled attention upon the object of my incertitude. Ah, must I confess it? That exquisite perfection of bodily form, although purified and made sacred by the shadow of death, affected me more voluptuously than it should have done, and that repose so closely resembled slumber that one might well have mistaken it for such. I forgot that I had come there to perform a funeral ceremony; I fancied myself a young bridegroom entering the chamber of the bride, who all modestly hides her fair face, and through coyness seeks to keep herself wholly veiled. Heartbroken with grief, yet wild with hope, shuddering at once with fear and pleasure, I bent over her and grasped the corner of the sheet. I lifted it back, holding my breath all the while through fear of waking her. My arteries throbbed with such violence that I felt them hiss through my temples, and the sweat poured from my forehead in streams, as though I had lifted a mighty slab of marble. There, indeed, lay Clarimonde, even as I had seen her at the church on the day of my ordination. She was not less charming than then. With her, death seemed but a last coquetry. The pallor of her cheeks, the less brilliant carnation of her lips, her long eyelashes lowered and relieving their dark fringe against that white skin, lent her an unspeakably seductive aspect of melancholy chastity and mental suffering; her long loose hair, still intertwined with some little blue flowers, made a shining pillow for her head, and veiled the nudity of her shoulders with its thick ringlets; her beautiful hands, purer, more diaphanous than the Host, were crossed on her bosom in an attitude of pious rest and silent prayer, which served to counteract all that might have proven otherwise too alluring – even after death – in the exquisite roundness and ivory polish of her bare arms from which the pearl bracelets had not yet been removed. I remained long in mute contemplation, and the more I gazed, the less could I persuade myself that life had really abandoned that beautiful body forever. I do not know whether it was an illusion or a reflection of the lamplight, but it seemed to me that the blood was again commencing to circulate under that lifeless pallor, although she remained all motionless. I laid my hand lightly on her arm; it was cold, but not colder than her hand on the day when it touched mine at the portals of the church. I resumed my position, bending my face above her, and bathing her cheeks with the warm dew of my tears. Ah, what bitter feelings of despair and helplessness, what agonies unutterable did I endure in that long watch! Vainly did I wish that I could have gathered all my life into one mass that I might give it all to her, and breathe into her chill remains the flame which devoured me. The night advanced, and feeling the moment of eternal separation approach, I could not deny myself the last sad sweet pleasure of imprinting a kiss upon the dead lips of her who had been my only love…. Oh, miracle! A faint breath mingled itself with my breath, and the mouth of Clarimonde responded to the passionate pressure of mine. Her eyes unclosed, and lighted up with something of their former brilliancy; she uttered a long sigh, and uncrossing her arms, passed them around my neck with a look of ineffable delight. 'Ah, it is thou, Romuald;' she murmured in a voice languishingly sweet as the last vibrations of a harp. 'What ailed thee, dearest? I waited so long for thee that I am dead; but we are now betrothed; I can see thee and visit thee. Adieu, Romuald, adieu! I love thee. That is all I wished to tell thee, and I give thee back the life which thy kiss for a moment recalled. We shall soon meet again.'

Her head fell back, but her arms yet encircled me, as though to retain me still. A furious whirlwind suddenly burst in that window, and entered the chamber. The last remaining leaf of the white rose for a moment palpitated at the extremity of the stalk like a butterfly's wing, then it detached itself and flew forth through the open casement, bearing with it the soul of Clarimonde. The lamp was extinguished, and I fell insensible upon the bosom of the beautiful dead.

When I came to myself again I was lying on the bed in my little room at the presbytery, and the old dog of the former curé was licking my hand which had been hanging down outside of the covers. Afterward I learned that I had lain thus for three days, giving no evidence of life beyond the faintest respiration. Barbara told me that the same coppery-complexioned man who came to seek me on the night of my departure from the presbytery, had brought me back the next morning in a close litter, and departed immediately afterward; but none knew of any castle in the neighbourhood answering to the description of that in which I had again found Clarimonde.

One morning I found the Abbé Sérapion in my room. While he inquired after my health in hypocritically honeyed accents, he constantly kept his two great yellow lion-eyes fixed upon me, and plunged his look into my soul like a sounding lead. Suddenly he said, in a clear vibrant voice, which rang in my ears like the trumpets of the Last Judgment:

'The great courtesan Clarimonde died a few days ago, at the close of an orgie which lasted eight days and eight nights. It was something infernally splendid. The abominations of the banquets of Belshazzar and Cleopatra were re-enacted there. Good God, what age are we living in? The guests were served by swarthy slaves who spoke an unknown tongue, and who seemed to me to be veritable demons. The livery of the very least among them would have served for the gala-dress of an emperor. There have always been very strange stories told of this Clarimonde, and all her lovers came to a violent or miserable end. They used to say that she was a ghoul, a female vampire; but I believe she was none other than Beelzebub himself.'

He ceased to speak and commenced to regard me more attentively than ever, as though to observe the effect of his words on me. I could not refrain from starting when I heard him utter the name of Clarimonde, and this news of her death, in addition to the pain it caused me by reason of its coincidence with the nocturnal scenes I had witnessed, filled me with an agony and terror which my face betrayed, despite my utmost endeavours to appear composed. Sérapion fixed an anxious and severe look upon me, and then observed: 'My son, I must warn you that you are standing with foot raised upon the brink of an abyss; take heed lest you fall therein.

Satan's claws are long, and tombs are not always true to their trust. The tombstone of Clarimonde should be sealed down with a triple seal, for, if report be true, it is not the first time she has died. May God watch over you, Romuald!'

And with these words the Abbé walked slowly to the door. I did not see him again at that time, for he left for S—— almost immediately.

I became completely restored to health and resumed my accustomed duties. The memory of Clarimonde and the words of the old Abbé were constantly in my mind; nevertheless no extraordinary event had occurred to verify the funereal predictions of Sérapion, and I had commenced to believe that his fears and my own terrors were over-exaggerated, when one night I had a strange dream. I had hardly fallen asleep when I heard my bed-curtains drawn apart, as their rings slid back upon the curtain rod with a sharp sound. I rose up quickly upon my elbow, and beheld the shadow of a woman standing erect before me. I recognized Clarimonde immediately. She bore in her hand a little lamp, shaped like those which are placed in tombs, and its light lent her fingers a rosy transparency, which extended itself by lessening degrees even to the opaque and milky whiteness of her bare arm. Her only garment was the linen winding-sheet which had shrouded her when lying upon the bed of death. She sought to gather its folds over her bosom as though ashamed of being so scantily clad, but her little hand was not equal to the task. She was so white that the colour of the drapery blended with that of her flesh under the pallid rays of the lamp. Enveloped with this subtle tissue which betrayed all the contour of her body, she seemed rather the marble statue of some fair antique rather than a woman endowed with life. But dead or living, statue or woman, shadow or body, her beauty was still the same, only that the green light of her eyes was less brilliant, and her mouth, once so warmly crimson, was only tinted with a faint tender rosiness, like that of her cheeks. The little blue flowers which I had noticed entwined in her hair were withered and dry, and had lost nearly all their leaves, but this did not prevent her from being charming – so charming that notwithstanding the strange character of the adventure, and the unexplainable manner in which she had entered my room, I felt not even for a moment the least fear.

She placed the lamp on the table and seated herself at the foot of my bed; then bending toward me, she said, in that voice at once silvery clear and yet velvety in its sweet softness, such as I never heard from any lips save hers:

'I have kept thee long in waiting, dear Romuald, and it must have seemed to thee that I had forgotten thee. But I come from afar off, very far off, and from a land whence no other has ever yet returned. There is neither sun nor moon in that land whence I come: all is but space and shadow; there is neither road nor pathway: no earth for the foot, no air for the wing; and nevertheless behold me here, for Love is stronger than Death and must conquer him in the end. Oh what sad faces and fearful things I have seen on my way hither! What difficulty my soul, returned to earth through the power of will alone, has had in finding its body and reinstating itself therein! What terrible efforts I had to make ere I could lift the ponderous slab with which they had covered me! See, the palms of my poor hands are all bruised! Kiss them, sweet love, that they may be healed!' She laid the cold palms of her hands upon my mouth, one after the other. I kissed them, indeed, many times, and she the while watched me with a smile of ineffable affection.

I confess to my shame that I had entirely forgotten the advice of the Abbé Sérapion and the sacred office wherewith I had been invested. I had fallen without resistance, and at the first assault. I had not even made the least effort to repel the tempter. The fresh coolness of Clarimonde's skin penetrated my own, and I felt voluptuous tremors pass over my whole body. Poor child! in spite of all I saw afterward, I can hardly yet believe she was a demon; at least she had no appearance of being such, and never did Satan so skilfully conceal his claws and horns. She had drawn her feet up beneath her, and squatted down on the edge of the couch in an attitude full of negligent coquetry. From time to time she passed her little hand through my hair and twisted it into curls, as though trying how a new style of wearing it would become my face. I abandoned myself to her hands with the most guilty pleasure, while she accompanied her gentle play with the prettiest prattle. The most remarkable fact was that I felt no astonishment whatever at so extraordinary an adventure, and as in dreams one finds no difficulty in accepting the most fantastic events as simple facts, so all these circumstances seemed to me perfectly natural in themselves.

'I loved thee long ere I saw thee, dear Romuald, and sought thee everywhere. Thou wast my dream, and I first saw thee in the church at the fatal moment. I said at once, 'It is he!' I gave thee a look into which I threw all the love I ever had, all the love I now have, all the love I shall ever have for thee – a look that would have damned a cardinal or brought a king to his knees at my feet in view of all his court. Thou remainedst unmoved, preferring thy God to me!

'Ah, how jealous I am of that God whom thou didst love and still lovest more than me!

'Woe is me, unhappy one that I am! I can never have thy heart all to myself, I whom thou didst recall to life with a kiss – dead Clarimonde, who for thy sake bursts asunder the gates of the tomb, and comes to consecrate to thee a life which she has resumed only to make thee happy!'

All her words were accompanied with the most impassioned caresses, which bewildered my sense and my reason to such an extent, that I did not fear to utter a frightful blasphemy for the sake of consoling her, and to declare that I loved her as much as God.

Her eyes rekindled and shone like chrysoprases. 'In truth? – in very truth? as much as God!' she cried, flinging her beautiful arms around me. 'Since it is so, thou wilt come with me; thou wilt follow me whithersoever I desire. Thou wilt cast away thy ugly black habit. Thou shalt be the proudest and most envied of cavaliers; thou shalt be my lover! To be the acknowledged lover of Clarimonde, who has refused even a Pope, that will be something to feel proud of! Ah, the fair, unspeakably happy existence, the beautiful golden life we shall live together! And when shall we depart, my fair sir?'

'Tomorrow! Tomorrow!' I cried in my delirium.

'Tomorrow, then, so let it be!' she answered. 'In the meanwhile I shall have opportunity to change my toilet, for this is a little too light and in nowise suited for a voyage. I must also forthwith notify all my friends who believe me dead, and mourn for me as deeply as they are capable of doing. The money, the dresses, the carriages – all will be ready. I shall call for thee at this same hour. Adieu, dear heart!' And she lightly touched my forehead with her lips. The lamp went out, the curtains closed again, and all became dark; a leaden, dreamless sleep fell on me and held me unconscious until the morning following.

I awoke later than usual, and the recollection of this singular adventure troubled me during the whole day. I finally persuaded myself that it was a mere vapour of my heated imagination. Nevertheless its sensations had been so vivid that it was difficult to persuade myself that they were not real, and it was not without some presentiment of what was going to happen that I got into bed at last, after having prayed God to drive far from me all thoughts of evil, and to protect the chastity of my slumber.

I soon fell into a deep sleep, and my dream was continued. The curtains again parted, and I beheld Clarimonde, not as on the former occasion, pale in her pale winding-sheet, with the violets of death upon her cheeks but gay, sprightly, jaunty, in a superb travelling dress of green velvet, trimmed with gold lace, and looped up on either side to allow a glimpse of satin petticoat. Her blond hair escaped in thick ringlets from beneath a broad black felt hat, decorated with white feathers whimsically twisted into various shapes. In one hand she held a little riding whip terminated by a golden whistle. She tapped me lightly with it, and exclaimed: 'Well, my fine sleeper, is this the way you make your preparations? I thought I would find you up and dressed. Arise quickly, we have no time to lose.'

I leaped out of bed at once.

'Come, dress yourself, and let us go,' she continued, pointing to a little package she had brought with her. 'The horses are becoming impatient of delay and champing their bits at the door. We ought to have been by this time at least ten leagues distant from here.'

I dressed myself hurriedly, and she handed me the articles of apparel herself one by one, bursting into laughter from time to time at my awkwardness, as she explained to me the use of a garment when I had made a mistake. She hurriedly arranged my hair, and this done, held up before me a little pocket mirror of Venetian crystal, rimmed with silver filigree-work, and playfully asked: 'How dost find thyself now? Wilt engage me for thy valet de chambre?'

I was no longer the same person, and I could not even recognize myself. I resembled my former self no more than a finished statue resembles a block of stone. My old face seemed but a coarse daub of the one reflected in the mirror. I was handsome, and my vanity was sensibly tickled by the metamorphosis. That elegant apparel, that richly embroidered vest had made of me a totally different personage, and I marvelled at the power of transformation owned by a few yards of cloth cut after a certain pattern. The spirit of my costume penetrated my very skin, and within ten minutes more I had become something of a coxcomb.

In order to feel more at ease in my new attire, I took several turns up and down the room. Clarimonde watched me with an air of maternal pleasure, and appeared well satisfied with her work. 'Come, enough of this child's-play! Let us start, Romuald, dear. We have far to go, and we may not get there in time.' She took my hand and led me forth. All the doors opened before her at a touch, and we passed by the dog without awaking him.

At the gate we found Margheritone waiting, the same swarthy groom who had once before been my escort. He held the bridles of three horses, all black like those which bore us to the castle – one for me, one for him, one for Clarimonde. Those horses must have been Spanish genets born of mares fecundated by a zephyr, for they were fleet as the wind itself, and the moon, which had just risen at our departure to light us on our way, rolled over the sky like a wheel detached from her own chariot. We beheld her on the right leaping from tree to tree, and putting herself out of breath in the effort to keep up with us. Soon we came upon a level plain where, hard by a clump of trees, a carriage with four vigorous horses awaited us. We entered it, and the postilions urged their animals into a mad gallop. I had one arm around Clarimonde's waist, and one of her hands clasped in mine; her head leaned upon my shoulder, and I felt her bosom, half bare, lightly pressing against my arm. I had never known such intense happiness. In that hour I had forgotten everything, and I no more remembered having ever been a priest than I remembered what I had been doing in my mother's womb, so great was the fascination which the evil spirit exerted upon me. From that night my nature seemed in some sort to have become halved, and there were two men within me, neither of whom knew the other. At one moment I believed myself a priest who dreamed nightly that he was a gentleman, at another that I was a gentleman who dreamed he was a priest. I could no longer distinguish the dream from the reality, nor could I discover where the reality began or where ended the dream. The exquisite young lord and libertine railed at the priest, the priest loathed the dissolute habits of the young lord. I always retained with extreme vividness all the perceptions of my two lives. Only there was one absurd fact which I could not explain to myself – namely, that the consciousness of the same individuality existed in two men so opposite in character. It was an anomaly for which I could not account – whether I believed myself to be the curé of the little village of C——, or *Il Signor Romualdo*, the titled lover of Clarimonde.

Be that as it may, I lived, at least I believed that I lived, in Venice. I have never been able to discover rightly how much of illusion and how much of reality there was in this fantastic adventure. We dwelt in a great palace on the Canaleio, filled with frescoes and statues, and containing two Titians in the noblest style of the great master, which were hung in Clarimonde's chamber. It was a palace well worthy of a king. We had each our gondola, our *barcarolli* in family livery, our music hall, and our special poet. Clarimonde always lived upon a magnificent scale; there was something of Cleopatra in her nature. As for me, I had the retinue of a prince's son, and I was regarded with as much reverential respect as though I had been of the family of one of the twelve Apostles or the four Evangelists of the Most Serene Republic. I would not have turned aside to allow even the Doge to pass, and I do not believe that since Satan fell from heaven, any creature was ever prouder or more insolent than I. I went to the Ridotto, and played with a luck which seemed absolutely infernal. I received the best of all society – the sons of ruined families, women of the theatre, shrewd knaves, parasites, hectoring swashbucklers. But notwithstanding the dissipation of such a life, I always remained faithful to Clarimonde. I loved her wildly. She would have excited satiety itself, and chained inconstancy. To have Clarimonde was to have twenty mistresses; aye, to possess all women: so mobile, so varied of aspect, so fresh in new charms was she all in herself – a very chameleon of a woman, in sooth. She made you commit with her the infidelity you would have committed with another, by donning to perfection the character, the attraction, the style of beauty of the woman who appeared to please you. She returned my love a hundredfold, and it was in vain that the young patricians and even the Ancients of the Council of Ten made her the most magnificent proposals. A Foscari even went so far as to offer to espouse her. She rejected all his overtures. Of gold she had enough. She wished no longer for anything but love – a love youthful, pure, evoked by herself, and which should be a first and last passion. I would have been perfectly happy but for a cursed nightmare which recurred every night, and in which I believed myself to be a poor village curé, practising mortification and penance for my excesses during the day. Reassured by my constant association with her, I never thought further of the strange manner in which I had become acquainted with Clarimonde. But the words of the Abbé Sérapion concerning her recurred often to my memory, and never ceased to cause me uneasiness.

For some time the health of Clarimonde had not been so good as usual; her complexion grew paler day by day. The physicians who were summoned could not comprehend the nature of her malady and knew not how to treat it. They all prescribed some insignificant remedies, and never called a second time. Her paleness, nevertheless, visibly increased, and she became colder and colder, until she seemed almost as white and dead as upon that memorable night in the unknown castle. I grieved with anguish unspeakable to behold her thus slowly perishing; and she, touched by my agony, smiled upon me sweetly and sadly with the fateful smile of those who feel that they must die.

One morning I was seated at her bedside, after breakfasting from a little table placed close at hand, so that I might not be obliged to leave her for a single instant. In the act of cutting some fruit I accidentally inflicted rather a deep gash on my finger. The blood immediately gushed forth in a little purple jet, and a few drops spurted upon Clarimonde. Her eyes flashed, her face suddenly assumed an expression of savage and ferocious joy such as I had never before observed in her. She leaped out of her bed with animal agility – the agility, as it were, of an ape or a cat – and sprang upon my wound, which she commenced to suck with an air of unutterable pleasure. She swallowed the blood in little mouthfuls, slowly and carefully, like a connoisseur tasting a wine from Xeres or Syracuse. Gradually her eyelids half closed, and the pupils of her green eyes became oblong instead of round. From time to time she paused in order to kiss my hand, then she would recommence to press her lips to the lips of the wound in order to coax forth a few more ruddy drops. When she found that the blood would no longer come, she arose with eyes liquid and brilliant, rosier than a May dawn; her face full and fresh, her hand warm and moist – in fine, more beautiful than ever, and in the most perfect health.

'I shall not die! I shall not die!' she cried, clinging to my neck, half mad with joy. 'I can love thee yet for a long time. My life is thine, and all that is of me comes from thee. A few drops of thy rich and noble blood, more precious and more potent than all the elixirs of the earth, have given me back life.'

This scene long haunted my memory, and inspired me with strange doubts in regard to Clarimonde; and the same evening, when slumber had transported me to my presbytery, I beheld the Abbé Sérapion, graver and more anxious of aspect than ever. He gazed attentively at me, and sorrowfully exclaimed: 'Not content with losing your soul, you now desire also to lose your body. Wretched young man, into how terrible a plight have you fallen!' The tone in which he uttered these words powerfully affected me, but in spite of its vividness even that impression was soon dissipated, and a thousand other cares erased it from my mind. At last one evening, while looking into a mirror whose traitorous position she had not taken into account, I saw Clarimonde in the act of emptying a powder into the cup of spiced wine which she had long been in the habit of preparing after our repasts. I took the cup, feigned to carry it to my lips, and then placed it on the nearest article of furniture as though intending to finish it at my leisure. Taking advantage of a moment when the fair one's back was turned, I threw the contents under the table, after which I retired to my chamber and went to bed, fully resolved not to sleep, but to watch and discover what should come of all this mystery. I did not have to wait long. Clarimonde entered in her night-dress, and having removed her apparel, crept into bed and lay down beside me. When she felt assured that I was asleep, she bared my arm, and drawing a gold pin from her hair, commenced to murmur in a low voice:

'One drop, only one drop! One ruby at the end of my needle.... Since thou lovest me yet, I must not die!... Ah, poor love! His beautiful blood, so brightly purple, I must drink it. Sleep, my only treasure! Sleep, my god, my child! I will do thee no harm; I will only take of thy life what I must to keep my own from being forever extinguished. But that I love thee so much, I could well resolve to have other lovers whose veins I could drain; but since I have known thee all other men have become hateful to me.... Ah, the beautiful arm! How round it is! How white it is! How shall I ever dare to prick this pretty blue vein!' And while thus murmuring to herself she wept, and I felt her tears raining on my arm as she clasped it with her hands. At last she took the resolve, slightly punctured me with her pin, and commenced to suck up the blood which oozed from the place. Although she swallowed only a few drops, the fear of weakening me soon seized her, and she carefully tied a little band around my arm, afterward rubbing the wound with an unguent which immediately cicatrized it.

Further doubts were impossible. The Abbé Sérapion was right. Notwithstanding this positive knowledge, however, I could not cease to love Clarimonde, and I would gladly of my own accord have given her all the blood she required to sustain her factitious life. Moreover, I felt but little fear of her. The woman seemed to plead with me for the vampire, and what I had already heard and seen sufficed to reassure me completely. In those days I had plenteous veins, which would not have been so easily exhausted as at present; and I would not have thought of bargaining for my blood, drop by drop. I would rather have opened myself the veins of my arm and said to her: 'Drink, and may my love infiltrate itself throughout thy body together with my blood!' I carefully avoided ever making the least reference to the narcotic drink she had prepared for me, or to the incident of the pin, and we lived in the most perfect harmony.

Yet my priestly scruples commenced to torment me more than ever, and I was at a loss to imagine what new penance I could invent in order to mortify and subdue my flesh. Although these visions were involuntary, and though I did not actually participate in anything relating to them, I could not dare to touch the body of Christ with hands so impure and a mind defiled by such debauches whether real or imaginary. In the effort to avoid falling under the influence of these wearisome hallucinations, I strove to prevent myself from being overcome by sleep. I held my eyelids open with my fingers, and stood for hours together leaning upright against the wall, fighting sleep with all my might; but the dust of drowsiness invariably gathered upon my eyes at last, and finding all resistance useless, I would have to let my arms fall in the extremity of despairing weariness, and the current of slumber would again bear me away to the perfidious shores. Sérapion addressed me with the most vehement exhortations, severely reproaching me for my softness and want of fervour. Finally, one day when I was more wretched than usual, he said to me: 'There is but one way by which you can obtain relief from this continual torment, and though it is an extreme measure it must be made use of; violent diseases require violent remedies. I know where Clarimonde is buried. It is necessary that we shall disinter her remains, and that you shall behold in how pitiable a state the object of your love is. Then you will no longer be tempted to lose your soul for the sake of an unclean corpse devoured by worms, and ready to crumble into dust. That will assuredly restore you to yourself.' For my part, I was so tired of this double life that I at once consented, desiring to ascertain beyond a doubt whether a priest or a gentleman had been the victim of delusion. I had become fully resolved either to kill one of the two men within me for the benefit of the other, or else to kill both, for so terrible an existence could not last long and be endured. The Abbé Sérapion provided himself with a mattock, a lever, and a lantern, and at midnight we wended our way to the cemetery of ——, the location and place of which were perfectly familiar to him. After having directed the rays of the dark lantern upon the inscriptions of several tombs, we came at last upon a great slab, half concealed by huge weeds and devoured by mosses and parasitic plants, whereupon we deciphered the opening lines of the epitaph:

Here lies Clarimonde
Who was famed in her life-time
As the fairest of women.*

'It is here without a doubt,' muttered Sérapion, and placing his lantern on the ground, he forced the point of the lever under the edge of the stone and commenced to raise it. The stone yielded, and he proceeded to work with the mattock. Darker and more silent than the night itself, I stood by and watched him do it, while he, bending over his dismal toil, streamed with sweat, panted, and his hard-coming breath seemed to have the harsh tone of a death rattle. It was a weird scene, and had any persons from without beheld us, they would assuredly have taken us rather for profane wretches and shroud-stealers than for priests of God. There was something grim and fierce in Sérapion's zeal which lent him the air of a demon rather than of an apostle or an angel, and his great aquiline face, with all its stern features brought out in strong relief by the lantern-light, had something

* *Ici git Clarimonde*
Qui fut de son vivant
La plus belle du monde.

The broken beauty of the lines is unavoidably lost in the translation.

fearsome in it which enhanced the unpleasant fancy. I felt an icy sweat come out upon my forehead in huge beads, and my hair stood up with a hideous fear. Within the depths of my own heart I felt that the act of the austere Sérapion was an abominable sacrilege; and I could have prayed that a triangle of fire would issue from the entrails of the dark clouds, heavily rolling above us, to reduce him to cinders. The owls which had been nestling in the cypress trees, startled by the gleam of the lantern, flew against it from time to time, striking their dusty wings against its panes, and uttering plaintive cries of lamentation; wild foxes yelped in the far darkness, and a thousand sinister noises detached themselves from the silence. At last Sérapion's mattock struck the coffin itself, making its planks re-echo with a deep sonorous sound, with that terrible sound nothingness utters when stricken. He wrenched apart and tore up the lid, and I beheld Clarimonde, pallid as a figure of marble, with hands joined; her white winding-sheet made but one fold from her head to her feet. A little crimson drop sparkled like a speck of dew at one corner of her colourless mouth. Sérapion, at this spectacle, burst into fury: 'Ah, thou art here, demon! Impure courtesan! Drinker of blood and gold!' And he flung holy water upon the corpse and the coffin, over which he traced the sign of the cross with his sprinkler. Poor Clarimonde had no sooner been touched by the blessed spray than her beautiful body crumbled into dust, and became only a shapeless and frightful mass of cinders and half-calcined bones.

'Behold your mistress, my Lord Romuald!' cried the inexorable priest, as he pointed to these sad remains. 'Will you be easily tempted after this to promenade on the Lido or at Fusina with your beauty?' I covered my face with my hands, a vast ruin had taken place within me. I returned to my presbytery, and the noble Lord Romuald, the lover of Clarimonde, separated himself from the poor priest with whom he had kept such strange company so long. But once only, the following night, I saw Clarimonde. She said to me, as she had said the first time at the portals of the church: 'Unhappy man! Unhappy man! What hast thou done? Wherefore have hearkened to that imbecile priest? Wert thou not happy? And what harm had I ever done thee that thou shouldst violate my poor tomb, and lay bare the miseries of my nothingness? All communication between our souls and our bodies is henceforth forever broken. Adieu! Thou will yet regret me!' She vanished in air as smoke, and I never saw her more.

Alas! she spoke truly indeed. I have regretted her more than once, and I regret her still. My soul's peace has been very dearly bought. The love of God was not too much to replace such a love as hers. And this, brother, is the story of my youth. Never gaze upon a woman, and walk abroad only with eyes ever fixed upon the ground; for however chaste and watchful one may be, the error of a single moment is enough to make one lose eternity.

The House and the Brain

Lord Edward Bulwer-Lytton

A friend of mine, who is a man of letters and a philosopher, said to me one day, as if between jest and earnest: 'Fancy! since we last met, I have discovered a haunted house in the midst of London.'

'Really haunted?—and by what—ghosts?'

'Well, I can't answer that question; all I know is this: six weeks ago my wife and I were in search of a furnished apartment. Passing a quiet street, we saw on the window of one of the houses a bill, 'Apartments, Furnished.' The situation suited us: we entered the house—liked the rooms—engaged them by the week—and left them the third day. No power on earth could have reconciled my wife to stay longer; and I don't wonder at it.'

'What did you see?'

'It was not so much what we saw or heard that drove us away, as it was an undefinable terror which seized both of us whenever we passed by the door of a certain unfurnished room, in which we neither saw nor heard anything. Accordingly, on the fourth morning I summoned the woman who kept the house and attended on us, and told her that the rooms did not quite suit us, and we would not stay out our week. She said, dryly: "I know why; you have stayed longer than any other lodger. Few ever stayed a second night; none before you a third. But I take it they have been very kind to you."

'"They—who?" I asked, affecting to smile.

'"Why, they who haunt the house, whoever they are. I don't mind them; I remember them many years ago, when I lived in this house, not as a servant; but I know they will be the death of me some day. I don't care – I'm old, and must die soon anyhow; and then I shall be with them, and in this house still." The woman spoke with so dreary a calmness that really it was a sort of awe that prevented my conversing with her further. I paid for my week, and too happy were my wife and I to get off so cheaply.'

'You excite my curiosity,' said I; 'nothing I should like better than to sleep in a haunted house. Pray give me the address of the one which you left so ignominiously.'

My friend gave me the address; and when we parted, I walked straight toward the house thus indicated.

It is situated on the north side of Oxford Street, in a dull but respectable thoroughfare. I found the house shut up – no bill at the window, and no response to my knock. As I was turning away, a beer-boy, collecting pewter pots at the neighbouring areas, said to me, 'Do you want any one at that house, sir?'

'Yes, I heard it was to be let.'

'Let!—Mr J. offered mother, who chars for him, a pound a week just to open and shut the windows, and she would not.'

'Would not!—and why?'

'The house is haunted; and the old woman who kept it was found dead in her bed, with her eyes wide open. They say the devil strangled her.'

'Pooh!—you speak of Mr J——. Is he the owner of the house?'

'Yes.'

'Where does he live?'

'In G—— Street, No. —.'

I gave the pot-boy the gratuity earned by his liberal information, and I was lucky enough to find Mr J—— at home – an elderly man, with intelligent countenance and prepossessing manners.

I communicated my name and my business frankly. I said I heard the house was considered to be haunted – that I had a strong desire to examine a house with so equivocal a reputation – that I should be greatly obliged if he would allow me to hire it, though only for a night. I was willing to pay for that privilege whatever he might be inclined to ask. 'Sir,' said Mr J——, with great courtesy, 'the house is at your service, for as short or as long a time as you please. Rent is out of the question. The poor old woman who died in it three weeks ago was a pauper whom I took out of a workhouse, for in her childhood she had been known to some of my family, and had once been in such good circumstances that she had rented that house of my uncle. She was a woman of superior education and strong mind, and was the only person I could ever induce to remain in the house. Indeed, since her death, which was sudden, and the coroner's inquest which gave it a notoriety in the neighbourhood, I have so despaired of finding any person to take charge of the house, much more a tenant, that I would willingly let it rent free for a year to any one who would pay its rates and taxes.'

'How long is it since the house acquired this sinister character?'

'That I can scarcely tell you, but very many years since. The old woman I spoke of said it was haunted when she rented it between thirty and forty years ago. I never had one lodger who stayed more than three days. I do not tell you their stories – to no two lodgers have there been exactly the same phenomena repeated. It is better that you should judge for yourself than enter the house with an imagination influenced by previous narratives; only be prepared to see and to hear something or other, and take whatever precautions you yourself please.'

'Have you never had a curiosity yourself to pass a night in that house?'

'Yes. I passed not a night, but three hours in broad daylight alone in that house. My curiosity is not satisfied, but it is quenched. I have no desire to renew the experiment. You can not complain, you see, sir, that I am not sufficiently candid; and unless your interest be exceedingly eager and your nerves unusually strong, I honestly add, that I advise you *not* to pass a night in that house.'

'My interest *is* exceedingly keen,' said I, 'and though only a coward will boast of his nerves in situations wholly unfamiliar to him, yet my nerves have been seasoned in such variety of danger that I have the right to rely on them—even in a haunted house.'

Mr J—— said very little more; he took the keys of his house out of his bureau, gave them to me – and, thanking him cordially for his frankness, and his urbane concession to my wish, I carried off my prize.

Impatient for the experiment, as soon as I reached home, I summoned my confidential servant – a young man of gay spirits, fearless temper, and as free from superstitious prejudice as any one I could think of.

'F——,' said I, 'you remember in Germany how disappointed we were at not finding a ghost in that old castle, which was said to be haunted by a headless apparition? Well, I have heard of a house in London which, I have reason to hope, is decidedly haunted. I mean to sleep there tonight. From what I hear, there is no doubt that something will allow itself to be seen or to be heard—something perhaps, excessively horrible. Do you think, if I take you with me, I may rely on your presence of mind, whatever may happen?'

'Oh, sir! pray trust me,' answered F——, grinning with delight.

'Very well; then here are the keys of the house—this is the address. Go now – select for me any bedroom you please; and since the house has not been inhabited for weeks make up a good fire – air the bed well – see, of course, that there are candles as well as fuel. Take with you my revolver and my dagger – so much for my weapons – arm yourself equally well; and if we are not a match for a dozen ghosts we shall be but a sorry couple of Englishmen.'

I was engaged for the rest of the day on business so urgent that I had not leisure to think much on the nocturnal adventure to which I had plighted my honour. I dined alone, and very late, and while dining read, as is my habit. I selected one of the volumes of Macaulay's essays. I thought to myself that I would take the book with me; there was so much of healthfulness in the style and practical life in the subjects, that it would serve as an antidote against the influence of superstitious fancy.

Accordingly, about half-past nine, I put the book into my pocket and strolled leisurely toward the haunted house. I took with me a favourite dog – an exceedingly sharp, bold, and vigilant bull-terrier – a dog fond of prowling about strange ghostly corners and passages at night in search of rats – a dog of dogs for a ghost.

It was a summer night, but chilly, the sky somewhat gloomy and overcast. Still there was a moon – faint and sickly, but still a moon – and, if the clouds permitted after midnight it would be brighter.

I reached the house, knocked, and my servant opened the door with a cheerful smile.

'All right, sir, and very comfortable.'

'Oh!' said I, rather disappointed; 'have you not seen nor heard anything remarkable?'

'Well, sir, I must own I have heard something queer.'

'What? – what?'

'The sound of feet pattering behind me; and once or twice small noises like whispers close at my ear – nothing more.'

'You are not at all frightened?'

'I! not a bit of it, sir;' and the man's bold look reassured me on one point – viz.: that happen what might, he would not desert me.

We were in the hall, the street door closed, and my attention was now drawn to my dog. He had at first run in eagerly enough but had sneaked back to the door, and was scratching and whining to get out. After patting him on the head, and encouraging him gently, the dog seemed to reconcile himself to the situation and followed me and F—— through the house, but keeping close at my heels instead of hurrying inquisitively in advance, which was his usual and normal habit in all strange places. We first visited the subterranean apartments, the kitchen, and other offices, and especially the cellars in which last there were two or three bottles of wine still left in a bin, covered with cobwebs, and evidently, by their appearance, undisturbed for many years. It was clear that the ghosts were not wine-bibbers. For the rest, we discovered nothing of interest. There was a gloomy little back-yard, with very high walls. The stones of this yard were very damp; and what with the damp, and what with the dust and smoke-grime on the pavement, our feet left a slight impression where we passed. And now appeared the first strange phenomenon witnessed by myself in this strange abode. I saw, just before me, the print of a foot suddenly form itself, as it were. I stopped, caught hold of my servant, and pointed to it. In advance of that footprint as suddenly dropped another. We both saw it. I advanced quickly to the place; the footprint kept advancing before me, a small footprint – the foot of a child; the impression was too faint thoroughly to distinguish the shape, but it seemed to us both that it was the print of a naked foot.

This phenomenon ceased when we arrived at the opposite wall, nor did it repeat itself on returning. We remounted the stairs, and entered the rooms on the ground floor, a dining-parlour, a small back-parlour, and a still smaller third room that had been probably appropriated to a footman – all still as death. We then visited the drawing-rooms, which seemed fresh and new. In the front room I seated myself in an armchair. F—— placed on the table the candlestick with which he had lighted us. I told him to shut the door.

As he turned to do so, a chair opposite to me moved from the wall quickly and noiselessly, and dropped itself about a yard from my own, immediately fronting it.

'Why, this is better than the turning-tables,' said I, with a half-laugh; and as I laughed, my dog put back his head and howled.

F——, coming back, had not observed the movement of the chair. He employed himself now in stilling the dog. I continued to gaze on the chair, and fancied I saw on it a pale blue misty outline of a human figure, but an outline so indistinct that I could only distrust my own vision. The dog was now quiet.

'Put back that chair opposite to me,' said I to F——; 'put it back to the wall.'

F—— obeyed. 'Was that you, sir?' said he, turning abruptly.

'I! – what?'

'Why, something struck me. I felt it sharply on the shoulder – just here.'

'No,' said I. 'But we have jugglers present, and though we may not discover their tricks, we shall catch them before they frighten us.'

We did not stay long in the drawing-rooms – in fact, they felt so damp and so chilly that I was glad to get to the fire upstairs. We locked the doors of the drawing-rooms – a precaution which, I should observe, we had taken with all the rooms we had searched below. The bedroom my servant had selected for me was the best on the floor – a large one, with two windows fronting the street. The four-posted bed, which took up no inconsiderable space, was opposite to the fire, which burnt clear and bright; a door in the wall to the left, between the bed and the window, communicated with the room which my servant appropriated to himself. This last was a small room with a sofa-bed, and had no communication with the landing-place – no other door but that which conducted to the bedroom I was to occupy. On either side of my fireplace was a cupboard, without locks, flush with the wall, and covered with the same dull-brown paper. We examined these cupboards – only hooks to suspend female dresses – nothing else; we sounded the walls – evidently solid – the outer walls of the building. Having finished the survey of these apartments, warmed myself a few moments, and lighted my cigar, I then, still accompanied by F——, went forth to complete my reconnoitre. In the landing-place there was another door; it was closed firmly. 'Sir,' said my servant, in surprise, 'I unlocked this door with all the others when I first came; it can not have got locked from the inside, for—'

Before he had finished his sentence, the door, which neither of us then was touching, opened quietly of itself. We looked at each other a single instant. The same thought seized both – some human agency might be detected here. I rushed in first – my servant followed. A small blank dreary room without furniture – a few empty boxes and hampers in a corner – a small window – the shutters closed – not even a fireplace – no other door but that by which we had entered – no carpet on the floor, and the floor seemed very old, uneven, worm-eaten, mended here and there, as was shown by the whiter patches on the wood; but no living being, and no visible place in which a living being could have hidden. As we stood gazing around, the door by which we had entered closed as quietly as it had before opened; we were imprisoned.

For the first time I felt a creep of undefinable horror. Not so my servant. 'Why, they don't think to trap us, sir; I could break that trumpery door with a kick of my foot.'

'Try first if it will open to your hand,' said I, shaking off the vague apprehension that had seized me, 'while I unclose the shutters and see what is without.'

I unbarred the shutters – the window looked on the little back-yard I have before described; there was no ledge without – nothing to break the sheer descent of the wall. No man getting out of that window would have found any footing till he had fallen on the stones below.

F——, meanwhile, was vainly attempting to open the door. He now turned round to me and asked my permission to use force. And I should here state, in justice to the servant, that far from evincing any superstitious terrors, his nerve, composure, and even gaiety amid circumstances so extraordinary, compelled my admiration, and made me congratulate myself on having secured a companion in every way fitted to the occasion. I willingly gave him the permission he required. But though he was a remarkably strong man, his force was as idle as his milder efforts; the door did not even shake to his stoutest kick. Breathless and panting, he desisted. I then tried the door myself, equally in vain. As I ceased from the effort, again that creep of horror came over me; but this time it was more cold and stubborn. I felt as if some strange and ghastly exhalation were rising up from the chinks of that rugged floor, and filling the atmosphere with a venomous influence hostile to human life. The door now very slowly and quietly opened as of its own accord. We precipitated ourselves into the landing-place. We both saw a large pale light – as large as the human figure, but shapeless and unsubstantial – move before us, and ascend the stairs that led from the landing into the attic. I followed the light, and my servant followed me. It entered to the right of the landing, a small garret, of which the door stood open. I entered in the same instant. The light then collapsed into a small globule, exceedingly brilliant and vivid; rested a moment on a bed in the corner, quivered, and vanished. We approached the bed and examined it – a half-tester, such as is commonly found in attics devoted to servants. On the drawers that stood near it we perceived an old faded silk handkerchief, with the needle still left in a rent half repaired. The kerchief was covered with dust; probably it had belonged to the old woman who had last died in that house, and this might have been her sleeping-room. I had sufficient curiosity to open the drawers: there were a few odds and ends of female dress, and two letters tied round with a narrow ribbon of faded yellow. I took the liberty to possess myself of the letters. We found nothing else in the room worth noticing – nor did the light reappear; but we distinctly heard, as we turned to go, a pattering footfall on the floor – just before us. We went through the other attics (in all four), the footfall still preceding us. Nothing to be seen – nothing but the footfall heard. I had the letters in my hand: just as I was descending the stairs I distinctly felt my wrist seized, and a faint soft effort made to draw the letters from my clasp. I only held them the more tightly, and the effort ceased.

We regained the bed-chamber appropriated to myself, and I then remarked that my dog had not followed us when we had left it. He was thrusting himself close to the fire, and trembling. I was impatient to examine the letters; and while I read them, my servant opened a little box in which he had deposited the weapons I had ordered him to bring; took them out, placed them on a table close at my bed-head, and he occupied himself in soothing the dog, who, however, seemed to heed him very little.

The letters were short – they were dated; the dates exactly thirty-five years ago. They were evidently from a lover to his mistress, or a husband to some young wife. Not only the terms of expression, but a distinct reference to a former voyage, indicated the writer to have been a seafarer. The spelling and handwriting were those of a man imperfectly educated, but still the language itself was forcible. In the expressions of endearment there was a kind of rough wild love; but here and there were dark unintelligible hints at some secret not of love – some secret that seemed of crime. 'We ought to love each other,' was one of the sentences I remember, 'for how every one else would execrate us if all was known.' Again: 'Don't let any one be in the same room with you at night—you talk in your sleep.' And again: 'What's done can't be undone; and I tell you there's nothing against us unless the dead could come to life.' Here there was underlined in a better handwriting (a female's): 'They do!' At the end of the letter latest in date the same female hand had written these words: 'Lost at sea the 4th of June, the same day as—'

I put down the letters, and began to muse over their contents.

Fearing, however, that the train of thought into which I fell might unsteady my nerves, I fully determined to keep my mind in a fit state to cope with whatever of marvellous the advancing night might bring forth. I roused myself – laid the letters on the table – stirred up the fire, which was still bright and cheering, and opened my volume of Macaulay. I read quietly enough till about half-past eleven. I then threw myself dressed upon the bed, and told my servant he might retire to his own room, but must keep himself awake. I bade him leave open the door between the two rooms. Thus alone, I kept two candles burning on the table by my bed-head. I placed my watch beside the weapons, and calmly resumed my Macaulay. Opposite to me the fire burned clear; and on the hearth-rug, seemingly asleep, lay the dog. In about twenty minutes I felt an exceedingly cold air pass by my cheek, like a sudden draft. I fancied the door to my right, communicating with the landing-place, must have got open; but no – it was closed. I then turned my glance to my left, and saw the flame of the candles violently swayed as by a wind. At the same moment the watch beside the revolver softly slid from the table – softly, softly – no visible hand – it was gone. I sprang up, seizing the revolver with one hand, the dagger with the other: I was not willing that my weapons should share the fate of the watch. Thus armed, I looked round the floor – no sign of the watch. Three slow, loud, distinct knocks were now heard at the bed-head; my servant called out: 'Is that you, sir?'

'No; be on your guard.'

The dog now roused himself and sat on his haunches, his ears moving quickly backward and forward. He kept his eyes fixed on me with a look so strange that he concentrated all my attention on himself. Slowly, he rose up, all his hair bristling, and stood perfectly rigid, and with the same wild stare. I had not time, however, to examine the dog. Presently my servant emerged from his room; and if ever I saw horror in the human face, it was then. I should not have recognized him had we met in the street, so altered was every lineament. He passed by me quickly, saying in a whisper that seemed scarcely to come from his lips: 'Run – run! it is after me!' He gained the door to the landing, pulled it open, and rushed forth. I followed him into the landing involuntarily, calling him to stop; but, without heeding me, he bounded down the stairs, clinging to the balusters, and taking several steps at a time. I heard, where I stood, the street-door open – heard it again clap to. I was left alone in the haunted house.

It was but for a moment that I remained undecided whether or not to follow my servant; pride and curiosity alike forbade so dastardly a flight. I re-entered my room, closing the door after me, and proceeded cautiously into the interior chamber. I encountered nothing to justify my servant's terror. I again carefully examined the walls, to see if there were any concealed door. I could find no trace of one – not even a seam in the dull-brown paper with which the room was hung. How, then, had the Thing, whatever it was, which had so scared him, obtained ingress except through my own chamber?

I returned to my room, shut and locked the door that opened upon the interior one, and stood on the hearth, expectant and prepared. I now perceived that the dog had slunk into an angle of the wall, and was pressing himself close against it, as if literally striving to force his way into it. I approached the animal and spoke to it; the poor brute was evidently beside itself with terror. It showed all its teeth, the slaver dropping from its jaws, and would certainly have bitten me if I had touched it. It did not seem to recognize me. Whoever has seen at the Zoological Gardens a rabbit, fascinated by a serpent, cowering in a corner, may form some idea of the anguish which the dog exhibited. Finding all efforts to soothe the animal in vain, and fearing that his bite might be as venomous in that state as in the madness of hydrophobia, I left him alone, placed my weapons on the table beside the fire, seated myself, and recommenced my Macaulay.

I now became aware that something interposed between the page and the light – the page was overshadowed; I looked up, and I saw what I shall find it very difficult, perhaps impossible, to describe.

It was a darkness shaping itself forth from the air in very undefined outline. I can not say it was of a human form, and yet it had more resemblance to a human form, or rather shadow, than to anything else. As it stood, wholly apart and distinct from the air and the light around it, its dimensions seemed gigantic, the summit nearly touching the ceiling. While I gazed, a feeling of intense cold seized me. An iceberg before me could not more have chilled me; nor could the cold of an iceberg have been more purely physical. I feel convinced that it was not the cold caused by fear. As I continued to gaze, I thought – but this I can not say with precision – that I distinguished two eyes looking down on me from the height. One moment I fancied that I distinguished them clearly, the next they seemed gone; but still two rays of a pale-blue light frequently shot through the darkness, as from the height on which I half-believed, half-doubted, that I had encountered the eyes.

I strove to speak – my voice utterly failed me; I could only think to myself: 'Is this fear? it is *not* fear!' I strove to rise – in vain; I felt as if weighed down by an irresistible force. Indeed, my impression was that of an immense and overwhelming power opposed to my volition – that sense of utter inadequacy to cope with a force beyond man's, which one may feel *physically* in a storm at sea, in a conflagration, or when confronting some terrible wild beast, or rather, perhaps, the shark of the ocean, I felt *morally*. Opposed to my will was another will, as far superior to its strength as storm, fire, and shark are superior in material force to the force of man.

And now, as this impression grew on me – now came, at last, horror – horror to a degree that no words can convey. Still I retained pride, if not courage; and in my own mind I said: 'This is horror, but it is not fear; unless I fear I can not be harmed; my reason rejects this thing; it is an illusion – I do not fear.' With a violent effort I succeeded at last in stretching out my hand toward the weapon on the table: as I did so, on the arm and shoulder I received a strange shock, and my arm fell to my side powerless. And now, to add to my horror, the light began slowly to wane from the candles – they were not, as it were, extinguished, but their flame seemed very gradually withdrawn; it was the same with the fire – the light was extracted from the fuel; in a few minutes the room was in utter darkness. The dread that came over me, to be thus in the dark with that dark Thing, whose power was so intensely felt, brought a reaction of nerve. In fact, terror had reached that climax, that either my senses must have deserted me, or I must have burst through the spell. I did burst through it. I found voice, though the voice was a shriek. I remembered that I broke forth with words like these: 'I do not fear, my soul does not fear'; and at the same time I found strength to rise. Still in that profound gloom I rushed to one of the windows – tore aside the curtain – flung open the shutters; my first thought was – Light. And when I saw the moon high, clear, and calm, I felt a joy that almost compensated for the previous terror. There was the moon, there was also the light from the gas-lamps in the deserted slumberous street. I turned to look back into the room; the moon penetrated its shadow very palely and partially – but still there was light. The dark Thing, whatever it might be, was gone – except that I could yet see a dim shadow, which seemed the shadow of that shade, against the opposite wall.

My eye now rested on the table, and from under the table (which was without cloth or cover – an old mahogany round table) there rose a hand, visible as far as the wrist. It was a hand, seemingly, as much of flesh and blood as my own, but the hand of an aged person – lean, wrinkled, small, too – a woman's hand. That hand very softly closed on the two letters that lay on the table; the hand and letters both vanished. Then there came the same three loud measured knocks I had heard at the bed-head before this extraordinary drama had commenced.

As those sounds slowly ceased, I felt the whole room vibrate sensibly; and at the far end there rose, as from the floor, sparks or globules like bubbles of light, many coloured – green, yellow, fire-red, azure. Up and down, to and fro, hither, thither, as tiny Will-o'-the-Wisps, the sparks moved, slow or swift, each at its own caprice. A chair (as in the drawing-room below) was now advanced from the wall without apparent agency, and placed at the opposite side of the table. Suddenly, as forth from the chair, there grew a shape – a woman's shape. It was distinct as a shape of life – ghastly as a shape of death. The face was that of youth, with a strange mournful beauty; the throat and shoulders were bare, the rest of the form in a loose robe of cloudy white. It began sleeking its long yellow hair, which fell over its shoulders; its eyes were not turned toward me, but to the door; it seemed listening, watching, waiting. The shadow of the shade in the background grew darker; and again I thought I beheld the eyes gleaming out from the summit of the shadow – eyes fixed upon that shape.

As if from the door, though it did not open, there grew out another shape, equally distinct, equally ghastly – a man's shape – a young man's. It was in the dress of the last century, or rather in a likeness of such dress (for both the male shape and the female, though defined, were evidently unsubstantial, impalpable – simulacra – phantasms); and there was something incongruous, grotesque, yet fearful, in the contrast between the elaborate finery, the courtly precision of that old-fashioned garb, with its ruffles and lace and buckles, and the corpse-like stillness of the flitting wearer. Just as the male shape approached the female, the dark Shadow started from the wall, all three for a moment wrapped in darkness. When the pale light returned, the two phantoms were as if in the grasp of the Shadow that towered between them; and there was a blood-stain on the breast of the female; and the phantom male was leaning on its phantom sword, and blood seemed trickling fast from the ruffles, from the lace; and the darkness of the intermediate Shadow swallowed them up – they were gone. And again the bubbles of light shot, and sailed, and undulated, growing thicker and thicker and more wildly confused in their movements.

The closet door to the right of the fireplace now opened, and from the aperture there came forth the form of an aged woman. In her hand she held letters – the very letters over which I had seen the Hand close; and behind her I heard a footstep. She turned round as if to listen, and then she opened the letters and seemed to read; and over her shoulder I saw a livid face, the face as of a man long drowned – bloated, bleached – seaweed tangled in his dripping hair; and at her feet lay a form as of a corpse, and beside the corpse there cowered a child, a miserable squalid child, with famine in its cheeks and fear in its eyes. And as I looked in the old woman's face, the wrinkles and lines vanished, and it became a face of youth – hard-eyed, stony, but still youth; and the Shadow darted forth, and darkened over those phantoms as it had darkened over the last.

Nothing now was left but the Shadow, and on that my eyes were intently fixed, till again eyes grew out of the Shadow – malignant, serpent eyes. And the bubbles of light again rose and fell, and in their disordered, irregular, turbulent maze, mingled with the wan moonlight. And now from these globules themselves, as from the shell of an egg, monstrous things burst out; the air grew filled with them; larvæ so bloodless and so hideous that I can in no way describe them except to remind the reader of the swarming life which the solar microscope brings before his eyes in a drop of water – things transparent, supple, agile, chasing each other, devouring each other – forms like naught ever beheld by the naked eye. As the shapes were without symmetry, so their movements were without order. In their very vagrancies there was no sport; they came round me and round, thicker and faster and swifter, swarming over my head, crawling over my right arm, which was outstretched in involuntary command against all evil beings. Sometimes I felt myself touched, but not by them; invisible hands touched me. Once I felt the clutch as of cold soft fingers at my throat. I was still equally conscious that if I gave way to fear I should be in bodily peril; and I concentrated all my faculties in the single focus of resisting, stubborn will. And I turned my sight from the Shadow – above all, from those strange serpent eyes – eyes that had now become distinctly visible. For there, though in naught else around me, I was aware that there was a WILL, and a will of intense, creative, working evil, which might crush down my own.

The pale atmosphere in the room began now to redden as if in the air of some near conflagration. The larvæ grew lurid as things that live in fire. Again the moon vibrated; again were heard the three measured knocks; and again all things were swallowed up in the darkness of the dark Shadow, as if out of that darkness all had come, into that darkness all returned.

As the gloom receded, the Shadow was wholly gone. Slowly, as it had been withdrawn, the flame grew again into the candles on the table, again into the fuel in the grate. The whole room came once more calmly, healthfully into sight.

The two doors were still closed, the door communicating with the servant's room still locked. In the corner of the wall, into which he had so convulsively niched himself, lay the dog. I called to him – no movement; I approached – the animal was dead; his eyes protruded; his tongue out of his mouth; the froth gathered round his jaws. I took him in my arms; I brought him to the fire; I felt acute grief for the loss of my poor favourite – acute self-reproach; I accused myself of his death; I imagined he had died of fright. But what was my surprise on finding that his neck was actually broken. Had this been done in the dark? – must it not have been by a hand human as mine? – must there not have been a human agency all the while in that room? Good cause to suspect it. I can not tell. I can not do more than state the fact fairly; the reader may draw his own inference.

Another surprising circumstance – my watch was restored to the table from which it had been so mysteriously withdrawn; but it had stopped at the very moment it was so withdrawn; nor, despite all the skill of the watchmaker, has it ever gone since – that is, it will go in a strange erratic way for a few hours, and then come to a dead stop – it is worthless.

Nothing more chanced for the rest of the night. Nor, indeed, had I long to wait before the dawn broke. Nor till it was broad daylight did I quit the haunted house. Before I did so, I revisited the little blind room in which my servant and myself had been for a time imprisoned. I had a strong impression – for which I could not account – that from that room had originated the mechanism of the phenomena – if I may use the term – which had been experienced in my chamber. And though I entered it now in the clear day, with the sun peering through the filmy window, I still felt, as I stood on its floors, the creep of the horror which I had first there experienced the night before, and which had been so aggravated by what had passed in my own chamber. I could not, indeed, bear to stay more than half a minute within those walls. I descended the stairs, and again I heard the footfall before me; and when I opened the street door, I thought I could distinguish a very low laugh. I gained my own house, expecting to find my runaway servant there. But he had not presented himself, nor did I hear more of him for three days, when I received a letter from him, dated from Liverpool to this effect:

> Honoured Sir: – I humbly entreat your pardon, though I can scarcely hope that you will think that I deserve it, unless—which Heaven forbid! – you saw what I did. I feel that it will be years before I can recover myself; and as to being fit for service, it is out of the question. I am therefore going to my brother-in-law at Melbourne. The ship sails tomorrow. Perhaps the long voyage may set me up. I do nothing now but start and tremble, and fancy It is behind me. I humbly beg you, honoured sir, to order my clothes, and whatever wages are due to me, to be sent to my mother's, at Walworth – John knows her address.

The letter ended with additional apologies, somewhat incoherent, and explanatory details as to effects that had been under the writer's charge.

This flight may perhaps warrant a suspicion that the man wished to go to Australia, and had been somehow or other fraudulently mixed up with the events of the night. I say nothing in refutation of that conjecture; rather, I suggest it as one that would seem to many persons the most probable solution of improbable occurrences. My belief in my own theory remained unshaken. I returned in the evening to the house, to bring away in a hack cab the things I had left there, with my poor dog's body. In this task I was not disturbed, nor did any incident worth note befall me, except that still, on ascending and descending the stairs, I heard the same footfall in advance. On leaving the house, I went to Mr J——'s. He was at home. I returned him the keys, told him that my curiosity was sufficiently gratified, and was about to relate quickly what had passed, when he stopped me, and said, though with much politeness, that he had no longer any interest in a mystery which none had ever solved.

I determined at least to tell him of the two letters I had read, as well as of the extraordinary manner in which they had disappeared, and I then inquired if he thought they had been addressed to the woman who had died in the house, and if there were anything in her early history which could possibly confirm the dark suspicions to which the letters gave rise. Mr J—— seemed startled, and, after musing a few moments, answered: 'I am but little acquainted with the woman's earlier history, except, as I before told you, that her family were known to mine. But you revive some vague reminiscences to her prejudice. I will make inquiries, and inform you of their result. Still, even if we could admit the popular superstition that a person who had been either the perpetrator or the victim of dark crimes in life could revisit, as a restless spirit, the scene in which those crimes had been committed, I should observe that the house was infested by strange sights and sounds before the old woman died—you smile—what would you say?'

'I would say this, that I am convinced, if we could get to the bottom of these mysteries, we should find a living human agency.'

'What! you believe it is all an imposture? for what object?'

'Not an imposture in the ordinary sense of the word. If suddenly I were to sink into a deep sleep, from which you could not awake me, but in that sleep could answer questions with an accuracy which I could not pretend to when awake—tell you what money you had in your pocket—nay, describe your very thoughts—it is not necessarily an imposture, any more than it is necessarily supernatural. I should be, unconsciously to myself, under a mesmeric influence, conveyed to me from a distance by a human being who had acquired power over me by previous *rapport*.'

'But if a mesmerizer could so affect another living being, can you suppose that a mesmerizer could also affect inanimate objects; move chairs – open and shut doors?'

'Or impress our senses with the belief in such effects – we never having been *en rapport* with the person acting on us? No. What is commonly called mesmerism could not do this; but there may be a power akin to mesmerism and superior to it – the power that in the old days was called Magic. That such a power may extend to all inanimate objects of matter, I do not say; but if so, it would not be against nature – it would only be a rare power in nature which might be given to constitutions with certain peculiarities, and cultivated by practise to an extraordinary degree.

'That such a power might extend over the dead – that is, over certain thoughts and memories that the dead may still retain – and compel, not that which ought properly to be called the Soul, and which is far beyond human reach, but rather a phantom of what has been most earth-stained on earth to make itself apparent to our senses – is a very ancient though obsolete theory, upon which I will hazard no opinion. But I do not conceive the power to be supernatural. Let me illustrate what I mean from an experiment which Paracelsus describes as not difficult, and which the author of the 'Curiosities of Literature' cites as credible: A flower perishes; you burn it. Whatever were the elements of that flower while it lived are gone, dispersed, you know not whither; you can never discover nor re-collect them. But you can, by chemistry, out of the burned dust of that flower, raise a spectrum of the flower, just as it seemed in life. It may be the same with the human being. The soul has as much escaped you as the essence or elements of the flower. Still you may make a spectrum of it. And this phantom, though in the popular superstition it is held to be the soul of the departed, must not be confounded with the true soul; it is but the *eidolon* of the dead form. Hence, like the best attested stories of ghosts or spirits, the thing that most strikes us is the absence of what we hold to be the soul; that is, of superior emancipated intelligence. These apparitions come for little or no object – they seldom speak when they do come; if they speak, they utter no ideas above those of an ordinary person on earth. Wonderful, therefore, as such phenomena may be (granting them to be truthful), I see much that philosophy may question, nothing that it is incumbent on philosophy to deny – viz., nothing supernatural. They are but ideas conveyed somehow or other (we have not yet discovered the means) from one mortal brain to another. Whether, in so doing, tables walk by their own accord, or fiend-like shapes appear in a magic circle, or bodyless hands rise and remove material objects, or a Thing of Darkness, such as presented itself to me, freeze our blood – still am I persuaded that these are but agencies conveyed, as by electric wires, to my own brain from the brain of another. In some constitutions there is a natural chemistry, and those constitutions may produce chemic wonders – in others a natural fluid, call it electricity, and these may produce electric wonders. But the wonders differ from Natural Science in this – they are alike objectless, purposeless, puerile, frivolous. They lead on to no grand results; and therefore the world does not heed, and true sages have not cultivated them. But sure I am, that of all I saw or heard, a man, human as myself, was the remote originator; and I believe unconsciously to himself as to the exact effects produced, for this reason: no two persons, you say, have ever experienced exactly the same thing. Well, observe, no two persons ever experience exactly the same dream. If this were an ordinary imposture, the machinery would be arranged for results that would but little vary; if it were a supernatural agency permitted by the Almighty, it would surely be for some definite end. These phenomena belong to neither class; my persuasion is that they originate in some brain now far distant; that that brain had no distinct volition in anything that occurred; that what does occur reflects but its devious, motley, ever-shifting, half-formed thoughts; in short, that it has been but the dreams of such a brain put in action and invested with a semi-substance. That this brain is of immense power, that it can set matter into movement, that it is malignant and destructive, I believe; some material force must have killed my dog; the same force might, for aught I know, have sufficed to kill myself, had I been as subjugated by terror as the dog – had my intellect or my spirit given me no countervailing resistance in my will.'

'It killed your dog! that is fearful! indeed it is strange that no animal can be induced to stay in that house; not even a cat. Rats and mice are never found in it.'

'The instincts of the brute creation detect influences deadly to their existence. Man's reason has a sense less subtle, because it has a resisting power more supreme. But enough; do you comprehend my theory?'

'Yes, though imperfectly – and I accept any crotchet (pardon the word), however odd, rather than embrace at once the notion of ghosts and hobgoblins we imbibed in our nurseries. Still, to my unfortunate house the evil is the same. What on earth can I do with the house?'

'I will tell you what I would do. I am convinced from my own internal feelings that the small unfurnished room at right angles to the door of the bedroom which I occupied forms a starting-point or receptacle for the influences which haunt the house; and I strongly advise you to have the walls opened, the floor removed – nay, the whole room pulled down. I observe that it is detached from the body of the house, built over the small back-yard, and could be removed without injury to the rest of the building.'

'And you think, if I did that—'

'You would cut off the telegraph wires. Try it. I am so persuaded that I am right that I will pay half the expense if you will allow me to direct the operations.'

'Nay, I am well able to afford the cost; for the rest, allow me to write to you.'

About ten days after I received a letter from Mr J——, telling me that he had visited the house since I had seen him; that he had found the two letters I had described, replaced in the drawer from which I had taken them; that he had read them with misgivings like my own; that he had instituted a cautious inquiry about the woman to whom I rightly conjectured they had been written. It seemed that thirty-six years ago (a year before the date of the letters) she had married, against the wish of her relations, an American of very suspicious character; in fact, he was generally believed to have been a pirate. She herself was the daughter of very respectable tradespeople, and had served in the capacity of a nursery governess before her marriage. She had a brother, a widower, who was considered wealthy, and who had one child of about six years old. A month after the marriage, the body of this brother was found in the Thames, near London Bridge; there seemed some marks of violence about his throat, but they were not deemed sufficient to warrant the inquest in any other verdict than that of 'found drowned.'

The American and his wife took charge of the little boy, the deceased brother having by his will left his sister the guardianship of his only child – and in the event of the child's death, the sister inherited. The child died about six months afterward – it was supposed to have been neglected and ill-treated. The neighbours deposed to having heard it shriek at night. The surgeon who had examined it after death said that it was emaciated as if from want of nourishment, and the body was covered with livid bruises. It seemed that one winter night the child had sought to escape – crept out into the back-yard – tried to scale the wall – fallen back exhausted, and had been found at morning on the stones in a dying state. But though there was some evidence of cruelty, there was none of murder; and the aunt and her husband had sought to palliate cruelty by alleging the exceeding stubbornness and perversity of the child, who was declared to be half-witted. Be that as it may, at the orphan's death the aunt inherited her brother's fortune. Before the first wedded year was out, the American quitted England abruptly, and never returned to it. He obtained a cruising vessel, which was lost in the Atlantic two years afterward. The widow was left in affluence; but reverses of various kinds had befallen her; a bank broke – an investment failed – she went into a small business and became insolvent – then she entered into service, sinking lower and lower, from housekeeper down to maid-of-all-work – never long retaining a place, though nothing decided against her character was ever alleged. She was considered sober, honest, and peculiarly quiet in her ways; still nothing prospered with her. And so she had dropped into the workhouse, from which Mr J—— had taken her, to be placed in charge of the very house which she had rented as mistress in the first year of her wedded life.

Mr J—— added that he had passed an hour alone in the unfurnished room which I had urged him to destroy, and that his impressions of dread while there were so great, though he had neither heard nor seen anything, that he was eager to have the walls bared and the floors removed as I had suggested. He had engaged persons for the work, and would commence any day I would name.

The day was accordingly fixed. I repaired to the haunted house – we went into the blind dreary room, took up the skirting, and then the floors. Under the rafters, covered with rubbish, was found a trap-door, quite large enough to admit a man. It was closely nailed down, with clamps and rivets of iron. On removing these we descended into a room below, the existence of which had never been suspected. In this room there had been a window and a flue, but they had been bricked over, evidently for many years. By the help of candles we examined this place; it still retained some mouldering furniture – three chairs, an oak settle, a table – all of the fashion of about eighty years ago. There was a chest of drawers against the wall, in which we found, half-rotted away, old-fashioned articles of a man's dress, such as might have been worn eighty or a hundred years ago by a gentleman of some rank – costly steel buttons and buckles, like those yet worn in court-dresses, a handsome court sword – in a waistcoat which had once been rich with gold lace, but which was now blackened and foul with damp, we found five guineas, a few silver coins, and an ivory ticket, probably for some place of entertainment long since passed away. But our main discovery was in a kind of iron safe fixed to the wall, the lock of which it cost us much trouble to get picked.

In this safe were three shelves, and two small drawers. Ranged on the shelves were several small bottles of crystal, hermetically stoppered. They contained colourless volatile essences, of the nature of which I shall only say that they were not poisonous – phosphor and ammonia entered into some of them. There were also some very curious glass tubes, and a small pointed rod of iron, with a large lump of rock crystal, and another of amber – also a lodestone of great power.

In one of the drawers we found a miniature portrait set in gold, and retaining the freshness of its colours most remarkably, considering the length of time it had probably been there. The portrait was that of a man who might be somewhat advanced in middle life, perhaps forty-seven or forty-eight.

It was a remarkable face – a most impressive face. If you could fancy some mighty serpent transformed into a man, preserving in the human lineaments the old serpent type, you would have a better idea of that countenance than long descriptions can convey; the width and flatness of frontal – the tapering elegance of contour disguising the strength of the deadly jaw – the long, large, terrible eye, glittering and green as the emerald – and withal a certain ruthless calm, as if from the consciousness of an immense power.

Mechanically I turned round the miniature to examine the back of it, and on the back was engraved a pentacle; in the middle of the pentacle a ladder, and the third step of the ladder was formed by the date 1765. Examining still more minutely, I detected a spring; this, on being pressed, opened the back of the miniature as a lid. Withinside the lid was engraved, 'Marianna to thee – Be faithful in life and in death to ——.' Here follows a name that I will not mention, but it was not unfamiliar to me. I had heard it spoken of by old men in my childhood as the name borne by a dazzling charlatan who had made a great sensation in London for a year or so, and had fled the country on the charge of a double murder within his own house – that of his mistress and his rival. I said nothing of this to Mr J——, to whom reluctantly I resigned the miniature.

We had found no difficulty in opening the first drawer within the iron safe; we found great difficulty in opening the second: it was not locked, but it resisted all efforts, till we inserted in the chinks the edge of a chisel. When we had thus drawn it forth, we found a very singular apparatus in the nicest order. Upon a small thin book, or rather tablet, was placed a saucer of crystal; this saucer was filled with a clear liquid – on that liquid floated a kind of compass, with a needle shifting rapidly round; but instead of the usual points of the compass were seven strange characters, not very unlike those used by astrologers to denote the planets. A peculiar but not strong nor displeasing odour came from this drawer, which was lined with a wood that we afterward discovered to be hazel. Whatever the cause of this odour, it produced a material effect on the nerves. We all felt it, even the two workmen who were in the room – a creeping, tingling sensation from the tips of the fingers to the roots of the hair. Impatient to examine the tablet, I removed the saucer. As I did so the needle of the compass went round and round with exceeding swiftness, and I felt a shock that ran through my whole frame, so that I dropped the saucer on the floor. The liquid was spilled – the saucer was broken – the compass rolled to the end of the room – and at that instant the walls shook to and fro, as if a giant had swayed and rocked them.

The two workmen were so frightened that they ran up the ladder by which we had descended from the trap-door; but seeing that nothing more happened, they were easily induced to return.

Meanwhile I had opened the tablet: it was bound in plain red leather, with a silver clasp; it contained but one sheet of thick vellum, and on that sheet were inscribed, within a double pentacle, words in old monkish Latin, which are literally to be translated thus: 'On all that it can reach within these walls – sentient or inanimate, living or dead – as moves the needle, so work my will! Accursed be the house, and restless be the dwellers therein.'

We found no more. Mr J—— burned the tablet and its anathema. He razed to the foundations the part of the building containing the secret room with the chamber over it. He had then the courage to inhabit the house himself for a month, and a quieter, better-conditioned house could not be found in all London. Subsequently he let it to advantage, and his tenant has made no complaints.

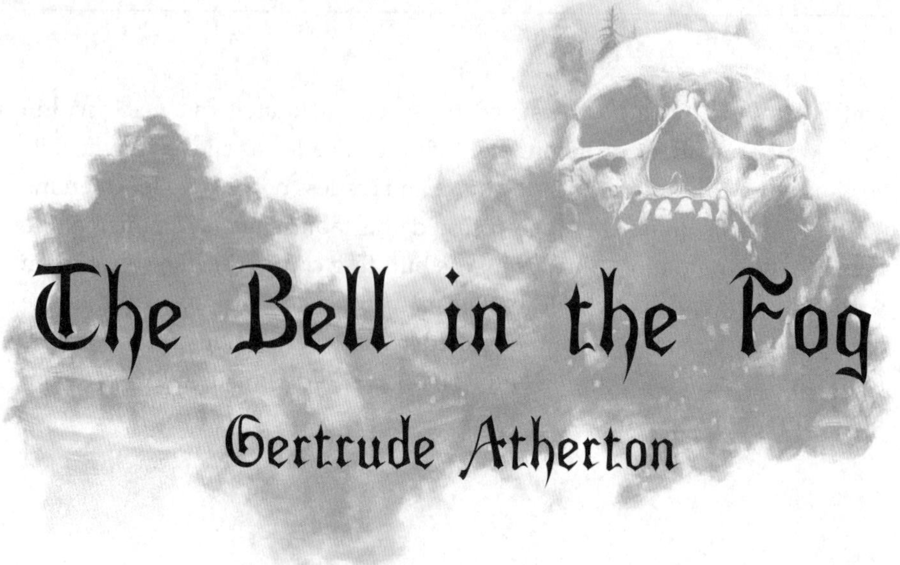

The Bell in the Fog

Gertrude Atherton

I

The great author had realized one of the dreams of his ambitious youth, the possession of an ancestral hall in England. It was not so much the good American's reverence for ancestors that inspired the longing to consort with the ghosts of an ancient line, as artistic appreciation of the mellowness, the dignity, the aristocratic aloofness of walls that have sheltered, and furniture that has embraced, generations and generations of the dead. To mere wealth, only his astute and incomparably modern brain yielded respect; his ego raised its goose-flesh at the sight of rooms furnished with a single check, conciliatory as the taste might be. The dumping of the old interiors of Europe into the glistening shells of the United States not only roused him almost to passionate protest, but offended his patriotism—which he classified among his unworked ideals. The average American was not an artist, therefore he had no excuse for even the affectation of cosmopolitanism. Heaven knew he was national enough in everything else, from his accent to his lack of repose; let his surroundings be in keeping.

Orth had left the United States soon after his first successes, and, his art being too great to be confounded with locality, he had long since ceased to be spoken of as an American author. All civilized Europe furnished stages for his puppets, and, if never picturesque nor impassioned, his originality was as overwhelming as his style. His subtleties might not always be understood—indeed, as a rule, they were not—but the musical mystery of his language and the penetrating charm of his lofty and cultivated mind induced raptures in the initiated, forever denied to those who failed to appreciate him.

His following was not a large one, but it was very distinguished. The aristocracies of the earth gave to it; and not to understand and admire Ralph Orth was deliberately to relegate one's self to the ranks. But the elect are few, and they frequently subscribe to the circulating libraries; on the Continent, they buy the Tauchnitz edition; and had not Mr Orth inherited a sufficiency of ancestral dollars to enable him to keep rooms in Jermyn Street, and the wardrobe of an Englishman of leisure, he might have been forced to consider the tastes of the middle-class at a desk in Hampstead. But, as it mercifully was, the fashionable and exclusive sets of London knew and sought him. He was too wary to become a fad, and too sophisticated to grate or bore; consequently, his popularity continued evenly from year to year, and long since he had come to be regarded as one of them. He was not keenly addicted to sport, but he could handle a gun, and all men respected his dignity and breeding. They cared less for his books than women did, perhaps because patience is not a characteristic of their sex. I am alluding, however, in this instance, to men-of-the-world. A group of young literary men—and one or two women—put him on a pedestal and kissed the earth before it. Naturally, they imitated him, and as this flattered him, and he had a kindly heart deep among the cere-cloths of his formalities, he sooner or later wrote "appreciations" of them all, which nobody living could understand, but which owing to the sub-title and signature answered every purpose.

With all this, however, he was not utterly content. From the 12th of August until late in the winter—when he did not go to Homburg and the Riviera—he visited the best houses in England, slept in state chambers, and meditated in historic parks; but the country was his one passion, and he longed for his own acres.

He was turning fifty when his great-aunt died and made him her heir: "as a poor reward for his immortal services to literature," read the will of this phenomenally appreciative relative. The estate was a large one. There was a rush for his books; new editions were announced. He smiled with cynicism, not unmixed with sadness; but he was very grateful for the money, and as soon as his fastidious taste would permit he bought him a country-seat.

The place gratified all his ideals and dreams—for he had romanced about his sometime English possession as he had never dreamed of woman. It had once been the property of the Church, and the ruin of cloister and chapel above the ancient wood was sharp against the low pale sky. Even the house itself was Tudor, but wealth from generation to generation had kept it in repair; and the lawns were as velvety, the hedges as rigid, the trees as aged as any in his own works. It was not a castle nor a great property, but it was quite perfect; and for a long while he felt like a bridegroom on a succession of honeymoons. He often laid his hand against the rough ivied walls in a lingering caress.

After a time, he returned the hospitalities of his friends, and his invitations, given with the exclusiveness of his great distinction, were never refused. Americans visiting England eagerly sought for letters to him; and if they were sometimes benumbed by that cold and formal presence, and awed by the silences of Chillingsworth—the few who entered there—they thrilled in anticipation of verbal triumphs, and forthwith bought an entire set of his books. It was characteristic that they dared not ask him for his autograph.

Although women invariably described him as "brilliant," a few men affirmed that he was gentle and lovable, and any one of them was well content to spend weeks at Chillingsworth with no other companion. But, on the whole, he was rather a lonely man.

It occurred to him how lonely he was one gay June morning when the sunlight was streaming through his narrow windows, illuminating tapestries and armor, the family portraits of the young profligate from whom he had made this splendid purchase, dusting its gold on the black wood of wainscot and floor. He was in the gallery at the moment, studying one of his two favorite portraits, a gallant little lad in the green costume of Robin Hood. The boy's expression was imperious and radiant, and he had that perfect beauty which in any disposition appealed so powerfully to the author. But as Orth stared today at the brilliant youth, of whose life he knew nothing, he suddenly became aware of a human stirring at the foundations of his aesthetic pleasure.

"I wish he were alive and here," he thought, with a sigh. "What a jolly little companion he would be! And this fine old mansion would make a far more complementary setting for him than for me."

He turned away abruptly, only to find himself face to face with the portrait of a little girl who was quite unlike the boy, yet so perfect in her own way, and so unmistakably painted by the same hand, that he had long since concluded they had been brother and sister. She was angelically fair, and, young as she was—she could not have been more than six years old—her dark-blue eyes had a beauty of mind which must have been remarkable twenty years later. Her pouting mouth was like a little scarlet serpent, her skin almost transparent, her pale hair fell waving—not curled with the orthodoxy of childhood—about her tender bare shoulders. She wore a long white frock, and clasped tightly against her breast a doll far more gorgeously arrayed than herself. Behind her were the ruins and the woods of Chillingsworth.

Orth had studied this portrait many times, for the sake of an art which he understood almost as well as his own; but today he saw only the lovely child. He forgot even the boy in the intensity of this new and personal absorption.

"Did she live to grow up, I wonder?" he thought. "She should have made a remarkable, even a famous woman, with those eyes and that brow, but—could the spirit within that ethereal frame stand the enlightenments of maturity? Would not that mind—purged, perhaps, in a long probation from the dross of other existences—flee in disgust from the commonplace problems of a woman's life? Such perfect beings should die while they are still perfect. Still, it is possible that this little girl, whoever she was, was idealized by the artist, who painted into her his own dream of exquisite childhood."

Again he turned away impatiently. "I believe I am rather fond of children," he admitted. "I catch myself watching them on the street when they are pretty enough. Well, who does not like them?" he added, with some defiance.

He went back to his work; he was chiselling a story which was to be the foremost excuse of a magazine as yet unborn. At the end of half an hour he threw down his wondrous instrument—which looked not unlike an ordinary pen—and making no attempt to disobey the desire that possessed him, went back to the gallery. The dark splendid boy, the angelic little girl were all he saw—even of the several children in that roll-call of the past—

and they seemed to look straight down his eyes into depths where the fragmentary ghosts of unrecorded ancestors gave faint musical response.

"The dead's kindly recognition of the dead," he thought. "But I wish these children were alive."

For a week he haunted the gallery, and the children haunted him. Then he became impatient and angry. "I am mooning like a barren woman," he exclaimed. "I must take the briefest way of getting those youngsters off my mind."

With the help of his secretary, he ransacked the library, and finally brought to light the gallery catalogue which had been named in the inventory. He discovered that his children were the Viscount Tancred and the Lady Blanche Mortlake, son and daughter of the second Earl of Teignmouth. Little wiser than before, he sat down at once and wrote to the present earl, asking for some account of the lives of the children. He awaited the answer with more restlessness than he usually permitted himself, and took long walks, ostentatiously avoiding the gallery.

"I believe those youngsters have obsessed me," he thought, more than once. "They certainly are beautiful enough, and the last time I looked at them in that waning light they were fairly alive. Would that they were, and scampering about this park."

Lord Teignmouth, who was intensely grateful to him, answered promptly.

"I am afraid," he wrote, "that I don't know much about my ancestors—those who didn't do something or other; but I have a vague remembrance of having been told by an aunt of mine, who lives on the family traditions—she isn't married—that the little chap was drowned in the river, and that the little girl died too—I mean when she was a little girl—wasted away, or something—I'm such a beastly idiot about expressing myself, that I wouldn't dare to write to you at all if you weren't really great. That is actually all I can tell you, and I am afraid the painter was their only biographer."

The author was gratified that the girl had died young, but grieved for the boy. Although he had avoided the gallery of late, his practised imagination had evoked from the throngs of history the high-handed and brilliant, surely adventurous career of the third Earl of Teignmouth. He had pondered upon the deep delights of directing such a mind and character, and had caught himself envying the dust that was older still. When he read of the lad's early death, in spite of his regret that such promise should have come to naught, he admitted to a secret thrill of satisfaction that the boy had so soon ceased to belong to any one. Then he smiled with both sadness and humor.

"What an old fool I am!" he admitted. "I believe I not only wish those children were alive, but that they were my own."

The frank admission proved fatal. He made straight for the gallery. The boy, after the interval of separation, seemed more spiritedly alive than ever, the little girl to suggest, with her faint appealing smile, that she would like to be taken up and cuddled.

"I must try another way," he thought, desperately, after that long communion. "I must write them out of me."

He went back to the library and locked up the *tour de force* which had ceased to command his classic faculty. At once, he began to write the story of the brief lives of the children, much to the amazement of that faculty, which was little accustomed to the simplicities. Nevertheless, before he had written three chapters, he knew that he was at work upon a masterpiece—and more: he was experiencing a pleasure so keen that once and again his hand trembled, and he saw the page through a mist. Although his characters had always been objective to himself and his more patient readers, none knew better than he—a man of no delusions—that they were so remote and exclusive as barely to escape being mere mentalities; they were never the pulsing living creations of the more full-blooded genius. But he had been content to have it so. His creations might find and leave him cold, but he had known his highest satisfaction in chiselling the statuettes, extracting subtle and elevating harmonies, while combining words as no man of his tongue had combined them before.

But the children were not statuettes. He had loved and brooded over them long ere he had thought to tuck them into his pen, and on its first stroke they danced out alive. The old mansion echoed with their laughter, with their delightful and original pranks. Mr Orth knew nothing of children, therefore all the pranks he invented were as original as his faculty. The little girl clung to his hand or knee as they both followed the adventurous course of their common idol, the boy. When Orth realized how alive they were, he opened each room of his home to them in turn, that evermore he might have sacred and poignant memories with all parts of the stately mansion where he must dwell alone to the end. He selected their bedrooms, and hovered over them—not through infantile disorders, which were beyond even his imagination,—but through those painful intervals incident upon the enterprising spirit of the boy and the devoted obedience of the girl to fraternal command. He ignored the second Lord Teignmouth; he was himself their father, and he admired himself extravagantly for the first time; art had chastened him long since. Oddly enough, the children had no mother, not even the memory of one.

He wrote the book more slowly than was his wont, and spent delightful hours pondering upon the chapter of the morrow. He looked forward to the conclusion with a sort of terror, and made up his mind that when the inevitable last word was written he should start at once for Homburg. Incalculable times a day he went to the gallery, for he no longer had any desire to write the children out of his mind, and his eyes hungered for them. They were his now. It was with an effort that he sometimes humorously reminded himself that another man had fathered them, and that their little skeletons were under the choir of the chapel. Not even for peace of mind would he have descended into the vaults of the lords of Chillingsworth and looked upon the marble effigies of his children. Nevertheless, when in a superhumorous mood, he dwelt upon his high satisfaction in having been enabled by his great-aunt to purchase all that was left of them.

For two months he lived in his fool's paradise, and then he knew that the book must end. He nerved himself to nurse the little girl through her wasting illness, and when he clasped her hands, his own shook, his knees trembled. Desolation settled upon the house, and he wished he had left one corner of it to which he could retreat unhaunted by the child's presence. He took long tramps, avoiding the river with a sensation next to panic. It was two days before he got back to his table, and then he had made up his mind to let the boy live. To kill him off, too, was more than his augmented stock of human nature could endure. After all, the lad's death had been purely accidental, wanton. It was just that he should live—with one of the author's inimitable suggestions of future greatness; but, at the end, the parting was almost as bitter as the other. Orth knew then how men feel when their sons go forth to encounter the world and ask no more of the old companionship.

The author's boxes were packed. He sent the manuscript to his publisher an hour after it was finished—he could not have given it a final reading to have saved it from failure—directed his secretary to examine the proof under a microscope, and left the next morning for Homburg. There, in inmost circles, he forgot his children. He visited in several of the great houses of the Continent until November; then returned to London to find his book the literary topic of the day. His secretary handed him the reviews; and for once in a way he read the finalities of the nameless. He found himself hailed as a genius, and compared in astonished phrases to the prodigiously clever talent which the world for twenty years had isolated under the name of Ralph Orth. This pleased him, for every writer is human enough to wish to be hailed as a genius, and immediately. Many are, and many wait; it depends upon the fashion of the moment, and the needs and bias of those who write of writers. Orth had waited twenty years; but his past was bedecked with the headstones of geniuses long since forgotten. He was gratified to come thus publicly into his estate, but soon reminded himself that all the adulation of which a belated world was capable could not give him one thrill of the pleasure which the companionship of that book had given him, while creating. It was the keenest pleasure in his memory, and when a man is fifty and has written many books, that is saying a great deal.

He allowed what society was in town to lavish honors upon him for something over a month, then cancelled all his engagements and went down to Chillingsworth.

His estate was in Hertfordshire, that county of gentle hills and tangled lanes, of ancient oaks and wide wild heaths, of historic houses, and dark woods, and green fields innumerable—a Wordsworthian shire, steeped in the deepest peace of England. As Orth drove towards his own gates he had the typical English sunset to gaze upon, a red streak with a church spire against it. His woods were silent. In the fields, the cows stood as if conscious of their part. The ivy on his old gray towers had been young with his children.

He spent a haunted night, but the next day stranger happenings began.

II

He rose early, and went for one of his long walks. England seems to cry out to be walked upon, and Orth, like others of the transplanted, experienced to the full the country's gift of foot-restlessness and mental calm. Calm flees, however, when the ego is rampant, and today, as upon others too recent, Orth's soul was as restless as his feet. He had walked for two hours when he entered the wood of his neighbor's estate, a domain seldom honored by him, as it, too, had been bought by an American—a flighty hunting widow, who displeased the fastidious taste of the author. He heard children's voices, and turned with the quick prompting of retreat.

As he did so, he came face to face, on the narrow path, with a little girl. For the moment he was possessed by the most hideous sensation which can visit a man's being—abject terror. He believed that body and soul were disintegrating. The child before him was his child, the original of a portrait in which the artist, dead two centuries ago, had missed exact fidelity, after all. The difference, even his rolling vision took note, lay in the warm pure living whiteness and the deeper spiritual suggestion of the child in his path. Fortunately for his self-respect, the surrender lasted but a moment. The little girl spoke.

"You look real sick," she said. "Shall I lead you home?"

The voice was soft and sweet, but the intonation, the vernacular, were American, and not of the highest class. The shock was, if possible, more agonizing than the other, but this time Orth rose to the occasion.

"Who are you?" he demanded, with asperity. "What is your name? Where do you live?"

The child smiled, an angelic smile, although she was evidently amused. "I never had so many questions asked me all at once," she said. "But I don't mind, and I'm glad you're not sick. I'm Mrs Jennie Root's little girl—my father's dead. My name is Blanche—you *are* sick! No?—and I live in Rome, New York State. We've come over here to visit pa's relations."

Orth took the child's hand in his. It was very warm and soft.

"Take me to your mother," he said, firmly; "now, at once. You can return and play afterwards. And as I wouldn't have you disappointed for the world, I'll send to town today for a beautiful doll."

The little girl, whose face had fallen, flashed her delight, but walked with great dignity beside him. He groaned in his depths as he saw they were pointing for the widow's house, but made up his mind that he would know the history of the child and of all her ancestors, if he had to sit down at table with his obnoxious neighbor. To his surprise, however, the child did not lead him into the park, but towards one of the old stone houses of the tenantry.

"Pa's great-great-great-grandfather lived there," she remarked, with all the American's pride of ancestry. Orth did not smile, however. Only the warm clasp of the hand in his, the soft thrilling voice of his still mysterious companion, prevented him from feeling as if moving through the mazes of one of his own famous ghost stories.

The child ushered him into the dining-room, where an old man was seated at the table reading his Bible. The room was at least eight hundred years old. The ceiling was supported by the trunk of a tree, black, and probably petrified. The windows had still their diamond panes, separated, no doubt, by the original lead. Beyond was a large kitchen in which were several women. The old man, who looked patriarchal enough to have laid the foundations of his dwelling, glanced up and regarded the visitor without hospitality. His expression softened as his eyes moved to the child.

"Who 'ave ye brought?" he asked. He removed his spectacles. "Ah!" He rose, and offered the author a chair. At the same moment, the women entered the room.

"Of course you've fallen in love with Blanche, sir," said one of them. "Everybody does."

"Yes, that is it. Quite so." Confusion still prevailing among his faculties, he clung to the naked truth. "This little girl has interested and startled me because she bears a precise resemblance to one of the portraits in Chillingsworth—painted about two hundred years ago. Such extraordinary likenesses do not occur without reason, as a rule, and, as I admired my portrait so deeply that I have written a story about it, you will not think it unnatural if I am more than curious to discover the reason for this resemblance. The little girl tells me that her ancestors lived in this very house, and as my little girl lived next door, so to speak, there undoubtedly is a natural reason for the resemblance."

His host closed the Bible, put his spectacles in his pocket, and hobbled out of the house.

"He'll never talk of family secrets," said an elderly woman, who introduced herself as the old man's daughter, and had placed bread and milk before the guest. "There are secrets in every family, and we have ours, but he'll never tell those old tales. All I can tell you is that an ancestor of little Blanche went to wreck and ruin because of some fine lady's doings, and killed himself. The story is that his boys turned out bad. One of them saw his crime, and never got over the shock; he was foolish like, after. The mother was a poor scared sort of creature, and hadn't much influence over the other boy. There seemed to be a blight on all the man's descendants, until one of them went to America. Since then, they haven't prospered, exactly, but they've done better, and they don't drink so heavy."

"They haven't done so well," remarked a worn patient-looking woman. Orth typed her as belonging to the small middle-class of an interior town of the eastern United States.

"You are not the child's mother?"

"Yes, sir. Everybody is surprised; you needn't apologize. She doesn't look like any of us, although her brothers and sisters are good enough for anybody to be proud of. But we all think she strayed in by mistake, for she looks like any lady's child, and, of course, we're only middle-class."

Orth gasped. It was the first time he had ever heard a native American use the term middle-class with a personal application. For the moment, he forgot the child. His analytical mind raked in the new specimen. He questioned, and learned that the woman's husband had kept a hat store in Rome, New York; that her boys were clerks, her girls in stores, or type-writing. They kept her and little Blanche—who had come after her other children were well grown—in comfort; and they were all very happy together. The boys broke out, occasionally; but, on the whole, were the best in the world, and her girls were worthy of far better than they had. All were robust, except Blanche. "She coming so late, when I was no longer young, makes her delicate," she remarked, with a slight blush, the signal of her chaste Americanism; "but I guess she'll get along all right. She couldn't have better care if she was a queen's child."

Orth, who had gratefully consumed the bread and milk, rose. "Is that really all you can tell me?" he asked.

"That's all," replied the daughter of the house. "And you couldn't pry open father's mouth."

Orth shook hands cordially with all of them, for he could be charming when he chose. He offered to escort the little girl back to her playmates in the wood, and she took prompt possession of his hand. As he was leaving, he turned suddenly to Mrs Root. "Why did you call her Blanche?" he asked.

"She was so white and dainty, she just looked it."

Orth took the next train for London, and from Lord Teignmouth obtained the address of the aunt who lived on the family traditions, and a cordial note of introduction to her. He then spent an hour anticipating, in a toy shop, the whims and pleasures of a child—an incident of paternity which his book-children had not inspired. He bought the finest doll, piano, French dishes, cooking apparatus, and playhouse in the shop, and signed a check for thirty pounds with a sensation of positive rapture. Then he took the train for Lancashire, where the Lady Mildred Mortlake lived in another ancestral home.

Possibly there are few imaginative writers who have not a leaning, secret or avowed, to the occult. The creative gift is in very close relationship with the Great Force behind the universe; for aught we know, may be an atom thereof. It is not strange, therefore, that the lesser and closer of the unseen forces should send their vibrations to it occasionally; or, at all events, that the imagination should incline its ear to the most mysterious and picturesque of all beliefs. Orth frankly dallied with the old dogma. He formulated no personal faith of any sort, but his creative faculty, that ego within an ego, had made more than one excursion into the invisible and brought back literary treasure.

The Lady Mildred received with sweetness and warmth the generous contributor to the family sieve, and listened with fluttering interest to all he had not told the world—she had read the book—and to the strange, Americanized sequel.

"I am all at sea," concluded Orth. "What had my little girl to do with the tragedy? What relation was she to the lady who drove the young man to destruction—?"

"The closest," interrupted Lady Mildred. "She was herself!"

Orth stared at her. Again he had a confused sense of disintegration. Lady Mildred, gratified by the success of her bolt, proceeded less dramatically:

"Wally was up here just after I read your book, and I discovered he had given you the wrong history of the picture. Not that he knew it. It is a story we have left untold as often as possible, and I tell it to you only because you would probably become a monomaniac if I didn't. Blanche Mortlake—that Blanche—there had been several of her name, but there has not been one since—did not die in childhood, but lived to be twenty-four. She was an angelic child, but little angels sometimes grow up into very naughty girls. I believe she was delicate as a child, which probably gave her that spiritual look. Perhaps she was spoiled and flattered, until her poor little soul was stifled, which is likely. At all events, she was the coquette of her day—she seemed to care for nothing but breaking hearts; and she did not stop when she married, either. She hated her husband, and became reckless. She had no children. So far, the tale is not an uncommon one; but the worst, and what makes the ugliest stain in our annals, is to come.

"She was alone one summer at Chillingsworth—where she had taken temporary refuge from her husband—and she amused herself—some say, fell in love—with a young man of the yeomanry, a tenant of the next estate. His name was Root. He, so it comes down to us, was a magnificent specimen of his kind, and in those days the yeomanry gave us our great soldiers. His beauty of face was quite as remarkable as his physique; he led all the rural youth in sport, and was a bit above his class in every way. He had a wife in no way remarkable, and two little boys, but was always more with his friends than his family. Where he and Blanche Mortlake met I don't know—in the woods, probably, although it has been said that he had the run of the house. But, at all events, he was wild about her, and she pretended to be about him. Perhaps she was, for women have stooped before and since. Some women can be stormed by a fine man in any circumstances; but, although I am a woman of the world, and not easy to shock, there are some things I tolerate so hardly that it is all I can do to bring myself to believe in them; and stooping is one. Well, they were the scandal of the county for months, and then, either because she had tired of her new toy, or his grammar grated after the first glamour, or because she feared her husband, who was returning from the Continent, she broke off with him and returned to town. He followed her, and forced his way into her house. It is said she melted, but made him swear never to attempt to see her again. He returned to his home, and killed himself. A few months later she took her own life. That is all I know."

"It is quite enough for me," said Orth.

The next night, as his train travelled over the great wastes of Lancashire, a thousand chimneys were spouting forth columns of fire. Where the sky was not red it was black. The place looked like hell. Another time Orth's imagination would have gathered immediate inspiration from this wildest region of England. The fair and peaceful counties of the south had nothing to compare in infernal grandeur with these acres of flaming columns. The chimneys were invisible in the lower darkness of the night; the fires might have leaped straight from the angry caldron of the earth.

But Orth was in a subjective world, searching for all he had ever heard of occultism. He recalled that the sinful dead are doomed, according to this belief, to linger for vast reaches of time in that borderland which is close to earth, eventually sent back to work out their final salvation; that they work it out among the descendants of the people they have wronged; that suicide is held by the devotees of occultism to be a cardinal sin, abhorred and execrated.

Authors are far closer to the truths enfolded in mystery than ordinary people, because of that very audacity of imagination which irritates their plodding critics. As only those who dare to make mistakes succeed greatly, only those who shake free the wings of their imagination brush, once in a way, the secrets of the great pale world. If such writers go wrong, it is not for the mere brains to tell them so.

Upon Orth's return to Chillingsworth, he called at once upon the child, and found her happy among his gifts. She put her arms about his neck, and covered his serene unlined face with soft kisses. This completed the conquest. Orth from that moment adored her as a child, irrespective of the psychological problem.

Gradually he managed to monopolize her. From long walks it was but a step to take her home for luncheon. The hours of her visits lengthened. He had a room fitted up as a nursery and filled with the wonders of toyland. He took her to London to see the pantomimes; two days before Christmas, to buy presents for her relatives; and together they strung them upon the most wonderful Christmas tree that the old hall of Chillingsworth had ever embraced. She had a donkey-cart, and a trained nurse, disguised as a maid, to wait upon her. Before a month had passed she was living in state at Chillingsworth and paying daily visits to her mother. Mrs Root was deeply flattered, and apparently well content. Orth told her plainly that he should make the child independent, and educate her, meanwhile. Mrs Root intended to spend six months in England, and Orth was in no hurry to alarm her by broaching his ultimate design.

He reformed Blanche's accent and vocabulary, and read to her out of books which would have addled the brains of most little maids of six; but she seemed to enjoy them, although she seldom made a comment. He was always ready to play games with her, but she was a gentle little thing, and, moreover, tired easily. She preferred to sit in the depths of a big chair, toasting her bare toes at the log-fire in the hall, while her friend read or talked to her. Although she was thoughtful, and, when left to herself, given to dreaming, his patient observation could detect nothing uncanny about her. Moreover, she had a quick sense of humor, she was easily amused, and could laugh as merrily as any child in the world. He was resigning all hope of further development on the shadowy side when one day he took her to the picture-gallery.

It was the first warm day of summer. The gallery was not heated, and he had not dared to take his frail visitor into its chilly spaces during the winter and spring. Although he had wished to see the effect of the picture on the child, he had shrunk from the bare possibility of the very developments the mental part of him craved; the other was warmed and satisfied for the first time, and held itself aloof from disturbance. But one day the sun streamed through the old windows, and, obeying a sudden impulse, he led Blanche to the gallery.

It was some time before he approached the child of his earlier love. Again he hesitated. He pointed out many other fine pictures, and Blanche smiled appreciatively at his remarks, that were wise in criticism and interesting in matter. He never knew just how much she understood, but the very fact that there were depths in the child beyond his probing riveted his chains.

Suddenly he wheeled about and waved his hand to her prototype. "What do you think of that?" he asked. "You remember, I told you of the likeness the day I met you."

She looked indifferently at the picture, but he noticed that her color changed oddly; its pure white tone gave place to an equally delicate gray.

"I have seen it before," she said. "I came in here one day to look at it. And I have been quite often since. You never forbade me," she added, looking at him appealingly, but dropping her eyes quickly. "And I like the little girl—and the boy—very much."

"Do you? Why?"

"I don't know"—a formula in which she had taken refuge before. Still her candid eyes were lowered; but she was quite calm. Orth, instead of questioning, merely fixed his eyes upon her, and waited. In a moment she stirred uneasily, but she did not laugh nervously, as another child would have done. He had never seen her self-possession ruffled, and he had begun to doubt he ever should. She was full of human warmth and affection. She seemed made for love, and every creature who came within her ken adored her, from the author himself down to the litter of puppies presented to her by the stable-boy a few weeks since; but her serenity would hardly be enhanced by death.

She raised her eyes finally, but not to his. She looked at the portrait.

"Did you know that there was another picture behind?" she asked.

"No," replied Orth, turning cold. "How did you know it?"

"One day I touched a spring in the frame, and this picture came forward. Shall I show you?"

"Yes!" And crossing curiosity and the involuntary shrinking from impending phenomena was a sensation of aesthetic disgust that *he* should be treated to a secret spring.

The little girl touched hers, and that other Blanche sprang aside so quickly that she might have been impelled by a sharp blow from behind. Orth narrowed his eyes and stared at what she revealed. He felt that his own Blanche was watching him, and set his features, although his breath was short.

There was the Lady Blanche Mortlake in the splendor of her young womanhood, beyond a doubt. Gone were all traces of her spiritual childhood, except, perhaps, in the shadows of the mouth; but more than fulfilled were the promises of her mind. Assuredly, the woman had been as brilliant and gifted as she had been restless and passionate. She wore her very pearls with arrogance, her very hands were tense with eager life, her whole being breathed mutiny.

Orth turned abruptly to Blanche, who had transferred her attention to the picture.

"What a tragedy is there!" he exclaimed, with a fierce attempt at lightness. "Think of a woman having all that pent up within her two centuries ago! And at the mercy of a stupid family, no doubt, and a still stupider husband. No wonder—Today, a woman like that might not be a model for all the virtues, but she certainly would use her gifts and become famous, the while living her life too fully to have any place in it for yeomen and such, or even for the trivial business of breaking hearts." He put his finger under Blanche's chin, and raised her face, but he could not compel her gaze. "You are the exact image of that little girl," he said, "except that you are even purer and finer. She had no chance, none whatever. You live in the woman's age. Your opportunities will be infinite. I shall see to it that they are. What you wish to be you shall be. There will be no pent-up energies here to burst out into disaster for yourself and others. You shall be trained to self-control—that is, if you ever develop self-will, dear child—every faculty shall be educated, every school of life you desire knowledge through shall be opened to you. You shall become that finest flower of civilization, a woman who knows how to use her independence."

She raised her eyes slowly, and gave him a look which stirred the roots of sensation—a long look of unspeakable melancholy. Her chest rose once; then she set her lips tightly, and dropped her eyes.

"What do you mean?" he cried, roughly, for his soul was chattering. "Is—it—do you—?" He dared not go too far, and concluded lamely, "You mean you fear that your mother will not give you to me when she goes—you have divined that I wish to adopt you? Answer me, will you?"

But she only lowered her head and turned away, and he, fearing to frighten or repel her, apologized for his abruptness, restored the outer picture to its place, and led her from the gallery.

He sent her at once to the nursery, and when she came down to luncheon and took her place at his right hand, she was as natural and childlike as ever. For some days he restrained his curiosity, but one evening, as they were sitting before the fire in the hall listening to the storm, and just after he had told her the story of the erl-king, he took her on his knee and asked her gently if she would not tell him what had been in her thoughts when he had drawn her brilliant future. Again her face turned gray, and she dropped her eyes.

"I cannot," she said. "I—perhaps—I don't know."

"Was it what I suggested?"

She shook her head, then looked at him with a shrinking appeal which forced him to drop the subject.

He went the next day alone to the gallery, and looked long at the portrait of the woman. She stirred no response in him. Nor could he feel that the woman of Blanche's future would stir the man in him. The paternal was all he had to give, but that was hers forever.

He went out into the park and found Blanche digging in her garden, very dirty and absorbed. The next afternoon, however, entering the hall noiselessly, he saw her sitting in her big chair, gazing out into nothing visible, her whole face settled in melancholy. He asked her if she were ill, and she recalled herself at once, but confessed to feeling tired. Soon after this he noticed that she lingered longer in the comfortable depths of her chair, and seldom went out, except with himself. She insisted that she was quite well, but after he had surprised her again looking as sad as if she had renounced every joy of childhood, he summoned from London a doctor renowned for his success with children.

The scientist questioned and examined her. When she had left the room he shrugged his shoulders.

"She might have been born with ten years of life in her, or she might grow up into a buxom woman," he said. "I confess I cannot tell. She appears to be sound enough, but I have no X-rays in my eyes, and for all I know she may be on the verge of decay. She certainly has the look of those who die young. I have never seen so spiritual a child. But I can put my finger on nothing. Keep her out-of-doors, don't give her sweets, and don't let her catch anything if you can help it."

Orth and the child spent the long warm days of summer under the trees of the park, or driving in the quiet lanes. Guests were unbidden, and his pen was idle. All that was human in him had gone out to Blanche. He loved her, and she was a perpetual delight to him. The rest of the world received the large measure of his indifference. There was no further change in her, and apprehension slept and let him sleep. He had persuaded Mrs Root to remain in England for a year. He sent her theatre tickets every week, and placed a horse and phaeton at her disposal. She was enjoying herself and seeing less and less of Blanche. He took the child to Bournemouth for a fortnight, and again to Scotland, both of which outings benefited as much as they pleased her. She had begun to tyrannize over him amiably, and she carried herself quite royally. But she was always sweet and truthful, and these qualities, combined with that something in the depths of her mind which defied his explorations, held him captive. She was devoted to him, and cared for no other companion, although she was demonstrative to her mother when they met.

It was in the tenth month of this idyl of the lonely man and the lonely child that Mrs Root flurriedly entered the library of Chillingsworth, where Orth happened to be alone.

"Oh, sir," she exclaimed, "I must go home. My daughter Grace writes me—she should have done it before—that the boys are not behaving as well as they should—she didn't tell me, as I was having such a good time she just hated to worry me—Heaven knows I've had enough worry—but now I must go—I just couldn't stay—boys are an awful responsibility—girls ain't a circumstance to them, although mine are a handful sometimes."

Orth had written about too many women to interrupt the flow. He let her talk until she paused to recuperate her forces. Then he said quietly:

"I am sorry this has come so suddenly, for it forces me to broach a subject at once which I would rather have postponed until the idea had taken possession of you by degrees—"

"I know what it is you want to say, sir," she broke in, "and I've reproached myself that I haven't warned you before, but I didn't like to be the one to speak first. You want Blanche—of course, I couldn't help seeing that; but I can't let her go, sir, indeed, I can't."

"Yes," he said, firmly, "I want to adopt Blanche, and I hardly think you can refuse, for you must know how greatly it will be to her advantage. She is a wonderful child; you have never been blind to that; she should have every opportunity, not only of money, but of association. If I adopt her legally, I shall, of course, make her my heir, and—there is no reason why she should not grow up as great a lady as any in England."

The poor woman turned white, and burst into tears. "I've sat up nights and nights, struggling," she said, when she could speak. "That, and missing her. I couldn't stand in her light, and I let her stay. I know I oughtn't to, now—I mean, stand in her light—but, sir, she is dearer than all the others put together."

"Then live here in England—at least, for some years longer. I will gladly relieve your children of your support, and you can see Blanche as often as you choose."

"I can't do that, sir. After all, she is only one, and there are six others. I can't desert them. They all need me, if only to keep them together—three girls unmarried and out in the world, and three boys just a little inclined to be wild. There is another point, sir—I don't exactly know how to say it."

"Well?" asked Orth, kindly. This American woman thought him the ideal gentleman, although the mistress of the estate on which she visited called him a boor and a snob.

"It is—well—you must know—you can imagine—that her brothers and sisters just worship Blanche. They save their dimes to buy her everything she wants—or used to want. Heaven knows what will satisfy her now, although I can't see that she's one bit spoiled. But she's just like a religion to them; they're not much on church. I'll tell you, sir, what I couldn't say to any one else, not even to these relations who've been so kind to me—but there's wildness, just a streak, in all my children, and I believe, I know, it's Blanche that keeps them straight. My girls get bitter, sometimes; work all the week and little fun, not caring for common men and no chance to marry gentlemen; and sometimes they break out and talk dreadful; then, when they're over it, they say they'll live for Blanche—they've said it over and over, and they mean it. Every sacrifice they've made for her—and they've made many—has done them good. It isn't that Blanche ever says a word of the preachy sort, or has anything of the Sunday-school child about her, or even tries to smooth them down when they're excited. It's just herself. The only thing she ever does is sometimes to draw herself up and look scornful, and that nearly kills them. Little as she is, they're crazy about having her respect. I've grown superstitious about her. Until she came I used to get frightened, terribly, sometimes, and I believe she came for that. So—you see! I know Blanche is too fine for us and ought to have the best; but, then, they are to be considered, too. They have their rights, and they've got much more good than bad in them. I don't know! I don't know! It's kept me awake many nights."

Orth rose abruptly. "Perhaps you will take some further time to think it over," he said. "You can stay a few weeks longer—the matter cannot be so pressing as that."

The woman rose. "I've thought this," she said; "let Blanche decide. I believe she knows more than any of us. I believe that whichever way she decided would be right. I won't say anything to her, so you won't think I'm working on her feelings; and I can trust you. But she'll know."

"Why do you think that?" asked Orth, sharply. "There is nothing uncanny about the child. She is not yet seven years old. Why should you place such a responsibility upon her?"

"Do you think she's like other children?"

"I know nothing of other children."

"I do, sir. I've raised six. And I've seen hundreds of others. I never was one to be a fool about my own, but Blanche isn't like any other child living—I'm certain of it."

"What *do* you think?"

And the woman answered, according to her lights: "I think she's an angel, and came to us because we needed her."

"And I think she is Blanche Mortlake working out the last of her salvation," thought the author; but he made no reply, and was alone in a moment.

It was several days before he spoke to Blanche, and then, one morning, when she was sitting on her mat on the lawn with the light full upon her, he told her abruptly that her mother must return home.

To his surprise, but unutterable delight, she burst into tears and flung herself into his arms.

"You need not leave me," he said, when he could find his own voice. "You can stay here always and be my little girl. It all rests with you."

"I can't stay," she sobbed. "I can't!"

"And that is what made you so sad once or twice?" he asked, with a double eagerness.

She made no reply.

"Oh!" he said, passionately, "give me your confidence, Blanche. You are the only breathing thing that I love."

"If I could I would," she said. "But I don't know—not quite."

"How much do you know?"

But she sobbed again and would not answer. He dared not risk too much. After all, the physical barrier between the past and the present was very young.

"Well, well, then, we will talk about the other matter. I will not pretend to disguise the fact that your mother is distressed at the idea of parting from you, and thinks it would be as sad for your brothers and sisters, whom she says you influence for their good. Do you think that you do?"

"Yes."

"How do you know this?"

"Do you know why you know everything?"

"No, my dear, and I have great respect for your instincts. But your sisters and brothers are now old enough to take care of themselves. They must be of poor stuff if they cannot live properly without the aid of a child. Moreover, they will be marrying soon. That will also mean that your mother will have many little grandchildren to console her for your loss. I will be the one bereft, if you leave me. I am the only one who really needs you. I don't say I will go to the bad, as you may have very foolishly persuaded yourself your family will do without you, but I trust to your instincts to make you realize how unhappy, how inconsolable I shall be. I shall be the loneliest man on earth!"

She rubbed her face deeper into his flannels, and tightened her embrace. "Can't you come, too?" she asked.

"No; you must live with me wholly or not at all. Your people are not my people, their ways are not my ways. We should not get along. And if you lived with me over there you might as well stay here, for your influence over them would be quite as removed. Moreover, if they are of the right stuff, the memory of you will be quite as potent for good as your actual presence."

"Not unless I died."

Again something within him trembled. "Do you believe you are going to die young?" he blurted out.

But she would not answer.

He entered the nursery abruptly the next day and found her packing her dolls. When she saw him, she sat down and began to weep hopelessly. He knew then that his fate was sealed. And when, a year later, he received her last little scrawl, he was almost glad that she went when she did.

The Striding Place

Gertrude Atherton

Weigall, continental and detached, tired early of grouse-shooting. To stand propped against a sod fence while his host's workmen routed up the birds with long poles and drove them towards the waiting guns, made him feel himself a parody on the ancestors who had roamed the moors and forests of this West Riding of Yorkshire in hot pursuit of game worth the killing. But when in England in August he always accepted whatever proffered for the season, and invited his host to shoot pheasants on his estates in the South. The amusements of life, he argued, should be accepted with the same philosophy as its ills.

It had been a bad day. A heavy rain had made the moor so spongy that it fairly sprang beneath the feet. Whether or not the grouse had haunts of their own, wherein they were immune from rheumatism, the bag had been small. The women, too, were an unusually dull lot, with the exception of a new-minded débutante who bothered Weigall at dinner by demanding the verbal restoration of the vague paintings on the vaulted roof above them.

But it was no one of these things that sat on Weigall's mind as, when the other men went up to bed, he let himself out of the castle and sauntered down to the river. His intimate friend, the companion of his boyhood, the chum of his college days, his fellow-traveller in many lands, the man for whom he possessed stronger affection than for all men, had mysteriously disappeared two days ago, and his track might have sprung to the upper air for all trace he had left behind him. He had been a guest on the adjoining estate during the past week, shooting with the fervor of the true sportsman, making love in the intervals to Adeline Cavan, and apparently in the best of spirits. As far as was known there was nothing to lower his mental mercury, for his rent-roll was a large one, Miss Cavan blushed whenever he looked at her, and, being one of the best shots in England, he was never happier than in August. The suicide theory was preposterous, all agreed, and there was as little reason to believe him murdered. Nevertheless, he had walked out of March Abbey two nights ago without hat or overcoat, and had not been seen since.

The country was being patrolled night and day. A hundred keepers and workmen were beating the woods and poking the bogs on the moors, but as yet not so much as a handkerchief had been found.

Weigall did not believe for a moment that Wyatt Gifford was dead, and although it was impossible not to be affected by the general uneasiness, he was disposed to be more angry than frightened. At Cambridge Gifford had been an incorrigible practical joker, and by no means had outgrown the habit; it would be like him to cut across the country in his evening clothes, board a cattle-train, and amuse himself touching up the picture of the sensation in West Riding.

However, Weigall's affection for his friend was too deep to companion with tranquillity in the present state of doubt, and, instead of going to bed early with the other men, he determined to walk until ready for sleep. He went down to the river and followed the path through the woods. There was no moon, but the stars sprinkled their cold light upon the pretty belt of water flowing placidly past wood and ruin, between green masses of overhanging rocks or sloping banks tangled with tree and shrub, leaping occasionally over stones with the harsh notes of an angry scold, to recover its equanimity the moment the way was clear again.

It was very dark in the depths where Weigall trod. He smiled as he recalled a remark of Gifford's: "An English wood is like a good many other things in life—very promising at a distance, but a hollow mockery when you get within. You see daylight on both sides, and the sun freckles the very bracken. Our woods need the night to make them seem what they ought to be—what they once were, before our ancestors' descendants demanded so much more money, in these so much more various days."

Weigall strolled along, smoking, and thinking of his friend, his pranks—many of which had done more credit to his imagination than this—and recalling conversations that had lasted the night through. Just before the end of the London season they had walked the streets one hot night after a party, discussing the various theories of the soul's destiny. That afternoon they had met at the coffin of a college friend whose mind had been a blank for the past three years. Some months previously they had called at the asylum to see him. His expression had been senile, his face imprinted with the record of debauchery. In death the face was placid, intelligent, without ignoble lineation—the face of the man they had known at college. Weigall and Gifford had had no time to comment there, and the afternoon and evening were full; but, coming forth from the house of festivity together, they had reverted almost at once to the topic.

"I cherish the theory," Gifford had said, "that the soul sometimes lingers in the body after death. During madness, of course, it is an impotent prisoner, albeit a conscious one. Fancy its agony, and its horror! What more natural than that, when the life-spark goes out, the tortured soul should take possession of the vacant skull and triumph once more for a few hours while old friends look their last? It has had time to repent while compelled to crouch and behold the result of its work, and it has shrived itself into a state of comparative purity. If I had my way, I should stay inside my bones until the coffin had gone into its niche, that I might obviate for my poor old comrade the tragic impersonality of death. And I should like to see justice done to it, as it were—to see it lowered among its ancestors with the ceremony and solemnity that are its due. I am afraid that if I dissevered myself too quickly, I should yield to curiosity and hasten to investigate the mysteries of space."

"You believe in the soul as an independent entity, then—-that it and the vital principle are not one and the same?"

"Absolutely. The body and soul are twins, life comrades—sometimes friends, sometimes enemies, but always loyal in the last instance. Some day, when I am tired of the world, I shall go to India and become a mahatma, solely for the pleasure of receiving proof during life of this independent relationship."

"Suppose you were not sealed up properly, and returned after one of your astral flights to find your earthly part unfit for habitation? It is an experiment I don't think I should care to try, unless even juggling with soul and flesh had palled."

"That would not be an uninteresting predicament. I should rather enjoy experimenting with broken machinery."

The high wild roar of water smote suddenly upon Weigall's ear and checked his memories. He left the wood and walked out on the huge slippery stones which nearly close the River Wharfe at this point, and watched the waters boil down into the narrow pass with their furious untiring energy. The black quiet of the woods rose high on either side. The stars seemed colder and whiter just above. On either hand the perspective of the river might have run into a rayless cavern. There was no lonelier spot in England, nor one which had the right to claim so many ghosts, if ghosts there were.

Weigall was not a coward, but he recalled uncomfortably the tales of those that had been done to death in the Strid.* Wordsworth's Boy of Egremond had been disposed of by the practical Whitaker; but countless others, more venturesome than wise, had gone down into that narrow boiling course, never to appear in the still pool a few yards beyond. Below the great rocks which form the walls of the Strid was believed to be a natural vault, on to whose shelves the dead were drawn. The spot had an ugly fascination. Weigall stood, visioning skeletons, uncoffined and green, the home of the eyeless things which had devoured all that had covered and filled that rattling symbol of man's mortality; then fell to wondering if any one had attempted to leap the Strid of late. It was covered with slime; he had never seen it look so treacherous.

He shuddered and turned away, impelled, despite his manhood, to flee the spot. As he did so, something tossing in the foam below the fall—something as white, yet independent of it—caught his eye and arrested his step. Then he saw that it was describing a contrary motion to the rushing water—an upward backward motion. Weigall stood rigid, breathless; he fancied he heard the crackling of his hair. Was that a hand? It thrust itself still higher above the boiling foam, turned sidewise, and four frantic fingers were distinctly visible against the black rock beyond.

---

* "This striding place is called the 'Strid,'
A name which it took of yore;
A thousand years hath it borne the name,
And it shall a thousand more."

Weigall's superstitious terror left him. A man was there, struggling to free himself from the suction beneath the Strid, swept down, doubtless, but a moment before his arrival, perhaps as he stood with his back to the current.

He stepped as close to the edge as he dared. The hand doubled as if in imprecation, shaking savagely in the face of that force which leaves its creatures to immutable law; then spread wide again, clutching, expanding, crying for help as audibly as the human voice.

Weigall dashed to the nearest tree, dragged and twisted off a branch with his strong arms, and returned as swiftly to the Strid. The hand was in the same place, still gesticulating as wildly; the body was undoubtedly caught in the rocks below, perhaps already half-way along one of those hideous shelves. Weigall let himself down upon a lower rock, braced his shoulder against the mass beside him, then, leaning out over the water, thrust the branch into the hand. The fingers clutched it convulsively. Weigall tugged powerfully, his own feet dragged perilously near the edge. For a moment he produced no impression, then an arm shot above the waters.

The blood sprang to Weigall's head; he was choked with the impression that the Strid had him in her roaring hold, and he saw nothing. Then the mist cleared. The hand and arm were nearer, although the rest of the body was still concealed by the foam. Weigall peered out with distended eyes. The meagre light revealed in the cuffs links of a peculiar device. The fingers clutching the branch were as familiar.

Weigall forgot the slippery stones, the terrible death if he stepped too far. He pulled with passionate will and muscle. Memories flung themselves into the hot light of his brain, trooping rapidly upon each other's heels, as in the thought of the drowning. Most of the pleasures of his life, good and bad, were identified in some way with this friend. Scenes of college days, of travel, where they had deliberately sought adventure and stood between one another and death upon more occasions than one, of hours of delightful companionship among the treasures of art, and others in the pursuit of pleasure, flashed like the changing particles of a kaleidoscope. Weigall had loved several women; but he would have flouted in these moments the thought that he had ever loved any woman as he loved Wyatt Gifford. There were so many charming women in the world, and in the thirty-two years of his life he had never known another man to whom he had cared to give his intimate friendship.

He threw himself on his face. His wrists were cracking, the skin was torn from his hands. The fingers still gripped the stick. There was life in them yet.

Suddenly something gave way. The hand swung about, tearing the branch from Weigall's grasp. The body had been liberated and flung outward, though still submerged by the foam and spray.

Weigall scrambled to his feet and sprang along the rocks, knowing that the danger from suction was over and that Gifford must be carried straight to the quiet pool. Gifford was a fish in the water and could live under it longer than most men. If he survived this, it would not be the first time that his pluck and science had saved him from drowning.

Weigall reached the pool. A man in his evening clothes floated on it, his face turned towards a projecting rock over which his arm had fallen, upholding the body. The hand that had held the branch hung limply over the rock, its white reflection visible in the black water. Weigall plunged into the shallow pool, lifted Gifford in his arms and returned to the bank. He laid the body down and threw off his coat that he might be the freer to practise the methods of resuscitation. He was glad of the moment's respite. The valiant life in the man might have been exhausted in that last struggle. He had not dared to look at his face, to put his ear to the heart. The hesitation lasted but a moment. There was no time to lose.

He turned to his prostrate friend. As he did so, something strange and disagreeable smote his senses. For a half-moment he did not appreciate its nature. Then his teeth clacked together, his feet, his outstretched arms pointed towards the woods. But he sprang to the side of the man and bent down and peered into his face. There was no face.

The Water Ghost of Harrowby Hall

John Kendrick Bangs

The trouble with Harrowby Hall was that it was haunted, and, what was worse, the ghost did not content itself with merely appearing at the bedside of the afflicted person who saw it, but persisted in remaining there for one mortal hour before it would disappear.

It never appeared except on Christmas Eve, and then as the clock was striking twelve, in which respect alone was it lacking in that originality which in these days is a *sine qua non* of success in spectral life. The owners of Harrowby Hall had done their utmost to rid themselves of the damp and dewy lady who rose up out of the best bedroom floor at midnight, but without avail. They had tried stopping the clock, so that the ghost would not know when it was midnight; but she made her appearance just the same, with that fearful miasmatic personality of hers, and there she would stand until everything about her was thoroughly saturated.

Then the owners of Harrowby Hall caulked up every crack in the floor with the very best quality of hemp, and over this were placed layers of tar and canvas; the walls were made waterproof, and the doors and windows likewise, the proprietors having conceived the notion that the unexorcised lady would find it difficult to leak into the room after these precautions had been taken; but even this did not suffice. The following Christmas Eve she appeared as promptly as before, and frightened the occupant of the room quite out of his senses by sitting down alongside of him and gazing with her cavernous blue eyes into his; and he noticed, too, that in her long, aqueously bony fingers bits of dripping seaweed were entwined, the ends hanging down, and these ends she drew across his forehead until he became like one insane. And then he swooned away, and was found unconscious in his bed the next morning by his host, simply saturated with seawater and fright, from the combined effects of which he never recovered, dying four years later of pneumonia and nervous prostration at the age of seventy-eight.

The next year the master of Harrowby Hall decided not to have the best spare bedroom opened at all, thinking that perhaps the ghost's thirst for making herself disagreeable would be satisfied by haunting the furniture, but the plan was as unavailing as the many that had preceded it.

The ghost appeared as usual in the room—that is, it was supposed she did, for the hangings were dripping wet the next morning, and in the parlor below the haunted room a great damp spot appeared on the ceiling. Finding no one there, she immediately set out to learn the reason why, and she chose none other to haunt than the owner of the Harrowby himself. She found him in his own cosey room drinking whiskey—whiskey undiluted—and felicitating himself upon having foiled her ghost-ship, when all of a sudden the curl went out of his hair, his whiskey bottle filled and overflowed, and he was himself in a condition similar to that of a man who has fallen into a water-butt. When he recovered from the shock, which was a painful one, he saw before him the lady of the cavernous eyes and seaweed fingers. The sight was so unexpected and so terrifying that he fainted, but immediately came to, because of the vast amount of water in his hair, which, trickling down over his face, restored his consciousness.

Now it so happened that the master of Harrowby was a brave man, and while he was not particularly fond of interviewing ghosts, especially such quenching ghosts as the one before him, he was not to be daunted by an apparition. He had paid the lady the compliment of fainting from the effects of his first surprise, and now that he had come to he intended to find out a few things he felt he had a right to know. He would have liked to put on a dry suit of clothes first, but the apparition declined to leave him for an instant until her hour was up, and he was forced to deny himself that pleasure. Every time he would move she would follow him, with the result that everything she came in contact with got a ducking. In an effort to warm himself up he approached the fire, an unfortunate move as it turned out, because it brought the ghost directly over the fire, which immediately was extinguished. The whiskey became utterly valueless as a comforter to his chilled system, because it was by this time diluted to a proportion of ninety per cent of water. The only thing he could do to ward off the evil effects of his encounter he did, and that was to swallow ten two-grain quinine pills, which he managed to put into his mouth before the ghost had time to interfere. Having done this, he turned with some asperity to the ghost, and said:

"Far be it from me to be impolite to a woman, madam, but I'm hanged if it wouldn't please me better if you'd stop these infernal visits of yours to this house. Go sit out on the lake, if you like that sort of thing; soak the water-butt, if you wish; but do not, I implore you, come into a gentleman's house and saturate him and his possessions in this way. It is damned disagreeable."

"Henry Hartwick Oglethorpe," said the ghost, in a gurgling voice, "you don't know what you are talking about."

"Madam," returned the unhappy householder, "I wish that remark were strictly truthful. I was talking about you. It would be shillings and pence—nay, pounds, in my pocket, madam, if I did not know you."

"That is a bit of specious nonsense," returned the ghost, throwing a quart of indignation into the face of the master of Harrowby. "It may rank high as repartee, but as a comment upon my statement that you do not know what you are talking about, it savors of irrelevant impertinence. You do not know that I am compelled to haunt this place year after year by inexorable fate. It is no pleasure to me to enter this house, and ruin and mildew everything I touch. I never aspired to be a shower-bath, but it is my doom. Do you know who I am?"

"No, I don't," returned the master of Harrowby. "I should say you were the Lady of the Lake, or Little Sallie Waters."

"You are a witty man for your years," said the ghost.

"Well, my humor is drier than yours ever will be," returned the master.

"No doubt. I'm never dry. I am the Water Ghost of Harrowby Hall, and dryness is a quality entirely beyond my wildest hope. I have been the incumbent of this highly unpleasant office for two hundred years tonight."

"How the deuce did you ever come to get elected?" asked the master.

"Through a suicide," replied the specter. "I am the ghost of that fair maiden whose picture hangs over the mantelpiece in the drawing-room. I should have been your great-great-great-great-great-aunt if I had lived, Henry Hartwick Oglethorpe, for I was the own sister of your great-great-great-great-grandfather."

"But what induced you to get this house into such a predicament?"

"I was not to blame, sir," returned the lady. "It was my father's fault. He it was who built Harrowby Hall, and the haunted chamber was to have been mine. My father had it furnished in pink and yellow, knowing well that blue and gray formed the only combination of color I could tolerate. He did it merely to spite me, and, with what I deem a proper spirit, I declined to live in the room; whereupon my father said I could live there or on the lawn, he didn't care which. That night I ran from the house and jumped over the cliff into the sea."

"That was rash," said the master of Harrowby.

"So I've heard," returned the ghost. "If I had known what the consequences were to be I should not have jumped; but I really never realized what I was doing until after I was drowned. I had been drowned a week when a sea-nymph came to me and informed me that I was to be one of her followers forever afterwards, adding that it should be my doom to haunt Harrowby Hall for one hour every Christmas Eve throughout the rest of eternity. I was to haunt that room on such Christmas Eves as I found it inhabited; and if it should turn out not to be inhabited, I was and am to spend the allotted hour with the head of the house."

"I'll sell the place."

"That you cannot do, for it is also required of me that I shall appear as the deeds are to be delivered to any purchaser, and divulge to him the awful secret of the house."

"Do you mean to tell me that on every Christmas Eve that I don't happen to have somebody in that guest-chamber, you are going to haunt me wherever I may be, ruining my whiskey, taking all the curl out of my hair, extinguishing my fire, and soaking me through to the skin?" demanded the master.

"You have stated the case, Oglethorpe. And what is more," said the water ghost, "it doesn't make the slightest difference where you are, if I find that room empty, wherever you may be I shall douse you with my spectral pres—"

Here the clock struck one, and immediately the apparition faded away.

It was perhaps more of a trickle than a fade, but as a disappearance it was complete.

"By St George and his Dragon!" ejaculated the master of Harrowby, wringing his hands. "It is guineas to hot-cross buns that next Christmas there's an occupant of the spare room, or I spend the night in a bathtub."

But the master of Harrowby would have lost his wager had there been anyone there to take him up, for when Christmas Eve came again he was in his grave, never having recovered from the cold contracted that awful night. Harrowby Hall was closed, and the heir to the estate was in London, where to him in his chambers came the same experience that his father had gone through, saving only that, being younger and stronger, he survived the shock. Everything in his rooms was ruined—his clocks were rusted in the works; a fine collection of water-color drawings was entirely obliterated by the onslaught of the water ghost; and what was worse, the apartments below his were drenched with the water soaking through the floors, a damage for which he was compelled to pay, and which resulted in his being requested by his landlady to vacate the premises immediately.

The story of the visitation inflicted upon his family had gone abroad, and no one could be got to invite him out to any function save afternoon teas and receptions. Fathers of daughters declined to permit him to remain in their houses later than eight o'clock at night, not knowing but that some emergency might arise in the supernatural world which would require the unexpected appearance of the water ghost in this on nights other than Christmas Eve, and before the mystic hour when weary churchyards, ignoring the rules which are supposed to govern polite society, begin to yawn. Nor would the maids themselves have aught to do with him, fearing the destruction by the sudden incursion of aqueous femininity of the costumes which they held most dear.

So the heir of Harrowby Hall resolved, as his ancestors for several generations before him had resolved, that something must be done. His first thought was to make one of his servants occupy the haunted room at the crucial moment; but in this he failed, because the servants themselves knew the history of that room and rebelled. None of his friends would consent to sacrifice their personal comfort to his, nor was there to be found in all England a man so poor as to be willing to occupy the doomed chamber on Christmas Eve for pay.

Then the thought came to the heir to have the fireplace in the room enlarged, so that he might evaporate the ghost at its first appearance, and he was felicitating himself upon the ingenuity of his plan, when he remembered what his father had told him—how that no fire could withstand the lady's extremely contagious dampness. And then he bethought him of steam-pipes. These, he remembered, could lie hundreds of feet deep in water, and still retain sufficient heat to drive the water away in vapor; and as a result of this thought the haunted room was heated by steam to a withering degree, and the heir for six months attended daily the Turkish baths, so that when Christmas Eve came he could himself withstand the awful temperature of the room.

The scheme was only partially successful. The water ghost appeared at the specified time, and found the heir of Harrowby prepared; but hot as the room was, it shortened her visit by no more than five minutes in the hour, during which time the nervous system of the young master was well-nigh shattered, and the room itself was cracked and warped to an extent which required the outlay of a large sum of money to remedy. And worse than this, as the last drop of the water ghost was slowly sizzling itself out on the floor, she whispered to her would-be conqueror that his scheme would avail him nothing, because there was still water in great plenty where she came from, and that next year would find her rehabilitated and as exasperatingly saturating as ever.

It was then that the natural action of the mind, in going from one extreme to the other, suggested to the ingenious heir of Harrowby the means by which the water ghost was ultimately conquered, and happiness once more came within the grasp of the house of Oglethorpe.

The heir provided himself with a warm suit of fur under-clothing. Donning this with the furry side in, he placed over it a rubber garment, tight-fitting, which he wore just as a woman wears a jersey. On top of this he placed another set of under-clothing, this suit made of wool, and over this was a second rubber garment like the first. Upon his head he placed a light and comfortable diving helmet, and so clad, on the following Christmas Eve he awaited the coming of his tormentor.

It was a bitterly cold night that brought to a close this twenty-fourth day of December. The air outside was still, but the temperature was below zero. Within all was quiet, the servants of Harrowby Hall awaiting with beating hearts the outcome of their master's campaign against his supernatural visitor.

The master himself was lying on the bed in the haunted room, clad as has already been indicated, and then—

The clock clanged out the hour of twelve.

There was a sudden banging of doors, a blast of cold air swept through the halls, the door leading into the haunted chamber flew open, a splash was heard, and the water ghost was seen standing at the side of the heir of Harrowby, from whose outer dress there streamed rivulets of water, but whose own person deep down under the various garments he wore was as dry and as warm as he could have wished.

"Ha!" said the young master of Harrowby. "I'm glad to see you."

"You are the most original man I've met, if that is true," returned the ghost. "May I ask where did you get that hat?"

"Certainly, madam," returned the master, courteously. "It is a little portable observatory I had made for just such emergencies as this. But, tell me, is it true that you are doomed to follow me about for one mortal hour—to stand where I stand, to sit where I sit?"

"That is my delectable fate," returned the lady.

"We'll go out on the lake," said the master, starting up.

"You can't get rid of me that way," returned the ghost. "The water won't swallow me up; in fact, it will just add to my present bulk."

"Nevertheless," said the master, firmly, "we will go out on the lake."

"But, my dear sir," returned the ghost, with a pale reluctance, "it is fearfully cold out there. You will be frozen hard before you've been out ten minutes."

"Oh no, I'll not," replied the master. "I am very warmly dressed. Come!" This last in a tone of command that made the ghost ripple.

And they started.

They had not gone far before the water ghost showed signs of distress.

"You walk too slowly," she said. "I am nearly frozen. My knees are so stiff now I can hardly move. I beseech you to accelerate your step."

"I should like to oblige a lady," returned the master, courteously, "but my clothes are rather heavy, and a hundred yards an hour is about my speed. Indeed, I think we would better sit down here on this snowdrift, and talk matters over."

"Do not! Do not do so, I beg!" cried the ghost. "Let me move on. I feel myself growing rigid as it is. If we stop here, I shall be frozen stiff."

"That, madam," said the master slowly, and seating himself on an ice-cake—"that is why I have brought you here. We have been on this spot just ten minutes; we have fifty more. Take your time about it, madam, but freeze, that is all I ask of you."

"I cannot move my right leg now," cried the ghost, in despair, "and my overskirt is a solid sheet of ice. Oh, good, kind Mr Oglethorpe, light a fire, and let me go free from these icy fetters."

"Never, madam. It cannot be. I have you at last."

"Alas!" cried the ghost, a tear trickling down her frozen cheek. "Help me, I beg. I congeal!"

"Congeal, madam, congeal!" returned Oglethorpe, coldly. "You have drenched me and mine for two hundred and three years, madam. Tonight you have had your last drench."

"Ah, but I shall thaw out again, and then you'll see. Instead of the comfortably tepid, genial ghost I have been in my past, sir, I shall be iced-water," cried the lady, threateningly.

"No, you won't, either," returned Oglethorpe; "for when you are frozen quite stiff, I shall send you to a cold-storage warehouse, and there shall you remain an icy work of art forever more."

"But warehouses burn."

"So they do, but this warehouse cannot burn. It is made of asbestos and surrounding it are fireproof walls, and within those walls the temperature is now and shall forever be 416 degrees below the zero point; low enough to make an icicle of any flame in this world—or the next," the master added, with an ill-suppressed chuckle.

"For the last time let me beseech you. I would go on my knees to you, Oglethorpe, were they not already frozen. I beg of you do not doo——"

Here even the words froze on the water-ghost's lips and the clock struck one. There was a momentary tremor throughout the ice-bound form, and the moon, coming out from behind a cloud, shone down on the rigid figure of a beautiful woman sculptured in clear, transparent ice. There stood the ghost of Harrowby Hall, conquered by the cold, a prisoner for all time.

The heir of Harrowby had won at last, and today in a large storage house in London stands the frigid form of one who will never again flood the house of Oglethorpe with woe and sea-water.

As for the heir of Harrowby, his success in coping with a ghost has made him famous, a fame that still lingers about him, although his victory took place some twenty years ago; and so far from being unpopular with the fair sex, as he was when we first knew him, he has not only been married twice, but is to lead a third bride to the altar before the year is out.

The Apparition of Mrs Veal

Daniel Defoe

The Preface

This relation is matter of fact, and attended with such circumstances, as may induce any reasonable man to believe it. It was sent by a gentleman, a justice of peace, at Maidstone, in Kent, and a very intelligent person, to his friend in London, as it is here worded; which discourse is attested by a very sober and understanding gentlewoman, a kinswoman of the said gentleman's, who lives in Canterbury, within a few doors of the house in which the within-named Mrs Bargrave lives; who believes his kinswoman to be of so discerning a spirit, as not to be put upon by any fallacy; and who positively assured him that the whole matter, as it is related and laid down, is really true; and what she herself had in the same words, as near as may be, from Mrs Bargrave's own mouth, who, she knows, had no reason to invent and publish such a story, or any design to forge and tell a lie, being a woman of much honesty and virtue, and her whole life a course, as it were, of piety. The use which we ought to make of it, is to consider, that there is a life to come after this, and a just God, who will retribute to every one according to the deeds done in the body; and therefore to reflect upon our past course of life we have led in the world; that our time is short and uncertain; and that if we would escape the punishment of the ungodly, and receive the reward of the righteous, which is the laying hold of eternal life, we ought, for the time to come, to return to God by a speedy repentance, ceasing to do evil, and learning to do well: to seek after God early, if happily He may be found of us, and lead such lives for the future, as may be well pleasing in His sight.

A Relation of the Apparition of Mrs Veal

This thing is so rare in all its circumstances, and on so good authority, that my reading and conversation has not given me anything like it: it is fit to gratify the most ingenious and serious inquirer. Mrs Bargrave is the person to whom Mrs Veal appeared after her death; she is my intimate friend, and I can avouch for her reputation, for these last fifteen or sixteen years, on my own knowledge; and I can confirm the good character she had from her youth, to the time of my acquaintance. Though, since this relation, she is calumniated by some people, that are friends to the brother of this Mrs Veal, who appeared; who think the relation of this appearance to be a reflection, and endeavor what they can to blast Mrs Bargrave's reputation, and to laugh the story out of countenance. But by the circumstances thereof, and the cheerful disposition of Mrs Bargrave, notwithstanding the ill-usage of a very wicked husband, there is not yet the least sign of dejection in her face; nor did I ever hear her let fall a desponding or murmuring expression; nay, not when actually under her husband's barbarity; which I have been witness to, and several other persons of undoubted reputation.

Now you must know, Mrs Veal was a maiden gentlewoman of about thirty years of age, and for some years last past had been troubled with fits; which were perceived coming on her, by her going off from her discourse very abruptly to some impertinence. She was maintained by an only brother, and kept his house in Dover. She was a very pious woman, and her brother a very sober man to all appearance; but now he does all he can to null or quash the story. Mrs Veal was intimately acquainted with Mrs Bargrave from her childhood. Mrs Veal's circumstances were then mean; her father did not take care of his children as he ought, so that they were exposed to hardships; and Mrs Bargrave, in those days, had as unkind a father, though she wanted neither for food nor clothing, whilst Mrs Veal wanted for both; insomuch that she would often say, Mrs Bargrave, you are not only the best, but the only friend I have in the world, and no circumstances of life shall ever dissolve my friendship. They would often condole each other's adverse fortunes, and read together Drelincourt upon Death, and other good books; and so, like two Christian friends, they comforted each other under their sorrow.

Some time after, Mr Veal's friends got him a place in the custom-house at Dover, which occasioned Mrs Veal, by little and little, to fall off from her intimacy with Mrs Bargrave, though there was never any such thing as a quarrel; but an indifferency came on by degrees, till at last Mrs Bargrave had not seen her in two years and a half; though above a twelvemonth of the time Mrs Bargrave hath been absent from Dover, and this last half year has been in Canterbury about two months of the time, dwelling in a house of her own.

In this house, on the 8th of September, 1705, she was sitting alone in the forenoon, thinking over her unfortunate life, and arguing herself into a due resignation to providence, though her condition seemed hard. And, said she, I have been provided for hitherto, and doubt not but I shall be still; and am well satisfied that my afflictions shall end when it is most fit for me: and then took up her sewing-work, which she had no sooner done, but she hears a knocking at the door. She went to see who was there, and this proved to be Mrs Veal, her old friend, who was in a riding-habit. At that moment of time the clock struck twelve at noon.

Madam, says Mrs Bargrave, I am surprised to see you, you have been so long a stranger; but told her, she was glad to see her, and offered to salute her; which Mrs Veal complied with, till their lips almost touched; and then Mrs Veal drew her hand across her own eyes, and said, I am not very well; and so waived it. She told Mrs Bargrave, she was going a journey, and had a great mind to see her first. But, says Mrs Bargrave, how came you to take a journey alone? I am amazed at it, because I know you have a fond brother. Oh! says Mrs Veal, I gave my brother the slip, and came away because I had so great a desire to see you before I took my journey. So Mrs Bargrave went in with her, into another room within the first, and Mrs Veal sat her down in an elbow-chair, in which Mrs Bargrave was sitting when she heard Mrs Veal knock. Then says Mrs Veal, My dear friend, I am come to renew our old friendship again, and beg your pardon for my breach of it; and if you can forgive me, you are the best of women. O, says Mrs Bargrave, do not mention such a thing; I have not had an uneasy thought about it; I can easily forgive it. What did you think of me? said Mrs Veal. Says Mrs Bargrave, I thought you were like the rest of the world, and that prosperity had made you forget yourself and me. Then Mrs Veal reminded Mrs Bargrave of the many friendly offices she did her in former days, and much of the conversation they had with each other in the times of their adversity; what books they read, and what comfort, in particular, they received from Drelincourt's Book of Death, which was the best, she said, on that subject ever written. She also mentioned Dr Sherlock, the two Dutch books which were translated, written upon death, and several others. But Drelincourt, she said, had the clearest notions of death, and of the future state, of any who had handled that subject. Then she asked Mrs Bargrave, whether she had Drelincourt. She said, Yes. Says Mrs Veal, Fetch it. And so Mrs Bargrave goes up stairs and brings it down. Says Mrs Veal, Dear Mrs Bargrave, if the eyes of our faith were as open as the eyes of our body, we should see numbers of angels about us for our guard. The notions we have of heaven now, are nothing like what it is, as Drelincourt says; therefore be comforted under your afflictions, and believe that the Almighty has a particular regard to you; and that your afflictions are marks of God's favour; and when they have done the business they are sent for, they shall be removed from you. And believe me, my dear friend, believe what I say to you, one minute of future happiness will infinitely reward you for all your sufferings. For, I can never believe (and claps her hand upon her knee with great earnestness, which indeed ran through most of her discourse), that ever God will suffer you to spend all your days in this afflicted state; but be assured, that your afflictions shall leave you, or you them, in a short time. She spake in that pathetical and heavenly manner, that Mrs Bargrave wept several times, she was so deeply affected with it.

Then Mrs Veal mentioned Dr Kenrick's Ascetick, at the end of which he gives an account of the lives of the primitive Christians. Their pattern she recommended to our imitation, and said, their conversation was not like this of our age: For now, says she, there is nothing but frothy, vain discourse, which is far different from theirs. Theirs was to edification, and to build one another up in faith; so that they were not as we are, nor are we as they were: but, says she, we ought to do as they did. There was a hearty friendship among them; but where is it now to be found? Says Mrs Bargrave, It is hard indeed to find a true friend in these days. Says Mrs Veal, Mr Norris has a fine copy of verses, called Friendship in Perfection, which I wonderfully admire. Have you seen the book? says Mrs Veal. No, says Mrs Bargrave, but I have the verses of my own writing out. Have you? says Mrs Veal, then fetch them. Which she did from above stairs, and offered them to Mrs Veal to read, who refused, and waived the thing, saying, holding down her head would make it ache; and then desired Mrs Bargrave to read them to her, which she did. As they were admiring friendship, Mrs Veal said, Dear Mrs Bargrave, I shall love you for ever. In these verses there is twice used the word Elysian. Ah! says Mrs Veal, these poets have such names for heaven. She would often draw her hands across her own eyes, and say, Mrs Bargrave, do not you think I am mightily impaired by my fits? No, says Mrs Bargrave, I think you look as well as ever I knew you. After all this discourse, which the apparition put in much finer words than Mrs Bargrave said she could pretend to, and as much more than she can remember, (for it cannot be thought, that an hour and three quarters' conversation could all be retained, though the main of it she thinks she does,) she said to Mrs Bargrave, she would have her write a letter to her brother, and tell him, she would have him give rings to such and such; and that there was a purse of gold in her cabinet, and that she would have two broad pieces given to her cousin Watson.

Talking at this rate, Mrs Bargrave thought that a fit was coming upon her, and so placed herself in a chair just before her knees, to keep her from falling to the ground, if her fits should occasion it: for the elbow-chair, she thought, would keep her from falling on either side. And to divert Mrs Veal, as she thought, took hold of her gown-sleeve several times, and commended it. Mrs Veal told her, it was a scowered silk, and newly made up. But for all this, Mrs Veal persisted in her request, and told Mrs Bargrave, she must not deny her: and she would have her tell her brother all their conversation, when she had opportunity. Dear Mrs Veal, says Mrs Bargrave, this seems so impertinent, that I cannot tell how to comply with it; and what a mortifying story will our conversation be to a young gentleman? Why, says Mrs Bargrave, it is much better, methinks, to do it yourself. No, says Mrs Veal, though it seems impertinent to you now, you will see more reason for it hereafter. Mrs Bargrave then, to satisfy her importunity, was going to fetch a pen and ink; but Mrs Veal said, Let it alone now, but do it when I am gone; but you must be sure to do it: which was one of the last things she enjoined her at parting; and so she promised her.

Then Mrs Veal asked for Mrs Bargrave's daughter; she said, she was not at home: But if you have a mind to see her, says Mrs Bargrave, I'll send for her. Do, says Mrs Veal. On which she left her, and went to a neighbour's to seek for her; and by the time Mrs Bargrave was returning, Mrs Veal was got without the door in the street, in the face of the beast-market, on a Saturday, which is market-day, and stood ready to part, as soon as Mrs Bargrave came to her. She asked her, why she was in such haste. She said she must be going, though perhaps she might not go her journey till Monday; and told Mrs Bargrave, she hoped she should see her again at her cousin Watson's, before she went whither she was going. Then she said, she would take her leave of her, and walked from Mrs Bargrave in her view, till a turning interrupted the sight of her, which was three quarters after one in the afternoon.

Mrs Veal died the 7th of September, at twelve o'clock at noon of her fits, and had not above four hours' senses before her death, in which time she received the sacrament. The next day after Mrs Veal's appearing, being Sunday, Mrs Bargrave was mightily indisposed with a cold, and a sore throat, that she could not go out that day; but on Monday morning she sent a person to Captain Watson's, to know if Mrs Veal was there. They wondered at Mrs Bargrave's inquiry; and sent her word, that she was not there, nor was expected. At this answer Mrs Bargrave told the maid she had certainly mistook the name, or made some blunder. And though she was ill, she put on her hood, and went herself to Captain Watson's though she knew none of the family, to see if Mrs Veal was there or not. They said, they wondered at her asking, for that she had not been in town; they were sure, if she had, she would have been there. Says Mrs Bargrave, I am sure she was with me on Saturday almost two hours. They said, it was impossible; for they must have seen her if she had. In comes Captain Watson, while they were in dispute, and said, that Mrs Veal was certainly dead, and her escutcheons were making. This strangely surprised Mrs Bargrave, when she sent to the person immediately who had the care of them, and found it true. Then she related the whole story to Captain Watson's family, and what gown she had on, and how striped; and that Mrs Veal told her, it was scowered. Then Mrs Watson cried out, You have seen her indeed, for none knew, but Mrs

Veal and myself, that the gown was scowered. And Mrs Watson owned, that she described the gown exactly: For, said she, I helped her to make it up. This Mrs Watson blazed all about the town, and avouched the demonstration of the truth of Mrs Bargrave's seeing Mrs Veal's apparition. And Captain Watson carried two gentlemen immediately to Mrs Bargrave's house, to hear the relation of her own mouth. And when it spread so fast, that gentlemen and persons of quality, the judicious and skeptical part of the world, flocked in upon her, it at last became such a task, that she was forced to go out of the way. For they were, in general, extremely satisfied of the truth of the thing, and plainly saw that Mrs Bargrave was no hypochondraic; for she always appears with such a cheerful air, and pleasing mien, that she has gained the favour and esteem of all the gentry; and it is thought a great favour, if they can but get the relation from her own mouth. I should have told you before, that Mrs Veal told Mrs Bargrave, that her sister and brother-in-law were just come down from London to see her. Says Mrs Bargrave, How came you to order matters so strangely? It could not be helped, says Mrs Veal. And her brother and sister did come to see her, and entered the town of Dover just as Mrs Veal was expiring. Mrs Bargrave asked her whether she would drink some tea. Says Mrs Veal, I do not care if I do; but I'll warrant you, this mad fellow (meaning Mrs Bargrave's husband) has broke all your trinkets. But, says Mrs Bargrave, I'll get something to drink in for all that; but Mrs Veal waived it, and said, It is no matter, let it alone; and so it passed.

All the time I sat with Mrs Bargrave, which was some hours, she recollected fresh sayings of Mrs Veal. And one material thing more she told Mrs Bargrave, that old Mr Breton allowed Mrs Veal ten pounds a year; which was a secret, and unknown to Mrs Bargrave, till Mrs Veal told it her.

Mrs Bargrave never varies in her story; which puzzles those who doubt of the truth, or are unwilling to believe it. A servant in the neighbour's yard, adjoining to Mrs Bargrave's house, heard her talking to somebody an hour of the time Mrs Veal was with her. Mrs Bargrave went out to her next neighbour's the very moment she parted with Mrs Veal, and told her what ravishing conversation she had with an old friend, and told the whole of it. Drelincourt's Book of Death is, since this happened, bought up strangely. And it is to be observed, that notwithstanding all the trouble and fatigue Mrs Bargrave has undergone upon this account, she never took the value of a farthing, nor suffered her daughter to take anything of anybody, and therefore can have no interest in telling the story.

But Mr Veal does what he can to stifle the matter, and said he would see Mrs Bargrave; but yet it is certain matter of fact that he has been at Captain Watson's since the death of his sister, and yet never went near Mrs. Bargrave; and some of his friends report her to be a liar, and that she knew of Mr Breton's ten pounds a year. But the person who pretends to say so, has the reputation of a notorious liar, among persons whom I know to be of undoubted credit. Now Mr Veal is more of a gentleman than to say she lies; but says, a bad husband has crazed her. But she needs only present herself, and it will effectually confute that pretense. Mr Veal says, he asked his sister on her death bed, whether she had a mind to dispose of anything? And she said, No. Now, the things which Mrs Veal's apparition would have disposed of, were so trifling, and nothing of justice aimed at in their disposal, that the design of it appears to me to be only in order to make Mrs Bargrave so to demonstrate the truth of her appearance, as to satisfy the world of the reality thereof, as to what she had seen and heard; and to secure her reputation among the reasonable and understanding part of mankind. And then again, Mr Veal owns, that there was a purse of gold; but it was not found in her cabinet, but in a comb-box. This looks improbable; for that Mrs Watson owned, that Mrs Veal was so very careful of the key of the cabinet, that she would trust nobody with it. And if so, no doubt she would not trust her gold out of it. And Mrs Veal's often drawing her hand over her eyes, and asking Mrs Bargrave whether her fits had not impaired her, looks to me as if she did it on purpose to remind Mrs Bargrave of her fits, to prepare her not to think it strange that she should put her upon writing to her brother to dispose of rings and gold, which looked so much like a dying person's request; and it took accordingly with Mrs Bargrave, as the effects of her fits coming upon her; and was one of the many instances of her wonderful love to her, and care of her, that she should not be affrighted; which indeed appears in her whole management, particularly in her coming to her in the day time, waiving the salutation, and when she was alone; and then the manner of her parting, to prevent a second attempt to salute her.

Now, why Mr Veal should think this relation a reflection, as it is plain he does, by his endeavouring to stifle it, I cannot imagine; because the generality believe her to be a good spirit, her discourse was so heavenly. Her two great errands were to comfort Mrs Bargrave in her affliction, and to ask her forgiveness for the breach of friendship, and with a pious discourse to encourage her. So that, after all, to suppose that Mrs Bargrave could hatch such an invention as this from Friday noon till Saturday noon, supposing that she knew of Mrs Veal's death the very first moment, without jumbling circumstances, and without any interest too; she must be more witty, fortunate, and wicked too, than any indifferent person, I dare say, will allow. I asked Mrs Bargrave several times, if she was sure she felt the gown? She answered modestly, If my senses be to be relied on, I am sure of it. I asked her, if she heard a sound when she clapped her hand upon her knee? She said, she did not remember she did; but said she appeared to be as much a substance as I did, who talked with her. And I may, said she, be as soon persuaded, that your apparition is talking to me now, as that I did not really see her: for I was under no manner of fear, and received her as a friend, and parted with her as such. I would not, says she, give one farthing to make any one believe it: I have no interest in it; nothing but trouble is entailed upon me for a long time, for aught I know; and had it not come to light by accident, it would never have been made public. But now, she says, she will make her own private use of it, and keep herself out of the way as much as she can; and so she has done since. She says, She had a gentleman who came thirty miles to her to hear the relation; and that she had told it to a room full of people at a time. Several particular gentlemen have had the story from Mrs Bargrave's own mouth.

This thing has very much affected me, and I am as well satisfied, as I am of the best-grounded matter of fact. And why we should dispute matter of fact, because we cannot solve things of which we can have no certain or demonstrative notions, seems strange to me. Mrs Bargrave's authority and sincerity alone, would have been undoubted in any other case.

What was it?

Fitz James O'Brien

It is, I confess, with considerable diffidence that I approach the strange narrative which I am about to relate. The events which I purpose detailing are of so extraordinary a character that I am quite prepared to meet with an unusual amount of incredulity and scorn. I accept all such beforehand. I have, I trust, the literary courage to face unbelief. I have, after mature consideration, resolved to narrate, in as simple and straightforward a manner as I can compass, some facts that passed under my observation, in the month of July last, and which, in the annals of the mysteries of physical science, are wholly unparalleled.

I live at No. — Twenty-sixth Street, in New York. The house is in some respects a curious one. It has enjoyed for the last two years the reputation of being haunted. It is a large and stately residence, surrounded by what was once a garden, but which is now only a green enclosure used for bleaching clothes. The dry basin of what has been a fountain, and a few fruit trees ragged and unpruned, indicate that this spot in past days was a pleasant, shady retreat, filled with fruits and flowers and the sweet murmur of waters.

The house is very spacious. A hall of noble size leads to a large spiral staircase winding through its centre, while the various apartments are of imposing dimensions. It was built some fifteen or twenty years since by Mr A——, the well-known New York merchant, who five years ago threw the commercial world into convulsions by a stupendous bank fraud. Mr A——, as every one knows, escaped to Europe, and died not long after, of a broken heart. Almost immediately after the news of his decease reached this country and was verified, the report spread in Twenty-sixth Street that No. — was haunted. Legal measures had dispossessed the widow of its former owner, and it was inhabited merely by a caretaker and his wife, placed there by the house agent into whose hands it had passed for the purposes of renting or sale. These people declared that they were troubled with unnatural noises. Doors were opened without any visible agency. The remnants of furniture scattered through the various rooms were, during the night, piled one upon the other by unknown hands. Invisible feet passed up and down the stairs in broad daylight, accompanied by the rustle of unseen silk dresses, and the gliding of viewless hands along the massive balusters. The caretaker and his wife declared they would live there no longer. The house agent laughed, dismissed them, and put others in their place. The noises and supernatural manifestations continued. The neighbourhood caught up the story, and the house remained untenanted for three years. Several persons negotiated for it; but, somehow, always before the bargain was closed they heard the unpleasant rumours and declined to treat any further.

It was in this state of things that my landlady, who at that time kept a boarding-house in Bleecker Street, and who wished to move further up town, conceived the bold idea of renting No. — Twenty-sixth Street. Happening to have in her house rather a plucky and philosophical set of boarders, she laid her scheme before us, stating candidly everything she had heard respecting the ghostly qualities of the establishment to which she wished to remove us. With the exception of two timid persons,—a sea-captain and a returned Californian, who immediately gave notice that they would leave,—all of Mrs Moffat's guests declared that they would accompany her in her chivalric incursion into the abode of spirits.

Our removal was effected in the month of May, and we were charmed with our new residence. The portion of Twenty-sixth Street where our house is situated, between Seventh and Eighth avenues, is one of the pleasantest localities in New York. The gardens back of the houses, running down nearly to the Hudson, form, in the summer time, a perfect avenue of verdure. The air is pure and invigorating, sweeping, as it does, straight across the river from the Weehawken heights, and even the ragged garden which surrounded the house, although displaying on washing days rather too much clothesline, still gave us a piece of greensward to look at, and a cool retreat in the summer evenings, where we smoked our cigars in the dusk, and watched the fireflies flashing their dark lanterns in the long grass.

Of course we had no sooner established ourselves at No. — than we began to expect ghosts. We absolutely awaited their advent with eagerness. Our dinner conversation was supernatural. One of the boarders, who had purchased Mrs Crowe's "Night Side of Nature" for his own private delectation, was regarded as a public enemy by the entire household for not having bought twenty copies. The man led a life of supreme wretchedness while he was reading this volume. A system of espionage was established, of which he was the victim. If he incautiously laid the book down for an instant and left the room, it was immediately seized and read aloud in secret places to a select few. I found myself a person of immense importance, it having leaked out that I was tolerably well versed in the history of supernaturalism, and had once written a story the foundation of which was a ghost. If a table or a wainscot panel happened to warp when we were assembled in the large drawing-room, there was an instant silence, and every one was prepared for an immediate clanking of chains and a spectral form.

After a month of psychological excitement, it was with the utmost dissatisfaction that we were forced to acknowledge that nothing in the remotest degree approaching the supernatural had manifested itself. Once the black butler asseverated that his candle had been blown out by some invisible agency while he was undressing himself for the night; but as I had more than once discovered this coloured gentleman in a condition when one candle must have appeared to him like two, I thought it possible that, by going a step further in his potations, he might have reversed this phenomenon, and seen no candle at all where he ought to have beheld one.

Things were in this state when an accident took place so awful and inexplicable in its character that my reason fairly reels at the bare memory of the occurrence. It was the tenth of July. After dinner was over I repaired, with my friend Dr Hammond, to the garden to smoke my evening pipe. Independent of certain mental sympathies which existed between the Doctor and myself, we were linked together by a vice. We both smoked opium. We knew each other's secret, and respected it. We enjoyed together that wonderful expansion of thought, that marvellous intensifying of the perceptive faculties, that boundless feeling of existence when we seem to have points of contact with the whole universe,—in short, that unimaginable spiritual bliss, which I would not surrender for a throne, and which I hope you, reader, will never—never taste.

Those hours of opium happiness which the Doctor and I spent together in secret were regulated with a scientific accuracy. We did not blindly smoke the drug of paradise, and leave our dreams to chance. While smoking, we carefully steered our conversation through the brightest and calmest channels of thought. We talked of the East, and endeavoured to recall the magical panorama of its glowing scenery. We criticized the most sensuous poets,—those who painted life ruddy with health, brimming with passion, happy in the possession of youth and strength and beauty. If we talked of Shakespeare's "Tempest," we lingered over Ariel, and avoided Caliban. Like the Guebers, we turned our faces to the East, and saw only the sunny side of the world.

This skilful colouring of our train of thought produced in our subsequent visions a corresponding tone. The splendours of Arabian fairyland dyed our dreams. We paced the narrow strip of grass with the tread and port of kings. The song of the *rana arborea,* while he clung to the bark of the ragged plum-tree, sounded like the strains of divine musicians. Houses, walls, and streets melted like rain clouds, and vistas of unimaginable glory stretched away before us. It was a rapturous companionship. We enjoyed the vast delight more perfectly because, even in our most ecstatic moments, we were conscious of each other's presence. Our pleasures, while individual, were still twin, vibrating and moving in musical accord.

On the evening in question, the tenth of July, the Doctor and myself drifted into an unusually metaphysical mood. We lit our large meerschaums, filled with fine Turkish tobacco, in the core of which burned a little black nut of opium, that, like the nut in the fairy tale, held within its narrow limits wonders beyond the reach of kings; we paced to and fro, conversing. A strange perversity dominated the currents of our thought. They would *not* flow through the sun-lit channels into which we strove to divert them. For some unaccountable reason, they constantly diverged into dark and lonesome beds, where a continual gloom brooded. It was in vain that, after our old fashion, we flung ourselves on the shores of the East, and talked of its gay bazaars, of the splendours of the time of Haroun, of harems and golden palaces. Black afreets continually arose from the depths of our talk, and expanded, like the one the fisherman released from the copper vessel, until they blotted everything bright from our vision. Insensibly, we yielded to the occult force that swayed us, and indulged in gloomy speculation. We had talked some time upon the proneness of the human mind to mysticism, and the almost universal love of the terrible, when Hammond suddenly said to me, "What do you consider to be the greatest element of terror?"

The question puzzled me. That many things were terrible, I knew. Stumbling over a corpse in the dark; beholding, as I once did, a woman floating down a deep and rapid river, with wildly lifted arms, and awful, upturned face, uttering, as she drifted, shrieks that rent one's heart while we, spectators, stood frozen at a window which overhung the river at a height of sixty feet, unable to make the slightest effort to save her, but dumbly watching her last supreme agony and her disappearance. A shattered wreck, with no life visible, encountered floating listlessly on the ocean, is a terrible object, for it suggests a huge terror, the proportions of which are veiled. But it now struck me, for the first time, that there must be one great and ruling embodiment of fear,—a King of Terrors, to which all others must succumb. What might it be? To what train of circumstances would it owe its existence?

"I confess, Hammond," I replied to my friend, "I never considered the subject before. That there must be one Something more terrible than any other thing, I feel. I cannot attempt, however, even the most vague definition."

"I am somewhat like you, Harry," he answered. "I feel my capacity to experience a terror greater than anything yet conceived by the human mind;—something combining in fearful and unnatural amalgamation hitherto supposed incompatible elements. The calling of the voices in Brockden Brown's novel of 'Wieland' is awful; so is the picture of the Dweller of the Threshold, in Bulwer's 'Zanoni'; but," he added, shaking his head gloomily, "there is something more horrible still than those."

"Look here, Hammond," I rejoined, "let us drop this kind of talk, for Heaven's sake! We shall suffer for it, depend on it."

"I don't know what's the matter with me tonight," he replied, "but my brain is running upon all sorts of weird and awful thoughts. I feel as if I could write a story like Hoffman, tonight, if I were only master of a literary style."

"Well, if we are going to be Hoffmanesque in our talk, I'm off to bed.

Opium and nightmares should never be brought together. How sultry it is! Good night, Hammond."

"Good night, Harry. Pleasant dreams to you."

"To you, gloomy wretch, afreets, ghouls, and enchanters."

We parted, and each sought his respective chamber. I undressed quickly and got into bed, taking with me, according to my usual custom, a book, over which I generally read myself to sleep. I opened the volume as soon as I had laid my head upon the pillow, and instantly flung it to the other side of the room. It was Goudon's "History of Monsters,"—a curious French work, which I had lately imported from Paris, but which, in the state of mind I had then reached, was anything but an agreeable companion. I resolved to go to sleep at once; so, turning down my gas until nothing but a little blue point of light glimmered on the top of the tube, I composed myself to rest.

The room was in total darkness. The atom of gas that still remained alight did not illuminate a distance of three inches round the burner. I desperately drew my arm across my eyes, as if to shut out even the darkness, and tried to think of nothing. It was in vain. The confounded themes touched on by Hammond in the garden kept obtruding themselves on my brain. I battled against them. I erected ramparts of would-be blankness of intellect to keep them out. They still crowded upon me. While I was lying still as a corpse, hoping that by a perfect physical inaction I should hasten mental repose, an awful incident occurred. A Something dropped, as it seemed, from the ceiling, plumb upon my chest, and the next instant I felt two bony hands encircling my throat, endeavouring to choke me.

I am no coward, and am possessed of considerable physical strength. The suddenness of the attack, instead of stunning me, strung every nerve to its highest tension. My body acted from instinct, before my brain had time to realize the terrors of my position. In an instant I wound two muscular arms around the creature, and squeezed it, with all the strength of despair, against my chest. In a few seconds the bony hands that had fastened on my throat loosened their hold, and I was free to breathe once more. Then commenced a struggle of awful intensity. Immersed in the most profound darkness, totally ignorant of the nature of the Thing by which I was so suddenly attacked, finding my grasp slipping every moment, by reason, it seemed to me, of the entire nakedness of my assailant, bitten with sharp teeth in the shoulder, neck, and chest, having every moment to protect my throat against a pair of sinewy, agile hands, which my utmost efforts could not confine,—these were a combination of circumstances to combat which required all the strength, skill, and courage that I possessed.

At last, after a silent, deadly, exhausting struggle, I got my assailant under by a series of incredible efforts of strength. Once pinned, with my knee on what I made out to be its chest, I knew that I was victor. I rested for a moment to breathe. I heard the creature beneath me panting in the darkness, and felt the violent throbbing of a heart. It was apparently as exhausted as I was; that was one comfort. At this moment I remembered that I usually placed under my pillow, before going to bed, a large yellow silk pocket handkerchief. I felt for it instantly; it was there. In a few seconds more I had, after a fashion, pinioned the creature's arms.

I now felt tolerably secure. There was nothing more to be done but to turn on the gas, and, having first seen what my midnight assailant was like, arouse the household. I will confess to being actuated by a certain pride in not giving the alarm before; I wished to make the capture alone and unaided.

Never losing my hold for an instant, I slipped from the bed to the floor, dragging my captive with me. I had but a few steps to make to reach the gas-burner; these I made with the greatest caution, holding the creature in a grip like a vice. At last I got within arm's length of the tiny speck of blue light which told me where the gas-burner lay. Quick as lightning I released my grasp with one hand and let on the full flood of light. Then I turned to look at my captive.

I cannot even attempt to give any definition of my sensations the instant after I turned on the gas. I suppose I must have shrieked with terror, for in less than a minute afterward my room was crowded with the inmates of the house. I shudder now as I think of that awful moment. *I saw nothing!* Yes; I had one arm firmly clasped round a breathing, panting, corporeal shape, my other hand gripped with all its strength a throat as warm, as apparently fleshy, as my own; and yet, with this living substance in my grasp, with its body pressed against my own, and all in the bright glare of a large jet of gas, I absolutely beheld nothing! Not even an outline,—a vapour!

I do not, even at this hour, realize the situation in which I found myself. I cannot recall the astounding incident thoroughly. Imagination in vain tries to compass the awful paradox.

It breathed. I felt its warm breath upon my cheek. It struggled fiercely. It had hands. They clutched me. Its skin was smooth, like my own. There it lay, pressed close up against me, solid as stone,—and yet utterly invisible!

I wonder that I did not faint or go mad on the instant. Some wonderful instinct must have sustained me; for, absolutely, in place of loosening my hold on the terrible Enigma, I seemed to gain an additional strength in my moment of horror, and tightened my grasp with such wonderful force that I felt the creature shivering with agony.

Just then Hammond entered my room at the head of the household. As soon as he beheld my face—which, I suppose, must have been an awful sight to look at—he hastened forward, crying, "Great heaven, Harry! what has happened?"

"Hammond! Hammond!" I cried, "come here. O, this is awful! I have been attacked in bed by something or other, which I have hold of; but I can't see it,—I can't see it!"

Hammond, doubtless struck by the unfeigned horror expressed in my countenance, made one or two steps forward with an anxious yet puzzled expression. A very audible titter burst from the remainder of my visitors. This suppressed laughter made me furious. To laugh at a human being in my position! It was the worst species of cruelty. *Now*, I can understand why the appearance of a man struggling violently, as it would seem, with an airy nothing, and calling for assistance against a vision, should have appeared ludicrous. *Then*, so great was my rage against the mocking crowd that had I the power I would have stricken them dead where they stood.

"Hammond! Hammond!" I cried again, despairingly, "for God's sake come to me. I can hold the—the thing but a short while longer. It is overpowering me. Help me! Help me!"

"Harry," whispered Hammond, approaching me, "you have been smoking too much opium."

"I swear to you, Hammond, that this is no vision," I answered, in the same low tone. "Don't you see how it shakes my whole frame with its struggles? If you don't believe me, convince yourself. Feel it,—touch it."

Hammond advanced and laid his hand in the spot I indicated. A wild cry of horror burst from him. He had felt it!

In a moment he had discovered somewhere in my room a long piece of cord, and was the next instant winding it and knotting it about the body of the unseen being that I clasped in my arms.

"Harry," he said, in a hoarse, agitated voice, for, though he preserved his presence of mind, he was deeply moved, "Harry, it's all safe now. You may let go, old fellow, if you're tired. The Thing can't move."

I was utterly exhausted, and I gladly loosed my hold.

Hammond stood holding the ends of the cord that bound the Invisible, twisted round his hand, while before him, self-supporting as it were, he beheld a rope laced and interlaced, and stretching tightly around a vacant space. I never saw a man look so thoroughly stricken with awe. Nevertheless his face expressed all the courage and determination which I knew him to possess. His lips, although white, were set firmly, and one could perceive at a glance that, although stricken with fear, he was not daunted.

The confusion that ensued among the guests of the house who were witnesses of this extraordinary scene between Hammond and myself,—who beheld the pantomime of binding this struggling Something,—who beheld me almost sinking from physical exhaustion when my task of jailer was over,—the confusion and terror that took possession of the bystanders, when they saw all this, was beyond description. The weaker ones fled from the apartment. The few who remained clustered near the door and could not be induced to approach Hammond and his Charge. Still incredulity broke out through their terror. They had not the courage to satisfy themselves, and yet they doubted. It was in vain that I begged of some of the men to come near and convince themselves by touch of the existence in that room of a living being which was invisible. They were incredulous, but did not dare to undeceive themselves. How could a solid, living, breathing body be invisible, they asked. My reply was this. I gave a sign to Hammond, and both of us—conquering our fearful repugnance to touch the invisible creature—lifted it from the ground, manacled as it was, and took it to my bed. Its weight was about that of a boy of fourteen.

"Now, my friends," I said, as Hammond and myself held the creature suspended over the bed, "I can give you self-evident proof that here is a solid, ponderable body, which, nevertheless, you cannot see. Be good enough to watch the surface of the bed attentively."

I was astonished at my own courage in treating this strange event so calmly; but I had recovered from my first terror, and felt a sort of scientific pride in the affair, which dominated every other feeling.

The eyes of the bystanders were immediately fixed on my bed. At a given signal Hammond and I let the creature fall. There was a dull sound of a heavy body alighting on a soft mass. The timbers of the bed creaked. A deep impression marked itself distinctly on the pillow, and on the bed itself. The crowd who witnessed this gave a low cry, and rushed from the room. Hammond and I were left alone with our Mystery.

We remained silent for some time, listening to the low, irregular breathing of the creature on the bed, and watching the rustle of the bedclothes as it impotently struggled to free itself from confinement. Then Hammond spoke.

"Harry, this is awful."

"Ay, awful."

"But not unaccountable."

"Not unaccountable! What do you mean? Such a thing has never occurred since the birth of the world. I know not what to think, Hammond. God grant that I am not mad, and that this is not an insane fantasy!"

"Let us reason a little, Harry. Here is a solid body which we touch, but which we cannot see. The fact is so unusual that it strikes us with terror. Is there no parallel, though, for such a phenomenon? Take a piece of pure glass. It is tangible and transparent. A certain chemical coarseness is all that prevents its being so entirely transparent as to be totally invisible. It is not *theoretically impossible*, mind you, to make a glass which shall not reflect a single ray of light,—a glass so pure and homogeneous in its atoms that the rays from the sun will pass through it as they do through the air, refracted but not reflected. We do not see the air, and yet we feel it."

"That's all very well, Hammond, but these are inanimate substances. Glass does not breathe, air does not breathe. *This* thing has a heart that palpitates,—a will that moves it,—lungs that play, and inspire and respire."

"You forget the phenomena of which we have so often heard of late," answered the Doctor, gravely. "At the meetings called 'spirit circles,' invisible hands have been thrust into the hands of those persons round the table,—warm, fleshly hands that seemed to pulsate with mortal life."

"What? Do you think, then, that this thing is—"

"I don't know what it is," was the solemn reply; "but please the gods I will, with your assistance, thoroughly investigate it."

We watched together, smoking many pipes, all night long, by the bedside of the unearthly being that tossed and panted until it was apparently wearied out. Then we learned by the low, regular breathing that it slept.

The next morning the house was all astir. The boarders congregated on the landing outside my room, and Hammond and myself were lions. We had to answer a thousand questions as to the state of our extraordinary prisoner, for as yet not one person in the house except ourselves could be induced to set foot in the apartment.

The creature was awake. This was evidenced by the convulsive manner in which the bedclothes were moved in its efforts to escape. There was something truly terrible in beholding, as it were, those second-hand indications of the terrible writhings and agonized struggles for liberty which themselves were invisible.

Hammond and myself had racked our brains during the long night to discover some means by which we might realize the shape and general appearance of the Enigma. As well as we could make out by passing our hands over the creature's form, its outlines and lineaments were human. There was a mouth; a round, smooth head without hair; a nose, which, however, was little elevated above the cheeks; and its hands and feet felt like those of a boy. At first we thought of placing the being on a smooth surface and tracing its outlines with chalk, as shoemakers trace the outline of the foot. This plan was given up as being of no value. Such an outline would give not the slightest idea of its conformation.

A happy thought struck me. We would take a cast of it in plaster of Paris. This would give us the solid figure, and satisfy all our wishes. But how to do it? The movements of the creature would disturb the setting of the plastic covering, and distort the mould. Another thought. Why not give it chloroform? It had respiratory organs,—that was evident by its breathing. Once reduced to a state of insensibility, we could do with it what we would. Doctor X—— was sent for; and after the worthy physician had recovered from the first shock of amazement, he proceeded to administer the chloroform. In three minutes afterward we were enabled to remove the fetters from the creature's body, and a modeller was busily engaged in covering the invisible form with the moist clay. In five minutes more we had a mould, and before evening a rough facsimile of the Mystery. It was shaped like a man,—distorted, uncouth, and horrible, but still a man. It was small, not over four feet and some inches in height, and its limbs revealed a muscular development that was unparalleled. Its face surpassed in hideousness anything I had ever seen. Gustav Doré, or Callot, or Tony Johannot, never conceived anything so horrible. There is a face in one of the latter's illustrations to *Un Voyage où il vous plaira*, which somewhat approaches the countenance of this creature, but does not equal it. It was the physiognomy of what I should fancy a ghoul might be. It looked as if it was capable of feeding on human flesh.

Having satisfied our curiosity, and bound every one in the house to secrecy, it became a question what was to be done with our Enigma? It was impossible that we should keep such a horror in our house; it was equally impossible that such an awful being should be let loose upon the world. I confess that I would have gladly voted for the creature's destruction. But who would shoulder the responsibility? Who would undertake the execution of this horrible semblance of a human being? Day after day this question was deliberated gravely. The boarders all left the house. Mrs Moffat was in despair, and threatened Hammond and myself with all sorts of legal penalties if we did not remove the Horror. Our answer was, "We will go if you like, but we decline taking this creature with us. Remove it yourself if you please. It appeared in your house. On you the responsibility rests." To this there was, of course, no answer. Mrs Moffat could not obtain for love or money a person who would even approach the Mystery.

The most singular part of the affair was that we were entirely ignorant of what the creature habitually fed on. Everything in the way of nutriment that we could think of was placed before it, but was never touched. It was awful to stand by, day after day, and see the clothes toss, and hear the hard breathing, and know that it was starving.

Ten, twelve days, a fortnight passed, and it still lived. The pulsations of the heart, however, were daily growing fainter, and had now nearly ceased. It was evident that the creature was dying for want of sustenance. While this terrible life-struggle was going on, I felt miserable. I could not sleep. Horrible as the creature was, it was pitiful to think of the pangs it was suffering.

At last it died. Hammond and I found it cold and stiff one morning in the bed. The heart had ceased to beat, the lungs to inspire. We hastened to bury it in the garden. It was a strange funeral, the dropping of that viewless corpse into the damp hole. The cast of its form I gave to Doctor X——, who keeps it in his museum in Tenth Street.

As I am on the eve of a long journey from which I may not return, I have drawn up this narrative of an event the most singular that has ever come to my knowledge.

The Rival Ghosts

Brander Matthews

The good ship sped on her way across the calm Atlantic. It was an outward passage, according to the little charts which the company had charily distributed, but most of the passengers were homeward bound, after a summer of rest and recreation, and they were counting the days before they might hope to see Fire Island Light. On the lee side of the boat, comfortably sheltered from the wind, and just by the door of the captain's room (which was theirs during the day), sat a little group of returning Americans. The Duchess (she was down on the purser's list as Mrs Martin, but her friends and familiars called her the Duchess of Washington Square) and Baby Van Rensselaer (she was quite old enough to vote, had her sex been entitled to that duty, but as the younger of two sisters she was still the baby of the family)—the Duchess and Baby Van Rensselaer were discussing the pleasant English voice and the not unpleasant English accent of a manly young lordling who was going to America for sport. Uncle Larry and Dear Jones were enticing each other into a bet on the ship's run of the morrow.

"I'll give you two to one she don't make 420," said Dear Jones.

"I'll take it," answered Uncle Larry. "We made 427 the fifth day last year." It was Uncle Larry's seventeenth visit to Europe, and this was therefore his thirty-fourth voyage.

"And when did you get in?" asked Baby Van Rensselaer. "I don't care a bit about the run, so long as we get in soon."

"We crossed the bar Sunday night, just seven days after we left Queenstown, and we dropped anchor off Quarantine at three o'clock on Monday morning."

"I hope we shan't do that this time. I can't seem to sleep any when the boat stops."

"I can; but I didn't," continued Uncle Larry; "because my state-room was the most for'ard in the boat, and the donkey-engine that let down the anchor was right over my head."

"So you got up and saw the sunrise over the bay," said Dear Jones, "with the electric lights of the city twinkling in the distance, and the first faint flush of the dawn in the east just over Fort Lafayette, and the rosy tinge which spread softly upward, and—"

"Did you both come back together?" asked the Duchess.

"Because he has crossed thirty-four times you must not suppose that he has a monopoly in sunrises," retorted Dear Jones. "No, this was my own sunrise; and a mighty pretty one it was, too."

"I'm not matching sunrises with you," remarked Uncle Larry, calmly; "but I'm willing to back a merry jest called forth by my sunrise against any two merry jests called forth by yours."

"I confess reluctantly that my sunrise evoked no merry jest at all." Dear Jones was an honest man, and would scorn to invent a merry jest on the spur of the moment.

"That's where my sunrise has the call," said Uncle Larry, complacently.

"What was the merry jest?" was Baby Van Rensselaer's inquiry, the natural result of a feminine curiosity thus artistically excited.

"Well, here it is. I was standing aft, near a patriotic American and a wandering Irishman, and the patriotic American rashly declared that you couldn't see a sunrise like that anywhere in Europe, and this gave the Irishman his chance, and he said, 'Sure ye don't have 'em here till we're through with 'em over there.'"

"It is true," said Dear Jones, thoughtfully, "that they do have some things over there better than we do; for instance, umbrellas."

"And gowns," added the Duchess.

"And antiquities,"—this was Uncle Larry's contribution.

"And we do have some things so much better in America!" protested Baby Van Rensselaer, as yet uncorrupted by any worship of the effete monarchies of despotic Europe. "We make lots of things a great deal nicer than you can get them in Europe—especially ice-cream."

"And pretty girls," added Dear Jones; but he did not look at her.

"And spooks," remarked Uncle Larry casually.

"Spooks?" queried the Duchess.

"Spooks. I maintain the word. Ghosts, if you like that better, or specters. We turn out the best quality of spook—"

"You forget the lovely ghost stories about the Rhine, and the Black Forest," interrupted Miss Van Rensselaer, with feminine inconsistency.

"I remember the Rhine and the Black Forest and all the other haunts of elves and fairies and hobgoblins; but for good honest spooks there is no place like home. And what differentiates our spook—*Spiritus Americanus*—from the ordinary ghost of literature is that it responds to the American sense of humor. Take Irving's stories for example. *The Headless Horseman*, that's a comic ghost story. And Rip Van Winkle—consider what humor, and what good-humor, there is in the telling of his meeting with the goblin crew of Hendrik Hudson's men! A still better example of this American way of dealing with legend and mystery is the marvelous tale of the rival ghosts."

"The rival ghosts?" queried the Duchess and Baby Van Rensselaer together. "Who were they?"

"Didn't I ever tell you about them?" answered Uncle Larry, a gleam of approaching joy flashing from his eye.

"Since he is bound to tell us sooner or later, we'd better be resigned and hear it now," said Dear Jones.

"If you are not more eager, I won't tell it at all."

"Oh, do, Uncle Larry; you know I just dote on ghost stories," pleaded Baby Van Rensselaer.

"Once upon a time," began Uncle Larry—"in fact, a very few years ago—there lived in the thriving town of New York a young American called Duncan—Eliphalet Duncan. Like his name, he was half Yankee and half Scotch, and naturally he was a lawyer, and had come to New York to make his way. His father was a Scotchman, who had come over and settled in Boston, and married a Salem girl. When Eliphalet Duncan was about twenty he lost both of his parents. His father left him with enough money to give him a start, and a strong feeling of pride in his

Scotch birth; you see there was a title in the family in Scotland, and although Eliphalet's father was the younger son of a younger son, yet he always remembered, and always bade his only son to remember, that his ancestry was noble. His mother left him her full share of Yankee grit, and a little house in Salem which has belonged to her family for more than two hundred years. She was a Hitchcock, and the Hitchcocks had been settled in Salem since the year 1. It was a great-great-grandfather of Mr Eliphalet Hitchcock who was foremost in the time of the Salem witchcraft craze. And this little old house which she left to my friend Eliphalet Duncan was haunted.

"By the ghost of one of the witches, of course," interrupted Dear Jones.

"Now how could it be the ghost of a witch, since the witches were all burned at the stake? You never heard of anybody who was burned having a ghost, did you?"

"That's an argument in favor of cremation, at any rate," replied Jones, evading the direct question.

"It is, if you don't like ghosts; I do," said Baby Van Rensselaer.

"And so do I," added Uncle Larry. "I love a ghost as dearly as an Englishman loves a lord."

"Go on with your story," said the Duchess, majestically overruling all extraneous discussion.

"This little old house at Salem was haunted," resumed Uncle Larry. "And by a very distinguished ghost—or at least by a ghost with very remarkable attributes."

"What was he like?" asked Baby Van Rensselaer, with a premonitory shiver of anticipatory delight.

"It had a lot of peculiarities. In the first place, it never appeared to the master of the house. Mostly it confined its visitations to unwelcome guests. In the course of the last hundred years it had frightened away four successive mothers-in-law, while never intruding on the head of the household."

"I guess that ghost had been one of the boys when he was alive and in the flesh." This was Dear Jones's contribution to the telling of the tale.

"In the second place," continued Uncle Larry, "it never frightened anybody the first time it appeared. Only on the second visit were the ghost-seers scared; but then they were scared enough for twice, and they rarely mustered up courage enough to risk a third interview. One of the most curious characteristics of this well-meaning spook was that it had no face—or at least that nobody ever saw its face."

"Perhaps he kept his countenance veiled?" queried the Duchess, who was beginning to remember that she never did like ghost stories.

"That was what I was never able to find out. I have asked several people who saw the ghost, and none of them could tell me anything about its face, and yet while in its presence they never noticed its features, and never remarked on their absence or concealment. It was only afterward when they tried to recall calmly all the circumstances of meeting with the mysterious stranger, that they became aware that they had not seen its face. And they could not say whether the features were covered, or whether they were wanting, or what the trouble was. They knew only that the face was never seen. And no matter how often they might see it, they never fathomed this mystery. To this day nobody knows whether the ghost which used to haunt the little old house in Salem had a face, or what manner of face it had."

"How awfully weird!" said Baby Van Rensselaer. "And why did the ghost go away?"

"I haven't said it went away," answered Uncle Larry, with much dignity.

"But you said it *used* to haunt the little old house at Salem, so I supposed it had moved. Didn't it?"

"You shall be told in due time. Eliphalet Duncan used to spend most of his summer vacations at Salem, and the ghost never bothered him at all, for he was the master of the house—much to his disgust, too, because he wanted to see for himself the mysterious tenant at will of his property. But he never saw it, never. He arranged with friends to call him whenever it might appear, and he slept in the next room with the door open; and yet when their frightened cries waked him the ghost was gone, and his only reward was to hear reproachful sighs as soon as he went back to bed. You see, the ghost thought it was not fair of Eliphalet to seek an introduction which was plainly unwelcome."

Dear Jones interrupted the storyteller by getting up and tucking a heavy rug snugly around Baby Van Rensselaer's feet, for the sky was now overcast and gray, and the air was damp and penetrating.

"One fine spring morning," pursued Uncle Larry, "Eliphalet Duncan received great news. I told you that there was a title in the family in Scotland, and that Eliphalet's father was the younger son of a younger son. Well, it happened that all Eliphalet's father's brothers and uncles had died off without male issue except the eldest son of the eldest, and he, of course, bore the title, and was Baron Duncan of Duncan. Now the great news that Eliphalet Duncan received in New York one fine spring morning was that Baron Duncan and his only son had been yachting in the Hebrides, and they had been caught in a black squall, and they were both dead. So my friend Eliphalet Duncan inherited the title and the estates."

"How romantic!" said the Duchess. "So he was a baron!"

"Well," answered Uncle Larry, "he was a baron if he chose. But he didn't choose."

"More fool he," said Dear Jones sententiously.

"Well," answered Uncle Larry, "I'm not so sure of that. You see, Eliphalet Duncan was half Scotch and half Yankee, and he had two eyes to the main chance. He held his tongue about his windfall of luck until he could find out whether the Scotch estates were enough to keep up the Scotch title. He soon discovered that they were not, and that the late Lord Duncan, having married money, kept up such state as he could out of the revenues of the dowry of Lady Duncan. And Eliphalet, he decided that he would rather be a well-fed lawyer in New York, living comfortably on his practice, than a starving lord in Scotland, living scantily on his title."

"But he kept his title?" asked the Duchess.

"Well," answered Uncle Larry, "he kept it quiet. I knew it, and a friend or two more. But Eliphalet was a sight too smart to put Baron Duncan of Duncan, Attorney and Counselor at Law, on his shingle."

"What has all this got to do with your ghost?" asked Dear Jones pertinently.

"Nothing with that ghost, but a good deal with another ghost. Eliphalet was very learned in spirit lore—perhaps because he owned the haunted house at Salem, perhaps because he was a Scotchman by descent. At all events, he had made a special study of the wraiths and white ladies and banshees and bogies of all kinds whose sayings and doings and warnings are recorded in the annals of the Scottish nobility. In fact, he was acquainted with the habits of every reputable spook in the Scotch peerage. And he knew that there was a Duncan ghost attached to the person of the holder of the title of Baron Duncan of Duncan."

"So, besides being the owner of a haunted house in Salem, he was also a haunted man in Scotland?" asked Baby Van Rensselaer.

"Just so. But the Scotch ghost was not unpleasant, like the Salem ghost, although it had one peculiarity in common with its trans-Atlantic fellow-spook. It never appeared to the holder of the title, just as the other never was visible to the owner of the house. In fact, the Duncan ghost was never seen at all. It was a guardian angel only. Its sole duty was to be in personal attendance on Baron Duncan of Duncan, and to warn him of impending evil. The traditions of the house told that the Barons of Duncan had again and again felt a premonition of ill fortune. Some of them had yielded and withdrawn from the venture they had undertaken, and it had failed dismally. Some had been obstinate, and had hardened their hearts, and had gone on reckless of defeat and to death. In no case had a Lord Duncan been exposed to peril without fair warning."

"Then how came it that the father and son were lost in the yacht off the Hebrides?" asked Dear Jones.

"Because they were too enlightened to yield to superstition. There is extant now a letter of Lord Duncan, written to his wife a few minutes before he and his son set sail, in which he tells her how hard he has had to struggle with an almost overmastering desire to give up the trip. Had he obeyed the friendly warning of the family ghost, the latter would have been spared a journey across the Atlantic."

"Did the ghost leave Scotland for America as soon as the old baron died?" asked Baby Van Rensselaer, with much interest.

"How did he come over," queried Dear Jones—"in the steerage, or as a cabin passenger?"

"I don't know," answered Uncle Larry calmly, "and Eliphalet, he didn't know. For as he was in no danger, and stood in no need of warning, he couldn't tell whether the ghost was on duty or not. Of course he was on the watch for it all the time. But he never got any proof of its presence until he went down to the little old house of Salem, just before the Fourth of July. He took a friend down with him—a young fellow who had been in the regular army since the day Fort Sumter was fired on, and who thought that after four years of the little unpleasantness down South, including six months in Libby, and after ten years of fighting the bad Indians on the plains, he wasn't likely to be much frightened by a ghost. Well, Eliphalet and the officer sat out on the porch all the evening smoking and talking over points in military law. A little after twelve o'clock, just as they began to think it was about time to turn in, they heard the most ghastly noise in the house. It wasn't a shriek, or a howl, or a yell, or anything they could put a name to. It was an undeterminate, inexplicable shiver and shudder of sound, which went wailing out of the window. The officer had been at Cold Harbor, but he felt himself getting colder this time. Eliphalet knew it was the ghost who haunted the house. As this weird sound died away, it was followed by another, sharp, short, blood-curdling in its intensity. Something in this cry seemed familiar to Eliphalet, and he felt sure that it proceeded from the family ghost, the warning wraith of the Duncans."

"Do I understand you to intimate that both ghosts were there together?" inquired the Duchess anxiously.

"Both of them were there," answered Uncle Larry. "You see, one of them belonged to the house, and had to be there all the time, and the other was attached to the person of Baron Duncan, and had to follow him there; wherever he was there was the ghost also. But Eliphalet, he had scarcely time to think this out when he heard both sounds again, not one after another, but both together, and something told him—some sort of an instinct he had—that those two ghosts didn't agree, didn't get on together, didn't exactly hit it off; in fact, that they were quarreling."

"Quarreling ghosts! Well, I never!" was Baby Van Rensselaer's remark.

"It is a blessed thing to see ghosts dwell together in unity," said Dear Jones.

And the Duchess added, "It would certainly be setting a better example."

"You know," resumed Uncle Larry, "that two waves of light or of sound may interfere and produce darkness or silence. So it was with these rival spooks. They interfered, but they did not produce silence or darkness. On the contrary, as soon as Eliphalet and the officer went into the house, there began at once a series of spiritualistic manifestations, a regular dark séance. A tambourine was played upon, a bell was rung, and a flaming banjo went singing around the room."

"Where did they get the banjo?" asked Dear Jones skeptically.

"I don't know. Materialized it, maybe, just as they did the tambourine. You don't suppose a quiet New York lawyer kept a stock of musical instruments large enough to fit out a strolling minstrel troupe just on the chance of a pair of ghosts coming to give him a surprise party, do you? Every spook has its own instrument of torture. Angels play on harps, I'm informed, and spirits delight in banjos and tambourines. These spooks of Eliphalet Duncan's were ghosts with all the modern improvements, and I guess they were capable of providing their own musical weapons. At all events, they had them there in the little old house at Salem the night Eliphalet and his friend came down. And they played on them, and they rang the bell, and they rapped here, there, and everywhere. And they kept it up all night."

"All night?" asked the awe-stricken Duchess.

"All night long," said Uncle Larry solemnly; "and the next night, too. Eliphalet did not get a wink of sleep, neither did his friend. On the second night the house ghost was seen by the officer; on the third night it showed itself again; and the next morning the officer packed his grip-sack and took the first train to Boston. He was a New Yorker, but he said he'd sooner go to Boston than see that ghost again. Eliphalet, he wasn't scared at all, partly because he never saw either the domiciliary or the titular spook, and partly because he felt himself on friendly terms with the spirit world, and didn't scare easily. But after losing three nights' sleep and the society of his friend, he began to be a little impatient, and to think that the thing had gone far enough. You see, while in a way he was fond of ghosts, yet he liked them best one at a time. Two ghosts were one too many. He wasn't bent on making a collection of spooks. He and one ghost were company, but he and two ghosts were a crowd."

"What did he do?" asked Baby Van Rensselaer.

"Well, he couldn't do anything. He waited awhile, hoping they would get tired; but he got tired out first. You see, it comes natural to a spook to sleep in the daytime, but a man wants to sleep nights, and they wouldn't let him sleep nights. They kept on wrangling and quarreling incessantly; they manifested and they dark-séanced as regularly as the old clock on the stairs struck twelve; they rapped and they rang bells and they banged the tambourine and they threw the flaming banjo about the house, and worse than all, they swore."

"I did not know that spirits were addicted to bad language," said the Duchess.

"How did he know they were swearing? Could he hear them?" asked Dear Jones.

"That was just it," responded Uncle Larry; "he could not hear them—at least not distinctly. There were inarticulate murmurs and stifled rumblings. But the impression produced on him was that they were swearing. If they had only sworn right out, he would not have minded it so much, because he would have known the worst. But the feeling that the air was full of suppressed profanity was very wearing and after standing it for a week, he gave up in disgust and went to the White Mountains."

"Leaving them to fight it out, I suppose," interjected Baby Van Rensselaer.

"Not at all," explained Uncle Larry. "They could not quarrel unless he was present. You see, he could not leave the titular ghost behind him, and the domiciliary ghost could not leave the house. When he went away he took the family ghost with him, leaving the house ghost behind. Now spooks can't quarrel when they are a hundred miles apart any more than men can."

"And what happened afterward?" asked Baby Van Rensselaer, with a pretty impatience.

"A most marvelous thing happened. Eliphalet Duncan went to the White Mountains, and in the car of the railroad that runs to the top of Mount Washington he met a classmate whom he had not seen for years, and this classmate introduced Duncan to his sister, and this sister was a remarkably pretty girl, and Duncan fell in love with her at first sight, and by the time he got to the top of Mount Washington he was so deep in love that he began to consider his own unworthiness, and to wonder whether she might ever be induced to care for him a little—ever so little."

"I don't think that is so marvelous a thing," said Dear Jones glancing at Baby Van Rensselaer.

"Who was she?" asked the Duchess, who had once lived in Philadelphia.

"She was Miss Kitty Sutton, of San Francisco, and she was a daughter of old Judge Sutton, of the firm of Pixley and Sutton."

"A very respectable family," assented the Duchess.

"I hope she wasn't a daughter of that loud and vulgar old Mrs Sutton whom I met at Saratoga, one summer, four or five years ago?" said Dear Jones.

"Probably she was."

"She was a horrid old woman. The boys used to call her Mother Gorgon."

"The pretty Kitty Sutton with whom Eliphalet Duncan had fallen in love was the daughter of Mother Gorgon. But he never saw the mother, who was in 'Frisco, or Los Angeles, or Santa Fe, or somewhere out West, and he saw a great deal of the daughter, who was up in the White Mountains. She was traveling with her brother and his wife, and as they journeyed from hotel to hotel, Duncan went with them, and filled out the quartette. Before the end of the summer he began to think about proposing. Of course he had lots of chances, going on excursions as they were every day. He made up his mind to seize the first opportunity, and that very evening he took her out for a moonlight row on Lake Winnipiseogee. As he handed her into the boat he resolved to do it, and he had a glimmer of a suspicion that she knew he was going to do it, too."

"Girls," said Dear Jones, "never go out in a rowboat at night with a young man unless you mean to accept him."

"Sometimes it's best to refuse him, and get it over once for all," said Baby Van Rensselaer.

"As Eliphalet took the oars he felt a sudden chill. He tried to shake it off, but in vain. He began to have a growing consciousness of impending evil. Before he had taken ten strokes—and he was a swift oarsman—he was aware of a mysterious presence between him and Miss Sutton."

"Was it the guardian-angel ghost warning him off the match?" interrupted Dear Jones.

"That's just what it was," said Uncle Larry. "And he yielded to it, and kept his peace, and rowed Miss Sutton back to the hotel with his proposal unspoken."

"More fool he," said Dear Jones. "It will take more than one ghost to keep me from proposing when my mind is made up." And he looked at Baby Van Rensselaer.

"The next morning," continued Uncle Larry, "Eliphalet overslept himself, and when he went down to a late breakfast he found that the Suttons had gone to New York by the morning train. He wanted to follow them at once, and again he felt the mysterious presence overpowering his will. He struggled two days, and at last he roused himself to do what he wanted in spite of the spook. When he arrived in New York it was late in the evening. He dressed himself hastily and went to the hotel where the Suttons put up, in the hope of seeing at least her brother. The guardian angel fought every inch of the walk with him, until he began to wonder whether, if Miss Sutton were to take him, the spook would forbid the banns. At the hotel he saw no one that night, and he went home determined to call as early as he could the next afternoon, and make an end of it. When he left his office about two o'clock the next day to learn his fate, he had not walked five blocks before he discovered that the wraith of the Duncans had withdrawn his opposition to the suit. There was no feeling of impending evil, no resistance, no struggle, no consciousness of an opposing presence. Eliphalet was greatly encouraged. He walked briskly to the hotel; he found Miss Sutton alone. He asked her the question, and got his answer."

"She accepted him, of course," said Baby Van Rensselaer.

"Of course," said Uncle Larry. "And while they were in the first flush of joy, swapping confidences and confessions, her brother came into the parlor with an expression of pain on his face and a telegram in his hand. The former was caused by the latter, which was from 'Frisco, and which announced the sudden death of Mrs Sutton, their mother."

"And that was why the ghost no longer opposed the match?" questioned Dear Jones.

"Exactly. You see, the family ghost knew that Mother Gorgon was an awful obstacle to Duncan's happiness, so it warned him. But the moment the obstacle was removed, it gave its consent at once."

The fog was lowering its thick damp curtain, and it was beginning to be difficult to see from one end of the boat to the other. Dear Jones tightened the rug which enwrapped Baby Van Rensselaer, and then withdrew again into his own substantial coverings.

Uncle Larry paused in his story long enough to light another of the tiny cigars he always smoked.

"I infer that Lord Duncan"—the Duchess was scrupulous in the bestowal of titles—"saw no more of the ghosts after he was married."

"He never saw them at all, at any time, either before or since. But they came very near breaking off the match, and thus breaking two young hearts."

"You don't mean to say that they knew any just cause or impediment why they should not forever after hold their peace?" asked Dear Jones.

"How could a ghost, or even two ghosts, keep a girl from marrying the man she loved?" This was Baby Van Rensselaer's question.

"It seems curious, doesn't it?" and Uncle Larry tried to warm himself by two or three sharp pulls at his fiery little cigar. "And the circumstances are quite as curious as the fact itself. You see, Miss Sutton wouldn't be married for a year after her mother's death, so she and Duncan had lots of time to tell each other all they knew. Eliphalet, he got to know a good deal about the girls she went to school with, and Kitty, she learned all about his family. He didn't tell her about the title for a long time, as he wasn't one to brag. But he described to her the little old house at Salem. And one evening toward the end of the summer, the wedding-day having been appointed for early in September, she told him that she didn't want to bridal tour at all; she just wanted to go down to the little old house at Salem to spend her honeymoon in peace and quiet, with nothing to do and nobody to bother them. Well, Eliphalet jumped at the suggestion. It suited him down to the ground. All of a sudden he remembered the spooks, and it knocked him all of a heap. He had told her about the Duncan Banshee, and the idea of having an ancestral ghost in personal attendance on her husband tickled her immensely. But he had never said anything about the ghost which haunted the little old house at Salem. He knew she would be frightened out of her wits if the house ghost revealed itself to her, and he saw at once that it would be impossible to go to Salem on their wedding trip. So he told her all about it, and how whenever he went to Salem the two ghosts interfered, and gave dark séances and manifested and materialized and made the place absolutely impossible. Kitty, she listened in silence, and Eliphalet, he thought she had changed her mind. But she hadn't done anything of the kind."

"Just like a man—to think she was going to," remarked Baby Van Rensselaer.

"She just told him she could not bear ghosts herself, but she would not marry a man who was afraid of them."

"Just like a girl—to be so inconsistent," remarked Dear Jones.

Uncle Larry's tiny cigar had long been extinct. He lighted a new one, and continued: "Eliphalet protested in vain. Kitty said her mind was made up. She was determined to pass her honeymoon in the little old house at Salem, and she was equally determined not to go there as long as there were any ghosts there. Until he could assure her that the spectral tenants had received notice to quit, and that there was no danger of manifestations and materializing, she refused to be married at all. She did not intend to have her honeymoon interrupted by two wrangling ghosts, and the wedding could be postponed until he had made ready the house for her."

"She was an unreasonable young woman," said the Duchess.

"Well, that's what Eliphalet thought, much as he was in love with her. And he believed he could talk her out of her determination. But he couldn't. She was set. And when a girl is set, there's nothing to do but yield to the inevitable. And that's just what Eliphalet did. He saw he would either have to give her up or to get the ghosts out; and as he loved her and did not care for the ghosts, he resolved to tackle the ghosts. He had clear grit, Eliphalet had—he was half Scotch and half Yankee, and neither breed turns tail in a hurry. So he made his plans and he went down to Salem. As he said goodbye to Kitty he had an impression that she was sorry she had made him go, but she kept up bravely, and put a bold face on it, and saw him off, and went home and cried for an hour, and was perfectly miserable until he came back the next day."

"Did he succeed in driving the ghosts away?" asked Baby Van Rensselaer, with great interest.

"That's just what I'm coming to," said Uncle Larry, pausing at the critical moment, in the manner of the trained story teller. "You see, Eliphalet had got a rather tough job, and he would gladly have had an extension of time on the contract, but he had to choose between the girl and the ghosts, and he wanted the girl. He tried to invent or remember some short and easy way with ghosts, but he couldn't. He wished that somebody had invented a specific for spooks—something that would make the ghosts come out of the house and die in the yard. He wondered if he could not tempt the ghosts to run in debt, so that he might get the sheriff to help him. He wondered also whether the ghosts could not be overcome with strong drink—a dissipated spook, a spook with delirium tremens, might be committed to the inebriate asylum. But none of these things seemed feasible."

"What did he do?" interrupted Dear Jones. "The learned counsel will please speak to the point."

"You will regret this unseemly haste," said Uncle Larry, gravely, "when you know what really happened."

"What was it, Uncle Larry?" asked Baby Van Rensselaer. "I'm all impatience."

And Uncle Larry proceeded:

"Eliphalet went down to the little old house at Salem, and as soon as the clock struck twelve the rival ghosts began wrangling as before. Raps here, there, and everywhere, ringing bells, banging tambourines, strumming banjos sailing about the room, and all the other manifestations and materializations followed one another just as they had the summer before. The only difference Eliphalet could detect was a stronger flavor in the spectral profanity; and this, of course, was only a vague impression, for he did not actually hear a single word. He waited awhile in patience, listening and watching. Of course he never saw either of the ghosts, because neither of them could appear to him. At last he got his dander up, and he thought it was about time to interfere, so he rapped on the table, and asked for silence. As soon as he felt that the spooks were listening to him he explained the situation to them. He told them he was in love, and that he could not marry unless they vacated the house. He appealed to them as old friends, and he laid claim to their gratitude. The titular ghost had been sheltered by the Duncan family for hundreds of years, and the domiciliary ghost had had free lodging in the little old house at Salem for nearly two centuries. He implored them to settle their differences, and to get him out of his difficulty at once. He suggested they'd better fight it out then and there, and see who was master. He had brought down with him all needful weapons. And he pulled out his valise, and spread on the table a pair of navy revolvers, a pair of shot-guns, a pair of dueling swords, and a couple of bowie-knives. He offered to serve as second for both parties, and to give the word when to begin. He also took out of his valise a pack of cards and a bottle of poison, telling them that if they wished to avoid carnage they might cut the cards to see which one should take the poison. Then he waited anxiously for their reply. For a little space there was silence. Then he became conscious of a tremulous shivering in one corner of the room, and he remembered that he had heard from that direction what sounded like a frightened sigh when he made the first suggestion of the duel. Something told him that this was the domiciliary ghost, and that it was badly scared. Then he was impressed by a certain movement in the opposite corner of the room, as though the titular ghost were drawing himself up with offended dignity. Eliphalet couldn't exactly see these things, because he never saw the ghosts, but he felt them. After a silence of nearly a minute a voice came from the corner where the family ghost stood—a voice strong and full, but trembling slightly with suppressed passion. And this voice told Eliphalet it was plain enough that he had not long been the head of the Duncans, and that he had never properly considered the characteristics of his race if now he supposed that one of his blood could draw his sword against a woman. Eliphalet said he had never suggested that the Duncan ghost should raise his hand against a woman and all he wanted was that the Duncan ghost should fight the other ghost. And then the voice told Eliphalet that the other ghost was a woman."

"What?" said Dear Jones, sitting up suddenly. "You don't mean to tell me that the ghost which haunted the house was a woman?"

"Those were the very words Eliphalet Duncan used," said Uncle Larry; "but he did not need to wait for the answer. All at once he recalled the traditions about the domiciliary ghost, and he knew that what the titular ghost said was the fact. He had never thought of the sex of a spook, but there was no doubt whatever that the house ghost was a woman. No sooner was this firmly fixed in Eliphalet's mind than he saw his way out of the difficulty. The ghosts must be married!—for then there would be no more interference, no more quarreling, no more manifestations and materializations, no more dark séances, with their raps and bells and tambourines and banjos. At first the ghosts would not hear of it. The voice in the corner declared that the Duncan wraith had never thought of matrimony. But Eliphalet argued with them, and pleaded and persuaded and coaxed, and dwelt on the advantages of matrimony. He had to confess, of course, that he did not know how to get a clergyman to marry them; but the voice from the corner gravely told him that there need be no difficulty in regard to that, as there was no lack of spiritual chaplains. Then, for the first time, the house ghost spoke, in a low, clear, gentle voice, and with a quaint, old-fashioned New England accent, which contrasted sharply with the broad Scotch speech of the family ghost. She said that Eliphalet Duncan seemed to have forgotten that she was married. But this did not upset Eliphalet at all; he remembered the whole case clearly, and he told her she was not a married ghost, but a widow, since her husband had been hung for murdering her. Then the Duncan ghost drew attention to the great disparity of their ages, saying that he was nearly four hundred and fifty years old, while she was barely two hundred. But Eliphalet had not talked to juries for nothing; he just buckled to, and coaxed those ghosts into matrimony. Afterward he came to the conclusion that they were willing to be coaxed, but at the time he thought he had pretty hard work to convince them of the advantages of the plan."

"Did he succeed?" asked Baby Van Rensselaer, with a young lady's interest in matrimony.

"He did," said Uncle Larry. "He talked the wraith of the Duncans and the specter of the little old house at Salem into a matrimonial engagement. And from the time they were engaged he had no more trouble with them. They were rival ghosts no longer. They were married by their spiritual chaplain the very same day that Eliphalet Duncan met Kitty Sutton in front of the railing of Grace Church. The ghostly bride and bridegroom went away at once on their bridal tour, and Lord and Lady Duncan went down to the little old house at Salem to pass their honeymoon."

Uncle Larry stopped. His tiny cigar was out again. The tale of the rival ghosts was told. A solemn silence fell on the little party on the deck of the ocean steamer, broken harshly by the hoarse roar of the fog-horn.

The Prayer

Violet Hunt

'It is but giving over of a game.
That must be lost.'—PHILASTER

'Come, Mrs Arne – come, my dear, you must not give way like this! You can't stand it – you really can't! Let Miss Kate take you away – now do!' urged the nurse, with her most motherly of intonations.

'Yes, Alice, Mrs Joyce is right. Come away – do come away – you are only making yourself ill. It is all over; you can do nothing! Oh, oh, do come away!' implored Mrs Arne's sister, shivering with excitement and nervousness.

A few moments ago Dr Graham had relinquished his hold on the pulse of Edward Arne with the hopeless movement of the eyebrows that meant – the end.

The nurse had made the little gesture of resignation that was possibly a matter of form with her. The young sister-in-law had hidden her face in her hands. The wife had screamed a scream that had turned them all hot and cold – and flung herself on the bed over her dead husband. There she lay; her cries were terrible, her sobs shook her whole body.

The three gazed at her pityingly, not knowing what to do next. The nurse, folding her hands, looked towards the doctor for directions, and the doctor drummed with his fingers on the bedpost.

The young girl timidly stroked the shoulder that heaved and writhed under her touch.

'Go away! Go away!' her sister reiterated continually, in a voice hoarse with fatigue and passion.

'Leave her alone, Miss Kate,' whispered the nurse at last; 'she will work it off best herself, perhaps.'

She turned down the lamp as if to draw a veil over the scene. Mrs Arne raised herself on her elbow, showing a face stained with tears and purple with emotion.

'What! Not gone?' she said harshly. 'Go away, Kate, go away! It is my house. I don't want you, I want no one – I want to speak to my husband. Will you go away – all of you. Give me an hour, half-an-hour – five minutes!'

She stretched out her arms imploringly to the doctor.

'Well…' said he, almost to himself.

He signed to the two women to withdraw, and followed them out into the passage. 'Go and get something to eat,' he said peremptorily, 'while you can. We shall have trouble with her presently. I'll wait in the dressing-room.'

He glanced at the twisting figure on the bed, shrugged his shoulders, and passed into the adjoining room, without, however, closing the door of communication. Sitting down in an armchair drawn up to the fire, he stretched himself and closed his eyes. The professional aspects of the case of Edward Arne rose up before him in all its interesting forms of complication…

It was just this professional attitude that Mrs Arne unconsciously resented both in the doctor and in the nurse. Through all their kindness she had realised and resented their scientific interest in her husband, for to them he had been no more than a curious and complicated case; and now that the blow had fallen, she regarded them both in the light of executioners. Her one desire, expressed with all the shameless sincerity of blind and thoughtless misery, was to be free of their hateful presence and alone – alone with her dead!

She was weary of the doctor's subdued manly tones – of the nurse's commonplace motherliness, too habitually adapted to the needs of all to be appreciated by the individual – of the childish consolation of the young sister, who had never loved, never been married, did not know what sorrow was! Their expressions of sympathy struck her like blows, the touch of their hands on her body, as they tried to raise her, stung her in every nerve.

With a sigh of relief she buried her head in the pillow, pressed her body more closely against that of her husband, and lay motionless.

Her sobs ceased.

The lamp went out with a gurgle. The fire leaped up, and died. She raised her head and stared about her helplessly, then sinking down again she put her lips to the ear of the dead man.

'Edward – dear Edward!' she whispered, 'why have you left me? Darling, why have you left me? I can't stay behind – you know I can't. I am too young to be left. It is only a year since you married me. I never thought it was only for a year. "Till death us do part" Yes, I know that's in it, but nobody ever thinks of that! I never thought of living without you! I meant to die with you…

'No – no – I can't die – I must not – till my baby is born, You will never see it. Don't you want to see it? Don't you? Oh, Edward, speak! Say something, darling, one word – one little word! Edward! Edward! are you there? Answer me for God's sake, answer me!

'Darling, I am so tired of waiting. Oh, think, dearest. There is so little time. They only gave me half-an-hour. In half-an-hour they will come and take you away from me – take you where I can't come to you – with all my love I can't come to you! I know the place – I saw it once. A great lonely place full of graves, and little stunted trees dripping with dirty London rain… and gas-lamps flaring all round… but quite, quite dark where the grave is… a long grey stone just like the rest. How could you stay there? – all alone – all alone – without me?

'Do you remember, Edward, what we once said – that whichever of us died first should come back to watch over the other, in the spirit? I promised you, and you promised me. What children we were! Death is not what we thought. It comforted us to say that then.

'Now, it's nothing – nothing – worse than nothing – don't want your spirit – I can't see it – or feel it – I want you, you, your eyes that looked at me, your mouth that kissed me—'

She raised his arms and clasped them round her neck, and lay there very still, murmuring, 'Oh, hold me, hold me! Love me if you can. Am I hateful? This is me! These are your arms…

The doctor in the next room moved in his chair. The noise awoke her from her dream of contentment, and she unwound the dead arm from her neck, and, holding it up by the wrist, considered it ruefully.

'Yes, I can put it round me, but I have to hold it there. It is quite cold – it doesn't care. Ah, my dear, you don't care! You are dead. I kiss you, but you don't kiss me. Edward! Edward! Oh, for heaven's sake kiss me once. Just once!

'No, no, that won't do – that's not enough! that's nothing! worse than nothing! I want you back, you, all you… What shall I do?… I often pray… Oh, if there be a God in heaven, and if He ever answered a prayer, let Him answer mine – my only prayer. I'll never ask another – and give you back to me! As you were – as I loved you – as I adored you! He must listen. He must!

'My God, my God, he's mine – he's my husband, he's my lover – give him back to me!'

'Left alone for half-an-hour or more with the corpse! It's not right!'

The muttered expression of the nurse's revolted sense of professional decency came from the head of the staircase, where she had been waiting for the last few minutes. The doctor joined her.

'Hush, Mrs Joyce! I'll go to her now.'

The door creaked on its hinges as he gently pushed it open and went in.

'What's that? What's that?' screamed Mrs Arne. 'Doctor! Doctor! Don't touch me! Either I am dead or he is alive!'

'Do you want to kill yourself, Mrs Arne?' said Dr Graham, with calculated sternness, coming forward; 'come away!'

'Not dead! Not dead!' she murmured.

'He is dead, I assure you. Dead and cold an hour ago! Feel!' He took hold of her, as she lay face downwards, and in so doing he touched the dead man's cheek – it was not cold!

Instinctively his finger sought a pulse.

'Stop' Wait!' he cried in his intense excitement. 'My dear Mrs Arne, control yourself!'

But Mrs Arne had fainted, and fallen heavily off the bed on the other side. Her sister, hastily summoned, attended to her, while the man they had all given over for dead was, with faint gasps and sighs and reluctant moans, pulled, as it were, hustled and dragged back over the threshold of life.

Chapter II

'Why do you always wear black, Alice?' asked Esther Graham. 'You are not in mourning that I know of.'

She was Dr Graham's only daughter and Mrs Arne's only friend. She sat with Mrs Arne in the dreary drawing-room of the house in Chelsea. She had come to tea. She was the only person who ever did come to tea there.

She was brusque, kind, and blunt, and had a talent for making inappropriate remarks. Six years ago Mrs Arne had been a widow for an hour! Her husband had succumbed to an apparently modal illness, and for the space of an hour had lain dead. When suddenly and inexplicably he had revived from his trance, the shock, combined with six weeks' nursing, had nearly killed his wife. All this Esther had heard from her father. She herself had only come to know Mrs Arne after her child was born, and all the tragic circumstances of her husband's illness put aside, and it was hoped forgotten. And when her idle question received no answer from the pale absent woman who sat opposite, with listless lack-lustre eyes fixed on the green and blue flames dancing in the fire, she hoped it had passed unnoticed. She waited for five minutes for Mrs Arne to resume the conversation, then her natural impatience got the better of her.

'Do say something, Alice!' she implored.

'Esther, I beg your pardon!' said Mrs Arne. 'I was thinking.'

'What were you thinking of?'

'I don't know.'

'No, of course you don't. People who sit and stare into the fire never do think, really. They are only brooding and making themselves ill, and that is what you are doing. You mope, you take no interest in anything, you never go out – I am sure you have not been out of doors today?'

'No – yes – I believe not. It is so cold.'

'You are sure to feel the cold if you sit in the house all day, and sure to get ill! Just look at yourself!'

Mrs Arne rose and looked at herself in the Italian mirror over the chimney-piece. It reflected faithfully enough her even pallor, her dark hair and eyes, the sweeping length of her eyelashes, the sharp curves of her nostrils, and the delicate arch of her eyebrows, that formed a thin sharp black line, so clear as to seem almost unnatural.

'Yes, I do look ill,' she said with conviction.

'No wonder. You choose to bury yourself alive.'

'Sometimes I do feel as if I lived in a grave. I look up at the ceiling and fancy it is my coffin-lid.'

'Don't please talk like that!' expostulated Miss Graham, pointing to Mrs Arne's little girl. 'If only for Dolly's sake, I think you should not give way to such morbid fancies. It isn't good for her to see you like this always.'

'Oh, Esther,' the other exclaimed, stung into something like vivacity, 'don't reproach me! I hope I am a good mother to my child!'

'Yes, dear, you are a model mother – and model wife too. Father says the way you look after your husband is something wonderful, but don't you think for your own sake you might try to be a little gayer? You encourage these moods, don't you? What is it? Is it the house?'

She glanced around her – at the high ceiling, at the heavy damask portières, the tall cabinets of china, the dim oak panelling – it reminded her of a neglected museum. Her eye travelled into the farthest corners, where the faint filmy dusk was already gathering, lit only by the bewildering cross-lights of the glass panels of cabinet doors – to the tall narrow windows – then back again to the woman in her mourning dress, cowering by the fire. She said sharply – 'You should go out more.'

'I do not like to – leave my husband.'

'Oh, I know that he is delicate and all that, but still, does he never permit you to leave him? Does he never go out by himself?'

'Not often!'

'And you have no pets! It is very odd of you. I simply can't imagine a house without animals.'

'We did have a dog once,' answered Mrs Arne plaintively, 'but it howled so we had to give it away. It would not go near Edward… But please don't imagine that I am dull! I have my child.'

She laid her hand on the flaxen head at her knee.

Miss Graham rose, frowning.

'Ah, you are too bad!' she exclaimed. 'You are like a widow exactly, with one child, stroking its orphan head and saying, "Poor fatherless darling."'

Voices were heard outside. Miss Graham stopped talking quite suddenly, and sought her veil and gloves on the mantelpiece.

'You need not go, Esther,' said Mrs Arne. 'It is only my husband.'

'Oh, but it is getting late,' said the other, crumpling up her gloves in her muff, and shuffling her feet nervously.

'Come!' said her hostess, with a bitter smile, 'put your gloves on properly – if you must go – but it is quite early still.'

'Please don't go, Miss Graham,' put in the child.

'I must. Go and meet your papa, like a good girl.'

'I don't want to.'

'You mustn't talk like that, Dolly,' said the doctor's daughter absently, still looking towards the door. Mrs Arne rose and fastened the clasps of the big fur-cloak for her friend. The wife's white, sad, oppressed face came very close to the girl's cheerful one, as she murmured in a low voice – 'You don't like my husband, Esther? I can't help noticing it. Why don't you?'

'Nonsense!' retorted the other, with the emphasis of one who is repelling an overtrue accusation. 'I do, only—'

'Only what?'

'Well, dear, it is foolish of me, of course, but I am – a little afraid of him.'

'Afraid of Edward!' said his wife slowly. 'Why should you be?'

'Well, dear – you see – I – I suppose women can't help being a little afraid of their friends' husbands – they can spoil their friendships with their wives in a moment, if they choose to disapprove of them. I really must go! Goodbye, child; give me a kiss! Don't ring, Alice. Please don't! I can open the door for myself—'

'Why should you?' said Mrs Arne. 'Edward is in the hall; I heard him speaking to Foster.'

'No; he has gone into his study. Goodbye, you apathetic creature!' She gave Mrs Arne a brief kiss and dashed out of the room. The voices outside had ceased, and she had reasonable hopes of reaching the door without being intercepted by Mrs Arne's husband. But he met her on the stairs.

Mrs Arne, listening intently from her seat by the fire, heard her exchange a few shy sentences with him, the sound of which died away as they went downstairs together. A few moments after, Edward Arne came into the room and dropped into the chair just vacated by his wife's visitor.

He crossed his legs and said nothing. Neither did she.

His nearness had the effect of making the woman look at once several years older. Where she was pale he was well-coloured; the network of little filmy wrinkles that, on a close inspection, covered her face, had no parallel on his smooth skin. He was handsome; soft, well-groomed flakes of auburn hair lay over his forehead, and his steely blue eyes shone equably, a contrast to the sombre fire of hers, and the masses of dark crinkly hair that shaded her brow. The deep lines of permanent discontent furrowed that brow as she sat with her chin propped on her hands, and her elbows resting on her knees. Neither spoke. When the hands of the clock over Mrs Arne's head pointed to seven, the white-aproned figure of the nurse appeared in the doorway, and the little girl rose and kissed her mother very tenderly.

Mrs Arne's forehead contracted. Looking uneasily at her husband, she said to the child tentatively, yet boldly, as one grasps the nettle, 'Say good night to your father!'

The child obeyed, saying 'Good night' indifferently in her father's direction.

'Kiss him!'

'No, please – please not.'

Her mother looked down on her curiously, sadly.

'You are a naughty, spoilt child!' she said, but without conviction. 'Excuse her, Edward.'

He did not seem to have heard.

'Well, if you don't care—' said his wife bitterly. 'Come, child.' She caught the little girl by the hand and left the room.

At the door she half turned and looked fixedly at her husband. It was a strange ambiguous gaze; in it passion and dislike were strangely combined. Then she shivered and closed the door softly after her.

The man in the armchair sat with no perceptible change of attitude, his unspeculative eyes fixed on the fire, his hands clasped idly in front of him. The pose was obviously habitual. The servant brought lights and closed the shutters, drew the curtains, and made up the fire noisily, without, however, eliciting any reproof from his master.

Edward Arne was an ideal master, as far as Foster was concerned. He kept cases of cigars, but never smoked them, although the supply had often to be renewed. He did not care what he ate or drank, although he kept as good a cellar as most gentlemen – Foster knew that. He never interfered, he counted for nothing, he gave no trouble. Foster had no intention of ever leaving such an easy place. True, his master was not cordial; he very seldom addressed him or seemed to know whether he was there, but then neither did he grumble if the fire in the study was allowed to go out, or interfere with Foster's liberty in any way. He had a better place of it than Annette, Mrs Arne's maid, who would be called up in the middle of the night to bathe her mistress's forehead with eau-de-Cologne, or made to brush her long hair for hours together to soothe her.

Naturally enough Foster and Annette compared notes as to their respective situations, and drew unflattering parallels between this capricious wife and model husband.

Chapter III

Miss Graham was not a demonstrative woman. On her return home she somewhat startled her father, as he sat by his study table, deeply interested in his diagnosis book, by the sudden violence of her embrace.

'Why this excitement?' he asked, smiling and turning round. He was a young-looking man for his age; his thin wiry figure and clear colour belied the evidence of his hair, tinged with grey, and the tired wrinkles that gave value to the acuteness and brilliancy of the eyes they surrounded.

'I don't know!' she replied, 'only you are so nice and alive somehow. I always feel like this when I come back from seeing the Arnes.'

'Then don't go to see the Arnes.'

'I'm so fond of her, father, and she will never come here to me, as you know. Or else nothing would induce me to enter her tomb of a house, and talk to that walking funeral of a husband of hers. I managed to get away today without having to shake hands with him. I always try to avoid it. But, father, I do wish you would go and see Alice.'

'Is she ill?'

'Well, not exactly ill, I suppose, but her eyes make me quite uncomfortable, and she says such odd things! I don't know if it is you or the clergyman she wants, but she is all wrong somehow!

'She never goes out except to church; she never pays a call, or has any one to call on her! Nobody ever asks the Arnes to dinner, and I'm sure I don't blame them – the sight of that man at one's table would spoil any party – and they never entertain. She is always alone. Day after day I go in and find her sitting over the fire, with that same brooding expression. I shouldn't be surprised in the least if she were to go mad some day. Father, what is it? What is the tragedy of the house?

'There is one, I am convinced. And yet, though I have been the intimate friend of that woman for years, I know no more about her than the man in the street.'

'She keeps her skeleton safe in the cupboard,' said Dr Graham. 'I respect her for that. And please don't talk nonsense about tragedies. Alice Arne is only morbid – the malady of the age. And she is a very religious woman.'

'I wonder if she complains of her odious husband to Mr Bligh. She is always going to his services.'

'Odious?'

'Yes, odious.' Miss Graham shuddered. 'I cannot stand him! I cannot bear the touch of his cold froggy hands, and the sight of his fishy eyes! That inane smile of his simply makes me shrivel up. Father, honestly, do you like him yourself?'

'My dear, I hardly know him! It is his wife I have known ever since she was a child, and I a boy at college. Her father was my tutor. I never knew her husband till six years ago, when she called me in to attend him in a very serious illness. I suppose she never speaks of it? No? A very odd affair. For the life of me I cannot tell how he managed to recover. You needn't tell people, for it affects my reputation, but I didn't save him! Indeed I have never been able to account for it. The man was given over for dead!'

'He might as well be dead for all the good he is,' said Esther scornfully. 'I have never heard him say more than a couple of sentences in my life.'

'Yet he was an exceedingly brilliant young man; one of the best men of his year at Oxford – a good deal run after – poor Alice was wild to marry him!'

'In love with that spiritless creature? He is like a house with someone dead in it, and all the blinds down!'

'Come, Esther, don't be morbid – not to say silly! You are very hard on the poor man! What's wrong with him? He is the ordinary, common-place, cold-blooded specimen of humanity, a little stupid, a little selfish – people who have gone through a serious illness like that are apt to be – but on the whole, a good husband, a good father, a good citizen—'

'Yes, and his wife is afraid of him, and his child hates him!' exclaimed Esther.

'Nonsense!' said Dr Graham sharply. 'The child is spoilt. Only children are apt to be – and the mother wants a change or a tonic of some kind. I'll go and talk to her when I have time. Go along and dress. Have you forgotten that George Graham is coming to dinner?'

After she had gone the doctor made a note on the corner of his blotting-pad, 'Mem.: to go and see Mrs Arne,' and dismissed the subject of the memorandum entirely from his mind.

George Graham was the doctor's nephew, a tall, weedy, cumbrous young man, full of fads and fallacies, with a gentle manner that somehow inspired confidence. He was several years younger than Esther, who loved to listen to his semi-scientific, semi-romantic stories of things met with in the course of his profession. 'Oh, I come across very queer things!' he would say mysteriously.

'There's a queer little widow—!'

'Tell me about your little widow?' asked Esther that day after dinner, when, her father having gone back to his study, she and her cousin sat together as usual.

He laughed.

'You like to hear of my professional experiences? Well, she certainly interested me,' he said thoughtfully. 'She is an odd psychological study in her way. I wish I could come across her again.'

'Where did you come across her, and what is her name?'

'I don't know her name, I don't want to; she is not a personage to me, only a case. I hardly know her face even. I have never seen it except in the twilight. But I gathered that she lived somewhere in Chelsea, for she came out on to the Embankment with only a kind of lacy thing over her head; she can't live far off, I fancy.'

Esther became instantly attentive. 'Go on,' she said.

'It was three weeks ago,' said George Graham. 'I was coming along the Embankment about ten o'clock. I walked through that little grove, you know, just between Cheyne Walk and the river, and I heard in there someone sobbing very bitterly. I looked and saw a woman sitting on a seat, with her head in her hands, crying. I was most awfully sorry, of course, and I thought I could perhaps do something for her, get her a glass of water, or salts, or something. I took her for a woman of the people – it was quite dark, you know. So I asked her very politely if I could do anything for her, and then I noticed her hands – they were quite white and covered with diamonds.'

'You were sorry you spoke, I suppose,' said Esther.

'She raised her head and said – I believe she laughed – "Are you going to tell me to move on?"'

'She thought you were a policeman?'

'Probably – if she thought at all – but she was in a semi-dazed condition. I told her to wait till I came back, and dashed round the corner to the chemist's and bought a bottle of salts. She thanked me, and made a little effort to rise and go away. She seemed very weak. I told her I was a medical man, I started in and talked to her.'

'And she to you?'

'Yes, quite straight. Don't you know that women always treat a doctor as if he were one step removed from their father confessor – not human – not in the same category as themselves? It is not complimentary to one as a man, but one hears a good deal one would not otherwise hear. She ended by telling me all about herself – in a veiled way, of course. It soothed her – relieved her – she seemed not to have had an outlet for years!'

'To a mere stranger!'

'To a doctor. And she did not know what she was saying half the time. She was hysterical, of course. Heavens! what nonsense she talked! She spoke of herself as a person somehow haunted, cursed by some malign fate, a victim of some fearful spiritual catastrophe, don't you know? I let her run on. She was convinced of the reality of a sort of "doom" that she had fancied had befallen her. It was quite pathetic. Then it got rather chilly – she shivered – I suggested her going in. She shrank back; she said, "If you only knew what a relief it is, how much less miserable I am out here! I can breathe; I can live – it is my only glimpse of the world that is alive – I live in a grave – oh, let me stay!" She seemed positively afraid to go home.

'Perhaps someone bullied her at home.'

'I suppose so, but then – she had no husband. He died, she told me, years ago. She had adored him, she said—'

'Is she pretty?'

'Pretty! Well, I hardly noticed. Let me see! Oh, yes, I suppose she was pretty – no, now I think of it, she would be too worn and faded to be what you call pretty.'

Esther smiled.

'Well, we sat there together for quite an hour, then the clock of Chelsea church struck eleven, and she got up and said "Goodbye," holding out her hand quite naturally, as if our meeting and conversation had been nothing out of the common. There was a sound like a dead leaf trailing across the walk and she was gone.

'Didn't you ask if you should see her again?'

'That would have been a mean advantage to take.'

'You might have offered to see her home.'

'I saw she did not mean me to.'

'She was a lady, you say,' pondered Esther. 'How was she dressed?'

'Oh, all right, like a lady – in black – mourning, I suppose. She has dark crinkly hair, and her eyebrows are very thin and arched – I noticed that in the dusk.'

'Does this photograph remind you of her?' asked Esther suddenly, taking him to the mantelpiece.

'Rather!'

'Alice! Oh, it couldn't be – she is not a widow, her husband is alive – has your friend any children?'

'Yes, one, she mentioned it.'

'How old?'

'Six years old, I think she said. She talks of the "responsibility of bringing up an orphan".'

'George, what time is it?' Esther asked suddenly.

'About nine o'clock.'

'Would you mind coming out with me?'

'I should like it. Where shall we go?'

'To St Adhelm's! It is close by here. There is a special late service tonight, and Mrs Arne is sure to be there.'

'Oh, Esther – curiosity!'

'No, not mere curiosity. Don't you see if it is my Mrs Arne who talked to you like this, it is very serious? I have thought her ill for a long time; but as ill as that—'

At St Adhelm's Church, Esther Graham pointed out a woman who was kneeling beside a pillar in an attitude of intense devotion and abandonment. She rose from her knees, and turned her rapt face up towards the pulpit whence the Reverend Ralph Bligh was holding his impassioned discourse. George Graham touched his cousin on the shoulder, and motioned to her to leave her place on the outermost rank of worshippers.

'That is the woman!' said he.

Chapter IV

'Mem.: to go and see Mrs Arne.' The doctor came across this note in his blotting-pad one day six weeks later. His daughter was out of town. He had heard nothing of the Arnes since her departure. He had promised to go and see her. He was a little conscience-stricken. Yet another week elapsed before he found time to call upon the daughter of his old tutor.

At the corner of Tite Street he met Mrs Arne's husband, and stopped. A doctor's professional kindliness of manner is, or ought to be, independent of his personal likings and dislikings, and there was a pleasant cordiality about his greeting which should have provoked a corresponding fervour on the part of Edward Arne.

'How are you, Arne?' Graham said. 'I was on my way to call on your wife.'

'Ah – yes!' said Edward Arne, with the ascending inflection of polite acquiescence. A ray of blue from his eyes rested transitorily on the doctor's face, and in that short moment the latter noted its intolerable vacuity, and for the first time in his life he felt a sharp pang of sympathy for the wife of such a husband.

'I suppose you are off to your club? – er – good bye!' he wound up abruptly. With the best will in the world he somehow found it almost impossible to carry on a conversation with Edward Arne, who raised his hand to his hat-brim in token of salutation, smiled sweetly, and walked on.

'He really is extraordinarily good-looking,' reflected the doctor, as he watched him down the street and safely over the crossing with a certain degree of solicitude for which he could not exactly account. 'And yet one feels one's vitality ebbing out at the finger-ends as one talks to him. I shall begin to believe in Esther's absurd fancies about him soon. Ah, there's the little girl!' he exclaimed, as he turned into Cheyne Walk and caught sight of her with her nurse, making violent demonstrations to attract his attention. 'She is alive, at any rate. How is your mother, Dolly?' he asked.

'Quite well, thank you,' was the child's reply. She added, 'She's crying. She sent me away because I looked at her. So I did. Her cheeks are quite red.'

'Run away – run away and play!' said the doctor nervously. He ascended the steps of the house, and rang the bell very gently and neatly.

'Not at—' began Foster, with the intonation of polite falsehood, but stopped on seeing the doctor, who, with his daughter, was a privileged person. 'Mrs Arne will see you, Sir.'

'Mrs Arne is not alone?' he said interrogatively.

'Yes, Sir, quite alone. I have just taken tea in.'

Dr Graham's doubts were prompted by the low murmur as of a voice, or voices, which came to him through the open door of the room at the head of the stairs. He paused and listened while Foster stood by, merely remarking, 'Mrs Arne do talk to herself sometimes, Sir.'

It was Mrs Arne's voice – the doctor recognised it now. It was not the voice of a sane or healthy woman. He at once mentally removed his visit from the category of a morning call, and prepared for a semi-professional inquiry.

'Don't announce me,' he said to Foster, and quietly entered the back drawing-room, which was separated by a heavy tapestry portière from the room where Mrs Arne sat, with an open book on the table before her, from which she had been apparently reading aloud. Her hands were now clasped tightly over her face, and when, presently, she removed them and began feverishly to turn page after page of her book, the crimson of her cheeks was seamed with white where her fingers had impressed themselves.

The doctor wondered if she saw him, for though her eyes were fixed in his direction, there was no apprehension in them. She went on reading, and it was the text, mingled with passionate interjection and fragmentary utterances, of the Burial Service that met his ears.

'"For as in Adam all die!" All die! It says all! For he must reign… The last enemy that shall be destroyed is Death. What shall they do if the dead rise not at all!… I die daily…! Daily!

No, no, better get it over… dead and buried… out of sight, out of mind… under a stone. Dead men don't come back… Go on! Get it over. I want to hear the earth rattle on the coffin, and then I shall know it is done. "Flesh and blood cannot inherit!" Oh, what did I do? What have I done? Why did I wish it so fervently? Why did I pray for it so earnestly? God gave me my wish—'

'Alice! Alice!' groaned the doctor.

She looked up. '"When this corruptible shall have put on incorruption—" "Dust to dust, ashes to ashes, earth to earth—" Yes, that is it. "After death, though worms destroy this body—"'

She flung the book aside and sobbed.

'That is what I was afraid of. My God! My God! Down there – in the dark – for ever and ever and ever! I could not bear to think of it! My Edward! And so I interfered… and prayed… and prayed till… Oh! I am punished. Flesh and blood could not inherit! I kept him there – I would not let him go… I kept him… I prayed… I denied him Christian burial… Oh, how could I know.

'Good heavens, Alice!' said Graham, coming sensibly forward, 'what does this mean? I have heard of schoolgirls going through the marriage service by themselves, but the burial service—'

He laid down his hat and went on severely, 'What have you to do with such things? Your child is flourishing – your husband alive and here—'

'And who kept him here?' interrupted Alice Arne fiercely, accepting the fact of his appearance without comment.

'You did,' he answered quickly, 'with your care and tenderness. I believe the warmth of your body, as you lay beside him for that half-hour, maintained the vital heat during that extraordinary suspension of the heart's action, which made us all give him up for dead. You were his best doctor, and brought him back to us.'

'Yes, it was I – it was I – you need not tell me it was I!'

'Come, be thankful!' he said cheerfully. 'Put that book away, and give me some tea, I'm very cold.'

'Oh, Dr Graham, how thoughtless of me!' said Mrs Arne, rallying at the slight imputation on her politeness he had purposely made. She tottered to the bell and rang it before he could anticipate her.

'Another cup,' she said quite calmly to Foster, who answered it. Then she sat down quivering all over with the suddenness of the constraint put upon her.

'Yes, sit down and tell me all about it,' said Dr Graham good-humouredly, at the same time observing her with the closeness he gave to difficult cases.

'There is nothing to tell,' she said simply, shaking her head, and futilely altering the position of the tea-cups on the tray. 'It all happened years ago. Nothing can be done now. Will you have sugar?'

He drank his tea and made conversation. He talked to her of some Dante lectures she was attending; of some details connected with her child's Kindergarten classes. These subjects did not interest her. There was a subject she wished to discuss, he could see that a question trembled on her tongue, and tried to lead up to it.

She introduced it herself, quite quietly, over a second cup. 'Sugar, Dr Graham? I forget. Dr Graham, tell me, do you believe that prayers – wicked unreasonable prayers – are granted?'

He helped himself to another slice of bread and butter before answering.

'Well,' he said slowly, 'it seems hard to believe that every fool who has a voice to pray with, and a brain where to conceive idiotic requests with, should be permitted to interfere with the economy of the universe. As a rule, if people were long-sighted enough to see the result of their petitions, I fancy very few of us would venture to interfere.'

Mrs Arne groaned.

She was a good Churchwoman, Graham knew, and he did not wish to sap her faith in any way, so he said no more, but inwardly wondered if a too rigid interpretation of some of the religious dogmas of the Vicar of St Adhelm's, her spiritual adviser, was not the clue to her distress. Then she put another question – 'Eh! What?' he said. 'Do I believe in ghosts? I will believe you if you will tell me you have seen one.

'You know, Doctor,' she went on, 'I was always afraid of ghosts – of spirits – things unseen. I couldn't ever read about them. I could not bear the idea of someone in the room with me that I could not see. There was a text that always frightened me that hung up in my room: "Thou, God, seest me!" It frightened me when I was a child, whether I had been doing wrong or not. But now,' shuddering, 'I think there are worse things than ghosts.'

'Well, now, what sort of things?' he asked good-humouredly. 'Astral bodies—?'

She leaned forward and laid her hot hand on his.

'Oh, Doctor, tell me, if a spirit – without the body we know it by – is terrible, what of a body' – her voice sank to a whisper, 'a body – senseless – lonely – stranded on this earth – without a spirit?'

She was watching his face anxiously. He was divided between a morbid inclination to laugh and the feeling of intense discomfort provoked by this wretched scene. He longed to give the conversation a more cheerful turn, yet did not wish to offend her by changing it too abruptly.

'I have heard of people not being able to keep body and soul together,' he replied at last, 'but I am not aware that practically such a division of forces has ever been achieved. And if we could only accept the theory of the de-spiritualised body, what a number of antipathetic people now wandering about in the world it would account for!'

The piteous gaze of her eyes seemed to seek to ward off the blow of his misplaced jocularity.

He left his seat and sat down on the couch beside her.

'Poor child! poor girl! you are ill, you are over-excited. What is it? Tell me,' he asked her as tenderly as the father she had lost in early life might have done. Her head sank on his shoulder.

'Are you unhappy?' he asked her gently.

'Yes!'

'You are too much alone. Get your mother or your sister to come and stay with you.'

'They won't come,' she wailed. 'They say the house is like a grave. Edward has made himself a study in the basement. It's an impossible room – but he has moved all his things in, and I can't – I won't go to him there…'

'You're wrong. For it's only a fad,' said Graham, 'he'll tire of it. And you must see more people somehow. It's a pity my daughter is away. Had you any visitors today?'

'Not a soul has crossed the threshold for eighteen days.'

'We must change all that,' said the doctor vaguely. 'Meantime you must cheer up. Why, you have no need to think of ghosts and graves – no need to be melancholy – you have your husband and your child—'

'I have my child – yes.'

The doctor took hold of Mrs Arne by the shoulder and held her a little away from him. He thought he had found the cause of her trouble – a more commonplace one than he had supposed.

'I have known you, Alice, since you were a child,' he said gravely. 'Answer me! You love your husband, don't you?'

'Yes.' It was as if she were answering futile prefatory questions in the witness-box. Yet he saw by the intense excitement in her eyes that he had come to the point she feared, and yet desired to bring forward.

'And he loves you?'

She was silent.

'Well, then, if you love each other, what more can you want? Why do you say you have only your child in that absurd way?'

She was still silent, and he gave her a little shake.

'Tell me, have you and he had any difference lately? Is there any – coldness – any – temporary estrangement between you?'

He was hardly prepared for the burst of foolish laughter that proceeded from the demure Mrs Arne as she rose and confronted him, all the blood in her body seeming for the moment to rush to her usually pale cheeks.

'Coldness! Temporary estrangement! If that were all. Oh, is everyone blind but me? There is all the world between us! – all the difference between this world and the next!' She sat down again beside the doctor and whispered in his ear, and her words were like a breath of hot wind from some Gehenna of the soul.

'Oh, Doctor, I have borne it for six years, and I must speak. No other woman could bear what I have borne, and yet be alive! And I loved him so; you don't know how I loved him! That was it – that was my crime—'

'Crime?' repeated the doctor.

'Yes, crime! It was impious, don't you see? But I have been punished. Oh, Doctor, you don't know what my life is! Listen! Listen! I must tell you. To live with a – At first before I guessed when I used to put my arms round him, and he merely submitted – and then it dawned on me what I was kissing! It is enough to turn a living woman into stone – for I am living, though sometimes I forget it. Yes, I am a live woman, though I live in a grave. Think what it is! – to wonder every night if you will be alive in the morning, to lie down every night in an open grave – to smell death in every corner – every room – to breathe death – to touch it…'

The portière in front of the door shook, a hoopstick parted it, a round white clad bundle supported on a pair of mottled red legs peeped in, pushing a hoop in front of her. The child made no noise. Mrs Arne seemed to have heard her, however. She slewed round violently as she sat on the sofa beside Dr Graham, leaving her hot hands clasped in his.

'You ask Dolly,' she exclaimed. 'She knows it, too – she feels it.'

'No, no, Alice, this won't do!' the doctor adjured her very low. Then he raised his voice and ordered the child from the room. He had managed to lift Mrs Arne's feet and laid her full length on the sofa by the time the maid reappeared. She had fainted.

He pulled down her eyelids and satisfied himself as to certain facts he had up till now dimly apprehended. When Mrs Arne's maid returned, he gave her mistress over to her care and proceeded to Edward Arne's new study in the basement.

'Morphia!' he muttered to himself, as he stumbled and faltered through gaslit passages, where furtive servants eyed him and scuttled to their burrows.

'What is he burying himself down here for?' he thought. 'Is it to get out of her way? They are a nervous pair of them!'

Arne was sunk in a large armchair drawn up before the fire. There was no other light, except a faint reflection from the gas-lamp in the road, striking down past the iron bars of the window that was sunk below the level of the street. The room was comfortless and empty, there was little furniture in it except a large bookcase at Arne's right hand and a table with a Tantalus on it standing some way off. There was a faded portrait in pastel of Alice Arne over the mantelpiece, and beside it, a poor pendant, a pen and ink sketch of the master of the house. They were quite discrepant, in size and medium, but they appeared to look at each other with the stolid attentiveness of newly married people.

'Seedy, Arne?' Graham said.

'Rather, today. Poke the fire for me, will you?'

'I've known you quite seven years,' said the doctor cheerfully, 'so I presume I can do that…

'There, now!...And I'll presume further – What have we got here?'

He took a small bottle smartly out of Edward Arne's fingers and raised his eyebrows. Edward Arne had rendered it up agreeably; he did not seem upset or annoyed.

'Morphia. It isn't a habit. I only got hold of the stuff yesterday – found it about the house.

'Alice was very jumpy all day, and communicated her nerves to me, I suppose. I've none as a rule, but do you know, Graham, I seem to be getting them – feel things a good deal more than I did, and want to talk about them.'

'What, are you growing a soul?' said the doctor carelessly, lighting a cigarette.

'Heaven forbid!' Arne answered equably. 'I've done very well without it all these years. But I'm fond of old Alice, you know, in my own way. When I was a young man, I was quite different. I took things hardly and got excited about them. Yes, excited. I was wild about Alice, wild! Yes, by Jove! though she has forgotten all about it.'

'Not that, but still it's natural she should long for some little demonstration of affection now and then… and she'd be awfully distressed if she saw you fooling with a bottle of morphia!

'You know, Arne, after that narrow squeak you had of it six years ago, Alice and I have a good right to consider that your life belongs to us!'

Edward Arne settled in his chair and replied, rather fretfully – 'All very well, but you didn't manage to do the job thoroughly. You didn't turn me out lively enough to please Alice. She's annoyed because when I take her in my arms, I don't hold her tight enough. I'm too quiet, too languid!... Hang it all, Graham, I believe she'd like me to stand for Parliament!… Why can't she let me just go along my own way? Surely a man who's come through an illness like mine can be let off parlour tricks? All this worry – it culminated the other day when I said I wanted to colonise a room down here, and did, with a spurt that took it out of me horribly, – all this worry, I say, seeing her upset and so on, keeps me low, and so I feel as if I wanted to take drugs to soothe me.'

'Soothe!' said Graham. 'This stuff is more than soothing if you take enough of it. I'll send you something more like what you want, and I'll take this away, by your leave.'

'I really can't argue!' replied Arne...' If you see Alice, tell her you find me fairly comfortable and don't put her off this room. I really like it best. She can come and see me here, I keep a good fire, tell her... I feel as if I wanted to sleep...' he added brusquely.

You have been indulging already,' said Graham softly. Arne had begun to doze off. His cushion had sagged down, the doctor stooped to rearrange it, carelessly laying the little phial for the moment in a crease of the rug covering the man's knees.

Mrs Arne in her mourning dress was crossing the hall as he came to the top of the basement steps and pushed open the swing door. She was giving some orders to Foster, the butler, who disappeared as the doctor advanced.

'You're about again,' he said, 'good girl!'

'Too silly of me,' she said, 'to be hysterical! After all these years! One should be able to keep one's own counsel. But it is over now, I promise I will never speak of it again.'

'We frightened poor Dolly dreadfully. I had to order her out like a regiment of soldiers.'

'Yes, I know. I'm going to her now.'

On his suggestion that she should look in on her husband first she looked askance.

'Down there!'

'Yes, that's his fancy. Let him be. He is a good deal depressed about himself and you. He notices a great deal more than you think. He isn't quite as apathetic as you describe him to be...

'Come here!' He led her into the unlit dining-room a little way. 'You expect too much, my dear. You do really! You make too many demands on the vitality you saved.'

'What did one save him for?' she asked fiercely. She continued more quietly, 'I know. I am going to be different.'

'Not you,' said Graham fondly. He was very partial to Alice Arne in spite of her silliness.

'You'll worry about Edward till the end of the chapter. I know you. And' – he turned her round by the shoulder so that she fronted the light in the hall – 'you elusive thing, let me have a good look at you... Hum! Your eyes, they're a bit starey...'

He let her go again with a sigh of impotence. Something must be done...

soon... he must think... He got hold of his coat and began to get into it Mrs Arne smiled, buttoned a button for him and then opened the front door, like a good hostess, a very little way. With a quick flirt of his hat he was gone, and she heard the clap of his brougham door and the order 'Home'.

'Been saying goodbye to that thief Graham?' said her husband gently, when she entered his room, her pale eyes staring a little, her thin hand busy at the front of her dress.

'Thief? Why? One moment! Where's your switch?'

She found it and turned on a blaze of light from which her husband seemed to shrink.

'Well, he carried off my drops. Afraid of my poisoning myself, I suppose?'

'Or acquiring the morphia habit,' said his wife in a dull level voice, 'as I have.'

She paused. He made no comment. Then, picking up the little phial Dr Graham had left in the crease of the rug, she spoke – 'You are the thief, Edward, as it happens, this is mine.'

'Is it? I found it knocking about: I didn't know it was yours. Well, will you give me some?'

'I will, if you like.'

'Well, dear, decide. You know I am in your hands and Graham's. He was rubbing that into me today.'

'Poor lamb!' she said derisively; 'I'd not allow my doctor, or my wife either, to dictate to me whether I should put an end to myself, or not.'

'Ah, but you've got a spirit, you see!' Arne yawned. 'However, let me have a go at the stuff and then you put it on top of the wardrobe or a shelf, where I shall know it is, but never reach out to get it, I promise you.'

'No, you wouldn't reach out a hand to keep yourself alive, let alone kill yourself,' said she. 'That is you all over, Edward.'

'And don't you see that is why I did die,' he said, with earnestness unexpected by her. 'And then, unfortunately, you and Graham bustled up and wouldn't let Nature take its course... I rather wish you hadn't been so officious.'

'And let you stay dead,' said she carelessly. 'But at the time I cared for you so much that I should have had to kill myself, or commit suttee like a Bengali widow. Ah, well!'

She reached out for a glass half-full of water that stood on the low ledge of a bookcase close by the arm of his chair… 'Will this glass do? What's in it? Only water? How much morphia shall I give you? An overdose?'

'I don't care if you do, and that's a fact.'

'It was a joke, Edward,' she said piteously.

'No joke to me. This fag end of life I've clawed hold of, doesn't interest me. And I'm bound to be interested in what I'm doing or I'm no good. I'm no earthly good now. I don't enjoy life, I've nothing to enjoy it with – in here—' he struck his breast. 'It's like a dull party one goes to by accident. All I want to do is to get into a cab and go home.'

His wife stood over him with the half-full glass in one hand and the little bottle in the other.

Her eyes dilated… her chest heaved.

'Edward!' she breathed. 'Was it all so useless?'

'Was what useless? Yes, as I was telling you, I go as one in a dream – a bad, bad dream, like the dreams I used to have when I overworked at college. I was brilliant, Alice, brilliant, do you hear? At some cost, I expect! Now I hate people – my fellow creatures. I've left them. They come and go, jostling me, and pushing me, on the pavements as I go along, avoiding them. Do you know where they should be, really, in relation to me?'

He rose a little in his seat – she stepped nervously aside, made as if to put down the bottle and the glass she was holding, then thought better of it and continued to extend them mechanically.

'They should be over my head. I've already left them and their petty nonsense of living. They mean nothing to me, no more than if they were ghosts walking. Or perhaps, it's I who am a ghost to them?… You don't understand it. It's because I suppose you have no imagination. You just know what you want and do your best to get it. You blurt out your blessed petition to your Deity and the idea that you're irrelevant never enters your head, soft, persistent, High Church thing that you are!…'

Alice Arne smiled, and balanced the objects she was holding. He motioned her to pour out the liquid from one to the other, but she took no heed; she was listening with all her ears. It was the nearest approach to the language of compliment, to anything in the way of loverlike personalities that she had heard fall from his lips since his illness. He went on, becoming as it were lukewarm to his subject – 'But the worst of it is that once break the cord that links you to humanity – it can't be mended.

Man doesn't live by bread alone… or lives to disappoint you. What am I to you, without my own poor personality?… Don't stare so, Alice! I haven't talked so much or so intimately for ages, have I? Let me try and have it out… Are you in any sort of hurry?'

'No, Edward.'

'Pour that stuff out and have done… Well, Alice, it's a queer feeling, I tell you. One goes about with one's looks on the ground, like a man who eyes the bed he is going to lie down in, and longs for. Alice, the crust of the earth seems a barrier between me and my own place. I want to scratch the boardings with my nails and shriek something like this: "Let me get down to you all, there where I belong!" It's a horrible sensation, like a vampire reversed!…'

'Is that why you insisted on having this room in the basement?' she asked breathlessly.

'Yes, I can't bear being upstairs, somehow. Here, with these barred windows and stone-cold floors… I can see the people's feet walking above there in the street… one has some sort of illusion…'

'Oh!' She shivered and her eyes travelled like those of a caged creature round the bare room and fluttered when they rested on the sombre windows imperiously barred. She dropped her gaze to the stone flags that showed beyond the oasis of Turkey carpet on which Arne's chair stood…

Then to the door, the door that she had closed on entering. It had heavy bolts, but they were not drawn against her, though by the look of her eyes it seemed she half imagined they were…

She made a step forward and moved her hands slightly. She looked down on them and what they held… then changed the relative positions of the two objects and held the bottle over the glass…

'Yes, come along!' her husband said. 'Are you going to be all day giving it me?'

With a jerk, she poured the liquid out into a glass and handed it to him. She looked away – towards the door…

'Ah, your way of escape!' said he, following her eyes. Then he drank, painstakingly.

The empty bottle fell out of her hands. She wrung them, murmuring – 'Oh, if I had only known!'

'Known what? That I should go near to cursing you for bringing me back?'

He fixed his cold eyes on her, as the liquid passed slowly over his tongue.

' – Or that you would end by taking back the gift you gave?'

No. 1 Branch Line: The Signalman

Charles Dickens

'Halloa! Below there!'

When he heard a voice thus calling to him, he was standing at the door of his box, with a flag in his hand, furled round its short pole. One would have thought, considering the nature of the ground, that he could not have doubted from what quarter the voice came; but instead of looking up to where I stood on the top of the steep cutting nearly over his head, he turned himself about, and looked down the Line. There was something remarkable in his manner of doing so, though I could not have said for my life what. But I know it was remarkable enough to attract my notice, even though his figure was foreshortened and shadowed, down to the deep trench, and mine was high above him, so steeped in the glow of an angry sunset, that I had shaded my eyes with my hand before I saw him at all.

'Hallow! Bellow!'

From looking down the Line, he turned himself about again, and, raising his eyes, saw my figure high above him.

'Is there any path by which I can come down and speak to you?'

He looked up at me without replying, and I looked down at him without pressing him too soon with a repetition of my idle question. Just then there came a vague vibration in the earth and air, quickly changing into a violent pulsation, and an oncoming rush that caused me to start back, as though it had force to draw me down. When such vapour as rose to my height from this rapid train had passed me, and was skimming away over the landscape, I looked down again, and saw him refurling the flag he had shown while the train went by.

I repeated my inquiry. After a pause, during which he seemed to regard me with fixed attention, he motioned with his rolled-up flag towards a point on my level, some two or three hundred yards distant. I called down to him, 'All right!' and made for that point. There, by dint of looking closely about me, I found a rough zigzag descending path notched out, which I followed.

The cutting was extremely deep, and unusually precipitate. It was made through a clammy stone, that became oozier and wetter as I went down. For these reasons, I found the way long enough to give me time to recall a singular aid of reluctance or compulsion with which he had pointed out the path.

When I came down low enough upon the zigzag descent to see him again, I saw that he was standing between the rails on the way by which the train had lately passed, in an attitude as if he were waiting for me to appear. He had his left hand at his chin, and that left elbow rested on his right hand, crossed over his breast. His attitude was one of such expectation and watchfulness that I stopped a moment, wondering at it.

I resumed my downward way, and stepping out upon the level of the railroad, and drawing nearer to him, saw that he was a dark sallow man, with a dark beard and rather heavy eyebrows. His post was in as solitary and dismal a place as ever I saw. On either side, a dripping-wet wall of jagged stone, excluding all view but a strip of sky; the perspective one way only a crooked prolongation of this great dungeon; the shorter perspective in the other direction terminating in a gloomy red light, and the gloomier entrance to a black tunnel, in whose massive architecture there was a barbarous, depressing, and forbidding air. So little sunlight ever found its way to this spot, that it had an earthy, deadly smell; and so much cold wind rushed through it, that it struck chill to me, as if I had left the natural world.

Before he stirred, I was near enough to him to have touched him. Not even then removing his eyes from mine, he stepped back one step, and lifted his hand.

This was a lonesome post to occupy (I said), and it had riveted my attention when I looked down from up yonder. A visitor was a rarity, I should suppose; not an unwelcome rarity, I hoped? In me, he merely saw a man, who had been shut up within narrow limits all his life, and who, being at last set free, had a newly-awakened interest in these great works. To such purpose I spoke to him; but I am far from sure of the terms I used; for, besides that I am not happy in opening any conversation, there was something in the man that daunted me.

He directed a most curious look towards the red light near the tunnel's mouth, and looked all about it, as if something were missing from it, and then he looked at me.

That light was part of his charge? Was it not?

He answered in a low voice, – 'Don't you know it is?'

The monstrous thought came into my mind, as I perused the fixed eyes and the saturnine face, that this was a spirit not a man. I have speculated since, whether there may not have been infection in his mind.

In my turn, I stepped back. But in making the action, I detected in his eyes some latent fear of me. This put the monstrous thought to flight. 'You look at me,' I said, forcing a smile, 'as if you had a dread of me.'

'I was doubtful,' he returned, 'whether I had seen you before.'

'Where?'

He pointed to the red light he had looked at.

'There?' I said.

Intently watchful of me, he replied (but without sound), 'Yes.'

'My good fellow, what should I do there? However, be that as it may, I never was there, you may swear.'

'I think I may,' he rejoined. 'Yes; I am sure I may.'

His manner cleared, like my own. He replied to my remarks with readiness, and in well-chosen words. Had he much to do there? Yes; that was to say, he had enough responsibility to bear; but exactness and watchfulness were what was required of him, and of actual work – manual labour – he had next to none. To change that signal, to trim those lights, and to turn this iron handle now and then, was all he had to do under that head. Regarding those many long and lonely hours of which I seemed to make so much, he could only say that the routine of his life had shaped itself into that form, and he had grown used to it. He had taught himself a language down here, – if only to know it by sight, and to have formed his own crude ideas of its pronunciation, could be called learning it. He had also worked at fractions and decimals, and tried a little algebra; but he was, and had been as a boy, a poor hand at figures. Was it necessary for him when on duty always to remain in that channel of damp air, and could he never rise into the sunshine from between those high stone walls? Why, that depended upon times and circumstances. Under some conditions there would be less upon the Line than under others, and the same held good as to certain hours of the day and night. In bright weather, he did choose occasions for getting a little above these lower shadows; but, being at all times liable to be called by his electric bell, and at such times listening for it with redoubled anxiety, the relief was less than I would suppose.

He took me into his box, where there was a fire, a desk for an official book in which he had to make certain entries, a telegraphic instrument with its dial, face, and needles, and the little bell of which he had spoken. On my trusting that he would excuse the remark that he had been well educated, and (I hoped I might say without offence), perhaps educated above the station, he observed that instances of slight incongruity in such wise would rarely be found wanting among large bodies of men; that he had heard it was so in workhouses, in the police force, even in that last desperate resource, the army; and that he knew it was so, more or less, in any great railway staff. He had been, when young (if I could believe it, sitting in that hut, – he scarcely could), a student of natural philosophy, and had attended lectures; but he had run wild, misused his opportunities, gone down, and never risen again. He had no complaint to offer about that. He had made his bed, and he lay upon it. It was far too late to make another.

All that I have here condensed he said in a quiet manner, with his grave dark regards divided between me and the fire. He threw in the word, 'Sir,' from time to time, and especially when he referred to his youth – as though to request me to understand that he claimed to be nothing but what I found him. He was several times interrupted by the little bell, and had to read off messages, and send replies. Once he had to stand without the door, and display a flag as a train passed, and make some verbal communication to the driver. In the discharge of his duties, I observed him to be remarkably exact and vigilant, breaking off his discourse at a syllable, and remaining silent until what he had to do was done.

In a word, I should have set this man down as one of the safest of men to be employed in that capacity, but for the circumstance that while he was speaking to me he twice broke off with a fallen colour, turned his face towards the little bell when it did NOT ring, opened the door of the hut (which was kept shut to exclude the unhealthy damp), and looked out towards the red light near the mouth of the tunnel. On both of those occasions, he came back to the fire with the inexplicable air upon him which I had remarked, without being able to define, when we were so far asunder.

Said I, when I rose to leave, 'You almost make me think that I have met with a contented man.'

(I am afraid I must acknowledge that I said it to lead him on.)

'I believe I used to be so,' he rejoined, in the low voice in which he had first spoken; 'but I am troubled, Sir, I am troubled.'

He would have recalled the words if he could. He had said them, however, and I took them up quickly.

'With what? What is your trouble?'

'It is very difficult to impart, Sir. It is very, very difficult to speak of. If ever you make me another visit, I will try to tell you.'

'But I expressly intend to make you another visit. Say, when shall it be?'

'I go off early in the morning and I shall be on again at ten tomorrow night, Sir.'

'I will come at eleven.'

He thanked me, and went out at the door with me. 'I'll show my white light, Sir,' he said, in his peculiar low voice, 'till you have found the way up. When you have found it, don't call out! And when you are at the top, don't call out!'

His manner seemed to make the place strike colder to me, but I said no more than, 'Very well.'

'And when you come down tomorrow night, don't call out! Let me ask you a parting question. What made you cry, "Halloa! Below there!" tonight?"

'Heavens knows,' said I. 'I cried something to that effect …'

'Not to that effect, Sir. Those were the very words. I know them well.'

'I admit those were the very words. I said them no doubt, because I saw you below.'

'For no other reason?'

'What other reason could I possibly have?'

'You had no feeling that they were conveyed to you in any supernatural way?'

'No.'

He wished me good night, and held up his light. I walked by the side of the down Line of rails (with a very disagreeable sensation of a train coming behind me) until I found the path. It was easier to mount than to descend, and I got back to my inn without any adventure.

Punctual to my appointment, I placed my foot on the first notch of the zigzag next night, as the distant clocks were striking eleven. He was waiting for me at the bottom, with his white light on. 'I have not called out,' I said, when we came close together; 'may I speak now?'

'By all means, Sir.'

'Goodnight, then, and here's my hand.'

'Goodnight, Sir, and here's mine.' With that we walked side by side to his box, entered it, closed the door, and sat down by the fire.

'I have made up my mind, Sir,' he began, bending forward as soon as we were seated, and speaking in a tone but a little above a whisper, 'that you shall not have to ask me twice what troubles me. I took you for someone else yesterday evening. That troubles me.'

'That mistake?'

'No. That someone else.'

'Who is it?'

'I don't know.'

'Like me?'

'I don't know. I never saw the face. The left arm is across the face and the right arm is waved – violently waved. This way.'

I followed his action with my eyes, and it was the action of an arm gesticulating with the utmost passion and vehemence, 'For God's sake, clear the way!'

'One moonlight night,' said the man, 'I was sitting here, when I heard a voice cry, "Halloa! Below there!" I started up, looked from that door, and saw this Someone else standing by the red light near the tunnel, waving as I just now showed you. The voice seemed hoarse with shouting, and it cried, "Look out! Look out!" And then again, "Halloa! Below there! Look out!" I caught up my lamp, turned it on red, and ran towards the figure, calling "What's wrong? What has happened? Where?" It stood just outside the blackness of the tunnel. I advanced so close upon it that I wondered at its keeping the sleeve across its eyes. I ran right up at it, and had my hand stretched out to pull the sleeve away, when it was gone.'

'Into the tunnel?' said I.

'No. I ran on into the tunnel, five hundred yards. I stopped, and held my lamp above my head, and saw the figures of the measured distance, and saw the wet stains stealing down the walls and trickling through the arch. I ran out again faster than I had run in (for I had a mortal abhorrence of the place upon me), and I looked all round the red light with my own red light, and I went up the iron ladder to the gallery atop of it, and I came down again, and ran back here. I telegraphed both ways. "An alarm has been given. Is anything wrong?" The answer came back, both ways, "All well."'

Resisting the slow touch of a frozen finger tracing out my spine, I showed him how that this figure must be a deception of his sense of sight; and how that figures, originating in disease of the delicate nerves that minister to the functions of the eye, were known to have become conscious of the nature of their affliction, and had even proved it by experimenting upon themselves. 'As to an imaginary cry,' said I, 'do but listen for a moment to the wind in this unnatural valley while we speak so low, and to the wild harp it makes of the telegraph wires.'

That was all very well, he returned, after we had sat listening for a while, and he ought to know something of the wind and the wires, – he who so often passed long winter nights there, alone and watching. But he would beg to remark that he had not finished.

I asked his pardon, and he slowly added these words, touching my arm,—

'Within six hours after the Appearance, the memorable accident on this Line happened, and within ten hours the dead and wounded were brought along through the tunnel over the spot where the figure had stood.'

A disagreeable shudder crept over me, but I did my best against it. It was not to be denied, I rejoined, that this was a remarkable coincidence, calculated deeply to impress his mind. But it was unquestionable that remarkable coincidence did continually occur, and they must be taken into account in dealing with such a subject. Though to be sure I must admit, I added (for I thought I saw that he was going to bring the objection to bear upon me), men of common sense did not allow much for coincidences in making the ordinary calculations of life.

He again begged to remark that he had not finished.

I again begged his pardon for being betrayed into interruptions.

'This,' he said, again laying his hand upon my arm, and glancing over his shoulder with hollow eyes, 'was just a year ago. Six or seven months passed, and I had recovered from the surprise and shock, when one morning, as the day was breaking, I, standing at the door, looked towards the red light, and saw the spectre again.' He stopped, with a fixed look at me.

'Did it cry out?'

'No. It was silent.'

'Did it wave its arm?'

'No. It leaned against the shaft of light, with both hands before the face. Like this.'

Once more I followed his action with my eyes. It was an action of mourning. I have seen such an attitude in stone figures on tombs.

'Did you go up to it?'

'I came in and sat down, partly to collect my thoughts, partly because it had turned me faint. When I went to the door again, daylight was above me, and the ghost was gone.'

'But nothing followed? Nothing came of this?'

He touched me on the arm with his forefinger twice or thrice, giving a ghastly nod each time:

'That very day, as a train came out of the tunnel, I noticed, at a carriage window on my side, what looked like a confusion of hands and heads, and something waved. I saw it just in time to signal the driver, Stop! He shut off, and put his brake on, but the train drifted past here a hundred and fifty yards or more. I ran after it, and, as I went along, heard terrible screams and cries. A beautiful young lady had died instantaneously in one of the compartments, and was brought in here, and laid down on this floor between us.'

Involuntarily I pushed my chair back, as I looked from the boards at which he pointed to himself.

'True, Sir. True. Precisely as it happened, so I tell it you.'

I could think of nothing to say, to any purpose, and my mouth was very dry. The wind and wires took up the story with a long lamenting wail.

He resumed. 'Now, Sir, mark this, and judge how my mind is troubled. The spectre came back a week ago. Ever since, it has been there, now and again, by fits and starts.'

'At the light?'

'At the Danger-light.'

'What does it seem to do?'

He repeated, if possible with increased passion and vehemence, that former gesticulation of 'For God's sake, clear the way!'

Then he went on. 'I have no peace or rest for it. It calls to me, for many minutes together, in an agonised manner, "Below there! Look out!" It stands waving to me. It rings my little bell …'

I caught at that. 'Did it ring your bell yesterday evening when I was here, and you went to the door?'

'Twice.'

'Why, see,' said I, 'how your imagination misleads you. My eyes were on the bell, and my ears open to the bell, and if I am a living man, it did NOT ring at those times. No, nor at any other time, except when it was rung in the natural course of physical things by the station communicating with you.'

He shook his head. 'I have never made a mistake as to that yet, Sir. I have never confused the spectre's ring with the man's. The ghost's ring is a strange vibration in the bell that it derives from nothing else, and I have not asserted that the bell stirs to the eye. I don't wonder that you failed to hear it. But I heard it.'

'And did the spectre seem to be there, when you looked out?'

'It WAS there.'

'Both times?'

He repeated firmly: 'Both times.'

'Will you come to the door with me, and look for it now?'

He bit his under-lip as though he were somewhat unwilling, but he arose. I opened the door, and stood on the step, while he stood in the doorway. There was the Danger-light. There was the dismal mouth of the tunnel. There were the high, wet stone walls of the cutting. There were the stars above them.

'Do you see it?' I asked him, taking particular note of his face. His eyes were prominent and strained, but not very much more so, perhaps, than my own had been when I had directed them earnestly towards the same spot.

'No,' he answered. 'It is not there.'

'Agreed,' said I.

We went in again, shut the door, and resumed our seats. I was thinking how best to improve this advantage, if it might be called one, when he took up the conversation in such a matter-of-course way, so assuming that there could be no serious question of the fact between us, that I felt myself placed in the weakest of positions.

'By this time you will fully understand, Sir,' he said, 'that what troubles me so dreadfully is the question, What does the spectre mean?'

I was not sure, I told him, that I did fully understand.

'What is its warning against?' he said, ruminating, with his eyes on the fire, and only by times turning them on me. 'What is the danger? Where is the danger? There is danger overhanging somewhere on the Line. Some dreadful calamity will happen. It is not to be doubted this third time, after what has gone before. But surely this is a cruel haunting of me. What can I do?'

He pulled out his handkerchief, and wiped the drops from his heated forehead.

'If I telegraph Danger, on either side of me, or on both, I can give no reason for it,' he went on, wiping the palms of his hands. 'I should get into trouble, and do no good. They would think I was mad. That is the way it would work: – Message: "Danger! Take care!" Answer. "What danger? Where?" Message: "Don't know. But for God's sake, take care!" They would displace me. What else could they do?'

His pain of mind was most pitiable to see. It was the mental torture of a conscientious man, oppressed beyond endurance by an unintelligible responsibility involving life.

'When it first stood under the Danger-light,' he went on, putting his dark hair back from his head, and drawing his hands outward and across his temples in an extremity of feverish distress, 'why not tell me where that accident was to happen, – if it must happen? Why not tell me how it could be averted, – if it could have been averted? When on its second coming it hid its face, why not tell me, instead, "She is going to die. Let them keep her at home"? If it came, on those two occasions, only to show me that its warnings were true, and so to prepare me for a third, why not warn me plainly now? And I, Lord help me! A mere poor signal-man on this solitary station! Why not go to somebody with credit to be believed, and power to act?'

When I saw him in this state, I saw that for the poor man's sake, as well as for public safety, what I had to do for the time was to compose his mind. Therefore, setting aside all question of reality or unreality between us, I represented to him that whoever thoroughly discharged his duty must do well, and that at least it was his comfort that he understood his duty, though he did not understand these confounding Appearances. In this effort I succeeded far better than in the attempt to reason him out of his conviction. He became calm; the occupations incidental to his post as the night advanced began to make larger demands on his attention: and I left him at two in the morning. I had offered to stay through the night, but he would not hear of it.

That I more than once looked back at the red light as I ascended the pathway, that I did not like the red light, and that I should have slept poorly if my bed had been under it, I see no reason to conceal. Nor did I like the two sequences of the accident and the dead girl. I see no reason to conceal that either.

But what ran most in my thoughts was the consideration how ought I to act, having become the recipient of this disclosure? I had proved the man to be intelligent, vigilant, painstaking, and exact; but how long might he remain so, in his state of mind? Though in a subordinate position, still he held a most important trust, and would I (for instance) like to stake my own life on the chances of his continuing to execute it with precision?

Unable to overcome a feeling that there would be something treacherous in my communicating what he had told me to his superiors in the Company, without first being plain with himself and proposing a middle course to him, I ultimately resolved to offer to accompany him (otherwise keeping his secret for the present) to the wisest medical practitioner we could hear of in those parts, and to take his opinion. A change in his time of duty would come round next night, he had apprised me, and he would be off an hour or two after sunrise, and on again soon after sunset. I had appointed to return accordingly.

Next evening was a lovely evening, and I walked out early to enjoy it. The sun was not yet quite down when I traversed the field-path near the top of the deep cutting. I would extend my walk for an hour, I said to myself, half an hour on and half an hour back, and it would then be time to go to my signal-man's box.

Before pursuing my stroll, I stepped to the brink, and mechanically looked down, from the point from which I had first seen him. I cannot describe the thrill that seized me, when, close at the mouth of the tunnel, I saw the appearance of a man, with his left sleeve across his eyes, passionately waving his right arm.

The nameless horror that oppressed me passed in a moment, for in a moment I saw that this appearance of a man was a man indeed, and that there was a little group of other men, standing at a short distance, to whom he seemed to be rehearsing the gesture he made. The Danger-light was not yet lighted. Against its shaft, a little low hut, entirely new to me, had been made of some wooden supports and tarpaulin. It looked no bigger than a bed.

With an irresistible sense that something was wrong, – with a flashing self-reproachful fear that fatal mischief had come of my leaving the man there, and causing no one to be sent to overlook or correct what he did, – I descended the notched path with all the speed I could make.

'What is the matter?' I asked the men.

'Signal-man killed this morning, Sir.'

'Not the man belonging to that box?'

'Yes, Sir.'

'Not the man I know?'

'You will recognise him, Sir, if you knew him,' said the man who spoke for the others, solemnly uncovering his own head, and raising an end of the tarpaulin, 'for his face is quite composed.'

'O, how did this happen, how did this happen?' I asked, turning from one to another as the hut closed in again.

'He was cut down by an engine, Sir. No man in England knew his work better. But somehow he was not clear of the outer rail. It was just at broad day. He had struck the light, and had the lamp in his hand. As the engine came out of the tunnel, his back was towards her, and she cut him down. That man drove her, and was showing how it happened. Show the gentleman, Tom.'

The man, who wore a rough dark dress, stepped back to his former place at the mouth of the tunnel.

'Coming round the curve in the tunnel, Sir,' he said, 'I saw him at the end, like as if I saw him down a perspective-glass. There was no time to check speed, and I knew him to be very careful. As he didn't seem to take heed of the whistle, I shut it off when we were running down upon him, and called to him as loud as I could call.'

'What did you say?'

'I said, "Below there! Look out! Look out! For God's sake, clear the way!"'

I started.

'Ah! it was a dreadful time, Sir. I never left off calling to him. I put this arm before my eyes not to see, and I waved this arm to the last; but it was of no use.'

†

Without prolonging the narrative to dwell on any one of its curious circumstances more than on any other, I may, in closing it, point out the coincidence that the warning of the Engine-Driver included, not only the words which the unfortunate Signal-man had repeated to me as haunting him, but also the words which I myself – not he – had attached, and that only in my own mind, to the gesticulation he had imitated.

From *All the Year Round, 1866*

Strange Event in the Life of Schalken the Painter

Sheridan Le Fanu

Being a Seventh Extract from the Legacy of the late Francis Purcell, P. P. of Drumcoolagh.

You will no doubt be surprised, my dear friend, at the subject of the following narrative. What had I to do with Schalken, or Schalken with me? He had returned to his native land, and was probably dead and buried, before I was born; I never visited Holland nor spoke with a native of that country. So much I believe you already know. I must, then, give you my authority, and state to you frankly the ground upon which rests the credibility of the strange story which I am about to lay before you.

I was acquainted, in my early days, with a Captain Vandael, whose father had served King William in the Low Countries, and also in my own unhappy land during the Irish campaigns. I know not how it happened that I liked this man's society, spite of his politics and religion: but so it was; and it was by means of the free intercourse to which our intimacy gave rise that I became possessed of the curious tale which you are about to hear.

I had often been struck, while visiting Vandael, by a remarkable picture, in which, though no connoisseur myself, I could not fail to discern some very strong peculiarities, particularly in the distribution of light and shade, as also a certain oddity in the design itself, which interested my curiosity. It represented the interior of what might be a chamber in some antique religious building – the foreground was occupied by a female figure, arrayed in a species of white robe, part of which is arranged so as to form a veil. The dress, however, is not strictly that of any religious order. In its hand the figure bears a lamp, by whose light alone the form and face are illuminated; the features are marked by an arch smile, such as pretty women wear when engaged in successfully practising some roguish trick; in the background, and, excepting where the dim red light of an expiring fire serves to define the form, totally in the shade, stands the figure of a man equipped in the old fashion, with doublet and so forth, in an attitude of alarm, his hand being placed upon the hilt of his sword, which he appears to be in the act of drawing.

'There are some pictures,' said I to my friend, 'which impress one, I know not how, with a conviction that they represent not the mere ideal shapes and combinations which have floated through the imagination of the artist, but scenes, faces, and situations which have actually existed. When I look upon that picture, something assures me that I behold the representation of a reality.'

Vandael smiled, and, fixing his eyes upon the painting musingly, he said:

'Your fancy has not deceived you, my good friend, for that picture is the record, and I believe a faithful one, of a remarkable and mysterious occurrence. It was painted by Schalken, and contains, in the face of the female figure, which occupies the most prominent place in the design, an accurate portrait of Rose Velderkaust, the niece of Gerard Douw, the first and, I believe, the only love of Godfrey Schalken. My father knew the painter well, and from Schalken himself he learned the story of the mysterious drama, one scene of which the picture has embodied. This painting, which is accounted a fine specimen of Schalken's style, was bequeathed to my father by the artist's will, and, as you have observed, is a very striking and interesting production.'

I had only to request Vandael to tell the story of the painting in order to be gratified; and thus it is that I am enabled to submit to you a faithful recital of what I heard myself, leaving you to reject or to allow the evidence upon which the truth of the tradition depends, with this one assurance, that Schalken was an honest, blunt Dutchman, and, I believe, wholly incapable of committing a flight of imagination; and further, that Vandael, from whom I heard the story, appeared firmly convinced of its truth.

There are few forms upon which the mantle of mystery and romance could seem to hang more ungracefully than upon that of the uncouth and clownish Schalken – the Dutch boor – the rude and dogged, but most cunning worker in oils, whose pieces delight the initiated of the present day almost as much as his manners disgusted the refined of his own; and yet this man, so rude, so dogged, so slovenly, I had almost said so savage, in mien and manner, during his after successes, had been selected by the capricious goddess, in his early life, to figure as the hero of a romance by no means devoid of interest or of mystery.

Who can tell how meet he may have been in his young days to play the part of the lover or of the hero – who can say that in early life he had been the same harsh, unlicked, and rugged boor that, in his maturer age, he proved – or how far the neglected rudeness which afterwards marked his air, and garb, and manners, may not have been the growth of that reckless apathy not unfrequently produced by bitter misfortunes and disappointments in early life?

These questions can never now be answered.

We must content ourselves, then, with a plain statement of facts, or what have been received and transmitted as such, leaving matters of speculation to those who like them.

When Schalken studied under the immortal Gerard Douw, he was a young man; and in spite of the phlegmatic constitution and unexcitable manner which he shared, we believe, with his countrymen, he was not incapable of deep and vivid impressions, for it is an established fact that the young painter looked with considerable interest upon the beautiful niece of his wealthy master.

Rose Velderkaust was very young, having, at the period of which we speak, not yet attained her seventeenth year, and, if tradition speaks truth, possessed all the soft dimpling charms of the fail; light-haired Flemish maidens. Schalken had not studied long in the school of Gerard Douw, when he felt this interest deepening into something of a keener and intenser feeling than was quite consistent with the tranquillity of his honest Dutch heart; and at the same time he perceived, or thought he perceived, flattering symptoms of a reciprocity of liking, and this was quite sufficient to determine whatever indecision he might have heretofore experienced, and to lead him to devote exclusively to her every hope and feeling of his heart. In short, he was as much in love as a Dutchman could be. He was not long in making his passion known to the pretty maiden herself, and his declaration was followed by a corresponding confession upon her part.

Schalken, however, was a poor man, and he possessed no counterbalancing advantages of birth or position to induce the old man to consent to a union which must involve his niece and ward in the strugglings and difficulties of a young and nearly friendless artist. He was, therefore, to wait until time had furnished him with opportunity, and accident with success; and then, if his labours were found sufficiently lucrative, it was to be hoped that his proposals might at least be listened to by her jealous guardian. Months passed away, and, cheered by the smiles of the little Rose, Schalken's labours were redoubled, and with such effect and improvement as reasonably to promise the realisation of his hopes, and no contemptible eminence in his art, before many years should have elapsed.

The even course of this cheering prosperity was, however, destined to experience a sudden and formidable interruption, and that, too, in a manner so strange and mysterious as to baffle all investigation, and throw upon the events themselves a shadow of almost supernatural horror.

Schalken had one evening remained in the master's studio considerably longer than his more volatile companions, who had gladly availed themselves of the excuse which the dusk of evening afforded, to withdraw from their several tasks, in order to finish a day of labour in the jollity and conviviality of the tavern.

But Schalken worked for improvement, or rather for love. Besides, he was now engaged merely in sketching a design, an operation which, unlike that of colouring, might be continued as long as there was light sufficient to distinguish between canvas and charcoal. He had not then, nor, indeed, until long after, discovered the peculiar powers of his pencil, and he was engaged in composing a group of extremely roguish-looking and grotesque imps and demons, who were inflicting various ingenious torments upon a perspiring and pot-bellied St Anthony, who reclined in the midst of them, apparently in the last stage of drunkenness.

The young artist, however, though incapable of executing, or even of appreciating, anything of true sublimity, had nevertheless discernment enough to prevent his being by any means satisfied with his work; and many were the patient erasures and corrections which the limbs and features of saint and devil underwent, yet all without producing in their new arrangement anything of improvement or increased effect.

The large, old-fashioned room was silent, and, with the exception of himself, quite deserted by its usual inmates. An hour had passed – nearly two – without any improved result. Daylight had already declined, and twilight was fast giving way to the darkness of night. The patience of the young man was exhausted, and he stood before his unfinished production, absorbed in no very pleasing ruminations, one hand buried in the folds of his long dark hair, and the other holding the piece of charcoal which had so ill executed its office, and which he now rubbed, without much regard to the sable streaks which it produced, with irritable pressure upon his ample Flemish inexpressibles.

'Pshaw!' said the young man aloud, 'would that picture, devils, saint, and all, were where they should be – in hell!'

A short, sudden laugh, uttered startlingly close to his ear, instantly responded to the ejaculation.

The artist turned sharply round, and now for the first time became aware that his labours had been overlooked by a stranger.

Within about a yard and a half, and rather behind him, there stood what was, or appeared to be, the figure of an elderly man: he wore a short cloak, and broad-brimmed hat with a conical crown, and in his hand, which was protected with a heavy, gauntlet-shaped glove, he carried a long ebony walking-stick, surmounted with what appeared, as it glittered dimly in the twilight, to be a massive head of gold, and upon his breast, through the folds of the cloak, there shone what appeared to be the links of a rich chain of the same metal.

The room was so obscure that nothing further of the appearance of the figure could be ascertained, and the face was altogether overshadowed by the heavy flap of the beaver which overhung it, so that not a feature could be discerned. A quantity of dark hair escaped from beneath this sombre hat, a circumstance which, connected with the firm, upright carriage of the intruder, proved that his years could not yet exceed threescore or thereabouts.

There was an air of gravity and importance about the garb of this person, and something indescribably odd, I might say awful, in the perfect, stone-like movelessness of the figure, that effectually checked the testy comment which had at once risen to the lips of the irritated artist. He therefore, as soon as he had sufficiently recovered the surprise, asked the stranger, civilly, to be seated, and desired to know if he had any message to leave for his master.

'Tell Gerard Douw,' said the unknown, without altering his attitude in the smallest degree, 'that Mynher Vanderhauseny of Rotterdam, desires to speak with him to-morrow evening at this hour, and, if he please, in this room, upon matters of weight – that is all. Good-night.'

The stranger, having finished this message, turned abruptly, and, with a quick but silent step, quitted the room, before Schalken had time to say a word in reply.

The young man felt a curiosity to see in what direction the burgher of Rotterdam would turn on quitting the studio, and for that purpose he went directly to the window which commanded the door.

A lobby of considerable extent intervened between the inner door of the painter's room and the street entrance, so that Schalken occupied the post of observation before the old man could possibly have reached the street.

He watched in vain, however. There was no other mode of exit.

Had the old man vanished, or was he lurking about the recesses of the lobby for some bad purpose? This last suggestion filled the mind of Schalken with a vague horror, which was so unaccountably intense as to make him alike afraid to remain in the room alone and reluctant to pass through the lobby.

However, with an effort which appeared very disproportioned to the occasion, he summoned resolution to leave the room, and, having double-locked the door and thrust the key in his pocket, without looking to the right or left, he traversed the passage which had so recently, perhaps still, contained the person of his mysterious visitant, scarcely venturing to breathe till he had arrived in the open street.

'Mynher Vanderhausen,' said Gerard Douw within himself, as the appointed hour approached, 'Mynher Vanderhausen of Rotterdam! I never heard of the man till yesterday. What can he want of me? A portrait, perhaps, to be painted; or a younger son or a poor relation to be apprenticed; or a collection to be valued; or – pshaw I there's no one in Rotterdam to leave me a legacy. Well, whatever the business may be, we shall soon know it all.'

It was now the close of day, and every easel, except that of Schalken, was deserted. Gerard Douw was pacing the apartment with the restless step of impatient expectation, every now and then humming a passage from a piece of music which he was himself composing; for, though no great proficient, he admired the art; sometimes pausing to glance over the work of one of his absent pupils, but more frequently placing himself at the window, from whence he might observe the passengers who threaded the obscure by-street in which his studio was placed.

'Said you not, Godfrey,' exclaimed Douw, after a long and fruitless gaze from his post of observation, and turning to Schalken —'said you not the hour of appointment was at about seven by the clock of the Stadhouse?'

'It had just told seven when I first saw him, sir,' answered the student.

'The hour is close at hand, then,' said the master, consulting a horologe as large and as round as a full-grown orange. 'Mynher Vanderhausen, from Rotterdam – is it not so?'

'Such was the name.'

'And an elderly man, richly clad?' continued Douw.

'As well as I might see,' replied his pupil; 'he could not be young, nor yet very old neither, and his dress was rich and grave, as might become a citizen of wealth and consideration.'

At this moment the sonorous boom of the Stadhouse clock told, stroke after stroke, the hour of seven; the eyes of both master and student were directed to the door; and it was not until the last peal of the old bell had ceased to vibrate, that Douw exclaimed:

'So, so; we shall have his worship presently – that is, if he means to keep his hour; if not, thou mayst wait for him, Godfrey, if you court the acquaintance of a capricious burgomaster. As for me, I think our old Leyden contains a sufficiency of such commodities, without an importation from Rotterdam.'

Schalken laughed, as in duty bound; and after a pause of some minutes, Douw suddenly exclaimed:

'What if it should all prove a jest, a piece of mummery got up by Vankarp, or some such worthy! I wish you had run all risks, and cudgelled the old burgomaster, stadholder, or whatever else he may be, soundly. I would wager a dozen of Rhenish, his worship would have pleaded old acquaintance before the third application.'

'Here he comes, sir,' said Schalken, in a low admonitory tone; and instantly, upon turning towards the door, Gerard Douw observed the same figure which had, on the day before, so unexpectedly greeted the vision of his pupil Schalken.

There was something in the air and mien of the figure which at once satisfied the painter that there was no mummery in the case, and that he really stood in the presence of a man of worship; and so, without hesitation, he doffed his cap, and courteously saluting the stranger, requested him to be seated.

The visitor waved his hand slightly, as, if in acknowledgment of the courtesy, but remained standing.

'I have the honour to see Mynher Vanderhausen, of Rotterdam?' said Gerard Douw.

'The same,' was the laconic reply of his visitant.

'I understand your worship desires to speak with me,' continued Douw, 'and I am here by appointment to wait your commands.'

'Is that a man of trust?' said Vanderhausen, turning towards Schalken, who stood at a little distance behind his master.

'Certainly,' replied Gerard.

'Then let him take this box and get the nearest jeweller or goldsmith to value its contents, and let him return hither with a certificate of the valuation.'

At the same time he placed a small case, about nine inches square, in the hands of Gerard Douw, who was as much amazed at its weight as at the strange abruptness with which it was handed to him.

In accordance with the wishes of the stranger, he delivered it into the hands of Schalken, and repeating HIS directions, despatched him upon the mission.

Schalken disposed his precious charge securely beneath the folds of his cloak, and rapidly traversing two or three narrow streets, he stopped at a corner house, the lower part of which was then occupied by the shop of a Jewish goldsmith.

Schalken entered the shop, and calling the little Hebrew into the obscurity of its back recesses, he proceeded to lay before him Vanderhausen's packet.

On being examined by the light of a lamp, it appeared entirely cased with lead, the outer surface of which was much scraped and soiled, and nearly white with age. This was with difficulty partially removed, and disclosed beneath a box of some dark and singularly hard wood; this, too, was forced, and after the removal of two or three folds of linen, its contents proved to be a mass of golden ingots, close packed, and, as the Jew declared, of the most perfect quality.

Every ingot underwent the scrutiny of the little Jew, who seemed to feel an epicurean delight in touching and testing these morsels of the glorious metal; and each one of them was replaced in the box with the exclamation:

'Mein Gott, how very perfect! not one grain of alloy – beautiful, beautiful!'

The task was at length finished, and the Jew certified under his hand the value of the ingots submitted to his examination to amount to many thousand rix-dollars.

With the desired document in his bosom, and the rich box of gold carefully pressed under his arm, and concealed by his cloak, he retraced his way, and entering the studio, found his master and the stranger in close conference.

Schalken had no sooner left the room, in order to execute the commission he had taken in charge, than Vanderhausen addressed Gerard Douw in the following terms:

'I may not tarry with you tonight more than a few minutes, and so I shall briefly tell you the matter upon which I come. You visited the town of Rotterdam some four months ago, and then I saw in the church of St Lawrence your niece, Rose Velderkaust. I desire to marry her, and if I satisfy you as to the fact that I am very wealthy – more wealthy than any husband you could dream of for her – I expect that you will forward my views to the utmost of your authority. If you approve my proposal, you must close with it at once, for I cannot command time enough to wait for calculations and delays.'

Gerard Douw was, perhaps, as much astonished as anyone could be by the very unexpected nature of Mynher Vanderhausen's communication; but he did not give vent to any unseemly expression of surprise, for besides the motives supplied by prudence and politeness, the painter experienced a kind of chill and oppressive sensation, something like that which is supposed to affect a man who is placed unconsciously in immediate contact with something to which he has a natural antipathy – an undefined horror and dread while standing in the presence of the eccentric stranger, which made him very unwilling to say anything which might reasonably prove offensive.

'I have no doubt,' said Gerard, after two or three prefatory hems, 'that the connection which you propose would prove alike advantageous and honourable to my niece; but you must be aware that she has a will of her own, and may not acquiesce in what WE may design for her advantage.'

'Do not seek to deceive me, Sir Painter,' said Vanderhausen; 'you are her guardian – she is your ward. She is mine if YOU like to make her so.'

The man of Rotterdam moved forward a little as he spoke, and Gerard Douw, he scarce knew why, inwardly prayed for the speedy return of Schalken.

'I desire,' said the mysterious gentleman, 'to place in your hands at once an evidence of my wealth, and a security for my liberal dealing with your niece. The lad will return in a minute or two with a sum in value five times the fortune which she has a right to expect from a husband. This shall lie in your hands, together with her dowry, and you may apply the united sum as suits her interest best; it shall be all exclusively hers while she lives. Is that liberal?'

Douw assented, and inwardly thought that fortune had been extraordinarily kind to his niece. The stranger, he thought, must be both wealthy and generous, and such an offer was not to be despised, though made by a humourist, and one of no very prepossessing presence.

Rose had no very high pretensions, for she was almost without dowry; indeed, altogether so, excepting so far as the deficiency had been supplied by the generosity of her uncle. Neither had she any right to raise any scruples against the match on the score of birth, for her own origin was by no means elevated; and as to other objections, Gerard resolved, and, indeed, by the usages of the time was warranted in resolving, not to listen to them for a moment.

'Sir,' said he, addressing the stranger, 'your offer is most liberal, and whatever hesitation I may feel in closing with it immediately, arises solely from my not having the honour of knowing anything of your family or station. Upon these points you can, of course, satisfy me without difficulty?'

'As to my respectability,' said the stranger, drily, 'you must take that for granted at present; pester me with no inquiries; you can discover nothing more about me than I choose to make known. You shall have sufficient security for my respectability – my word, if you are honourable: if you are sordid, my gold.'

'A testy old gentleman,' thought Douw; 'he must have his own way. But, all things considered, I am justified in giving my niece to him. Were she my own daughter, I would do the like by her. I will not pledge myself unnecessarily, however.'

'You will not pledge yourself unnecessarily,' said Vanderhausen, strangely uttering the very words which had just floated through the mind of his companion; 'but you will do so if it IS necessary, I presume; and I will show you that I consider it indispensable. If the gold I mean to leave in your hands satisfy you, and if you desire that my proposal shall not be at once withdrawn, you must, before I leave this room, write your name to this engagement.'

Having thus spoken, he placed a paper in the hands of Gerard, the contents of which expressed an engagement entered into by Gerard Douw, to give to Wilken Vanderhausen, of Rotterdam, in marriage, Rose Velderkaust, and so forth, within one week of the date hereof.

While the painter was employed in reading this covenant, Schalken, as we have stated, entered the studio, and having delivered the box and the valuation of the Jew into the hands of the stranger, he was about to retire, when Vanderhausen called to him to wait; and, presenting the case and the certificate to Gerard Douw, he waited in silence until he had satisfied himself by an inspection of both as to the value of the pledge left in his hands. At length he said:

'Are you content?'

The painter said he would fain have another day to consider.

'Not an hour,' said the suitor, coolly.

'Well, then,' said Douw, 'I am content; it is a bargain.'

'Then sign at once,' said Vanderhausen; 'I am weary.'

At the same time he produced a small case of writing materials, and Gerard signed the important document.

'Let this youth witness the covenant,' said the old man; and Godfrey Schalken unconsciously signed the instrument which bestowed upon another that hand which he had so long regarded as the object and reward of all his labours.

The compact being thus completed, the strange visitor folded up the paper, and stowed it safely in an inner pocket.

'I will visit you tomorrow night, at nine of the clock, at your house,

Gerard Douw, and will see the subject of our contract. Farewell.' And so saying, Wilken Vanderhausen moved stiffly, but rapidly out of the room.

Schalken, eager to resolve his doubts, had placed himself by the window in order to watch the street entrance; but the experiment served only to support his suspicions, for the old man did not issue from the door. This was very strange, very odd, very fearful. He and his master returned together, and talked but little on the way, for each had his own subjects of reflection, of anxiety, and of hope.

Schalken, however, did not know the ruin which threatened his cherished schemes.

Gerard Douw knew nothing of the attachment which had sprung up between his pupil and his niece; and even if he had, it is doubtful whether he would have regarded its existence as any serious obstruction to the wishes of Mynher Vanderhausen.

Marriages were then and there matters of traffic and calculation; and it would have appeared as absurd in the eyes of the guardian to make a mutual attachment an essential element in a contract of marriage, as it would have been to draw up his bonds and receipts in the language of chivalrous romance.

The painter, however, did not communicate to his niece the important step which he had taken on her behalf, and his resolution arose not from any anticipation of opposition on her part, but solely from a ludicrous consciousness that if his ward were, as she very naturally might do, to ask him to describe the appearance of the bridegroom whom he destined for her, he would be forced to confess that he had not seen his face, and, if called upon, would find it impossible to identify him.

Upon the next day, Gerard Douw having dined, called his niece to him, and having scanned her person with an air of satisfaction, he took her hand, and looking upon her pretty, innocent face with a smile of kindness, he said:

'Rose, my girl, that face of yours will make your fortune.' Rose blushed and smiled. 'Such faces and such tempers seldom go together, and, when they do, the compound is a love-potion which few heads or hearts can resist. Trust me, thou wilt soon be a bride, girl. But this is trifling, and I am pressed for time, so make ready the large room by eight o'clock tonight, and give directions for supper at nine. I expect a friend tonight; and observe me, child, do thou trick thyself out handsomely. I would not have him think us poor or sluttish.'

With these words he left the chamber, and took his way to the room to which we have already had occasion to introduce our readers – that in which his pupils worked.

When the evening closed in, Gerard called Schalken, who was about to take his departure to his obscure and comfortless lodgings, and asked him to come home and sup with Rose and Vanderhausen.

The invitation was of course accepted, and Gerard Douw and his pupil soon found themselves in the handsome and somewhat antique-looking room which had been prepared for the reception of the stranger.

A cheerful wood-fire blazed in the capacious hearth; a little at one side an old-fashioned table, with richly-carved legs, was placed – destined, no doubt, to receive the supper, for which preparations were going forward; and ranged with exact regularity, stood the tall-backed chairs, whose ungracefulness was more than counterbalanced by their comfort.

The little party, consisting of Rose, her uncle, and the artist, awaited the arrival of the expected visitor with considerable impatience.

Nine o'clock at length came, and with it a summons at the street-door, which, being speedily answered, was followed by a slow and emphatic tread upon the staircase; the steps moved heavily across the lobby, the door of the room in which the party which we have described were assembled slowly opened, and there entered a figure which startled, almost appalled, the phlegmatic Dutchmen, and nearly made Rose scream with affright; it was the form, and arrayed in the garb, of Mynher Vanderhausen; the air, the gait, the height was the same, but the features had never been seen by any of the party before.

The stranger stopped at the door of the room, and displayed his form and face completely. He wore a dark-coloured cloth cloak, which was short and full, not falling quite to the knees; his legs were cased in dark purple silk stockings, and his shoes were adorned with roses of the same colour. The opening of the cloak in front showed the under-suit to consist of some very dark, perhaps sable material, and his hands were enclosed in a pair of heavy leather gloves which ran up considerably above the wrist, in the manner of a gauntlet. In one hand he carried his walking-stick and his hat, which he had removed, and the other hung heavily by his side. A quantity of grizzled hair descended in long tresses from his head, and its folds rested upon the plaits of a stiff ruff, which effectually concealed his neck.

So far all was well; but the face! – all the flesh of the face was coloured with the bluish leaden hue which is sometimes produced by the operation of metallic medicines administered in excessive quantities; the eyes were enormous, and the white appeared both above and below the iris, which gave to them an expression of insanity, which was heightened by their glassy fixedness; the nose was well enough, but the mouth was writhed considerably to one side, where it opened in order to give egress to two long, discoloured fangs, which projected from the upper jaw, far below the lower lip; the hue of the lips themselves bore the usual relation to that of the face, and was consequently nearly black. The character of the face was malignant, even satanic, to the last degree; and, indeed, such a combination of horror could hardly be accounted for, except by supposing the corpse of some atrocious malefactor, which had long hung blackening upon the gibbet, to have at length become the habitation of a demon – the frightful sport of Satanic possession.

It was remarkable that the worshipful stranger suffered as little as possible of his flesh to appear, and that during his visit he did not once remove his gloves.

Having stood for some moments at the door, Gerard Douw at length found breath and collectedness to bid him welcome, and, with a mute inclination of the head, the stranger stepped forward into the room.

There was something indescribably odd, even horrible, about all his motions, something undefinable, that was unnatural, un-human – it was as if the limbs were guided and directed by a spirit unused to the management of bodily machinery.

The stranger said hardly anything during his visit, which did not exceed half an hour; and the host himself could scarcely muster courage enough to utter the few necessary salutations and courtesies: and, indeed, such was the nervous terror which the presence of Vanderhausen inspired, that very little would have made all his entertainers fly bellowing from the room.

They had not so far lost all self-possession, however, as to fail to observe two strange peculiarities of their visitor.

During his stay he did not once suffer his eyelids to close, nor even to move in the slightest degree; and further, there was a death-like stillness in his whole person, owing to the total absence of the heaving motion of the chest, caused by the process of respiration.

These two peculiarities, though when told they may appear trifling, produced a very striking and unpleasant effect when seen and observed. Vanderhausen at length relieved the painter of Leyden of his inauspicious presence; and with no small gratification the little party heard the street-door close after him.

'Dear uncle,' said Rose, 'what a frightful man! I would not see him again for the wealth of the States!'

'Tush, foolish girl!' said Douw, whose sensations were anything but comfortable. 'A man may be as ugly as the devil, and yet if his heart and actions are good, he is worth all the pretty-faced, perfumed puppies that walk the Mall. Rose, my girl, it is very true he has not thy pretty face, but I know him to be wealthy and liberal; and were he ten times more ugly—'

'Which is inconceivable,' observed Rose.

'These two virtues would be sufficient,' continued her uncle, 'to counterbalance all his deformity; and if not of power sufficient actually to alter the shape of the features, at least of efficacy enough to prevent one thinking them amiss.'

'Do you know, uncle,' said Rose, 'when I saw him standing at the door, I could not get it out of my head that I saw the old, painted, wooden figure that used to frighten me so much in the church of St Laurence of Rotterdam.'

Gerard laughed, though he could not help inwardly acknowledging the justness of the comparison. He was resolved, however, as far as he could, to check his niece's inclination to ridicule the ugliness of her intended bridegroom, although he was not a little pleased to observe that she appeared totally exempt from that mysterious dread of the stranger which, he could not disguise it from himself, considerably affected him, as also his pupil Godfrey Schalken.

Early on the next day there arrived, from various quarters of the town, rich presents of silks, velvets, jewellery, and so forth, for Rose; and also a packet directed to Gerard Douw, which, on being opened, was found to contain a contract of marriage, formally drawn up, between Wilken Vanderhausen of the Boom-quay, in Rotterdam, and Rose Velderkaust of Leyden, niece to Gerard Douw, master in the art of painting, also of the same city; and containing engagements on the part of Vanderhausen to make settlements upon his bride, far more splendid than he had before led her guardian to believe likely, and which were to be secured to her use in the most unexceptionable manner possible – the money being placed in the hands of Gerard Douw himself.

I have no sentimental scenes to describe, no cruelty of guardians, or magnanimity of wards, or agonies of lovers. The record I have to make is one of sordidness, levity, and interest. In less than a week after the first interview which we have just described, the contract of marriage was fulfilled, and Schalken saw the prize which he would have risked anything to secure, carried off triumphantly by his formidable rival.

For two or three days he absented himself from the school; he then returned and worked, if with less cheerfulness, with far more dogged resolution than before; the dream of love had given place to that of ambition.

Months passed away, and, contrary to his expectation, and, indeed, to the direct promise of the parties, Gerard Douw heard nothing of his niece, or her worshipful spouse. The interest of the money, which was to have been demanded in quarterly sums, lay unclaimed in his hands. He began to grow extremely uneasy.

Mynher Vanderhausen's direction in Rotterdam he was fully possessed of. After some irresolution he finally determined to journey thither – a trifling undertaking, and easily accomplished – and thus to satisfy himself of the safety and comfort of his ward, for whom he entertained an honest and strong affection.

His search was in vain, however. No one in Rotterdam had ever heard of Mynher Vanderhausen.

Gerard Douw left not a house in the Boom-quay untried; but all in vain. No one could give him any information whatever touching the object of his inquiry; and he was obliged to return to Leyden, nothing wiser than when he had left it.

On his arrival he hastened to the establishment from which Vanderhausen had hired the lumbering though, considering the times, most luxurious vehicle which the bridal party had employed to convey them to Rotterdam. From the driver of this machine he learned, that having proceeded by slow stages, they had late in the evening approached Rotterdam; but that before they entered the city, and while yet nearly a mile from it, a small party of men, soberly clad, and after the old fashion, with peaked beards and moustaches, standing in the centre of the road, obstructed the further progress of the carriage. The driver reined in his horses, much fearing, from the obscurity of the hour, and the loneliness of the road, that some mischief was intended.

His fears were, however, somewhat allayed by his observing that these strange men carried a large litter, of an antique shape, and which they immediately set down upon the pavement, whereupon the bridegroom, having opened the coach-door from within, descended, and having assisted his bride to do likewise, led her, weeping bitterly and wringing her hands, to the litter, which they both entered. It was then raised by the men who surrounded it, and speedily carried towards the city, and before it had proceeded many yards the darkness concealed it from the view of the Dutch charioteer.

In the inside of the vehicle he found a purse, whose contents more than thrice paid the hire of the carriage and man. He saw and could tell nothing more of Mynher Vanderhausen and his beautiful lady. This mystery was a source of deep anxiety and almost of grief to Gerard Douw.

There was evidently fraud in the dealing of Vanderhausen with him, though for what purpose committed he could not imagine. He greatly doubted how far it was possible for a man possessing in his countenance so strong an evidence of the presence of the most demoniac feelings, to be in reality anything but a villain; and every day that passed without his hearing from or of his niece, instead of inducing him to forget his fears, on the contrary tended more and more to exasperate them.

The loss of his niece's cheerful society tended also to depress his spirits; and in order to dispel this despondency, which often crept upon his mind after his daily employment was over, he was wont frequently to prevail upon Schalken to accompany him home, and by his presence to dispel, in some degree, the gloom of his otherwise solitary supper.

One evening, the painter and his pupil were sitting by the fire, having accomplished a comfortable supper, and had yielded to that silent pensiveness sometimes induced by the process of digestion, when their reflections were disturbed by a loud sound at the street-door, as if occasioned by some person rushing forcibly and repeatedly against it. A domestic had run without delay to ascertain the cause of the disturbance, and they heard him twice or thrice interrogate the applicant for admission, but without producing an answer or any cessation of the sounds.

They heard him then open the hall-door, and immediately there followed a light and rapid tread upon the staircase. Schalken laid his hand on his sword, and advanced towards the door. It opened before he reached it, and Rose rushed into the room. She looked wild and haggard, and pale with exhaustion and terror; but her dress surprised them as much even as her unexpected appearance. It consisted of a kind of white woollen wrapper, made close about the neck, and descending to the very ground. It was much deranged and travel-soiled. The poor creature had hardly entered the chamber when she fell senseless on the floor. With some difficulty they succeeded in reviving her, and on recovering her senses she instantly exclaimed, in a tone of eager, terrified impatience:

'Wine, wine, quickly, or I'm lost!'

Much alarmed at the strange agitation in which the call was made, they at once administered to her wishes, and she drank some wine with a haste and eagerness which surprised them. She had hardly swallowed it, when she exclaimed, with the same urgency:

'Food, food, at once, or I perish!'

A considerable fragment of a roast joint was upon the table, and Schalken immediately proceeded to cut some, but he was anticipated; for no sooner had she become aware of its presence than she darted at it with the rapacity of a vulture, and, seizing it in her hands she tore off the flesh with her teeth and swallowed it.

When the paroxysm of hunger had been a little appeased, she appeared suddenly to become aware how strange her conduct had been, or it may have been that other more agitating thoughts recurred to her mind, for she began to weep bitterly and to wring her hands.

'Oh! send for a minister of God,' said she; 'I am not safe till he comes; send for him speedily.'

Gerard Douw despatched a messenger instantly, and prevailed on his niece to allow him to surrender his bedchamber to her use; he also persuaded her to retire to it at once and to rest; her consent was extorted upon the condition that they would not leave her for a moment.

'Oh that the holy man were here!' she said; 'he can deliver me. The dead and the living can never be one – God has forbidden it.'

With these mysterious words she surrendered herself to their guidance, and they proceeded to the chamber which Gerard Douw had assigned to her use.

'Do not – do not leave me for a moment,' said she. 'I am lost for ever if you do.'

Gerard Douw's chamber was approached through a spacious apartment, which they were now about to enter. Gerard Douw and Schalken each carried a was candle, so that a sufficient degree of light was cast upon all surrounding objects. They were now entering the large chamber, which, as I have said, communicated with Douw's apartment, when Rose suddenly stopped, and, in a whisper which seemed to thrill with horror, she said:

'O God! he is here – he is here! See, see – there he goes!'

She pointed towards the door of the inner room, and Schalken thought he saw a shadowy and ill-defined form gliding into that apartment. He drew his sword, and raising the candle so as to throw its light with increased distinctness upon the objects in the room, he entered the chamber into which the shadow had glided. No figure was there – nothing but the furniture which belonged to the room, and yet he could not be deceived as to the fact that something had moved before them into the chamber.

A sickening dread came upon him, and the cold perspiration broke out in heavy drops upon his forehead; nor was he more composed when he heard the increased urgency, the agony of entreaty, with which Rose implored them not to leave her for a moment.

'I saw him,' said she. 'He's here! I cannot be deceived – I know him. He's by me – he's with me – he's in the room. Then, for God's sake, as you would save, do not stir from beside me!'

They at length prevailed upon her to lie down upon the bed, where she continued to urge them to stay by her. She frequently uttered incoherent sentences, repeating again and again, 'The dead and the living cannot be one – God has forbidden it!' and then again, 'Rest to the wakeful – sleep to the sleep-walkers.'

These and such mysterious and broken sentences she continued to utter until the clergyman arrived.

Gerard Douw began to fear, naturally enough, that the poor girl, owing to terror or ill-treatment, had become deranged; and he half suspected, by the suddenness of her appearance, and the unseasonableness of the hour, and, above all, from the wildness and terror of her manner, that she had made her escape from some place of confinement for lunatics, and was in immediate fear of pursuit. He resolved to summon medical advice as soon as the mind of his niece had been in some measure set at rest by the offices of the clergyman whose attendance she had so earnestly desired; and until this object had been attained, he did not venture to put any questions to her, which might possibly, by reviving painful or horrible recollections, increase her agitation.

The clergyman soon arrived – a man of ascetic countenance and venerable age – one whom Gerard Douw respected much, forasmuch as he was a veteran polemic, though one, perhaps, more dreaded as a combatant than beloved as a Christian – of pure morality, subtle brain, and frozen heart. He entered the chamber which communicated with that in which Rose reclined, and immediately on his arrival she requested him to pray for her, as for one who lay in the hands of Satan, and who could hope for deliverance – only from heaven.

That our readers may distinctly understand all the circumstances of the event which we are about imperfectly to describe, it is necessary to state the relative position of the parties who were engaged in it. The old clergyman and Schalken were in the anteroom of which we have already spoken; Rose lay in the inner chamber, the door of which was open; and by the side of the bed, at her urgent desire, stood her guardian; a candle burned in the bedchamber, and three were lighted in the outer apartment.

The old man now cleared his voice, as if about to commence; but before he had time to begin, a sudden gust of air blew out the candle which served to illuminate the room in which the poor girl lay, and she, with hurried alarm, exclaimed:

'Godfrey, bring in another candle; the darkness is unsafe.'

Gerard Douw, forgetting for the moment her repeated injunctions in the immediate impulse, stepped from the bedchamber into the other, in order to supply what she desired.

'O God I do not go, dear uncle!' shrieked the unhappy girl; and at the same time she sprang from the bed and darted after him, in order, by her grasp, to detain him.

But the warning came too late, for scarcely had he passed the threshold, and hardly had his niece had time to utter the startling exclamation, when the door which divided the two rooms closed violently after him, as if swung to by a strong blast of wind.

Schalken and he both rushed to the door, but their united and desperate efforts could not avail so much as to shake it.

Shriek after shriek burst from the inner chamber, with all the piercing loudness of despairing terror. Schalken and Douw applied every energy and strained every nerve to force open the door; but all in vain.

There was no sound of struggling from within, but the screams seemed to increase in loudness, and at the same time they heard the bolts of the latticed window withdrawn, and the window itself grated upon the sill as if thrown open.

One LAST shriek, so long and piercing and agonised as to be scarcely human, swelled from the room, and suddenly there followed a death-like silence.

A light step was heard crossing the floor, as if from the bed to the window; and almost at the same instant the door gave way, and, yielding to the pressure of the external applicants, they were nearly precipitated into the room. It was empty. The window was open, and Schalken sprang to a chair and gazed out upon the street and canal below. He saw no form, but he beheld, or thought he beheld, the waters of the broad canal beneath settling ring after ring in heavy circular ripples, as if a moment before disturbed by the immersion of some large and heavy mass.

No trace of Rose was ever after discovered, nor was anything certain respecting her mysterious wooer detected or even suspected; no clue whereby to trace the intricacies of the labyrinth and to arrive at a distinct conclusion was to be found. But an incident occurred, which, though it will not be received by our rational readers as at all approaching to evidence upon the matter, nevertheless produced a strong and a lasting impression upon the mind of Schalken.

Many years after the events which we have detailed, Schalken, then remotely situated, received an intimation of his father's death, and of his intended burial upon a fixed day in the church of Rotterdam. It was necessary that a very considerable journey should be performed by the funeral procession, which, as it will readily be believed, was not very numerously attended. Schalken with difficulty arrived in Rotterdam late in the day upon which the funeral was appointed to take place. The procession had not then arrived. Evening closed in, and still it did not appear.

Schalken strolled down to the church – he found it open – notice of the arrival of the funeral had been given, and the vault in which the body was to be laid had been opened. The official who corresponds to our sexton, on seeing a well-dressed gentleman, whose object was to attend the expected funeral, pacing the aisle of the church, hospitably invited him to share with him the comforts of a blazing wood fire, which, as was his custom in winter time upon such occasions, he had kindled on the hearth of a chamber which communicated, by a flight of steps, with the vault below.

In this chamber Schalken and his entertainer seated themselves, and the sexton, after some fruitless attempts to engage his guest in conversation, was obliged to apply himself to his tobacco-pipe and can to solace his solitude.

In spite of his grief and cares, the fatigues of a rapid journey of nearly forty hours gradually overcame the mind and body of Godfrey Schalken, and he sank into a deep sleep, from which he was awakened by someone shaking him gently by the shoulder. He first thought that the old sexton had called him, but HE was no longer in the room.

He roused himself, and as soon as he could clearly see what was around him, he perceived a female form, clothed in a kind of light robe of muslin, part of which was so disposed as to act as a veil, and in her hand she carried a lamp. She was moving rather away from him, and towards the flight of steps which conducted towards the vaults.

Schalken felt a vague alarm at the sight of this figure, and at the same time an irresistible impulse to follow its guidance. He followed it towards the vaults, but when it reached the head of the stairs, he paused; the figure paused also, and, turning gently round, displayed, by the light of the lamp it carried, the face and features of his first love, Rose Velderkaust. There was nothing horrible, or even sad, in the countenance. On the contrary, it wore the same arch smile which used to enchant the artist long before in his happy days.

A feeling of awe and of interest, too intense to be resisted, prompted him to follow the spectre, if spectre it were. She descended the stairs – he followed; and, turning to the left, through a narrow passage, she led him, to his infinite surprise, into what appeared to be an old-fashioned Dutch apartment, such as the pictures of Gerard Douw have served to immortalise.

Abundance of costly antique furniture was disposed about the room, and in one corner stood a four-post bed, with heavy black-cloth curtains around it; the figure frequently turned towards him with the same arch smile; and when she came to the side of the bed, she drew the curtains, and by the light of the lamp which she held towards its contents, she disclosed to the horror-stricken painter, sitting bolt upright in the bed, the livid and demoniac form of Vanderhausen. Schalken had hardly seen him when he fell senseless upon the floor, where he lay until discovered, on the next morning, by persons employed in closing the passages into the vaults. He was lying in a cell of considerable size, which had not been disturbed for a long time, and he had fallen beside a large coffin which was supported upon small stone pillars, a security against the attacks of vermin.

To his dying day Schalken was satisfied of the reality of the vision which he had witnessed, and he has left behind him a curious evidence of the impression which it wrought upon his fancy, in a painting executed shortly after the event we have narrated, and which is valuable as exhibiting not only the peculiarities which have made Schalken's pictures sought after, but even more so as presenting a portrait, as close and faithful as one taken from memory can be, of his early love, Rose Velderkaust, whose mysterious fate must ever remain matter of speculation.

The picture represents a chamber of antique masonry, such as might be found in most old cathedrals, and is lighted faintly by a lamp carried in the hand of a female figure, such as we have above attempted to describe; and in the background, and to the left of him who examines the painting, there stands the form of a man apparently aroused from sleep, and by his attitude, his hand being laid upon his sword, exhibiting considerable alarm: this last figure is illuminated only by the expiring glare of a wood or charcoal fire.

The whole production exhibits a beautiful specimen of that artful and singular distribution of light and shade which has rendered the name of Schalken immortal among the artists of his country. This tale is traditionary, and the reader will easily perceive, by our studiously omitting to heighten many points of the narrative, when a little additional colouring might have added effect to the recital, that we have desired to lay before him, not a figment of the brain, but a curious tradition connected with, and belonging to, the biography of a famous artist.

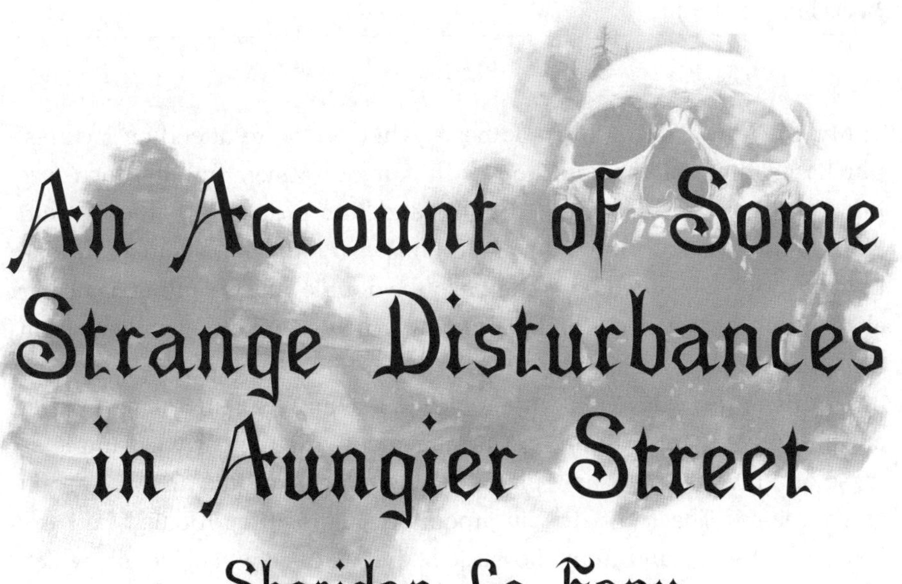

An Account of Some Strange Disturbances in Aungier Street

Sheridan Le Fanu

It is not worth telling, this story of mine – at least, not worth writing. Told, indeed, as I have sometimes been called upon to tell it, to a circle of intelligent and eager faces, lighted up by a good after-dinner fire on a winter's evening, with a cold wind rising and wailing outside, and all snug and cosy within, it has gone off – though I say it, who should not – indifferent well. But it is a venture to do as you would have me. Pen, ink, and paper are cold vehicles for the marvellous, and a 'reader' decidedly a more critical animal than a 'listener'. If, however, you can induce your friends to read it after nightfall, and when the fireside talk has run for a while on thrilling tales of shapeless terror; in short, if you will secure me the *mollia tempora fandi,* I will go to my work, and say my say, with better heart. Well, then, these conditions presupposed, I shall waste no more words, but tell you simply how it all happened.

My cousin (Tom Ludlow) and I studied medicine together. I think he would have succeeded, had he stuck to the profession; but he preferred the Church, poor fellow, and died early, a sacrifice to contagion, contracted in the noble discharge of his duties. For my present purpose, I say enough of his character when I mention that he was of a sedate but frank and cheerful nature; very exact in his observance of truth, and not by any means like myself – of an excitable or nervous temperament.

My Uncle Ludlow – Tom's father – while we were attending lectures, purchased three or four old houses in Aungier Street, one of which was unoccupied. *He* resided in the country, and Tom proposed that we should take up our abode in the untenanted house, so long as it should continue unlet; a move which would accomplish the double end of settling us nearer alike to our lecture-rooms and to our amusements, and of relieving us from the weekly charge of rent for our lodgings.

Our furniture was very scant – our whole equipage remarkably modest and primitive; and, in short, our arrangements pretty nearly as simple as those of a bivouac. Our new plan was, therefore, executed almost as soon as conceived. The front drawing-room was our sitting-room. I had the bedroom over it, and Tom the back bedroom on the same floor, which nothing could have induced me to occupy.

The house, to begin with, was a very old one. It had been, I believe, newly fronted about fifty years before; but with this exception, it had nothing modern about it. The agent who bought it and looked into the titles for my uncle, told me that it was sold, along with much other forfeited property, at Chichester House, I think, in 1702; and had belonged to Sir Thomas Hacket, who was Lord Mayor of Dublin in James II's time. How old it was *then*, I can't say; but, at all events, it had seen years and changes enough to have contracted all that mysterious and saddened air, at once exciting and depressing, which belongs to most old mansions.

There had been very little done in the way of modernising details; and, perhaps, it was better so; for there was something queer and by-gone in the very walls and ceilings – in the shape of doors and windows – in the odd diagonal site of the chimney-pieces – in the beams and ponderous cornices – not to mention the singular solidity of all the woodwork, from the banisters to the window-frames, which hopelessly defied disguise, and would have emphatically proclaimed their antiquity through any conceivable amount of modern finery and varnish.

An effort had, indeed, been made, to the extent of papering the drawing-rooms; but somehow, the paper looked raw and out of keeping; and the old woman, who kept a little dirt-pie of a shop in the lane, and whose daughter – a girl of two and fifty – was our solitary handmaid, coming in at sunrise, and chastely receding again as soon as she had made all ready for tea in our state apartment; – this woman, I say, remembered it, when old Judge Horrocks (who, having earned the reputation of a particularly 'hanging judge', ended by hanging himself, as the coroner's jury found, under an impulse of 'temporary insanity', with a child's skipping-rope, over the massive old bannisters) resided there, entertaining good company, with fine venison and rare old port. In those halcyon days, the drawing-rooms were hung with gilded leather, and, I dare say, cut a good figure, for they were really spacious rooms.

The bedrooms were wainscoted, but the front one was not gloomy; and in it the cosiness of antiquity quite overcame its sombre associations. But the back bedroom, with its two queerly-placed melancholy windows, staring vacantly at the foot of the bed, and with the shadowy recess to be found in most old houses in Dublin, like a large ghostly closet, which, from congeniality of temperament, had amalgamated with the bedchamber, and dissolved the partition. At night-time, this 'alcove' – as our 'maid' was wont to call it – had, in my eyes, a specially sinister and suggestive character. Tom's distant and solitary candle glimmered vainly into its darkness. *There* it was always overlooking him – always itself impenetrable. But this was only part of the effect. The whole room was, I can't tell how, repulsive to me. There was, I suppose, in its proportions and features, a latent discord – a certain mysterious and indescribable relation, which jarred indistinctly upon some secret sense of the fitting and the safe, and raised indefinable suspicions and apprehensions of the imagination. On the whole, as I began by saying, nothing could have induced me to pass a night alone in it.

I had never pretended to conceal from poor Tom my superstitious weakness; and he, on the other hand, most unaffectedly ridiculed my tremors. The sceptic was, however, destined to receive a lesson, as you shall hear.

We had not been very long in occupation of our respective dormitories, when I began to complain of uneasy nights and disturbed sleep. I was, I suppose, the more impatient under this annoyance, as I was usually a sound sleeper, and by no means prone to nightmares. It was now, however, my destiny, instead of enjoying my customary repose, every night to 'sup full of horrors'. After a preliminary course of disagreeable and frightful dreams, my troubles took a definite form, and the same vision, without an appreciable variation in a single detail, visited me at least (on an average) every second night in the week.

Now, this dream, nightmare, or infernal illusion – which you please – of which I was the miserable sport, was on this wise:—

I saw, or thought I saw, with the most abominable distinctness, although at the time in profound darkness, every article of furniture and accidental arrangement of the chamber in which I lay. This, as you know, is incidental to ordinary nightmare. Well, while in this clairvoyant condition, which seemed but the lighting up of the theatre in which was to be exhibited the monotonous tableau of horror, which made my nights insupportable, my attention invariably became, I know not why, fixed upon the windows opposite the foot of my bed; and, uniformly with the same effect, a sense of dreadful anticipation always took slow but sure possession of me. I became somehow conscious of a sort of horrid but undefined preparation going forward in some unknown quarter, and by some unknown agency, for my torment; and, after an interval, which always seemed to me of the same length, a picture suddenly flew up to the window, where it remained fixed, as if by an electrical attraction, and my discipline of horror then commenced, to last perhaps for hours. The picture thus mysteriously glued to the window-panes, was the portrait of an old man, in a crimson flowered silk dressing-gown, the folds of which I could now describe, with a countenance embodying a strange mixture of intellect, sensuality, and power, but withal sinister and full of malignant omen. His nose was hooked, like the beak of a vulture; his eyes large, grey, and prominent, and lighted up with a more than mortal cruelty and coldness. These features were surmounted by a crimson velvet cap, the hair that peeped from under which was white with age, while the eyebrows retained their original blackness. Well I remember every line, hue, and shadow of that stony countenance, and well I may! The gaze of this hellish visage was fixed upon me, and mine returned it with the inexplicable fascination of nightmare, for what appeared to me to be hours of agony. At last—

The cock he crew, away then flew the fiend who had enslaved me through the awful watches of the night; and, harassed and nervous, I rose to the duties of the day.

I had – I can't say exactly why, but it may have been from the exquisite anguish and profound impressions of unearthly horror, with which this strange phantasmagoria was associated – an insurmountable antipathy to describing the exact nature of my nightly troubles to my friend and comrade. Generally, however, I told him that I was haunted by abominable dreams; and, true to the imputed materialism of medicine, we put our heads together to dispel my horrors, not by exorcism, but by a tonic.

I will do this tonic justice, and frankly admit that the accursed portrait began to intermit its visits under its influence. What of that? Was this singular apparition – as full of character as of terror – therefore the creature of my fancy, or the invention of my poor stomach? Was it, in short, *subjective* (to borrow the technical slang of the day) and not the palpable aggression and intrusion of an external agent? That, good friend, as we will both admit, by no means follows. The evil spirit, who enthralled my senses in the shape of that portrait, may have been just as near me, just as energetic, just as malignant, though I saw him not. What means the whole moral code of revealed religion regarding the due keeping of our own bodies, soberness, temperance, etc.? here is an obvious connexion between the material and the invisible; the healthy tone of the system, and its unimpaired energy, may, for aught we can tell, guard us against influences which would otherwise render life itself terrific. The mesmerist and the electro-biologist will fail upon an average with nine patients out of ten – so may the evil spirit. Special conditions of the corporeal system are indispensable to the production of certain spiritual phenomena. The operation succeeds sometimes – sometimes fails – that is all.

I found afterwards that my would-be sceptical companion had his troubles too. But of these I knew nothing yet. One night, for a wonder, I was sleeping soundly, when I was roused by a step on the lobby outside my room, followed by the loud clang of what turned out to be a large brass candlestick, flung with all his force by poor Tom Ludlow over the banisters, and rattling with a rebound down the second flight of stairs; and almost concurrently with this, Tom burst open my door, and bounced into my room backwards, in a state of extraordinary agitation.

I had jumped out of bed and clutched him by the arm before I had any distinct idea of my own whereabouts. There we were – in our shirts – standing before the open door – staring through the great old banister opposite, at the lobby window, through which the sickly light of a clouded moon was gleaming.

'What's the matter, Tom? What's the matter with you? What the devil's the matter with you, Tom?' I demanded, shaking him with nervous impatience.

He took a long breath before he answered me, and then it was not very coherently.

'It's nothing, nothing at all – did I speak? – what did I say? – where's the candle, Richard? It's dark; I – I had a candle!'

'Yes, dark enough,' I said; 'but what's the matter? – what *is* it? – why don't you speak, Tom? – have you lost your wits? – what is the matter?'

'The matter? – oh, it is all over. It must have been a dream – nothing at all but a dream – don't you think so? It could not be anything more than a dream.'

'Of *course*,' said I, feeling uncommonly nervous, 'it *was* a dream.'

'I thought,' he said, 'there was a man in my room, and – and I jumped out of bed; and – and – where's the candle?'

'In your room, most likely,' I said, 'shall I go and bring it?'

'No; stay here – don't go; it's no matter – don't, I tell you; it was all a dream. Bolt the door, Dick; I'll stay here with you – I feel nervous. So, Dick, like a good fellow, light your candle and open the window – I am in a *shocking state*.'

I did as he asked me, and robing himself like Granuaile in one of my blankets, he seated himself close beside my bed.

Every body knows how contagious is fear of all sorts, but more especially that particular kind of fear under which poor Tom was at that moment labouring. I would not have heard, nor I believe would he have recapitulated, just at that moment, for half the world, the details of the hideous vision which had so unmanned him.

'Don't mind telling me anything about your nonsensical dream, Tom,' said I, affecting contempt, really in a panic; 'let us talk about something else; but it is quite plain that this dirty old house disagrees with us both, and hang me if I stay here any longer, to be pestered with indigestion and – and – bad nights, so we may as well look out for lodgings – don't you think so? – at once.'

Tom agreed, and, after an interval, said—

'I have been thinking, Richard, that it is a long time since I saw my father, and I have made up my mind to go down tomorrow and return in a day or two, and you can take rooms for us in the meantime.'

I fancied that this resolution, obviously the result of the vision which had so profoundly scared him, would probably vanish next morning with the damps and shadows of night. But I was mistaken. Off went Tom at peep of day to the country, having agreed that so soon as I had secured suitable lodgings, I was to recall him by letter from his visit to my Uncle Ludlow.

Now, anxious as I was to change my quarters, it so happened, owing to a series of petty procrastinations and accidents, that nearly a week elapsed before my bargain was made and my letter of recall on the wing to Tom; and, in the meantime, a trifling adventure or two had occurred to your humble servant, which, absurd as they now appear, diminished by distance, did certainly at the time serve to whet my appetite for change considerably.

A night or two after the departure of my comrade, I was sitting by my bedroom fire, the door locked, and the ingredients of a tumbler of hot whisky-punch upon the crazy spider-table; for, as the best mode of keeping the

Black spirits and white,
Blue spirits and grey,

with which I was environed, at bay, I had adopted the practice recommended by the wisdom of my ancestors, and 'kept my spirits up by pouring spirits down'. I had thrown aside my volume of Anatomy, and was treating myself by way of a tonic, preparatory to my punch and bed, to half-a-dozen pages of the *Spectator*, when I heard a step on the flight of stairs descending from the attics. It was two o'clock, and the streets were as silent as a churchyard – the sounds were, therefore, perfectly distinct. There was a slow, heavy tread, characterised by the emphasis and deliberation of age, descending by the narrow staircase from above; and, what made the sound more singular, it was plain that the feet which produced it were perfectly bare, measuring the descent with something between a pound and a flop, very ugly to hear.

I knew quite well that my attendant had gone away many hours before, and that nobody but myself had any business in the house. It was quite plain also that the person who was coming down stairs had no intention whatever of concealing his movements; but, on the contrary, appeared disposed to make even more noise, and proceed more deliberately, than was at all necessary. When the step reached the foot of the stairs outside my room, it seemed to stop; and I expected every moment to see my door open spontaneously, and give admission to the original of my detested portrait. I was, however, relieved in a few seconds by hearing the descent renewed, just in the same manner, upon the staircase leading down to the drawing-rooms, and thence, after another pause, down the next flight, and so on to the hall, whence I heard no more.

Now, by the time the sound had ceased, I was wound up, as they say, to a very unpleasant pitch of excitement. I listened, but there was not a stir. I screwed up my courage to a decisive experiment – opened my door, and in a stentorian voice bawled over the banisters, 'Who's there?' There was no answer but the ringing of my own voice through the empty old house – no renewal of the movement; nothing, in short, to give my unpleasant sensations a definite direction. There is, I think, something most disagreeably disenchanting in the sound of one's own voice under such circumstances, exerted in solitude, and in vain. It redoubled my sense of isolation, and my misgivings increased on perceiving that the door, which I certainly thought I had left open, was closed behind me; in a vague alarm, lest my retreat should be cut off, I got again into my room as quickly as I could, where I remained in a state of imaginary blockade, and very uncomfortable indeed, till morning.

Next night brought no return of my barefooted fellow-lodger; but the night following, being in my bed, and in the dark – somewhere, I suppose, about the same hour as before, I distinctly heard the old fellow again descending from the garrets.

This time I had had my punch, and the *morale* of the garrison was consequently excellent. I jumped out of bed, clutched the poker as I passed the expiring fire, and in a moment was upon the lobby. The sound had ceased by this time – the dark and chill were discouraging; and, guess my horror, when I saw, or thought I saw, a black monster, whether in the shape of a man or a bear I could not say, standing, with its back to the wall, on the lobby, facing me, with a pair of great greenish eyes shining dimly out. Now, I must be frank, and confess that the cupboard which displayed our plates and cups stood just there, though at the moment I did not recollect it. At the same time I must honestly say, that making every allowance for an excited imagination, I never could satisfy myself that I was made the dupe of my own fancy in this matter; for this apparition, after one or two shiftings of shape, as if in the act of incipient transformation, began, as it seemed on second thoughts, to advance upon me in its original form. From an instinct of terror rather than of courage, I hurled the poker, with all my force, at its head; and to the music of a horrid crash made my way into my room, and double-locked the door. Then, in a minute more, I heard the horrid bare feet walk down the stairs, till the sound ceased in the hall, as on the former occasion.

If the apparition of the night before was an ocular delusion of my fancy sporting with the dark outlines of our cupboard, and if its horrid eyes were nothing but a pair of inverted teacups, I had, at all events, the satisfaction of having launched the poker with admirable effect, and in true 'fancy' phrase, 'knocked its two daylights into one', as the commingled fragments of my tea-service testified. I did my best to gather comfort and courage from these evidences; but it would not do. And then what could I say of those horrid bare feet, and the regular tramp, tramp, tramp, which measured the distance of the entire staircase through the solitude of my haunted dwelling, and at an hour when no good influence was stirring? Confound it! – the whole affair was abominable. I was out of spirits, and dreaded the approach of night.

It came, ushered ominously in with a thunder-storm and dull torrents of depressing rain. Earlier than usual the streets grew silent; and by twelve o'clock nothing but the comfortless pattering of the rain was to be heard.

I made myself as snug as I could. I lighted *two* candles instead of one. I forswore bed, and held myself in readiness for a sally, candle in hand; for, *coûte qui coûte,* I was resolved to *see* the being, if visible at all, who troubled the nightly stillness of my mansion. I was fidgetty and nervous and tried in vain to interest myself with my books. I walked up and down my room, whistling in turn martial and hilarious music, and listening ever and anon for the dreaded noise. I sate down and stared at the square label on the solemn and reserved-looking black bottle, until 'FLANAGAN & CO'S BEST OLD MALT WHISKY' grew into a sort of subdued accompaniment to all the fantastic and horrible speculations which chased one another through my brain.

Silence, meanwhile, grew more silent, and darkness darker. I listened in vain for the rumble of a vehicle, or the dull clamour of a distant row. There was nothing but the sound of a rising wind, which had succeeded the thunder-storm that had travelled over the Dublin mountains quite out of hearing. In the middle of this great city I began to feel myself alone with nature, and Heaven knows what beside. My courage was ebbing. Punch, however, which makes beasts of so many, made a man of me again – just in time to hear with tolerable nerve and firmness the lumpy, flabby, naked feet deliberately descending the stairs again.

I took a candle, not without a tremor. As I crossed the floor I tried to extemporise a prayer, but stopped short to listen, and never finished it. The steps continued. I confess I hesitated for some seconds at the door before I took heart of grace and opened it. When I peeped out the lobby was perfectly empty – there was no monster standing on the staircase; and as the detested sound ceased, I was reassured enough to venture forward nearly to the banisters. Horror of horrors! within a stair or two beneath the spot where I stood the unearthly tread smote the floor. My eye caught something in motion; it was about the size of Goliath's foot – it was grey, heavy, and flapped with a dead weight from one step to another. As I am alive, it was the most monstrous grey rat I ever beheld or imagined.

Shakespeare says – 'Some men there are cannot abide a gaping pig, and some that are mad if they behold a cat.' I went well-nigh out of my wits when I beheld this *rat'*; for, laugh at me as you may, it fixed upon me, I thought, a perfectly human expression of malice; and, as it shuffled about and looked up into my face almost from between my feet, I saw, I could swear it – I felt it then, and know it now, the infernal gaze and the accursed countenance of my old friend in the portrait, transfused into the visage of the bloated vermin before me.

I bounced into my room again with a feeling of loathing and horror I cannot describe, and locked and bolted my door as if a lion had been at the other side. D—n him or *it*; curse the portrait and its original! I felt in my soul that the rat – yes, the *rat*, the RAT I had just seen, was that evil being in masquerade, and rambling through the house upon some infernal night lark.

Next morning I was early trudging through the miry streets; and, among other transactions, posted a peremptory note recalling Tom. On my return, however, I found a note from my absent 'chum', announcing his intended return next day. I was doubly rejoiced at this, because I had succeeded in getting rooms; and because the change of scene and return of my comrade were rendered specially pleasant by the last night's half ridiculous half horrible adventure.

I slept extemporaneously in my new quarters in Digges' Street that night, and next morning returned for breakfast to the haunted mansion, where I was certain Tom would call immediately on his arrival.

I was quite right – he came; and almost his first question referred to the primary object of our change of residence.

'Thank God,' he said with genuine fervour, on hearing that all was arranged. 'On *your* account I am delighted. As to myself, I assure you that no earthly consideration could have induced me ever again to pass a night in this disastrous old house.'

'Confound the house!' I ejaculated, with a genuine mixture of fear and detestation, 'we have not had a pleasant hour since we came to live here'; and so I went on, and related incidentally my adventure with the plethoric old rat.

'Well, if that were *all*,' said my cousin, affecting to make light of the matter, 'I don't think I should have minded it very much.'

'Ay, but its eye – its countenance, my dear Tom,' urged I; 'if you had seen *that*, you would have felt it might be *anything* but what it seemed.'

'I am inclined to think the best conjurer in such a case would be an able-bodied cat,' he said, with a provoking chuckle.

'But let us hear your own adventure,' I said tartly.

At this challenge he looked uneasily round him. I had poked up a very unpleasant recollection.

'You shall hear it, Dick; I'll tell it to you,' he said. 'Begad, sir, I should feel quite queer, though, telling it *here*, though we are too strong a body for ghosts to meddle with just now.'

Though he spoke this like a joke, I think it was serious calculation. Our Hebe was in a corner of the room, packing our cracked delft tea and dinner-services in a basket. She soon suspended operations, and with mouth and eyes wide open became an absorbed listener. Tom's experiences were told nearly in these words:—

'I saw it three times, Dick – three distinct times; and I am perfectly certain it meant me some infernal harm. I was, I say, in danger – in *extreme* danger;

for, if nothing else had happened, my reason would most certainly have failed me, unless I had escaped so soon. Thank God. I *did* escape.

'The first night of this hateful disturbance, I was lying in the attitude of sleep, in that lumbering old bed. I hate to think of it. I was really wide awake, though I had put out my candle, and was lying as quietly as if I had been asleep; and although accidentally restless, my thoughts were running in a cheerful and agreeable channel.

'I think it must have been two o'clock at least when I thought I heard a sound in that – that odious dark recess at the far end of the bedroom. It was as if someone was drawing a piece of cord slowly along the floor, lifting it up, and dropping it softly down again in coils. I sate up once or twice in my bed, but could see nothing, so I concluded it must be mice in the wainscot. I felt no emotion graver than curiosity, and after a few minutes ceased to observe it.

'While lying in this state, strange to say; without at first a suspicion of anything supernatural, on a sudden I saw an old man, rather stout and square, in a sort of roan-red dressing-gown, and with a black cap on his head, moving stiffly and slowly in a diagonal direction, from the recess, across the floor of the bedroom, passing my bed at the foot, and entering the lumber-closet at the left. He had something under his arm; his head hung a little at one side; and, merciful God! when I saw his face.'

Tom stopped for a while, and then said—

'That awful countenance, which living or dying I never can forget, disclosed what he was. Without turning to the right or left, he passed beside me, and entered the closet by the bed's head.

'While this fearful and indescribable type of death and guilt was passing, I felt that I had no more power to speak or stir than if I had been myself a corpse. For hours after it had disappeared, I was too terrified and weak to move. As soon as daylight came, I took courage, and examined the room, and especially the course which the frightful intruder had seemed to take, but there was not a vestige to indicate anybody's having passed there; no sign of any disturbing agency visible among the lumber that strewed the floor of the closet.

'I now began to recover a little. I was fagged and exhausted, and at last, overpowered by a feverish sleep. I came down late; and finding you out of spirits, on account of your dreams about the portrait, whose *original* I am now certain disclosed himself to me, I did not care to talk about the infernal vision. In fact, I was trying to persuade myself that the whole thing was an illusion, and I did not like to revive in their intensity the hated impressions of the past night – or to risk the constancy of my scepticism, by recounting the tale of my sufferings.

'It required some nerve, I can tell you, to go to my haunted chamber next night, and lie down quietly in the same bed,' continued Tom. 'I did so with a degree of trepidation, which, I am not ashamed to say, a very little matter would have sufficed to stimulate to downright panic. This night, however, passed off quietly enough, as also the next; and so too did two or three more. I grew more confident, and began to fancy that I believed in the theories of spectral illusions, with which I had at first vainly tried to impose upon my convictions.

'The apparition had been, indeed, altogether anomalous. It had crossed the room without any recognition of my presence: I had not disturbed *it*, and *it* had no mission to *me*. What, then, was the imaginable use of its crossing the room in a visible shape at all? Of course it might have *been* in the closet instead of *going* there, as easily as it introduced itself into the recess without entering the chamber in a shape discernible by the senses. Besides, how the deuce *had* I seen it? It was a dark night; I had no candle; there was no fire; and yet I saw it as distinctly, in colouring and outline, as ever I beheld human form! A cataleptic dream would explain it all; and I was determined that a dream it should be.

'One of the most remarkable phenomena connected with the practice of mendacity is the vast number of deliberate lies we tell ourselves, whom, of all persons, we can least expect to deceive. In all this, I need hardly tell you, Dick, I was simply lying to myself, and did not believe one word of the wretched humbug. Yet I went on, as men will do, like persevering charlatans and impostors, who tire people into credulity by the mere force of reiteration; so I hoped to win myself over at last to a comfortable scepticism about the ghost.

'He had not appeared a second time – that certainly was a comfort; and what, after all, did I care for him, and his queer old toggery and strange looks? Not a fig! I was nothing the worse for having seen him, and a good story the better. So I tumbled into bed, put out my candle, and, cheered by a loud drunken quarrel in the back lane, went fast asleep.

'From this deep slumber I awoke with a start. I knew I had had a horrible dream; but what it was I could not remember. My heart was thumping furiously; I felt bewildered and feverish; I sat up in the bed and looked about the room. A broad flood of moonlight came in through the curtainless window; everything was as I had last seen it; and though the domestic squabble in the back lane was, unhappily for me, allayed, I yet could hear a pleasant fellow singing, on his way home, the then popular comic ditty called, 'Murphy Delany'. Taking advantage of this diversion I lay down again, with my face towards the fireplace, and closing my eyes, did my best to think of nothing else but the song, which was every moment growing fainter in the distance:—

''Twas Murphy Delany, so funny and frisky,
Stept into a shebeen shop to get his skin full;
He reeled out again pretty well lined with whiskey,
As fresh as a shamrock, as blind as a bull.'

'The singer, whose condition I dare say resembled that of his hero, was soon too far off to regale my ears any more; and as his music died away, I myself sank into a doze, neither sound nor refreshing. Somehow the song had got into my head, and I went meandering on through the adventures of my respectable fellow-countryman, who, on emerging from the "shebeen shop", fell into a river, from which he was fished up to be "sat upon" by a coroner's jury, who having learned from a "horse-doctor" that he was "dead as a door-nail, so there was an end", returned their verdict accordingly, just as he returned to his senses, when an angry altercation and a pitched battle between the body and the coroner winds up the lay with due spirit and pleasantry.

'Through this ballad I continued with a weary monotony to plod, down to the very last line, and then *da capo*, and so on, in my uncomfortable half-sleep, for how long, I can't conjecture. I found myself at last, however, muttering, "*dead* as a door-nail, so there was an end"; and something like another voice within me, seemed to say, very faintly, but sharply, "dead! dead! *dead*! and may the Lord have mercy on your soul!" and instantaneously I was wide awake, and staring right before me from the pillow.

'Now – will you believe it, Dick? – I saw the same accursed figure standing full front, and gazing at me with its stony and fiendish countenance, not two yards from the bedside.'

Tom stopped here, and wiped the perspiration from his face. I felt very queer. The girl was as pale as Tom; and, assembled as we were in the very scene of these adventures, we were all, I dare say, equally grateful for the clear daylight and the resuming bustle out of doors.

'For about three seconds only I saw it plainly; then it grew indistinct; but, for a long time, there was something like a column of dark vapour where it had been standing, between me and the wall; and I felt sure that he was still there. After a good while, this appearance went too. I took my clothes downstairs to the hall, and dressed there, with the door half open; then went out into the street, and walked about the town till morning, when I came back, in a miserable state of nervousness and exhaustion. I was such a fool, Dick, as to be ashamed to tell you how I came to be so upset. I thought you would laugh at me; especially as I had always talked philosophy, and treated *your* ghosts with contempt. I concluded you would give me no quarter; and so kept my tale of horror to myself.

'Now, Dick, you will hardly believe me, when I assure you, that for many nights after this last experience, I did not go to my room at all. I used to sit up for a while in the drawing-room after you had gone up to your bed; and then steal down softly to the hall-door, let myself out, and sit in the 'Robin Hood' tavern until the last guest went off; and then I got through the night like a sentry, pacing the streets till morning.

'For more than a week I never slept in bed. I sometimes had a snooze on a form in the 'Robin Hood', and sometimes a nap in a chair during the day; but regular sleep I had absolutely none.

'I was quite resolved that we should get into another house; but I could not bring myself to tell you the reason, and I somehow put it off from day to day, although my life was, during every hour of this procrastination, rendered as miserable as that of a felon with the constables on his track. I was growing absolutely ill from this wretched mode of life.

'One afternoon I determined to enjoy an hour's sleep upon your bed. I hated mine; so that I had never, except in a stealthy visit every day to unmake it, lest Martha should discover the secret of my nightly absence, entered the ill-omened chamber.

'As ill-luck would have it, you had locked your bedroom, and taken away the key. I went into my own to unsettle the bedclothes, as usual, and give the bed the appearance of having been slept in. Now, a variety of circumstances concurred to bring about the dreadful scene through which I was that night to pass. In the first place, I was literally overpowered with fatigue, and longing for sleep; in the next place, the effect of this extreme exhaustion upon my nerves resembled that of a narcotic, and rendered me less susceptible than, perhaps, I should in any other condition have been, of the exciting fears which had become habitual to me. Then again, a little bit of the window was open, a pleasant freshness pervaded the room, and, to crown all, the cheerful sun of day was making the room quite pleasant. What was to prevent my enjoying an hour's nap *here*? The whole air was resonant with the cheerful hum of life, and the broad matter-of-fact light of day filled every corner of the room.

'I yielded – stifling my qualms – to the almost overpowering temptation; and merely throwing off my coat, and loosening my cravat, I lay down, limiting myself to *half*-an-hour's doze in the unwonted enjoyment of a feather bed, a coverlet, and a bolster.

'It was horribly insidious; and the demon, no doubt, marked my infatuated preparations. Dolt that I was, I fancied, with mind and body worn out for want of sleep, and an arrear of a full week's rest to my credit, that such measure as *half*-an-hour's sleep, in such a situation, was possible. My sleep was death-like, long, and dreamless.

'Without a start or fearful sensation of any kind, I waked gently, but completely. It was, as you have good reason to remember, long past midnight – I believe, about two o'clock. When sleep has been deep and long enough to satisfy nature thoroughly, one often wakens in this way, suddenly, tranquilly, and completely.

'There was a figure seated in that lumbering, old sofa-chair, near the fireplace. Its back was rather towards me, but I could not be mistaken; it turned slowly round, and, merciful heavens! there was the stony face, with its infernal lineaments of malignity and despair, gloating on me. There was now no doubt as to its consciousness of my presence, and the hellish malice with which it was animated, for it arose, and drew close to the bedside. There was a rope about its neck, and the other end, coiled up, it held stiffly in its hand.

'My good angel nerved me for this horrible crisis. I remained for some seconds transfixed by the gaze of this tremendous phantom. He came close to the bed, and appeared on the point of mounting upon it. The next instant I was upon the floor at the far side, and in a moment more was, I don't know how, upon the lobby.

'But the spell was not yet broken; the valley of the shadow of death was not yet traversed. The abhorred phantom was before me there; it was standing near the banisters, stooping a little, and with one end of the rope round its own neck, was poising a noose at the other, as if to throw over mine; and while engaged in this baleful pantomime, it wore a smile so sensual, so unspeakably dreadful, that my senses were nearly overpowered. I saw and remember nothing more, until I found myself in your room.

'I had a wonderful escape, Dick – there is no disputing *that* – an escape for which, while I live, I shall bless the mercy of heaven. No one can conceive or imagine what it is for flesh and blood to stand in the presence of such a thing, but one who has had the terrific experience. Dick, Dick, a shadow has passed over me – a chill has crossed my blood and marrow, and I will never be the same again – never, Dick – never!'

Our handmaid, a mature girl of two-and-fifty, as I have said, stayed her hand, as Tom's story proceeded, and by little and little drew near to us, with open mouth, and her brows contracted over her little, beady black eyes, till stealing a glance over her shoulder now and then, she established herself close behind us. During the relation, she had made various earnest comments, in an undertone; but these and her ejaculations, for the sake of brevity and simplicity, I have omitted in my narration.

'It's often I heard tell of it,' she now said, 'but I never believed it rightly till now – though, indeed, why should not I? Does not my mother, down there in the lane, know quare stories, God bless us, beyant telling about it? But you ought not to have slept in the back bedroom. She was loath to let me be going in and out of that room even in the day time, let alone for any Christian to spend the night in it; for sure she says it was his own bedroom.'

'*Whose* own bedroom?' we asked, in a breath.

'Why, *his* – the ould Judge's – Judge Horrock's, to be sure, God rest his sowl'; and she looked fearfully round.

'Amen!' I muttered. 'But did he die there?'

'Die there! No, not quite *there*,' she said. 'Shure, was not it over the banisters he hung himself, the ould sinner, God be merciful to us all? and was not it in the alcove they found the handles of the skipping-rope cut off, and the knife where he was settling the cord, God bless us, to hang himself with? It was his housekeeper's daughter owned the rope, my mother often told me, and the child never throve after, and used to be starting up out of her sleep, and screeching in the night time, wid dhrames and frights that cum an her; and they said how it was the speerit of the ould Judge that was tormentin' her; and she used to be roaring and yelling out to hould back the big ould fellow with the crooked neck; and then she'd screech 'Oh, the master! the master! he's stampin' at me, and beckoning to me! Mother, darling, don't let me go!' And so the poor crathure died at last, and the docthers said it was wather on the brain, for it was all they could say.'

'How long ago was all this?' I asked.

'Oh, then, how would I know?' she answered. 'But it must be a wondherful long time ago, for the housekeeper was an ould woman, with a pipe in her mouth, and not a tooth left, and better nor eighty years ould when my mother was first married; and they said she was a rale buxom, fine-dressed woman when the ould Judge come to his end; an', indeed, my mother's not far from eighty years ould herself this day; and what made it worse for the unnatural ould villain, God rest his soul, to frighten the little girl out of the world the way he did, was what was mostly thought and believed by every one. My mother says how the poor little crathure was his own child; for he was by all accounts an ould villain every way, an' the hangin'est judge that ever was known in Ireland's ground.'

'From what you said about the danger of sleeping in that bedroom,' said I, 'I suppose there were stories about the ghost having appeared there to others.'

'Well, there was things said – quare things, surely,' she answered, as it seemed, with some reluctance. 'And why would not there? Sure was it not up in that same room he slept for more than twenty years? and was it not in the *alcove* he got the rope ready that done his own business at last, the way he done many a betther man's in his lifetime? – and was not the body lying in the same bed after death, and put in the coffin there, too, and carried out to his grave from it in Pether's churchyard, after the coroner was done? But there was quare stories – my mother has them all – about how one Nicholas Spaight got into trouble on the head of it.'

'And what did they say of this Nicholas Spaight?' I asked.

'Oh, for that matther, it's soon told,' she answered.

And she certainly did relate a very strange story, which so piqued my curiosity, that I took occasion to visit the ancient lady, her mother, from whom I learned many very curious particulars. Indeed, I am tempted to tell the tale, but my fingers are weary, and I must defer it. But if you wish to hear it another time, I shall do my best.

When we had heard the strange tale I have *not* told you, we put one or two further questions to her about the alleged spectral visitations, to which the house had, ever since the death of the wicked old Judge, been subjected.

'No one ever had luck in it,' she told us. 'There was always cross accidents, sudden deaths, and short times in it. The first that tuck, it was a family – I forget their name – but at any rate there was two young ladies and their papa. He was about sixty, and a stout healthy gentleman as you'd wish to see at that age. Well, he slept in that unlucky back bedroom; and, God between us an' harm! sure enough he was found dead one morning, half out of the bed, with his head as black as a sloe, and swelled like a puddin', hanging down near the floor. It was a fit, they said. He was as dead as a mackerel, and so *he* could not say what it was; but the ould people was all sure that it was nothing at all but the ould Judge, God bless us! that frightened him out of his senses and his life together.

'Some time after there was a rich old maiden lady took the house. I don't know which room *she* slept in, but she lived alone; and at any rate, one morning, the servants going down early to their work, found her sitting on the passage-stairs, shivering and talkin' to herself, quite mad; and never a word more could any of *them* or her friends get from her ever afterwards but, 'Don't ask me to go, for I promised to wait for him.' They never made out from her who it was she meant by *him*, but of course those that knew all about the ould house were at no loss for the meaning of all that happened to her.

'Then afterwards, when the house was let out in lodgings, there was Micky Byrne that took the same room, with his wife and three little children; and sure I heard Mrs Byrne myself telling how the children used to be lifted up in the bed at night, she could not see by what mains; and how they were starting and screeching every hour, just all as one as the housekeeper's little girl that died, till at last one night poor Micky had a dhrop in him, the way he used now and again; and what do you think in the middle of the night he thought he heard a noise on the stairs, and being in liquor, nothing less id do him but out he must go himself to see what was wrong. Well, after that, all she ever heard of him was himself sayin', 'Oh, God!' and a tumble that shook the very house; and there, sure enough, he was lying on the lower stairs, under the lobby, with his neck smashed double undher him, where he was flung over the banisters.'

Then the handmaiden added—

'I'll go down to the lane, and send up Joe Gavvey to pack up the rest of the taythings, and bring all the things across to your new lodgings.'

And so we all sallied out together, each of us breathing more freely, I have no doubt, as we crossed that ill-omened threshold for the last time.

Now, I may add thus much, in compliance with the immemorial usage of the realm of fiction, which sees the hero not only through his adventures, but fairly out of the world. You must have perceived that what the flesh, blood, and bone hero of romance proper is to the regular compounder of fiction, this old house of brick, wood, and mortar is to the humble recorder of this true tale. I, therefore, relate, as in duty bound, the catastrophe which ultimately befell it, which was simply this – that about two years subsequently to my story it was taken by a quack doctor, who called himself Baron Duhlstoerf, and filled the parlour windows with bottles of indescribable horrors preserved in brandy, and the newspapers with the usual grandiloquent and mendacious advertisements. This gentleman among his virtues did not reckon sobriety, and one night, being overcome with much wine, he set fire to his bed curtains, partially burned himself, and totally consumed the house. It was afterwards rebuilt, and for a time an undertaker established himself in the premises.

I have now told you my own and Tom's adventures, together with some valuable collateral particulars; and having acquitted myself of my engagement, I wish you a very good night, and pleasant dreams.

The Clock

William Fryer Harvey

I liked your description of the people at the *pension*. I can just picture that rather sinister Miss Cornelius, with her toupee and clinking bangles. I don't wonder you felt frightened that night when you found her sleepwalking in the corridor. But after all, why shouldn't she sleepwalk? As to the movements of the furniture in the lounge on the Sunday, you are, I suppose, in an earthquake zone, though an earthquake seems too big an explanation for the ringing of that little handbell on the mantelpiece. It's rather as if our parlour maid – another new one! – were to call a stray elephant to account for the teapot we found broken yesterday. You have at least, in Italy, escaped the eternal problem of maids.

Yes, my dear, I most certainly believe you. I have never had experiences quite like yours, but your mention of Miss Cornelius has reminded me of something rather similar that happened nearly twenty years ago, soon after I left school. I was staying with my aunt in Hampstead. You remember her, I expect; or, if not her, the poodle, Monsieur, that she used to make perform such pathetic tricks. There was another guest, whom I had never met before, a Mrs Caleb. She lived in Lewes and had been staying with my aunt for about a fortnight, recuperating after a series of domestic upheavals, which had culminated in her two servants leaving her at an hour's notice – without any reason, according to Mrs Caleb, but I wondered. I had never seen the maids; I had seen Mrs Caleb and, frankly, I disliked her. She left the same sort of impression on me as I gather your Miss Cornelius leaves on you – something queer and secretive; underground, if you can use the expression, rather than underhand. And I could feel in my body that she did not like me.

It was summer. Joan Denton – you remember her; her husband was killed in Gallipoli – had suggested that I should go down to spend the day with her. Her people had rented a little cottage some three miles out of Lewes. We arranged a day. It was gloriously fine for a wonder, and I had planned to leave that stuffy old Hampstead house before the old ladies were astir. But Mrs Caleb waylaid me in the hall, just as I was going out.

'I wonder,' she said, 'I wonder if you could do me a small favour. If you *do* have any time to spare in Lewes – only if you do – would you be so kind as to call at my house? I left a little travelling-clock there in the hurry of parting. If it's not in the drawing-room, it will be in my bedroom or in one of the maids' bedrooms. I know I lent it to the cook, who was a poor riser, but I can't remember if she returned it. Would it be too much to ask? The house has been locked up for twelve days, but everything is in order. I have the keys here. The large one is for the garden gate, the small one for the front door.'

I could only accept, and she proceeded to tell me how I could find Ash Grove House.

'You will feel quite like a burglar,' she said. 'But mind, it's only if you have time to spare.'

As a matter of fact I found myself glad of any excuse to kill time. Poor old Joan had been taken suddenly ill in the night – they feared appendicitis – and though her people were very kind and asked me to stay to lunch, I could see that I should only be in the way, and made Mrs Caleb's commission an excuse for an early departure.

I found Ash Grove without difficulty. It was a medium-sized red-brick house, standing by itself in a high walled garden that bounded a narrow lane. A flagged path led from the gate to the front door, in front of which grew, not an ash, but a monkey-puzzle, that must have made the rooms unnecessarily gloomy. The side door, as I expected, was locked. The dining-room and drawing-room lay on either side of the hall and, as the windows of both were shuttered, I left the hall door open, and in the dim light looked round hurriedly for the clock, which, from what Mrs Caleb had said, I hardly expected to find in either of the downstairs rooms. It was neither on table nor mantelpiece. The rest of the furniture was carefully covered over with white dust-sheets. Then I went upstairs. But, before doing so, I closed the front door. I did in fact feel rather like a burglar, and I thought that if anyone did happen to see the front door open, I might have difficulty in explaining things.

Happily the upstairs windows were not shuttered. I made a hurried search of the principal bedrooms. They had been left in apple-pie order; nothing was out of place; but there was no sign of Mrs Caleb's clock. The impression that the house gave me – you know the sense of personality that a house conveys – was neither pleasing nor displeasing, but it was stuffy, stuffy from the absence of fresh air, with an additional stuffiness added, that seemed to come out from the hangings and quilts and anti-macassars. The corridor, onto which the bedrooms I had examined opened, communicated with a smaller wing, an older part of the house, I imagined, which contained a box-room and the maids' sleeping-quarters. The last door that I unlocked (I should say that the doors of all the rooms were locked, and relocked by me after I had glanced inside them) contained the object of my search. Mrs Caleb's travelling-clock was on the mantelpiece, ticking away merrily.

That was how I thought of it at first. And then for the first time I realised that there was something wrong. The clock had no business to be ticking. The house had been shut up for twelve days. No one had come in to air it or to light fires. I remember how Mrs Caleb had told my aunt that if she left the keys with a neighbour, she was never sure who might get hold of them. And yet the clock was going.

I wondered if some vibration had set the mechanism in motion, and pulled out my watch to see the time. It was five minutes to one. The clock on the mantelpiece said four minutes to the hour. Then, without quite knowing why, I shut the door on to the landing, locked myself in, and again looked round the room. Nothing was out of place. The only thing that might have called for remark was that there appeared to be a slight indentation on the pillow and the bed; but the mattress was a feather mattress, and you know how difficult it is to make them perfectly smooth. You won't need to be told that I gave a hurried glance under the bed – do you remember your supposed burglar in Number Six at St Ursula's? – and then, and much more reluctantly, opened the doors of two horribly capacious cupboards, both happily empty, except for a framed text with its face to the wall.

By this time I really was frightened. The clock went ticking on. I had a horrible feeling that an alarm might go off at any moment, and the thought of being in that empty house was almost too much for me. However, I made an attempt to pull myself together. It might after all be a fourteen-day clock. If it were, then it would be almost run down. I could roughly find out how long the clock had been going by winding it up. I hesitated to put the matter to the test, but the uncertainty was too much for me. I took it out of its case and began to wind. I had scarcely turned the winding-screw twice when it stopped. The clock clearly was not running down; the hands had been set in motion probably only an hour or two before.

I felt cold and faint and, going to the window, threw up the sash, letting in the sweet, live air of the garden. I knew now that the house was queer, horribly queer. Could someone be living in the house? Was someone else in the house now? I thought that I had been in all the rooms, but had I? I had only just opened the bathroom door, and I had certainly not opened any cupboards, except those in the room in which I was.

Then, as I stood by the open window, wondering what I should do next and feeling that I just couldn't go down that corridor into the darkened hall to fumble at the latch of the front door with I don't know what behind me, I heard a noise. It was very faint at first, and seemed to be coming from the stairs. It was a curious noise – not the noise of anyone climbing up the stairs, but – you will laugh if this letter reaches you by a morning post – of something hopping up the stairs, like a very big bird would hop. I heard it on the landing; it stopped. Then there was a curious scratching noise against one of the bedroom doors, the sort of noise you can make with the nail of your little finger scratching polished wood. Whatever it was, was coming slowly down the corridor, scratching at the doors as it went. I could stand it no longer. Nightmare pictures of locked doors opening filled my brain. I took up the clock, wrapped it in my Macintosh, and dropped it out of the window on to a flower-bed. Then I managed to crawl out of the window and, getting a grip of the sill, 'successfully negotiated', as the journalists would say, 'a twelve-foot drop.' So much for our much abused Gym at St Ursula's. Picking up the Macintosh, I ran round to the front door and locked it. Then I felt I could breathe, but not until I was on the far side of the gate in the garden wall did I feel safe.

Then I remembered that the bedroom window was open. What was I to do? Wild horses wouldn't have dragged me into that house again unaccompanied. I made up my mind to go to the police station and tell them everything. I should be laughed at, of course, and they might easily refuse to believe my story of Mrs Caleb's commission. I had actually begun to walk down the lane in the direction of the town when I chanced to look back at the house. The window that I had left open was shut.

No, my dear, I didn't see any face or anything dreadful like that… and, of course, it may have shut by itself. It was an ordinary sash-window, and you know they are often difficult to keep open.

And the rest? Why, there's really nothing more to tell. I didn't even see Mrs Caleb again. She had had some sort of fainting fit just before lunchtime, my aunt informed me on my return, and had had to go to bed. Next morning I travelled down to Cornwall to join mother and the children. I thought I had forgotten all about it, but when three years later Uncle Charles suggested giving me a travelling-clock for a twenty-first birthday present, I was foolish enough to prefer the alternative that he offered, a collected edition of the works of Thomas Carlyle.

The Beast with Five Fingers

William Fryer Harvey

When I was a little boy I once went with my father to call on Adrian Borlsover. I played on the floor with a black spaniel while my father appealed for a subscription. Just before we left my father said, 'Mr Borlsover, may my son here shake hands with you? It will be a thing to look back upon with pride when he grows to be a man.'

I came up to the bed on which the old man was lying and put my hand in his, awed by the still beauty of his face. He spoke to me kindly, and hoped that I should always try to please my father. Then he placed his right hand on my head and asked for a blessing to rest upon me. 'Amen!' said my father, and I followed him out of the room, feeling as if I wanted to cry. But my father was in excellent spirits.

'That old gentleman, Jim,' said he, 'is the most wonderful man in the whole town. For ten years he has been quite blind.'

'But I saw his eyes,' I said. 'They were ever so black and shiny; they weren't shut up like Nora's puppies. Can't he see at all?'

And so I learnt for the first time that a man might have eyes that looked dark and beautiful and shining without being able to see.

'Just like Mrs Tomlinson has big ears,' I said, 'and can't hear at all except when Mr Tomlinson shouts.'

'Jim,' said my father, 'it's not right to talk about a lady's ears. Remember what Mr Borlsover said about pleasing me and being a good boy.'

That was the only time I saw Adrian Borlsover. I soon forgot about him and the hand which he laid in blessing on my head. But for a week I prayed that those dark tender eyes might see.

'His spaniel may have puppies,' I said in my prayers, 'and he will never be able to know how funny they look with their eyes all closed up. Please let old Mr Borlsover see.'

Adrian Borlsover, as my father had said, was a wonderful man. He came of an eccentric family. Borlsovers' sons, for some reason, always seemed to marry very ordinary women, which perhaps accounted for the fact that no Borlsover had been a genius, and only one Borlsover had been mad. But they were great champions of little causes, generous patrons of odd sciences, founders of querulous sects, trustworthy guides to the bypath meadows of erudition.

Adrian was an authority on the fertilization of orchids. He had held at one time the family living at Borlsover Conyers, until a congenital weakness of the lungs obliged him to seek a less rigorous climate in the sunny south coast watering-place where I had seen him. Occasionally he would relieve one or other of the local clergy. My father described him as a fine preacher, who gave long and inspiring sermons from what many men would have considered unprofitable texts. 'An excellent proof,' he would add, 'of the truth of the doctrine of direct verbal inspiration.'

Adrian Borlsover was exceedingly clever with his hands. His penmanship was exquisite. He illustrated all his scientific papers, made his own woodcuts, and carved the reredos that is at present the chief feature of interest in the church at Borlsover Conyers. He had an exceedingly clever knack in cutting silhouettes for young ladies and paper pigs and cows for little children, and made more than one complicated wind instrument of his own devising.

When he was fifty years old Adrian Borlsover lost his sight. In a wonderfully short time he had adapted himself to the new conditions of life. He quickly learned to read Braille. So marvellous indeed was his sense of touch that he was still able to maintain his interest in botany. The mere passing of his long supple fingers over a flower was sufficient means for its identification, though occasionally he would use his lips. I have found several letters of his among my father's correspondence. In no case was there anything to show that he was afflicted with blindness and this in spite of the fact that he exercised undue economy in the spacing of lines. Towards the close of his life the old man was credited with powers of touch that seemed almost uncanny: it has been said that he could tell at once the colour of a ribbon placed between his fingers. My father would neither confirm nor deny the story.

I

Adrian Borlsover was a bachelor. His elder brother George had married late in life, leaving one son, Eustace, who lived in the gloomy Georgian mansion at Borlsover Conyers, where he could work undisturbed in collecting material for his great book on heredity.

Like his uncle, he was a remarkable man. The Borlsovers had always been born naturalists, but Eustace possessed in a special degree the power of systematizing his knowledge. He had received his university education in Germany, and then, after post-graduate work in Vienna and Naples, had travelled for four years in South America and the East, getting together a huge store of material for a new study into the processes of variation.

He lived alone at Borlsover Conyers with Saunders his secretary, a man who bore a somewhat dubious reputation in the district, but whose powers as a mathematician, combined with his business abilities, were invaluable to Eustace.

Uncle and nephew saw little of each other. The visits of Eustace were confined to a week in the summer or autumn: long weeks, that dragged almost as slowly as the bath-chair in which the old man was drawn along the sunny sea front. In their way the two men were fond of each other, though their intimacy would doubtless have been greater had they shared the same religious views. Adrian held to the old-fashioned evangelical dogmas of his early manhood; his nephew for many years had been thinking of embracing Buddhism. Both men possessed, too, the reticence the Borlsovers had always shown, and which their enemies sometimes called hypocrisy. With Adrian it was a reticence as to the things he had left undone; but with Eustace it seemed that the curtain which he was so careful to leave undrawn hid something more than a half-empty chamber.

Two years before his death Adrian Borlsover developed, unknown to himself, the not uncommon power of automatic writing. Eustace made the discovery by accident. Adrian was sitting reading in bed, the forefinger of his left hand tracing the Braille characters, when his nephew noticed that a pencil the old man held in his right hand was moving slowly along the opposite page. He left his seat in the window and sat down beside the bed. The right hand continued to move, and now he could see plainly that they were letters and words which it was forming.

'Adrian Borlsover,' wrote the hand, 'Eustace Borlsover, George Borlsover, Francis Borlsover, Sigismund Borlsover, Adrian Borlsover, Eustace Borlsover, Saville Borlsover. B, for Borlsover. Honesty is the Best Policy. Beautiful Belinda Borlsover.'

'What curious nonsense!' said Eustace to himself.

'King George the Third ascended the throne in 1760,' wrote the hand. 'Crowd, a noun of multitude; a collection of individuals – Adrian Borlsover, Eustace Borlsover.'

'It seems to me,' said his uncle, closing the book, 'that you had much better make the most of the afternoon sunshine and take your walk now.' 'I think perhaps I will,' Eustace answered as he picked up the volume. 'I won't go far, and when I come back I can read to you those articles in *Nature* about which we were speaking.'

He went along the promenade, but stopped at the first shelter, and seating himself in the corner best protected from the wind, he examined the book at leisure. Nearly every page was scored with a meaningless jungle of pencil marks: rows of capital letters, short words, long words, complete sentences, copy-book tags. The whole thing, in fact, had the appearance of a copy-book, and on a more careful scrutiny Eustace thought that there was ample evidence to show that the handwriting at the beginning of the book, good though it was, was not nearly so good as the handwriting at the end.

He left his uncle at the end of October, with a promise to return early in December. It seemed to him quite clear that the old man's power of automatic writing was developing rapidly, and for the first time he looked forward to a visit that combined duty with interest.

But on his return he was at first disappointed. His uncle, he thought, looked older. He was listless too, preferring others to read to him and dictating nearly all his letters. Not until the day before he left had Eustace an opportunity of observing Adrian Borlsover's new-found faculty.

The old man, propped up in bed with pillows, had sunk into a light sleep. His two hands lay on the coverlet, his left hand tightly clasping his right. Eustace took an empty manuscript book and placed a pencil within reach of the fingers of the right hand. They snatched at it eagerly; then dropped the pencil to unloose the left hand from its restraining grasp.

'Perhaps to prevent interference I had better hold that hand,' said Eustace to himself, as he watched the pencil. Almost immediately it began to write.

'Blundering Borlsovers, unnecessarily unnatural, extraordinarily eccentric, culpably curious.'

'Who are you?' asked Eustace, in a low voice.

'Never you mind,' wrote the hand of Adrian.

'Is it my uncle who is writing?'

'Oh, my prophetic soul, mine uncle.'

'Is it anyone I know?'

'Silly Eustace, you'll see me very soon.'

'When shall I see you?'

'When poor old Adrian's dead.'

'Where shall I see you?'

'Where shall you not?'

Instead of speaking his next question, Borlsover wrote it. 'What is the time?'

The fingers dropped the pencil and moved three or four times across the paper. Then, picking up the pencil, they wrote:

'Ten minutes before four. Put your book away, Eustace. Adrian mustn't find us working at this sort of thing. He doesn't know what to make of it, and I won't have poor old Adrian disturbed. *Au revoir*.'

Adrian Borlsover awoke with a start.

'I've been dreaming again,' he said; 'such queer dreams of leaguered cities and forgotten towns. You were mixed up in this one, Eustace, though I can't remember how. Eustace, I want to warn you. Don't walk in doubtful paths. Choose your friends well. Your poor grandfather—'

A fit of coughing put an end to what he was saying, but Eustace saw that the hand was still writing. He managed unnoticed to draw the book away. 'I'll light the gas,' he said, 'and ring for tea.' On the other side of the bed curtain he saw the last sentences that had been written.

'It's too late, Adrian,' he read. 'We're friends already; aren't we, Eustace Borlsover?'

On the following day Eustace Borlsover left. He thought his uncle looked ill when he said goodbye, and the old man spoke despondently of the failure his life had been.

'Nonsense, uncle!' said his nephew. 'You have got over your difficulties in a way not one in a hundred thousand would have done. Every one marvels at your splendid perseverance in teaching your hand to take the place of your lost sight. To me it's been a revelation of the possibilities of education.'

'Education,' said his uncle dreamily, as if the word had started a new train of thought, 'education is good so long as you know to whom and for what purpose you give it. But with the lower orders of men, the base and more sordid spirits, I have grave doubts as to its results. Well, goodbye, Eustace, I may not see you again. You are a true Borlsover, with all the Borlsover faults. Marry, Eustace. Marry some good, sensible girl. And if by any chance I don't see you again, my will is at my solicitor's. I've not left you any legacy, because I know you're well provided for, but I thought you might like to have my books. Oh, and there's just one other thing. You know, before the end people often lose control over themselves and make absurd requests. Don't pay any attention to them, Eustace. Goodbye!' and he held out his hand. Eustace took it. It remained in his a fraction of a second longer than he had expected, and gripped him with a virility that was surprising. There was, too, in its touch a subtle sense of intimacy.

'Why, uncle!' he said, 'I shall see you alive and well for many long years to come.'

Two months later Adrian Borlsover died.

II

Eustace Borlsover was in Naples at the time. He read the obituary notice in the *Morning Post* on the day announced for the funeral.

'Poor old fellow!' he said. 'I wonder where I shall find room for all his books.'

The question occurred to him again with greater force when three days later he found himself standing in the library at Borlsover Conyers, a huge room built for use, and not for beauty, in the year of Waterloo by a Borlsover who was an ardent admirer of the great Napoleon. It was arranged on the plan of many college libraries, with tall, projecting bookcases forming deep recesses of dusty silence, fit graves for the old hates of forgotten controversy, the dead passions of forgotten lives. At the end of the room, behind the bust of some unknown eighteenth-century divine, an ugly iron corkscrew stair led to a shelf-lined gallery. Nearly every shelf was full.

'I must talk to Saunders about it,' said Eustace. 'I suppose that it will be necessary to have the billiard-room fitted up with book cases.'

The two men met for the first time after many weeks in the dining-room that evening.

'Hullo!' said Eustace, standing before the fire with his hands in his pockets. 'How goes the world, Saunders? Why these dress togs?' He himself was wearing an old shooting-jacket. He did not believe in mourning, as he had told his uncle on his last visit; and though he usually went in for quiet-coloured ties, he wore this evening one of an ugly red, in order to shock Morton the butler, and to make them thrash out the whole question of mourning for themselves in the servants' hall. Eustace was a true Borlsover. 'The world,' said Saunders, 'goes the same as usual, confoundedly slow. The dress togs are accounted for by an invitation from Captain Lockwood to bridge.'

'How are you getting there?'

'I've told your coachman to drive me in your carriage. Any objection?'

'Oh, dear me, no! We've had all things in common for far too many years for me to raise objections at this hour of the day.'

'You'll find your correspondence in the library,' went on Saunders. 'Most of it I've seen to. There are a few private letters I haven't opened. There's also a box with a rat, or something, inside it that came by the evening post. Very likely it's the six-toed albino. I didn't look, because I didn't want to mess up my things but I should gather from the way it's jumping about that it's pretty hungry.'

'Oh, I'll see to it,' said Eustace, 'while you and the Captain earn an honest penny.'

Dinner over and Saunders gone, Eustace went into the library. Though the fire had been lit the room was by no means cheerful.

'We'll have all the lights on at any rate,' he said, as he turned the switches. 'And, Morton,' he added, when the butler brought the coffee, 'get me a screwdriver or something to undo this box. Whatever the animal is, he's kicking up the deuce of a row. What is it? Why are you dawdling?'

'If you please, sir, when the postman brought it he told me that they'd bored the holes in the lid at the post-office. There were no breathin' holes in the lid, sir, and they didn't want the animal to die. That is all, sir.'

'It's culpably careless of the man, whoever he was,' said Eustace, as he removed the screws, 'packing an animal like this in a wooden box with no means of getting air. Confound it all! I meant to ask Morton to bring me a cage to put it in. Now I suppose I shall have to get one myself.'

He placed a heavy book on the lid from which the screws had been removed, and went into the billiard-room. As he came back into the library with an empty cage in his hand he heard the sound of something falling, and then of something scuttling along the floor.

'Bother it! The beast's got out. How in the world am I to find it again in this library!'

To search for it did indeed seem hopeless. He tried to follow the sound of the scuttling in one of the recesses where the animal seemed to be running behind the books in the shelves, but it was impossible to locate it. Eustace resolved to go on quietly reading. Very likely the animal might gain confidence and show itself. Saunders seemed to have dealt in his usual methodical manner with most of the correspondence. There were still the private letters.

What was that? Two sharp clicks and the lights in the hideous candelabra that hung from the ceiling suddenly went out.

'I wonder if something has gone wrong with the fuse,' said Eustace, as he went to the switches by the door. Then he stopped. There was a noise at the other end of the room, as if something was crawling up the iron corkscrew stair. 'If it's gone into the gallery,' he said, 'well and good.' He hastily turned on the lights, crossed the room, and climbed up the stair. But he could see nothing. His grandfather had placed a little gate at the top of the stair, so that children could run and romp in the gallery without fear of accident. This Eustace closed, and having considerably narrowed the circle of his search, returned to his desk by the fire.

How gloomy the library was! There was no sense of intimacy about the room. The few busts that an eighteenth-century Borlsover had brought back from the grand tour, might have been in keeping in the old library. Here they seemed out of place. They made the room feel cold, in spite of the heavy red damask curtains and great gilt cornices.

With a crash two heavy books fell from the gallery to the floor; then, as Borlsover looked, another and yet another.

'Very well; you'll starve for this, my beauty!' he said. 'We'll do some little experiments on the metabolism of rats deprived of water. Go on! Chuck them down! I think I've got the upper hand.' He turned once again to his correspondence. The letter was from the family solicitor. It spoke of his uncle's death and of the valuable collection of books that had been left to him in the will.

'There was one request,' he read, 'which certainly came as a surprise to me. As you know, Mr Adrian Borlsover had left instructions that his body was to be buried in as simple a manner as possible at Eastbourne. He expressed a desire that there should be neither wreaths nor flowers of any kind, and hoped that his friends and relatives would not consider it necessary to wear mourning. The day before his death we received a letter cancelling these instructions. He wished his body to be embalmed (he gave us the address of the man we were to employ – Pennifer, Ludgate Hill), with orders that his right hand was to be sent to you, stating that it was at your special request. The other arrangements as to the funeral remained unaltered.'

'Good Lord!' said Eustace; 'what in the world was the old boy driving at? And what in the name of all that's holy is that?'

Someone was in the gallery. Someone had pulled the cord attached to one of the blinds, and it had rolled up with a snap. Someone must be in the gallery, for a second blind did the same. Someone must be walking round the gallery, for one after the other the blinds sprang up, letting in the moonlight.

'I haven't got to the bottom of this yet,' said Eustace, 'but I will do before the night is very much older,' and he hurried up the corkscrew stair. He had just got to the top when the lights went out a second time, and he heard again the scuttling along the floor. Quickly he stole on tiptoe in the dim moonshine in the direction of the noise, feeling as he went for one of the switches. His fingers touched the metal knob at last. He turned on the electric light.

About ten yards in front of him, crawling along the floor, was a man's hand. Eustace stared at it in utter astonishment. It was moving quickly, in the manner of a geometer caterpillar, the fingers humped up one moment, flattened out the next; the thumb appeared to give a crab-like motion to the whole. While he was looking, too surprised to stir, the hand disappeared round the corner. Eustace ran forward. He no longer saw it, but he could hear it as it squeezed its way behind the books on one of the shelves. A heavy volume had been displaced. There was a gap in the row of books where it had got in. In his fear lest it should escape him again, he seized the first book that came to his hand and plugged it into the hole. Then, emptying two shelves of their contents, he took the wooden boards and propped them up in front to make his barrier doubly sure.

'I wish Saunders was back,' he said; 'one can't tackle this sort of thing alone.' It was after eleven, and there seemed little likelihood of Saunders returning before twelve. He did not dare to leave the shelf unwatched, even to run downstairs to ring the bell. Morton the butler often used to come round about eleven to see that the windows were fastened, but he might not come. Eustace was thoroughly unstrung. At last he heard steps down below.

'Morton!' he shouted; 'Morton!'

'Sir?'

'Has Mr Saunders got back yet?'

'Not yet, sir.'

'Well, bring me some brandy, and hurry up about it. I'm up here in the gallery, you duffer.'

'Thanks,' said Eustace, as he emptied the glass. 'Don't go to bed yet, Morton. There are a lot of books that have fallen down by accident; bring them up and put them back in their shelves.'

Morton had never seen Borlsover in so talkative a mood as on that night. 'Here,' said Eustace, when the books had been put back and dusted, 'you might hold up these boards for me, Morton. That beast in the box got out, and I've been chasing it all over the place.'

'I think I can hear it chawing at the books, sir. They're not valuable, I hope? I think that's the carriage, sir; I'll go and call Mr Saunders.'

It seemed to Eustace that he was away for five minutes, but it could hardly have been more than one when he returned with Saunders. 'All right, Morton, you can go now. I'm up here, Saunders.'

'What's all the row?' asked Saunders, as he lounged forward with his hands in his pockets. The luck had been with him all the evening. He was completely satisfied, both with himself and with Captain Lockwood's taste in wines. 'What's the matter? You look to me to be in an absolute blue funk.'

'That old devil of an uncle of mine,' began Eustace – 'oh, I can't explain it all. It's his hand that's been playing old Harry all the evening. But I've got it cornered behind these books. You've got to help me catch it.'

'What's up with you, Eustace? What's the game?'

'It's no game, you silly idiot! If you don't believe me take out one of those books and put your hand in and feel.'

'All right,' said Saunders; 'but wait till I've rolled up my sleeve. The accumulated dust of centuries, eh?' He took off his coat, knelt down, and thrust his arm along the shelf.

'There's something there right enough,' he said. 'It's got a funny stumpy end to it, whatever it is, and nips like a crab. Ah, no, you don't!' He pulled his hand out in a flash. 'Shove in a book quickly. Now it can't get out.'

'What was it?' asked Eustace.

'It was something that wanted very much to get hold of me. I felt what seemed like a thumb and forefinger. Give me some brandy.'

'How are we to get it out of there?'

'What about a landing net?'

'No good. It would be too smart for us. I tell you, Saunders, it can cover the ground far faster than I can walk. But I think I see how we can manage it. The two books at the end of the shelf are big ones that go right back against the wall. The others are very thin. I'll take out one at a time, and you slide the rest along until we have it squashed between the end two.'

It certainly seemed to be the best plan. One by one, as they took out the books, the space behind grew smaller and smaller. There was something in it that was certainly very much alive. Once they caught sight of fingers pressing outward for a way of escape. At last they had it pressed between the two big books.

'There's muscle there, if there isn't flesh and blood,' said Saunders, as he held them together. 'It seems to be a hand right enough, too. I suppose this is a sort of infectious hallucination. I've read about such cases before.'

'Infectious fiddlesticks!' said Eustace, his face white with anger; 'bring the thing downstairs. We'll get it back into the box.'

It was not altogether easy, but they were successful at last. 'Drive in the screws,' said Eustace, 'we won't run any risks. Put the box in this old desk of mine. There's nothing in it that I want. Here's the key. Thank goodness, there's nothing wrong with the lock.'

'Quite a lively evening,' said Saunders. 'Now let's hear more about your uncle.'

They sat up together until early morning. Saunders had no desire for sleep. Eustace was trying to explain and to forget: to conceal from himself a fear that he had never felt before – the fear of walking alone down the long corridor to his bedroom.

III

'Whatever it was,' said Eustace to Saunders on the following morning, 'I propose that we drop the subject. There's nothing to keep us here for the next ten days. We'll motor up to the Lakes and get some climbing.'

'And see nobody all day, and sit bored to death with each other every night. Not for me thanks. Why not run up to town? Run's the exact word in this case, isn't it? We're both in such a blessed funk. Pull yourself together Eustace, and let's have another look at the hand.'

'As you like,' said Eustace; 'there's the key.' They went into the library and opened the desk. The box was as they had left it on the previous night.

'What are you waiting for?' asked Eustace.

'I am waiting for you to volunteer to open the lid. However, since you seem to funk it, allow me. There doesn't seem to be the likelihood of any rumpus this morning, at all events.' He opened the lid and picked out the hand.

'Cold?' asked Eustace.

'Tepid. A bit below blood-heat by the feel. Soft and supple too. If it's the embalming, it's a sort of embalming I've never seen before. Is it your uncle's hand?'

'Oh, yes, it's his all right,' said Eustace. 'I should know those long thin fingers anywhere. Put it back in the box, Saunders. Never mind about the screws. I'll lock the desk, so that there'll be no chance of its getting out.

We'll compromise by motoring up to town for a week. If we get off soon after lunch we ought to be at Grantham or Stamford by night.'

'Right,' said Saunders; 'and tomorrow – Oh, well, by tomorrow we shall have forgotten all about this beastly thing.'

If when the morrow came they had not forgotten, it was certainly true that at the end of the week they were able to tell a very vivid ghost story at the little supper Eustace gave on Hallow E'en.

'You don't want us to believe that it's true, Mr Borlsover? How perfectly awful!'

'I'll take my oath on it, and so would Saunders here; wouldn't you, old chap?'

'Any number of oaths,' said Saunders. 'It was a long thin hand, you know, and it gripped me just like that.'

'Don't Mr Saunders! Don't! How perfectly horrid! Now tell us another one, do. Only a really creepy one, please!'

'Here's a pretty mess!' said Eustace on the following day as he threw a letter across the table to Saunders. 'It's your affair, though. Mrs Merrit, if I understand it, gives a month's notice.'

'Oh, that's quite absurd on Mrs Merrit's part,' Saunders replied. 'She doesn't know what she's talking about. Let's see what she says.'

> 'DEAR SIR,' he read, 'this is to let you know that I must give you a month's notice as from Tuesday the 13th. For a long time I've felt the place too big for me, but when Jane Parfit, and Emma Laidlaw go off with scarcely as much as an 'if you please,' after frightening the wits out of the other girls, so that they can't turn out a room by themselves or walk alone down the stairs for fear of treading on half-frozen toads or hearing it run along the passages at night, all I can say is that it's no place for me. So I must ask you, Mr Borlsover, sir, to find a new housekeeper that has no objection to large and lonely houses, which some people do say, not that I believe them for a minute, my poor mother always having been a Wesleyan, are haunted.
>
> 'Yours faithfully,
>
> ELIZABETH MERRIT.
>
> 'P.S. – I should be obliged if you would give my respects to Mr Saunders. I hope that he won't run no risks with his cold.'

'Saunders,' said Eustace, 'you've always had a wonderful way with you in dealing with servants. You mustn't let poor old Merrit go.'

'Of course she shan't go,' said Saunders. 'She's probably only angling for a rise in salary. I'll write to her this morning.'

'No; there's nothing like a personal interview. We've had enough of town. We'll go back tomorrow, and you must work your cold for all it's worth. Don't forget that it's got on to the chest, and will require weeks of feeding up and nursing.'

'All right. I think I can manage Mrs Merrit.'

But Mrs Merrit was more obstinate than he had thought. She was very sorry to hear of Mr Saunders's cold, and how he lay awake all night in London coughing; very sorry indeed. She'd change his room for him gladly, and get the south room aired. And wouldn't he have a basin of hot bread and milk last thing at night? But she was afraid that she would have to leave at the end of the month.

'Try her with an increase of salary,' was the advice of Eustace.

It was no use. Mrs Merrit was obdurate, though she knew of a Mrs Handyside who had been housekeeper to Lord Gargrave, who might be glad to come at the salary mentioned.

'What's the matter with the servants, Morton?' asked Eustace that evening when he brought the coffee into the library. 'What's all this about Mrs Merrit wanting to leave?'

'If you please, sir, I was going to mention it myself. I have a confession to make, sir. When I found your note asking me to open that desk and take out the box with the rat, I broke the lock as you told me, and was glad to do it, because I could hear the animal in the box making a great noise, and I thought it wanted food. So I took out the box, sir, and got a cage, and was going to transfer it, when the animal got away.'

'What in the world are you talking about? I never wrote any such note.'

'Excuse me, sir, it was the note I picked up here on the floor on the day you and Mr Saunders left. I have it in my pocket now.'

It certainly seemed to be in Eustace's handwriting. It was written in pencil, and began somewhat abruptly.

'Get a hammer, Morton,' he read, 'or some other tool, and break open the lock in the old desk in the library. Take out the box that is inside. You need not do anything else. The lid is already open. Eustace Borlsover.'

'And you opened the desk?'

'Yes, sir; and as I was getting the cage ready the animal hopped out.'

'What animal?'

'The animal inside the box, sir.'

'What did it look like?'

'Well, sir, I couldn't tell you,' said Morton nervously; 'my back was turned, and it was halfway down the room when I looked up.'

'What was its colour?' asked Saunders; 'black?'

'Oh, no, sir, a grayish white. It crept along in a very funny way, sir. I don't think it had a tail.'

'What did you do then?'

'I tried to catch it, but it was no use. So I set the rat-traps and kept the library shut. Then that girl Emma Laidlaw left the door open when she was cleaning, and I think it must have escaped.'

'And you think it was the animal that's been frightening the maids?'

'Well, no, sir, not quite. They said it was—you'll excuse me, sir—a hand that they saw. Emma trod on it once at the bottom of the stairs. She thought then it was a half-frozen toad, only white. And then Parfit was washing up the dishes in the scullery. She wasn't thinking about anything in particular. It was close on dusk. She took her hands out of the water and was drying them absent-minded like on the roller towel, when she found that she was drying someone else's hand as well, only colder than hers.'

'What nonsense!' exclaimed Saunders.

'Exactly, sir; that's what I told her; but we couldn't get her to stop.'

'You don't believe all this?' said Eustace, turning suddenly towards the butler.

'Me, sir? Oh, no, sir! I've not seen anything.'

'Nor heard anything?'

'Well, sir, if you must know, the bells do ring at odd times, and there's nobody there when we go; and when we go round to draw the blinds of a night, as often as not somebody's been there before us. But as I says to Mrs Merrit, a young monkey might do wonderful things, and we all know that Mr Borlsover has had some strange animals about the place.'

'Very well, Morton, that will do.'

'What do you make of it?' asked Saunders when they were alone. 'I mean of the letter he said you wrote.'

'Oh, that's simple enough,' said Eustace. 'See the paper it's written on? I stopped using that years ago, but there were a few odd sheets and envelopes left in the old desk. We never fastened up the lid of the box before locking it in. The hand got out, found a pencil, wrote this note, and shoved it through a crack on to the floor where Morton found it. That's plain as daylight.'

'But the hand couldn't write?'

'Couldn't it? You've not seen it do the things I've seen,' and he told Saunders more of what had happened at Eastbourne.

'Well,' said Saunders, 'in that case we have at least an explanation of the legacy. It was the hand which wrote unknown to your uncle that letter to your solicitor, bequeathing itself to you. Your uncle had no more to do with that request than I. In fact, it would seem that he had some idea of this automatic writing, and feared it.'

'Then if it's not my uncle, what is it?'

'I suppose some people might say that a disembodied spirit had got your uncle to educate and prepare a little body for it. Now it's got into that little body and is off on its own.'

'Well, what are we to do?'

'We'll keep our eyes open,' said Saunders, 'and try to catch it. If we can't do that, we shall have to wait till the bally clockwork runs down. After all, if it's flesh and blood, it can't live for ever.'

For two days nothing happened. Then Saunders saw it sliding down the banister in the hall. He was taken unawares, and lost a full second before he started in pursuit, only to find that the thing had escaped him. Three days later, Eustace, writing alone in the library at night, saw it sitting on an open book at the other end of the room. The fingers crept over the page, feeling the print as if it were reading; but before he had time to get up from his seat, it had taken the alarm and was pulling itself up the curtains. Eustace watched it grimly as it hung on to the cornice with three fingers, flicking thumb and forefinger at him in an expression of scornful derision.

'I know what I'll do,' he said. 'If I only get it into the open I'll set the dogs on to it.'

He spoke to Saunders of the suggestion.

'It's jolly good idea,' he said; 'only we won't wait till we find it out of doors. We'll get the dogs. There are the two terriers and the under-keeper's

Irish mongrel that's on to rats like a flash. Your spaniel has not got spirit enough for this sort of game.' They brought the dogs into the house, and the keeper's Irish mongrel chewed up the slippers, and the terriers tripped up Morton as he waited at table; but all three were welcome. Even false security is better than no security at all.

For a fortnight nothing happened. Then the hand was caught, not by the dogs, but by Mrs Merrit's grey parrot. The bird was in the habit of periodically removing the pins that kept its seed and water tins in place, and of escaping through the holes in the side of the cage. When once at liberty Peter would show no inclination to return, and would often be about the house for days. Now, after six consecutive weeks of captivity, Peter had again discovered a new means of unloosing his bolts and was at large, exploring the tapestried forests of the curtains and singing songs in praise of liberty from cornice and picture rail.

'It's no use your trying to catch him,' said Eustace to Mrs Merrit, as she came into the study one afternoon towards dusk with a step-ladder. 'You'd much better leave Peter alone. Starve him into surrender, Mrs Merrit, and don't leave bananas and seed about for him to peck at when he fancies he's hungry. You're far too softhearted.'

'Well, sir, I see he's right out of reach now on that picture rail, so if you wouldn't mind closing the door, sir, when you leave the room, I'll bring his cage in tonight and put some meat inside it. He's that fond of meat, though it does make him pull out his feathers to suck the quills. They *do* say that if you cook—'

'Never mind, Mrs Merrit,' said Eustace, who was busy writing. 'That will do; I'll keep an eye on the bird.'

There was silence in the room, unbroken but for the continuous whisper of his pen.

'Scratch poor Peter,' said the bird. 'Scratch poor old Peter!'

'Be quiet, you beastly bird!'

'Poor old Peter! Scratch poor Peter, do.'

'I'm more likely to wring your neck if I get hold of you.' He looked up at the picture rail, and there was the hand holding on to a hook with three fingers, and slowly scratching the head of the parrot with the fourth. Eustace ran to the bell and pressed it hard; then across to the window, which he closed with a bang. Frightened by the noise the parrot shook its wings preparatory to flight, and as it did so the fingers of the hand got hold of it by the throat. There was a shrill scream from Peter as he fluttered across the room, wheeling round in circles that ever descended, borne down under the weight that clung to him. The bird dropped at last quite suddenly, and Eustace saw fingers and feathers rolled into an inextricable mass on the floor. The struggle abruptly ceased as finger and thumb squeezed the neck; the bird's eyes rolled up to show the whites, and there was a faint, half-choked gurgle. But before the fingers had time to loose their hold, Eustace had them in his own.

'Send Mr Saunders here at once,' he said to the maid who came in answer to the bell. 'Tell him I want him immediately.'

Then he went with the hand to the fire. There was a ragged gash across the back where the bird's beak had torn it, but no blood oozed from the wound. He noticed with disgust that the nails had grown long and discoloured.

'I'll burn the beastly thing,' he said. But he could not burn it. He tried to throw it into the flames, but his own hands, as if restrained by some old primitive feeling, would not let him. And so Saunders found him pale and irresolute, with the hand still clasped tightly in his fingers.

'I've got it at last,' he said in a tone of triumph.

'Good; let's have a look at it.'

'Not when it's loose. Get me some nails and a hammer and a board of some sort.'

'Can you hold it all right?'

'Yes, the thing's quite limp; tired out with throttling poor old Peter, I should say.'

'And now,' said Saunders when he returned with the things, 'what are we going to do?'

'Drive a nail through it first, so that it can't get away; then we can take our time over examining it.'

'Do it yourself,' said Saunders. 'I don't mind helping you with guinea-pigs occasionally when there's something to be learned; partly because I don't fear a guinea-pig's revenge. This thing's different.'

'All right, you miserable skunk. I won't forget the way you've stood by me.'

He took up a nail, and before Saunders had realised what he was doing had driven it through the hand, deep into the board.

'Oh, my aunt,' he giggled hysterically, 'look at it now,' for the hand was writhing in agonized contortions, squirming and wriggling upon the nail like a worm upon the hook.

'Well,' said Saunders, 'you've done it now. I'll leave you to examine it.'

'Don't go, in heaven's name. Cover it up, man, cover it up! Shove a cloth over it! Here!' and he pulled off the antimacassar from the back of a chair and wrapped the board in it. 'Now get the keys from my pocket and open the safe. Chuck the other things out. Oh, Lord, it's getting itself into frightful knots! and open it quick!' He threw the thing in and banged the door.

'We'll keep it there till it dies,' he said. 'May I burn in hell if I ever open the door of that safe again.'

Mrs Merrit departed at the end of the month. Her successor certainly was more successful in the management of the servants. Early in her rule she declared that she would stand no nonsense, and gossip soon withered and died. Eustace Borlsover went back to his old way of life. Old habits crept over and covered his new experience. He was, if anything, less morose, and showed a greater inclination to take his natural part in country society.

'I shouldn't be surprised if he marries one of these days,' said Saunders. 'Well, I'm in no hurry for such an event. I know Eustace far too well for the future Mrs Borlsover to like me. It will be the same old story again: a long friendship slowly made – marriage – and a long friendship quickly forgotten.'

IV

But Eustace Borlsover did not follow the advice of his uncle and marry. He was too fond of old slippers and tobacco. The cooking, too, under Mrs Handyside's management was excellent, and she seemed, too, to have a heaven-sent faculty in knowing when to stop dusting.

Little by little the old life resumed its old power. Then came the burglary. The men, it was said, broke into the house by way of the conservatory. It was really little more than an attempt, for they only succeeded in carrying away a few pieces of plate from the pantry. The safe in the study was certainly found open and empty, but, as Mr Borlsover informed the police inspector, he had kept nothing of value in it during the last six months.

'Then you're lucky in getting off so easily, sir,' the man replied. 'By the way they have gone about their business, I should say they were experienced cracksmen. They must have caught the alarm when they were just beginning their evening's work.'

'Yes,' said Eustace, 'I suppose I am lucky.'

'I've no doubt,' said the inspector, 'that we shall be able to trace the men. I've said that they must have been old hands at the game. The way they got in and opened the safe shows that. But there's one little thing that puzzles me. One of them was careless enough not to wear gloves, and I'm bothered if I know what he was trying to do. I've traced his finger-marks on the new varnish on the window sashes in every one of the downstairs rooms. They are very distinct ones too.'

'Right hand or left, or both?' asked Eustace.

'Oh, right every time. That's the funny thing. He must have been a foolhardy fellow, and I rather think it was him that wrote that.' He took out a slip of paper from his pocket. 'That's what he wrote, sir. 'I've got out, Eustace Borlsover, but I'll be back before long.' Some gaol bird just escaped, I suppose. It will make it all the easier for us to trace him. Do you know the writing, sir?'

'No,' said Eustace; 'it's not the writing of anyone I know.'

'I'm not going to stay here any longer,' said Eustace to Saunders at luncheon. 'I've got on far better during the last six months than ever I expected, but I'm not going to run the risk of seeing that thing again. I shall go up to town this afternoon. Get Morton to put my things together, and join me with the car at Brighton on the day after tomorrow. And bring the proofs of those two papers with you. We'll run over them together.'

'How long are you going to be away?'

'I can't say for certain, but be prepared to stay for some time. We've stuck to work pretty closely through the summer, and I for one need a holiday. I'll engage the rooms at Brighton. You'll find it best to break the journey at Hitchin. I'll wire to you there at the Crown to tell you the Brighton address.'

The house he chose at Brighton was in a terrace. He had been there before. It was kept by his old college gyp, a man of discreet silence, who was admirably partnered by an excellent cook. The rooms were on the first floor. The two bedrooms were at the back, and opened out of each other. 'Saunders can have the smaller one, though it is the only one with a fire-place,' he said. 'I'll stick to the larger of the two, since it's got a bathroom adjoining. I wonder what time he'll arrive with the car.'

Saunders came about seven, cold and cross and dirty. 'We'll light the fire in the dining-room,' said Eustace, 'and get Prince to unpack some of the things while we are at dinner. What were the roads like?'

'Rotten; swimming with mud, and a beastly cold wind against us all day. And this is July. Dear old England!'

'Yes,' said Eustace, 'I think we might do worse than leave dear old England for a few months.'

They turned in soon after twelve.

'You oughtn't to feel cold, Saunders,' said Eustace, 'when you can afford to sport a great cat-skin lined coat like this. You do yourself very well, all things considered. Look at those gloves, for instance. Who could possibly feel cold when wearing them?'

'They are far too clumsy though for driving. Try them on and see,' and he tossed them through the door on to Eustace's bed, and went on with his unpacking. A minute later he heard a shrill cry of terror. 'Oh, Lord,' he heard, 'it's in the glove! Quick, Saunders, quick!' Then came a smacking thud. Eustace had thrown it from him. 'I've chucked it into the bathroom,' he gasped, 'it's hit the wall and fallen into the bath. Come now if you want to help.' Saunders, with a lighted candle in his hand, looked over the edge of the bath. There it was, old and maimed, dumb and blind, with a ragged hole in the middle, crawling, staggering, trying to creep up the slippery sides, only to fall back helpless.

'Stay there,' said Saunders. 'I'll empty a collar box or something, and we'll jam it in. It can't get out while I'm away.'

'Yes, it can,' shouted Eustace. 'It's getting out now. It's climbing up the plug chain. No, you brute, you filthy brute, you don't! Come back, Saunders, it's getting away from me. I can't hold it; it's all slippery. Curse its claw! Shut the window, you idiot! The top too, as well as the bottom. You utter idiot! It's got out!' There was the sound of something dropping on to the hard flagstones below, and Eustace fell back fainting.

For a fortnight he was ill.

'I don't know what to make of it,' the doctor said to Saunders. 'I can only suppose that Mr Borlsover has suffered some great emotional shock. You had better let me send someone to help you nurse him. And by all means indulge that whim of his never to be left alone in the dark. I would keep a light burning all night if I were you. But he *must* have more fresh air. It's perfectly absurd this hatred of open windows.'

Eustace, however, would have no one with him but Saunders. 'I don't want the other men,' he said. 'They'd smuggle it in somehow. I know they would.'

'Don't worry about it, old chap. This sort of thing can't go on indefinitely. You know I saw it this time as well as you. It wasn't half so active. It won't go on living much longer, especially after that fall. I heard it hit the flags myself. As soon as you're a bit stronger we'll leave this place; not bag and baggage, but with only the clothes on our backs, so that it won't be able to hide anywhere. We'll escape it that way. We won't give any address, and we won't have any parcels sent after us. Cheer up, Eustace! You'll be well enough to leave in a day or two. The doctor says I can take you out in a chair tomorrow.'

'What have I done?' asked Eustace. 'Why does it come after me? I'm no worse than other men. I'm no worse than you, Saunders; you know I'm not. It was you who were at the bottom of that dirty business in San Diego, and that was fifteen years ago.'

'It's not that, of course,' said Saunders. 'We are in the twentieth century, and even the parsons have dropped the idea of your old sins finding you out. Before you caught the hand in the library it was filled with pure malevolence—to you and all mankind. After you spiked it through with that nail it naturally forgot about other people, and concentrated its attention on you. It was shut up in the safe, you know, for nearly six months. That gives plenty of time for thinking of revenge.'

Eustace Borlsover would not leave his room, but he thought that there might be something in Saunders's suggestion to leave Brighton without notice. He began rapidly to regain his strength.

'We'll go on the first of September,' he said.

The evening of August 31st was oppressively warm. Though at midday the windows had been wide open, they had been shut an hour or so before dusk. Mrs Prince had long since ceased to wonder at the strange habits of the gentlemen on the first floor. Soon after their arrival she had been told to take down the heavy window curtains in the two bedrooms, and day by day the rooms had seemed to grow more bare. Nothing was left lying about.

'Mr Borlsover doesn't like to have any place where dirt can collect,' Saunders had said as an excuse. 'He likes to see into all the corners of the room.'

'Couldn't I open the window just a little?' he said to Eustace that evening. 'We're simply roasting in here, you know.'

'No, leave well alone. We're not a couple of boarding-school misses fresh from a course of hygiene lectures. Get the chessboard out.'

They sat down and played. At ten o'clock Mrs Prince came to the door with a note. 'I am sorry I didn't bring it before,' she said, 'but it was left in the letter-box.'

'Open it, Saunders, and see if it wants answering.'

It was very brief. There was neither address nor signature.

'Will eleven o'clock tonight be suitable for our last appointment?'

'Who is it from?' asked Borlsover.

'It was meant for me,' said Saunders. 'There's no answer, Mrs Prince,' and he put the paper into his pocket. 'A dunning letter from a tailor; I suppose he must have got wind of our leaving.'

It was a clever lie, and Eustace asked no more questions. They went on with their game.

On the landing outside Saunders could hear the grandfather's clock whispering the seconds, blurting out the quarter-hours.

'Check!' said Eustace. The clock struck eleven. At the same time there was a gentle knocking on the door; it seemed to come from the bottom panel.

'Who's there?' asked Eustace.

There was no answer.

'Mrs Prince, is that you?'

'She is up above,' said Saunders; 'I can hear her walking about the room.'

'Then lock the door; bolt it too. Your move, Saunders.'

While Saunders sat with his eyes on the chessboard, Eustace walked over to the window and examined the fastenings. He did the same in Saunders's room and the bathroom. There were no doors between the three rooms, or he would have shut and locked them too.

'Now, Saunders,' he said, 'don't stay all night over your move. I've had time to smoke one cigarette already. It's bad to keep an invalid waiting. There's only one possible thing for you to do. What was that?'

'The ivy blowing against the window. There, it's your move now, Eustace.'

'It wasn't the ivy, you idiot. It was someone tapping at the window,' and he pulled up the blind. On the outer side of the window, clinging to the sash, was the hand.

'What is it that it's holding?'

'It's a pocket-knife. It's going to try to open the window by pushing back the fastener with the blade.'

'Well, let it try,' said Eustace. 'Those fasteners screw down; they can't be opened that way. Anyhow, we'll close the shutters. It's your move, Saunders. I've played.'

But Saunders found it impossible to fix his attention on the game. He could not understand Eustace, who seemed all at once to have lost his fear. 'What do you say to some wine?' he asked. 'You seem to be taking things coolly, but I don't mind confessing that I'm in a blessed funk.'

'You've no need to be. There's nothing supernatural about that hand, Saunders. I mean it seems to be governed by the laws of time and space. It's not the sort of thing that vanishes into thin air or slides through oaken doors. And since that's so, I defy it to get in here. We'll leave the place in the morning. I for one have bottomed the depths of fear. Fill your glass, man! The windows are all shuttered, the door is locked and bolted. Pledge me my uncle Adrian! Drink, man! What are you waiting for?'

Saunders was standing with his glass half raised. 'It can get in,' he said hoarsely; 'it can get in! We've forgotten. There's the fireplace in my bedroom. It will come down the chimney.'

'Quick!' said Eustace, as he rushed into the other room; 'we haven't a minute to lose. What can we do? Light the fire, Saunders. Give me a match, quick!'

'They must be all in the other room. I'll get them.'

'Hurry, man, for goodness' sake! Look in the bookcase! Look in the bathroom! Here, come and stand here; I'll look.'

'Be quick!' shouted Saunders. 'I can hear something!'

'Then plug a sheet from your bed up the chimney. No, here's a match.' He had found one at last that had slipped into a crack in the floor.

'Is the fire laid? Good, but it may not burn. I know—the oil from that old reading-lamp and this cotton-wool. Now the match, quick! Pull the sheet away, you fool! We don't want it now.'

There was a great roar from the grate as the flames shot up. Saunders had been a fraction of a second too late with the sheet. The oil had fallen on to it. It, too, was burning.

'The whole place will be on fire!' cried Eustace, as he tried to beat out the flames with a blanket. 'It's no good! I can't manage it. You must open the door, Saunders, and get help.'

Saunders ran to the door and fumbled with the bolts. The key was stiff in the lock.

'Hurry!' shouted Eustace; 'the whole place is ablaze!'

The key turned in the lock at last. For half a second Saunders stopped to look back. Afterwards he could never be quite sure as to what he had seen, but at the time he thought that something black and charred was creeping slowly, very slowly, from the mass of flames towards Eustace Borlsover. For a moment he thought of returning to his friend, but the noise and the smell of the burning sent him running down the passage crying, 'Fire! Fire!' He rushed to the telephone to summon help, and then back to the bathroom – he should have thought of that before – for water. As he burst open the bedroom door there came a scream of terror which ended suddenly, and then the sound of a heavy fall.

The Haunted Orchard

Richard Le Gallienne

Spring was once more in the world. As she sang to herself in the faraway woodlands her voice reached even the ears of the city, weary with the long winter. Daffodils flowered at the entrances to the Subway, furniture removing vans blocked the side streets, children clustered like blossoms on the doorsteps, the open cars were running, and the cry of the 'cash clo'' man was once more heard in the land.

Yes, it was the spring, and the city dreamed wistfully of lilacs and the dewy piping of birds in gnarled old apple-trees, of dogwood lighting up with sudden silver the thickening woods, of water-plants unfolding their glossy scrolls in pools of morning freshness.

On Sunday mornings, the outbound trains were thronged with eager pilgrims, hastening out of the city, to behold once more the ancient marvel of the spring; and, on Sunday evenings, the railway termini were aflower with banners of blossom from rifled woodland and orchard carried in the hands of the returning pilgrims, whose eyes still shone with the spring magic, in whose ears still sang the fairy music.

And as I beheld these signs of the vernal equinox I knew that I, too, must follow the music, forsake awhile the beautiful siren we call the city, and in the green silences meet once more my sweetheart Solitude.

As the train drew out of the Grand Central, I hummed to myself,

'I've a neater, sweeter maiden, in a greener, cleaner land'

and so I said goodbye to the city, and went forth with beating heart to meet the spring.

I had been told of an almost forgotten corner on the south coast of Connecticut, where the spring and I could live in an inviolate loneliness – a place uninhabited save by birds and blossoms, woods and thick grass, and an occasional silent farmer, and pervaded by the breath and shimmer of the Sound.

Nor had rumour lied, for when the train set me down at my destination I stepped out into the most wonderful green hush, a leafy Sabbath silence through which the very train, as it went farther on its way, seemed to steal as noiselessly as possible for fear of breaking the spell.

After a winter in the town, to be dropped thus suddenly into the intense quiet of the countryside makes an almost ghostly impression upon one, as of an enchanted silence, a silence that listens and watches but never speaks, finger on lip. There is a spectral quality about everything upon which the eye falls: the woods, like great green clouds, the wayside flowers, the still farm-houses half lost in orchard bloom – all seem to exist in a dream. Everything is so still, everything so supernaturally green. Nothing moves or talks, except the gentle susurrus of the spring wind swaying the young buds high up in the quiet sky, or a bird now and again, or a little brook singing softly to itself among the crowding rushes.

Though, from the houses one notes here and there, there are evidently human inhabitants of this green silence, none are to be seen. I have often wondered where the countryfolk hide themselves, as I have walked hour after hour, past farm and croft and lonely door-yards, and never caught sight of a human face. If you should want to ask the way, a farmer is as shy as a squirrel, and if you knock at a farm-house door, all is as silent as a rabbit-warren.

As I walked along in the enchanted stillness, I came at length to a quaint old farm-house – 'old Colonial' in its architecture – embowered in white lilacs, and surrounded by an orchard of ancient apple-trees which cast a rich shade on the deep spring grass. The orchard had the impressiveness of those old religious groves, dedicated to the strange worship of sylvan gods, gods to be found now only in Horace or Catullus, and in the hearts of young poets to whom the beautiful antique Latin is still dear.

The old house seemed already the abode of Solitude. As I lifted the latch of the white gate and walked across the forgotten grass, and up on to the veranda already festooned with wistaria, and looked into the window, I saw Solitude sitting by an old piano, on which no composer later than Bach had ever been played.

In other words, the house was empty; and going round to the back, where old barns and stables leaned together as if falling asleep, I found a broken pane, and so climbed in and walked through the echoing rooms. The house was very lonely. Evidently no one had lived in it for a long time. Yet it was all ready for some occupant, for whom it seemed to be waiting. Quaint old four-poster bedsteads stood in three rooms – dimity curtains and spotless linen – old oak chests and mahogany presses; and, opening drawers in Chippendale sideboards, I came upon beautiful frail old silver and exquisite china that set me thinking of a beautiful grandmother of mine, made out of old lace and laughing wrinkles and mischievous old blue eyes.

There was one little room that particularly interested me, a tiny bedroom all white, and at the window the red roses were already in bud. But what caught my eye with peculiar sympathy was a small bookcase, in which were some twenty or thirty volumes, wearing the same forgotten expression – forgotten and yet cared for – which lay like a kind of memorial charm upon everything in the old house. Yes, everything seemed forgotten and yet everything, curiously – even religiously – remembered. I took out book after book from the shelves, once or twice flowers fell out from the pages – and I caught sight of a delicate handwriting here and there and frail markings. It was evidently the little intimate library of a young girl. What surprised me most was to find that quite half the books were in French – French poets and French romancers: a charming, very rare edition of Ronsard, a beautifully printed edition of Alfred de Musset, and a copy of Théophile Gautier's *Mademoiselle de Maupin*. How did these exotic books come to be there alone in a deserted New England farm-house?

This question was to be answered later in a strange way. Meanwhile I had fallen in love with the sad, old, silent place, and as I closed the white gate and was once more on the road, I looked about for someone who could tell me whether or not this house of ghosts might be rented for the summer by a comparatively living man.

I was referred to a fine old New England farm-house shining white through the trees a quarter of a mile away. There I met an ancient couple, a typical New England farmer and his wife; the old man, lean, chin-bearded, with keen grey eyes flickering occasionally with a shrewd humour, the old lady with a kindly old face of the withered-apple type and ruddy. They were evidently prosperous people, but their minds – for some reason I could not at the moment divine – seemed to be divided between their New England desire to drive a hard bargain and their disinclination to let the house at all.

Over and over again they spoke of the loneliness of the place. They feared I would find it very lonely. No one had lived in it for a long time, and so on. It seemed to me that afterwards I understood their curious hesitation, but at the moment only regarded it as a part of the circuitous New England method of bargaining. At all events, the rent I offered finally overcame their disinclination, whatever its cause, and so I came into possession – for four months – of that silent old house, with the white lilacs, and the drowsy barns, and the old piano, and the strange orchard; and, as the summer came on, and the year changed its name from May to June, I used to lie under the apple-trees in the afternoons, dreamily reading some old book, and through half-sleepy eyelids watching the silken shimmer of the Sound.

I had lived in the old house for about a month, when one afternoon a strange thing happened to me. I remember the date well. It was the afternoon of Tuesday, June 13th. I was reading, or rather dipping here and there, in Burton's *Anatomy of Melancholy*. As I read, I remember that a little unripe apple, with a petal or two of blossom still clinging to it, fell upon the old yellow page. Then I suppose I must have fallen into a dream, though it seemed to me that both my eyes and my ears were wide open, for I suddenly became aware of a beautiful young voice singing very softly somewhere among the leaves. The singing was very frail, almost imperceptible, as though it came out of the air. It came and went fitfully, like the elusive fragrance of sweetbrier – as though a girl was walking to and fro, dreamily humming to herself in the still afternoon. Yet there was no one to be seen. The orchard had never seemed more lonely. And another fact that struck me as strange was that the words that floated to me out of the aerial music were French, half sad, half gay snatches of some long-dead singer of old France, I looked about for the origin of the sweet sounds, but in vain. Could it be the birds that were singing in French in this strange orchard? Presently the voice seemed to come quite close to me, so near that it might have been the voice of a dryad singing to me out of the tree against which I was leaning. And this time I distinctly caught the words of the sad little song:

'Chante, rossignol, chante,
Toi qui as le cœur gai;
Tu as le cœur à rire,
Moi, je l'ai-t-à pleurer.'

But, though the voice was at my shoulder, I could see no one, and then the singing stopped with what sounded like a sob; and a moment or two later I seemed to hear a sound of sobbing far down the orchard. Then there followed silence, and I was left to ponder on the strange occurrence. Naturally, I decided that it was just a day-dream between sleeping and waking over the pages of an old book; yet when next day and the day after the invisible singer was in the orchard again, I could not be satisfied with such mere matter-of-fact explanation.

'A la claire fontaine,'

went the voice to and fro through the thick orchard boughs,

'M'en allant promener,
J'ai trouvé l'eau si belle
Que je m'y suis baigné,
Lui y a longtemps que je t'aime,
Jamais je ne t'oubliai.'

It was certainly uncanny to hear that voice going to and fro the orchard, there somewhere amid the bright sun-dazzled boughs – yet not a human creature to be seen – not another house even within half a mile. The most materialistic mind could hardly but conclude that here was something 'not dreamed of in our philosophy.' It seemed to me that the only reasonable explanation was the entirely irrational one – that my orchard was haunted: haunted by some beautiful young spirit, with some sorrow of lost joy that would not let her sleep quietly in her grave.

And next day I had a curious confirmation of my theory. Once more I was lying under my favorite apple-tree, half reading and half watching the Sound, lulled into a dream by the whir of insects and the spices called up from the earth by the hot sun. As I bent over the page, I suddenly had the startling impression that someone was leaning over my shoulder and reading with me, and that a girl's long hair was falling over me down on to the page. The book was the Ronsard I had found in the little bedroom. I turned, but again there was nothing there. Yet this time I knew that I had not been dreaming, and I cried out:

'Poor child! tell me of your grief – that I may help your sorrowing heart to rest.'

But, of course, there was no answer; yet that night I dreamed a strange dream. I thought I was in the orchard again in the afternoon and once again heard the strange singing – but this time, as I looked up, the singer was no longer invisible. Coming toward me was a young girl with wonderful blue eyes filled with tears and gold hair that fell to her waist. She wore a straight, white robe that might have been a shroud or a bridal dress. She appeared not to see me, though she came directly to the tree where I was sitting. And there she knelt and buried her face in the grass and sobbed as if her heart would break. Her long hair fell over her like a mantle, and in my dream I stroked it pityingly and murmured words of comfort for a sorrow I did not understand.... Then I woke suddenly as one does from dreams. The moon was shining brightly into the room. Rising from my bed, I looked out into the orchard. It was almost as bright as day. I could plainly see the tree of which I had been dreaming, and then a fantastic notion possessed me. Slipping on my clothes, I went out into one of the old barns and found a spade. Then I went to the tree where I had seen the girl weeping in my dream and dug down at its foot.

I had dug little more than a foot when my spade struck upon some hard substance, and in a few more moments I had uncovered and exhumed a small box, which, on examination, proved to be one of those pretty old-fashioned Chippendale work-boxes used by our grandmothers to keep their thimbles and needles in, their reels of cotton and skeins of silk. After smoothing down the little grave in which I had found it, I carried the box into the house, and under the lamplight examined its contents.

Then at once I understood why that sad young spirit went to and fro the orchard singing those little French songs – for the treasure-trove I had found under the apple-tree, the buried treasure of an unquiet, suffering soul, proved to be a number of love-letters written mostly in French in a very picturesque hand – letters, too, written but some five or six years before. Perhaps I should not have read them – yet I read them with such reverence for the beautiful, impassioned love that animated them, and literally made them 'smell sweet and blossom in the dust,' that I felt I had the sanction of the dead to make myself the confidant of their story. Among the letters were little songs, two of which I had heard the strange young voice singing in the orchard, and, of course, there were many withered flowers and such like remembrances of bygone rapture.

Not that night could I make out all the story, though it was not difficult to define its essential tragedy, and later on a gossip in the neighbourhood and a headstone in the churchyard told me the rest. The unquiet young soul that had sung so wistfully to and fro the orchard was my landlord's daughter. She was the only child of her parents, a beautiful, willful girl, exotically unlike those from whom she was sprung and among whom she lived with a disdainful air of exile. She was, as a child, a little creature of fairy fancies, and as she grew up it was plain to her father and mother that she had come from another world than theirs. To them she seemed like a child in an old fairy-tale strangely found on his hearth by some shepherd as he returns from the fields at evening – a little fairy girl swaddled in fine linen, and dowered with a mysterious bag of gold.

Soon she developed delicate spiritual needs to which her simple parents were strangers. From long truancies in the woods she would come home laden with mysterious flowers, and soon she came to ask for books and pictures and music, of which the poor souls that had given her birth had never heard. Finally she had her way, and went to study at a certain fashionable college; and there the brief romance of her life began. There she met a romantic young Frenchman who had read Ronsard to her and written her those picturesque letters I had found in the old mahogany work-box. And after a while the young Frenchman had gone back to France, and the letters had ceased. Month by month went by, and at length one day, as she sat wistful at the window, looking out at the foolish sunlit road, a message came. He was dead. That headstone in the village churchyard tells the rest. She was very young to die – scarcely nineteen years; and the dead who have died young, with all their hopes and dreams still like unfolded buds within their hearts, do not rest so quietly in the grave as those who have gone through the long day from morning until evening and are only too glad to sleep.

†

Next day I took the little box to a quiet corner of the orchard, and made a little pyre of fragrant boughs – for so I interpreted the wish of that young, unquiet spirit – and the beautiful words are now safe, taken up again into the aerial spaces from which they came.

But since then the birds sing no more little French songs in my old orchard.

The Messenger

Robert W. Chambers

Little gray messenger,
Robed like painted Death,
Your robe is dust.
Whom do you seek
Among lilies and closed buds
　　At dusk?

Among lilies and closed buds
　　At dusk,
Whom do you seek,
Little gray messenger,
Robed in the awful panoply
Of painted Death?

R.W.C.

All-wise,
Hast thou seen all there is to see with thy two eyes?
Dost thou know all there is to know, and so,
Omniscient,
Darest thou still to say thy brother lies?

R.W.C.

I

"The bullet entered here," said Max Fortin, and he placed his middle finger over a smooth hole exactly in the center of the forehead.

I sat down upon a mound of dry seaweed and unslung my fowling piece.

The little chemist cautiously felt the edges of the shot-hole, first with his middle finger, and then with his thumb.

"Let me see the skull again," said I.

Max Fortin picked it up from the sod.

"It's like all the others," he repeated, wiping his glasses on his handkerchief. "I thought you might care to see one of the skulls, so I brought this over from the gravel pit. The men from Bannalec are digging yet. They ought to stop."

"How many skulls are there altogether?" I inquired.

"They found thirty-eight skulls; there are thirty-nine noted in the list. They lie piled up in the gravel pit on the edge of Le Bihan's wheat field. The men are at work yet. Le Bihan is going to stop them."

"Let's go over," said I; and I picked up my gun and started across the cliffs, Portin on one side, Môme on the other.

"Who has the list?" I asked, lighting my pipe. "You say there is a list?"

"The list was found rolled up in a brass cylinder," said the chemist. He added: "You should not smoke here. You know that if a single spark drifted into the wheat—"

"Ah, but I have a cover to my pipe," said I, smiling.

Fortin watched me as I closed the pepper-box arrangement over the glowing bowl of the pipe. Then he continued:

"The list was made out on thick yellow paper; the brass tube has preserved it. It is as fresh today as it was in 1760. You shall see it."

"Is that the date?"

"The list is dated 'April, 1760.' The Brigadier Durand has it. It is not written in French."

"Not written in French!" I exclaimed.

"No," replied Fortin solemnly, "it is written in Breton."

"But," I protested, "the Breton language was never written or printed in 1760."

"Except by priests," said the chemist.

"I have heard of but one priest who ever wrote the Breton language," I began.

Fortin stole a glance at my face.

"You mean—the Black Priest?" he asked.

I nodded.

Fortin opened his mouth to speak again, hesitated, and finally shut his teeth obstinately over the wheat stem that he was chewing.

"And the Black Priest?" I suggested encouragingly. But I knew it was useless; for it is easier to move the stars from their courses than to make an obstinate Breton talk. We walked on for a minute or two in silence.

"Where is the Brigadier Durand?" I asked, motioning Môme to come out of the wheat, which he was trampling as though it were heather. As I spoke we came in sight of the farther edge of the wheat field and the dark, wet mass of cliffs beyond.

"Durand is down there—you can see him; he stands just behind the mayor of St Gildas."

"I see," said I; and we struck straight down, following a sun-baked cattle path across the heather.

When we reached the edge of the wheat field, Le Bihan, the mayor of St Gildas, called to me, and I tucked my gun under my arm and skirted the wheat to where he stood.

"Thirty-eight skulls," he said in his thin, high-pitched voice; "there is but one more, and I am opposed to further search. I suppose Fortin told you?"

I shook hands with him, and returned the salute of the Brigadier Durand.

"I am opposed to further search," repeated Le Bihan, nervously picking at the mass of silver buttons which covered the front of his velvet and broadcloth jacket like a breastplate of scale armor.

Durand pursed up his lips, twisted his tremendous mustache, and hooked his thumbs in his saber belt.

"As for me," he said, "I am in favor of further search."

"Further search for what—for the thirty-ninth skull?" I asked.

Le Bihan nodded. Durand frowned at the sunlit sea, rocking like a bowl of molten gold from the cliffs to the horizon. I followed his eyes. On the dark glistening cliffs, silhouetted against the glare of the sea, sat a cormorant, black, motionless, its horrible head raised toward heaven.

"Where is that list, Durand?" I asked.

The gendarme rummaged in his despatch pouch and produced a brass cylinder about a foot long. Very gravely he unscrewed the head and dumped out a scroll of thick yellow paper closely covered with writing on both sides. At a nod from Le Bihan he handed me the scroll. But I could make nothing of the coarse writing, now faded to a dull brown.

"Come, come, Le Bihan," I said impatiently, "translate it, won't you? You and Max Fortin make a lot of mystery out of nothing, it seems."

Le Bihan went to the edge of the pit where the three Bannalec men were digging, gave an order or two in Breton, and turned to me.

As I came to the edge of the pit the Bannalec men were removing a square piece of sailcloth from what appeared to be a pile of cobblestones.

"Look!" said Le Bihan shrilly. I looked. The pile below was a heap of skulls. After a moment I clambered down the gravel sides of the pit and walked over to the men of Bannalec. They saluted me gravely, leaning on their picks and shovels, and wiping their sweating faces with sunburned hands.

"How many?" said I in Breton.

"Thirty-eight," they replied.

I glanced around. Beyond the heap of skulls lay two piles of human bones. Beside these was a mound of broken, rusted bits of iron and steel. Looking closer, I saw that this mound was composed of rusty bayonets, saber blades, scythe blades, with here and there a tarnished buckle attached to a bit of leather hard as iron.

I picked up a couple of buttons and a belt plate. The buttons bore the royal arms of England; the belt plate was emblazoned with the English arms and also with the number "27."

"I have heard my grandfather speak of the terrible English regiment, the 27th Foot, which landed and stormed the fort up there," said one of the Bannalec men.

"Oh!" said I; "then these are the bones of English soldiers?"

"Yes," said the men of Bannalec.

Le Bihan was calling to me from the edge of the pit above, and I handed the belt plate and buttons to the men and climbed the side of the excavation.

"Well," said I, trying to prevent Môme from leaping up and licking my face as I emerged from the pit, "I suppose you know what these bones are. What are you going to do with them?"

"There was a man," said Le Bihan angrily, "an Englishman, who passed here in a dog-cart on his way to Quimper about an hour ago, and what do you suppose he wished to do?"

"Buy the relics?" I asked, smiling.

"Exactly—the pig!" piped the mayor of St Gildas. "Jean Marie Tregunc, who found the bones, was standing there where Max Fortin stands, and do you know what he answered? He spat upon the ground, and said: 'Pig of an Englishman, do you take me for a desecrator of graves?'"

I knew Tregunc, a sober, blue-eyed Breton, who lived from one year's end to the other without being able to afford a single bit of meat for a meal.

"How much did the Englishman offer Tregunc?" I asked.

"Two hundred francs for the skulls alone."

I thought of the relic hunters and the relic buyers on the battlefields of our civil war.

"Seventeen hundred and sixty is long ago," I said.

"Respect for the dead can never die," said Fortin.

"And the English soldiers came here to kill your fathers and burn your homes," I continued.

"They were murderers and thieves, but—they are dead," said Tregunc, coming up from the beach below, his long sea rake balanced on his dripping jersey.

"How much do you earn every year, Jean Marie?" I asked, turning to shake hands with him.

"Two hundred and twenty francs, monsieur."

"Forty-five dollars a year," I said. "Bah! you are worth more, Jean. Will you take care of my garden for me? My wife wished me to ask you. I think it would be worth one hundred francs a month to you and to me. Come on, Le Bihan—come along, Fortin—and you, Durand. I want somebody to translate that list into French for me."

Tregunc stood gazing at me, his blue eyes dilated.

"You may begin at once," I said, smiling, "if the salary suits you?"

"It suits," said Tregunc, fumbling for his pipe in a silly way that annoyed Le Bihan.

"Then go and begin your work," cried the mayor impatiently; and Tregunc started across the moors toward St Gildas, taking off his velvet-ribboned cap to me and gripping his sea rake very hard.

"You offer him more than my salary," said the mayor, after a moment's contemplation of his silver buttons.

"Pooh!" said I, "what do you do for your salary except play dominoes with Max Portin at the Groix Inn?"

Le Bihan turned red, but Durand rattled his saber and winked at Max Fortin, and I slipped my arm through the arm of the sulky magistrate, laughing.

"There's a shady spot under the cliff," I said; "come on, Le Bihan, and read me what is in the scroll."

In a few moments we reached the shadow of the cliff, and I threw myself upon the turf, chin on hand, to listen.

The gendarme, Durand, also sat down, twisting his mustache into needle-like points. Fortin leaned against the cliff, polishing his glasses and examining us with vague, near-sighted eyes; and Le Bihan, the mayor, planted himself in our midst, rolling up the scroll and tucking it under his arm.

"First of all," he began in a shrill voice, "I am going to light my pipe, and while lighting it I shall tell you what I have heard about the attack on the fort yonder. My father told me; his father told him."

He jerked his head in the direction of the ruined fort, a small, square stone structure on the sea cliff, now nothing but crumbling walls. Then he slowly produced a tobacco pouch, a bit of flint and tinder, and a long-stemmed pipe fitted with a microscopical bowl of baked clay. To fill such a pipe requires ten minutes' close attention. To smoke it to a finish takes but four puffs. It is very Breton, this Breton pipe. It is the crystallization of everything Breton.

"Go on," said I, lighting a cigarette.

"The fort," said the mayor, "was built by Louis XIV, and was dismantled twice by the English. Louis XV restored it in 1730. In 1760 it was carried by assault by the English. They came across from the island of Groix—three shiploads, and they stormed the fort and sacked St Julien yonder, and they started to burn St Gildas—you can see the marks of their bullets on my house yet; but the men of Bannalec and the men of Lorient fell upon them with pike and scythe and blunderbuss, and those who did not run away lie there below in the gravel pit now—thirty-eight of them."

"And the thirty-ninth skull?" I asked, finishing my cigarette.

The mayor had succeeded in filling his pipe, and now he began to put his tobacco pouch away.

"The thirty-ninth skull," he mumbled, holding the pipe stem between his defective teeth—"the thirty-ninth skull is no business of mine. I have told the Bannalec men to cease digging."

"But what is—whose is the missing skull?" I persisted curiously.

The mayor was busy trying to strike a spark to his tinder. Presently he set it aglow, applied it to his pipe, took the prescribed four puffs, knocked the ashes out of the bowl, and gravely replaced the pipe in his pocket.

"The missing skull?" he asked.

"Yes," said I, impatiently.

The mayor slowly unrolled the scroll and began to read, translating from the Breton into French. And this is what he read:

> "On the Cliffs of St Gildas,
> April 13, 1760.
>
> "On this day, by order of the Count of Soisic, general in chief of the Breton forces now lying in Kerselec Forest, the bodies of thirty-eight English soldiers of the 27th, 50th, and 72d regiments of Foot were buried in this spot, together with their arms and equipments."

The mayor paused and glanced at me reflectively.

"Go on, Le Bihan," I said.

"With them," continued the mayor, turning the scroll and reading on the other side, "was buried the body of that vile traitor who betrayed the fort to the English. The manner of his death was as follows: By order of the most noble Count of Soisic, the traitor was first branded upon the forehead with the brand of an arrowhead. The iron burned through the flesh and was pressed heavily so that the brand should even burn into the bone of the skull. The traitor was then led out and bidden to kneel. He admitted having guided the English from the island of Groix. Although a priest and a Frenchman, he had violated his priestly office to aid him in discovering the password to the fort. This password he extorted during confession from a young Breton girl who was in the habit of rowing across from the island of Groix to visit her husband in the fort. When the fort fell, this young girl, crazed by the death of her husband, sought the Count of Soisic and told how the priest had forced her to confess to him all she knew about the fort. The priest was arrested at St Gildas as he was about to cross the river to Lorient. When arrested he cursed the girl, Marie Trevec——"

"What!" I exclaimed, "Marie Trevec!"

"Marie Trevec," repeated Le Bihan; "the priest cursed Marie Trevec, and all her family and descendants. He was shot as he knelt, having a mask of leather over his face, because the Bretons who composed the squad of execution refused to fire at a priest unless his face was concealed. The priest was l'Abbé Sorgue, commonly known as the Black Priest on account of his dark face and swarthy eyebrows. He was buried with a stake through his heart."

Le Bihan paused, hesitated, looked at me, and handed the manuscript back to Durand. The gendarme took it and slipped it into the brass cylinder.

"So," said I, "the thirty-ninth skull is the skull of the Black Priest."

"Yes," said Fortin. "I hope they won't find it."

"I have forbidden them to proceed," said the mayor querulously. "You heard me, Max Fortin."

I rose and picked up my gun. Môme came and pushed his head into my hand.

"That's a fine dog," observed Durand, also rising.

"Why don't you wish to find his skull?" I asked Le Bihan. "It would be curious to see whether the arrow brand really burned into the bone."

"There is something in that scroll that I didn't read to you," said the mayor grimly. "Do you wish to know what it is?"

"Of course," I replied in surprise.

"Give me the scroll again, Durand," he said; then he read from the bottom: "I, l'Abbé Sorgue, forced to write the above by my executioners, have written it in my own blood; and with it I leave my curse. My curse on St Gildas, on Marie Trevec, and on her descendants. I will come back to St Gildas when my remains are disturbed. Woe to that Englishman whom my branded skull shall touch!"

"What rot!" I said. "Do you believe it was really written in his own blood?"

"I am going to test it," said Fortin, "at the request of Monsieur le Maire. I am not anxious for the job, however."

"See," said Le Bihan, holding out the scroll to me, "it is signed, 'L'Abbé Sorgue.'"

I glanced curiously over the paper.

"It must be the Black Priest," I said. "He was the only man who wrote in the Breton language. This is a wonderfully interesting discovery, for now, at last, the mystery of the Black Priest's disappearance is cleared up. You will, of course, send this scroll to Paris, Le Bihan?"

"No," said the mayor obstinately, "it shall be buried in the pit below where the rest of the Black Priest lies."

I looked at him and recognized that argument would be useless. But still I said, "It will be a loss to history, Monsieur Le Bihan."

"All the worse for history, then," said the enlightened Mayor of St Gildas.

We had sauntered back to the gravel pit while speaking. The men of Bannalec were carrying the bones of the English soldiers toward the St Gildas cemetery, on the cliffs to the east, where already a knot of white-coiffed women stood in attitudes of prayer; and I saw the somber robe of a priest among the crosses of the little graveyard.

"They were thieves and assassins; they are dead now," muttered Max Fortin.

"Respect the dead," repeated the Mayor of St Gildas, looking after the Bannalec men.

"It was written in that scroll that Marie Trevec, of Groix Island, was cursed by the priest—she and her descendants," I said, touching Le Bihan on the arm. "There was a Marie Trevec who married an Yves Trevec of St Gildas—"

"It is the same," said Le Bihan, looking at me obliquely.

"Oh!" said I; "then they were ancestors of my wife."

"Do you fear the curse?" asked Le Bihan.

"What?" I laughed.

"There was the case of the Purple Emperor," said Max Fortin timidly.

Startled for a moment, I faced him, then shrugged my shoulders and kicked at a smooth bit of rock which lay near the edge of the pit, almost embedded in gravel.

"Do you suppose the Purple Emperor drank himself crazy because he was descended from Marie Trevec?" I asked contemptuously.

"Of course not," said Max Fortin hastily.

"Of course not," piped the mayor. "I only—Hellow! what's that you're kicking?"

"What?" said I, glancing down, at the same time involuntarily giving another kick. The smooth bit of rock dislodged itself and rolled out of the loosened gravel at my feet.

"The thirty-ninth skull!" I exclaimed. "By jingo, it's the noddle of the Black Priest! See! there is the arrowhead branded on the front!"

The mayor stepped back. Max Fortin also retreated. There was a pause, during which I looked at them, and they looked anywhere but at me.

"I don't like it," said the mayor at last, in a husky, high voice. "I don't like it! The scroll says he will come back to St Gildas when his remains are disturbed. I—I don't like it, Monsieur Darrel—"

"Bosh!" said I; "the poor wicked devil is where he can't get out. For Heaven's sake, Le Bihan, what is this stuff you are talking in the year of grace 1896?"

The mayor gave me a look.

"And he says 'Englishman.' You are an Englishman, Monsieur Darrel," he announced.

"You know better. You know I'm an American."

"It's all the same," said the Mayor of St Gildas, obstinately.

"No, it isn't!" I answered, much exasperated, and deliberately pushed the skull till it rolled into the bottom of the gravel pit below.

"Cover it up," said I; "bury the scroll with it too, if you insist, but I think you ought to send it to Paris. Don't look so gloomy, Fortin, unless you believe in werewolves and ghosts. Hey! what the—what the devil's the matter with you, anyway? What are you staring at, Le Bihan?"

"Come, come," muttered the mayor in a low, tremulous voice, "it's time we got out of this. Did you see? Did you see, Fortin?"

"I saw," whispered Max Fortin, pallid with fright.

The two men were almost running across the sunny pasture now, and I hastened after them, demanding to know what was the matter.

"Matter!" chattered the mayor, gasping with exasperation and terror. "The skull is rolling up hill again," and he burst into a terrified gallop, Max Fortin followed close behind.

I watched them stampeding across the pasture, then turned toward the gravel pit, mystified, incredulous. The skull was lying on the edge of the pit, exactly where it had been before I pushed it over the edge. For a second I stared at it; a singular chilly feeling crept up my spinal column, and I turned and walked away, sweat starting from the root of every hair on my head. Before I had gone twenty paces the absurdity of the whole thing struck me. I halted, hot with shame and annoyance, and retraced my steps.

There lay the skull.

"I rolled a stone down instead of the skull," I muttered to myself. Then with the butt of my gun I pushed the skull over the edge of the pit and watched it roll to the bottom; and as it struck the bottom of the pit, Môme, my dog, suddenly whipped his tail between his legs, whimpered, and made off across the moor.

"Môme!" I shouted, angry and astonished; but the dog only fled the faster, and I ceased calling from sheer surprise.

"What the mischief is the matter with that dog!" I thought. He had never before played me such a trick.

Mechanically I glanced into the pit, but I could not see the skull. I looked down. The skull lay at my feet again, touching them.

"Good heavens!" I stammered, and struck at it blindly with my gunstock. The ghastly thing flew into the air, whirling over and over, and rolled again down the sides of the pit to the bottom. Breathlessly I stared at it, then, confused and scarcely comprehending, I stepped back from the pit, still facing it, one, ten, twenty paces, my eyes almost starting from my head, as though I expected to see the thing roll up from the bottom of the pit under my very gaze. At last I turned my back to the pit and strode out across the gorse-covered moorland toward my home. As I reached the road that winds from St Gildas to St Julien I gave one hasty glance at the pit over my shoulder. The sun shone hot on the sod about the excavation. There was something white and bare and round on the turf at the edge of the pit. It might have been a stone; there were plenty of them lying about.

II

When I entered my garden I saw Môme sprawling on the stone doorstep. He eyed me sideways and flopped his tail.

"Are you not mortified, you idiot dog?" I said, looking about the upper windows for Lys.

Môme rolled over on his back and raised one deprecating forepaw, as though to ward off calamity.

"Don't act as though I was in the habit of beating you to death," I said, disgusted. I had never in my life raised whip to the brute. "But you are a fool dog," I continued. "No, you needn't come to be babied and wept over; Lys can do that, if she insists, but I am ashamed of you, and you can go to the devil."

Môme slunk off into the house, and I followed, mounting directly to my wife's boudoir. It was empty.

"Where has she gone?" I said, looking hard at Môme, who had followed me. "Oh! I see you don't know. Don't pretend you do. Come off that lounge! Do you think Lys wants tan-colored hairs all over her lounge?"

I rang the bell for Catherine and Fine, but they didn't know where "madame" had gone; so I went into my room, bathed, exchanged my somewhat grimy shooting clothes for a suit of warm, soft knickerbockers, and, after lingering some extra moments over my toilet—for I was particular, now that I had married Lys—I went down to the garden and took a chair out under the fig-trees.

"Where can she be?" I wondered, Môme came sneaking out to be comforted, and I forgave him for Lys's sake, whereupon he frisked.

"You bounding cur," said I, "now what on earth started you off across the moor? If you do it again I'll push you along with a charge of dust shot."

As yet I had scarcely dared think about the ghastly hallucination of which I had been a victim, but now I faced it squarely, flushing a little with mortification at the thought of my hasty retreat from the gravel pit.

"To think," I said aloud, "that those old woman's tales of Max Fortin and Le Bihan should have actually made me see what didn't exist at all! I lost my nerve like a schoolboy in a dark bedroom." For I knew now that I had mistaken a round stone for a skull each time, and had pushed a couple of big pebbles into the pit instead of the skull itself.

"By jingo!" said I, "I'm nervous; my liver must be in a devil of a condition if I see such things when I'm awake! Lys will know what to give me."

I felt mortified and irritated and sulky, and thought disgustedly of Le Bihan and Max Fortin.

But after a while I ceased speculating, dismissed the mayor, the chemist, and the skull from my mind, and smoked pensively, watching the sun low dipping in the western ocean. As the twilight fell for a moment over ocean and moorland, a wistful, restless happiness filled my heart, the happiness that all men know—all men who have loved.

Slowly the purple mist crept out over the sea; the cliffs darkened; the forest was shrouded.

Suddenly the sky above burned with the afterglow, and the world was alight again.

Cloud after cloud caught the rose dye; the cliffs were tinted with it; moor and pasture, heather and forest burned and pulsated with the gentle flush. I saw the gulls turning and tossing above the sand bar, their snowy wings tipped with pink; I saw the sea swallows sheering the surface of the still river, stained to its placid depths with warm reflections of the clouds. The twitter of drowsy hedge birds broke out in the stillness; a salmon rolled its shining side above tidewater.

The interminable monotone of the ocean intensified the silence. I sat motionless, holding my breath as one who listens to the first low rumor of an organ. All at once the pure whistle of a nightingale cut the silence, and the first moonbeam silvered the wastes of mist-hung waters.

I raised my head.

Lys stood before me in the garden.

When we had kissed each other, we linked arms and moved up and down the gravel walks, watching the moonbeams sparkle on the sand bar as the tide ebbed and ebbed. The broad beds of white pinks about us were atremble with hovering white moths; the October roses hung all abloom, perfuming the salt wind.

"Sweetheart," I said, "where is Yvonne? Has she promised to spend Christmas with us?"

"Yes, Dick; she drove me down from Plougat this afternoon. She sent her love to you. I am not jealous. What did you shoot?"

"A hare and four partridges. They are in the gun room. I told Catherine not to touch them until you had seen them."

Now I suppose I knew that Lys could not be particularly enthusiastic over game or guns; but she pretended she was, and always scornfully denied that it was for my sake and not for the pure love of sport. So she dragged me off to inspect the rather meager game bag, and she paid me pretty compliments, and gave a little cry of delight and pity as I lifted the enormous hare out of the sack by his ears.

"He'll eat no more of our lettuce," I said attempting to justify the assassination.

"Unhappy little bunny—and what a beauty! O Dick, you are a splendid shot, are you not?"

I evaded the question and hauled out a partridge.

"Poor little dead things'" said Lys in a whisper; "it seems a pity—doesn't it, Dick? But then you are so clever—"

"We'll have them broiled," I said guardedly, "tell Catherine."

Catherine came in to take away the game, and presently 'Fine Lelocard, Lys's maid, announced dinner, and Lys tripped away to her boudoir.

I stood an instant contemplating her blissfully, thinking, "My boy, you're the happiest fellow in the world—you're in love with your wife'"

I walked into the dining-room, beamed at the plates, walked out again; met Tregunc in the hallway, beamed on him; glanced into the kitchen, beamed at Catherine, and went up stairs, still beaming.

Before I could knock at Lys's door it opened, and Lys came hastily out. When she saw me she gave a little cry of relief, and nestled close to my breast.

"There is something peering in at my window," she said.

"What!" I cried angrily.

"A man, I think, disguised as a priest, and he has a mask on. He must have climbed up by the bay tree."

I was down the stairs and out of doors in no time. The moonlit garden was absolutely deserted. Tregunc came up, and together we searched the hedge and shrubbery around the house and out to the road.

"Jean Marie," said I at length, "loose my bulldog—he knows you—and take your supper on the porch where you can watch. My wife says the fellow is disguised as a priest, and wears a mask."

Tregunc showed his white teeth in a smile. "He will not care to venture in here again, I think, Monsieur Darrel."

I went back and found Lys seated quietly at the table.

"The soup is ready, dear," she said. "Don't worry; it was only some foolish lout from Bannalec. No one in St Gildas or St Julien would do such a thing."

I was too much exasperated to reply at first, but Lys treated it as a stupid joke, and after a while I began to look at it in that light.

Lys told me about Yvonne, and reminded me of my promise to have Herbert Stuart down to meet her.

"You wicked diplomat!" I protested. "Herbert is in Paris, and hard at work for the Salon."

"Don't you think he might spare a week to flirt with the prettiest girl in Finistere?" inquired Lys innocently.

"Prettiest girl! Not much!" I said.

"Who is, then?" urged Lys.

I laughed a trifle sheepishly.

"I suppose you mean me, Dick," said Lys, coloring up.

"Now I bore you, don't I?"

"Bore me? Ah, no, Dick."

After coffee and cigarettes were served I spoke about Tregunc, and Lys approved.

"Poor Jean! He will be glad, won't he? What a dear fellow you are!"

"Nonsense," said I; "we need a gardener; you said so yourself, Lys."

But Lys leaned over and kissed me, and then bent down and hugged Môme—who whistled through his nose in sentimental appreciation.

"I am a very happy woman," said Lys.

"Môme was a very bad dog today," I observed.

"Poor Môme!" said Lys, smiling.

When dinner was over and Môme lay snoring before the blaze—for the October nights are often chilly in Finistere—Lys curled up in the chimney corner with her embroidery, and gave me a swift glance from under her dropping lashes.

"You look like a schoolgirl, Lys," I said teasingly. "I don't believe you are sixteen yet."

She pushed back her heavy burnished hair thoughtfully. Her wrist was as white as surf foam.

"Have we been married four years? I don't believe it," I said.

She gave me another swift glance and touched the embroidery on her knee, smiling faintly.

"I see," said I, also smiling at the embroidered garment. "Do you think it will fit?"

"Fit?" repeated Lys. Then she laughed

"And," I persisted, "are you perfectly sure that you—er—we shall need it?"

"Perfectly," said Lys. A delicate color touched her cheeks and neck. She held up the little garment, all fluffy with misty lace and wrought with quaint embroidery.

"It is very gorgeous," said I; "don't use your eyes too much, dearest. May I smoke a pipe?"

"Of course," she said selecting a skein of pale blue silk.

For a while I sat and smoked in silence, watching her slender fingers among the tinted silks and thread of gold.

Presently she spoke: "What did you say your crest is, Dick?"

"My crest? Oh, something or other rampant on a something or other—"

"Dick!"

"Dearest?"

"Don't be flippant."

"But I really forget. It's an ordinary crest; everybody in New York has them. No family should be without 'em."

"You are disagreeable, Dick. Send Josephine upstairs for my album."

"Are you going to put that crest on the—the—whatever it is?"

"I am; and my own crest, too."

I thought of the Purple Emperor and wondered a little.

"You didn't know I had one, did you?" she smiled.

"What is it?" I replied evasively.

"You shall see. Ring for Josephine."

I rang, and, when 'Fine appeared, Lys gave her some orders in a low voice, and Josephine trotted away, bobbing her white-coiffed head with a "Bien, Madame!"

After a few minutes she returned, bearing a tattered, musty volume, from which the gold and blue had mostly disappeared.

I took the book in my hands and examined the ancient emblazoned covers.

"Lilies!" I exclaimed.

"Fleur-de-lis," said my wife demurely.

"Oh!" said I, astonished, and opened the book.

"You have never before seen this book?" asked Lys, with a touch of malice in her eyes.

"You know I haven't. Hello! What's this? Oho! So there should be a de before Trevec? Lys de Trevec? Then why in the world did the Purple Emperor——"

"Dick!" cried Lys.

"All right," said I. "Shall I read about the Sieur de Trevec who rode to Saladin's tent alone to seek for medicine for St Louise? Or shall I read about—what is it? Oh, here it is, all down in black and white—about the Marquis de Trevec who drowned himself before Alva's eyes rather than surrender the banner of the fleur-de-lis to Spain? It's all written here. But, dear, how about that soldier named Trevec who was killed in the old fort on the cliff yonder?"

"He dropped the de, and the Trevecs since then have been Republicans," said Lys—"all except me."

"That's quite right," said I; "it is time that we Republicans should agree upon some feudal system. My dear, I drink to the king!" and I raised my wine glass and looked at Lys.

"To the king," said Lys, flushing. She smoothed out the tiny garment on her knees; she touched the glass with her lips; her eyes were very sweet. I drained the glass to the king.

After a silence I said: "I will tell the king stories. His majesty shall be amused."

"His majesty," repeated Lys softly.

"Or hers," I laughed. "Who knows?"

"Who knows?" murmured Lys; with a gentle sigh.

"I know some stories about Jack the Giant-Killer," I announced. "Do you, Lys?"

"I? No, not about a giant-killer, but I know all about the werewolf, and Jeanne-la-Flamme, and the Man in Purple Tatters, and—O dear me, I know lots more."

"You are very wise," said I. "I shall teach his majesty, English."

"And I Breton," cried Lys jealously.

"I shall bring playthings to the king," said I—"big green lizards from the gorse, little gray mullets to swim in glass globes, baby rabbits from the forest of Kerselec—"

"And I," said Lys, "will bring the first primrose, the first branch of aubepine, the first jonquil, to the king—my king."

"Our king," said I; and there was peace in Finistere.

I lay back, idly turning the leaves of the curious old volume.

"I am looking," said I, "for the crest."

"The crest, dear? It is a priest's head with an arrow-shaped mark on the forehead, on a field——"

I sat up and stared at my wife.

"Dick, whatever is the matter?" she smiled. "The story is there in that book. Do you care to read it? No? Shall I tell it to you? Well, then: It happened in the third crusade. There was a monk whom men called the Black Priest. He turned apostate, and sold himself to the enemies of Christ. A Sieur de Trevec burst into the Saracen camp, at the head of only one hundred lances, and carried the Black Priest away out of the very midst of their army."

"So that is how you come by the crest," I said quietly; but I thought of the branded skull in the gravel pit, and wondered.

"Yes," said Lys. "The Sieur de Trevec cut the Black Priest's head off, but first he branded him with an arrow mark on the forehead. The book says it was a pious action, and the Sieur de Trevec got great merit by it. But I think it was cruel, the branding," she sighed.

"Did you ever hear of any other Black Priest?"

"Yes. There was one in the last century, here in St Gildas. He cast a white shadow in the sun. He wrote in the Breton language. Chronicles, too, I believe. I never saw them. His name was the same as that of the old chronicler, and of the other priest, Jacques Sorgue. Some said he was a lineal descendant of the traitor. Of course the first Black Priest was bad enough for anything. But if he did have a child, it need not have been the ancestor of the last Jacques Sorgue. They say he was so good he was not allowed to die, but was caught up to heaven one day," added Lys, with believing eyes.

I smiled.

"But he disappeared," persisted Lys.

"I'm afraid his journey was in another direction," I said jestingly, and thoughtlessly told her the story of the morning. I had utterly forgotten the masked man at her window, but before I finished I remembered him fast enough, and realized what I had done as I saw her face whiten.

"Lys," I urged tenderly, "that was only some clumsy clown's trick. You said so yourself. You are not superstitious, my dear?"

Her eyes were on mine. She slowly drew the little gold cross from her bosom and kissed it. But her lips trembled as they pressed the symbol of faith.

III

About nine o'clock the next morning I walked into the Groix Inn and sat down at the long discolored oaken table, nodding good-day to Marianne Bruyere, who in turn bobbed her white coiffe at me.

"My clever Bannalec maid," said I, "what is good for a stirrup-cup at the Groix Inn?"

"Schist?" she inquired in Breton.

"With a dash of red wine, then," I replied.

She brought the delicious Quimperle cider, and I poured a little Bordeaux into it. Marianne watched me with laughing black eyes.

"What makes your cheeks so red, Marianne?" I asked. "Has Jean Marie been here?"

"We are to be married, Monsieur Darrel," she laughed.

"Ah! Since when has Jean Marie Tregunc lost his head?"

"His head? Oh, Monsieur Darrel—his heart, you mean!"

"So I do," said I. "Jean Marie is a practical fellow."

"It is all due to your kindness—" began the girl, but I raised my hand and held up the glass.

"It's due to himself. To your happiness, Marianne"; and I took a hearty draught of the schist. "Now," said I, "tell me where I can find Le Bihan and Max Fortin."

"Monsieur Le Bihan and Monsieur Fortin are above in the broad room. I believe they are examining the Red Admiral's effects."

"To send them to Paris? Oh, I know. May I go up, Marianne?"

"And God go with you," smiled the girl.

When I knocked at the door of the broad room above little Max Fortin opened it. Dust covered his spectacles and nose; his hat, with the tiny velvet ribbons fluttering, was all awry.

"Come in, Monsieur Darrel," he said; "the mayor and I are packing up the effects of the Purple Emperor and of the poor Red Admiral."

"The collections?" I asked, entering the room. "You must be very careful in packing those butterfly cases; the slightest jar might break wings and antennas, you know."

Le Bihan shook hands with me and pointed to the great pile of boxes.

"They're all cork lined," he said, "but Fortin and I are putting felt around each box. The Entomological Society of Paris pays the freight."

The combined collection of the Red Admiral and the Purple Emperor made a magnificent display.

I lifted and inspected case after case set with gorgeous butterflies and moths, each specimen carefully labelled with the name in Latin. There were cases filled with crimson tiger moths all aflame with color; cases devoted to the common yellow butterflies; symphonies in orange and pale yellow; cases of soft gray and dun-colored sphinx moths; and cases of grayish nettle-bed butterflies of the numerous family of Vanessa.

All alone in a great case by itself was pinned the purple emperor, the Apatura Iris, that fatal specimen that had given the Purple Emperor his name and quietus.

I remembered the butterfly, and stood looking at it with bent eyebrows.

Le Bihan glanced up from the floor where he was nailing down the lid of a box full of cases.

"It is settled, then," said he, "that madame, your wife, gives the Purple Emperor's entire Collection to the city of Paris?"

I nodded.

"Without accepting anything for it?"

"It is a gift," I said.

"Including the purple emperor there in the case? That butterfly is worth a great deal of money," persisted Le Bihan.

"You don't suppose that we would wish to sell that specimen, do you?" I answered a trifle sharply.

"If I were you I should destroy it," said the mayor in his high-pitched voice.

"That would be nonsense," said I, "like your burying the brass cylinder and scroll yesterday."

"It was not nonsense," said Le Bihan doggedly, "and I should prefer not to discuss the subject of the scroll."

I looked at Max Portin, who immediately avoided my eyes.

"You are a pair of superstitious old women," said I, digging my hands into my pockets; "you swallow every nursery tale that is invented."

"What of it?" said Le Bihan sulkily; "there's more truth than lies in most of 'em."

"Oh!" I sneered, "does the Mayor of St Gildas and St Julien believe in the loup-garou?"

"No, not in the loup-garou."

"In what, then—Jeanne-la-Flamme?"

"That," said Le Bihan with conviction, "is history."

"The devil it is!" said I; "and perhaps, Monsieur the mayor, your faith in giants is unimpaired?"

"There were giants—everybody knows it," growled Max Fortin.

"And you a chemist!" I observed scornfully.

"Listen, Monsieur Darrel," squeaked Le Bihan; "you know yourself that the Purple Emperor was a scientific man. Now suppose I should tell you that he always refused to include in his collection a Death's Messenger?"

"A what?" I exclaimed.

"You know what I mean—that moth that flies by night; some call it the Death's Head, but in St Gildas we call it 'Death's Messenger.'"

"Oh!" said I, "you mean that big sphinx moth that is commonly known as the 'death's-head moth.' Why the mischief should the people here call it death's messenger?"

"For hundreds of years it has been known as death's messenger in St Gildas," said Max Fortin. "Even Froissart speaks of it in his commentaries on Jacques Sorgue's *Chronicles*. The book is in your library."

"Sorgue? And who was Jacques Sorgue? I never read his book."

"Jacques Sorgue was the son of some unfrocked priest—I forget. It was during the crusades."

"Good Heavens!" I burst out, "I've been hearing of nothing but crusades and priests and death and sorcery ever since I kicked that skull into the gravel pit, and I am tired of it, I tell you frankly. One would think we lived in the dark ages. Do you know what year of our Lord it is, Le Bihan?"

"Eighteen hundred and ninety-six," replied the mayor.

"And yet you two hulking men are afraid of a death's-head moth."

"I don't care to have one fly into the window," said Max Fortin; "it means evil to the house and the people in it."

"God alone knows why he marked one of his creatures with a yellow death's head on the back," observed Le Bihan piously, "but I take it that he meant it as a warning; and I propose to profit by it," he added triumphantly.

"See here, Le Bihan," I said; "by a stretch of imagination one can make out a skull on the thorax of a certain big sphinx moth. What of it?"

"It is a bad thing to touch," said the mayor wagging his head.

"It squeaks when handled," added Max Fortin.

"Some creatures squeak all the time," I observed, looking hard at Le Bihan.

"Pigs," added the mayor.

"Yes, and asses," I replied. "Listen, Le Bihan: do you mean to tell me that you saw that skull roll uphill yesterday?"

The mayor shut his mouth tightly and picked up his hammer.

"Don't be obstinate," I said; "I asked you a question."

"And I refuse to answer," snapped Le Bihan. "Fortin saw what I saw; let him talk about it."

I looked searchingly at the little chemist.

"I don't say that I saw it actually roll up out of the pit, all by itself," said Fortin with a shiver, "but—but then, how did it come up out of the pit, if it didn't roll up all by itself?"

"It didn't come up at all; that was a yellow cobblestone that you mistook for the skull again," I replied. "You were nervous, Max."

"A—a very curious cobblestone, Monsieur Darrel," said Fortin.

"I also was a victim to the same hallucination," I continued, "and I regret to say that I took the trouble to roll two innocent cobblestones into the gravel pit, imagining each time that it was the skull I was rolling."

"It was," observed Le Bihan with a morose shrug.

"It just shows," said I, ignoring the mayor's remark, "how easy it is to fix up a train of coincidences so that the result seems to savor of the supernatural. Now, last night my wife imagined that she saw a priest in a mask peer in at her window—"

Fortin and Le Bihan scrambled hastily from their knees, dropping hammer and nails.

"W-h-a-t—what's that?" demanded the mayor.

I repeated what I had said. Max Fortin turned livid.

"My God!" muttered Le Bihan, "the Black Priest is in St Gildas!"

"D-don't you—you know the old prophecy?" stammered Fortin; "Froissart quotes it from Jacques Sorgue:

"'When the Black Priest rises from the dead,
St Gildas folk shall shriek in bed;
When the Black Priest rises from his grave,
May the good God St Gildas save!'"

"Aristide Le Bihan," I said angrily, "and you, Max Fortin, I've got enough of this nonsense! Some foolish lout from Bannalec has been in St Gildas playing tricks to frighten old fools like you. If you have nothing better to talk about than nursery legends I'll wait until you come to your senses. Good morning." And I walked out, more disturbed than I cared to acknowledge to myself.

The day had become misty and overcast. Heavy, wet clouds hung in the east. I heard the surf thundering against the cliffs, and the gray gulls squealed as they tossed and turned high in the sky. The tide was creeping across the river sands, higher, higher, and I saw the seaweed floating on the beach, and the lancons springing from the foam, silvery threadlike flashes in the gloom. Curlew were flying up the river in twos and threes; the timid sea swallows skimmed across the moors toward some quiet, lonely pool, safe from the coming tempest. In every hedge field birds were gathering, huddling together, twittering restlessly.

When I reached the cliffs I sat down, resting my chin on my clenched hands. Already a vast curtain of rain, sweeping across the ocean miles away, hid the island of Groix. To the east, behind the white semaphore on the hills, black clouds crowded up over the horizon. After a little the thunder boomed, dull, distant, and slender skeins of lightning unraveled across the crest of the coming storm. Under the cliff at my feet the surf rushed foaming over the shore, and the lancons jumped and skipped and quivered until they seemed to be but the reflections of the meshed lightning.

I turned to the east. It was raining over Groix, it was raining at Sainte Barbe, it was raining now at the semaphore. High in the storm whirl a few gulls pitched; a nearer cloud trailed veils of rain in its wake; the sky was spattered with lightning; the thunder boomed.

As I rose to go, a cold raindrop fell upon the back of my hand, and another, and yet another on my face. I gave a last glance at the sea, where the waves were bursting into strange white shapes that seemed to fling out menacing arms toward me. Then something moved on the cliff, something black as the black rock it clutched—a filthy cormorant, craning its hideous head at the sky.

Slowly I plodded homeward across the somber moorland, where the gorse stems glimmered with a dull metallic green, and the heather, no longer violet and purple, hung drenched and dun-colored among the dreary rocks. The wet turf creaked under my heavy boots, the black-thorn scraped and grated against knee and elbow. Over all lay a strange light, pallid, ghastly, where the sea spray whirled across the landscape and drove into my face until it grew numb with the cold. In broad bands, rank after rank, billow on billow, the rain burst out across the endless moors, and yet there was no wind to drive it at such a pace.

Lys stood at the door as I turned into the garden, motioning me to hasten; and then for the first time I became conscious that I was soaked to the skin.

"However in the world did you come to stay out when such a storm threatened?" she said. "Oh, you are dripping! Go quickly and change; I have laid your warm underwear on the bed, Dick."

I kissed my wife, and went upstairs to change my dripping clothes for something more comfortable.

When I returned to the morning room there was a driftwood fire on the hearth, and Lys sat in the chimney corner embroidering.

"Catherine tells me that the fishing fleet from Lorient is out. Do you think they are in danger, dear?" asked Lys, raising her blue eyes to mine as I entered.

"There is no wind, and there will be no sea," said I, looking out of the window. Far across the moor I could see the black cliffs looming in the mist.

"How it rains!" murmured Lys; "come to the fire, Dick."

I threw myself on the fur rug, my hands in my pockets, my head on Lys's knees.

"Tell me a story," I said. "I feel like a boy of ten."

Lys raised a finger to her scarlet lips. I always waited for her to do that.

"Will you be very still, then?" she said.

"Still as death."

"Death," echoed a voice, very softly.

"Did you speak, Lys?" I asked, turning so that I could see her face.

"No; did you, Dick?"

"Who said 'death'?" I asked, startled.

"Death," echoed a voice, softly.

I sprang up and looked about. Lys rose too, her needles and embroidery falling to the floor. She seemed about to faint, leaning heavily on me, and I led her to the window and opened it a little way to give her air. As I did so the chain lightning split the zenith, the thunder crashed, and a sheet of rain swept into the room, driving with it something that fluttered—something that flapped, and squeaked, and beat upon the rug with soft, moist wings.

We bent over it together, Lys clinging to me, and we saw that it was a death's-head moth drenched with rain.

The dark day passed slowly as we sat beside the fire, hand in hand, her head against my breast, speaking of sorrow and mystery and death. For Lys believed that there were things on earth that none might understand, things that must be nameless forever and ever, until God rolls up the scroll of life and all is ended. We spoke of hope and fear and faith, and the mystery of the saints; we spoke of the beginning and the end, of the shadow of sin, of omens, and of love. The moth still lay on the floor quivering its somber wings in the warmth of the fire, the skull and ribs clearly etched upon its neck and body.

"If it is a messenger of death to this house," I said, "why should we fear, Lys?"

"Death should be welcome to those who love God," murmured Lys, and she drew the cross from her breast and kissed it.

"The moth might die if I threw it out into the storm," I said after a silence.

"Let it remain," sighed Lys.

Late that night my wife lay sleeping, and I sat beside her bed and read in the Chronicle of Jacques Sorgue. I shaded the candle, but Lys grew restless, and finally I took the book down into the morning room, where the ashes of the fire rustled and whitened on the hearth.

The death's-head moth lay on the rug before the fire where I had left it. At first I thought it was dead, but when I looked closer I saw a lambent fire in its amber eyes. The straight white shadow it cast across the floor wavered as the candle flickered.

The pages of the Chronicle of Jacques Sorgue were damp and sticky; the illuminated gold and blue initials left flakes of azure and gilt where my hand brushed them.

"It is not paper at all; it is thin parchment," I said to myself; and I held the discolored page close to the candle flame and read, translating laboriously:

> "I, Jacques Sorgue, saw all these things. And I saw the Black Mass celebrated in the chapel of St Gildas-on-the-Cliff. And it was said by the Abbé Sorgue, my kinsman: for which deadly sin the apostate priest was seized by the most noble Marquis of Plougastel and by him condemned to be burned with hot irons, until his seared soul quit its body and fly to its master the devil. But when the Black Priest lay in the crypt of Plougastel, his master Satan came at night and set him free, and carried him across land and sea to Mahmoud, which is Soldan or Saladin. And I, Jacques Sorgue, traveling afterward by sea, beheld with my own eyes my kinsman, the Black Priest of St Gildas, borne along in the air upon a vast black wing, which was the wing of his master Satan. And this was seen also by two men of the crew."

I turned the page. The wings of the moth on the floor began to quiver. I read on and on, my eyes blurring under the shifting candle flame. I read of battles and of saints, and I learned how the Great Soldan made his pact with Satan, and then I came to the Sieur de Trevec, and read how he seized the Black Priest in the midst of Saladin's tents and carried him away and cut off his head first branding him on the forehead. "And before he suffered," said the Chronicle, "he cursed the Sieur de Trevec and his descendants, and he said he would surely return to St Gildas. 'For the violence you do to me, I will do violence to you. For the evil I suffer at your hands, I will work evil on you and your descendants. Woe to your children, Sieur de Trevec!'" There was a whirr, a beating of strong wings, and my candle flashed up as in a sudden breeze. A humming filled the room; the great moth darted hither and thither, beating, buzzing, on ceiling and wall. I flung down my book and stepped forward. Now it lay fluttering upon the window sill, and for a moment I had it under my hand, but the thing squeaked and I shrank back. Then suddenly it darted across the candle flame; the light flared and went out, and at the same moment a shadow moved in the darkness outside. I raised my eyes to the window. A masked face was peering in at me.

Quick as thought I whipped out my revolver and fired every cartridge, but the face advanced beyond the window, the glass melting away before it like mist, and through the smoke of my revolver I saw something creep swiftly into the room. Then I tried to cry out, but the thing was at my throat, and I fell backward among the ashes of the hearth.

When my eyes unclosed I was lying on the hearth, my head among the cold ashes. Slowly I got on my knees, rose painfully, and groped my way to a chair. On the floor lay my revolver, shining in the pale light of early morning. My mind clearing by degrees, I looked, shuddering, at the window. The glass was unbroken. I stooped stiffly, picked up my revolver and opened the cylinder. Every cartridge had been fired. Mechanically I closed the cylinder and placed the revolver in my pocket. The book, the Chronicles of Jacques Sorgue, lay on the table beside me, and as I started to close it I glanced at the page. It was all splashed with rain, and the lettering had run, so that the page was merely a confused blur of gold and red and black. As I stumbled toward the door I cast a fearful glance over my shoulder. The death's-head moth crawled shivering on the rug.

IV

The sun was about three hours high. I must have slept, for I was aroused by the sudden gallop of horses under our window. People were shouting and calling in the road. I sprang up and opened the sash. Le Bihan was there, an image of helplessness, and Max Fortin stood beside him polishing his glasses. Some gendarmes had just arrived from Quimperle, and I could hear them around the corner of the house, stamping, and rattling their sabres and carbines, as they led their horses into my stable.

Lys sat up, murmuring half-sleepy, half-anxious questions.

"I don't know," I answered. "I am going out to see what it means."

"It is like the day they came to arrest you," Lys said, giving me a troubled look. But I kissed her and laughed at her until she smiled too. Then I flung on coat and cap and hurried down the stairs.

The first person I saw standing in the road was the Brigadier Durand.

"Hello!" said I, "have you come to arrest me again? What the devil is all this fuss about, anyway?"

"We were telegraphed for an hour ago," said Durand briskly, "and for a sufficient reason, I think. Look there, Monsieur Darrel!"

He pointed to the ground almost under my feet.

"Good heavens!" I cried, "where did that puddle of blood come from?"

"That's what I want to know, Monsieur Darrel. Max Fortin found it at daybreak. See, it's splashed all over the grass, too. A trail of it leads into your garden, across the flower beds to your very window, the one that opens from the morning room. There is another trail leading from this spot across the road to the cliffs, then to the gravel pit, and thence across the moor to the forest of Kerselec. We are going to mount in a minute and search the bosquets. Will you join us? Bon Dieu! but the fellow bled like an ox. Max Fortin says it's human blood, or I should not have believed it."

The little chemist of Quimperle came up at that moment, rubbing his glasses with a colored handkerchief.

"Yes, it is human blood," he said, "but one thing puzzles me: the corpuscles are yellow. I never saw any human blood before with yellow corpuscles. But your English Doctor Thompson asserts that he has—"

"Well, it's human blood, anyway—isn't it?" insisted Durand, impatiently.

"Ye-es," admitted Max Fortin.

"Then it's my business to trail it," said the big gendarme, and he called his men and gave the order to mount.

"Did you hear anything last night?" asked Durand of me.

"I heard the rain. I wonder the rain did not wash away these traces."

"They must have come after the rain ceased. See this thick splash, how it lies over and weighs down the wet grass blades. Pah!"

It was a heavy, evil-looking clot, and I stepped back from it, my throat closing in disgust.

"My theory," said the brigadier, "is this: Some of those Biribi fishermen, probably the Icelanders, got an extra glass of cognac into their hides and quarreled on the road. Some of them were slashed, and staggered to your house. But there is only one trail, and yet—and yet, how could all that blood come from only one person? Well, the wounded man, let us say, staggered first to your house and then back here, and he wandered off, drunk and dying, God knows where. That's my theory."

"A very good one," said I calmly. "And you are going to trail him?"

"Yes."

"When?"

"At once. Will you come?"

"Not now. I'll gallop over by-and-bye. You are going to the edge of the Kerselec forest?"

"Yes; you will hear us calling. Are you coming, Max Fortin? And you, Le Bihan? Good; take the dog-cart."

The big gendarme tramped around the corner to the stable and presently returned mounted on a strong gray horse, his sabre shone on his saddle; his pale yellow and white facings were spotless. The little crowd of white-coiffed women with their children fell back as Durand touched spurs and clattered away followed by his two troopers. Soon after Le Bihan and Max Fortin also departed in the mayor's dingy dog-cart.

"Are you coming?" piped Le Bihan shrilly.

"In a quarter of an hour," I replied, and went back to the house.

When I opened the door of the morning room the death's-head moth was beating its strong wings against the window. For a second I hesitated, then walked over and opened the sash. The creature fluttered out, whirred over the flower beds a moment, then darted across the moorland toward the sea. I called the servants together and questioned them. Josephine, Catherine, Jean Marie Tregunc, not one of them had heard the slightest disturbance during the night. Then I told Jean Marie to saddle my horse, and while I was speaking Lys came down.

"Dearest," I began, going to her.

"You must tell me everything you know, Dick," she interrupted, looking me earnestly in the face.

"But there is nothing to tell—only a drunken brawl, and someone wounded."

"And you are going to ride—where, Dick?"

"Well, over to the edge of Kerselec forest. Durand and the mayor, and Max Fortin, have gone on, following a—a trail."

"What trail?"

"Some blood."

"Where did they find it?"

"Out in the road there." Lys crossed herself.

"Does it come near our house?"

"Yes."

"How near?"

"It comes up to the morning room window," said I, giving in.

Her hand on my arm grew heavy. "I dreamed last night—"

"So did I—" but I thought of the empty cartridges in my revolver, and stopped.

"I dreamed that you were in great danger, and I could not move hand or foot to save you; but you had your revolver, and I called out to you to fire—"

"I did fire!" I cried excitedly.

"You—you fired?"

I took her in my arms. "My darling," I said "something strange has happened—something that I cannot understand as yet. But, of course, there is an explanation. Last night I thought I fired at the Black Priest."

"Ah!" gasped Lys.

"Is that what you dreamed?"

"Yes, yes, that was it! I begged you to fire—"

"And I did."

Her heart was beating against my breast. I held her close in silence.

"Dick," she said at length, "perhaps you killed the—the thing."

"If it was human I did not miss," I answered grimly. "And it was human," I went on, pulling myself together, ashamed of having so nearly gone to pieces. "Of course it was human! The whole affair is plain enough. Not a drunken brawl, as Durand thinks; it was a drunken lout's practical joke, for which he has suffered. I suppose I must have filled him pretty full of bullets, and he has crawled away to die in Kerselec forest. It's a terrible affair; I'm sorry I fired so hastily; but that idiot Le Bihan and Max Fortin have been working on my nerves till I am as hysterical as a schoolgirl," I ended angrily.

"You fired—but the window glass was not shattered," said Lys in a low voice.

"Well, the window was open, then. And as for the—the rest—I've got nervous indigestion, and a doctor will settle the Black Priest for me, Lys."

I glanced out of the window at Tregunc waiting with my horse at the gate.

"Dearest, I think I had better go to join Durand and the others."

"I will go, too."

"Oh, no!"

"Yes, Dick."

"Don't, Lys."

"I shall suffer every moment you are away."

"The ride is too fatiguing, and we can't tell what unpleasant sight you may come upon. Lys, you don't really think there is anything supernatural in this affair?"

"Dick," she answered gently, "I am a Bretonne." With both arms around my neck, my wife said, "Death is the gift of God. I do not fear it when we are together. But alone—oh, my husband, I should fear a God who could take you away from me!"

We kissed each other soberly, simply, like two children. Then Lys hurried away to change her gown, and I paced up and down the garden waiting for her.

She came, drawing on her slender gauntlets. I swung her into the saddle, gave a hasty order to Jean Marie, and mounted.

Now, to quail under thoughts of terror on a morning like this, with Lys in the saddle beside me, no matter what had happened or might happen was impossible. Moreover, Môme came sneaking after us. I asked Tregunc to catch him, for I was afraid he might be brained by our horses' hoofs if he followed, but the wily puppy dodged and bolted after Lys, who was trotting along the highroad. "Never mind," I thought; "if he's hit he'll live, for he has no brains to lose."

Lys was waiting for me in the road beside the Shrine of Our Lady of St Gildas when I joined her. She crossed herself, I doffed my cap, then we shook out our bridles and galloped toward the forest of Kerselec.

We said very little as we rode. I always loved to watch Lys in the saddle. Her exquisite figure and lovely face were the incarnation of youth and grace; her curling hair glistened like threaded gold.

Out of the corner of my eye I saw the spoiled puppy Môme come bounding cheerfully alongside, oblivious of our horses' heels. Our road swung close to the cliffs. A filthy cormorant rose from the black rocks and flapped heavily across our path. Lys's horse reared, but she pulled him down, and pointed at the bird with her riding crop.

"I see," said I; "it seems to be going our way. Curious to see a cormorant in a forest, isn't it?"

"It is a bad sign," said Lys. "You know the Morbihan proverb: 'When the cormorant turns from the sea, Death laughs in the forest, and wise woodsmen build boats.'"

"I wish," said I sincerely, "that there were fewer proverbs in Brittany."

We were in sight of the forest now; across the gorse I could see the sparkle of gendarmes' trappings, and the glitter of Le Bihan's silver-buttoned jacket. The hedge was low and we took it without difficulty, and trotted across the moor to where Le Bihan and Durand stood gesticulating.

They bowed ceremoniously to Lys as we rode up.

"The trail is horrible—it is a river," said the mayor in his squeaky voice. "Monsieur Darrel, I think perhaps madame would scarcely care to come any nearer."

Lys drew bridle and looked at me.

"It is horrible!" said Durand, walking up beside me; "it looks as though a bleeding regiment had passed this way. The trail winds and winds about here in the thickets; we lose it at times, but we always find it again. I can't understand how one man—no, nor twenty—could bleed like that!"

A halloo, answered by another, sounded from the depths of the forest.

"It's my men; they are following the trail," muttered the brigadier. "God alone knows what is at the end!"

"Shall we gallop back, Lys?" I asked.

"No; let us ride along the western edge of the woods and dismount. The sun is so hot now, and I should like to rest for a moment," she said.

"The western forest is clear of anything disagreeable," said Durand.

"Very well," I answered; "call me, Le Bihan, if you find anything."

Lys wheeled her mare, and I followed across the springy heather, Môme trotting cheerfully in the rear.

We entered the sunny woods about a quarter of a kilometer from where we left Durand. I took Lys from her horse, flung both bridles over a limb, and, giving my wife my arm, aided her to a flat mossy rock which overhung a shallow brook gurgling among the beech trees. Lys sat down and drew off her gauntlets. Môme pushed his head into her lap, received an undeserved caress, and came doubtfully toward me. I was weak enough to condone his offense, but I made him lie down at my feet, greatly to his disgust.

I rested my head on Lys's knees, looking up at the sky through the crossed branches of the trees.

"I suppose I have killed him," I said. "It shocks me terribly, Lys."

"You could not have known, dear. He may have been a robber, and—if—not—did—have you ever fired your revolver since that day four years ago when the Red Admiral's son tried to kill you? But I know you have not."

"No," said I, wondering. "It's a fact, I have not. Why?"

"And don't you remember that I asked you to let me load it for you the day when Yves went off, swearing to kill you and his father?"

"Yes, I do remember. Well?"

"Well, I—I took the cartridges first to St Gildas chapel and dipped them in holy water. You must not laugh, Dick," said Lys gently, laying her cool hands on my lips.

"Laugh, my darling!"

Overhead the October sky was pale amethyst, and the sunlight burned like orange flame through the yellow leaves of beech and oak. Gnats and midges danced and wavered overhead; a spider dropped from a twig halfway to the ground and hung suspended on the end of his gossamer thread.

"Are you sleepy, dear?" asked Lys, bending over me.

"I am—a little; I scarcely slept two hours last night," I answered.

"You may sleep, if you wish," said Lys, and touched my eyes caressingly.

"Is my head heavy on your knees?"

"No, Dick."

I was already in a half doze; still I heard the brook babbling under the beeches and the humming of forest flies overhead. Presently even these were stilled.

The next thing I knew I was sitting bolt upright, my ears ringing with a scream, and I saw Lys cowering beside me, covering her white face with both hands.

As I sprang to my feet she cried again and clung to my knees. I saw my dog rush growling into a thicket, then I heard him whimper, and he came backing out, whining, ears flat, tail down. I stooped and disengaged Lys's hand.

"Don't go, Dick!" she cried. "O God, it's the Black Priest!"

In a moment I had leaped across the brook and pushed my way into the thicket. It was empty. I stared about me; I scanned every tree trunk, every bush. Suddenly I saw him. He was seated on a fallen log, his head resting in his hands, his rusty black robe gathered around him. For a moment my hair stirred under my cap; sweat started on forehead and cheek bone; then I recovered my reason, and understood that the man was human and was probably wounded to death. Ay, to death; for there at my feet, lay the wet trail of blood, over leaves and stones, down into the little hollow, across to the figure in black resting silently under the trees.

I saw that he could not escape even if he had the strength, for before him, almost at his very feet, lay a deep, shining swamp.

As I stepped forward my foot broke a twig. At the sound the figure started a little, then its head fell forward again. Its face was masked. Walking up to the man, I bade him tell where he was wounded. Durand and the others broke through the thicket at the same moment and hurried to my side.

"Who are you who hide a masked face in a priest's robe?" said the gendarme loudly.

There was no answer.

"See—see the stiff blood all over his robe," muttered Le Bihan to Fortin.

"He will not speak," said I.

"He may be too badly wounded," whispered Le Bihan.

"I saw him raise his head," I said, "my wife saw him creep up here."

Durand stepped forward and touched the figure.

"Speak!" he said.

"Speak!" quavered Fortin.

Durand waited a moment, then with a sudden upward movement he stripped off the mask and threw back the man's head. We were looking into the eye sockets of a skull. Durand stood rigid; the mayor shrieked. The skeleton burst out from its rotting robes and collapsed on the ground before us. From between the staring ribs and the grinning teeth spurted a torrent of black blood, showering the shrinking grasses; then the thing shuddered, and fell over into the black ooze of the bog. Little bubbles of iridescent air appeared from the mud; the bones were slowly engulfed, and, as the last fragments sank out of sight, up from the depths and along the bank crept a creature, shiny, shivering, quivering its wings.

It was a death's-head moth.

†

I wish I had time to tell you how Lys outgrew superstitions—for she never knew the truth about the affair, and she never will know, since she has promised not to read this book. I wish I might tell you about the king and his coronation, and how the coronation robe fitted. I wish that I were able to write how Yvonne and Herbert Stuart rode to a boar hunt in Quimperle, and how the hounds raced the quarry right through the town, overturning three gendarmes, the notary, and an old woman. But I am becoming garrulous and Lys is calling me to come and hear the king say that he is sleepy. And his highness shall not be kept waiting.

THE KING'S CRADLE SONG

Seal with a seal of gold
The scroll of a life unrolled;
Swathe him deep in his purple stole;
Ashes of diamonds, crystalled coal,
Drops of gold in each scented fold.
Crimson wings of the Little Death,
Stir his hair with your silken breath;
Flaming wings of sins to be,
Splendid pinions of prophecy,
Smother his eyes with hues and dyes,
While the white moon spins and the winds arise,
And the stars drip through the skies.
Wave, O wings of the Little Death!
Seal his sight and stifle his breath,
Cover his breast with the gemmed shroud pressed;

From north to north, from west to west,
Wave, O wings of the Little Death!
Till the white moon reels in the cracking skies,
And the ghosts of God arise.

The Bridal Pair

Robert W. Chambers

"If I were you," said the elder man, "I should take three months' solid rest."

"A month is enough," said the younger man. "Ozone will do it; the first brace of grouse I bag will do it—" He broke off abruptly, staring at the line of dimly lighted cars, where negro porters stood by the vestibuled sleepers, directing passengers to staterooms and berths.

"Dog all right, doctor?" inquired the elder man pleasantly. "All right, doctor," replied the younger; "I spoke to the baggage master." There was a silence; the elder man chewed an unlighted cigar reflectively, watching his companion with keen narrowing eyes.

The younger physician stood full in the white electric light, lean head lowered, apparently preoccupied with a study of his own shadow swimming and quivering on the asphalt at his feet.

"So you fear I may break down?" he observed, without raising his head.

"I think you're tired out," said the other.

"That's a more agreeable way of expressing it," said the young fellow. "I hear"— he hesitated, with a faint trace of irritation—"I understand that Forbes Stanly thinks me mentally unsound."

"He probably suspects what you're up to," said the elder man soberly.

"Well, what will he do when I announce my germ theory? Put me in a strait-jacket?"

"He'll say you're mad, until you prove it; every physician will agree with him—until your radium test shows us the microbe of insanity."

"Doctor," said the young man abruptly, "I'm going to admit something—to you."

"All right; go ahead and admit it."

"Well, I am a bit worried about my own condition."

"It's time you were," observed the other.

"Yes—it's about time. Doctor, I am seriously affected."

The elder man looked up sharply.

"Yes, I'm—in love."

"Ah!" muttered the elder physician, amused and a trifle disgusted; "so that's your malady, is it?"

"A malady—yes; not explainable by our germ theory—not affected by radio-activity. Doctor, I'm speaking lightly enough, but there's no happiness in it."

"Never is," commented the other, striking a match and lighting his ragged cigar. After a puff or two the cigar went out. "All I have to say," he added, "is, don't do it just now. Show me a scale of pure radium and I'll give you leave to marry every spinster in New York. In the mean time go and shoot a few dozen harmless, happy grouse; they can't shoot back. But let love alone . . . By the way, who is she?"

"I don't know."

"You know her name, I suppose?"

The young fellow shook his head. "I don't even know where she lives," he said finally.

After a pause the elder man took him gently by the arm: "Are you subject to this sort of thing? Are you susceptible?"

"No, not at all."

"Ever before in love?"

"Yes—once."

"When?"

"When I was about ten years old. Her name was Rosamund—aged eight. I never had the courage to speak to her. She died recently, I believe."

The reply was so quietly serious, so destitute of any suspicion of humor, that the elder man's smile faded; and again he cast one of his swift, keen glances at his companion.

"Won't you stay away three months?" he asked patiently.

But the other only shook his head, tracing with the point of his walking stick the outline of his own shadow on the asphalt.

A moment later he glanced at his watch, closed it with a snap, silently shook hands with his equally silent friend, and stepped aboard the sleeping car.

Neither had noticed the name of the sleeping car.

It happened to be the Rosamund.

Loungers and passengers on Wildwood station drew back from the platform's edge as the towering locomotive shot by them, stunning their ears with the clangor of its melancholy bell.

Slower, slower glided the dusty train, then stopped, jolting; eddying circles of humanity closed around the cars, through which descending passengers pushed.

"Wildwood! Wildwood!" cried the trainmen; trunks tumbling out of the forward car descended with a bang!—a yelping, wagging setter dog landed on the platform, hysterically grateful to be free; and at the same moment a young fellow in tweed shooting clothes, carrying gripsack and gun case, made his way forward toward the baggage master, who was being jerked all over the platform by the frantic dog.

"Much obliged; I'll take the dog," he said, slipping a bit of silver into the official's hand, and receiving the dog's chain in return.

"Hope you'll have good sport," replied the baggage master. "There's a lot o' birds in this country, they tell me. You've got a good dog there."

The young man smiled and nodded, released the chain from his dog's collar, and started off up the dusty village street, followed by an urchin carrying his luggage.

The landlord of the Wildwood Inn stood on the veranda, prepared to receive guests. When a young man, a white setter dog, and a small boy loomed up, his speculative eyes became suffused with benevolence.

"How-de-so, sir?" he said cordially. "Guess you was with us three year since—stayed to supper. Ain't that so?"

"It certainly is," said his guest cheerfully. "I am surprised that you remember me."

"Be ye?" rejoined the landlord, gratified. "Say! I can tell the name of every man, woman, an' child that has ever set down to eat with us. You was here with a pair o' red bird dawgs; shot a mess o' birds before dark, come back pegged out, an' took the ten-thirty to Noo York. Hey? Yaas, an' you was cussin' round because you couldn't stay an' shoot for a month."

"I had to work hard in those days," laughed the young man. "You are right; it was three years ago this month."

"Time's a flyer; it's fitted with triple screws these days," said the landlord. "Come right in an' make yourself to home. Ed! O Ed! Take this bag to 13! We're all full, sir. You ain't scared at No. 13, be ye? Say! if I ain't a liar you had 13 three years ago! Waal, now!—ain't that the dumbdest— But you can have what you want Monday. How long was you calkerlatin' to stay?"

"A month—if the shooting is good."

"It's all right. Orrin Plummet come in last night with a mess o pa'tridges. He says the woodcock is droppin' in to the birches south o' Sweetbrier Hill."

The young man nodded, and began to remove his gun from the service-worn case of sole leather.

"Ain't startin' right off, be ye?" inquired his host, laughing.

"I can't begin too quickly," said the young man, busy locking barrels to stock, while the dog looked on, thumping the veranda floor with his plumy tail.

The landlord admired the slim, polished weapon. "That's the instrooment!" he observed. "That there's a slick bird dawg, too. Guess I'd better fill my ice box. Your limit's thirty of each—cock an' parridge. After that there's ducks."

"It's a good, sane law," said the young man, dropping his gun under one arm.

The landlord scratched his ear reflectively. "Lemme see," he mused; "wasn't you a doctor? I heard tell that you made up pieces for the papers about the idjits an' loonyticks of Rome an' Roosia an' furrin climes."

"I have written a little on European and Asiatic insanity," replied the doctor good-humoredly.

"Was you over to them parts?"

"For three years." He whistled the dog in from the road, where several yellow curs were walking round and round him, every hair on end.

The landlord said: "You look a little peaked yourself. Take it easy the fust, is my advice."

His guest nodded abstractedly, lingering on the veranda, preoccupied with the beauty of the village street, which stretched away westward under tall elms. Autumn-tinted hills closed the vista; beyond them spread the blue sky.

"The cemetery lies that way, does it not?" inquired the young man.

"Straight ahead," said the landlord. "Take the road to the Holler."

"Do you"— the doctor hesitated—"do you recall a funeral there three years ago?"

"Whose?" asked his host bluntly.

"I don't know."

"I'll ask my woman; she saves them funeral pieces an' makes a album."

"Friend o' yours buried there?"

"No."

The landlord sauntered toward the barroom, where two fellow taxpayers stood shuffling their feet impatiently.

"Waal, good luck, Doc," he said, without intentional offense; "supper's at six. We'll try an' make you comfortable."

"Thank you," replied the doctor, stepping out into the road, and motioning the white setter to heel.

"I remember now," he muttered, as he turned northward, where the road forked; "the cemetery lies to the westward; there should be a lane at the next turning—"

He hesitated and stopped, then resumed his course, mumbling to himself: "I can pass the cemetery later; she would not be there; I don't think I shall ever see her again... I— I wonder whether I am—perfectly—well—"

The words were suddenly lost in a sharp indrawn breath; his heart ceased beating, fluttered, then throbbed on violently; and he shook from head to foot.

There was a glimmer of a summer gown under the trees; a figure passed from shadow to sunshine, and again into the cool dusk of a leafy lane.

The pallor of the young fellow's face changed; a heavy flush spread from forehead to neck; he strode forward, dazed, deafened by the tumult of his drumming pulses. The dog, alert, suspicious, led the way, wheeling into the bramble-bordered lane, only to halt, turn back, and fall in behind his master again.

In the lane ahead the light summer gown fluttered under the foliage, bright in the sunlight, almost lost in the shadows. Then he saw her on the hill's breezy crest, poised for a moment against the sky.

When at length he reached the hill, he found her seated in the shade of a pine. She looked up serenely, as though she had expected him, and they faced each other. A moment later his dog left him, sneaking away without a sound.

When he strove to speak, his voice had an unknown tone to him. Her upturned face was his only answer. The breeze in the pinetops, which had been stirring lazily and monotonously, ceased.

Her delicate face was like a blossom lifted in the still air; her upward glance chained him to silence. The first breeze broke the spell: he spoke a word, then speech died on his lips; he stood twisting his shooting cap, confused, not daring to continue.

The girl leaned back, supporting her weight on one arm, fingers almost buried in the deep green moss.

"It is three years today," he said, in the dull voice of one who dreams; "three years today. May I not speak?"

In her lowered head and eyes he read acquiescence; in her silence, consent.

"Three years ago today," he repeated; "the anniversary has given me courage to speak to you. Surely you will not take offense; we have traveled so far together!—from the end of the world to the end of it, and back again, here—to this place of all places in the world! And now to find you here on this day of all days—here within a step of our first meeting place—three years ago today! And all the world we have traveled over since never speaking, yet ever passing on paths parallel—paths which for thousands of miles ran almost within arm's distance—"

She raised her head slowly, looking out from the shadows of the pines into the sunshine. Her dreamy eyes rested on acres of golden-rod and hill-side brambles quivering in the September heat; on fern-choked gullies edged with alder; on brown and purple grasses; on pine thickets where slim silver birches glimmered.

"Will you speak to me?" he asked. "I have never even heard the sound of your voice."

She turned and looked at him, touching with idle fingers the soft hair curling on her temples. Then she bent her head once more, the faintest shadow of a smile in her eyes.

"Because," he said humbly, "these long years of silent recognition count for something! And then the strangeness of it!—the fate of it—the quiet destiny that ruled our lives—that rules them now—now as I am speaking, weighting every second with its tiny burden of fate."

She straightened up, lifting her half-buried hand from the moss; and he saw the imprint there where the palm and fingers had rested.

"Three years that end today—end with the new moon," he said. "Do you remember?"

"Yes," she said.

He quivered at the sound of her voice. "You were there, just beyond those oaks," he said eagerly; "we can see them from here. The road turns there—"

"Turns by the cemetery," she murmured.

"Yes, yes, by the cemetery! You had been there, I think."

"Do you remember that?" she asked.

"I have never forgotten—never!" he repeated, striving to hold her eyes to his own; "it was not twilight; there was a glimmer of day in the west, but the woods were darkening, and the new moon lay in the sky, and the evening was very clear and still."

Impulsively he dropped on one knee beside her to see her face; and as he spoke, curbing his emotion and impatience with that subtle deference which is inbred in men or never acquired, she stole a glance at him; and his worn visage brightened as though touched with sunlight.

"The second time I saw you was in New York," he said—"only a glimpse of your face in the crowd—but I knew you."

"I saw you," she mused.

"Did you?" he cried, enchanted. "I dared not believe that you recognized me."

"Yes, I knew you... Tell me more."

The thrilling voice set him aflame; faint danger signals tinted her face and neck.

"In December," he went on unsteadily, "I saw you in Paris—I saw only you amid the thousand faces in the candlelight of Notre Dame."

"And I saw you... And then?"

"And then two months of darkness... And at last a light—moonlight—and you on the terrace at Amara."

"There was only a flower bed—a few spikes of white hyacinths between us," she said dreamily.

He strove to speak coolly. "Day and night have built many a wall between us; was that you who passed me in the starlight, so close that our shoulders touched, in that narrow street in Samarkand? And the dark figure with you—"

"Yes, it was I and my attendant."

"And… you, there in the fog—"

"At Archangel? Yes, it was I."

"On the Goryn?"

"It was I… And I am here at last—with you. It is our destiny."

So, kneeling there beside her in the shadow of the pines, she absolved him in their dim confessional, holding him guiltless under the destiny that awaits us all.

Again that illumination touched his haggard face as though brightened by a sun ray stealing through the still foliage above. He grew younger under the level beauty of her gaze; care fell from him like a mask; the shadows that had haunted his eyes faded; youth awoke, transfiguring him and all his eyes beheld.

Made prisoner by love, adoring her, fearing her, he knelt beside her, knowing already that she had surrendered, though fearful yet by word or gesture or a glance to claim what destiny was holding for him holding securely, inexorably, for him alone.

He spoke of her kindness in understanding him, and of his gratitude; of her generosity, of his wonder that she had ever noticed him on his way through the world.

"I cannot believe that we have never before spoken to each other," he said; "that I do not even know your name. Surely there was once a corner in the land of childhood where we sat together when the world was younger."

She said, dreamily: "Have you forgotten?"

"Forgotten?"

"That sunny corner in the land of childhood."

"Had you been there, I should not have forgotten," he replied, troubled.

"Look at me," she said. Her lovely eyes met his; under the penetrating sweetness of her gaze his heart quickened and grew restless and his uneasy soul stirred, awaking memories.

"There was a child," she said, "years ago; a child at school. You sometimes looked at her, you never spoke. Do you remember?"

He rose to his feet, staring down at her.

"Do you remember?" she asked again.

"Rosamund! Do you mean Rosamund? How should you know that?" he faltered.

The struggle for memory focused all his groping senses; his eyes seemed to look her through and through.

"How can you know?" he repeated unsteadily. "You are not Rosamund... Are you?... She is dead. I heard that she was dead... Are you Rosamund?"

"Do you not know?"

"Yes; you are not Rosamund... What do you know of her?"

"I think she loved you."

"Is she dead?"

The girl looked up at him, smiling, following with delicate perception the sequence of his thoughts; and already his thoughts were far from the child Rosamund, a sweetheart of a day long since immortal; already he had forgotten his question, though the question was of life or death.

Sadness and unrest and the passing of souls concerned not him; she knew that all his thoughts were centered on her; that he was already living over once more the last three years, with all their mystery and charm, savoring their fragrance anew in the exquisite enchantment of her presence.

Through the autumn silence the pines began to sway in a wind unfelt below. She raised her eyes and saw their green crests shimmering and swimming in a cool current; a thrilling sound stole out, and with it floated the pine perfume, exhaling in the sunshine. He heard the dreamy harmony above, looked up; then, troubled, somber, moved by he knew not what, he knelt once more in the shadow beside her—close beside her.

She did not stir. Their destiny was close upon them. It came in the guise of love.

He bent nearer. "I love you," he said. "I loved you from the first. And shall forever. You knew it long ago."

She did not move.

"You knew I loved you?"

"Yes, I knew it."

The emotion in her voice, in every delicate contour of her face, pleaded for mercy. He gave her none, and she bent her head in silence, clasped hands tightening.

And when at last he had had his say, the burning words still rang in her ears through the silence. A curious faintness stole upon her, coming stealthily like a hateful thing. She strove to put it from her, to listen, to remember and understand the words he had spoken, but the dull confusion grew with the sound of the pines.

"Will you love me? Will you try to love me?"

"I love you," she said; "I have loved you so many, many years; I— I am Rosamund—"

She bowed her head and covered her face with both hands… "Rosamund! Rosamund!" he breathed, enraptured.

She dropped her hands with a little cry; the frightened sweetness of her eyes held back his outstretched arms. "Do not touch me," she whispered; "you will not touch me, will you?—not yet—not now. Wait till I understand!" She pressed her hands to her eyes, then again let them fall, staring straight at him. "I loved you so!" she whispered. "Why did you wait?"

"Rosamund! Rosamund!" he cried sorrowfully, "what are you saying? I do not understand; I can understand nothing save that I worship you. May I not touch you?—touch your hand, Rosamund? I love you so."

"And I love you. I beg you not to touch me—not yet. There is something—some reason why—"

"Tell me, sweetheart."

"Do you not know?"

"By Heaven, I do not!" he said, troubled and amazed.

She cast one desperate, unhappy glance at him, then rose to her full height, gazing out over the hazy valleys to where the mountains began, piled up like dim sun-tipped clouds in the north.

The hill wind stirred her hair and fluttered the white ribbons at waist and shoulder. The golden-rod swayed in the sunshine. Below, amid yellow treetops, the roofs and chimneys of the village glimmered.

"Dear, do you not understand?" she said. "How can I make you understand that I love you—too late?"

"Give yourself to me, Rosamund; let me touch you—let me take you—"

"Will you love me always?"

"In life, in death, which cannot part us. Will you marry me, Rosamund?"

She looked straight into his eyes. "Dear, do you not understand? Have you forgotten? I died three years ago today."

The unearthly sweetness of her white face startled him. A terrible light broke in on him; his heart stood still.

In his dull brain words were sounding—his own words, written years ago: "When God takes the mind and leaves the body alive, there grows in it, sometimes, a beauty almost supernatural."

He had seen it in his practice. A thrill of fright penetrated him, piercing every vein with its chill. He strove to speak; his lips seemed frozen; he stood there before her, a ghastly smile stamped on his face, and in his heart, terror.

"What do you mean, Rosamund?" he said at last.

"That I am dead, dear. Did you not understand that? I— I thought you knew it—when you first saw me at the cemetery, after all those years since childhood.... Did you not know it?" she asked wistfully. "I must wait for my bridal."

Misery whitened his face as he raised his head and looked out across the sunlit world.

Something had smeared and marred the fair earth; the sun grew gray as he stared.

Stupefied by the crash, the ruins of life around him, he stood mute, erect, facing the west.

She whispered, "Do you understand?"

"Yes," he said; "we will wed later. You have been ill, dear; but it is all right now—and will always be—God help us! Love is stronger than all—stronger than death."

"I know it is stronger than death," she said, looking out dreamily over the misty valley.

He followed her gaze, calmly, serenely reviewing all that he must renounce, the happiness of wedlock, children—all that a man desires.

Suddenly instinct stirred, awaking man's only friend—hope. A lifetime for the battle!—for a cure! Hopeless? He laughed in his excitement. Despair?—when the cure lay almost within his grasp! the work he had given his life to! A month more in the laboratory—two months—three—perhaps a year. What of it? It must surely come—how could he fail when the work of his life meant all in life for her?

The light of exaltation slowly faded from his face; ominous, foreboding thoughts crept in; fear laid a shaky hand on his head which fell heavily forward on his breast.

Science and man's cunning and the wisdom of the world!

"O God," he groaned, "for Him who cured by laying on His hands!"

Now that he had learned her name, and that her father was alive, he stood mutely beside her, staring steadily at the chimneys and stately dormered roof almost hidden behind the crimson maple foliage across the valley—her home.

She had seated herself once more upon the moss, hands clasped upon one knee, looking out into the west with dreamy eyes.

"I shall not be long," he said gently. "Will you wait here for me? I will bring your father with me."

"I will wait for you. But you must come before the new moon. Will you? I must go when the new moon lies in the west."

"Go, dearest? Where?"

"I may not tell you," she sighed, "but you will know very soon—very soon now. And there will be no more sorrow, I think," she added timidly.

"There will be no more sorrow," he repeated quietly.

"For the former things are passing away," she said.

He broke a heavy spray of golden-rod and laid it across her knees; she held out a blossom to him—a blind gentian, blue as her eyes. He kissed it.

"Be with me when the new moon comes," she whispered. "It will be so sweet. I will teach you how divine is death, if you will come."

"You shall teach me the sweetness of life," he said tremulously.

"Yes—life. I did not know you called it by its truest name."

So he went away, trudging sturdily down the lane, gun glistening on his shoulder.

Where the lane joins the shadowy village street his dog skulked up to him, sniffing at his heels.

A mill whistle was sounding; through the red rays of the setting sun people were passing.

Along the row of village shops loungers followed him with vacant eyes. He saw nothing, heard nothing, though a kindly voice called after him, and a young girl smiled at him on her short journey through the world.

The landlord of the Wildwood Inn sat sunning himself in the red evening glow.

"Well, doctor," he said, "you look tired to death. Eh? What's that you say?"

The young man repeated his question in a low voice. The landlord shook his head.

"No, sir. The big house on the hill is empty—been empty these three years. No, sir, there ain't no family there now. The old gentleman moved away three years ago."

"You are mistaken," said the doctor; "his daughter tells me he lives there."

"His—his daughter?" repeated the landlord. "Why, doctor, she's dead." He turned to his wife, who sat sewing by the open window: "Ain't it three years, Marthy?"

"Three years today," said the woman, biting off her thread. "She's buried in the family vault over the hill. She was a right pretty little thing, too."

"Turned nineteen," mused the landlord, folding his newspaper reflectively.

The great gray house on the hill was closed, windows and doors boarded over, lawn, shrubbery, and hedges tangled with weeds. A few scarlet poppies glimmered above the brown grass. Save for these, and clumps of tall wild phlox, there were no blossoms among the weeds.

His dog, which had sneaked after him, cowered as he turned northward across the fields.

Swifter and swifter he strode; and as he stumbled on, the long sunset clouds faded, the golden light in the west died out, leaving a calm, clear sky tinged with the faintest green.

Pines hid the west as he crept toward the hill where she awaited him. As he climbed through dusky purple grasses, higher, higher, he saw the new moon's crescent tipping above the hills; and he crushed back the deathly fright that clutched at him and staggered on.

"Rosamund!"

The pines answered him.

"Rosamund!"

The pines replied, answering together. Then the wind died away, and there was no answer when he called.

East and south the darkening thickets, swaying, grew still. He saw the slim silver birches glimmering like the ghosts of young trees dead; he saw on the moss at his feet a broken stalk of golden-rod.

The new moon had drawn a veil across her face; sky and earth were very still.

While the moon lasted he lay, eyes open, listening, his face pillowed on the moss. It was long after sunrise when his dog came to him; later still when men came.

And at first they thought he was asleep.

A Pleasant Evening

Robert W. Chambers

Et pis, doucett'ment on s'endort. On fait sa carne, on fait sa sorgue. On ronfle, et, comme un tuyan d'orgue. L'tuyan s'met à ronfler pus fort…
Aristide Bruant

Chapter I

As I stepped upon the platform of a Broadway cable-car at Forty-second Street, somebody said:

"Hello, Hilton, Jamison's looking for you."

"Hello, Curtis," I replied, "what does Jamison want?"

"He wants to know what you've been doing all the week," said Curtis, hanging desperately to the railing as the car lurched forward; "he says you seem to think that the *Manhattan Illustrated Weekly* was created for the sole purpose of providing salary and vacations for you."

"The shifty old tom-cat!" I said, indignantly, "he knows well enough where I've been. Vacation! Does he think the State Camp in June is a snap?"

"Oh," said Curtis, "you've been to Peekskill?"

"I should say so," I replied, my wrath rising as I thought of my assignment.

"Hot?" inquired Curtis, dreamily.

"One hundred and three in the shade," I answered. "Jamison wanted three full pages and three half pages, all for process work, and a lot of line drawings into the bargain. I could have faked them—I wish I had. I was fool enough to hustle and break my neck to get some honest drawings, and that's the thanks I get!"

"Did you have a camera?"

"No. I will next time—I'll waste no more conscientious work on Jamison," I said sulkily.

"It doesn't pay," said Curtis. "When I have military work assigned me, I don't do the dashing sketch-artist act, you bet; I go to my studio, light my pipe, pull out a lot of old *Illustrated London News*, select several suitable battle scenes by Caton Woodville—and use 'em too."

The car shot around the neck-breaking curve at Fourteenth Street.

"Yes," continued Curtis, as the car stopped in front of the Morton House for a moment, then plunged forward again amid a furious clanging of gongs, "it doesn't pay to do decent work for the fat-headed men who run the Manhattan Illustrated. They don't appreciate it."

"I think the public does," I said, "but I'm sure Jamison doesn't. It would serve him right if I did what most of you fellows do—take a lot of Caton Woodville's and Thulstrup's drawings, change the uniforms, 'chic' a figure or two, and turn in a drawing labelled 'from life.' I'm sick of this sort of thing anyway. Almost every day this week I've been chasing myself over that tropical camp, or galloping in the wake of those batteries. I've got a full page of the 'camp by moonlight,' full pages of 'artillery drill' and 'light battery in action,' and a dozen smaller drawings that cost me more groans and perspiration than Jamison ever knew in all his lymphatic life!"

"Jamison's got wheels," said Curtis—"more wheels than there are bicycles in Harlem. He wants you to do a full page by Saturday."

"A what?" I exclaimed, aghast.

"Yes he does. He was going to send Jim Crawford, but Jim expects to go to California for the winter fair, and you've got to do it."

"What is it?" I demanded savagely.

"The animals in Central Park," chuckled Curtis.

I was furious. The animals! Indeed! I'd show Jamison that I was entitled to some consideration! This was Thursday; that gave me a day and a half to finish a full-page drawing for the paper, and, after my work at the State Camp I felt that I was entitled to a little rest. Anyway I objected to the subject. I intended to tell Jamison so—I intended to tell him firmly. However, many of the things that we often intended to tell Jamison were never told. He was a peculiar man, fat-faced, thin-lipped, gentle-voiced, mild-mannered, and soft in his movements as a pussy-cat.

Just why our firmness should give way when we were actually in his presence, I have never quite been able to determine. He said very little—so did we, although we often entered his presence with other intentions.

The truth was that the *Manhattan Illustrated Weekly* was the best paying, best illustrated paper in America, and we young fellows were not anxious to be cast adrift. Jamison's knowledge of art was probably as extensive as the knowledge of any 'Art editor' in the city. Of course that was saying nothing, but the fact merited careful consideration on our part, and we gave it much consideration.

This time, however, I decided to let Jamison know that drawings are not produced by the yard, and that I was neither a floor-walker nor a hand-me-down. I would stand up for my rights; I'd tell old Jamison a few things to set the wheels under his silk hat spinning, and if he attempted any of his pussy-cat ways on me, I'd give him a few plain facts that would curl what hair he had left.

Glowing with a splendid indignation I jumped off the car at the City Hall, followed by Curtis, and a few minutes later entered the office of the *Manhattan Illustrated News*.

"Mr Jamison would like to see you, sir," said one of the compositors as I passed into the long hallway. I threw my drawings on the table and passed a handkerchief over my forehead.

"Mr Jamison would like to see you, sir," said a small freckle-faced boy with a smudge of ink on his nose.

"I know it," I said, and started to remove my gloves.

"Mr Jamison would like to see you, sir," said a lank messenger who was carrying a bundle of proofs to the floor below.

"The deuce take Jamison," I said to myself I started toward the dark passage that leads to the abode of Jamison, running over in my mind the neat and sarcastic speech which I had been composing during the last ten minutes.

Jamison looked up and nodded softly as I entered the room. I forgot my speech.

"Mr Hilton," he said, "we want a full page of the Zoo before it is removed to Bronx Park. Saturday afternoon at three o'clock the drawing must be in the engraver's hands. Did you have a pleasant week in camp?"

"It was hot," I muttered, furious to find that I could not remember my little speech.

"The weather," said Jamison, with soft courtesy, "is oppressive everywhere. Are your drawings in, Mr Hilton?"

"Yes. It was infernally hot and I worked like a n****r—"

"I suppose you were quite overcome. Is that why you took a two days' trip to the Catskills? I trust the mountain air restored you—but—was it prudent to go to Cranston's for the cotillion Tuesday? Dancing in such uncomfortable weather is really unwise. Good-morning, Mr Hilton, remember the engraver should have your drawings on Saturday by three."

I walked out, half hypnotized, half enraged. Curtis grinned at me as I passed—I could have boxed his ears.

"Why the mischief should I lose my tongue whenever that old tom-cat purrs!" I asked myself as I entered the elevator and was shot down to the first floor. "I'll not put up with this sort of thing much longer—how in the name of all that's foxy did he know that I went to the mountains? I suppose he thinks I'm lazy because I don't wish to be boiled to death. How did he know about the dance at Cranston's? Old cat!"

The roar and turmoil of machinery and busy men filled my ears as I crossed the avenue and turned into the City Hall Park.

From the staff on the tower the flag drooped in the warm sunshine with scarcely a breeze to lift its crimson bars. Overhead stretched a splendid cloudless sky, deep, deep blue, thrilling, scintillating in the gemmed rays of the sun.

Pigeons wheeled and circled about the roof of the grey Post Office or dropped out of the blue above to flutter around the fountain in the square.

On the steps of the City Hall the unlovely politician lounged, exploring his heavy under jaw with wooden toothpick, twisting his drooping black moustache, or distributing tobacco juice over marble steps and close-clipped grass.

My eyes wandered from these human vermin to the calm scornful face of Nathan Hale, on his pedestal, and then to the grey-coated Park policeman whose occupation was to keep little children from the cool grass.

A young man with thin hands and blue circles under his eyes was slumbering on a bench by the fountain, and the policeman walked over to him and struck him on the soles of his shoes with a short club.

The young man rose mechanically, stared about, dazed by the sun, shivered, and limped away.

I saw him sit down on the steps of the white marble building, and I went over and spoke to him.

He neither looked at me, nor did he notice the coin I offered.

"You're sick," I said, "you had better go to the hospital."

"Where?" he asked vacantly—"I've been, but they wouldn't receive me."

He stooped and tied the bit of string that held what remained of his shoe to his foot.

"You are French," I said.

"Yes."

"Have you no friends? Have you been to the French Consul?"

"The Consul!" he replied; "no, I haven't been to the French Consul."

After a moment I said, "You speak like a gentleman."

He rose to his feet and stood very straight, looking me, for the first time, directly in the eyes.

"Who are you?" I asked abruptly.

"An outcast," he said, without emotion, and limped off thrusting his hands into his ragged pockets.

"Huh!" said the Park policeman who had come up behind me in time to hear my question and the vagabond's answer; "don't you know who that hobo is?—An' you a newspaper man!"

"Who is he, Cusick?" I demanded, watching the thin shabby figure moving across Broadway toward the river.

"On the level you don't know, Mr Hilton?" repeated Cusick, suspiciously.

"No, I don't; I never before laid eyes on him."

"Why," said the sparrow policeman, "that's 'Soger Charlie';—you remember—that French officer what sold secrets to the Dutch Emperor."

"And was to have been shot? I remember now, four years ago—and he escaped—you mean to say that is the man?"

"Everybody knows it," sniffed Cusick, "I'd a-thought you newspaper gents would have knowed it first."

"What was his name?" I asked after a moment's thought.

"Soger Charlie—"

"I mean his name at home."

"Oh, some French dago name. No Frenchman will speak to him here; sometimes they curse him and kick him. I guess he's dyin' by inches."

I remembered the case now. Two young French cavalry officers were arrested, charged with selling plans of fortifications and other military secrets to the Germans. On the eve of their conviction, one of them, Heaven only knows how, escaped and turned up in New York. The other was duly shot. The affair had made some noise, because both young men were of good families. It was a painful episode, and I had hastened to forget it. Now that it was recalled to my mind, I remembered the newspaper accounts of the case, but I had forgotten the names of the miserable young men.

"Sold his country," observed Cusick, watching a group of children out of the corner of his eyes—"you can't trust no Frenchman nor dagoes nor Dutchmen either. I guess Yankees are about the only white men."

I looked at the noble face of Nathan Hale and nodded.

"Nothin' sneaky about us, eh, Mr Hilton?"

I thought of Benedict Arnold and looked at my boots.

Then the policeman said, "Well, so long, Mr Hilton," and went away to frighten a pasty-faced little girl who had climbed upon the railing and was leaning down to sniff the fragrant grass.

"Cheese it, de cop!" cried her shrill-voiced friends, and the whole bevy of small ragamuffins scuttled away across the square.

With a feeling of depression I turned and walked toward Broadway, where the long yellow cable-cars swept up and down, and the din of gongs and the deafening rumble of heavy trucks echoed from the marble walls of the Court House to the granite mass of the Post Office.

Throngs of hurrying busy people passed up town and down town, slim sober-faced clerks, trim cold-eyed brokers, here and there a red-necked politician linking arms with some favourite heeler, here and there a City Hall lawyer, sallow-faced and saturnine. Sometimes a fireman, in his severe blue uniform, passed through the crowd, sometimes a blue-coated policeman, mopping his clipped hair, holding his helmet in his white-gloved hand. There were women too, pale-faced shop girls with pretty eyes, tall blonde girls who might be typewriters and might not, and many, many older women whose business in that part of the city no human being could venture to guess, but who hurried up town and down town, all occupied with something that gave to the whole restless throng a common likeness—the expression of one who hastens toward a hopeless goal.

I knew some of those who passed me. There was little Jocelyn of the Mail and Express; there was Hood, who had more money than he wanted and was going to have less than he wanted when he left Wall Street; there was Colonel Tidmouse of the 45th Infantry, N.G.S.N.Y, probably coming from the office of the Army and Navy Journal, and there was Dick Harding who wrote the best stories of New York life that have been printed. People said his hat no longer fitted— especially people who also wrote stories of New York life and whose hats threatened to fit as long as they lived.

I looked at the statue of Nathan Hale, then at the human stream that flowed around his pedestal.

"Quand même," I muttered and walked out into Broadway, signalling to the gripman of an uptown cable-car.

Chapter II

I passed into the Park by the Fifth Avenue and 59th Street gate; I could never bring myself to enter it through the gate that is guarded by the hideous pigmy statue of Thorwaldsen.

The afternoon sun poured into the windows of the New Netherlands Hotel, setting every orange-curtained pane a-glitter, and tipping the wings of the bronze dragons with flame.

Gorgeous masses of flowers blazed in the sunshine from the grey terraces of the Savoy, from the high grilled court of the Vanderbilt palace, and from the balconies of the Plaza opposite.

The white marble façade of the Metropolitan Club was a grateful relief in the universal glare, and I kept my eyes on it until I had crossed the dusty street and entered the shade of the trees.

Before I came to the Zoo, I smelled it. Next week it was to be removed to the fresh cool woods and meadows in Bronx Park, far from the stifling air of the city, far from the infernal noise of the Fifth Avenue omnibuses.

A noble stag stared at me from his enclosure among the trees as I passed down the winding asphalt walk. "Never mind, old fellow," said I, "you will be splashing about in the Bronx River next week and cropping maple shoots to your heart's content."

On I went, past herds of staring deer, past great lumbering elk, and moose, and long-faced African antelopes, until I came to the dens of the great carnivora.

The tigers sprawled in the sunshine, blinking and licking their paws; the lions slept in the shade or squatted on their haunches, yawning gravely. A slim panther travelled to and fro behind her barred cage, pausing at times to peer wistfully out into the free sunny world. My heart ached for caged wild things, and I walked on, glancing up now and then to encounter the blank stare of a tiger or the mean shifty eyes of some ill-smelling hyena.

Across the meadow I could see the elephants swaying and swinging their great heads, the sober bison solemnly slobbering over their cuds, the sarcastic countenances of camels, the wicked little zebras, and a lot more animals of the camel and llama tribe, all resembling each other, all equally ridiculous, stupid, deadly uninteresting.

Somewhere behind the old arsenal an eagle was screaming, probably a Yankee eagle; I heard the "rchug! rchug!" of a blowing hippopotamus, the squeal of a falcon, and the snarling yap! of quarrelling wolves.

"A pleasant place for a hot day!" I pondered bitterly, and I thought some things about Jamison that I shall not insert in this volume. But I lighted a cigarette to deaden the aroma from the hyenas, unclasped my sketching block, sharpened my pencil, and fell to work on a family group of hippopotami.

They may have taken me for a photographer, for they all wore smiles as if "welcoming a friend," and my sketch block presented a series of wide open jaws, behind which shapeless bulky bodies vanished in alarming perspective.

The alligators were easy; they looked to me as though they had not moved since the founding of the Zoo, but I had a bad time with the big bison, who persistently turned his tail to me, looking stolidly around his flank to see how I stood it. So I pretended to be absorbed in the antics of two bear cubs, and the dreary old bison fell into the trap, for I made some good sketches of him and laughed in his face as I closed the book.

There was a bench by the abode of the eagles, and I sat down on it to draw the vultures and condors, motionless as mummies among the piled rocks. Gradually I enlarged the sketch, bringing in the gravel plaza, the steps leading up to Fifth Avenue, the sleepy park policeman in front of the arsenal—and a slim, white-browed girl, dressed in shabby black, who stood silently in the shade of the willow trees.

After a while I found that the sketch, instead of being a study of the eagles, was in reality a composition in which the girl in black occupied the principal point of interest. Unwittingly I had subordinated everything else to her, the brooding vultures, the trees and walks, and the half indicated groups of sun-warmed loungers.

She stood very still, her pallid face bent, her thin white hands loosely clasped before her.

"Rather dejected reverie," I thought, "probably she's out of work." Then I caught a glimpse of a sparkling diamond ring on the slender third finger of her left hand.

"She'll not starve with such a stone as that about her," I said to myself, looking curiously at her dark eyes and sensitive mouth. They were both beautiful, eyes and mouth—beautiful, but touched with pain.

After a while I rose and walked back to make a sketch or two of the lions and tigers. I avoided the monkeys—I can't stand them, and they never seem funny to me, poor dwarfish, degraded caricatures of all that is ignoble in ourselves.

"I've enough now," I thought; "I'll go home and manufacture a full page that will probably please Jamison." So I strapped the elastic band around my sketching block, replaced pencil and rubber in my waistcoat pocket, and strolled off toward the Mall to smoke a cigarette in the evening glow before going back to my studio to work until midnight, up to the chin in charcoal grey and Chinese white.

Across the long meadow I could see the roofs of the city faintly looming above the trees. A mist of amethyst, ever deepening, hung low on the horizon, and through it, steeple and dome, roof and tower, and the tall chimneys where thin fillets of smoke curled idly, were transformed into pinnacles of beryl and flaming minarets, swimming in filmy haze. Slowly the enchantment deepened; all that was ugly and shabby and mean had fallen away from the distant city, and now it towered into the evening sky, splendid, gilded, magnificent, purified in the fierce furnace of the setting sun.

The red disk was half hidden now; the tracery of trees, feathery willow and budding birch, darkened against the glow; the fiery rays shot far across the meadow, gilding the dead leaves, staining with soft crimson the dark moist tree trunks around me.

Far across the meadow a shepherd passed in the wake of a huddling flock, his dog at his heels, faint moving blots of grey.

A squirrel sat up on the gravel walk in front of me, ran a few feet, and sat up again, so close that I could see the palpitation of his sleek flanks.

Somewhere in the grass a hidden field insect was rehearsing last summer's solos; I heard the tap! tap! tat-tat-t-t-tat! of a woodpecker among the branches overhead and the querulous note of a sleepy robin.

The twilight deepened; out of the city the music of bells floated over wood and meadow; faint mellow whistles sounded from the river craft along the north shore, and the distant thunder of a gun announced the close of a June day.

The end of my cigarette began to glimmer with a redder light; shepherd and flock were blotted out in the dusk, and I only knew they were still moving when the sheep bells tinkled faintly.

Then suddenly that strange uneasiness that all have known—that half-awakened sense of having seen it all before, of having been through it all, came over me, and I raised my head and slowly turned.

A figure was seated at my side. My mind was struggling with the instinct to remember.

Something so vague and yet so familiar—something that eluded thought yet challenged it, something—God knows what! troubled me. And now, as I looked, without interest, at the dark figure beside me, an apprehension, totally involuntary, an impatience to understand, came upon me, and I sighed and turned restlessly again to the fading west.

I thought I heard my sigh re-echoed—I scarcely heeded; and in a moment I sighed again, dropping my burned-out cigarette on the gravel beneath my feet.

"Did you speak to me?" said someone in a low voice, so close that I swung around rather sharply.

"No," I said after a moment's silence.

It was a woman. I could not see her face clearly, but I saw on her clasped hands, which lay listlessly in her lap, the sparkle of a great diamond. I knew her at once. It did not need a glance at the shabby dress of black, the white face, a pallid spot in the twilight, to tell me that I had her picture in my sketch-book.

"Do—do you mind if I speak to you?" she asked timidly. The hopeless sadness in her voice touched me, and I said: "Why, no, of course not. Can I do anything for you?"

"Yes," she said, brightening a little, "if you—you only would."

"I will if I can," said I, cheerfully; "what is it? Out of ready cash?"

"No, not that," she said, shrinking back.

I begged her pardon, a little surprised, and withdrew my hand from my change pocket.

"It is only—only that I wish you to take these,"— she drew a thin packet from her breast—"these two letters."

"I?" I asked astonished.

"Yes, if you will."

"But what am I to do with them?" I demanded.

"I can't tell you; I only know that I must give them to you. Will you take them?"

"Oh, yes, I'll take them," I laughed, "am I to read them?" I added to myself, "It's some clever begging trick."

"No," she answered slowly, "you are not to read them; you are to give them to somebody."

"To whom? Anybody?"

"No, not to anybody. You will know whom to give them to when the time comes.

"Then I am to keep them until further instructions?"

"Your own heart will instruct you," she said, in a scarcely audible voice. She held the thin packet toward me, and to humor her I took it. It was wet.

"The letters fell into the sea," she said; "there was a photograph which should have gone with them but the salt water washed it blank. Will you care if I ask you something else?"

"I? Oh, no."

"Then give me the picture that you made of me today." I laughed again, and demanded how she knew I had drawn her.

"Is it like me?" she said.

"I think it is very like you," I answered truthfully.

"Will you not give it to me?"

Now it was on the tip of my tongue to refuse, but I reflected that I had enough sketches for a full page without that one, so I handed it to her, nodded that she was welcome, and stood up. She rose also, the diamond flashing on her finger.

"You are sure that you are not in want?" I asked, with a tinge of good-natured sarcasm.

"Hark!" she whispered; "listen!—do you hear the bells of the convent!" I looked out into the misty night.

"There are no bells sounding," I said, "and anyway there are no convent bells here. We are in New York, mademoiselle"— I had noticed her French accent—"we are in Protestant Yankee-land, and the bells that ring are much less mellow than the bells of France."

I turned pleasantly to say good-night. She was gone.

Chapter III

"Have you ever drawn a picture of a corpse?" inquired Jamison next morning as I walked into his private room with a sketch of the proposed full page of the Zoo.

"No, and I don't want to," I replied, sullenly.

"Let me see your Central Park page," said Jamison in his gentle voice, and I displayed it. It was about worthless as an artistic production, but it pleased Jamison, as I knew it would.

"Can you finish it by this afternoon?" he asked, looking up at me with persuasive eyes.

"Oh, I suppose so," I said, wearily; "anything else, Mr Jamison?"

"The corpse," he replied, "I want a sketch by tomorrow—finished."

"What corpse?" I demanded, controlling my indignation as I met Jamison's soft eyes.

There was a mute duel of glances. Jamison passed his hand across his forehead with a slight lifting of the eyebrows.

"I shall want it as soon as possible," he said in his caressing voice.

What I thought was, "Damned purring pussy-cat!" What I said was, "Where is this corpse?"

"In the Morgue—have you read the morning papers? No? Ah—as you very rightly observe you are too busy to read the morning papers. Young men must learn industry first, of course, of course. What you are to do is this: the San Francisco police have sent out an alarm regarding the disappearance of a Miss Tufft—the millionaire's daughter, you know. Today a body was brought to the Morgue here in New York, and it has been identified as the missing young lady— by a diamond ring. Now I am convinced that it isn't, and I'll show you why, Mr Hilton."

He picked up a pen and made a sketch of a ring on a margin of that morning's Tribune.

"That is the description of her ring as sent on from San Francisco. You notice the diamond is set in the centre of the ring where the two gold serpents' tails cross!

"Now the ring on the finger of the woman in the Morgue is like this," and he rapidly sketched another ring where the diamond rested in the fangs of the two gold serpents.

"That is the difference," he said in his pleasant, even voice.

"Rings like that are not uncommon," said I, remembering that I had seen such a ring on the finger of the white-faced girl in the Park the evening before. Then a sudden thought took shape—perhaps that was the girl whose body lay in the Morgue!

"Well," said Jamison, looking up at me, "what are you thinking about?"

"Nothing," I answered, but the whole scene was before my eyes, the vultures brooding among the rocks, the shabby black dress, and the pallid face—and the ring, glittering on that slim white hand!

"Nothing," I repeated, "when shall I go, Mr Jamison? Do you want a portrait—or what?"

"Portrait—careful drawing of the ring, and—er—a centre piece of the Morgue at night. Might as well give people the horrors while we're about it."

"But," said I, "the policy of this paper—"

"Never mind, Mr Hilton," purred Jamison, "I am able to direct the policy of this paper."

"I don't doubt you are," I said angrily.

"I am," he repeated, undisturbed and smiling; "you see this Tufft case interests society. I am— er—also interested."

He held out to me a morning paper and pointed to a heading.

I read: "Miss Tufft Dead! Her Fiancé was Mr Jamison, the well known Editor."

"What!" I cried in horrified amazement. But Jamison had left the room, and I heard him chatting and laughing softly with some visitors in the press-room outside.

I flung down the paper and walked out.

"The cold-blooded toad!" I exclaimed again and again;—"making capital out of his fiancée's disappearance! Well, I—I'm d—nd! I knew he was a bloodless, heartless grip-penny, but I never thought—I never imagined—" Words failed me.

Scarcely conscious of what I did I drew a Herald from my pocket and saw the column entitled:

"Miss Tufft Found! Identified by a Ring. Wild Grief of Mr Jamison, her Fiancé."

That was enough. I went out into the street and sat down in City Hall Park. And, as I sat there, a terrible resolution came to me; I would draw that dead girl's face in such a way that it would chill Jamison's sluggish blood, I would crowd the black shadows of the Morgue with forms and ghastly faces, and every face should bear something in it of Jamison. Oh, I'd rouse him from his cold snaky apathy! I'd confront him with Death in such an awful form, that, passionless, base, inhuman as he was, he'd shrink from it as he would from a dagger thrust. Of course I'd lose my place, but that did not bother me, for I had decided to resign anyway, not having a taste for the society of human reptiles. And, as I sat there in the sunny park, furious, trying to plan a picture whose sombre horror should leave in his mind an ineffaceable scar, I suddenly thought of the pale black-robed girl in Central Park. Could it be her poor slender body that lay among the shadows of the grim Morgue! If ever brooding despair was stamped on any face, I had seen its print on hers when she spoke to me in the Park and gave me the letters. The letters! I had not thought of them since, but now I drew them from my pocket and looked at the addresses.

"Curious," I thought, "the letters are still damp; they smell of salt water too."

I looked at the address again, written in the long fine hand of an educated woman who had been bred in a French convent. Both letters bore the same address, in French:

"Captain d'Yniol.
(Kindness of a Stranger.)"

"Captain d'Yniol," I repeated aloud—"confound it, I've heard that name! Now, where the deuce—where in the name of all that's queer—" Somebody who had sat down on the bench beside me placed a heavy hand on my shoulder.

It was the Frenchman, "Soger Charlie."

"You spoke my name," he said in apathetic tones.

"Your name!"

"Captain d'Yniol," he repeated; "it is my name."

I recognized him in spite of the black goggles he was wearing, and, at the same moment, it flashed into my mind that d'Yniol was the name of the traitor who had escaped. Ah, I remembered now!

"I am Captain d'Yniol," he said again, and I saw his fingers closing on my coat sleeve.

It may have been my involuntary movement of recoil—I don't know—but the fellow dropped my coat and sat straight up on the bench.

"I am Captain d'Yniol." he said for the third time, "charged with treason and under sentence of death."

"And innocent!" I muttered, before I was even conscious of having spoken. What was it that wrung those involuntary words from my lips, I shall never know, perhaps—but it was I, not he, who trembled, seized with a strange agitation, and it was I, not he, whose hand was stretched forth impulsively, touching his.

Without a tremor he took my hand, pressed it almost imperceptibly, and dropped it. Then I held both letters toward him, and, as he neither looked at them nor at me, I placed them in his hand. Then he started.

"Read them," I said, "they are for you."

"Letters!" he gasped in a voice that sounded like nothing human.

"Yes, they are for you—I know it now—"

"Letters!—letters directed to me?"

"Can you not see?" I cried.

Then he raised one frail hand and drew the goggles from his eyes, and, as I looked, I saw two tiny white specks exactly in the centre of both pupils.

"Blind!" I faltered.

"I have been unable to read for two years," he said.

After a moment he placed the tip of one finger on the letters.

"They are wet," I said; "shall—would you like to have me read them?" For a long time he sat silently in the sunshine, fumbling with his cane, and I watched him without speaking. At last he said, "Read, Monsieur," and I took the letters and broke the seals.

The first letter contained a sheet of paper, damp and discoloured, on which a few lines were written:

> "My darling, I knew you were innocent—" Here the writing ended, but, in the blur beneath, I read: "Paris shall know—France shall know, for at last I have the proofs and I am coming to find you, my soldier, and to place them in your own dear brave hands. They know, now, at the War Ministry—they have a copy of the traitor's confession— but they dare not make it public—they dare not withstand the popular astonishment and rage. Therefore I sail on Monday from Cherbourg by the Green Cross Line, to bring you back to your own again, where you will stand before all the world, without fear, without reproach."
>
> "Aline."

"This—this is terrible!" I stammered; "can God live and see such things done!"

But with his thin hand he gripped my arm again, bidding me read the other letter; and I shuddered at the menace in his voice.

Then, with his sightless eyes on me, I drew the other letter from the wet, stained envelope. And before I was aware—before I understood the purport of what I saw, I had read aloud these half effaced lines:

> "The *Lorient* is sinking—an iceberg—mid-ocean—goodbye you are innocent—I love—"

"The *Lorient*!" I cried; "it was the French steamer that was never heard from—the *Lorient* of the Green Cross Line! I had forgotten—I—"

The loud crash of a revolver stunned me; my ears rang and ached with it as I shrank back from a ragged dusty figure that collapsed on the bench beside me, shuddered a moment, and tumbled to the asphalt at my feet.

The trampling of the eager hard-eyed crowd, the dust and taint of powder in the hot air, the harsh alarm of the ambulance clattering up Mail Street—these I remember, as I knelt there, helplessly holding the dead man's hands in mine.

"Soger Charlie," mused the sparrow policeman, "shot his-self, didn't he, Mr Hilton? You seen him, sir—blowed the top of his head off, didn't he, Mr Hilton?"

"Soger Charlie," they repeated, "a French dago what shot his-self;" and the words echoed in my ears long after the ambulance rattled away, and the increasing throng dispersed, sullenly, as a couple of policemen cleared a space around the pool of thick blood on the asphalt.

They wanted me as a witness, and I gave my card to one of the policemen who knew me. The rabble transferred its fascinated stare to me, and I turned away and pushed a path between frightened shop girls and ill-smelling loafers, until I lost myself in the human torrent of Broadway.

The torrent took me with it where it flowed—East? West?—I did not notice nor care, but I passed on through the throng, listless, deadly weary of attempting so solve God's justice— striving to understand His purpose—His laws—His judgments which are "true and righteous altogether."

Chapter IV

"More to be desired are they than gold, yea, than much fine gold. Sweeter also than honey and the honey-comb!"

I turned sharply toward the speaker who shambled at my elbow. His sunken eyes were dull and lustreless, his bloodless face gleamed pallid as a death mask above the blood-red jersey—the emblem of the soldiers of Christ.

I don't know why I stopped, lingering, but, as he passed, I said, "Brother, I also was meditating upon God's wisdom and His testimonies."

The pale fanatic shot a glance at me, hesitated, and fell into my own pace, walking by my side.

Under the peak of his Salvation Army cap his eyes shone in the shadow with a strange light.

"Tell me more," I said, sinking my voice below the roar of traffic, the clang! clang! of the cable-cars, and the noise of feet on the worn pavements—"tell me of His testimonies."

"Moreover by them is Thy servant warned and in keeping of them there is great reward. Who can understand His errors? Cleanse Thou me from secret faults. Keep back Thy servant also from presumptuous sins. Let them not have dominion over me. Then shall I be upright and I shall be innocent from the great transgression. Let the words of my mouth and the meditation of my heart be acceptable in Thy sight—O Lord! My strength and my Redeemer!"

"It is Holy Scripture that you quote," I said; "I also can read that when I choose. But it cannot clear for me the reasons—it cannot make me understand—"

"What?" he asked, and muttered to himself.

"That, for instance," I replied, pointing to a cripple, who had been born deaf and dumb and horridly misshapen—a wretched diseased lump on the sidewalk below St Paul's Churchyard—a sore-eyed thing that mouthed and mowed and rattled pennies in a tin cup as though the sound of copper could stem the human pack that passed hot on the scent of gold.

Then the man who shambled beside me turned and looked long and earnestly into my eyes.

And after a moment a dull recollection stirred within me—a vague something that seemed like the awakening memory of a past, long, long forgotten, dim, dark, too subtle, too frail, too indefinite— ah! the old feeling that all men have known—the old strange uneasiness, that useless struggle to remember when and where it all occurred before.

And the man's head sank on his crimson jersey, and he muttered, muttered to himself of God and love and compassion, until I saw that the fierce heat of the city had touched his brain, and I went away and left him prating of mysteries that none but such as he dare name.

So I passed on through dust and heat; and the hot breath of men touched my cheek and eager eyes looked into mine. Eyes, eyes—that met my own and looked through them, beyond—far beyond to where gold glittered amid the mirage of eternal hope. Gold! It was in the air where the soft sunlight gilded the floating motes, it was under foot in the dust that the sun made gilt, it glimmered from every window pane where the long red beams struck golden sparks above the gasping gold-hunting hordes of Wall Street.

High, high, in the deepening sky the tall buildings towered, and the breeze from the bay lifted the sun-dyed flags of commerce until they waved above the turmoil of the hives below—waved courage and hope and strength to those who lusted after gold.

The sun dipped low behind Castle William as I turned listlessly into the Battery, and the long straight shadows of the trees stretched away over greensward and asphalt walk.

Already the electric lights were glimmering among the foliage although the bay shimmered like polished brass and the topsails of the ships glowed with a deeper hue, where the red sun rays fell athwart the rigging.

Old men tottered along the sea-wall, tapping the asphalt with worn canes, old women crept to and fro in the coming twilight—old women who carried baskets that gaped for charity or bulged with mouldy stuffs—food, clothing?—I could not tell; I did not care to know.

The heavy thunder from the parapets of Castle William died away over the placid bay, the last red arm of the sun shot up out of the sea, and wavered and faded into the sombre tones of the afterglow. Then came the night, timidly at first, touching sky and water with grey fingers, folding the foliage into soft massed shapes, creeping onward, onward, more swiftly now, until colour and form had gone from all the earth and the world was a world of shadows.

And, as I sat there on the dusky sea-wall, gradually the bitter thoughts faded and I looked out into the calm night with something of that peace that comes to all when day is ended.

The death at my very elbow of the poor blind wretch in the Park had left a shock, but now my nerves relaxed their tension and I began to think about it all—about the letters and the strange woman who had given them to me. I wondered where she had found them—whether they really were carried by some vagrant current in to the shore from the wreck of the fated Lorient.

Nothing but these letters had human eyes encountered from the Lorient, although we believed that fire or berg had been her portion; for there had been no storms when the Lorient steamed away from Cherbourg.

And what of the pale-faced girl in black who had given these letters to me, saying that my own heart would teach me where to place them?

I felt in my pockets for the letters where I had thrust them all crumpled and wet. They were there, and I decided to turn them over to the police. Then I thought of Cusick and the City Hall Park and these set my mind running on Jamison and my own work—ah! I had forgotten that— I had forgotten that I had sworn to stir Jamison's cold, sluggish blood! Trading on his fiancée's reported suicide—or murder! True, he had told me that he was satisfied that the body at the Morgue was not Miss Tufft's because the ring did not correspond with his fiancée's ring. But what sort of a man was that!—to go crawling and nosing about morgues and graves for a full-page illustration which might sell a few extra thousand papers. I had never known he was such a man. It was strange too—for that was not the sort of illustration that the Weekly used; it was against all precedent— against the whole policy of the paper. He would lose a hundred subscribers where he would gain one by such work.

"The callous brute!" I muttered to myself, "I'll wake him up—I'll—"

I sat straight up on the bench and looked steadily at a figure which was moving toward me under the spluttering electric light.

It was the woman I had met in the Park.

She came straight up to me, her pale face gleaming like marble in the dark, her slim hands outstretched.

"I have been looking for you all day—all day," she said, in the same low thrilling tones—"I want the letters back; have you them here?"

"Yes," I said, "I have them here—take them in Heaven's name; they have done enough evil for one day!"

She took the letters from my hand; I saw the ring, made of the double serpents, flashing on her slim finger, and I stepped closer, and looked her in the eyes.

"Who are you?" I asked.

"I? My name is of no importance to you," she answered.

"You are right," I said, "I do not care to know your name. That ring of yours—"

"What of my ring?" she murmured.

"Nothing—a dead woman lying in the Morgue wears such a ring. Do you know what your letters have done? No? Well I read them to a miserable wretch and he blew his brains out!"

"You read them to a man!"

"I did. He killed himself."

"Who was that man?"

"Captain d'Yniol—"

With something between a sob and a laugh she seized my hand and covered it with kisses, and I, astonished and angry, pulled my hand away from her cold lips and sat down on the bench.

"You needn't thank me," I said sharply; "if I had known that—but no matter. Perhaps after all the poor devil is better off somewhere in other regions with his sweetheart who was drowned— yes, I imagine he is. He was blind and ill—and broken-hearted."

"Blind?" she asked gently.

"Yes. Did you know him?"

"I knew him."

"And his sweetheart, Aline?"

"Aline," she repeated softly—"she is dead. I come to thank you in her name."

"For what?—for his death?"

"Ah, yes, for that."

"Where did you get those letters?" I asked her, suddenly.

She did not answer, but stood fingering the wet letters.

Before I could speak again she moved away into the shadows of the trees, lightly, silently, and far down the dark walk I saw her diamond flashing.

Grimly brooding, I rose and passed through the Battery to the steps of the Elevated Road.

These I climbed, bought my ticket, and stepped out to the damp platform. When a train came I crowded in with the rest, still pondering on my vengeance, feeling and believing that I was to scourge the conscience of the man who speculated on death.

And at last the train stopped at 28th Street, and I hurried out and down the steps and away to the Morgue.

When I entered the Morgue, Skelton, the keeper, was standing before a slab that glistened faintly under the wretched gas jets. He heard my footsteps, and turned around to see who was coming. Then he nodded, saying:

"Mr Hilton, just take a look at this here stiff—I'll be back in a moment—this is the one that all the papers take to be Miss Tufft—but they're all off, because this stiff has been here now for two weeks."

I drew out my sketching-block and pencils.

"Which is it, Skelton?" I asked, fumbling for my rubber.

"This one, Mr Hilton, the girl what's smilin'. Picked up off Sandy Hook, too. Looks as if she was asleep, eh?"

"What's she got in her hand—clenched tight? Oh—a letter. Turn up the gas, Skelton, I want to see her face."

The old man turned the gas jet, and the flame blazed and whistled in the damp, fetid air. Then suddenly my eyes fell on the dead.

Rigid, scarcely breathing, I stared at the ring, made of two twisted serpents set with a great diamond—I saw the wet letters crushed in her slender hand—I looked, and—God help me!—I looked upon the dead face of the girl with whom I had been speaking on the Battery!

"Dead for a month at least," said Skelton, calmly.

Then, as I felt my senses leaving me, I screamed out, and at the same instant somebody from behind seized my shoulder and shook me savagely—shook me until I opened my eyes again and gasped and coughed.

"Now then, young feller!" said a Park policeman bending over me, "if you go to sleep on a bench, somebody'll lift your watch!"

I turned, rubbing my eyes desperately.

Then it was all a dream—and no shrinking girl had come to me with damp letters—I had not gone to the office—there was no such person as Miss Tufft—Jamison was not an unfeeling villain—no, indeed!—he treated us all much better than we deserved, and he was kind and generous too. And the ghastly suicide! Thank God that also was a myth—and the Morgue and the Battery at night where that pale-faced girl had—ugh!

I felt for my sketch-block, found it; turned the pages of all the animals that I had sketched, the hippopotami, the buffalo, the tigers—ah! where was that sketch in which I had made the woman in shabby black the principal figure, with the brooding vultures all around and the crowd in the sunshine—? It was gone.

I hunted everywhere, in every pocket. It was gone.

At last I rose and moved along the narrow asphalt path in the falling twilight.

And as I turned into the broader walk, I was aware of a group, a policeman holding a lantern, some gardeners, and a knot of loungers gathered about something—a dark mass on the ground.

"Found 'em just so," one of the gardeners was saying, "better not touch 'em until the coroner comes."

The policeman shifted his bull's-eye a little; the rays fell on two faces, on two bodies, half supported against a park bench. On the finger of the girl glittered a splendid diamond, set between the fangs of two gold serpents. The man had shot himself; he clasped two wet letters in his hand. The girl's clothing and hair were wringing wet, and her face was the face of a drowned person.

"Well, sir," said the policeman, looking at me; "you seem to know these two people—by your looks—"

"I never saw them before," I gasped, and walked on, trembling in every nerve.

For among the folds of her shabby black dress I had noticed the end of a paper—my sketch that I had missed!

Passeur

Robert W. Chambers

O friends, I've served ye food and bed;
O friends, the mist is rising wet;
Then bide a moment, O my dead,
Where, lonely, I must linger yet!

Passeur

Because man goeth to his long home,
And the mourners go about the streets.

When he had finished his pipe he tapped the brier bowl against the chimney until the ashes powdered the charred log smouldering across the andirons. Then he sank back in his chair, absently touching the hot pipe-bowl with the tip of each finger until it grew cool enough to be dropped into his coat pocket.

Twice he raised his eyes to the little American clock ticking upon the mantel. He had half an hour to wait.

The three candles that lighted the room might be trimmed to advantage; this would give him something to do. A pair of scissors lay open upon the bureau, and he rose and picked them up. For a while he stood dreamily shutting and opening the scissors, his eyes roaming about the room. There was an easel in the corner, and a pile of dusty canvases behind it; behind the canvases there was a shadow—that gray, menacing shadow that never moved.

When he had trimmed each candle he wiped the smoky scissors on a paint rag and flung them on the bureau again. The clock pointed to ten; he had been occupied exactly three minutes.

The bureau was littered with neckties, pipes, combs and brushes, matches, reels and fly-books, collars, shirt studs, a new pair of Scotch shooting stockings, and a woman's workbasket.

He picked out all the neckties, folded them once, and hung them over a bit of twine that stretched across the looking-glass; the shirt studs he shovelled into the top drawer along with brushes, combs, and stockings; the reels and fly-books he dusted with his handkerchief and placed methodically along the mantel shelf. Twice he stretched out his hand toward the woman's workbasket, but his hand fell to his side again, and he turned away into the room staring at the dying fire.

Outside the snow-sealed window a shutter broke loose and banged monotonously, until he flung open the panes and fastened it. The soft, wet snow, that had choked the window-panes all day, was frozen hard now, and he had to break the polished crust before he could find the rusty shutter hinge.

He leaned out for a moment, his numbed hands resting on the snow, the roar of a rising snow-squall in his ears; and out across the desolate garden and stark hedgerow he saw the flat black river spreading through the gloom.

A candle sputtered and snapped behind him; a sheet of drawing-paper fluttered across the floor, and he closed the panes and turned back into the room, both hands in his worn pockets.

The little American clock on the mantel ticked and ticked, but the hands lagged, for he had not been occupied five minutes in all. He went up to the mantel and watched the hands of the clock. A minute—longer than a year to him—crept by.

Around the room the furniture stood ranged—a chair or two of yellow pine, a table, the easel, and in one corner the broad curtained bed; and behind each lay shadows, menacing shadows that never moved.

A little pale flame started up from the smoking log on the andirons; the room sang with the sudden hiss of escaping wood gases. After a little the back of the log caught fire; jets of blue flared up here and there with mellow sounds like the lighting of gas-burners in a row, and in a moment a thin sheet of yellow flame wrapped the whole charred log.

Then the shadows moved; not the shadows behind the furniture—they never moved—but other shadows, thin, gray, confusing, that came and spread their slim patterns all around him, and trembled and trembled.

He dared not step or tread upon them, they were too real; they meshed the floor around his feet, they ensnared his knees, they fell across his breast like ropes. Some night, in the silence of the moors, when wind and river were still, he feared these strands of shadow might tighten—creep higher around his throat and tighten. But even then he knew that those other shadows would never move, those gray shapes that knelt crouching in every corner.

When he looked up at the clock again ten minutes had straggled past. Time was disturbed in the room; the strands of shadow seemed entangled among the hands of the clock, dragging them back from their rotation. He wondered if the shadows would strangle Time, some still night when the wind and the flat river were silent.

There grew a sudden chill across the floor; the cracks of the boards let it in. He leaned down and drew his sabots toward him from their place near the andirons, and slipped them over his chaussons; and as he straightened up, his eyes mechanically sought the mantel above, where in the dusk another pair of sabots stood, little, slender, delicate sabots, carved from red beech. A year's dust grayed their surface; a year's rust dulled the silver band across the instep. He said this to himself aloud, knowing that it was within a few minutes of the year.

His own sabots came from Mort-Dieu; they were shaved square and banded with steel. But in days past he had thought that no sabot in Mort-Dieu was delicate enough to touch the instep of the Mort-Dieu passeur. So he sent to the shore lighthouse, and they sent to Lorient, where the women are coquettish and show their hair under the coiffe, and wear dainty sabots; and in this town, where vanity corrupts and there is much lace on coiffe and collarette, a pair of delicate sabots was found, banded with silver and chiselled in red beech. The sabots stood on the mantel above the fire now, dusty and tarnished.

There was a sound from the window, the soft murmur of snow blotting glass panes. The wind, too, muttered under the roof eaves. Presently it would begin to whisper to him from the chimney—he knew it—and he held his hands over his ears and stared at the clock.

In the hamlet of Mort-Dieu the pines sing all day of the sea secrets, but in the night the ghosts of little gray birds fill the branches, singing of the sunshine of past years. He heard the song as he sat, and he crushed his hands over his ears; but the gray birds joined with the wind in the chimney, and he heard all that he dared not hear, and he thought all that he dared not hope or think, and the swift tears scalded his eyes.

In Mort-Dieu the nights are longer than anywhere on earth; he knew it—why should he not know? This had been so for a year; it was different before. There were so many things different before; days and nights vanished like minutes then; the pines told no secrets of the sea, and the gray birds had not yet come to Mort-Dieu. Also, there was Jeanne, passeur at the Carmes.

When he first saw her she was poling the square, flat-bottomed ferry skiff from the Carmes to Mort-Dieu, a red handkerchief bound across her silky black hair, a red skirt fluttering just below her knees. The next time he saw her he had to call to her across the placid river, "Ohé! Ohé, passeur!" She came, poling the flat skiff, her deep blue eyes fixed pensively on him, the scarlet skirt and kerchief idly flapping in the April wind. Then day followed day when the far call "Passeur!" grew clearer and more joyous, and the faint answering cry, "I come!" rippled across the water like music tinged with laughter. Then spring came, and with spring came love—love, carried free across the ferry from the Carmes to Mort-Dieu.

The flame above the charred log whistled, flickered, and went out in a jet of wood vapour, only to play like lightning above the gas and relight again. The clock ticked more loudly, and the song from the pines filled the room. But in his straining eyes a summer landscape was reflected, where white clouds sailed and white foam curled under the square bow of a little skiff. And he pressed his numbed hands tighter to his ears to drown the cry, "Passeur! Passeur!"

And now for a moment the clock ceased ticking. It was time to go—who but he should know it, he who went out into the night swinging his lantern? And he went. He had gone each night from the first—from that first strange winter evening when a strange voice had answered him across the river, the voice of the new passeur. He had never heard *her* voice again.

So he passed down the windy wooden stairs, lantern hanging lighted in his hand, and stepped out into the storm. Through sheets of drifting snow, over heaps of frozen seaweed and icy drift he moved, shifting his lantern right and left, until its glimmer on the water warned him. Then he called out into the night, "Passeur!" The frozen spray spattered his face and crusted the lantern; he heard the distant boom of breakers beyond the bar, and the noise of mighty winds among the seaward cliffs.

"Passeur!"

Across the broad flat river, black as a sea of pitch, a tiny light sparkled a moment. Again he cried, "Passeur!"

"I come!"

He turned ghastly white, for it was her voice—or was he crazy?—and he sprang waist deep into the icy current and cried out again, but his voice ended in a sob.

Slowly through the snow the flat skiff took shape, creeping nearer and nearer. But she was not at the pole—he saw that; there was only a tall, thin man, shrouded to the eyes in oilskin; and he leaped into the boat and bade the ferryman hasten.

Halfway across he rose in the skiff, and called, "Jeanne!" But the roar of the storm and the thrashing of icy waves drowned his voice. Yet he heard her again, and she called to him by name.

When at last the boat grated upon the invisible shore, he lifted his lantern, trembling, stumbling among the rocks, and calling to her, as though his voice could silence the voice that had spoken a year ago that night. And it could not. He sank shivering upon his knees, and looked out into the darkness, where an ocean rolled across a world. Then his stiff lips moved, and he repeated her name; but the hand of the ferryman fell gently upon his head.

And when he raised his eyes he saw that the ferryman was Death.

Number Ninety

Bithia Mary Croker

For a period extending over some years, a notice appeared periodically in various daily papers. It read:

'To let furnished, for a term of years, at a very low rental, a large old-fashioned family residence, comprising eleven bedrooms, four reception rooms, dressing rooms, two staircases, complete servants' offices, ample accommodation for a Gentleman's establishment, including six-stall stable, coach-house, etc.'

This advertisement referred to number ninety.

Occasionally you saw it running for a week or a fortnight at a stretch, as if it were resolved to force itself into consideration by sheer persistency. Sometimes for months I looked for it in vain. Other folk might possibly fancy that the effort of the house agent had been crowned at last with success – that it was let, and no longer in the market.

I knew better. I knew that it would never, never find a tenant. I knew that it was passed on as a hopeless case, from house-agent to house-agent. I knew that it would never be occupied, save by rats – and, more than this, I knew the reason why!

I will not say in what square, street, or road number ninety may be found, nor will I divulge to human being its precise and exact locality, but this I'm prepared to state, that it is positively in existence, is in Charleston, and is still empty.

Twenty years ago, this very Christmas, I was down from New York visiting my friend John Hollyoak, a civil engineer from Charleston. We were guests at a little dinner party in the neighbourhood of the South Battery. Conversation became very brisk as the champagne circulated, and many topics were started, discussed, and dismissed.

We talked on an extraordinary variety of subjects.

I distinctly recollect a long argument on mushrooms – mushrooms, murders, racing, cholera; from cholera we came to sudden death, from sudden death to churchyards, and from churchyards, it was naturally but a step to ghosts.

John Hollyoak, who was the most vehement, the most incredulous, the most jocular, and the most derisive of the anti-ghost faction, brought matters to a climax by declaring that nothing would give him greater pleasure than to pass a night in a haunted house – and the worse its character, the better he would be pleased!

His challenge was instantly taken up by our somewhat ruffled host, who warmly assured him that his wishes could be easily satisfied, and that he would be accommodated with a night's lodging in a haunted house within twenty-four hours – in fact, in a house of such a desperate reputation, that even the adjoining mansions stood vacant.

He then proceeded to give a brief outline of the history of number ninety. It had once been the residence of a well-known county family, but what evil events had happened therein tradition did not relate.

On the death of the last owner – a diabolical-looking aged person, much resembling the typical wizard – it had passed into the hands of a kinsman, resident abroad, who had no wish to return to Charleston, and who desired his agents to let it, if they could – a most significant condition!

Year by year went by, and still this 'Highly desirable family mansion' could find no tenant, although the rent was reduced, and reduced, and again reduced, to almost zero!

The most ghastly whispers were afloat – the most terrible experiences were actually proclaimed on the housetops!

No tenant would remain, even gratis; and for the last ten years, this, 'handsome, desirable town family residence' had been the abode of rats by day, and something else by night – so said the neighbours.

Of course it was the very thing for John, and he snatched up the gauntlet on the spot. He scoffed at its evil repute, and solemnly promised to rehabilitate its character within a week.

I was charged by our host to serve as a witness – to verify that John Hollyoak did indeed spend the night at number ninety. The next night at ten o' clock, I found myself standing with John on the steps of the notorious abode; but I was not going to remain; the carriage that brought us was to take me back to my respectable chambers.

This ill-fated house was large, solemn-looking, and gloomy. A heavy portico frowned down on neighbouring barefaced hall-doors. The elderly caretaker was prudently awaiting us outside with a key, which said key he turned in the lock, and admitted us into a great echoing hall, black as night, saying as he did so: 'My missus has made the bed, and stoked up a good fire in the first front, Sir. Your things is all laid out, and I hope you'll have a comfortable night, Sir.'

'No, Sir! Thank you, Sir! Excuse me, I'll not come in! Goodnight!' and with the words still on his lips, he clattered down the steps with most indecent haste, and vanished.

'And of course you will not come in either?' said John. 'It is not in the bond, and I prefer to face them alone!' and he laughed contemptuously, a laugh that had a curious echo, it struck me at the time. A laugh strangely repeated, with an unpleasant mocking emphasis. 'Call for me, alive or dead, at eight o'clock tomorrow morning!' he added, pushing me forcibly out into the porch, and closing the door with a heavy, reverberating clang, that sounded halfway down the street.

I did call for him the next morning as desired, with the caretaker, who stared at John's commonplace, self-possessed appearance, with an expression of respectful astonishment.

'So it was all humbug, of course,' I said, as he took my arm, and we set off for our club.

'You shall have the whole story whenever we have had something to eat,' he replied somewhat impatiently. 'It will keep till after breakfast—I'm famishing!'

I remarked that he looked unusually grave as we chatted over our broiled fish and omlette, and that occasionally his attention seemed wandering, to say the least. The moment he had brought out his cigar case and lit up he turned to me and said:

'I see you are just quivering to know my experience, and I won't keep you in suspense any longer. In four words—I have seen them!'

I merely looked at him with widely parted mouth and staring interrogative eyes.

I believe I had best endeavour to give the narrative without comment, and in John Hollyoak's own way. This is, as well as I can recollect, his experience word for word:

'I proceeded upstairs, after I had shut you out, lighting my way by a match, and found the front room easily, as the door was ajar, and it was lit up by a roaring and most cheerful-looking fire, and two wax candles. It was a comfortable apartment, furnished with old-fashioned chairs and tables, and the traditional four-poster bed. There were numerous doors, which proved to be cupboards; and when I had executed a rigorous search in each of these closets and locked them, and investigated the bed above and beneath, sounded the walls, and bolted the door, I sat down before the fire, lit a cigar, opened a book, and felt that I was going to be master of the situation, and most thoroughly and comfortably "at home". My novel proved absorbing. I read on greedily, chapter after chapter, and so interested was I, and amused – for it was a lively book – that I positively lost sight of my whereabouts, and fancied myself reading in my own chamber! There was not a sound. The coals dropping from the grate occasionally broke the silence, till a neighboring church-clock slowly boomed twelve! "The hour!" I said to myself, with a laugh, as I gave the fire a rousing poke, and commenced a new chapter; but ere I had read three pages I had occasion to pause and listen. What was that distinct sound now coming nearer and nearer? "Rats, of course," said Common-sense – "it was just the house for vermin." Then a longish silence. Again a stir, sounds approaching, as if apparently caused by many feet passing down the corridor – high-heeled shoes, the sweeping switch of silken trains! Of course it was all imagination, I assured myself – or rats! Rats were capable of making such curious improbable noises!

'Then another silence. No sound but cinders and the ticking of my watch, which I had laid upon the table.'

'I resumed my book, rather ashamed, and a little indignant with myself for having neglected it, and calmly dismissed my late interruption as "rats – nothing but rats".'

'I had been reading and smoking for some time in a placid and highly incredulous frame of mind, when I was somewhat rudely startled by a loud single knock at my room door. I took no notice of it, but merely laid down my novel and sat tight. Another knock more imperious this time – After a moment's mental deliberation I arose, armed myself with the poker, prepared to brain any number of rats, and threw the door open with a violent swing that strained its very hinges, and beheld, to my amazement, a tall powdered footman in a laced scarlet uniform, who, making a formal inclination of his head, astonished me still further by saying:

'"Dinner is ready!"

'"I'm not coming!"' I replied, without a moment's hesitation, and thereupon I slammed the door in his face, locked it, and resumed my seat, also my book; but reading was a farce; my ears were aching for the next sound.

'It came soon – rapid steps running up the stairs, and again a single knock. I went over to the door, and once more discovered the tall butler, who repeated, with a studied courtesy:

'"Dinner is ready, and the company are waiting."

'"I told you I was not coming. Be off, and be hanged!" I cried again, shutting the door violently.

'This time I did not make even a pretence at reading. I merely sat and waited for the next move.

'I had not long to sit. In ten minutes I heard a third loud summons. I rose, went to the door, and tore it open. There, as I expected, was the servant again, with his parrot speech:

'"Dinner is ready, the company are waiting, and the master says you must come!"

'"All right, then, I'll come," I replied, wearied by reason of his importunity, and feeling suddenly fired with a desire to see the end of the adventure.

'He accordingly led the way downstairs, and I followed him, noting as I went the gold buttons on his coat, also that the hall and passages were now brilliantly illuminated by glowing candles, and hung with living green, the crisp leaves of holly, mistletoe and ivy reflecting back the light. There were several uniformed servants passing to and fro, and from the dining room, there issued a buzz of tongues, loud volleys of laughter, many hilarious voices, and a clatter of knives and forks. I was not left much time for speculation, as in another second I found myself inside the door, and my escort announced me in a loud voice as "Mr Hollyoak".

'I could hardly credit my senses, as I looked round and saw about two dozen people, dressed in a fashion of the 18th century, seated at the table, set for a sumptuous Christmas dinner, and lighted up by a blaze of wax candles in massive candelabra.

'A swarthy elderly gentleman, who presided at the head of the board, rose deliberately as I entered. He was dressed in a crimson coat, braided with silver. He wore a white wig, had the most piercing black eyes I ever encountered, made me the finest bow I ever received in all my life, and with a polite wave of his hand, indicated my seat – a vacant chair between two powdered and embroided beauties, with overflowing white shoulders and necks sparkling with diamonds.

'At first I was fully convinced that the whole affair was a superbly matured practical joke. Everything looked so real, so truly flesh and blood, so complete in every detail; but I gazed around in vain for one familiar face.

'I saw young, old, and elderly, handsome and the reverse. On all faces there was a similar expression – reckless, hardened defiance, and something else that made me shudder, but that I could not classify or define.

'Were they a secret community? Burglars or counterfeiters? But no; in one rapid glance I noticed that they belonged exclusively to the upper stratum of society – bygone society. The jabber of talking had momentarily ceased, and the host, imperiously hammering the table with a knife-handle, said in a singularly harsh grating voice:

'"Ladies and gentlemen, permit me to give you a toast! Our guest!" looking straight at me with his glittering coal-black eyes.

'Every glass was immediately raised. Twenty faces were turned towards mine, when, happily, a sudden impulse seized me. I sprang to my feet and said:

'"Ladies and gentlemen, I beg to thank you for your kind hospitality, but before I accept it, allow me to say grace!"

'I did not wait for permission, but hurriedly repeated a Latin benediction. Ere the last syllable was uttered, in an instant there was a violent crash, an uproar, a sound of running, of screams, groans and curses, and then utter darkness.

'I found myself standing alone by a big mahogany table which I could just dimly discern by the aid of a street-lamp that threw its meager rays into the great empty dining room from two deep and narrow windows.

'I must confess that I felt my nerves a little shaken by this instantaneous change from light to darkness-from a crowd of gay and noisy companions, to utter solitude and silence. I stood for a moment trying to recover my mental balance. I rubbed my eyes hard to assure myself that I was wide awake, and then I placed this very cigar-case in the middle of the table, as a sign and token that I had been downstairs – which cigar-case I found exactly where I left it this morning – and then went and groped my way into the hall and regained my room.

'I met with no obstacle en route. I saw no one, but as I closed and double-locked my door I distinctly heard a low laugh outside the keyhole – a sort of suppressed, malicious titter, that made me furious.

'I opened the door at once. There was nothing to be seen. I waited and listened – dead silence. I then undressed and went to bed, resolved that a whole army of butlers would fail to allure me once more to that Christmas feast. I was determined not to lose my night's rest – ghosts or no ghosts.

'Just as I was dozing off I remember hearing the neighboring clock chime two. It was the last sound I was aware of, the house was now as silent as a vault. My fire burnt away cheerfully. I was no longer in the least degree inclined for reading, and I fell fast asleep and slept soundly till I heard the cabs and milk-carts beginning their morning career.

'I then rose, dressed at my leisure, and found you, my good, faithful friend, awaiting me, rather anxiously, on the hall-door steps.

'I have not done with that house yet. I'm determined to find out who these people are, and where they come from. I shall sleep there again tonight, along with my bulldog; and you will see that I shall have news for you tomorrow morning-if I am still alive to tell the tale,' he added with a laugh.

In vain I would have dissuaded him. I protested, argued, and implored. I declared that rashness was not courage; that he had seen enough; that I, who had seen nothing, and only listened to his experiences, was convinced that number ninety was a house to be avoided.

I might just as well have talked to my umbrella! So, once more, I reluctantly accompanied him to his previous night's lodging. Once more I saw him swallowed up inside the gloomy, forbidding-looking, re-echoing hall.

I then went home in an unusually anxious, semi-excited, nervous state of mind. I lay wide awake, tumbling and tossing hour after hour, a prey to the most foolish ideas – ideas I would have laughed to scorn in daylight.

More than once I was certain that I heard John Hollyoak distractedly calling me; and I sat up in bed and listened intently. Of course it was fancy, for the instant I did so, there was no sound.

At the first gleam of winter dawn, I rose, dressed, and swallowed a cup of good strong coffee to clear my brain from the misty notions it had harboured during the night. And then I invested myself in my warmest topcoat, and set off for number ninety. Early as it was – it was but half-past seven-I found the caretaker was before me, pacing the pavement, his face drawn with a melancholy expression.

I was not disposed to wait for eight o'clock. I was too uneasy, and too impatient for further particulars of the Christmas dinner-party. So I rang with all my might, and knocked with all my strength.

No sound within – no answer! But John was always a heavy steeper. I was resolved to arouse him all the same, and knocked and rang, and rang and knocked, incessantly for fully ten minutes.

I then stooped down and applied my eye to the keyhole; I looked steadily into the aperture, till I became accustomed to the darkness, and then it seemed to me that another eye – a very strange, fiery eye – was glaring into mine from the other side of the door!

I removed my eye and applied my mouth instead, and shouted with all the power of my lungs:

'John! John Hollyoak!'

How his name echoed and re-echoed up through that dark and empty house! 'He must hear that,' I said to myself as I pressed my ear closely against the lock, and listened with throbbing suspense.

The echo of 'Hollyoak' had hardly died away when I swear that distinctly heard a low, sniggering, mocking laugh – that was my only answer – that; and a vast unresponsive silence.

I was now quite desperate. I shook the door frantically, with all my strength. I broke the bell; in short, my behaviour was such that it excited the curiosity of a police officer, who crossed the road to know, 'What was up?'

'I want to get in!' I panted, breathless with my exertions.

'You'd better stay where you are!' said the police officer; 'the outside of this house is the best of it! There are terrible stories...'

'But there is a gentleman inside it!' I interrupted impatiently. 'He slept there last night, and I can't wake him. He has the key!'

'Oh, you can't wake him!' returned the police officer gravely. 'Then we must get a locksmith!'

But already the thoughtful caretaker had procured one; and already considerable and curious crowd surrounded the steps.

After five minutes of maddening delay, the great heavy door was opened and swung slowly back, and I instantly rushed in, followed less frantically by the police officer and the caretaker.

I had not far to seek John Hollyoak! He and his dog were lying at the foot of the stairs, both stone dead!

The Red Bungalow

Bithia Mary Croker

It is a considerable time since my husband's regiment ('The Snapshots') was stationed in Kulu, yet it seems as if it were but yesterday, when I look back on the days we spent in India. As I sit by the fire, or in the sunny corner of the garden, sometimes when my eyes are dim with reading I close them upon the world, and see, with vivid distinctness, events which happened years ago. Among various mental pictures, there is not one which stands forth with the same weird and lurid effect as the episode of 'The Red Bungalow.'

Robert was commanding his regiment, and we were established in a pretty spacious house at Kulu, and liked the station. It was a little off the beaten track, healthy and sociable. Memories of John Company and traces of ancient Empires still clung to the neighbourhood. Pig-sticking and rose-growing. Badminton and polo, helped the residents of the place to dispose of the long, long Indian day – never too long for me!

One morning I experienced an agreeable surprise, when, in reading the Gazette, I saw that my cousin, Tom Fellowes, had been appointed Quartermaster-General of the district, and was to take up the billet at once.

Tom had a wife and two dear little children (our nursery was empty), and as soon as I had put down the paper I wired to Netta to congratulate and beg them to come to us immediately. Indian moves are rapid. Within a week our small party had increased to six, Tom, Netta, little Guy, aged four, and Baba, a dark-eyed coquette of nearly two. They also brought with them an invaluable ayah – a Madrassi. She spoke English with a pretty foreign accent, and was entirely devoted to the children.

Netta was a slight young woman with brilliant eyes, jet black hair, and a firm mouth. She was lively, clever, and a capital helpmate for an army man, with marvellous energy, and enviable taste.

Tom, an easy-going individual in private life, a red-hot soldier. All financial and domestic affairs were left in the hands of his wife, and she managed him and them with conspicuous success.

†

Before Netta had been with us three days he began, in spite of my protestations, to clamour about 'getting a house'.

'Why, you have only just arrived,' I remonstrated. 'You are not even half unpacked. Wait here a few weeks, and make acquaintance with the place and people. It is such a pleasure to me to have you and the children.'

'You spoil them – especially Guy! 'she answered with a laugh. 'The sooner they are removed the better, and, seriously, I want to settle in. I am longing to do up my new house, and make it pretty, and have a garden – a humble imitation of yours – a Badminton court, and a couple of ponies. I'm like a child looking forward to a new toy, for, cooped up in Fort William in Calcutta, I never felt that I had a real home.'

'Even so,' I answered, 'there is plenty of time, and I think you might remain here till after Christmas.'

'Christmas!' she screamed. 'I shall be having Christmas parties myself, and a tree for the kids; and you, dear Liz, shall come and help me. I want to get into a house next week.'

'Then pray don't look to me for any assistance. If you make such a hasty exit the station will think we have quarrelled.'

'The station could not be so detestable, and no one could quarrel with you, you dear old thing,' and as she stooped down and patted my cheek, I realised that she was fully resolved to have her own way.

'I have yards and yards of the most lovely cretonne for cushions, and chairs, and curtains,' she continued, 'brought out from home, and never yet made up. Your Dirzee is bringing me two men tomorrow. When I was out riding this morning, I went to an auction-room – John Mahomed, they call the man – and inspected some sofas and chairs. Do let us drive there this afternoon on our way to the club, and I also wish to have a look round. I hear that nearly all the good bungalows are occupied.'

'Yes, they are,' I answered triumphantly. 'At present there is not one in the place to suit you! I have been running over them with my mind's eye, and either they are near the river, or too small, or – not healthy. After Christmas the Watsons are going home; there will be their bungalow – it is nice and large, and has a capital office, which would suit Tom.'

We drove down to John Mahomed's that afternoon, and selected some furniture – Netta exhibiting her usual taste and business capacity. On our way to the club I pointed out several vacant houses, and, among them, the Watsons' charming abode – with its celebrated gardens, beds of brilliant green lucerne, and verandah curtained in yellow roses.

'Oh yes,' she admitted, 'it is a fine, roomy sort of abode, but I hate a thatched roof – I want one with tiles – red tiles. They make such a nice bit of colour among trees.'

'I'm afraid you won't find many tiled roofs in Kulu,' I answered; 'this will limit you a good deal.'

For several mornings, together, we explored bungalows – and I was by no means sorry to find that, in the eyes of Netta, they were all more or less found wanting – too small, too damp, too near the river, too stuffy – and I had made up my mind that the Watsons' residence (despite its thatch) was to be Netta's fate, when one afternoon she hurried in, a little breathless and dusty, and announced, with a wild wave of her sunshade, 'I've found it!'

'Where? Do you mean a house?' I exclaimed.

'Yes. What moles we've been! At the back of this, down the next turn, at the cross roads! Most central and suitable. They call it the Red Bungalow.'

'The Red Bungalow,' I repeated reflectively. I had never cast a thought to it – what is always before one is frequently unnoticed. Also it had been unoccupied ever since we had come to the station, and as entirely overlooked as if it had no existence! I had a sort of recollection that there was some drawback – it was either too large, or too expensive, or too out of repair.

'It is strange that I never mentioned it,' I said.

'But it has had no tenant for years.'

'Unless I am greatly mistaken, it will have one before long,' rejoined

Netta, with her most definite air. 'It looks as if it were just waiting for us – and had been marked "reserved".'

'Then you have been over it?'

'No, I could not get in, the doors are all bolted, and there seems to be no chokedar. I wandered round the verandahs, and took stock of the size and proportions – it stands in an imposing compound. There are the ruins at the back, mixed up with the remains of a garden – old guava trees, lemon trees, a vine, and a well. There is a capital place at one side for two Badminton courts, and I have mentally laid out a rose-garden in front of the portico.'

'How quickly your mind travels!'

'Everything must travel quickly in these days,' she retorted. 'We all have to put on the pace. Just as I was leaving, I met a venerable coolie person, who informed me that John Mahomed had the keys, so I despatched him to bring them at once, and promised a rupee for his trouble. Now do, like a good soul, let us have tea, and start off immediately after to inspect my treasure-trove!'

'I can promise you a cup of tea in five minutes,' I replied, 'but I am not so certain of your treasure-trove.'

'I am. I generally can tell what suits me at first sight. The only thing I am afraid of is the rent. Still, in Tommy's position one must not consider that. He is obliged to live in a suitable style.'

'The Watsons' house has often had a staff-tenant. I believe it would answer all your requirements.'

'Too near the road, and too near the General,' she objected, with a gesture of impatience.

'Ah, here comes tea at last!'

It came, but before I had time to swallow my second cup, I found myself hustled out of the house by my energetic cousin and en route to her wonderful discovery – the Red Bungalow.

We had but a short distance to walk, and, often as I had passed the house, I now gazed at it for the first time with an air of critical interest. In Kulu, for some unexplained reason, this particular bungalow had never counted; it was boycotted – no, that is not the word – ignored, as if, like some undesirable character, it had no place in the station's thoughts.

Nevertheless, its position was sufficiently prominent – it stood at a point where four ways met. Two gateless entrances opened into different roads, as if determined to obtrude upon public attention. Standing aloof between the approaches was the house – large, red-tiled, and built back in the shape of the letter 'T' from an enormous pillared porch, which, with some tall adjacent trees, gave it an air of reserve and dignity.

'The coolie with the keys has not arrived,' said Netta, 'so I will just take you round and show you its capabilities myself. Here '– as we stumbled over some rough grass – 'is where I should make a couple of Badminton courts, and this'– as we came to the back of the bungalow – 'is the garden.'

Yes, here were old choked-up stone water-channels, the traces of walks, hoary guava and apricot trees, a stone pergola and a dead vine, also a well, with elaborate tracery, and odd, shapeless mounds of ancient masonry. As we stood we faced the back verandah of the house. To our right hand lay tall cork trees, a wide expanse of compound, and the road; to our left, at a distance, more trees, a high wall, and clustered beneath it the servants' quarters, the cookhouse, and a long range of stables.

It was a fine, important-looking residence, although the stables were almost roofless and the garden and compound a wilderness, given over to stray goats and tame lizards.

'Yes, there is only one thing I am afraid of,' exclaimed Netta.

'Snakes?' I suggested. 'It looks rather snaky.'

'No, the rent; and here comes the key at last,' and as she spoke a fat young clerk, on a small yellow pony, trotted quickly under the porch – a voluble person, who wore spotless white garments, and spoke English with much fluency.

'I am abject. Please excuse being so tardy. I could not excavate the key; but at last I got it, and now I will hasten to exhibit premises. First of all, I go and open doors and windows, and call in the atmosphere – ladies kindly excuse.' Leaving his tame steed on its honour, the baboo hurried to the back, and presently we heard the grinding of locks, banging of shutters, and grating of bolts. Then the door was flung open and we entered, walked (as is usual) straight into the drawing-room, a fine, lofty, half-circular room, twice as large and well-proportioned as mine. The drawing room led into an equally excellent dining room. I saw Netta measuring it with her eye, and she said, 'One could easily seat thirty people here, and what a place for a Christmas tree!'

The dining room opened into an immense bedroom which gave directly on the back verandah, with a flight of shallow steps leading into the garden.

'The nursery,' she whispered; 'capital!'

At either side were two other rooms, with bath and dressing rooms complete. Undoubtedly it was an exceedingly commodious and well-planned house.

As we stood once more in the nursery – all the wide doors being open – we could see directly through the bungalow out into the porch, as the three large apartments were en suite.

'A draught right through, you see!' she said.

'So cool in the hot weather.'

Then we returned to the drawing room, where I noticed that Netta was already arranging the furniture with her mental eye. At last she turned to the baboo and said, 'And what is the rent?'

After a moment's palpable hesitation he replied, 'Ninety rupees a month. If you take it for some time it will be all put in repair and done up.'

'Ninety!' I mentally echoed – and we paid one hundred and forty!

'Does it belong to John Mahomed?' I asked.

'No – to a client.'

'Does he live here?'

'No – he lives far away, in another region; we have never seen him.'

'How long is it since this was occupied?'

'Oh, a good while.'

'Some years?'

'Perhaps,' with a wag of his head.

'Why has it stood empty? Is it unhealthy?' asked Netta.

'Oh no, no. I think it is too majestic, too gigantic for insignificant people. They like something more altogether and cosy; it is not cosy – it is suitable to persons like a lady on the General's staff,' and he bowed himself to Netta.

I believe she was secretly of his opinion, for already she had assumed the air of the mistress of the house, and said briskly, 'Now I wish to see the kitchen, and servants' quarters,' and, picking up her dainty skirts, she led the way thither through loose stones and hard yellow grass. As I have a rooted antipathy to dark and uninhabited places, possibly the haunt of snakes and scorpions, I failed to attend her, but, leaving the baboo to continue his duty, turned back into the house alone.

I paced the drawing room, dining room, the nursery, and as I stood surveying the long vista of apartments, with the sun pouring into the porch on one hand, and on the green foliage and baked yellow earth of the garden on the other, I confessed to myself that Netta was a miracle!

She, a new arrival, had hit upon this excellent and suitable residence; and a bargain. But, then, she always found bargains; their discovery was her metier!

As I stood reflecting thus, gazing absently into the outer glare, a dark and mysterious cloud seemed to fall upon the place, the sun was suddenly obscured, and from the portico came a sharp little gust of wind that gradually increased into a long-drawn wailing cry – surely the cry of some lost soul! What could have put such a hideous idea in my head ? But the cry rang in my ears with such piercing distinctness that I felt myself trembling from head to foot; in a second the voice had, as it were, passed forth into the garden and was stifled among the tamarind trees in an agonised wail. I roused myself from a condition of frightful obsession, and endeavoured to summon my common sense and self-command. Here was I, a middle-aged Scotchwoman, standing in this empty bungalow, clutching my garden umbrella, and imagining horrors!

Such thoughts I must keep exclusively to myself, lest I become the laughing-stock of a station with a keen sense of the ridiculous.

Yes, I was an imaginative old goose, but I walked rather quickly back into the porch, and stepped into the open air, with a secret but invincible prejudice against the Red Bungalow. This antipathy was not shared by Netta, who had returned from her quest all animation and satisfaction.

'The stables require repair, and some of the go-downs,' she said, 'and the whole house must be re-coloured inside, and matted. I will bring my husband round tomorrow morning,' she announced, dismissing the baboo. 'We will be here at eight o'clock sharp.'

By this I knew – and so did the baboo – that the Red Bungalow was let at last!

'Well, what do you think of it?' asked Netta triumphantly, as we were walking home together.

'It is a roomy house,' I admitted, 'but there is no office for Tom.'

'Oh, he has the Brigade Office. – Any more objections? '

'A bungalow so long vacant, so entirely overlooked, must have *something* against it – and it is not the rent.'

'Nor is it unhealthy,' she argued. 'It is quite high, higher than your bungalow – no water near it, and the trees not too close. I can see that you don't like it. Can you give me a good reason?'

'I really wish I could. No, I do not like it – there is something about it that repels me. You know I'm a Highlander, and am sensitive to impressions.'

'My dear Liz,' and here she came to a dead halt, 'you don't mean me to suppose that you think it is haunted? Why, this is the twentieth century!'

'I did not say it was haunted' – (I dared not voice my fears) – 'but I declare that I do not like it, and I wish you'd wait; wait only a couple of days, and I'll take you to see the Watsons' bungalow – so sunny, so lived in – always so cheerful, with a lovely garden, and an office for Tom.'

'I'm not sure that *that* is an advantage!' she exclaimed with a smile. 'It is not always agreeable to have a man on the premises for twenty-four hours out of the twenty-four hours!'

'But the Watsons—'

'My dear Liz, if you say another word about the Watsons' bungalow I shall have a bad attack of the sulks, and go straight to bed!'

It is needless to mention that Tom was delighted with the bungalow selected by his ever-clever little wife, and for the next week our own abode was the resort of tailors, hawkers, butchers, milkmen, furniture-makers, ponies and cows on sale, and troops of servants in quest of places.

Every day Netta went over to the house to inspect, and to give directions, to see how the mallees were laying out the garden and Badminton courts, and the matting people and whitewashers were progressing indoors.

Many hands make light work, and within a week the transformation of the Red Bungalow was astonishing. Within a fortnight it was complete; the stables were again occupied – also the new spick-and-span servants' quarters; Badminton courts were ready to be played upon; the verandah and porch were gay with palms and plants and parrots, and the drawing room was the admiration of all Kulu. Netta introduced plants in pots – pots actually dressed up in pongee silk – to the station ladies; her sofa cushions were frilled, she had quantities of pretty pictures and photos, silver knick-knacks, and gay rugs.

But before Netta had had the usual name-board – 'Major Fellowes, A.Q.M.G.'– attached to the gate piers of the Red Bungalow, there had been some demur and remonstrance. My ayah, an old Madrasi, long in my service, had ventured one day, as she held my hair in her hand, 'That new missus never taking the old Red Bungalow?'

'Yes.'

'My missus then telling her, *please*, that plenty bad place – oh, so bad! No one living there this many years.'

'Why – what is it?'

'I not never knowing, only the one word – bad. Oh, my missus! you speak, never letting these pretty little children go there.'

'But other people have lived there, Mary—'

'Never long – so people telling – the house man paint bungalow all so nice – same like now – they make great bargain – so pleased. One day they go away, away, away, never coming back. Please, please,' and she stooped and kissed my hand, 'speak that master, tell him – *bad* bungalow.'

Of course I pooh-poohed the subject to Mary, who actually wept, good kind creature, and as she did my hair had constantly to dry her eyes on her saree.

And, knowing how futile a word to Tom would prove, I once more attacked Netta. I said, 'Netta, I'm sure you think I'm an ignorant, superstitious imbecile, but I believe in presentiments. I have a presentiment, dear, about that Bungalow – *do* give it up to please and, yes, comfort me—'

'What! my beautiful find – the best house in Kulu – my *bargain*?'

'You may find it a dear bargain!'

'Not even to oblige you, dear Liz, can I break off my agreement, and I have really set my heart on your *bête noire*. I am so, so sorry,' and she came over and caressed me.

I wonder if Netta in her secret heart suspected that I, the Colonel's wife, might be a little jealous that the new arrival had secured a far more impressive looking abode than her own, and for this mean reason I endeavoured to persuade her to 'move on.'

However, her mind must have been entirely disabused of this by a lady on whom we were calling, who said:

'Oh, Mrs Fellowes, have you got a house yet, or will you wait for the Watsons'? Such a—'

'I am already suited,' interrupted Netta. 'We have found just the thing – not far from my cousin's, too – a fine, roomy, cheerful place, with a huge compound; we are already making the garden.'

'Roomy – large compound; near Mrs Drummond,' she repeated with knitted brow. 'No – oh, surely you do not mean the Red Bungalow? '

'Yes, that is its name; I am charmed with it, and so lucky to find it.'

'No difficulty in finding it, dear Mrs Fellowes, but I believe the difficulty is in remaining there.'

'Do you mean that it's haunted?' enquired Netta with a rather superior air.

'Something of that sort – the natives call it 'the devil's house.' A terrible tragedy happened there long ago – so long ago that it is forgotten; but you will find it almost impossible to keep servants!'

'You are certainly most discouraging, but I hope some day you will come and dine with us, and see how comfortable we are!'

There was a note of challenge in this invitation, and I could see with the traditional 'half-eye' that Mrs Dodd and Mrs Fellowes would scarcely be bosom friends.

Nor was this the sole warning.

At the club a very old resident, wife of a Government employee, who had spent twenty years in Kulu, came and seated herself by me one morning with the air of a person who desired to fulfil a disagreeable duty.

'I am afraid you will think me presuming, Mrs Drummond, but I feel that I ought to speak. Do you know that the house your cousin has taken is said to be unlucky? The last people only remained a month, though they got it for next to nothing – a mere song,'

'Yes, I've heard of these places, and read of them, too,' I replied, 'but it generally turns out that someone has an interest in keeping it empty; possibly natives live there.'

'*Any*where but there!' she exclaimed. 'Not a soul will go near it after nightfall – there is not even the usual chokedar—'

'What is it? What is the tale?'

'Something connected with those old mounds of brickwork, and the well. I think a palace or a temple stood on the spot thousands of years ago, when Kulu was a great native city.

'Do try and dissuade your cousin from going there; she will find her mistake sooner or later. I hope you won't think me very officious, but she is young and happy, and has two such dear children, especially the little boy.'

Yes, especially the little boy! I was devoted to Guy – my husband, too. We had bought him a pony and a tiny monkey, and were only too glad to keep him and Baba for a few days when their parents took the great step and moved into the Red Bungalow.

In a short time all was in readiness; the big end room made a delightful nursery; the children had also the run of the back verandah and the garden, and were soon completely and happily at home.

An inhabited house seems so different to the same when it stands silent, with closed doors – afar from the sound of voices and footsteps. I could scarcely recognise Netta's new home. It was the centre of half the station gaieties – Badminton parties twice a week, dinners, 'Chotah Hazra' gatherings on the great verandah, and rehearsals for a forthcoming play; the pattering of little feet, servants, horses, cows, goats, dogs, parrots, all contributed their share to the general life and stir. I went over to the Bungalow almost daily: I dined, I breakfasted, I had tea, and I never saw anything but the expected and the commonplace, yet I failed to eradicate my first instinct, my secret apprehension and aversion. Christmas was over, the parties, dinners and teas were among memories of the past; we were well advanced in the month of February, when Netta, the triumphant, breathed her first complaint. The servants – excellent servants, with long and bond fide characters – arrived, stayed one week, or perhaps two, and then came and said, 'Please I go!'

None of them remained in the compound at night, except the horsekeepers and an orderly; they retired to more congenial quarters in an adjoining bazaar, and the maddening part was that they would give no definite name or shape to their fears – they spoke of 'It' and a 'Thing'– a fearsome object, that dwelt within and around the Bungalow.

The children's ayah, a Madras woman, remained loyal and staunch; she laughed at the Bazaar tales and their reciters; and, as her husband was the cook, Netta was fairly independent of the cowardly crew who nightly fled to the Bazaar.

Suddenly the ayah, the treasure, fell ill of fever – the really virulent fever that occasionally seizes on natives of the country, and seems to lick up their very life. As my servants' quarters were more comfortable – and I am something of a nurse – I took the invalid home, and Netta promoted her understudy (a local woman) temporarily into her place. She was a chattering, gay, gaudy creature, that I had never approved, but Netta would not listen to any advice, whether with respect to medicines, servants, or bungalows. Her choice in the latter had undoubtedly turned out well, and she was not a little exultant, and bragged to me that she never left it in anyone's power to say, 'There – I told you so!'

It was Baba's birthday – she was two – a pretty, healthy child, but for her age backward: beyond 'Dadda', 'Mamma', and 'Ayah', she could not say one word. However, as Tom cynically remarked, 'she was bound to make up for it by and by!'

It was twelve o'clock on this very warm morning when I took my umbrella and topee and started off to help Netta with her preparations for the afternoon. The chief feature of the entertainment was to be a bran pie.

I found my cousin hard at work when I arrived. In the verandah a great bathtub full of bran had been placed on a table, and she was draping the said tub with elegant festoons of pink glazed calico – her implement a hammer and tacks – whilst I burrowed into the bran, and there interred the bodies of dolls and cats and horses, and all manner of pleasant surprises. We were making a dreadful litter, and a considerable noise, when suddenly above the hammering I heard a single sharp cry.

'Listen!' I said.

'Oh, Baba is awake – naughty child – and she will disturb her brother,' replied the mother, selecting a fresh tack. 'The ayah is there. Don't go.'

'But it had such an odd, uncanny sound,' I protested.

'Dear old Liz! how nervous you are! Baba's scream is something between a whistle of an express and a fog-horn. She has abnormal lung power – and today she is restless and upset by her birthday – and her teeth. Your fears.'

Then she stopped abruptly, for a loud, frantic shriek, the shriek of extreme mortal terror, now rose high above her voice, and, throwing the hammer from her, Netta fled into the drawing room, over-turning chairs in her route, dashed across the drawing room, and burst into the nursery, from whence came these most appalling cries. There, huddled together, we discovered the two children on the table which stood in the middle of the apartment. Guy had evidently climbed up by a chair, and dragged his sister along with him. It was a beautiful afternoon, the sun streamed in upon them, and the room, as far as we could see, was empty. Yes, but not empty to the trembling little creatures on the table, for with wide, mad eyes they seemed to follow the motion of a something that was creeping round the room close to the wall, and I noticed that their gaze went up and down, as they accompanied its progress with starting pupils and gasping breaths.

'Oh! what is it, my darling?' cried Netta, seizing Guy, whilst I snatched at Baba.

He stretched himself stiffly in her arms, and, pointing with a trembling finger to a certain spot, gasped, 'Oh, Mummy! look, look, look!' and with the last word, which was a shriek of horror, he fell into violent convulsions.

But look as we might, we could see nothing, save the bare matting and the bare wall. What frightful object had made itself visible to these innocent children has never been discovered to the present day.

Little Guy, in spite of superhuman efforts to save him, died of brain fever, unintelligible to the last; the only words we could distinguish among his ravings were, 'Look, look, look! Oh, Mummy! look, look, look!' and as for Baba, whatever was seen by her is locked within her lips, for she remains dumb to the present day.

The ayah had nothing to disclose; she could only beat her head upon the ground and scream, and declare that she had just left the children for a moment to speak to the milkman.

But other servants confessed that the ayah had been gossiping in the cookhouse for more than half an hour. The sole living creature that had been with the children when 'It' had appeared to them, was Guy's little pet monkey, which was subsequently found under the table quite dead.

At first I was afraid that after the shock of Guy's death poor Netta would lose her reason. Of course they all came to us, that same dreadful afternoon, leaving the birthday feast already spread, the bran pie in the verandah, the music on the piano; never had there been such a hasty flight, such a domestic earthquake. We endeavoured to keep the mysterious tragedy to ourselves. Little Guy had brain fever; surely it was natural that relations should be together in their trouble, and I declared that I, being a noted nurse, had bodily carried off the child, who was followed by the whole family.

People talked of 'A stroke of the sun', but I believe something of the truth filtered into the Bazaar – where all things are known. Shortly after little Guy's death Netta took Baba home, declaring she would never, never return to India, and Tom applied for and obtained a transfer to another station. He sold off the household furniture, the pretty knick-knacks, the pictures, all that had gone to make Netta's house so attractive, for she could not endure to look on them again. They had been in that house. As for the Red Bungalow, it is once more closed, and silent. The squirrels and hoo-poos share the garden, the stables are given over to scorpions, the house to white ants. On application to John Mahomed, anyone desirous of becoming a tenant will certainly find that it is still to be had for a mere song!

The Pale Man

Julius Long

Have not yet met the man in No. 212. I do not even know his name. He never patronizes the hotel restaurant, and he does not use the lobby. On the three occasions when we passed each other by, we did not speak, although we nodded in a semi-cordial, noncommittal way. I should like very much to make his acquaintance. It is lonesome in this dreary place. With the exception of the aged lady down the corridor, the only permanent guests are the man in No. 212 and myself. However, I should not complain, for this utter quiet is precisely what the doctor prescribed.

I wonder if the man in No. 212, too, has come here for a rest. He is so very pale. Yet I can not believe that he is ill, for his paleness is not of a sickly cast, but rather wholesome in its ivory clarity. His carriage is that of a man enjoying the best of health. He is tall and straight. He walks erectly and with a brisk, athletic stride. His pallor is no doubt congenital, else he would quickly tan under this burning, summer sun.

He must have traveled here by auto, for he certainly was not a passenger on the train that brought me, and he checked in only a short time after my arrival. I had briefly rested in my room and was walking down the stairs when I encountered him ascending with his bag. It is odd that our venerable bell-boy did not show him to his room.

It is odd, too, that, with so many vacant rooms in the hotel, he should have chosen No. 212 at the extreme rear. The building is a long, narrow affair three stories high. The rooms are all on the east side, as the west wall is flush with a decrepit business building. The corridor is long and drab, and its stiff, bloated paper exudes a musty, unpleasant odor. The feeble electric bulbs that light it shine dimly as from a tomb. Revolted by this corridor, I insisted vigorously upon being given No. 201, which is at the front and blessed with southern exposure. The room clerk, a disagreeable fellow with a Hitler mustache, was very reluctant to let me have it, as it is ordinarily reserved for his more profitable transient trade. I fear my stubborn insistence has made him an enemy.

If only I had been as self-assertive thirty years ago! I should now be a full-fledged professor instead of a broken-down assistant. I still smart from the cavalier manner in which the president of the university summarily recommended my vacation. No doubt he acted for my best interests. The people who have dominated my poor life invariably have.

Oh, well, the summer's rest will probably do me considerable good. It is pleasant to be away from the university. There is something positively gratifying about the absence of the graduate student face.

If only it were not so lonely! I must devise a way of meeting the pale man in No. 212. Perhaps the room clerk can arrange matters.

†

I have been here exactly a week, and if there is a friendly soul in this miserable little town, he has escaped my notice. Although the tradespeople accept my money with flattering eagerness, they studiously avoid even the most casual conversation. I am afraid I can never cultivate their society unless I can arrange to have my ancestors recognized as local residents for the last hundred and fifty years.

Despite the coolness of my reception, I have been frequently venturing abroad. In the back of my mind I have cherished hopes that I might encounter the pale man in No. 211. Incidentally, I wonder why he has moved from No. 212. There is certainly little advantage in coming only one room nearer to the front. I noticed the change yesterday when I saw him coming out of his new room.

We nodded again, and this time I thought I detected a certain malign satisfaction in his somber, black eyes. He must know that I am eager to make his acquaintance, yet his manner forbids overtures. If he wants to make me go all the way, he can go to the devil. I am not the sort to run after anybody. Indeed, the surly diffidence of the room clerk has been enough to prevent me from questioning him about his mysterious guest.

†

I wonder where the pale man takes his meals. I have been absenting myself from the hotel restaurant and patronizing the restaurants outside. At each I have ventured inquiries about the man in No. 210. No one at any restaurant remembered his having been there. Perhaps he has entrée into the Brahmin homes of this town. And again, he may have found a boarding-house. I shall have to learn if there be one.

The pale man must be difficult to please, for he has again changed his room. I am baffled by his conduct. If he is so desirous of locating himself more conveniently in the hotel, why does he not move to No. 202, which is the nearest available room to the front?

Perhaps I can make his inability to locate himself permanently an excuse for starting a conversation. "I see we are closer neighbors now," I might casually say. But that is too banal. I must await a better opportunity.

†

He has done it again! He is now occupying No. 209. I am intrigued by his little game. I waste hours trying to fathom its point. What possible motive could he have? I should think he would get on the hotel people's nerves. I wonder what our combination bellhop-chambermaid thinks of having to prepare four rooms for a single guest. If he were not stone-deaf, I would ask him. At present I feel too exhausted to attempt such an enervating conversation.

I am tremendously interested in the pale man's next move. He must either skip a room or remain where he is, for a permanent guest, a very old lady, occupies No. 208. She has not budged from her room since I have been here, and I imagine that she does not intend to.

I wonder what the pale man will do. I await his decision with the nervous excitement of a devotee of the track on the eve of a big race. After all, I have so little diversion.

†

Well, the mysterious guest was not forced to remain where he was, nor did he have to skip a room. The lady in No. 208 simplified matters by conveniently dying. No one knows the cause of her death, but it is generally attributed to old age. She was buried this morning. I was among the curious few who attended her funeral. When I returned home from the mortuary, I was in time to see the pale man leaving her room. Already he has moved in.

He favored me with a smile whose meaning I have tried in vain to decipher. I can not but believe that he meant it to have some significance. He acted as if there were between us some secret that I failed to appreciate. But, then, perhaps his smile was meaningless after all and only ambiguous by chance, like that of the Mona Lisa.

†

My man of mystery now resides in No. 207, and I am not the least surprized. I would have been astonished if he had not made his scheduled move, I have almost given up trying to understand his eccentric conduct. I do not know a single thing more about him than I knew the day he arrived. I wonder whence he came. There is something indefinably foreign about his manner. I am curious to hear his voice. I like to imagine that he speaks the exotic tongue of some far-away country. If only I could somehow inveigle him into conversation! I wish that I were possessed of the glib assurance of a college boy, who can address himself to the most distinguished celebrity without batting an eye. It is no wonder that I am only an assistant professor.

†

I am worried. This morning I awoke to find myself lying prone upon the floor. I was fully clothed. I must have fallen exhausted there after I returned to my room last night.

I wonder if my condition is more serious than I had suspected. Until now I have been inclined to discount the fears of those who have pulled a long face about me. For the first time I recall the prolonged hand-clasp of the president when he bade me goodbye from the university. Obviously he never expected to see me alive again.

Of course I am not that unwell. Nevertheless, I must be more careful. Thank heaven I have no dependents to worry about. I have not even a wife, for I was never willing to exchange the loneliness of a bachelor for the loneliness of a husband.

I can say in all sincerity that the prospect of death does not frighten me. Speculation about life beyond the grave has always bored me. Whatever it is, or is not, I'll try to get along.

I have been so preoccupied about the sudden turn of my own affairs that I have neglected to make note of a most extraordinary incident. The pale man has done an astounding thing. He has skipped three rooms and moved all the way to No. 203. We are now very close neighbors. We shall meet oftener, and my chances for making his acquaintance are now greater.

†

I have confined myself to my bed during the last few days and have had my food brought to me. I even called a local doctor, whom I suspect to be a quack. He looked me over with professional indifference and told me not to leave my room. For some reason he does not want me to climb stairs. For this bit of information he received a ten-dollar bill which, as I directed him, he fished out of my coat pocket. A pickpocket could not have done it better.

He had not been gone long when I was visited by the room clerk. That worthy suggested with a great show of kindly concern that I use the facilities of the local hospital. It was so modern and all that. With more firmness than I have been able to muster in a long time, I gave him to understand that I intended to remain where I am. Frowning sullenly, he stiffly retired. The doctor must have paused long enough downstairs to tell him a pretty story. It is obvious that he is afraid I shall die in his best room.

The pale man is up to his old tricks. Last night, when I tottered down the hall, the door of No. 202 was ajar. Without thinking, I looked inside. The pale man sat in a rocking-chair idly smoking a cigarette. He looked up into my eyes and smiled that peculiar, ambiguous smile that has so deeply puzzled me. I moved on down the corridor, not so much mystified as annoyed. The whole mystery of the man's conduct is beginning to irk me. It is all so inane, so utterly lacking in motive.

I feel that I shall never meet the pale man. But, at least, I am going to learn his identity. Tomorrow I shall ask for the room clerk and deliberately interrogate him.

†

I know now. I know the identity of the pale man, and I know the meaning of his smile.

Early this afternoon I summoned the room clerk to my bedside.

"Please tell me," I asked abruptly, "who is the man in No. 202?"

The clerk stared wearily and uncomprehendingly.

"You must be mistaken. That room is unoccupied."

"Oh, but it is," I snapped in irritation. "I myself saw the man there only two nights ago. He is a tall, handsome fellow with dark eyes and hair. He is unusually pale. He checked in the day that I arrived."

The hotel man regarded me dubiously, as if I were trying to impose upon him.

"But I assure you there is no such person in the house. As for his checking in when you did, you were the only guest we registered that day."

"What? Why, I've seen him twenty times! First he had No. 212 at the end of the corridor. Then he kept moving toward the front. Now he's next door in No. 202."

The room clerk threw up his hands.

"You're crazy!" he exclaimed, and I saw that he meant what he said.

I shut up at once and dismissed him. After he had gone, I heard him rattling the knob of the pale man's door. There is no doubt that he believes the room to be empty.

Thus it is that I can now understand the events of the past few weeks. I now comprehend the significance of the death in No. 207. I even feel partly responsible for the old lady's passing. After all, I brought the pale man with me. But it was not I who fixed his path. Why he chose to approach me room after room through the length of this dreary hotel, why his path crossed the threshold of the woman in No. 207, those mysteries I can not explain.

I suppose I should have guessed his identity when he skipped the three rooms the night I fell unconscious upon the floor. In a single night of triumph he advanced until he was almost to my door.

He will be coming by and by to inhabit this room, his ultimate goal. When he comes, I shall at least be able to return his smile of grim recognition.

Meanwhile, I have only to wait beyond my bolted door.

†

The door swings slowly open....

The Damned Thing

Ambrose Bierce

I – One Does Not Always Eat What is on the Table

By the light of a tallow candle which had been placed on one end of a rough table a man was reading something written in a book. It was an old account book, greatly worn; and the writing was not, apparently, very legible, for the man sometimes held the page close to the flame of the candle to get a stronger light on it. The shadow of the book would then throw into obscurity a half of the room, darkening a number of faces and figures; for besides the reader, eight other men were present. Seven of them sat against the rough log walls, silent, motionless, and the room being small, not very far from the table. By extending an arm any one of them could have touched the eighth man, who lay on the table, face upward, partly covered by a sheet, his arms at his sides. He was dead.

The man with the book was not reading aloud, and no one spoke; all seemed to be waiting for something to occur; the dead man only was without expectation. From the blank darkness outside came in, through the aperture that served for a window, all the ever unfamiliar noises of night in the wilderness—the long nameless note of a distant coyote; the stilly pulsing thrill of tireless insects in trees; strange cries of night birds, so different from those of the birds of day; the drone of great blundering beetles, and all that mysterious chorus of small sounds that seem always to have been but half heard when they have suddenly ceased, as if conscious of an indiscretion. But nothing of all this was noted in that company; its members were not overmuch addicted to idle interest in matters of no practical importance; that was obvious in every line of their rugged faces—obvious even in the dim light of the single candle. They were evidently men of the vicinity—farmers and woodsmen.

The person reading was a trifle different; one would have said of him that he was of the world, worldly, albeit there was that in his attire which attested a certain fellowship with the organisms of his environment. His coat would hardly have passed muster in San Francisco; his foot-gear was not of urban origin, and the hat that lay by him on the floor (he was the only one uncovered) was such that if one had considered it as an article of mere personal adornment he would have missed its meaning. In countenance the man was rather prepossessing, with just a hint of sternness; though that he may have assumed or cultivated, as appropriate to one in authority. For he was a coroner. It was by virtue of his office that he had possession of the book in which he was reading; it had been found among the dead man's effects—in his cabin, where the inquest was now taking place.

When the coroner had finished reading he put the book into his breast pocket. At that moment the door was pushed open and a young man entered. He, clearly, was not of mountain birth and breeding: he was clad as those who dwell in cities. His clothing was dusty, however, as from travel. He had, in fact, been riding hard to attend the inquest.

The coroner nodded; no one else greeted him.

"We have waited for you," said the coroner. "It is necessary to have done with this business tonight."

The young man smiled. "I am sorry to have kept you," he said. "I went away, not to evade your summons, but to post to my newspaper an account of what I suppose I am called back to relate."

The coroner smiled.

"The account that you posted to your newspaper," he said, "differs, probably, from that which you will give here under oath."

"That," replied the other, rather hotly and with a visible flush, "is as you please. I used manifold paper and have a copy of what I sent. It was not written as news, for it is incredible, but as fiction. It may go as a part of my testimony under oath."

"But you say it is incredible."

"That is nothing to you, sir, if I also swear that it is true."

The coroner was silent for a time, his eyes upon the floor. The men about the sides of the cabin talked in whispers, but seldom withdrew their gaze from the face of the corpse. Presently the coroner lifted his eyes and said: "We will resume the inquest."

The men removed their hats. The witness was sworn.

"What is your name?" the coroner asked.

"William Harker."

"Age?"

"Twenty-seven."

"You knew the deceased, Hugh Morgan?"

"Yes."

"You were with him when he died?"

"Near him."

"How did that happen—your presence, I mean?"

"I was visiting him at this place to shoot and fish. A part of my purpose, however, was to study him and his odd, solitary way of life. He seemed a good model for a character in fiction. I sometimes write stories."

"I sometimes read them."

"Thank you."

"Stories in general—not yours."

Some of the jurors laughed. Against a somber background humor shows high lights. Soldiers in the intervals of battle laugh easily, and a jest in the death chamber conquers by surprise.

"Relate the circumstances of this man's death," said the coroner. "You may use any notes or memoranda that you please."

The witness understood. Pulling a manuscript from his breast pocket he held it near the candle and turning the leaves until he found the passage that he wanted began to read.

II - What May Happen in a Field of Wild Oats

"The sun had hardly risen when we left the house. We were looking for quail, each with a shotgun, but we had only one dog. Morgan said that our best ground was beyond a certain ridge that he pointed out, and we crossed it by a trail through the *chaparral*.

On the other side was comparatively level ground, thickly covered with wild oats. As we emerged from the *chaparral* Morgan was but a few yards in advance. Suddenly we heard, at a little distance to our right and partly in front, a noise as of some animal thrashing about in the bushes, which we could see were violently agitated.

"'We've started a deer,' I said. 'I wish we had brought a rifle.'

"Morgan, who had stopped and was intently watching the agitated *chaparral,* said nothing, but had cocked both barrels of his gun and was holding it in readiness to aim. I thought him a trifle excited, which surprised me, for he had a reputation for exceptional coolness, even in moments of sudden and imminent peril.

"'O, come,' I said. 'You are not going to fill up a deer with quail-shot, are you?'

"Still he did not reply; but catching a sight of his face as he turned it slightly toward me I was struck by the intensity of his look. Then I understood that we had serious business in hand and my first conjecture was that we had 'jumped' a grizzly. I advanced to Morgan's side, cocking my piece as I moved.

"The bushes were now quiet and the sounds had ceased, but Morgan was as attentive to the place as before.

"'What is it? What the devil is it?' I asked.

"'That Damned Thing!' he replied, without turning his head. His voice was husky and unnatural. He trembled visibly.

"I was about to speak further, when I observed the wild oats near the place of the disturbance moving in the most inexplicable way. I can hardly describe it. It seemed as if stirred by a streak of wind, which not only bent it, but pressed it down—crushed it so that it did not rise; and this movement was slowly prolonging itself directly toward us.

"Nothing that I had ever seen had affected me so strangely as this unfamiliar and unaccountable phenomenon, yet I am unable to recall any sense of fear. I remember—and tell it here because, singularly enough, I recollected it then—that once in looking carelessly out of an open window I momentarily mistook a small tree close at hand for one of a group of larger trees at a little distance away. It looked the same size as the others, but being more distinctly and sharply defined in mass and detail seemed out of harmony with them. It was a mere falsification of the law of aerial perspective, but it startled, almost terrified me. We so rely upon the orderly operation of familiar natural laws that any seeming suspension of them is noted as a menace to our safety, a warning of unthinkable calamity. So now the apparently causeless movement of the herbage and the slow, undeviating approach of the line of disturbances were distinctly disquieting. My companion appeared actually frightened, and I could hardly credit my senses when I saw him suddenly throw his gun to his shoulder and fire both barrels at the agitated grain! Before the smoke of the discharge had cleared away I heard a loud savage cry—a scream like that of a wild animal—and flinging his gun upon the ground Morgan sprang away and ran swiftly from the spot. At the same instant I was thrown violently to the ground by the impact of something unseen in the smoke—some soft, heavy substance that seemed thrown against me with great force.

"Before I could get upon my feet and recover my gun, which seemed to have been struck from my hands, I heard Morgan crying out as if in mortal agony, and mingling with his cries were such hoarse, savage sounds as one hears from fighting dogs. Inexpressibly terrified, I struggled to my feet and looked in the direction of Morgan's retreat; and may Heaven in mercy spare me from another sight like that! At a distance of less than thirty yards was my friend, down upon one knee, his head thrown back at a frightful angle, hatless, his long hair in disorder and his whole body in violent movement from side to side, backward and forward. His right arm was lifted and seemed to lack the hand—at least, I could see none. The other arm was invisible. At times, as my memory now reports this extraordinary scene, I could discern but a part of his body; it was as if he had been partly blotted out—I cannot otherwise express it—then a shifting of his position would bring it all into view again.

"All this must have occurred within a few seconds, yet in that time Morgan assumed all the postures of a determined wrestler vanquished by superior weight and strength. I saw nothing but him, and him not always distinctly. During the entire incident his shouts and curses were heard, as if through an enveloping uproar of such sounds of rage and fury as I had never heard from the throat of man or brute!

"For a moment only I stood irresolute, then throwing down my gun I ran forward to my friend's assistance. I had a vague belief that he was suffering from a fit, or some form of convulsion. Before I could reach his side he was down and quiet. All sounds had ceased, but with a feeling of such terror as even these awful events had not inspired I now saw again the mysterious movement of the wild oats, prolonging itself from the trampled area about the prostrate man toward the edge of a wood. It was only when it had reached the wood that I was able to withdraw my eyes and look at my companion. He was dead."

III – A Man Though Naked May Be in Rags

The coroner rose from his seat and stood beside the dead man. Lifting an edge of the sheet he pulled it away, exposing the entire body, altogether naked and showing in the candle-light a claylike yellow. It had, however, broad maculations of bluish black, obviously caused by extravasated blood from contusions. The chest and sides looked as if they had been beaten with a bludgeon. There were dreadful lacerations; the skin was torn in strips and shreds.

The coroner moved round to the end of the table and undid a silk handkerchief which had been passed under the chin and knotted on the top of the head. When the handkerchief was drawn away it exposed what had been the throat. Some of the jurors who had risen to get a better view repented their curiosity and turned away their faces. Witness Harker went to the open window and leaned out across the sill, faint and sick. Dropping the handkerchief upon the dead man's neck the coroner stepped to an angle of the room and from a pile of clothing produced one garment after another, each of which he held up a moment for inspection. All were torn, and stiff with blood. The jurors did not make a closer inspection. They seemed rather uninterested. They had, in truth, seen all this before; the only thing that was new to them being Harker's testimony.

"Gentlemen," the coroner said, "we have no more evidence, I think. Your duty has been already explained to you; if there is nothing you wish to ask you may go outside and consider your verdict."

The foreman rose—a tall, bearded man of sixty, coarsely clad.

"I should like to ask one question, Mr Coroner," he said. "What asylum did this yer last witness escape from?"

"Mr Harker," said the coroner, gravely and tranquilly, "from what asylum did you last escape?"

Harker flushed crimson again, but said nothing, and the seven jurors rose and solemnly filed out of the cabin.

"If you have done insulting me, sir," said Harker, as soon as he and the officer were left alone with the dead man, "I suppose I am at liberty to go?"

"Yes."

Harker started to leave, but paused, with his hand on the door latch. The habit of his profession was strong in him—stronger than his sense of personal dignity. He turned about and said:

"The book that you have there—I recognize it as Morgan's diary. You seemed greatly interested in it; you read in it while I was testifying. May I see it? The public would like——"

"The book will cut no figure in this matter," replied the official, slipping it into his coat pocket; "all the entries in it were made before the writer's death."

As Harker passed out of the house the jury re-entered and stood about the table, on which the now covered corpse showed under the sheet with sharp definition. The foreman seated himself near the candle, produced from his breast pocket a pencil and scrap of paper and wrote rather laboriously the following verdict, which with various degrees of effort all signed:

"We, the jury, do find that the remains come to their death at the hands of a mountain lion, but some of us thinks, all the same, they had fits."

IV – An Explanation From The Tomb

In the diary of the late Hugh Morgan are certain interesting entries having, possibly, a scientific value as suggestions. At the inquest upon his body the book was not put in evidence; possibly the coroner thought it not worth while to confuse the jury. The date of the first of the entries mentioned cannot be ascertained; the upper part of the leaf is torn away; the part of the entry remaining follows:

" …would run in a half-circle, keeping his head turned always toward the center, and again he would stand still, barking furiously. At last he ran away into the brush as fast as he could go. I thought at first that he had gone mad, but on returning to the house found no other alteration in his manner than what was obviously due to fear of punishment.

"Can a dog see with his nose? Do odors impress some cerebral center with images of the thing that emitted them?...

"Sept. 2.—Looking at the stars last night as they rose above the crest of the ridge east of the house, I observed them successively disappear—from left to right. Each was eclipsed but an instant, and only a few at the same time, but along the entire length of the ridge all that were within a degree or two of the crest were blotted out. It was as if something had passed along between me and them; but I could not see it, and the stars were not thick enough to define its outline. Ugh! I don't like this."...

Several weeks' entries are missing, three leaves being torn from the book.

"Sept. 27.—It has been about here again—I find evidences of its presence every day. I watched again all last night in the same cover, gun in hand, double-charged with buckshot. In the morning the fresh footprints were there, as before. Yet I would have sworn that I did not sleep—indeed, I hardly sleep at all. It is terrible, insupportable! If these amazing experiences are real I shall go mad; if they are fanciful I am mad already.

"Oct. 3.—I shall not go—it shall not drive me away. No, this is *my* house, *my* land. God hates a coward....

"Oct. 5.—I can stand it no longer; I have invited Harker to pass a few weeks with me—he has a level head. I can judge from his manner if he thinks me mad.

"Oct. 7.—I have the solution of the mystery; it came to me last night—suddenly, as by revelation. How simple—how terribly simple!

"There are sounds that we cannot hear. At either end of the scale are notes that stir no chord of that imperfect instrument, the human ear. They are too high or too grave. I have observed a flock of blackbirds occupying an entire tree-top—the tops of several trees—and all in full song. Suddenly—in a moment—at absolutely the same instant—all spring into the air and fly away. How? They could not all see one another—whole tree-tops intervened. At no point could a leader have been visible to all. There must have been a signal of warning or command, high and shrill above the din, but by me unheard. I have observed, too, the same simultaneous flight when all were silent, among not only blackbirds, but other birds—quail, for example, widely separated by bushes—even on opposite sides of a hill.

"It is known to seamen that a school of whales basking or sporting on the surface of the ocean, miles apart, with the convexity of the earth between, will sometimes dive at the same instant—all gone out of sight in a moment. The signal has been sounded—too grave for the ear of the sailor at the masthead and his comrades on the deck—who nevertheless feel its vibrations in the ship as the stones of a cathedral are stirred by the bass of the organ.

"As with sounds, so with colors. At each end of the solar spectrum the chemist can detect the presence of what are known as 'actinic' rays. They represent colors—integral colors in the composition of light—which we are unable to discern. The human eye is an imperfect instrument; its range is but a few octaves of the real 'chromatic scale.' I am not mad; there are colors that we cannot see.

"And, God help me! the Damned Thing is of such a color!"

Afterward

Edith Wharton

"Oh, there *is* one, of course, but you'll never know it."

The assertion, laughingly flung out six months earlier in a bright June garden, came back to Mary Boyne with a sharp perception of its latent significance as she stood, in the December dusk, waiting for the lamps to be brought into the library.

The words had been spoken by their friend Alida Stair, as they sat at tea on her lawn at Pangbourne, in reference to the very house of which the library in question was the central, the pivotal "feature." Mary Boyne and her husband, in quest of a country place in one of the southern or southwestern counties, had, on their arrival in England, carried their problem straight to Alida Stair, who had successfully solved it in her own case; but it was not until they had rejected, almost capriciously, several practical and judicious suggestions that she threw it out: "Well, there's Lyng, in Dorsetshire. It belongs to Hugo's cousins, and you can get it for a song."

The reasons she gave for its being obtainable on these terms—its remoteness from a station, its lack of electric light, hot-water pipes, and other vulgar necessities—were exactly those pleading in its favor with two romantic Americans perversely in search of the economic drawbacks which were associated, in their tradition, with unusual architectural felicities.

"I should never believe I was living in an old house unless I was thoroughly uncomfortable," Ned Boyne, the more extravagant of the two, had jocosely insisted; "the least hint of 'convenience' would make me think it had been bought out of an exhibition, with the pieces numbered, and set up again." And they had proceeded to enumerate, with humorous precision, their various suspicions and exactions, refusing to believe that the house their cousin recommended was *really* Tudor till they learned it had no heating system, or that the village church was literally in the grounds till she assured them of the deplorable uncertainty of the water-supply.

"It's too uncomfortable to be true!" Edward Boyne had continued to exult as the avowal of each disadvantage was successively wrung from her; but he had cut short his rhapsody to ask, with a sudden relapse to distrust: "And the ghost? You've been concealing from us the fact that there is no ghost!"

Mary, at the moment, had laughed with him, yet almost with her laugh, being possessed of several sets of independent perceptions, had noted a sudden flatness of tone in Alida's answering hilarity.

"Oh, Dorsetshire's full of ghosts, you know."

"Yes, yes; but that won't do. I don't want to have to drive ten miles to see somebody else's ghost. I want one of my own on the premises. Is there a ghost at Lyng?"

His rejoinder had made Alida laugh again, and it was then that she had flung back tantalizingly: "Oh, there *is* one, of course, but you'll never know it."

"Never know it?" Boyne pulled her up. "But what in the world constitutes a ghost except the fact of its being known for one?"

"I can't say. But that's the story."

"That there's a ghost, but that nobody knows it's a ghost?"

"Well—not till afterward, at any rate."

"Till afterward?"

"Not till long, long afterward."

"But if it's once been identified as an unearthly visitant, why hasn't its *signalement* been handed down in the family? How has it managed to preserve its incognito?"

Alida could only shake her head. "Don't ask me. But it has."

"And then suddenly—" Mary spoke up as if from some cavernous depth of divination—"suddenly, long afterward, one says to one's self, *'That was it?'* "

She was oddly startled at the sepulchral sound with which her question fell on the banter of the other two, and she saw the shadow of the same surprise flit across Alida's clear pupils. "I suppose so. One just has to wait."

"Oh, hang waiting!" Ned broke in. "Life's too short for a ghost who can only be enjoyed in retrospect. Can't we do better than that, Mary?"

But it turned out that in the event they were not destined to, for within three months of their conversation with Mrs Stair they were established at Lyng, and the life they had yearned for to the point of planning it out in all its daily details had actually begun for them.

It was to sit, in the thick December dusk, by just such a wide-hooded fireplace, under just such black oak rafters, with the sense that beyond the mullioned panes the downs were darkening to a deeper solitude: it was for the ultimate indulgence in such sensations that Mary Boyne had endured for nearly fourteen years the soul-deadening ugliness of the Middle West, and that Boyne had ground on doggedly at his engineering till, with a suddenness that still made her blink, the prodigious windfall of the Blue Star Mine had put them at a stroke in possession of life and the leisure to taste it. They had never for a moment meant their new state to be one of idleness; but they meant to give themselves only to harmonious activities. She had her vision of painting and gardening (against a background of gray walls), he dreamed of the production of his long-planned book on the "Economic Basis of Culture"; and with such absorbing work ahead no existence could be too sequestered; they could not get far enough from the world, or plunge deep enough into the past.

Dorsetshire had attracted them from the first by a semblance of remoteness out of all proportion to its geographical position. But to the Boynes it was one of the ever-recurring wonders of the whole incredibly compressed island—a nest of counties, as they put it—that for the production of its effects so little of a given quality went so far: that so few miles made a distance, and so short a distance a difference.

"It's that," Ned had once enthusiastically explained, "that gives such depth to their effects, such relief to their least contrasts. They've been able to lay the butter so thick on every exquisite mouthful."

The butter had certainly been laid on thick at Lyng: the old gray house, hidden under a shoulder of the downs, had almost all the finer marks of commerce with a protracted past. The mere fact that it was neither large nor exceptional made it, to the Boynes, abound the more richly in its special sense—the sense of having been for centuries a deep, dim reservoir of life. The life had probably not been of the most vivid order: for long periods, no doubt, it had fallen as noiselessly into the past as the quiet drizzle of autumn fell, hour after hour, into the green fish-pond between the yews; but these back-waters of existence sometimes breed, in their sluggish depths, strange acuities of emotion, and Mary Boyne had felt from the first the occasional brush of an intenser memory.

The feeling had never been stronger than on the December afternoon when, waiting in the library for the belated lamps, she rose from her seat and stood among the shadows of the hearth. Her husband had gone off, after luncheon, for one of his long tramps on the downs. She had noticed of late that he preferred to be unaccompanied on these occasions; and, in the tried security of their personal relations, had been driven to conclude that his book was bothering him, and that he needed the afternoons to turn over in solitude the problems left from the morning's work. Certainly the book was not going as smoothly as she had imagined it would, and the lines of perplexity between his eyes had never been there in his engineering days. Then he had often looked fagged to the verge of illness, but the native demon of "worry" had never branded his brow. Yet the few pages he had so far read to her—the introduction, and a synopsis of the opening chapter—gave evidences of a firm possession of his subject, and a deepening confidence in his powers.

The fact threw her into deeper perplexity, since, now that he had done with "business" and its disturbing contingencies, the one other possible element of anxiety was eliminated. Unless it were his health, then? But physically he had gained since they had come to Dorsetshire, grown robuster, ruddier, and fresher-eyed. It was only within a week that she had felt in him the undefinable change that made her restless in his absence, and as tongue-tied in his presence as though it were *she* who had a secret to keep from him!

The thought that there *was* a secret somewhere between them struck her with a sudden smart rap of wonder, and she looked about her down the dim, long room.

"Can it be the house?" she mused.

The room itself might have been full of secrets. They seemed to be piling themselves up, as evening fell, like the layers and layers of velvet shadow dropping from the low ceiling, the dusky walls of books, the smoke-blurred sculpture of the hooded hearth. "Why, of course—the house is haunted!" she reflected.

The ghost—Alida's imperceptible ghost—after figuring largely in the banter of their first month or two at Lyng, had been gradually discarded as too ineffectual for imaginative use. Mary had, indeed, as became the tenant of a haunted house, made the customary inquiries among her few rural neighbors, but, beyond a vague, "They du say so, Ma'am," the villagers had nothing to impart. The elusive specter had apparently never had sufficient identity for a legend to crystallize about it, and after a time the Boynes had laughingly set the matter down to their profit-and-loss account, agreeing that Lyng was one of the few houses good enough in itself to dispense with supernatural enhancements.

"And I suppose, poor, ineffectual demon, that's why it beats its beautiful wings in vain in the void," Mary had laughingly concluded.

"Or, rather," Ned answered, in the same strain, "why, amid so much that's ghostly, it can never affirm its separate existence as *the* ghost." And thereupon their invisible housemate had finally dropped out of their references, which were numerous enough to make them promptly unaware of the loss.

Now, as she stood on the hearth, the subject of their earlier curiosity revived in her with a new sense of its meaning—a sense gradually acquired through close daily contact with the scene of the lurking mystery. It was the house itself, of course, that possessed the ghost-seeing faculty, that communed visually but secretly with its own past; and if one could only get into close enough communion with the house, one might surprise its secret, and acquire the ghost-sight on one's own account. Perhaps, in his long solitary hours in this very room, where she never trespassed till the afternoon, her husband *had* acquired it already, and was silently carrying the dread weight of whatever it had revealed to him. Mary was too well-versed in the code of the spectral world not to know that one could not talk about the ghosts one saw: to do so was almost as great a breach of good-breeding as to name a lady in a club. But this explanation did not really satisfy her. "What, after all, except for the fun of the *frisson*," she reflected, "would he really care for any of their old ghosts?" And thence she was thrown back once more on the fundamental dilemma: the fact that one's greater or less susceptibility to spectral influences had no particular bearing on the case, since, when one *did* see a ghost at Lyng, one did not know it.

"Not till long afterward," Alida Stair had said. Well, supposing Ned had seen one when they first came, and had known only within the last week what had happened to him? More and more under the spell of the hour, she threw back her searching thoughts to the early days of their tenancy, but at first only to recall a gay confusion of unpacking, settling, arranging of books, and calling to each other from remote corners of the house as treasure after treasure of their habitation revealed itself to them. It was in this particular connection that she presently recalled a certain soft afternoon of the previous October, when, passing from the first rapturous flurry of exploration to a detailed inspection of the old house, she had pressed (like a novel heroine) a panel that opened at her touch, on a narrow flight of stairs leading to an unsuspected flat ledge of the roof—the roof which, from below, seemed to slope away on all sides too abruptly for any but practised feet to scale.

The view from this hidden coign was enchanting, and she had flown down to snatch Ned from his papers and give him the freedom of her discovery. She remembered still how, standing on the narrow ledge, he had passed his arm about her while their gaze flew to the long, tossed horizon-line of the downs, and then dropped contentedly back to trace the arabesque of yew hedges about the fish-pond, and the shadow of the cedar on the lawn.

"And now the other way," he had said, gently turning her about within his arm; and closely pressed to him, she had absorbed, like some long, satisfying draft, the picture of the gray-walled court, the squat lions on the gates, and the lime-avenue reaching up to the highroad under the downs.

It was just then, while they gazed and held each other, that she had felt his arm relax, and heard a sharp "Hullo!" that made her turn to glance at him.

Distinctly, yes, she now recalled she had seen, as she glanced, a shadow of anxiety, of perplexity, rather, fall across his face; and, following his eyes, had beheld the figure of a man—a man in loose, grayish clothes, as it appeared to her—who was sauntering down the lime-avenue to the court with the tentative gait of a stranger seeking his way. Her short-sighted eyes had given her but a blurred impression of slightness and grayness, with something foreign, or at least unlocal, in the cut of the figure or its garb; but her husband had apparently seen more—seen enough to make him push past her with a sharp "Wait!" and dash down the twisting stairs without pausing to give her a hand for the descent.

A slight tendency to dizziness obliged her, after a provisional clutch at the chimney against which they had been leaning, to follow him down more cautiously; and when she had reached the attic landing she paused again for a less definite reason, leaning over the oak banister to strain her eyes through the silence of the brown, sun-flecked depths below. She lingered there till, somewhere in those depths, she heard the closing of a door; then, mechanically impelled, she went down the shallow flights of steps till she reached the lower hall.

The front door stood open on the mild sunlight of the court, and hall and court were empty. The library door was open, too, and after listening in vain for any sound of voices within, she quickly crossed the threshold, and found her husband alone, vaguely fingering the papers on his desk.

He looked up, as if surprised at her precipitate entrance, but the shadow of anxiety had passed from his face, leaving it even, as she fancied, a little brighter and clearer than usual.

"What was it? Who was it?" she asked.

"Who?" he repeated, with the surprise still all on his side.

"The man we saw coming toward the house."

He seemed honestly to reflect. "The man? Why, I thought I saw Peters; I dashed after him to say a word about the stable-drains, but he had disappeared before I could get down."

"Disappeared? Why, he seemed to be walking so slowly when we saw him."

Boyne shrugged his shoulders. "So I thought; but he must have got up steam in the interval. What do you say to our trying a scramble up Meldon Steep before sunset?"

That was all. At the time the occurrence had been less than nothing, had, indeed, been immediately obliterated by the magic of their first vision from Meldon Steep, a height which they had dreamed of climbing ever since they had first seen its bare spine heaving itself above the low roof of Lyng. Doubtless it was the mere fact of the other incident's having occurred on the very day of their ascent to Meldon that had kept it stored away in the unconscious fold of association from which it now emerged; for in itself it had no mark of the portentous. At the moment there could have been nothing more natural than that Ned should dash himself from the roof in the pursuit of dilatory tradesmen. It was the period when they were always on the watch for one or the other of the specialists employed about the place; always lying in wait for them, and dashing out at them with questions, reproaches, or reminders. And certainly in the distance the gray figure had looked like Peters.

Yet now, as she reviewed the rapid scene, she felt her husband's explanation of it to have been invalidated by the look of anxiety on his face. Why had the familiar appearance of Peters made him anxious? Why, above all, if it was of such prime necessity to confer with that authority on the subject of the stable-drains, had the failure to find him produced such a look of relief? Mary could not say that any one of these considerations had occurred to her at the time, yet, from the promptness with which they now marshaled themselves at her summons, she had a sudden sense that they must all along have been there, waiting their hour.

II

Weary with her thoughts, she moved toward the window. The library was now completely dark, and she was surprised to see how much faint light the outer world still held.

As she peered out into it across the court, a figure shaped itself in the tapering perspective of bare lines: it looked a mere blot of deeper gray in the grayness, and for an instant, as it moved toward her, her heart thumped to the thought, "It's the ghost!"

She had time, in that long instant, to feel suddenly that the man of whom, two months earlier, she had a brief distant vision from the roof was now, at his predestined hour, about to reveal himself as *not* having been Peters; and her spirit sank under the impending fear of the disclosure. But almost with the next tick of the clock the ambiguous figure, gaining substance and character, showed itself even to her weak sight as her husband's; and she turned away to meet him, as he entered, with the confession of her folly.

"It's really too absurd," she laughed out from the threshold, "but I never *can* remember!"

"Remember what?" Boyne questioned as they drew together.

"That when one sees the Lyng ghost one never knows it." Her hand was on his sleeve, and he kept it there, but with no response in his gesture or in the lines of his fagged, preoccupied face.

"Did you think you'd seen it?" he asked, after an appreciable interval.

"Why, I actually took *you* for it, my dear, in my mad determination to spot it!"

"Me—just now?" His arm dropped away, and he turned from her with a faint echo of her laugh. "Really, dearest, you'd better give it up, if that's the best you can do."

"Yes, I give it up—I give it up. Have *you*?" she asked, turning round on him abruptly.

The parlor-maid had entered with letters and a lamp, and the light struck up into Boyne's face as he bent above the tray she presented.

"Have *you*?" Mary perversely insisted, when the servant had disappeared on her errand of illumination.

"Have I what?" he rejoined absently, the light bringing out the sharp stamp of worry between his brows as he turned over the letters.

"Given up trying to see the ghost." Her heart beat a little at the experiment she was making.

Her husband, laying his letters aside, moved away into the shadow of the hearth.

"I never tried," he said, tearing open the wrapper of a newspaper.

"Well, of course," Mary persisted, "the exasperating thing is that there's no use trying, since one can't be sure till so long afterward."

He was unfolding the paper as if he had hardly heard her; but after a pause, during which the sheets rustled spasmodically between his hands, he lifted his head to say abruptly, "Have you any idea *how long*?"

Mary had sunk into a low chair beside the fireplace. From her seat she looked up, startled, at her husband's profile, which was darkly projected against the circle of lamplight.

"No; none. Have *you*?" she retorted, repeating her former phrase with an added keenness of intention.

Boyne crumpled the paper into a bunch, and then inconsequently turned back with it toward the lamp.

"Lord, no! I only meant," he explained, with a faint tinge of impatience, "is there any legend, any tradition, as to that?"

"Not that I know of," she answered; but the impulse to add, "What makes you ask?" was checked by the reappearance of the parlor-maid with tea and a second lamp.

With the dispersal of shadows, and the repetition of the daily domestic office, Mary Boyne felt herself less oppressed by that sense of something mutely imminent which had darkened her solitary afternoon. For a few moments she gave herself silently to the details of her task, and when she looked up from it she was struck to the point of bewilderment by the change in her husband's face. He had seated himself near the farther lamp, and was absorbed in the perusal of his letters; but was it something he had found in them, or merely the shifting of her own point of view, that had restored his features to their normal aspect? The longer she looked, the more definitely the change affirmed itself. The lines of painful tension had vanished, and such traces of fatigue as lingered were of the kind easily attributable to steady mental effort. He glanced up, as if drawn by her gaze, and met her eyes with a smile.

"I'm dying for my tea, you know; and here's a letter for you," he said.

She took the letter he held out in exchange for the cup she proffered him, and, returning to her seat, broke the seal with the languid gesture of the reader whose interests are all inclosed in the circle of one cherished presence.

Her next conscious motion was that of starting to her feet, the letter falling to them as she rose, while she held out to her husband a long newspaper clipping.

"Ned! What's this? What does it mean?"

He had risen at the same instant, almost as if hearing her cry before she uttered it; and for a perceptible space of time he and she studied each other, like adversaries watching for an advantage, across the space between her chair and his desk.

"What's what? You fairly made me jump!" Boyne said at length, moving toward her with a sudden, half-exasperated laugh. The shadow of apprehension was on his face again, not now a look of fixed foreboding, but a shifting vigilance of lips and eyes that gave her the sense of his feeling himself invisibly surrounded.

Her hand shook so that she could hardly give him the clipping.

"This article—from the *Waukesha Sentinel*—that a man named Elwell has brought suit against you—that there was something wrong about the Blue Star Mine. I can't understand more than half."

They continued to face each other as she spoke, and to her astonishment, she saw that her words had the almost immediate effect of dissipating the strained watchfulness of his look.

"Oh, *that*!" He glanced down the printed slip, and then folded it with the gesture of one who handles something harmless and familiar. "What's the matter with you this afternoon, Mary? I thought you'd got bad news."

She stood before him with her undefinable terror subsiding slowly under the reassuring touch of his composure.

"You knew about this, then—it's all right?"

"Certainly I knew about it; and it's all right."

"But what *is* it? I don't understand. What does this man accuse you of?"

"Oh, pretty nearly every crime in the calendar." Boyne had tossed the clipping down, and thrown himself comfortably into an armchair near the fire. "Do you want to hear the story? It's not particularly interesting—just a squabble over interests in the Blue Star."

"But who is this Elwell? I don't know the name."

"Oh, he's a fellow I put into it—gave him a hand up. I told you all about him at the time."

"I daresay. I must have forgotten." Vainly she strained back among her memories. "But if you helped him, why does he make this return?"

"Oh, probably some shyster lawyer got hold of him and talked him over. It's all rather technical and complicated. I thought that kind of thing bored you."

His wife felt a sting of compunction. Theoretically, she deprecated the American wife's detachment from her husband's professional interests, but in practice she had always found it difficult to fix her attention on Boyne's report of the transactions in which his varied interests involved him. Besides, she had felt from the first that, in a community where the amenities of living could be obtained only at the cost of efforts as arduous as her husband's professional labors, such brief leisure as they could command should be used as an escape from immediate preoccupations, a flight to the life they always dreamed of living. Once or twice, now that this new life had actually drawn its magic circle about them, she had asked herself if she had done right; but hitherto such conjectures had been no more than the retrospective excursions of an active fancy. Now, for the first time, it startled her a little to find how little she knew of the material foundation on which her happiness was built.

She glanced again at her husband, and was reassured by the composure of his face; yet she felt the need of more definite grounds for her reassurance.

"But doesn't this suit worry you? Why have you never spoken to me about it?"

He answered both questions at once: "I didn't speak of it at first because it *did* worry me—annoyed me, rather. But it's all ancient history now. Your correspondent must have got hold of a back number of the *Sentinel*."

She felt a quick thrill of relief. "You mean it's over? He's lost his case?"

There was a just perceptible delay in Boyne's reply. "The suit's been withdrawn—that's all."

But she persisted, as if to exonerate herself from the inward charge of being too easily put off. "Withdrawn because he saw he had no chance?"

"Oh, he had no chance," Boyne answered.

She was still struggling with a dimly felt perplexity at the back of her thoughts.

"How long ago was it withdrawn?"

He paused, as if with a slight return of his former uncertainty. "I've just had the news now; but I've been expecting it."

"Just now—in one of your letters?"

"Yes; in one of my letters."

She made no answer, and was aware only, after a short interval of waiting, that he had risen, and strolling across the room, had placed himself on the sofa at her side. She felt him, as he did so, pass an arm about her, she felt his hand seek hers and clasp it, and turning slowly, drawn by the warmth of his cheek, she met the smiling clearness of his eyes.

"It's all right—it's all right?" she questioned, through the flood of her dissolving doubts; and "I give you my word it never was righter!" he laughed back at her, holding her close.

III

One of the strangest things she was afterward to recall out of all the next day's incredible strangeness was the sudden and complete recovery of her sense of security.

It was in the air when she woke in her low-ceilinged, dusky room; it accompanied her down-stairs to the breakfast-table, flashed out at her from the fire, and re-duplicated itself brightly from the flanks of the urn and the sturdy flutings of the Georgian teapot. It was as if, in some roundabout way, all her diffused apprehensions of the previous day, with their moment of sharp concentration about the newspaper article,—as if this dim questioning of the future, and startled return upon the past,—had between them liquidated the arrears of some haunting moral obligation. If she had indeed been careless of her husband's affairs, it was, her new state seemed to prove, because her faith in him instinctively justified such carelessness; and his right to her faith had overwhelmingly affirmed itself in the very face of menace and suspicion. She had never seen him more untroubled, more naturally and unconsciously in possession of himself, than after the cross-examination to which she had subjected him: it was almost as if he had been aware of her lurking doubts, and had wanted the air cleared as much as she did.

It was as clear, thank Heaven! as the bright outer light that surprised her almost with a touch of summer when she issued from the house for her daily round of the gardens. She had left Boyne at his desk, indulging herself, as she passed the library door, by a last peep at his quiet face, where he bent, pipe in his mouth, above his papers, and now she had her own morning's task to perform. The task involved on such charmed winter days almost as much delighted loitering about the different quarters of her demesne as if spring were already at work on shrubs and borders. There were such inexhaustible possibilities still before her, such opportunities to bring out the latent graces of the old place, without a single irreverent touch of alteration, that the winter months were all too short to plan what spring and autumn executed. And her recovered sense of safety gave, on this particular morning, a peculiar zest to her progress through the sweet, still place. She went first to the kitchen-garden, where the espaliered pear-trees drew complicated patterns on the walls, and pigeons were fluttering and preening about the silvery-slated roof of their cot. There was something wrong about the piping of the hothouse, and she was expecting an authority from Dorchester, who was to drive out between trains and make a diagnosis of the boiler. But when she dipped into the damp heat of the greenhouses, among the spiced scents and waxy pinks and reds of old-fashioned exotics,—even the flora of Lyng was in the note!—she learned that the great man had not arrived, and the day being too rare to waste in an artificial atmosphere, she came out again and paced slowly along the springy turf of the bowling-green to the gardens behind the house. At their farther end rose a grass terrace, commanding, over the fish-pond and the yew hedges, a view of the long house-front, with its twisted chimney-stacks and the blue shadows of its roof angles, all drenched in the pale gold moisture of the air.

Seen thus, across the level tracery of the yews, under the suffused, mild light, it sent her, from its open windows and hospitably smoking chimneys, the look of some warm human presence, of a mind slowly ripened on a sunny wall of experience. She had never before had so deep a sense of her intimacy with it, such a conviction that its secrets were all beneficent, kept, as they said to children, "for one's good," so complete a trust in its power to gather up her life and Ned's into the harmonious pattern of the long, long story it sat there weaving in the sun.

She heard steps behind her, and turned, expecting to see the gardener, accompanied by the engineer from Dorchester. But only one figure was in sight, that of a youngish, slightly built man, who, for reasons she could not on the spot have specified, did not remotely resemble her preconceived notion of an authority on hot-house boilers. The new-comer, on seeing her, lifted his hat, and paused with the air of a gentleman —perhaps a traveler—desirous of having it immediately known that his intrusion is involuntary. The local fame of Lyng occasionally attracted the more intelligent sight-seer, and Mary half-expected to see the stranger dissemble a camera, or justify his presence by producing it. But he made no gesture of any sort, and after a moment she asked, in a tone responding to the courteous deprecation of his attitude: "Is there any one you wish to see?"

"I came to see Mr Boyne," he replied. His intonation, rather than his accent, was faintly American, and Mary, at the familiar note, looked at him more closely. The brim of his soft felt hat cast a shade on his face, which, thus obscured, wore to her short-sighted gaze a look of seriousness, as of a person arriving "on business," and civilly but firmly aware of his rights.

Past experience had made Mary equally sensible to such claims; but she was jealous of her husband's morning hours, and doubtful of his having given any one the right to intrude on them.

"Have you an appointment with Mr Boyne?" she asked.

He hesitated, as if unprepared for the question.

"Not exactly an appointment," he replied.

"Then I'm afraid, this being his working-time, that he can't receive you now. Will you give me a message, or come back later?"

The visitor, again lifting his hat, briefly replied that he would come back later, and walked away, as if to regain the front of the house. As his figure receded down the walk between the yew hedges, Mary saw him pause and look up an instant at the peaceful house-front bathed in faint winter sunshine; and it struck her, with a tardy touch of compunction, that it would have been more humane to ask if he had come from a distance, and to offer, in that case, to inquire if her husband could receive him. But as the thought occurred to her he passed out of sight behind a pyramidal yew, and at the same moment her attention was distracted by the approach of the gardener, attended by the bearded pepper-and-salt figure of the boiler-maker from Dorchester.

The encounter with this authority led to such far-reaching issues that they resulted in his finding it expedient to ignore his train, and beguiled Mary into spending the remainder of the morning in absorbed confabulation among the greenhouses. She was startled to find, when the colloquy ended, that it was nearly luncheon-time, and she half expected, as she hurried back to the house, to see her husband coming out to meet her. But she found no one in the court but an under-gardener raking the gravel, and the hall, when she entered it, was so silent that she guessed Boyne to be still at work behind the closed door of the library.

Not wishing to disturb him, she turned into the drawing room, and there, at her writing-table, lost herself in renewed calculations of the outlay to which the morning's conference had committed her. The knowledge that she could permit herself such follies had not yet lost its novelty; and somehow, in contrast to the vague apprehensions of the previous days, it now seemed an element of her recovered security, of the sense that, as Ned had said, things in general had never been "righter." She was still luxuriating in a lavish play of figures when the parlor-maid, from the threshold, roused her with a dubiously worded inquiry as to the expediency of serving luncheon. It was one of their jokes that Trimmle announced luncheon as if she were divulging a state secret, and Mary, intent upon her papers, merely murmured an absent-minded assent.

She felt Trimmle wavering expressively on the threshold as if in rebuke of such offhand acquiescence; then her retreating steps sounded down the passage, and Mary, pushing away her papers, crossed the hall, and went to the library door. It was still closed, and she wavered in her turn, disliking to disturb her husband, yet anxious that he should not exceed his normal measure of work. As she stood there, balancing her impulses, the esoteric Trimmle returned with the announcement of luncheon, and Mary, thus impelled, opened the door and went into the library.

Boyne was not at his desk, and she peered about her, expecting to discover him at the book-shelves, somewhere down the length of the room; but her call brought no response, and gradually it became clear to her that he was not in the library.

She turned back to the parlor-maid.

"Mr Boyne must be upstairs. Please tell him that luncheon is ready."

The parlor-maid appeared to hesitate between the obvious duty of obeying orders and an equally obvious conviction of the foolishness of the injunction laid upon her. The struggle resulted in her saying doubtfully, "If you please, Madam, Mr Boyne's not upstairs."

"Not in his room? Are you sure?"

"I'm sure, Madam."

Mary consulted the clock. "Where is he, then?"

"He's gone out," Trimmle announced, with the superior air of one who has respectfully waited for the question that a well-ordered mind would have first propounded.

Mary's previous conjecture had been right, then. Boyne must have gone to the gardens to meet her, and since she had missed him, it was clear that he had taken the shorter way by the south door, instead of going round to the court. She crossed the hall to the glass portal opening directly on the yew garden, but the parlor-maid, after another moment of inner conflict, decided to bring out recklessly, "Please, Madam, Mr Boyne didn't go that way."

Mary turned back. "Where *did* he go? And when?"

"He went out of the front door, up the drive, Madam." It was a matter of principle with Trimmle never to answer more than one question at a time.

"Up the drive? At this hour?" Mary went to the door herself, and glanced across the court through the long tunnel of bare limes. But its perspective was as empty as when she had scanned it on entering the house.

"Did Mr Boyne leave no message?" she asked.

Trimmle seemed to surrender herself to a last struggle with the forces of chaos.

"No, Madam. He just went out with the gentleman."

"The gentleman? What gentleman?" Mary wheeled about, as if to front this new factor.

"The gentleman who called, Madam," said Trimmle, resignedly.

"When did a gentleman call? Do explain yourself, Trimmle!"

Only the fact that Mary was very hungry, and that she wanted to consult her husband about the greenhouses, would have caused her to lay so unusual an injunction on her attendant; and even now she was detached enough to note in Trimmle's eye the dawning defiance of the respectful subordinate who has been pressed too hard.

"I couldn't exactly say the hour, Madam, because I didn't let the gentleman in," she replied, with the air of magnanimously ignoring the irregularity of her mistress's course.

"You didn't let him in?"

"No, Madam. When the bell rang I was dressing, and Agnes—"

"Go and ask Agnes, then," Mary interjected.

Trimmle still wore her look of patient magnanimity. "Agnes would not know, Madam, for she had unfortunately burnt her hand in trying the wick of the new lamp from town—" Trimmle, as Mary was aware, had always been opposed to the new lamp— "and so Mrs Dockett sent the kitchen-maid instead."

Mary looked again at the clock. "It's after two! Go and ask the kitchen-maid if Mr Boyne left any word."

She went into luncheon without waiting, and Trimmle presently brought her there the kitchen-maid's statement that the gentleman had called about one o'clock, that Mr Boyne had gone out with him without leaving any message. The kitchen-maid did not even know the caller's name, for he had written it on a slip of paper, which he had folded and handed to her, with the injunction to deliver it at once to Mr Boyne.

Mary finished her luncheon, still wondering, and when it was over, and Trimmle had brought the coffee to the drawing room, her wonder had deepened to a first faint tinge of disquietude. It was unlike Boyne to absent himself without explanation at so unwonted an hour, and the difficulty of identifying the visitor whose summons he had apparently obeyed made his disappearance the more unaccountable. Mary Boyne's experience as the wife of a busy engineer, subject to sudden calls and compelled to keep irregular hours, had trained her to the philosophic acceptance of surprises; but since Boyne's withdrawal from business he had adopted a Benedictine regularity of life. As if to make up for the dispersed and agitated years, with their "stand-up" lunches and dinners rattled down to the joltings of the dining-car, he cultivated the last refinements of punctuality and monotony, discouraging his wife's fancy for the unexpected; and declaring that to a delicate taste there were infinite gradations of pleasure in the fixed recurrences of habit.

Still, since no life can completely defend itself from the unforeseen, it was evident that all Boyne's precautions would sooner or later prove unavailable, and Mary concluded that he had cut short a tiresome visit by walking with his caller to the station, or at least accompanying him for part of the way.

This conclusion relieved her from farther preoccupation, and she went out herself to take up her conference with the gardener. Thence she walked to the village post-office, a mile or so away; and when she turned toward home, the early twilight was setting in.

She had taken a footpath across the downs, and as Boyne, meanwhile, had probably returned from the station by the highroad, there was little likelihood of their meeting on the way. She felt sure, however, of his having reached the house before her; so sure that, when she entered it herself, without even pausing to inquire of Trimmle, she made directly for the library. But the library was still empty, and with an unwonted precision of visual memory she immediately observed that the papers on her husband's desk lay precisely as they had lain when she had gone in to call him to luncheon.

Then of a sudden she was seized by a vague dread of the unknown. She had closed the door behind her on entering, and as she stood alone in the long, silent, shadowy room, her dread seemed to take shape and sound, to be there audibly breathing and lurking among the shadows. Her short-sighted eyes strained through them, half-discerning an actual presence, something aloof, that watched and knew; and in the recoil from that intangible propinquity she threw herself suddenly on the bell-rope and gave it a desperate pull.

The long, quavering summons brought Trimmle in precipitately with a lamp, and Mary breathed again at this sobering reappearance of the usual.

"You may bring tea if Mr Boyne is in," she said, to justify her ring.

"Very well, Madam. But Mr Boyne is not in," said Trimmle, putting down the lamp.

"Not in? You mean he's come back and gone out again?"

"No, Madam. He's never been back."

The dread stirred again, and Mary knew that now it had her fast.

"Not since he went out with—the gentleman?"

"Not since he went out with the gentleman."

"But who *was* the gentleman?" Mary gasped out, with the sharp note of someone trying to be heard through a confusion of meaningless noises.

"That I couldn't say, Madam." Trimmle, standing there by the lamp, seemed suddenly to grow less round and rosy, as though eclipsed by the same creeping shade of apprehension.

"But the kitchen-maid knows—wasn't it the kitchen-maid who let him in?"

"She doesn't know either, Madam, for he wrote his name on a folded paper."

Mary, through her agitation, was aware that they were both designating the unknown visitor by a vague pronoun, instead of the conventional formula which, till then, had kept their allusions within the bounds of custom. And at the same moment her mind caught at the suggestion of the folded paper.

"But he must have a name! Where is the paper?"

She moved to the desk, and began to turn over the scattered documents that littered it. The first that caught her eye was an unfinished letter in her husband's hand, with his pen lying across it, as though dropped there at a sudden summons.

"My dear Parvis,"—who was Parvis?—"I have just received your letter announcing Elwell's death, and while I suppose there is now no farther risk of trouble, it might be safer—"

She tossed the sheet aside, and continued her search; but no folded paper was discoverable among the letters and pages of manuscript which had been swept together in a promiscuous heap, as if by a hurried or a startled gesture.

"But the kitchen-maid *saw* him. Send her here," she commanded, wondering at her dullness in not thinking sooner of so simple a solution. Trimmle, at the behest, vanished in a flash, as if thankful to be out of the room, and when she reappeared, conducting the agitated underling, Mary had regained her self-possession, and had her questions pat.

The gentleman was a stranger, yes—that she understood. But what had he said? And, above all, what had he looked like? The first question was easily enough answered, for the disconcerting reason that he had said so little—had merely asked for Mr Boyne, and, scribbling something on a bit of paper, had requested that it should at once be carried in to him.

"Then you don't know what he wrote? You're not sure it was his name?"

The kitchen-maid was not sure, but supposed it was, since he had written it in answer to her inquiry as to whom she should announce.

"And when you carried the paper in to Mr Boyne, what did he say?"

The kitchen-maid did not think that Mr Boyne had said anything, but she could not be sure, for just as she had handed him the paper and he was opening it, she had become aware that the visitor had followed her into the library, and she had slipped out, leaving the two gentlemen together.

"But then, if you left them in the library, how do you know that they went out of the house?"

This question plunged the witness into momentary inarticulateness, from which she was rescued by Trimmle, who, by means of ingenious circumlocutions, elicited the statement that before she could cross the hall to the back passage she had heard the gentlemen behind her, and had seen them go out of the front door together.

"Then, if you saw the gentleman twice, you must be able to tell me what he looked like."

But with this final challenge to her powers of expression it became clear that the limit of the kitchen-maid's endurance had been reached. The obligation of going to the front door to "show in" a visitor was in itself so subversive of the fundamental disarray, and she could only stammer out, after various panting efforts at evocation, "His hat, mum, was different-like, as you might say—"

"Different? How different?" Mary flashed out at her, her own mind, in the same instant, leaping back to an image left on it that morning, but temporarily lost under layers of subsequent impressions.

"His hat had a wide brim, you mean? and his face was pale—a youngish face?" Mary pressed her, with a white-lipped intensity of interrogation. But if the kitchen-maid found any adequate answer to this challenge, it was swept away for her listener down the rushing current of her own convictions. The stranger—the stranger in the garden! Why had Mary not thought of him before? She needed no one now to tell her that it was he who had called for her husband and gone away with him. But who was he, and why had Boyne obeyed his call?

IV

It leaped out at her suddenly, like a grin out of the dark, that they had often called England so little—"such a confoundedly hard place to get lost in."

A confoundedly hard place to get lost in! That had been her husband's phrase. And now, with the whole machinery of official investigation sweeping its flashlights from shore to shore, and across the dividing straits; now, with Boyne's name blazing from the walls of every town and village, his portrait (how that wrung her!) hawked up and down the country like the image of a hunted criminal; now the little compact, populous island, so policed, surveyed, and administered, revealed itself as a Sphinx-like guardian of abysmal mysteries, staring back into his wife's anguished eyes as if with the malicious joy of knowing something they would never know!

In the fortnight since Boyne's disappearance there had been no word of him, no trace of his movements. Even the usual misleading reports that raise expectancy in tortured bosoms had been few and fleeting. No one but the bewildered kitchen-maid had seen him leave the house, and no one else had seen "the gentleman" who accompanied him. All inquiries in the neighborhood failed to elicit the memory of a stranger's presence that day in the neighborhood of Lyng. And no one had met Edward Boyne, either alone or in company, in any of the neighboring villages, or on the road across the downs, or at either of the local railway stations. The sunny English noon had swallowed him as completely as if he had gone out into Cimmerian night.

Mary, while every external means of investigation was working at its highest pressure, had ransacked her husband's papers for any trace of antecedent complications, of entanglements or obligations unknown to her, that might throw a faint ray into the darkness. But if any such had existed in the background of Boyne's life, they had disappeared as completely as the slip of paper on which the visitor had written his name. There remained no possible thread of guidance except—if it were indeed an exception—the letter which Boyne had apparently been in the act of writing when he received his mysterious summons. That letter, read and reread by his wife, and submitted by her to the police, yielded little enough for conjecture to feed on.

"I have just heard of Elwell's death, and while I suppose there is now no farther risk of trouble, it might be safer—" That was all. The "risk of trouble" was easily explained by the newspaper clipping which had apprised Mary of the suit brought against her husband by one of his associates in the Blue Star enterprise. The only new information conveyed in the letter was the fact of its showing Boyne, when he wrote it, to be still apprehensive of the results of the suit, though he had assured his wife that it had been withdrawn, and though the letter itself declared that the plaintiff was dead. It took several weeks of exhaustive cabling to fix the identity of the "Parvis" to whom the fragmentary communication was addressed, but even after these inquiries had shown him to be a Waukesha lawyer, no new facts concerning the Elwell suit were elicited. He appeared to have had no direct concern in it, but to have been conversant with the facts merely as an acquaintance, and possible intermediary; and he declared himself unable to divine with what object Boyne intended to seek his assistance.

This negative information, sole fruit of the first fortnight's feverish search, was not increased by a jot during the slow weeks that followed. Mary knew that the investigations were still being carried on, but she had a vague sense of their gradually slackening, as the actual march of time seemed to slacken. It was as though the days, flying horror-struck from the shrouded image of the one inscrutable day, gained assurance as the distance lengthened, till at last they fell back into their normal gait. And so with the human imaginations at work on the dark event. No doubt it occupied them still, but week by week and hour by hour it grew less absorbing, took up less space, was slowly but inevitably crowded out of the foreground of consciousness by the new problems perpetually bubbling up from the vaporous caldron of human experience.

Even Mary Boyne's consciousness gradually felt the same lowering of velocity. It still swayed with the incessant oscillations of conjecture; but they were slower, more rhythmical in their beat. There were moments of overwhelming lassitude when, like the victim of some poison which leaves the brain clear, but holds the body motionless, she saw herself domesticated with the Horror, accepting its perpetual presence as one of the fixed conditions of life.

These moments lengthened into hours and days, till she passed into a phase of stolid acquiescence. She watched the familiar routine of life with the incurious eye of a savage on whom the meaningless processes of civilization make but the faintest impression. She had come to regard herself as part of the routine, a spoke of the wheel, revolving with its motion; she felt almost like the furniture of the room in which she sat, an insensate object to be dusted and pushed about with the chairs and tables. And this deepening apathy held her fast at Lyng, in spite of the urgent entreaties of friends and the usual medical recommendation of "change." Her friends supposed that her refusal to move was inspired by the belief that her husband would one day return to the spot from which he had vanished, and a beautiful legend grew up about this imaginary state of waiting. But in reality she had no such belief: the depths of anguish inclosing her were no longer lighted by flashes of hope. She was sure that Boyne would never come back, that he had gone out of her sight as completely as if Death itself had waited that day on the threshold. She had even renounced, one by one, the various theories as to his disappearance which had been advanced by the press, the police, and her own agonized imagination. In sheer lassitude her mind turned from these alternatives of horror, and sank back into the blank fact that he was gone.

No, she would never know what had become of him—no one would ever know. But the house knew; the library in which she spent her long, lonely evenings knew. For it was here that the last scene had been enacted, here that the stranger had come, and spoken the word which had caused Boyne to rise and follow him. The floor she trod had felt his tread; the books on the shelves had seen his face; and there were moments when the intense consciousness of the old, dusky walls seemed about to break out into some audible revelation of their secret. But the revelation never came, and she knew it would never come. Lyng was not one of the garrulous old houses that betray the secrets intrusted to them. Its very legend proved that it had always been the mute accomplice, the incorruptible custodian of the mysteries it had surprised. And Mary Boyne, sitting face to face with its portentous silence, felt the futility of seeking to break it by any human means.

V

"I don't say it *wasn't* straight, yet don't say it *was* straight. It was business."

Mary, at the words, lifted her head with a start, and looked intently at the speaker.

When, half an hour before, a card with "Mr Parvis" on it had been brought up to her, she had been immediately aware that the name had been a part of her consciousness ever since she had read it at the head of Boyne's unfinished letter. In the library she had found awaiting her a small neutral-tinted man with a bald head and gold eye-glasses, and it sent a strange tremor through her to know that this was the person to whom her husband's last known thought had been directed.

Parvis, civilly, but without vain preamble,—in the manner of a man who has his watch in his hand, — had set forth the object of his visit. He had "run over" to England on business, and finding himself in the neighborhood of Dorchester, had not wished to leave it without paying his respects to Mrs Boyne; without asking her, if the occasion offered, what she meant to do about Bob Elwell's family.

The words touched the spring of some obscure dread in Mary's bosom. Did her visitor, after all, know what Boyne had meant by his unfinished phrase? She asked for an elucidation of his question, and noticed at once that he seemed surprised at her continued ignorance of the subject. Was it possible that she really knew as little as she said?

"I know nothing—you must tell me," she faltered out; and her visitor thereupon proceeded to unfold his story. It threw, even to her confused perceptions, and imperfectly initiated vision, a lurid glare on the whole hazy episode of the Blue Star Mine. Her husband had made his money in that brilliant speculation at the cost of "getting ahead" of someone less alert to seize the chance; the victim of his ingenuity was young Robert Elwell, who had "put him on" to the Blue Star scheme.

Parvis, at Mary's first startled cry, had thrown her a sobering glance through his impartial glasses.

"Bob Elwell wasn't smart enough, that's all; if he had been, he might have turned round and served Boyne the same way. It's the kind of thing that happens every day in business. I guess it's what the scientists call the survival of the fittest," said Mr Parvis, evidently pleased with the aptness of his analogy.

Mary felt a physical shrinking from the next question she tried to frame; it was as though the words on her lips had a taste that nauseated her.

"But then—you accuse my husband of doing something dishonorable?"

Mr Parvis surveyed the question dispassionately. "Oh, no, I don't. I don't even say it wasn't straight." He glanced up and down the long lines of books, as if one of them might have supplied him with the definition he sought. "I don't say it *wasn't* straight, and yet I don't say it *was* straight. It was business." After all, no definition in his category could be more comprehensive than that.

Mary sat staring at him with a look of terror. He seemed to her like the indifferent, implacable emissary of some dark, formless power.

"But Mr Elwell's lawyers apparently did not take your view, since I suppose the suit was withdrawn by their advice."

"Oh, yes, they knew he hadn't a leg to stand on, technically. It was when they advised him to withdraw the suit that he got desperate. You see, he'd borrowed most of the money he lost in the Blue Star, and he was up a tree. That's why he shot himself when they told him he had no show."

The horror was sweeping over Mary in great, deafening waves.

"He shot himself? He killed himself because of *that*?"

"Well, he didn't kill himself, exactly. He dragged on two months before he died." Parvis emitted the statement as unemotionally as a gramophone grinding out its "record."

"You mean that he tried to kill himself, and failed? And tried again?"

"Oh, he didn't have to *try* again," said Parvis, grimly.

They sat opposite each other in silence, he swinging his eye-glass thoughtfully about his finger, she, motionless, her arms stretched along her knees in an attitude of rigid tension.

"But if you knew all this," she began at length, hardly able to force her voice above a whisper, "how is it that when I wrote you at the time of my husband's disappearance you said you didn't understand his letter?"

Parvis received this without perceptible discomfiture. "Why, I didn't understand it—strictly speaking. And it wasn't the time to talk about it, if I had. The Elwell business was settled when the suit was withdrawn. Nothing I could have told you would have helped you to find your husband."

Mary continued to scrutinize him. "Then why are you telling me now?"

Still Parvis did not hesitate. "Well, to begin with, I supposed you knew more than you appear to—I mean about the circumstances of Elwell's death. And then people are talking of it now; the whole matter's been raked up again. And I thought, if you didn't know, you ought to."

She remained silent, and he continued: "You see, it's only come out lately what a bad state Elwell's affairs were in. His wife's a proud woman, and she fought on as long as she could, going out to work, and taking sewing at home, when she got too sick—something with the heart, I believe. But she had his bedridden mother to look after, and the children, and she broke down under it, and finally had to ask for help. That attracted attention to the case, and the papers took it up, and a subscription was started. Everybody out there liked Bob Elwell, and most of the prominent names in the place are down on the list, and people began to wonder why—"

Parvis broke off to fumble in an inner pocket. "Here," he continued, "here's an account of the whole thing from the *Sentinel*—a little sensational, of course. But I guess you'd better look it over."

He held out a newspaper to Mary, who unfolded it slowly, remembering, as she did so, the evening when, in that same room, the perusal of a clipping from the *Sentinel* had first shaken the depths of her security.

As she opened the paper, her eyes, shrinking from the glaring head-lines, "Widow of Boyne's Victim Forced to Appeal for Aid," ran down the column of text to two portraits inserted in it. The first was her husband's, taken from a photograph made the year they had come to England. It was the picture of him that she liked best, the one that stood on the writing-table upstairs in her bedroom. As the eyes in the photograph met hers, she felt it would be impossible to read what was said of him, and closed her lids with the sharpness of the pain.

"I thought if you felt disposed to put your name down—" she heard Parvis continue.

She opened her eyes with an effort, and they fell on the other portrait. It was that of a youngish man, slightly built, in rough clothes, with features somewhat blurred by the shadow of a projecting hat-brim. Where had she seen that outline before? She stared at it confusedly, her heart hammering in her throat and ears. Then she gave a cry.

"This is the man—the man who came for my husband!"

She heard Parvis start to his feet, and was dimly aware that she had slipped backward into the corner of the sofa, and that he was bending above her in alarm. With an intense effort she straightened herself, and reached out for the paper, which she had dropped.

"It's the man! I should know him anywhere!" she cried in a voice that sounded in her own ears like a scream.

Parvis's voice seemed to come to her from far off, down endless, fog-muffled windings.

"Mrs Boyne, you're not very well. Shall I call somebody? Shall I get a glass of water?"

"No, no, no!" She threw herself toward him, her hand frantically clenching the newspaper. "I tell you, it's the man! I know him! He spoke to me in the garden!"

Parvis took the journal from her, directing his glasses to the portrait. "It can't be, Mrs Boyne. It's Robert Elwell."

"Robert Elwell?" Her white stare seemed to travel into space. "Then it was Robert Elwell who came for him."

"Came for Boyne? The day he went away?" Parvis's voice dropped as hers rose. He bent over, laying a fraternal hand on her, as if to coax her gently back into her seat. "Why, Elwell was dead! Don't you remember?"

Mary sat with her eyes fixed on the picture, unconscious of what he was saying.

"Don't you remember Boyne's unfinished letter to me—the one you found on his desk that day? It was written just after he'd heard of Elwell's death." She noticed an odd shake in Parvis's unemotional voice. "Surely you remember that!" he urged her.

Yes, she remembered: that was the profoundest horror of it. Elwell had died the day before her husband's disappearance; and this was Elwell's portrait; and it was the portrait of the man who had spoken to her in the garden. She lifted her head and looked slowly about the library. The library could have borne witness that it was also the portrait of the man who had come in that day to call Boyne from his unfinished letter. Through the misty surgings of her brain she heard the faint boom of half-forgotten words—words spoken by Alida Stair on the lawn at Pangbourne before Boyne and his wife had ever seen the house at Lyng, or had imagined that they might one day live there.

"This was the man who spoke to me," she repeated.

She looked again at Parvis. He was trying to conceal his disturbance under what he imagined to be an expression of indulgent commiseration; but the edges of his lips were blue. "He thinks me mad; but I'm not mad," she reflected; and suddenly there flashed upon her a way of justifying her strange affirmation.

She sat quiet, controlling the quiver of her lips, and waiting till she could trust her voice to keep its habitual level; then she said, looking straight at Parvis: "Will you answer me one question, please? When was it that Robert Elwell tried to kill himself?"

"When—when?" Parvis stammered.

"Yes; the date. Please try to remember."

She saw that he was growing still more afraid of her. "I have a reason," she insisted gently.

"Yes, yes. Only I can't remember. About two months before, I should say."

"I want the date," she repeated.

Parvis picked up the newspaper. "We might see here," he said, still humoring her. He ran his eyes down the page. "Here it is. Last October—the—"

She caught the words from him. "The 20th, wasn't it?" With a sharp look at her, he verified. "Yes, the 20th. Then you *did* know?"

"I know now." Her white stare continued to travel past him. "Sunday, the 20th—that was the day he came first."

Parvis's voice was almost inaudible. "Came here first?"

"Yes."

"You saw him twice, then?"

"Yes, twice." She breathed it at him with dilated eyes. "He came first on the 20th of October. I remember the date because it was the day we went up Meldon Steep for the first time." She felt a faint gasp of inward laughter at the thought that but for that she might have forgotten.

Parvis continued to scrutinize her, as if trying to intercept her gaze.

"We saw him from the roof," she went on. "He came down the lime-avenue toward the house. He was dressed just as he is in that picture. My husband saw him first. He was frightened, and ran down ahead of me; but there was no one there. He had vanished."

"Elwell had vanished?" Parvis faltered.

"Yes." Their two whispers seemed to grope for each other. "I couldn't think what had happened. I see now. He *tried* to come then; but he wasn't dead enough—he couldn't reach us. He had to wait for two months; and then he came back again—and Ned went with him."

She nodded at Parvis with the look of triumph of a child who has successfully worked out a difficult puzzle. But suddenly she lifted her hands with a desperate gesture, pressing them to her bursting temples.

"Oh, my God! I sent him to Ned—I told him where to go! I sent him to this room!" she screamed out.

She felt the walls of the room rush toward her, like inward falling ruins; and she heard Parvis, a long way off, as if through the ruins, crying to her, and struggling to get at her. But she was numb to his touch, she did not know what he was saying. Through the tumult she heard but one clear note, the voice of Alida Stair, speaking on the lawn at Pangbourne.

"You won't know till afterward," it said. "You won't know till long, long afterward."

Kerfol

Edith Wharton

I

"You ought to buy it," said my host; "it's just the place for a solitary-minded devil like you. And it would be rather worth while to own the most romantic house in Brittany. The present people are dead broke, and it's going for a song—you ought to buy it."

It was not with the least idea of living up to the character my friend Lanrivain ascribed to me (as a matter of fact, under my unsociable exterior I have always had secret yearnings for domesticity) that I took his hint one autumn afternoon and went to Kerfol. My friend was motoring over to Quimper on business: he dropped me on the way, at a cross-road on a heath, and said: "First turn to the right and second to the left. Then straight ahead till you see an avenue. If you meet any peasants, don't ask your way. They don't understand French, and they would pretend they did and mix you up. I'll be back for you here by sunset—and don't forget the tombs in the chapel."

I followed Lanrivain's directions with the hesitation occasioned by the usual difficulty of remembering whether he had said the first turn to the right and second to the left, or the contrary. If I had met a peasant I should certainly have asked, and probably been sent astray; but I had the desert landscape to myself, and so stumbled on the right turn and walked across the heath till I came to an avenue. It was so unlike any other avenue I have ever seen that I instantly knew it must be *the* avenue. The grey-trunked trees sprang up straight to a great height and then interwove their pale-grey branches in a long tunnel through which the autumn light fell faintly. I know most trees by name, but I haven't to this day been able to decide what those trees were. They had the tall curve of elms, the tenuity of poplars, the ashen colour of olives under a rainy sky; and they stretched ahead of me for half a mile or more without a break in their arch. If ever I saw an avenue that unmistakably led to something, it was the avenue at Kerfol. My heart beat a little as I began to walk down it.

Presently the trees ended and I came to a fortified gate in a long wall. Between me and the wall was an open space of grass, with other grey avenues radiating from it. Behind the wall were tall slate roofs mossed with silver, a chapel belfry, the top of a keep. A moat filled with wild shrubs and brambles surrounded the place; the drawbridge had been replaced by a stone arch, and the portcullis by an iron gate. I stood for a long time on the hither side of the moat, gazing about me, and letting the influence of the place sink in. I said to myself: "If I wait long enough, the guardian will turn up and show me the tombs—" and I rather hoped he wouldn't turn up too soon.

I sat down on a stone and lit a cigarette. As soon as I had done it, it struck me as a puerile and portentous thing to do, with that great blind house looking down at me, and all the empty avenues converging on me. It may have been the depth of the silence that made me so conscious of my gesture. The squeak of my match sounded as loud as the scraping of a brake, and I almost fancied I heard it fall when I tossed it onto the grass. But there was more than that: a sense of irrelevance, of littleness, of futile bravado, in sitting there puffing my cigarette-smoke into the face of such a past.

I knew nothing of the history of Kerfol—I was new to Brittany, and Lanrivain had never mentioned the name to me till the day before—but one couldn't as much as glance at that pile without feeling in it a long accumulation of history. What kind of history I was not prepared to guess: perhaps only that sheer weight of many associated lives and deaths which gives a majesty to all old houses. But the aspect of Kerfol suggested something more—a perspective of stern and cruel memories stretching away, like its own grey avenues, into a blur of darkness.

Certainly no house had ever more completely and finally broken with the present. As it stood there, lifting its proud roofs and gables to the sky, it might have been its own funeral monument. "Tombs in the chapel? The whole place is a tomb!" I reflected. I hoped more and more that the guardian would not come. The details of the place, however striking, would seem trivial compared with its collective impressiveness; and I wanted only to sit there and be penetrated by the weight of its silence.

"It's the very place for you!" Lanrivain had said; and I was overcome by the almost blasphemous frivolity of suggesting to any living being that Kerfol was the place for him. "Is it possible that any one could *not* See—?" I wondered. I did not finish the thought: what I meant was undefinable. I stood up and wandered toward the gate. I was beginning to want to know more; not to *see* more—I was by now so sure it was not a question of seeing—but to feel more: feel all the place had to communicate. "But to get in one will have to rout out the keeper," I thought reluctantly, and hesitated. Finally I crossed the bridge and tried the iron gate. It yielded, and I walked through the tunnel formed by the thickness of the *chemin de ronde*. At the farther end, a wooden barricade had been laid across the entrance, and beyond it was a court enclosed in noble architecture. The main building faced me; and I now saw that one half was a mere ruined front, with gaping windows through which the wild growths of the moat and the trees of the park were visible. The rest of the house was still in its robust beauty. One end abutted on the round tower, the other on the small traceried chapel, and in an angle of the building stood a graceful well-head crowned with mossy urns. A few roses grew against the walls, and on an upper window-sill I remember noticing a pot of fuchsias.

My sense of the pressure of the invisible began to yield to my architectural interest. The building was so fine that I felt a desire to explore it for its own sake. I looked about the court, wondering in which corner the guardian lodged. Then I pushed open the barrier and went in. As I did so, a dog barred my way. He was such a remarkably beautiful little dog that for a moment he made me forget the splendid place he was defending. I was not sure of his breed at the time, but have since learned that it was Chinese, and that he was of a rare variety called the "Sleeve-dog." He was very small and golden brown, with large brown eyes and a ruffled throat: he looked like a large tawny chrysanthemum. I said to myself:

"These little beasts always snap and scream, and somebody will be out in a minute."

The little animal stood before me, forbidding, almost menacing: there was anger in his large brown eyes. But he made no sound, he came no nearer. Instead, as I advanced, he gradually fell back, and I noticed that another dog, a vague rough brindled thing, had limped up on a lame leg. "There'll be a hubbub now," I thought; for at the same moment a third dog, a long-haired white mongrel, slipped out of a doorway and joined the others. All three stood looking at me with grave eyes; but not a sound came from them. As I advanced they continued to fall back on muffled paws, still watching me. "At a given point, they'll all charge at my ankles: it's one of the jokes that dogs who live together put up on one," I thought. I was not alarmed, for they were neither large nor formidable. But they let me wander about the court as I pleased, following me at a little distance—always the same distance—and always keeping their eyes on me. Presently I looked across at the ruined facade, and saw that in one of its empty window-frames another dog stood: a white pointer with one brown ear. He was an old grave dog, much more experienced than the others; and he seemed to be observing me with a deeper intentness. "I'll hear from *him,*" I said to myself; but he stood in the window-frame, against the trees of the park, and continued to watch me without moving. I stared back at him for a time, to see if the sense that he was being watched would not rouse him. Half the width of the court lay between us, and we gazed at each other silently across it. But he did not stir, and at last I turned away. Behind me I found the rest of the pack, with a newcomer added: a small black greyhound with pale agate-coloured eyes. He was shivering a little, and his expression was more timid than that of the others. I noticed that he kept a little behind them. And still there was not a sound.

I stood there for fully five minutes, the circle about me—waiting, as they seemed to be waiting. At last I went up to the little golden-brown dog and stooped to pat him. As I did so, I heard myself give a nervous laugh. The little dog did not start, or growl, or take his eyes from me—he simply slipped back about a yard, and then paused and continued to look at me. "Oh, hang it!" I exclaimed, and walked across the court toward the well.

As I advanced, the dogs separated and slid away into different corners of the court. I examined the urns on the well, tried a locked door or two, and looked up and down the dumb façade; then I faced about toward the chapel. When I turned I perceived that all the dogs had disappeared except the old pointer, who still watched me from the window. It was rather a relief to be rid of that cloud of witnesses; and I began to look about me for a way to the back of the house. "Perhaps there'll be somebody in the garden," I thought. I found a way across the moat, scrambled over a wall smothered in brambles, and got into the garden. A few lean hydrangeas and geraniums pined in the flower-beds, and the ancient house looked down on them indifferently. Its garden side was plainer and severer than the other: the long granite front, with its few windows and steep roof, looked like a fortress-prison. I walked around the farther wing, went up some disjointed steps, and entered the deep twilight of a narrow and incredibly old box-walk. The walk was just wide enough for one person to slip through, and its branches met overhead. It was like the ghost of a box-walk, its lustrous green all turning to the shadowy greyness of the avenues. I walked on and on, the branches hitting me in the face and springing back with a dry rattle; and at length I came out on the grassy top of the *chemin de ronde*. I walked along it to the gate-tower, looking down into the court, which was just below me. Not a human being was in sight; and neither were the dogs. I found a flight of steps in the thickness of the wall and went down them; and when I emerged again into the court, there stood the circle of dogs, the golden-brown one a little ahead of the others, the black greyhound shivering in the rear.

"Oh, hang it—you uncomfortable beasts, you!" I exclaimed, my voice startling me with a sudden echo. The dogs stood motionless, watching me. I knew by this time that they would not try to prevent my approaching the house, and the knowledge left me free to examine them. I had a feeling that they must be horribly cowed to be so silent and inert. Yet they did not look hungry or ill-treated. Their coats were smooth and they were not thin, except the shivering greyhound. It was more as if they had lived a long time with people who never spoke to them or looked at them: as though the silence of the place had gradually benumbed their busy inquisitive natures. And this strange passivity, this almost human lassitude, seemed to me sadder than the misery of starved and beaten animals. I should have liked to rouse them for a minute, to coax them into a game or a scamper; but the longer I looked into their fixed and weary eyes the more preposterous the idea became. With the windows of that house looking down on us, how could I have imagined such a thing? The dogs knew better: *they* knew what the house would tolerate and what it would not. I even fancied that they knew what was passing through my mind, and pitied me for my frivolity. But even that feeling probably reached them through a thick fog of listlessness. I had an idea that their distance from me was as nothing to my remoteness from them. The impression they produced was that of having in common one memory so deep and dark that nothing that had happened since was worth either a growl or a wag.

"I say," I broke out abruptly, addressing myself to the dumb circle, "do you know what you look like, the whole lot of you? You look as if you'd seen a ghost—that's how you look! I wonder if there *is* a ghost here, and nobody but you left for it to appear to?" The dogs continued to gaze at me without moving....

†

It was dark when I saw Lanrivain's motor lamps at the cross-roads—and I wasn't exactly sorry to see them. I had the sense of having escaped from the loneliest place in the whole world, and of not liking loneliness—to that degree—as much as I had imagined I should. My friend had brought his solicitor back from Quimper for the night, and seated beside a fat and affable stranger I felt no inclination to talk of Kerfol....

But that evening, when Lanrivain and the solicitor were closeted in the study, Madame de Lanrivain began to question me in the drawing-room.

"Well—are you going to buy Kerfol?" she asked, tilting up her gay chin from her embroidery.

"I haven't decided yet. The fact is, I couldn't get into the house," I said, as if I had simply postponed my decision, and meant to go back for another look.

"You couldn't get in? Why, what happened? The family are mad to sell the place, and the old guardian has orders—"

"Very likely. But the old guardian wasn't there."

"What a pity! He must have gone to market. But his daughter—?"

"There was nobody about. At least I saw no one."

"How extraordinary! Literally nobody?"

"Nobody but a lot of dogs—a whole pack of them—who seemed to have the place to themselves."

Madame de Lanrivain let the embroidery slip to her knee and folded her hands on it. For several minutes she looked at me thoughtfully.

"A pack of dogs—you *saw* them?"

"Saw them? I saw nothing else!"

"How many?" She dropped her voice a little. "I've always wondered—"

I looked at her with surprise: I had supposed the place to be familiar to her. "Have you never been to Kerfol?" I asked.

"Oh, yes: often. But never on that day."

"What day?"

"I'd quite forgotten—and so had Hervé, I'm sure. If we'd remembered, we never should have sent you today—but then, after all, one doesn't half believe that sort of thing, does one?"

"What sort of thing?" I asked, involuntarily sinking my voice to the level of hers. Inwardly I was thinking: "I *knew* there was something...."

Madame de Lanrivain cleared her throat and produced a reassuring smile. "Didn't Hervé tell you the story of Kerfol? An ancestor of his was mixed up in it. You know every Breton house has its ghost-story; and some of them are rather unpleasant."

"Yes—but those dogs?"

"Well, those dogs are the ghosts of Kerfol. At least, the peasants say there's one day in the year when a lot of dogs appear there; and that day the keeper and his daughter go off to Morlaix and get drunk. The women in Brittany drink dreadfully." She stooped to match a silk; then she lifted her charming inquisitive Parisian face. "Did you *really* see a lot of dogs? There isn't one at Kerfol." she said.

II

Lanrivain, the next day, hunted out a shabby calf volume from the back of an upper shelf of his library.

"Yes—here it is. What does it call itself? *A History of the Assizes of the Duchy of Brittany. Quimper, 1702.* The book was written about a hundred years later than the Kerfol affair; but I believe the account is transcribed pretty literally from the judicial records. Anyhow, it's queer reading. And there's a Hervé de Lanrivain mixed up in it—not exactly *my* style, as you'll see. But then he's only a collateral. Here, take the book up to bed with you. I don't exactly remember the details; but after you've read it I'll bet anything you'll leave your light burning all night!"

I left my light burning all night, as he had predicted; but it was chiefly because, till near dawn, I was absorbed in my reading. The account of the trial of Anne de Cornault, wife of the lord of Kerfol, was long and closely printed. It was, as my friend had said, probably an almost literal transcription of what took place in the courtroom; and the trial lasted nearly a month. Besides, the type of the book was very bad…

At first I thought of translating the old record. But it is full of wearisome repetitions, and the main lines of the story are forever straying off into side issues. So I have tried to disentangle it, and give it here in a simpler form. At times, however, I have reverted to the text because no other words could have conveyed so exactly the sense of what I felt at Kerfol; and nowhere have I added anything of my own.

III

It was in the year 16— that Yves de Cornault, lord of the domain of Kerfol, went to the *pardon* of Locronan to perform his religious duties. He was a rich and powerful noble, then in his sixty-second year, but hale and sturdy, a great horseman and hunter and a pious man. So all his neighbours attested. In appearance he was short and broad, with a swarthy face, legs slightly bowed from the saddle, a hanging nose and broad hands with black hairs on them. He had married young and lost his wife and son soon after, and since then had lived alone at Kerfol. Twice a year he went to Morlaix, where he had a handsome house by the river, and spent a week or ten days there; and occasionally he rode to Rennes on business. Witnesses were found to declare that during these absences he led a life different from the one he was known to lead at Kerfol, where he busied himself with his estate, attended mass daily, and found his only amusement in hunting the wild boar and water-fowl. But these rumours are not particularly relevant, and it is certain that among people of his own class in the neighbourhood he passed for a stern and even austere man, observant of his religious obligations, and keeping strictly to himself. There was no talk of any familiarity with the women on his estate, though at that time the nobility were very free with their peasants. Some people said he had never looked at a woman since his wife's death; but such things are hard to prove, and the evidence on this point was not worth much.

Well, in his sixty-second year, Yves de Cornault went to the *pardon* at Locronan, and saw there a young lady of Douarnenez, who had ridden over pillion behind her father to do her duty to the saint. Her name was Anne de Barrigan, and she came of good old Breton stock, but much less great and powerful than that of Yves de Cornault; and her father had squandered his fortune at cards, and lived almost like a peasant in his little granite manor on the moors… I have said I would add nothing of my own to this bald statement of a strange case; but I must interrupt myself here to describe the young lady who rode up to the lych-gate of Locronan at the very moment when the Baron de Cornault was also dismounting there. I take my description from a faded drawing in red crayon, sober and truthful enough to be by a late pupil of the Clouets, which hangs in Lanrivain's study, and is said to be a portrait of Anne de Barrigan. It is unsigned and has no mark of identity but the initials A. B., and the date 16—, the year after her marriage. It represents a young woman with a small oval face, almost pointed, yet wide enough for a full mouth with a tender depression at the corners. The nose is small, and the eyebrows are set rather high, far apart, and as lightly pencilled as the eyebrows in a Chinese painting. The forehead is high and serious, and the hair, which one feels to be fine and thick and fair, is drawn off it and lies close like a cap. The eyes are neither large nor small, hazel probably, with a look at once shy and steady. A pair of beautiful long hands are crossed below the lady's breast…

The chaplain of Kerfol, and other witnesses, averred that when the Baron came back from Locronan he jumped from his horse, ordered another to be instantly saddled, called to a young page to come with him, and rode away that same evening to the south. His steward followed the next morning with coffers laden on a pair of pack mules. The following week Yves de Cornault rode back to Kerfol, sent for his vassals and tenants, and told them he was to be married at All Saints to Anne de Barrigan of Douarnenez. And on All Saints' Day the marriage took place.

As to the next few years, the evidence on both sides seems to show that they passed happily for the couple. No one was found to say that Yves de Cornault had been unkind to his wife, and it was plain to all that he was content with his bargain. Indeed, it was admitted by the chaplain and other witnesses for the prosecution that the young lady had a softening influence on her husband, and that he became less exacting with his tenants, less harsh to peasants and dependents, and less subject to the fits of gloomy silence which had darkened his widowhood. As to his wife, the only grievance her champions could call up in her behalf was that Kerfol was a lonely place, and that when her husband was away on business at Bennes or Morlaix—whither she was never taken—she was not allowed so much as to walk in the park unaccompanied. But no one asserted that she was unhappy, though one servant-woman said she had surprised her crying, and had heard her say that she was a woman accursed to have no child, and nothing in life to call her own. But that was a natural enough feeling in a wife attached to her husband; and certainly it must have been a great grief to Yves de Cornault that she bore no son. Yet he never made her feel her childlessness as a reproach—she admits this in her evidence—but seemed to try to make her forget it by showering gifts and favours on her. Rich though he was, he had never been openhanded; but nothing was too fine for his wife, in the way of silks or gems or linen, or whatever else she fancied. Every wandering merchant was welcome at Kerfol, and when the master was called away he never came back without bringing his wife a handsome present—something curious and particular—from Morlaix or Rennes or Quimper. One of the waiting-women gave, in cross-examination, an interesting list of one year's gifts, which I copy. From Morlaix, a carved ivory junk, with Chinamen at the oars, that a strange sailor had brought back as a votive offering for Notre Dame de la Clarté, above Ploumanac'h; from Quimper, an embroidered gown, worked by the nuns of the Assumption; from Rennes, a silver rose that opened and showed an amber Virgin with a crown of garnets; from Morlaix, again, a length of Damascus velvet shot with gold, bought of a Jew from Syria; and for Michaelmas that same year, from Rennes, a necklet or bracelet of round stones—emeralds and pearls and rubies—strung like beads on a fine gold chain. This was the present that pleased the lady best, the woman said. Later on, as it happened, it was produced at the trial, and appears to have struck the Judges and the public as a curious and valuable jewel.

The very same winter, the Baron absented himself again, this time as far as Bordeaux, and on his return he brought his wife something even odder and prettier than the bracelet. It was a winter evening when he rode up to Kerfol and, walking into the hall, found her sitting by the hearth, her chin on her hand, looking into the fire. He carried a velvet box in his hand and, setting it down, lifted the lid and let out a little golden-brown dog.

Anne de Cornault exclaimed with pleasure as the little creature bounded toward her. "Oh, it looks like a bird or a butterfly!" she cried as she picked it up; and the dog put its paws on her shoulders and looked at her with eyes "like a Christian's." After that she would never have it out of her sight, and petted and talked to it as if it had been a child—as indeed it was the nearest thing to a child she was to know. Yves de Cornault was much pleased with his purchase. The dog had been brought to him by a sailor from an East India merchantman, and the sailor had bought it of a pilgrim in a bazaar at Jaffa, who had stolen it from a nobleman's wife in China: a perfectly permissible thing to do, since the pilgrim was a Christian and the nobleman a heathen doomed to hell-fire.

Yves de Cornault had paid a long price for the dog, for they were beginning to be in demand at the French court, and the sailor knew he had got hold of a good thing; but Anne's pleasure was so great that, to see her laugh and play with the little animal, her husband would doubtless have given twice the sum.

†

So far, all the evidence is at one, and the narrative plain sailing; but now the steering becomes difficult. I will try to keep as nearly as possible to Anne's own statements; though toward the end, poor thing....

Well, to go back. The very year after the little brown dog was brought to Kerfol, Yves de Cornault, one winter night, was found dead at the head of a narrow flight of stairs leading down from his wife's rooms to a door opening on the court. It was his wife who found him and gave the alarm, so distracted, poor wretch, with fear and horror—for his blood was all over her—that at first the roused household could not make out what she was saying, and thought she had suddenly gone mad. But there, sure enough, at the top of the stairs lay her husband, stone dead, and head foremost, the blood from his wounds dripping down to the steps below him. He had been dreadfully scratched and gashed about the face and throat, as if with curious pointed weapons; and one of his legs had a deep tear in it which had cut an artery, and probably caused his death. But how did he come there, and who had murdered him?

His wife declared that she had been asleep in her bed, and hearing his cry had rushed out to find him lying on the stairs; but this was immediately questioned. In the first place, it was proved that from her room she could not have heard the struggle on the stairs, owing to the thickness of the walls and the length of the intervening passage; then it was evident that she had not been in bed and asleep, since she was dressed when she roused the house, and her bed had not been slept in. Moreover, the door at the bottom of the stairs was ajar, and it was noticed by the chaplain (an observant man) that the dress she wore was stained with blood about the knees, and that there were traces of small blood-stained hands low down on the staircase walls, so that it was conjectured that she had really been at the postern-door when her husband fell and, feeling her way up to him in the darkness on her hands and knees, had been stained by his blood dripping down on her. Of course it was argued on the other side that the blood-marks on her dress might have been caused by her kneeling down by her husband when she rushed out of her room; but there was the open door below, and the fact that the finger-marks in the staircase all pointed upward.

The accused held to her statement for the first two days, in spite of its improbability; but on the third day word was brought to her that Hervé de Lanrivain, a young nobleman of the neighbourhood, had been arrested for complicity in the crime. Two or three witnesses thereupon came forward to say that it was known throughout the country that Lanrivain had formerly been on good terms with the lady of Cornault; but that he had been absent from Brittany for over a year, and people had ceased to associate their names. The witnesses who made this statement were not of a very reputable sort. One was an old herb-gatherer suspected of witchcraft, another a drunken clerk from a neighbouring parish, the third a half-witted shepherd who could be made to say anything; and it was clear that the prosecution was not satisfied with its case, and would have liked to find more definite proof of Lanrivain's complicity than the statement of the herb-gatherer, who swore to having seen him climbing the wall of the park on the night of the murder. One way of patching out incomplete proofs in those days was to put some sort of pressure, moral or physical, on the accused person. It is not clear what pressure was put on Anne de Cornault; but on the third day, when she was brought in court, she "appeared weak and wandering," and after being encouraged to collect herself and speak the truth, on her honour and the wounds of her Blessed Redeemer, she confessed that she had in fact gone down the stairs to speak with Hervé de Lanrivain (who denied everything), and had been surprised there by the sound of her husband's fall. That was better; and the prosecution rubbed its hands with satisfaction. The satisfaction increased when various dependents living at Kerfol were induced to say—with apparent sincerity—that during the year or two preceding his death their master had once more grown uncertain and irascible, and subject to the fits of brooding silence which his household had learned to dread before his second marriage. This seemed to show that things had not been going well at Kerfol; though no one could be found to say that there had been any signs of open disagreement between husband and wife.

Anne de Cornault, when questioned as to her reason for going down at night to open the door to Hervé de Lanrivain, made an answer which must have sent a smile around the court. She said it was because she was lonely and wanted to talk with the young man. Was this the only reason? she was asked; and replied: "Yes, by the Cross over your Lordships' heads." "But why at midnight?" the court asked. "Because I could see him in no other way." I can see the exchange of glances across the ermine collars under the Crucifix.

Anne de Cornault, further questioned, said that her married life had been extremely lonely: "desolate" was the word she used. It was true that her husband seldom spoke harshly to her; but there were days when he did not speak at all. It was true that he had never struck or threatened her; but he kept her like a prisoner at Kerfol, and when he rode away to Morlaix or Quimper or Rennes he set so close a watch on her that she could not pick a flower in the garden without having a waiting-woman at her heels. "I am no Queen, to need such honours," she once said to him; and he had answered that a man who has a treasure does not leave the key in the lock when he goes out. "Then take me with you," she urged; but to this he said that towns were pernicious places, and young wives better off at their own firesides.

"But what did you want to say to Hervé de Lanrivain?" the court asked; and she answered: "To ask him to take me away."

"Ah—you confess that you went down to him with adulterous thoughts?"

"Then why did you want him to take you away?"

"Because I was afraid for my life."

"Of whom were you afraid?"

"Of my husband."

"Why were you afraid of your husband?"

"Because he had strangled my little dog."

Another smile must have passed around the courtroom: in days when any nobleman had a right to hang his peasants—and most of them exercised it—pinching a pet animal's wind-pipe was nothing to make a fuss about.

At this point one of the Judges, who appears to have had a certain sympathy for the accused, suggested that she should be allowed to explain herself in her own way; and she thereupon made the following statement.

The first years of her marriage had been lonely; but her husband had not been unkind to her. If she had had a child she would not have been unhappy; but the days were long, and it rained too much.

It was true that her husband, whenever he went away and left her, brought her a handsome present on his return; but this did not make up for the loneliness. At least nothing had, till he brought her the little brown dog from the East: after that she was much less unhappy. Her husband seemed pleased that she was so fond of the dog; he gave her leave to put her jewelled bracelet around its neck, and to keep it always with her.

One day she had fallen asleep in her room, with the dog at her feet, as his habit was. Her feet were bare and resting on his back. Suddenly she was waked by her husband: he stood beside her, smiling not unkindly.

"You look like my great-grandmother, Juliane de Cornault, lying in the chapel with her feet on a little dog," he said.

The analogy sent a chill through her, but she laughed and answered: "Well, when I am dead you must put me beside her, carved in marble, with my dog at my feet."

"Oho—we'll wait and see," he said, laughing also, but with his black brows close together. "The dog is the emblem of fidelity."

"And do you doubt my right to lie with mine at my feet?"

"When I'm in doubt I find out," he answered. "I am an old man," he added, "and people say I make you lead a lonely life. But I swear you shall have your monument if you earn it."

"And I swear to be faithful," she returned, "if only for the sake of having my little dog at my feet."

Not long afterward he went on business to the Quimper Assizes; and while he was away his aunt, the widow of a great nobleman of the duchy, came to spend a night at Kerfol on her way to the *pardon* of Ste. Barbe. She was a woman of piety and consequence, and much respected by Yves de Cornault, and when she proposed to Anne to go with her to Ste. Barbe no one could object, and even the chaplain declared himself in favour of the pilgrimage. So Anne set out for Ste. Barbe, and there for the first time she talked with Hervé de Lanrivain. He had come once or twice to Kerfol with his father, but she had never before exchanged a dozen words with him. They did not talk for more than five minutes now: it was under the chestnuts, as the procession was coming out of the chapel. He said: "I pity you," and she was surprised, for she had not supposed that any one thought her an object of pity. He added: "Call for me when you need me," and she smiled a little, but was glad afterward, and thought often of the meeting.

She confessed to having seen him three times afterward: not more. How or where she would not say—one had the impression that she feared to implicate someone. Their meetings had been rare and brief; and at the last he had told her that he was starting the next day for a foreign country, on a mission which was not without peril and might keep him for many months absent. He asked her for a remembrance, and she had none to give him but the collar about the little dog's neck. She was sorry afterward that she had given it, but he was so unhappy at going that she had not had the courage to refuse.

Her husband was away at the time. When he returned a few days later he picked up the animal to pet it, and noticed that its collar was missing. His wife told him that the dog had lost it in the undergrowth of the park, and that she and her maids had hunted a whole day for it. It was true, she explained to the court, that she had made the maids search for the necklet—they all believed the dog had lost it in the park…

Her husband made no comment, and that evening at supper he was in his usual mood, between good and bad: you could never tell which. He talked a good deal, describing what he had seen and done at Rennes; but now and then he stopped and looked hard at her, and when she went to bed she found her little dog strangled on her pillow. The little thing was dead, but still warm; she stooped to lift it, and her distress turned to horror when she discovered that it had been strangled by twisting twice round its throat the necklet she had given to Lanrivain.

The next morning at dawn she buried the dog in the garden, and hid the necklet in her breast. She said nothing to her husband, then or later, and he said nothing to her; but that day he had a peasant hanged for stealing a faggot in the park, and the next day he nearly beat to death a young horse he was breaking.

Winter set in, and the short days passed, and the long nights, one by one; and she heard nothing of Hervé de Lanrivain. It might be that her husband had killed him; or merely that he had been robbed of the necklet. Day after day by the hearth among the spinning maids, night after night alone on her bed, she wondered and trembled. Sometimes at table her husband looked across at her and smiled; and then she felt sure that Lanrivain was dead. She dared not try to get news of him, for she was sure her husband would find out if she did: she had an idea that he could find out anything. Even when a witchwoman who was a noted seer, and could show you the whole world in her crystal, came to the castle for a night's shelter, and the maids flocked to her, Anne held back.

The winter was long and black and rainy. One day, in Yves de Cornault's absence, some gypsies came to Kerfol with a troop of performing dogs. Anne bought the smallest and cleverest, a white dog with a feathery coat and one blue and one brown eye. It seemed to have been ill-treated by the gypsies, and clung to her plaintively when she took it from them. That evening her husband came back, and when she went to bed she found the dog strangled on her pillow.

After that she said to herself that she would never have another dog; but one bitter cold evening a poor lean greyhound was found whining at the castle-gate, and she took him in and forbade the maids to speak of him to her husband. She hid him in a room that no one went to, smuggled food to him from her own plate, made him a warm bed to lie on and petted him like a child.

Yves de Cornault came home, and the next day she found the greyhound strangled on her pillow. She wept in secret, but said nothing, and resolved that even if she met a dog dying of hunger she would never bring him into the castle; but one day she found a young sheepdog, a brindled puppy with good blue eyes, lying with a broken leg in the snow of the park. Yves de Cornault was at Bennes, and she brought the dog in, warmed and fed it, tied up its leg and hid it in the castle till her husband's return. The day before, she gave it to a peasant woman who lived a long way off, and paid her handsomely to care for it and say nothing; but that night she heard a whining and scratching at her door, and when she opened it the lame puppy, drenched and shivering, jumped up on her with little sobbing barks. She hid him in her bed, and the next morning was about to have him taken back to the peasant woman when she heard her husband ride into the court. She shut the dog in a chest, and went down to receive him. An hour or two later, when she returned to her room, the puppy lay strangled on her pillow…

After that she dared not make a pet of any other dog; and her loneliness became almost unendurable. Sometimes, when she crossed the court of the castle, and thought no one was looking, she stopped to pat the old pointer at the gate. But one day as she was caressing him her husband came out of the chapel; and the next day the old dog was gone…

This curious narrative was not told in one sitting of the court, or received without impatience and incredulous comment. It was plain that the Judges were surprised by its puerility, and that it did not help the accused in the eyes of the public. It was an odd tale, certainly; but what did it prove? That Yves de Cornault disliked dogs, and that his wife, to gratify her own fancy, persistently ignored this dislike. As for pleading this trivial disagreement as an excuse for her relations—whatever their nature—with her supposed accomplice, the argument was so absurd that her own lawyer manifestly regretted having let her make use of it, and tried several times to cut short her story. But she went on to the end, with a kind of hypnotized insistence, as though the scenes she evoked were so real to her that she had forgotten where she was and imagined herself to be reliving them.

At length the Judge who had previously shown a certain kindness to her said (leaning forward a little, one may suppose, from his row of dozing colleagues): "Then you would have us believe that you murdered your husband because he would not let you keep a pet dog?"

"I did not murder my husband."

"Who did, then? Hervé de Lanrivain?"

"No."

"Who then? Can you tell us?"

"Yes, I can tell you. The dogs—" At that point she was carried out of the court in a swoon.

†

It was evident that her lawyer tried to get her to abandon this line of defense. Possibly her explanation, whatever it was, had seemed convincing when she poured it out to him in the heat of their first private colloquy; but now that it was exposed to the cold daylight of judicial scrutiny, and the banter of the town, he was thoroughly ashamed of it, and would have sacrificed her without a scruple to save his professional reputation. But the obstinate Judge—who perhaps, after all, was more inquisitive than kindly—evidently wanted to hear the story out, and she was ordered, the next day, to continue her deposition.

She said that after the disappearance of the old watchdog nothing particular happened for a month or two. Her husband was much as usual: she did not remember any special incident. But one evening a pedlar woman came to the castle and was selling trinkets to the maids. She had no heart for trinkets, but she stood looking on while the women made their choice. And then, she did not know how, but the pedlar coaxed her into buying for herself a pear-shaped pomander with a strong scent in it—she had once seen something of the kind on a gypsy woman. She had no desire for the pomander, and did not know why she had bought it. The pedlar said that whoever wore it had the power to read the future; but she did not really believe that, or care much either. However, she bought the thing and took it up to her room, where she sat turning it about in her hand. Then the strange scent attracted her and she began to wonder what kind of spice was in the box. She opened it and found a grey bean rolled in a strip of paper; and on the paper she saw a sign she knew, and a message from Hervé de Lanrivain, saying that he was at home again and would be at the door in the court that night after the moon had set…

She burned the paper and sat down to think. It was nightfall, and her husband was at home… She had no way of warning Lanrivain, and there was nothing to do but to wait…

At this point I fancy the drowsy courtroom beginning to wake up. Even to the oldest hand on the bench there must have been a certain relish in picturing the feelings of a woman on receiving such a message at nightfall from a man living twenty miles away, to whom she had no means of sending a warning…

She was not a clever woman, I imagine; and as the first result of her cogitation she appears to have made the mistake of being, that evening, too kind to her husband. She could not ply him with wine, according to the traditional expedient, for though he drank heavily at times he had a strong head; and when he drank beyond its strength it was because he chose to, and not because a woman coaxed him. Not his wife, at any rate—she was an old story by now. As I read the case, I fancy there was no feeling for her left in him but the hatred occasioned by his supposed dishonour.

At any rate, she tried to call up her old graces; but early in the evening he complained of pains and fever, and left the hall to go up to the closet where he sometimes slept. His servant carried him a cup of hot wine, and brought back word that he was sleeping and not to be disturbed; and an hour later, when Anne lifted the tapestry and listened at his door, she heard his loud regular breathing. She thought it might be a feint, and stayed a long time barefooted in the passage, her ear to the crack; but the breathing went on too steadily and naturally to be other than that of a man in a sound sleep. She crept back to her room reassured, and stood in the window watching the moon set through the trees of the park. The sky was misty and starless, and after the moon went down the night was black as pitch. She knew the time had come, and stole along the passage, past her husband's door—where she stopped again to listen to his breathing—to the top of the stairs. There she paused a moment, and assured herself that no one was following her; then she began to go down the stairs in the darkness. They were so steep and winding that she had to go very slowly, for fear of stumbling. Her one thought was to get the door unbolted, tell Lanrivain to make his escape, and hasten back to her room. She had tried the bolt earlier in the evening, and managed to put a little grease on it; but nevertheless, when she drew it, it gave a squeak... not loud, but it made her heart stop; and the next minute, overhead, she heard a noise...

"What noise?" the prosecution interposed.

"My husband's voice calling out my name and cursing me."

"What did you hear after that?"

"A terrible scream and a fall."

"Where was Hervé de Lanrivain at this time?"

"He was standing outside in the court. I just made him out in the darkness. I told him for God's sake to go, and then I pushed the door shut."

"What did you do next?"

"I stood at the foot of the stairs and listened."

"What did you hear?"

"I heard dogs snarling and panting." (Visible discouragement of the bench, boredom of the public, and exasperation of the lawyer for the defense. Dogs again—! But the inquisitive Judge insisted.)

"What dogs?"

She bent her head and spoke so low that she had to be told to repeat her answer: "I don't know."

"How do you mean—you don't know?"

"I don't know what dogs..."

The Judge again intervened: "Try to tell us exactly what happened. How long did you remain at the foot of the stairs?"

"Only a few minutes."

"And what was going on meanwhile overhead?"

"The dogs kept on snarling and panting. Once or twice he cried out. I think he moaned once. Then he was quiet."

"Then what happened?"

"Then I heard a sound like the noise of a pack when the wolf is thrown to them—gulping and lapping."

(There was a groan of disgust and repulsion through the court, and another attempted intervention by the distracted lawyer. But the inquisitive Judge was still inquisitive.)

"And all the while you did not go up?"

"Yes—I went up then—to drive them off."

"The dogs?"

"Yes."

"Well—?"

"When I got there it was quite dark. I found my husband's flint and steel and struck a spark. I saw him lying there. He was dead."

"And the dogs?"

"The dogs were gone."

"Gone—where to?"

"I don't know. There was no way out—and there were no dogs at Kerfol."

She straightened herself to her full height, threw her arms above her head, and fell down on the stone floor with a long scream. There was a moment of confusion in the courtroom. Someone on the bench was heard to say: "This is clearly a case for the ecclesiastical authorities"—and the prisoner's lawyer doubtless jumped at the suggestion.

After this, the trial loses itself in a maze of cross-questioning and squabbling. Every witness who was called corroborated Anne de Cornault's statement that there were no dogs at Kerfol: had been none for several months. The master of the house had taken a dislike to dogs, there was no denying it. But, on the other hand, at the inquest, there had been long and bitter discussions as to the nature of the dead man's wounds. One of the surgeons called in had spoken of marks that looked like bites. The suggestion of witchcraft was revived, and the opposing lawyers hurled tomes of necromancy at each other.

At last Anne de Cornault was brought back into court—at the instance of the same Judge—and asked if she knew where the dogs she spoke of could have come from. On the body of her Redeemer she swore that she did not. Then the Judge put his final question: "If the dogs you think you heard had been known to you, do you think you would have recognized them by their barking?"

"Yes."

"Did you recognize them?"

"Yes."

"What dogs do you take them to have been?"

"My dead dogs," she said in a whisper... She was taken out of court, not to reappear there again. There was some kind of ecclesiastical investigation, and the end of the business was that the Judges disagreed with each other, and with the ecclesiastical committee, and that Anne de Cornault was finally handed over to the keeping of her husband's family, who shut her up in the keep of Kerfol, where she is said to have died many years later, a harmless madwoman.

So ends her story. As for that of Hervé de Lanrivain, I had only to apply to his collateral descendant for its subsequent details. The evidence against the young man being insufficient, and his family influence in the duchy considerable, he was set free, and left soon afterward for Paris. He was probably in no mood for a worldly life, and he appears to have come almost immediately under the influence of the famous M. Arnauld d'Andilly and the gentlemen of Port Royal. A year or two later he was received into their Order, and without achieving any particular distinction he followed its good and evil fortunes till his death some twenty years later. Lanrivain showed me a portrait of him by a pupil of Philippe de Champaigne: sad eyes, an impulsive mouth and a narrow brow. Poor Hervé de Lanrivain: it was a grey ending. Yet as I looked at his stiff and sallow effigy, in the dark dress of the Janséniste, I almost found myself envying his fate. After all, in the course of his life two great things had happened to him: he had loved romantically, and he must have talked with Pascal…

The Room in the Tower

Edward Frederic Benson

It is probable that everybody who is at all a constant dreamer has had at least one experience of an event or a sequence of circumstances which have come to his mind in sleep being subsequently realized in the material world. But, in my opinion, so far from this being a strange thing, it would be far odder if this fulfilment did not occasionally happen, since our dreams are, as a rule, concerned with people whom we know and places with which we are familiar, such as might very naturally occur in the awake and daylit world. True, these dreams are often broken into by some absurd and fantastic incident, which puts them out of court in regard to their subsequent fulfilment, but on the mere calculation of chances, it does not appear in the least unlikely that a dream imagined by anyone who dreams constantly should occasionally come true. Not long ago, for instance, I experienced such a fulfilment of a dream which seems to me in no way remarkable and to have no kind of psychical significance. The manner of it was as follows.

A certain friend of mine, living abroad, is amiable enough to write to me about once in a fortnight. Thus, when fourteen days or thereabouts have elapsed since I last heard from him, my mind, probably, either consciously or subconsciously, is expectant of a letter from him. One night last week I dreamed that as I was going upstairs to dress for dinner I heard, as I often heard, the sound of the postman's knock on my front door, and diverted my direction downstairs instead. There, among other correspondence, was a letter from him. Thereafter the fantastic entered, for on opening it I found inside the ace of diamonds, and scribbled across it in his well-known handwriting, 'I am sending you this for safe custody, as you know it is running an unreasonable risk to keep aces in Italy.' The next evening I was just preparing to go upstairs to dress when I heard the postman's knock, and did precisely as I had done in my dream. There, among other letters, was one from my friend. Only it did not contain the ace of diamonds. Had it done so, I should have attached more weight to the matter, which, as it stands, seems to me a perfectly ordinary coincidence. No doubt I consciously or subconsciously expected a letter from him, and this suggested to me my dream. Similarly, the fact that my friend had not written to me for a fortnight suggested to him that he should do so. But occasionally it is not so easy to find such an explanation, and for the following story I can find no explanation at all. It came out of the dark, and into the dark it has gone again.

All my life I have been a habitual dreamer: the nights are few, that is to say, when I do not find on awaking in the morning that some mental experience has been mine, and sometimes, all night long, apparently, a series of the most dazzling adventures befall me. Almost without exception these adventures are pleasant, though often merely trivial. It is of an exception that I am going to speak.

It was when I was about sixteen that a certain dream first came to me, and this is how it befell. It opened with my being set down at the door of a big red-brick house, where, I understood, I was going to stay. The servant who opened the door told me that tea was being served in the garden, and led me through a low dark-panelled hall, with a large open fireplace, on to a cheerful green lawn set round with flower beds. There were grouped about the tea-table a small party of people, but they were all strangers to me except one, who was a schoolfellow called Jack Stone, clearly the son of the house, and he introduced me to his mother and father and a couple of sisters. I was, I remember, somewhat astonished to find myself here, for the boy in question was scarcely known to me, and I rather disliked what I knew of him; moreover, he had left school nearly a year before. The afternoon was very hot, and an intolerable oppression reigned. On the far side of the lawn ran a red-brick wall, with an iron gate in its centre, outside which stood a walnut tree. We sat in the shadow of the house opposite a row of long windows, inside which I could see a table with cloth laid, glimmering with glass and silver. This garden front of the house was very long, and at one end of it stood a tower of three storeys, which looked to me much older than the rest of the building.

Before long, Mrs Stone, who, like the rest of the party, had sat in absolute silence, said to me, 'Jack will show you your room: I have given you the room in the tower.'

Quite inexplicably my heart sank at her words. I felt as if I had known that I should have the room in the tower, and that it contained something dreadful and significant. Jack instantly got up, and I understood that I had to follow him. In silence we passed through the hall, and mounted a great oak staircase with many corners, and arrived at a small landing with two doors set in it. He pushed one of these open for me to enter, and without coming in himself, closed it after me. Then I knew that my conjecture had been right: there was something awful in the room, and with the terror of nightmare growing swiftly and enveloping me, I awoke in a spasm of terror.

Now that dream or variations on it occurred to me intermittently for fifteen years. Most often it came in exactly this form, the arrival, the tea laid out on the lawn, the deadly silence succeeded by that one deadly sentence, the mounting with Jack Stone up to the room in the tower where horror dwelt, and it always came to a close in the nightmare of terror at that which was in the room, though I never saw what it was. At other times I experienced variations on this same theme. Occasionally, for instance, we would be sitting at dinner in the dining-room, into the windows of which I had looked on the first night when the dream of this house visited me, but wherever we were, there was the same silence, the same sense of dreadful oppression and foreboding. And the silence I knew would always be broken by Mrs Stone saying to me, 'Jack will show you your room: I have given you the room in the tower.' Upon which (this was invariable) I had to follow him up the oak staircase with many corners, and enter the place that I dreaded more and more each time that I visited it in sleep. Or, again, I would find myself playing cards still in silence in a drawing-room lit with immense chandeliers, that gave a blinding illumination. What the game was I have no idea; what I remember, with a sense of miserable anticipation, was that soon Mrs Stone would get up and say to me, 'Jack will show you your room: I have given you the room in the tower.' This drawing room where we played cards was next to the dining room, and, as I have said, was always brilliantly illuminated, whereas the rest of the house was full of dusk and shadows. And yet, how often, in spite of those bouquets of lights, have I not pored over the cards that were dealt me, scarcely able for some reason to see them. Their designs, too, were strange: there were no red suits, but all were black, and among them there were certain cards which were black all over. I hated and dreaded those.

As this dream continued to recur, I got to know the greater part of the house. There was a smoking room beyond the drawing room, at the end of a passage with a green baize door. It was always very dark there, and as often as I went there I passed somebody whom I could not see in the doorway coming out. Curious developments, too, took place in the characters that peopled the dream as might happen to living persons. Mrs Stone, for instance, who, when I first saw her, had been black-haired, became grey, and instead of rising briskly, as she had done at first when she said, 'Jack will show you your room: I have given you the room in the tower,' got up very feebly, as if the strength was leaving her limbs. Jack also grew up, and became a rather ill-looking young man, with a brown moustache, while one of the sisters ceased to appear, and I understood she was married.

Then it so happened that I was not visited by this dream for six months or more, and I began to hope, in such inexplicable dread did I hold it, that it had passed away for good. But one night after this interval I again found myself being shown out onto the lawn for tea, and Mrs Stone was not there, while the others were all dressed in black. At once I guessed the reason, and my heart leaped at the thought that perhaps this time I should not have to sleep in the room in the tower, and though we usually all sat in silence, on this occasion the sense of relief made me talk and laugh as I had never yet done. But even then matters were not altogether comfortable, for no one else spoke, but they all looked secretly at each other. And soon the foolish stream of my talk ran dry, and gradually an apprehension worse than anything I had previously known gained on me as the light slowly faded.

Suddenly a voice which I knew well broke the stillness, the voice of Mrs Stone, saying, 'Jack will show you your room: I have given you the room in the tower.' It seemed to come from near the gate in the red-brick wall that bounded the lawn, and looking up, I saw that the grass outside was sown thick with gravestones. A curious greyish light shone from them, and I could read the lettering on the grave nearest me, and it was, 'In evil memory of Julia Stone.' And as usual Jack got up, and again I followed him through the hall and up the staircase with many corners. On this occasion it was darker than usual, and when I passed into the room in the tower I could only just see the furniture, the position of which was already familiar to me. Also there was a dreadful odour of decay in the room, and I woke screaming.

The dream, with such variations and developments as I have mentioned, went on at intervals for fifteen years. Sometimes I would dream it two or three nights in succession; once, as I have said, there was an intermission of six months, but taking a reasonable average, I should say that I dreamed it quite as often as once in a month. It had, as is plain, something of nightmare about it, since it always ended in the same appalling terror, which so far from getting less, seemed to me to gather fresh fear every time that I experienced it. There was, too, a strange and dreadful consistency about it. The characters in it, as I have mentioned, got regularly older, death and marriage visited this silent family, and I never in the dream, after Mrs Stone had died, set eyes on her again. But it was always her voice that told me that the room in the tower was prepared for me, and whether we had tea out on the lawn, or the scene was laid in one of the rooms overlooking it, I could always see her gravestone standing just outside the iron gate. It was the same, too, with the married daughter; usually she was not present, but once or twice she returned again, in company with a man, whom I took to be her husband. He, too, like the rest of them, was always silent. But, owing to the constant repetition of the dream, I had ceased to attach, in my waking hours, any significance to it. I never met Jack Stone again during all those years, nor did I ever see a house that resembled this dark house of my dream. And then something happened.

I had been in London in this year, up till the end of the July, and during the first week in August went down to stay with a friend in a house he had taken for the summer months, in the Ashdown Forest district of Sussex. I left London early, for John Clinton was to meet me at Forest Row Station, and we were going to spend the day golfing, and go to his house in the evening. He had his motor with him, and we set off, about five of the afternoon, after a thoroughly delightful day, for the drive, the distance being some ten miles. As it was still so early we did not have tea at the club house, but waited till we should get home. As we drove, the weather, which up till then had been, though hot, deliciously fresh, seemed to me to alter in quality, and become very stagnant and oppressive, and I felt that indefinable sense of ominous apprehension that I am accustomed to before thunder. John, however, did not share my views, attributing my loss of lightness to the fact that I had lost both my matches. Events proved, however, that I was right, though I do not think that the thunderstorm that broke that night was the sole cause of my depression.

Our way lay through deep high-banked lanes, and before we had gone very far I fell asleep, and was only awakened by the stopping of the motor. And with a sudden thrill, partly of fear but chiefly of curiosity, I found myself standing in the doorway of my house of dream. We went, I half wondering whether or not I was dreaming still, through a low oak-panelled hall, and out onto the lawn, where tea was laid in the shadow of the house. It was set in flower beds, a red-brick wall, with a gate in it, bounded one side, and out beyond that was a space of rough grass with a walnut tree. The facade of the house was very long, and at one end stood a three-storeyed tower, markedly older than the rest.

Here for the moment all resemblance to the repeated dream ceased. There was no silent and somehow terrible family, but a large assembly of exceedingly cheerful persons, all of whom were known to me. And in spite of the horror with which the dream itself had always filled me, I felt nothing of it now that the scene of it was thus reproduced before me. But I felt intensest curiosity as to what was going to happen.

Tea pursued its cheerful course, and before long Mrs Clinton got up. And at that moment I think I knew what she was going to say. She spoke to me, and what she said was:

'Jack will show you your room: I have given you the room in the tower.'

At that, for half a second, the horror of the dream took hold of me again. But it quickly passed, and again I felt nothing more than the most intense curiosity. It was not very long before it was amply satisfied.

John turned to me.

'Right up at the top of the house,' he said, 'but I think you'll be comfortable. We're absolutely full up. Would you like to go and see it now? By Jove, I believe that you are right, and that we are going to have a thunderstorm. How dark it has become.'

I got up and followed him. We passed through the hall, and up the perfectly familiar staircase. Then he opened the door, and I went in. And at that moment sheer unreasoning terror again possessed me. I did not know what I feared: I simply feared. Then like a sudden recollection, when one remembers a name which has long escaped the memory,

I knew what I feared. I feared Mrs Stone, whose grave with the sinister inscription, 'In evil memory,' I had so often seen in my dream, just beyond the lawn which lay below my window. And then once more the fear passed so completely that I wondered what there was to fear, and I found myself, sober and quiet and sane, in the room in the tower, the name of which I had so often heard in my dream, and the scene of which was so familiar.

I looked around it with a certain sense of proprietorship, and found that nothing had been changed from the dreaming nights in which I knew it so well. Just to the left of the door was the bed, lengthways along the wall, with the head of it in the angle. In a line with it was the fireplace and a small bookcase; opposite the door the outer wall was pierced by two lattice-paned windows, between which stood the dressing-table, while ranged along the fourth wall was the washing-stand and a big cupboard. My luggage had already been unpacked, for the furniture of dressing and undressing lay orderly on the wash-stand and toilet-table, while my dinner clothes were spread out on the coverlet of the bed. And then, with a sudden start of unexplained dismay, I saw that there were two rather conspicuous objects which I had not seen before in my dreams: one a life-sized oil painting of Mrs Stone, the other a black-and-white sketch of Jack Stone, representing him as he had appeared to me only a week before in the last of the series of these repeated dreams, a rather secret and evil-looking man of about thirty. His picture hung between the windows, looking straight across the room to the other portrait, which hung at the side of the bed. At that I looked next, and as I looked I felt once more the horror of nightmare seize me.

It represented Mrs Stone as I had seen her last in my dreams: old and withered and white-haired. But in spite of the evident feebleness of body, a dreadful exuberance and vitality shone through the envelope of flesh, an exuberance wholly malign, a vitality that foamed and frothed with unimaginable evil. Evil beamed from the narrow, leering eyes; it laughed in the demon-like mouth. The whole face was instinct with some secret and appalling mirth; the hands, clasped together on the knee, seemed shaking with suppressed and nameless glee. Then I saw also that it was signed in the left-hand bottom corner, and wondering who the artist could be, I looked more closely, and read the inscription, 'Julia Stone by Julia Stone.'

There came a tap at the door, and John Clinton entered.

'Got everything you want?' he asked.

'Rather more than I want,' said I, pointing to the picture.

He laughed.

'Hard-featured old lady,' he said. 'By herself, too, I remember. Anyhow she can't have flattered herself much.'

'But don't you see?' said I. 'It's scarcely a human face at all. It's the face of some witch, of some devil.'

He looked at it more closely.

'Yes; it isn't very pleasant,' he said. 'Scarcely a bedside manner, eh? Yes; I can imagine getting the nightmare if I went to sleep with that close by my bed. I'll have it taken down if you like.'

'I really wish you would,' I said. He rang the bell, and with the help of a servant we detached the picture and carried it out onto the landing, and put it with its face to the wall.

'By Jove, the old lady is a weight,' said John, mopping his forehead. 'I wonder if she had something on her mind.'

The extraordinary weight of the picture had struck me too. I was about to reply, when I caught sight of my own hand. There was blood on it, in considerable quantities, covering the whole palm.

'I've cut myself somehow,' said I.

John gave a little startled exclamation.

'Why, I have too,' he said.

Simultaneously the footman took out his handkerchief and wiped his hand with it. I saw that there was blood also on his handkerchief.

John and I went back into the tower room and washed the blood off; but neither on his hand nor on mine was there the slightest trace of a scratch or cut. It seemed to me that, having ascertained this, we both, by a sort of tacit consent, did not allude to it again. Something in my case had dimly occurred to me that I did not wish to think about. It was but a conjecture, but I fancied that I knew the same thing had occurred to him.

The heat and oppression of the air, for the storm we had expected was still undischarged, increased very much after dinner, and for some time most of the party, among whom were John Clinton and myself, sat outside on the path bounding the lawn, where we had had tea. The night was absolutely dark, and no twinkle of star or moon ray could penetrate the pall of cloud that overset the sky. By degrees our assembly thinned, the women went up to bed, men dispersed to the smoking or billiard room, and by eleven o'clock my host and I were the only two left. All the evening I thought that he had something on his mind, and as soon as we were alone he spoke.

'The man who helped us with the picture had blood on his hand, too, did you notice?' he said.

'I asked him just now if he had cut himself, and he said he supposed he had, but that he could find no mark of it. Now where did that blood come from?'

By dint of telling myself that I was not going to think about it, I had succeeded in not doing so, and I did not want, especially just at bedtime, to be reminded of it.

'I don't know,' said I, 'and I don't really care so long as the picture of Mrs Stone is not by my bed.'

He got up.

'But it's odd,' he said. 'Ha! Now you'll see another odd thing.'

A dog of his, an Irish terrier by breed, had come out of the house as we talked. The door behind us into the hall was open, and a bright oblong of light shone across the lawn to the iron gate which led on to the rough grass outside, where the walnut tree stood. I saw that the dog had all his hackles up, bristling with rage and fright; his lips were curled back from his teeth, as if he was ready to spring at something, and he was growling to himself. He took not the slightest notice of his master or me, but stiffly and tensely walked across the grass to the iron gate. There he stood for a moment, looking through the bars and still growling. Then of a sudden his courage seemed to desert him: he gave one long howl, and scuttled back to the house with a curious crouching sort of movement.

'He does that half-a-dozen times a day,' said John. 'He sees something which he both hates and fears.'

I walked to the gate and looked over it. Something was moving on the grass outside, and soon a sound which I could not instantly identify came to my ears. Then I remembered what it was: it was the purring of a cat. I lit a match, and saw the purrer, a big blue Persian, walking round and round in a little circle just outside the gate, stepping high and ecstatically, with tail carried aloft like a banner. Its eyes were bright and shining, and every now and then it put its head down and sniffed at the grass.

I laughed.

'The end of that mystery, I am afraid,' I said. 'Here's a large cat having Walpurgis night all alone.'

'Yes, that's Darius,' said John. 'He spends half the day and all night there. But that's not the end of the dog mystery, for Toby and he are the best of friends, but the beginning of the cat mystery. What's the cat doing there? And why is Darius pleased, while Toby is terror-stricken?'

At that moment I remembered the rather horrible detail of my dreams when I saw through the gate, just where the cat was now, the white tombstone with the sinister inscription. But before I could answer the rain began, as suddenly and heavily as if a tap had been turned on, and simultaneously the big cat squeezed through the bars of the gate, and came leaping across the lawn to the house for shelter. Then it sat in the doorway, looking out eagerly into the dark. It spat and struck at John with its paw, as he pushed it in, in order to close the door.

Somehow, with the portrait of Julia Stone in the passage outside, the room in the tower had absolutely no alarm for me, and as I went to bed, feeling very sleepy and heavy, I had nothing more than interest for the curious incident about our bleeding hands, and the conduct of the cat and dog. The last thing I looked at before I put out my light was the square empty space by my bed where the portrait had been. Here the paper was of its original full tint of dark red: over the rest of the walls it had faded. Then I blew out my candle and instantly fell asleep.

My awaking was equally instantaneous, and I sat bolt upright in bed under the impression that some bright light had been flashed in my face, though it was now absolutely pitch dark. I knew exactly where I was, in the room which I had dreaded in dreams, but no horror that I ever felt when asleep approached the fear that now invaded and froze my brain. Immediately after a peal of thunder crackled just above the house, but the probability that it was only a flash of lightning which awoke me gave no reassurance to my galloping heart. Something I knew was in the room with me, and instinctively I put out my right hand, which was nearest the wall, to keep it away. And my hand touched the edge of a picture-frame hanging close to me.

I sprang out of bed, upsetting the small table that stood by it, and I heard my watch, candle, and matches clatter onto the floor. But for the moment there was no need of light, for a blinding flash leaped out of the clouds, and showed me that by my bed again hung the picture of Mrs Stone. And instantly the room went into blackness again. But in that flash I saw another thing also, namely a figure that leaned over the end of my bed, watching me. It was dressed in some close-clinging white garment, spotted and stained with mould, and the face was that of the portrait.

Overhead the thunder cracked and roared, and when it ceased and the deathly stillness succeeded, I heard the rustle of movement coming nearer me, and, more horrible yet, perceived an odour of corruption and decay. And then a hand was laid on the side of my neck, and close beside my ear I heard quick-taken, eager breathing. Yet I knew that this thing, though it could be perceived by touch, by smell, by eye and by ear, was still not of this earth, but something that had passed out of the body and had power to make itself manifest. Then a voice, already familiar to me, spoke.

'I knew you would come to the room in the tower,' it said. 'I have been long waiting for you. At last you have come. Tonight I shall feast; before long we will feast together.'

And the quick breathing came closer to me; I could feel it on my neck.

At that the terror, which I think had paralysed me for the moment, gave way to the wild instinct of self-preservation. I hit wildly with both arms, kicking out at the same moment, and heard a little animal-squeal, and something soft dropped with a thud beside me. I took a couple of steps forward, nearly tripping up over whatever it was that lay there, and by the merest good-luck found the handle of the door. In another second I ran out on the landing, and had banged the door behind me. Almost at the same moment I heard a door open somewhere below, and John Clinton, candle in hand, came running upstairs.

'What is it?' he said. 'I sleep just below you, and heard a noise as if – Good heavens, there's blood on your shoulder.'

I stood there, so he told me afterwards, swaying from side to side, white as a sheet, with the mark on my shoulder as if a hand covered with blood had been laid there.

'It's in there,' I said, pointing. 'She, you know. The portrait is in there, too, hanging up on the place we took it from.'

At that he laughed.

'My dear fellow, this is mere nightmare,' he said.

He pushed by me, and opened the door, I standing there simply inert with terror, unable to stop him, unable to move.

'Phew! What an awful smell,' he said.

Then there was silence; he had passed out of my sight behind the open door. Next moment he came out again, as white as myself, and instantly shut it.

'Yes, the portrait's there,' he said, 'and on the floor is a thing – a thing spotted with earth, like what they bury people in. Come away, quick, come away.'

How I got downstairs I hardly know. An awful shuddering and nausea of the spirit rather than of the flesh had seized me, and more than once he had to place my feet upon the steps, while every now and then he cast glances of terror and apprehension up the stairs. But in time we came to his dressing-room on the floor below, and there I told him what I have here described.

The sequel can be made short; indeed, some of my readers have perhaps already guessed what it was, if they remember that inexplicable affair of the churchyard at West Fawley, some eight years ago, where an attempt was made three times to bury the body of a certain woman who had committed suicide. On each occasion the coffin was found in the course of a few days again protruding from the ground. After the third attempt, in order that the thing should not be talked about, the body was buried elsewhere in unconsecrated ground. Where it was buried was just outside the iron gate of the garden belonging to the house where this woman had lived.

She had committed suicide in a room at the top of the tower in that house. Her name was Julia Stone.

Subsequently the body was again secretly dug up, and the coffin was found to be full of blood.

The Man Who Went Too Far

Edward Frederic Benson

The little village of St Faith's nestles in a hollow of wooded hill up on the north bank of the river Fawn in the county of Hampshire, huddling close round its grey Norman church as if for spiritual protection against the fays and fairies, the trolls and 'little people', who might be supposed still to linger in the vast empty spaces of the New Forest, and to come after dusk and do their doubtful businesses. Once outside the hamlet you may walk in any direction (so long as you avoid the high road which leads to Brockenhurst) for the length of a summer afternoon without seeing sign of human habitation, or possibly even catching sight of another human being. Shaggy wild ponies may stop their feeding for a moment as you pass, the white scuts of rabbits will vanish into their burrows, a brown viper perhaps will glide from your path into a clump of heather, and unseen birds will chuckle in the bushes, but it may easily happen that for a long day you will see nothing human. But you will not feel in the least lonely; in summer, at any rate, the sunlight will be gay with butterflies, and the air thick with all those woodland sounds which like instruments in an orchestra combine to play the great symphony of the yearly festival of June. Winds whisper in the birches, and sigh among the firs; bees are busy with their redolent labour among the heather, a myriad birds chirp in the green temples of the forest trees, and the voice of the river prattling over stony places, bubbling into pools, chuckling and gulping round corners, gives you the sense that many presences and companions are near at hand.

Yet, oddly enough, though one would have thought that these benign and cheerful influences of wholesome air and spaciousness of forest were very healthful comrades for a man, in so far as nature can really influence this wonderful human genus which has in these centuries learned to defy her most violent storms in its well-established houses, to bridle her torrents and make them light its streets, to tunnel her mountains and plow her seas, the inhabitants of St Faith's will not willingly venture into the forest after dark. For in spite of the silence and loneliness of the hooded night it seems that a man is not sure in what company he may suddenly find himself, and though it is difficult to get from these villagers any very clear story of occult appearances, the feeling is widespread. One story indeed I have heard with some definiteness, the tale of a monstrous goat that has been seen to skip with hellish glee about the woods and shady places, and this perhaps is connected with the story which I have here attempted to piece together. It too is well-known to them; for all remember the young artist who died here not long ago, a young man, or so he struck the beholder, of great personal beauty, with something about him that made men's faces to smile and brighten when they looked on him. His ghost they will tell you 'walks' constantly by the stream and through the woods which he loved so, and in especial it haunts a certain house, the last of the village, where he lived, and its garden in which he was done to death. For my part I am inclined to think that the terror of the Forest dates chiefly from that day. So, such as the story is, I have set it forth in connected form. It is based partly on the accounts of the villagers, but mainly on that of Darcy, a friend of mine and a friend of the man with whom these events were chiefly concerned.

†

The day had been one of untarnished midsummer splendour, and as the sun drew near to its setting, the glory of the evening grew every moment more crystalline, more miraculous. Westward from St Faith's the beechwood which stretched for some miles toward the heathery upland beyond already cast its veil of clear shadow over the red roofs of the village, but the spire of the grey church, over-topping all, still pointed a flaming orange finger into the sky. The river Fawn, which runs below, lay in sheets of sky-reflected blue, and wound its dreamy devious course round the edge of this wood, where a rough two-planked bridge crossed from the bottom of the garden of the last house in the village, and communicated by means of a little wicker gate with the wood itself. Then once out of the shadow of the wood the stream lay in flaming pools of the molten crimson of the sunset, and lost itself in the haze of woodland distances.

This house at the end of the village stood outside the shadow, and the lawn which sloped down to the river was still flecked with sunlight. Garden-beds of dazzling colour lined its gravel walks, and down the middle of it ran a brick pergola, half-hidden in clusters of rambler-rose and purple with starry clematis. At the bottom end of it, between two of its pillars, was slung a hammock containing a shirt-sleeved figure.

The house itself lay somewhat remote from the rest of the village, and a footpath leading across two fields, now tall and fragrant with hay, was its only communication with the high road. It was low-built, only two stories in height, and like the garden, its walls were a mass of flowering roses. A narrow stone terrace ran along the garden front, over which was stretched an awning, and on the terrace a young silent-footed man-servant was busied with the laying of the table for dinner. He was neat-handed and quick with his job, and having finished it he went back into the house, and reappeared again with a large rough bath-towel on his arm. With this he went to the hammock in the pergola.

'Nearly eight, sir,' he said.

'Has Mr Darcy come yet?' asked a voice from the hammock.

'No, sir.'

'If I'm not back when he comes, tell him that I'm just having a bathe before dinner.'

The servant went back to the house, and after a moment or two Frank Halton struggled to a sitting posture, and slipped out on to the grass. He was of medium height and rather slender in build, but the supple ease and grace of his movements gave the impression of great physical strength: even his descent from the hammock was not an awkward performance. His face and hands were of very dark complexion, either from constant exposure to wind and sun, or, as his black hair and dark eyes tended to show, from some strain of southern blood. His head was small, his face of an exquisite beauty of modelling, while the smoothness of its contour would have led you to believe that he was a beardless lad still in his teens. But something, some look which living and experience alone can give, seemed to contradict that, and finding yourself completely puzzled as to his age, you would next moment probably cease to think about that, and only look at this glorious specimen of young manhood with wondering satisfaction.

He was dressed as became the season and the heat, and wore only a shirt open at the neck, and a pair of flannel trousers. His head, covered very thickly with a somewhat rebellious crop of short curly hair, was bare as he strolled across the lawn to the bathing-place that lay below. Then for a moment there was silence, then the sound of splashed and divided waters, and presently after, a great shout of ecstatic joy, as he swam up-stream with the foamed water standing in a frill round his neck. Then after some five minutes of limb-stretching struggle with the flood, he turned over on his back, and with arms thrown wide, floated down-stream, ripple-cradled and inert. His eyes were shut, and between half-parted lips he talked gently to himself.

'I am one with it,' he said to himself, 'the river and I, I and the river. The coolness and splash of it is I, and the water-herbs that wave in it are I also. And my strength and my limbs are not mine but the river's. It is all one, all one, dear Fawn.'

†

A quarter of an hour later he appeared again at the bottom of the lawn, dressed as before, his wet hair already drying into its crisp short curls again. There he paused a moment, looking back at the stream with the smile with which men look on the face of a friend, then turned towards the house. Simultaneously his servant came to the door leading on to the terrace, followed by a man who appeared to be some halfway through the fourth decade of his years. Frank and he saw each other across the bushes and garden-beds, and each quickening his step, they met suddenly face to face round an angle of the garden walk, in the fragrance of syringa.

'My dear Darcy,' cried Frank, 'I am charmed to see you.'

But the other stared at him in amazement.

'Frank!' he exclaimed.

'Yes, that is my name,' he said laughing, 'what is the matter?'

Darcy took his hand.

'What have you done to yourself?' he asked. 'You are a boy again.'

'Ah, I have a lot to tell you,' said Frank. 'Lots that you will hardly believe, but I shall convince you—'

He broke off suddenly, and held up his hand.

'Hush, there is my nightingale,' he said.

The smile of recognition and welcome with which he had greeted his friend faded from his face, and a look of rapt wonder took its place, as of a lover listening to the voice of his beloved. His mouth parted slightly, showing the white line of teeth, and his eyes looked out and out till they seemed to Darcy to be focused on things beyond the vision of man. Then something perhaps startled the bird, for the song ceased.

'Yes, lots to tell you,' he said. 'Really I am delighted to see you. But you look rather white and pulled down; no wonder after that fever. And there is to be no nonsense about this visit. It is June now, you stop here till you are fit to begin work again. Two months at least.'

'Ah, I can't trespass quite to that extent.'

Frank took his arm and walked him down the grass.

'Trespass? Who talks of trespass? I shall tell you quite openly when I am tired of you, but you know when we had the studio together, we used not to bore each other. However, it is ill talking of going away on the moment of your arrival. Just a stroll to the river, and then it will be dinner-time.'

Darcy took out his cigarette case, and offered it to the other.

Frank laughed.

'No, not for me. Dear me, I suppose I used to smoke once. How very odd!'

'Given it up?'

'I don't know. I suppose I must have. Anyhow I don't do it now. I would as soon think of eating meat.'

'Another victim on the smoking altar of vegetarianism?'

'Victim?' asked Frank. 'Do I strike you as such?'

He paused on the margin of the stream and whistled softly. Next moment a moor-hen made its splashing flight across the river, and ran up the bank. Frank took it very gently in his hands and stroked its head, as the creature lay against his shirt.

'And is the house among the reeds still secure?' he half-crooned to it. 'And is the missus quite well, and are the neighbours flourishing? There, dear, home with you,' and he flung it into the air.

'That bird's very tame,' said Darcy, slightly bewildered.

'It is rather,' said Frank, following its flight.

†

During dinner Frank chiefly occupied himself in bringing himself up-to-date in the movements and achievements of this old friend whom he had not seen for six years. Those six years, it now appeared, had been full of incident and success for Darcy; he had made a name for himself as a portrait painter which bade fair to outlast the vogue of a couple of seasons, and his leisure time had been brief. Then some four months previously he had been through a severe attack of typhoid, the result of which as concerns this story was that he had come down to this sequestered place to recruit.

'Yes, you've got on,' said Frank at the end. 'I always knew you would. A.R.A. with more in prospect. Money? You roll in it, I suppose, and, O Darcy, how much happiness have you had all these years? That is the only imperishable possession. And how much have you learned? Oh, I don't mean in Art. Even I could have done well in that.'

Darcy laughed.

'Done well? My dear fellow, all I have learned in these six years you knew, so to speak, in your cradle. Your old pictures fetch huge prices. Do you never paint now?'

Frank shook his head.

'No, I'm too busy,' he said.

'Doing what? Please tell me. That is what every one is for ever asking me.'

'Doing? I suppose you would say I do nothing.'

Darcy glanced up at the brilliant young face opposite him.

'It seems to suit you, that way of being busy,' he said. 'Now, it's your turn. Do you read? Do you study? I remember you saying that it would do us all – all us artists, I mean – a great deal of good if we would study any one human face carefully for a year, without recording a line. Have you been doing that?'

Frank shook his head again.

'I mean exactly what I say,' he said, 'I have been *doing* nothing. And I have never been so occupied. Look at me; have I not done something to myself to begin with?'

'You are two years younger than I,' said Darcy, 'at least you used to be. You therefore are thirty-five. But had I never seen you before I should say you were just twenty. But was it worth while to spend six years of greatly-occupied life in order to look twenty? Seems rather like a woman of fashion.'

Frank laughed boisterously.

'First time I've ever been compared to that particular bird of prey,' he said. 'No, that has not been my occupation – in fact I am only very rarely conscious that one effect of my occupation has been that. Of course, it must have been if one comes to think of it. It is not very important. Quite true my body has become young. But that is very little; I have become young.'

Darcy pushed back his chair and sat sideways to the table looking at the other.

'Has that been your occupation then?' he asked.

'Yes, that anyhow is one aspect of it. Think what youth means! It is the capacity for growth, mind, body, spirit, all grow, all get stronger, all have a fuller, firmer life every day. That is something, considering that every day that passes after the ordinary man reaches the full-blown flower of his strength, weakens his hold on life. A man reaches his prime, and remains, we say, in his prime, for ten years, or perhaps twenty. But after his primest prime is reached, he slowly, insensibly weakens. These are the signs of age in you, in your body, in your art probably, in your mind. You are less electric than you were. But I, when I reach my prime – I am nearing it – ah, you shall see.'

The stars had begun to appear in the blue velvet of the sky, and to the east the horizon seen above the black silhouette of the village was growing dove-coloured with the approach of moon-rise. White moths hovered dimly over the garden-beds, and the footsteps of night tip-toed through the bushes. Suddenly Frank rose.

'Ah, it is the supreme moment,' he said softly. 'Now more than at any other time the current of life, the eternal imperishable current runs so close to me that I am almost enveloped in it. Be silent a minute.'

He advanced to the edge of the terrace and looked out standing stretched with arms outspread. Darcy heard him draw a long breath into his lungs, and after many seconds expel it again. Six or eight times he did this, then turned back into the lamplight.

'It will sound to you quite mad, I expect,' he said, 'but if you want to hear the soberest truth I have ever spoken and shall ever speak, I will tell you about myself. But come into the garden if it is not too damp for you. I have never told anyone yet, but I shall like to tell you. It is long, in fact, since I have even tried to classify what I have learned.'

They wandered into the fragrant dimness of the pergola, and sat down. Then Frank began:

'Years ago, do you remember,' he said, 'we used often to talk about the decay of joy in the world. Many impulses, we settled, had contributed to this decay, some of which were good in themselves, others that were quite completely bad. Among the good things, I put what we may call certain Christian virtues, renunciation, resignation, sympathy with suffering, and the desire to relieve sufferers. But out of those things spring very bad ones, useless renunciations, asceticism for its own sake, mortification of the flesh with nothing to follow, no corresponding gain that is, and that awful and terrible disease which devastated England some centuries ago, and from which by heredity of spirit we suffer now, Puritanism. That was a dreadful plague, the brutes held and taught that joy and laughter and merriment were evil: it was a doctrine the most profane and wicked. Why, what is the commonest crime one sees? A sullen face. That is the truth of the matter.

'Now all my life I have believed that we are intended to be happy, that joy is of all gifts the most divine. And when I left London, abandoned my career, such as it was, I did so because I intended to devote my life to the cultivation of joy, and, by continuous and unsparing effort, to be happy. Among people, and in constant intercourse with others, I did not find it possible; there were too many distractions in towns and work-rooms, and also too much suffering. So I took one step backwards or forwards, as you may choose to put it, and went straight to Nature, to trees, birds, animals, to all those things which quite clearly pursue one aim only, which blindly follow the great native instinct to be happy without any care at all for morality, or human law or divine law. I wanted, you understand, to get all joy first-hand and unadulterated, and I think it scarcely exists among men; it is obsolete.'

Darcy turned in his chair.

'Ah, but what makes birds and animals happy?' he asked. 'Food, food and mating.'

Frank laughed gently in the stillness.

'Do not think I became a sensualist,' he said. 'I did not make that mistake. For the sensualist carries his miseries pick-a-back, and round his feet is wound the shroud that shall soon enwrap him. I may be mad, it is true, but I am not so stupid anyhow as to have tried that. No, what is it that makes puppies play with their own tails, that sends cats on their prowling ecstatic errands at night?'.

He paused a moment.

'So I went to Nature,' he said. 'I sat down here in this New Forest, sat down fair and square, and looked. That was my first difficulty, to sit here quiet without being bored, to wait without being impatient, to be receptive and very alert, though for a long time nothing particular happened. The change in fact was slow in those early stages.'

'Nothing happened?' asked Darcy rather impatiently, with the sturdy revolt against any new idea which to the English mind is synonymous with nonsense. 'Why, what in the world *should* happen?'

Now Frank as he had known him was the most generous but most quick-tempered of mortal men; in other words his anger would flare to a prodigious beacon, under almost no provocation, only to be quenched again under a gust of no less impulsive kindliness. Thus the moment Darcy had spoken, an apology for his hasty question was halfway up his tongue. But there was no need for it to have travelled even so far, for Frank laughed again with kindly, genuine mirth.

'Oh, how I should have resented that a few years ago,' he said. 'Thank goodness that resentment is one of the things I have got rid of. I certainly wish that you should believe my story – in fact, you are going to – but that you at this moment should imply that you do not, does not concern me.'

'Ah, your solitary sojournings have made you inhuman,' said Darcy, still very English.

'No, human,' said Frank. 'Rather more human, at least rather less of an ape.'

'Well, that was my first quest,' he continued, after a moment, 'the deliberate and unswerving pursuit of joy, and my method, the eager contemplation of Nature. As far as motive went, I daresay it was purely selfish, but as far as effect goes, it seems to me about the best thing one can do for one's fellow-creatures, for happiness is more infectious than small-pox. So, as I said, I sat down and waited; I looked at happy things, zealously avoided the sight of anything unhappy, and by degrees a little trickle of the happiness of this blissful world began to filter into me. The trickle grew more abundant, and now, my dear fellow, if I could for a moment divert from me into you one half of the torrent of joy that pours through me day and night, you would throw the world, art, everything aside, and just live, exist. When a man's body dies, it passes into trees and flowers. Well, that is what I have been trying to do with my soul before death.'

The servant had brought into the pergola a table with syphons and spirits, and had set a lamp upon it. As Frank spoke he leaned forward towards the other, and Darcy for all his matter-of-fact commonsense could have sworn that his companion's face shone, was luminous in itself. His dark brown eyes glowed from within, the unconscious smile of a child irradiated and transformed his face. Darcy felt suddenly excited, exhilarated.

'Go on,' he said. 'Go on. I can feel you are somehow telling me sober truth. I daresay you are mad; but I don't see that matters.'

Frank laughed again.

'Mad?' he said. 'Yes, certainly, if you wish. But I prefer to call it sane. However, nothing matters less than what anybody chooses to call things. God never labels his gifts; He just puts them into our hands; just as he put animals in the garden of Eden, for Adam to name if he felt disposed.'

'So by the continual observance and study of things that were happy,' continued he, 'I got happiness, I got joy. But seeking it, as I did, from Nature, I got much more which I did not seek, but stumbled upon originally by accident. It is difficult to explain, but I will try.

'About three years ago I was sitting one morning in a place I will show you tomorrow. It is down by the river brink, very green, dappled with shade and sun, and the river passes there through some little clumps of reeds. Well, as I sat there, doing nothing, but just looking and listening, I heard the sound quite distinctly of some flute-like instrument playing a strange unending melody. I thought at first it was some musical yokel on the highway and did not pay much attention. But before long the strangeness and indescribable beauty of the tune struck me. It never repeated itself, but it never came to an end, phrase after phrase ran its sweet course, it worked gradually and inevitably up to a climax, and having attained it, it went on; another climax was reached and another and another. Then with a sudden gasp of wonder I localized where it came from. It came from the reeds and from the sky and from the trees. It was everywhere, it was the sound of life. It was, my dear Darcy, as the Greeks would have said, it was Pan playing on his pipes, the voice of Nature. It was the life-melody, the world-melody.'

Darcy was far too interested to interrupt, though there was a question he would have liked to ask, and Frank went on:

'Well, for the moment I was terrified, terrified with the impotent horror of nightmare, and I stopped my ears and just ran from the place and got back to the house panting, trembling, literally in a panic. Unknowingly, for at that time I only pursued joy, I had begun, since I drew my joy from Nature, to get in touch with Nature. Nature, force, God, call it what you will, had drawn across my face a little gossamer web of essential life. I saw that when I emerged from my terror, and I went very humbly back to where I had heard the Pan-pipes. But it was nearly six months before I heard them again.'

'Why was that?' asked Darcy.

'Surely because I had revolted, rebelled, and worst of all been frightened. For I believe that just as there is nothing in the world which so injures one's body as fear, so there is nothing that so much shuts up the soul. I was afraid, you see, of the one thing in the world which has real existence. No wonder its manifestation was withdrawn.'

'And after six months?'

'After six months one blessed morning I heard the piping again. I wasn't afraid that time. And since then it has grown louder, it has become more constant. I now hear it often, and I can put myself into such an attitude towards Nature that the pipes will almost certainly sound. And never yet have they played the same tune, it is always something new, something fuller, richer, more complete than before.'

'What do you mean by "such an attitude towards Nature"?' asked Darcy.

'I can't explain that; but by translating it into a bodily attitude it is this.'

Frank sat up for a moment quite straight in his chair, then slowly sunk back with arms outspread and head drooped.

'That,' he said, 'an effortless attitude, but open, resting, receptive. It is just that which you must do with your soul.'

Then he sat up again.

'One word more,' he said, 'and I will bore you no further. Nor unless you ask me questions shall I talk about it again. You will find me, in fact, quite sane in my mode of life. Birds and beasts you will see behaving somewhat intimately to me, like that moor-hen, but that is all. I will walk with you, ride with you, play golf with you, and talk with you on any subject you like. But I wanted you on the threshold to know what has happened to me. And one thing more will happen.'

He paused again, and a slight look of fear crossed his eyes.

'There will be a final revelation,' he said, 'a complete and blinding stroke which will throw open to me, once and for all, the full knowledge, the full realization and comprehension that I am one, just as you are, with life. In reality there is no "me," no "you," no "it." Everything is part of the one and only thing which is life. I know that that is so, but the realization of it is not yet mine. But it will be, and on that day, so I take it, I shall see Pan. It may mean death, the death of my body, that is, but I don't care. It may mean immortal, eternal life lived here and now and for ever. Then having gained that, ah, my dear Darcy, I shall preach such a gospel of joy, showing myself as the living proof of the truth, that Puritanism, the dismal religion of sour faces, shall vanish like a breath of smoke, and be dispersed and disappear in the sunlit air. But first the full knowledge must be mine.'

Darcy watched his face narrowly.

'You are afraid of that moment,' he said.

Frank smiled at him.

'Quite true; you are quick to have seen that. But when it comes I hope I shall not be afraid.'

For some little time there was silence; then Darcy rose.

'You have bewitched me, you extraordinary boy,' he said. 'You have been telling me a fairy-story, and I find myself saying, "Promise me it is true."'

'I promise you that,' said the other.

'And I know I shan't sleep,' added Darcy.

Frank looked at him with a sort of mild wonder as if he scarcely understood.

'Well, what does that matter?' he said.

'I assure you it does. I am wretched unless I sleep.'

'Of course I can make you sleep if I want,' said Frank in a rather bored voice.

'Well, do.'

'Very good: go to bed. I'll come upstairs in ten minutes.'

Frank busied himself for a little after the other had gone, moving the table back under the awning of the veranda and quenching the lamp. Then he went with his quick silent tread upstairs and into Darcy's room. The latter was already in bed, but very wide-eyed and wakeful, and Frank with an amused smile of indulgence, as for a fretful child, sat down on the edge of the bed.

'Look at me,' he said, and Darcy looked.

'The birds are sleeping in the brake,' said Frank softly, 'and the winds are asleep. The sea sleeps, and the tides are but the heaving of its breast. The stars swing slow, rocked in the great cradle of the Heavens, and—'

He stopped suddenly, gently blew out Darcy's candle, and left him sleeping.

Morning brought to Darcy a flood of hard commonsense, as clear and crisp as the sunshine that filled his room. Slowly as he woke he gathered together the broken threads of the memories of the evening which had ended, so he told himself, in a trick of common hypnotism. That accounted for it all; the whole strange talk he had had was under a spell of suggestion from the extraordinary vivid boy who had once been a man; all his own excitement, his acceptance of the incredible had been merely the effect of a stronger, more potent will imposed on his own. How strong that will was, he guessed from his own instantaneous obedience to Frank's suggestion of sleep. And armed with impenetrable commonsense he came down to breakfast. Frank had already begun, and was consuming a large plateful of porridge and milk with the most prosaic and healthy appetite.

'Slept well?' he asked.

'Yes, of course. Where did you learn hypnotism?'

'By the side of the river.'

'You talked an amazing quantity of nonsense last night,' remarked Darcy, in a voice prickly with reason.

'Rather. I felt quite giddy. Look, I remembered to order a dreadful daily paper for you. You can read about money markets or politics or cricket matches.'

Darcy looked at him closely. In the morning light Frank looked even fresher, younger, more vital than he had done the night before, and the sight of him somehow dinted Darcy's armour of commonsense.

'You are the most extraordinary fellow I ever saw,' he said. 'I want to ask you some more questions.'

'Ask away,' said Frank.

†

For the next day or two Darcy plied his friend with many questions, objections and criticisms on the theory of life and gradually got out of him a coherent and complete account of his experience. In brief then, Frank believed that 'by lying naked', as he put it, to the force which controls the passage of the stars, the breaking of a wave, the budding of a tree, the love of a youth and maiden, he had succeeded in a way hitherto undreamed of in possessing himself of the essential principle of life. Day by day, so he thought, he was getting nearer to, and in closer union with the great power itself which caused all life to be, the spirit of nature, of force, or the spirit of God. For himself, he confessed to what others would call paganism; it was sufficient for him that there existed a principle of life. He did not worship it, he did not pray to it, he did not praise it. Some of it existed in all human beings, just as it existed in trees and animals; to realize and make living to himself the fact that it was all one, was his sole aim and object.

Here perhaps Darcy would put in a word of warning. 'Take care,' he said. 'To see Pan meant death, did it not?'

Frank's eyebrows would rise at this.

'What does that matter?' he said. 'True, the Greeks were always right, and they said so, but there is another possibility. For the nearer I get to it, the more living, the more vital and young I become.'

'What then do you expect the final revelation will do for you?'

'I have told you,' said he. 'It will make me immortal.'

But it was not so much from speech and argument that Darcy grew to grasp his friend's conception, as from the ordinary conduct of his life. They were passing, for instance, one morning down the village street, when an old woman, very bent and decrepit, but with an extraordinary cheerfulness of face, hobbled out from her cottage. Frank instantly stopped when he saw her.

'You old darling! How goes it all?' he said.

But she did not answer, her dim old eyes were riveted on his face; she seemed to drink in like a thirsty creature the beautiful radiance which shone there. Suddenly she put her two withered old hands on his shoulders.

'You're just the sunshine itself,' she said, and he kissed her and passed on.

But scarcely a hundred yards further a strange contradiction of such tenderness occurred. A child running along the path towards them fell on its face, and set up a dismal cry of fright and pain. A look of horror came into Frank's eyes, and, putting his fingers in his ears, he fled at full speed down the street, and did not pause till he was out of hearing. Darcy, having ascertained that the child was not really hurt, followed him in bewilderment.

'Are you without pity then?' he asked.

Frank shook his head impatiently.

'Can't you see?' he asked. 'Can't you understand that that sort of thing, pain, anger, anything unlovely throws me back, retards the coming of the great hour! Perhaps when it comes I shall be able to piece that side of life on to the other, on to the true religion of joy. At present I can't.'

'But the old woman. Was she not ugly?'

Frank's radiance gradually returned.

'Ah, no. She was like me. She longed for joy, and knew it when she saw it, the old darling.'

Another question suggested itself.

'Then what about Christianity?' asked Darcy.

'I can't accept it. I can't believe in any creed of which the central doctrine is that God who is Joy should have had to suffer. Perhaps it was so; in some inscrutable way I believe it may have been so, but I don't understand how it was possible. So I leave it alone; my affair is joy.'

They had come to the weir above the village, and the thunder of riotous cool water was heavy in the air. Trees dipped into the translucent stream with slender trailing branches, and the meadow where they stood was starred with midsummer blossomings. Larks shot up caroling into the crystal dome of blue, and a thousand voices of June sang round them. Frank, bare-headed as was his wont, with his coat slung over his arm and his shirt sleeves rolled up above the elbow, stood there like some beautiful wild animal with eyes half-shut and mouth half-open, drinking in the scented warmth of the air. Then suddenly he flung himself face downwards on the grass at the edge of the stream, burying his face in the daisies and cowslips, and lay stretched there in wide-armed ecstasy, with his long fingers pressing and stroking the dewy herbs of the field. Never before had Darcy seen him thus fully possessed by his idea; his caressing fingers, his half-buried face pressed close to the grass, even the clothed lines of his figure were instinct with a vitality that somehow was different from that of other men. And some faint glow from it reached Darcy, some thrill, some vibration from that charged recumbent body passed to him, and for a moment he understood as he had not understood before, despite his persistent questions and the candid answers they received, how real, and how realized by Frank, his idea was.

Then suddenly the muscles in Frank's neck became stiff and alert, and he half-raised his head, whispering, 'The Pan-pipes, the Pan-pipes. Close, oh, so close.'

Very slowly, as if a sudden movement might interrupt the melody, he raised himself and leaned on the elbow of his bent arm. His eyes opened wider, the lower lids drooped as if he focused his eyes on something very far away, and the smile on his face broadened and quivered like sunlight on still water, till the exultance of its happiness was scarcely human. So he remained motionless and rapt for some minutes, then the look of listening died from his face, and he bowed his head satisfied.

'Ah, that was good,' he said. 'How is it possible you did not hear? Oh, you poor fellow! Did you really hear nothing?'

A week of this outdoor and stimulating life did wonders in restoring to Darcy the vigour and health which his weeks of fever had filched from him, and as his normal activity and higher pressure of vitality returned, he seemed to himself to fall even more under the spell which the miracle of Frank's youth cast over him. Twenty times a day he found himself saying to himself suddenly at the end of some ten minutes' silent resistance to the absurdity of Frank's idea: 'But it isn't possible; it can't be possible,' and from the fact of his having to assure himself so frequently of this, he knew that he was struggling and arguing with a conclusion which already had taken root in his mind. For in any case a visible living miracle confronted him, since it was equally impossible that this youth, this boy, trembling on the verge of manhood, was thirty-five. Yet such was the fact.

July was ushered in by a couple of days of blustering and fretful rain, and Darcy, unwilling to risk a chill, kept to the house. But to Frank this weeping change of weather seemed to have no bearing on the behaviour of man, and he spent his days exactly as he did under the suns of June, lying in his hammock, stretched on the dripping grass, or making huge rambling excursions into the forest, the birds hopping from tree to tree after him, to return in the evening, drenched and soaked, but with the same unquenchable flame of joy burning within him.

'Catch cold?' he would ask, 'I've forgotten how to do it, I think. I suppose it makes one's body more sensible always to sleep out-of-doors. People who live indoors always remind me of something peeled and skinless.'

'Do you mean to say you slept out-of-doors last night in that deluge?' asked Darcy. 'And where, may I ask?'

Frank thought a moment.

'I slept in the hammock till nearly dawn,' he said. 'For I remember the light blinked in the east when I awoke. Then I went – where did I go? – oh, yes, to the meadow where the Pan-pipes sounded so close a week ago. You were with me, do you remember? But I always have a rug if it is wet.'

And he went whistling upstairs.

Somehow that little touch, his obvious effort to recall where he had slept, brought strangely home to Darcy the wonderful romance of which he was the still half-incredulous beholder. Sleep till close on dawn in a hammock, then the tramp – or probably scamper – underneath the windy and weeping heavens to the remote and lonely meadow by the weir! The picture of other such nights rose before him; Frank sleeping perhaps by the bathing-place under the filtered twilight of the stars, or the white blaze of moon-shine, a stir and awakening at some dead hour, perhaps a space of silent wide-eyed thought, and then a wandering through the hushed woods to some other dormitory, alone with his happiness, alone with the joy and the life that suffused and enveloped him, without other thought or desire or aim except the hourly and never-ceasing communion with the joy of nature.

They were in the middle of dinner that night, talking on indifferent subjects, when Darcy suddenly broke off in the middle of a sentence.

'I've got it,' he said. 'At last I've got it.'

'Congratulate you,' said Frank. 'But what?'

'The radical unsoundness of your idea. It is this: All nature from highest to lowest is full, crammed full of suffering; every living organism in nature preys on another, yet in your aim to get close to, to be one with nature, you leave suffering altogether out; you run away from it, you refuse to recognize it. And you are waiting, you say, for the final revelation.'

Frank's brow clouded slightly.

'Well?' he asked, rather wearily.

'Cannot you guess then when the final revelation will be? In joy you are supreme, I grant you that; I did not know a man could be so master of it. You have learned perhaps practically all that nature can teach. And if, as you think, the final revelation is coming to you, it will be the revelation of horror, suffering, death, pain in all its hideous forms. Suffering does exist: you hate it and fear it.'

Frank held up his hand.

'Stop; let me think,' he said.

There was silence for a long minute.

'That never struck me,' he said at length. 'It is possible that what you suggest is true. Does the sight of Pan mean that, do you think? Is it that nature, take it altogether, suffers horribly, suffers to a hideous inconceivable extent? Shall I be shown all the suffering?'

He got up and came round to where Darcy sat.

'If it is so, so be it,' he said. 'Because, my dear fellow, I am near, so splendidly near to the final revelation. Today the pipes have sounded almost without pause. I have even heard the rustle in the bushes, I believe, of Pan's coming. I have seen, yes, I saw today, the bushes pushed aside as if by a hand, and piece of a face, not human, peered through. But I was not frightened, at least I did not run away this time.'

He took a turn up to the window and back again.

'Yes, there is suffering all through,' he said, 'and I have left it all out of my search. Perhaps, as you say, the revelation will be that. And in that case, it will be goodbye. I have gone on one line. I shall have gone too far along one road, without having explored the other. But I can't go back now. I wouldn't if I could; not a step would I retrace! In any case, whatever the revelation is, it will be God. I'm sure of that.'

The rainy weather soon passed, and with the return of the sun Darcy again joined Frank in long rambling days. It grew extraordinarily hotter, and with the fresh bursting of life, after the rain, Frank's vitality seemed to blaze higher and higher. Then, as is the habit of the English weather, one evening clouds began to bank themselves up in the west, the sun went down in a glare of coppery thunder-rack, and the whole earth broiling under an unspeakable oppression and sultriness paused and panted for the storm. After sunset the remote fires of lightning began to wink and flicker on the horizon, but when bed-time came the storm seemed to have moved no nearer, though a very low unceasing noise of thunder was audible. Weary and oppressed by the stress of the day, Darcy fell at once into a heavy uncomforting sleep.

He woke suddenly into full consciousness, with the din of some appalling explosion of thunder in his ears, and sat up in bed with racing heart. Then for a moment, as he recovered himself from the panic-land which lies between sleeping and waking, there was silence, except for the steady hissing of rain on the shrubs outside his window. But suddenly that silence was shattered and shredded into fragments by a scream from somewhere close at hand outside in the black garden, a scream of supreme and despairing terror. Again, and once again it shrilled up, and then a babble of awful words was interjected. A quivering sobbing voice that he knew, said:

'My God, oh, my God; oh, Christ!'

And then followed a little mocking, bleating laugh. Then was silence again; only the rain hissed on the shrubs.

All this was but the affair of a moment, and without pause either to put on clothes or light a candle, Darcy was already fumbling at his door-handle. Even as he opened it he met a terror-stricken face outside, that of the man-servant who carried a light.

'Did you hear?' he asked.

The man's face was bleached to a dull shining whiteness.

'Yes, sir,' he said. 'It was the master's voice.'

†

Together they hurried down the stairs, and through the dining room where an orderly table for breakfast had already been laid, and out on to the terrace. The rain for the moment had been utterly stayed, as if the tap of the heavens had been turned off, and under the lowering black sky, not quite dark, since the moon rode somewhere serene behind the conglomerated thunder-clouds, Darcy stumbled into the garden, followed by the servant with the candle. The monstrous leaping shadow of himself was cast before him on the lawn; lost and wandering odours of rose and lily and damp earth were thick about him, but more pungent was some sharp and acrid smell that suddenly reminded him of a certain châlet in which he had once taken refuge in the Alps. In the blackness of the hazy light from the sky, and the vague tossing of the candle behind him, he saw that the hammock in which Frank so often lay was tenanted. A gleam of white shirt was there, as if a man sitting up in it, but across that there was an obscure dark shadow, and as he approached the acrid odour grew more intense.

He was now only some few yards away, when suddenly the black shadow seemed to jump into the air, then came down with tappings of hard hoofs on the brick path that ran down the pergola, and with frolicsome skippings galloped off into the bushes. When that was gone Darcy could see quite clearly that a shirted figure sat up in the hammock. For one moment, from sheer terror of the unseen, he hung on his step, and the servant joining him they walked together to the hammock.

It was Frank. He was in shirt and trousers only, and he sat up with braced arms. For one half-second he stared at them, his face a mask of horrible contorted terror. His upper lip was drawn back so that the gums of the teeth appeared, and his eyes were focused not on the two who approached him but on something quite close to him; his nostrils were widely expanded, as if he panted for breath, and terror incarnate and repulsion and deathly anguish ruled dreadful lines on his smooth cheeks and forehead. Then even as they looked the body sank backwards, and the ropes of the hammock wheezed and strained.

Darcy lifted him out and carried him indoors. Once he thought there was a faint convulsive stir of the limbs that lay with so dead a weight in his arms, but when they got inside, there was no trace of life. But the look of supreme terror and agony of fear had gone from his face, a boy tired with play but still smiling in his sleep was the burden he laid on the floor. His eyes had closed, and the beautiful mouth lay in smiling curves, even as when a few mornings ago, in the meadow by the weir, it had quivered to the music of the unheard melody of Pan's pipes. Then they looked further.

Frank had come back from his bath before dinner that night in his usual costume of shirt and trousers only. He had not dressed, and during dinner, so Darcy remembered, he had rolled up the sleeves of his shirt to above the elbow. Later, as they sat and talked after dinner on the close sultriness of the evening, he had unbuttoned the front of his shirt to let what little breath of wind there was play on his skin. The sleeves were rolled up now, the front of the shirt was unbuttoned, and on his arms and on the brown skin of his chest were strange discolourations which grew momently more clear and defined, till they saw that the marks were pointed prints, as if caused by the hoofs of some monstrous goat that had leaped and stamped upon him.

The Open Window

Saki

'My aunt will be down presently, Mr Nuttel,' said a very self-possessed young lady of fifteen; 'in the meantime you must try and put up with me.'

Framton Nuttel endeavoured to say the correct something which should duly flatter the niece of the moment without unduly discounting the aunt that was to come. Privately he doubted more than ever whether these formal visits on a succession of total strangers would do much towards helping the nerve cure which he was supposed to be undergoing.

'I know how it will be,' his sister had said when he was preparing to migrate to this rural retreat; 'you will bury yourself down there and not speak to a living soul, and your nerves will be worse than ever from moping. I shall just give you letters of introduction to all the people I know there. Some of them, as far as I can remember, were quite nice.'

Framton wondered whether Mrs Sappleton, the lady to whom he was presenting one of the letters of introduction, came into the nice division.

'Do you know many of the people round here?' asked the niece, when she judged that they had had sufficient silent communion.

'Hardly a soul,' said Framton. 'My sister was staying here, at the rectory, you know, some four years ago, and she gave me letters of introduction to some of the people here.'

He made the last statement in a tone of distinct regret.

'Then you know practically nothing about my aunt?' pursued the self-possessed young lady.

'Only her name and address,' admitted the caller. He was wondering whether Mrs Sappleton was in the married or widowed state. An undefinable something about the room seemed to suggest masculine habitation.

'Her great tragedy happened just three years ago,' said the child; 'that would be since your sister's time.'

'Her tragedy?' asked Framton; somehow in this restful country spot tragedies seemed out of place.

'You may wonder why we keep that window wide open on an October afternoon,' said the niece, indicating a large French window that opened on to a lawn.

'It is quite warm for the time of the year,' said Framton; 'but has that window got anything to do with the tragedy?'

'Out through that window, three years ago to a day, her husband and her two young brothers went off for their day's shooting. They never came back. In crossing the moor to their favourite snipe-shooting ground they were all three engulfed in a treacherous piece of bog. It had been that dreadful wet summer, you know, and places that were safe in other years gave way suddenly without warning. Their bodies were never recovered. That was the dreadful part of it.' Here the child's voice lost its self-possessed note and became falteringly human. 'Poor aunt always thinks that they will come back some day, they and the little brown spaniel that was lost with them, and walk in at that window just as they used to do. That is why the window is kept open every evening till it is quite dusk. Poor dear aunt, she has often told me how they went out, her husband with his white waterproof coat over his arm, and Ronnie, her youngest brother, singing 'Bertie, why do you bound?' as he always did to tease her, because she said it got on her nerves. Do you know, sometimes on still, quiet evenings like this, I almost get a creepy feeling that they will all walk in through that window—'

She broke off with a little shudder. It was a relief to Framton when the aunt bustled into the room with a whirl of apologies for being late in making her appearance.

'I hope Vera has been amusing you?' she said.

'She has been very interesting,' said Framton.

'I hope you don't mind the open window,' said Mrs Sappleton briskly; 'my husband and brothers will be home directly from shooting, and they always come in this way. They've been out for snipe in the marshes today, so they'll make a fine mess over my poor carpets. So like you menfolk, isn't it?'

She rattled on cheerfully about the shooting and the scarcity of birds, and the prospects for duck in the winter. To Framton it was all purely horrible. He made a desperate but only partially successful effort to turn the talk on to a less ghastly topic; he was conscious that his hostess was giving him only a fragment of her attention, and her eyes were constantly straying past him to the open window and the lawn beyond. It was certainly an unfortunate coincidence that he should have paid his visit on this tragic anniversary.

'The doctors agree in ordering me complete rest, an absence of mental excitement, and avoidance of anything in the nature of violent physical exercise,' announced Framton, who laboured under the tolerably widespread delusion that total strangers and chance acquaintances are hungry for the least detail of one's ailments and infirmities, their cause and cure. 'On the matter of diet they are not so much in agreement,' he continued.

'No?' said Mrs Sappleton, in a voice which only replaced a yawn at the last moment. Then she suddenly brightened into alert attention – but not to what Framton was saying.

'Here they are at last!' she cried. 'Just in time for tea, and don't they look as if they were muddy up to the eyes!'

Framton shivered slightly and turned towards the niece with a look intended to convey sympathetic comprehension. The child was staring out through the open window with dazed horror in her eyes. In a chill shock of nameless fear Framton swung round in his seat and looked in the same direction.

In the deepening twilight three figures were walking across the lawn towards the window; they all carried guns under their arms, and one of them was additionally burdened with a white coat hung over his shoulders. A tired brown spaniel kept close at their heels. Noiselessly they neared the house, and then a hoarse young voice chanted out of the dusk: 'I said, Bertie, why do you bound?'

Framton grabbed wildly at his stick and hat; the hall-door, the gravel-drive, and the front gate were dimly-noted stages in his headlong retreat. A cyclist coming along the road had to run into the hedge to avoid an imminent collision.

'Here we are, my dear,' said the bearer of the white mackintosh, coming in through the window; 'fairly muddy, but most of it's dry. Who was that who bolted out as we came up?'

'A most extraordinary man, a Mr Nuttel,' said Mrs Sappleton; 'could only talk about his illnesses, and dashed off without a word of goodbye or apology when you arrived. One would think he had seen a ghost.'

'I expect it was the spaniel,' said the niece calmly; 'he told me he had a horror of dogs. He was once hunted into a cemetery somewhere on the banks of the Ganges by a pack of pariah dogs, and had to spend the night in a newly dug grave with the creatures snarling and grinning and foaming just above him. Enough to make anyone their nerve.'

Romance at short notice was her speciality.

The Whistling Room

William Hope Hodgson

Carnacki shook a friendly fist at me as I entered, late. Then he opened the door into the dining room, and ushered the four of us – Jessop, Arkright, Taylor and myself – in to dinner.

We dined well, as usual, and, equally as usual, Carnacki was pretty silent during the meal. At the end, we took our wine and cigars to our usual positions, and Carnacki – having got himself comfortable in his big chair – began without any preliminary:—

'I have just got back from Ireland, again,' he said. 'And I thought you chaps would be interested to hear my news. Besides, I fancy I shall see the thing clearer, after I have told it all out straight. I must tell you this, though, at the beginning – up to the present moment, I have been utterly and completely "stumped". I have tumbled upon one of the most peculiar cases of "haunting" – or devilment of some sort – that I have come against. Now listen.

'I have been spending the last few weeks at Iastrae Castle, about twenty miles northeast of Galway. I got a letter about a month ago from a Mr Sid K. Tassoc, who it seemed had bought the place lately, and moved in, only to find that he had bought a very peculiar piece of property.

'When I got there, he met me at the station, driving a jaunting car, and drove me up to the castle, which, by the way, he called a "house shanty". I found that he was "pigging it" there with his boy brother and another American, who seemed to be half-servant and half-companion. It seems that all the servants had left the place, in a body, as you might say, and now they were managing among themselves, assisted by some day-help.

'The three of them got together a scratch feed, and Tassoc told me all about the trouble whilst we were at table. It is most extraordinary, and different from anything that I have had to do with; though that Buzzing Case was very queer, too.

'Tassoc began right in the middle of his story. "We've got a room in this shanty," he said, "which has got a most infernal whistling in it; sort of haunting it. The thing starts any time; you never know when, and it goes on until it frightens you. All the servants have gone, as you know. It's not ordinary whistling, and it isn't the wind. Wait till you hear it."

'"We're all carrying guns," said the boy; and slapped his coat pocket.

'"As bad as that?" I said; and the older boy nodded. "It may be soft," he replied; "but wait till you've heard it. Sometimes I think it's some infernal thing, and the next moment, I'm just as sure that someone's playing a trick on me."

'"Why?" I asked. "What is to be gained?"

'"You mean," he said, "that people usually have some good reason for playing tricks as elaborate as this. Well, I'll tell you. There's a lady in this province, by the name of Miss Donnehue, who's going to be my wife, this day two months. She's more beautiful than they make them, and so far as I can see, I've just stuck my head into an Irish hornet's nest. There's about a score of hot young Irishmen been courting her these two years gone, and now that I'm come along and cut them out, they feel raw against me. Do you begin to understand the possibilities?"

'"Yes," I said. "Perhaps I do in a vague sort of way; but I don't see how all this affects the room?"

'"Like this," he said. "When I'd fixed it up with Miss Donnehue, I looked out for a place, and bought this little house shanty. Afterward, I told her – one evening during dinner, that I'd decided to tie up here. And then she asked me whether I wasn't afraid of the whistling room. I told her it must have been thrown in gratis, as I'd heard nothing about it. There were some of her men friends present, and I saw a smile go 'round. I found out, after a bit of questioning, that several people have bought this place during the last twenty-odd years. And it was always on the market again, after a trial.

'"Well, the chaps started to bait me a bit, and offered to take bets after dinner that I'd not stay six months in the place. I looked once or twice to Miss Donnehue, so as to be sure I was 'getting the note' of the talkee-talkee; but I could see that she didn't take it as a joke, at all. Partly, I think, because there was a bit of a sneer in the way the men were tackling me, and partly because she really believes there is something in this yarn of the Whistling Room.

'"However, after dinner, I did what I could to even things up with the others. I nailed all their bets, and screwed them down hard and safe. I guess some of them are going to be hard hit, unless I lose; which I don't mean to. Well, there you have practically the whole yarn.'

'"Not quite," I told him. "All that I know, is that you have bought a castle with a room in it that is in some way 'queer', and that you've been doing some betting. Also, I know that your servants have got frightened and run away. Tell me something about the whistling?"

'"Oh, that!" said Tassoc; "that started the second night we were in. I'd had a good look 'round the room, in the daytime, as you can understand; for the talk up at Arlestrae – Miss Donnehue's place – had made me wonder a bit. But it seems just as usual as some of the other rooms in the old wing, only perhaps a bit more lonesome. But that may be only because of the talk about it, you know.

'"The whistling started about ten o'clock, on the second night, as I said. Tom and I were in the library, when we heard an awfully queer whistling, coming along the East Corridor – The room is in the East Wing, you know.

'"That's that blessed ghost!" I said to Tom, and we collared the lamps off the table, and went up to have a look. I tell you, even as we dug along the corridor, it took me a bit in the throat, it was so beastly queer. It was a sort of tune, in a way; but more as if a devil or some rotten thing were laughing at you, and going to get 'round at your back. That's how it makes you feel.

'"When we got to the door, we didn't wait; but rushed it open; and then I tell you the sound of the thing fairly hit me in the face. Tom said he got it the same way – sort of felt stunned and bewildered. We looked all 'round, and soon got so nervous, we just cleared out, and I locked the door.

'"We came down here, and had a stiff peg each. Then we got fit again, and began to think we'd been nicely had. So we took sticks, and went out into the grounds, thinking after all it must be some of these confounded Irishmen working the ghost-trick on us. But there was not a leg stirring.

'"We went back into the house, and walked over it, and then paid another visit to the room. But we simply couldn't stand it. We fairly ran out, and locked the door again. I don't know how to put it into words; but I had a feeling of being up against something that was rottenly dangerous. You know! We've carried our guns ever since.

'"Of course, we had a real turn out of the room next day, and the whole house place; and we even hunted 'round the grounds; but there was nothing queer. And now I don't know what to think; except that the sensible part of me tells me that it's some plan of these Wild Irishmen to try to take a rise out of me."

'"Done anything since?" I asked him.

'"Yes," he said – "watched outside of the door of the room at nights, and chased 'round the grounds, and sounded the walls and floor of the room. We've done everything we could think of; and it's beginning to get on our nerves; so we sent for you."

'By this, we had finished eating. As we rose from the table, Tassoc suddenly called out: – 'Ssh! Hark!'

'We were instantly silent, listening. Then I heard it, an extraordinary hooning whistle, monstrous and inhuman, coming from far away through corridors to my right.

'"By G—d!" said Tassoc; "and it's scarcely dark yet! Collar those candles, both of you, and come along."

'In a few moments, we were all out of the door and racing up the stairs. Tassoc turned into a long corridor, and we followed, shielding our candles as we ran. The sound seemed to fill all the passage as we drew near, until I had the feeling that the whole air throbbed under the power of some wanton Immense Force – a sense of an actual taint, as you might say, of monstrosity all about us.

'Tassoc unlocked the door; then, giving it a push with his foot, jumped back, and drew his revolver. As the door flew open, the sound beat out at us, with an effect impossible to explain to one who has not heard it – with a certain, horrible personal note in it; as if in there in the darkness you could picture the room rocking and creaking in a mad, vile glee to its own filthy piping and whistling and hooning. To stand there and listen, was to be stunned by Realization. It was as if someone showed you the mouth of a vast pit suddenly, and said: – That's Hell. And you knew that they had spoken the truth. Do you get it, even a little bit?

'I stepped back a pace into the room, and held the candle over my head, and looked quickly 'round. Tassoc and his brother joined me, and the man came up at the back, and we all held our candles high. I was deafened with the shrill, piping hoon of the whistling; and then, clear in my ear, something seemed to be saying to me: – "Get out of here – quick! Quick! Quick!"

'As you chaps know, I never neglect that sort of thing. Sometimes it may be nothing but nerves; but as you will remember, it was just such a warning that saved me in the "Grey Dog" Case, and in the "Yellow Finger" Experiments; as well as other times. Well, I turned sharp 'round to the others: "Out!" I said. "For God's sake, *out* quick." And in an instant I had them into the passage.

'There came an extraordinary yelling scream into the hideous whistling, and then, like a clap of thunder, an utter silence. I slammed the door, and locked it. Then, taking the key, I looked 'round at the others. They were pretty white, and I imagine I must have looked that way too. And there we stood a moment, silent.

'"Come down out of this, and have some whisky," said Tassoc, at last, in a voice he tried to make ordinary; and he led the way. I was the back man, and I know we all kept looking over our shoulders. When we got downstairs, Tassoc passed the bottle 'round. He took a drink, himself, and slapped his glass down on to the table. Then sat down with a thud.

'"That's a lovely thing to have in the house with you, isn't it!" he said. And directly afterward: – "What on earth made you hustle us all out like that, Carnacki?"

'"Something seemed to be telling me to get out, quick," I said. "Sounds a bit silly, superstitious, I know; but when you are meddling with this sort of thing, you've got to take notice of queer fancies, and risk being laughed at."

'I told him then about the "Grey Dog" business, and he nodded a lot to that. "Of course," I said, "this may be nothing more than those would-be rivals of yours playing some funny game; but, personally, though I'm going to keep an open mind, I feel that there is something beastly and dangerous about this thing."

'We talked for a while longer, and then Tassoc suggested billiards, which we played in a pretty half-hearted fashion, and all the time cocking an ear to the door, as you might say, for sounds; but none came, and later, after coffee, he suggested early bed, and a thorough overhaul of the room on the morrow.

'My bedroom was in the newer part of the castle, and the door opened into the picture gallery. At the East end of the gallery was the entrance to the corridor of the East Wing; this was shut off from the gallery by two old and heavy oak doors, which looked rather odd and quaint beside the more modern doors of the various rooms.

'When I reached my room, I did not go to bed; but began to unpack my instrument trunk, of which I had retained the key. I intended to take one or two preliminary steps at once, in my investigation of the extraordinary whistling.

'Presently, when the castle had settled into quietness, I slipped out of my room, and across to the entrance of the great corridor. I opened one of the low, squat doors, and threw the beam of my pocket searchlight down the passage. It was empty, and I went through the doorway, and pushed-to the oak behind me. Then along the great passageway, throwing my light before and behind, and keeping my revolver handy.

'I had hung a "protection belt" of garlic 'round my neck, and the smell of it seemed to fill the corridor and give me assurance; for, as you all know, it is a wonderful "protection" against the more usual Aeiirii forms of semi-materialization, by which I supposed the whistling might be produced; though, at that period of my investigation, I was quite prepared to find it due to some perfectly natural cause; for it is astonishing the enormous number of cases that prove to have nothing abnormal in them.

'In addition to wearing the necklet, I had plugged my ears loosely with garlic, and as I did not intend to stay more than a few minutes in the room, I hoped to be safe.

'When I reached the door, and put my hand into my pocket for the key, I had a sudden feeling of sickening funk. But I was not going to back out, if I could help it. I unlocked the door and turned the handle. Then I gave the door a sharp push with my foot, as Tassoc had done, and drew my revolver, though I did not expect to have any use for it, really.

'I shone the searchlight all 'round the room, and then stepped inside, with a disgustingly horrible feeling of walking slap into a waiting Danger.

I stood a few seconds, waiting, and nothing happened, and the empty room showed bare from corner to corner. And then, you know, I realized that the room was full of an abominable silence; can you understand that? A sort of purposeful silence, just as sickening as any of the filthy noises the Things have power to make. Do you remember what I told you about that "Silent Garden" business? Well, this room had just that same *malevolent* silence—the beastly quietness of a thing that is looking at you and not seeable itself, and thinks that it has got you. Oh, I recognized it instantly, and I whipped the top off my lantern, so as to have light over the *whole* room.

'Then I set-to, working like fury, and keeping my glance all about me. I sealed the two windows with lengths of human hair, right across, and sealed them at every frame. As I worked, a queer, scarcely perceptible tenseness stole into the air of the place, and the silence seemed, if you can understand me, to grow more solid. I knew then that I had no business there without "full protection"; for I was practically certain that this was no mere Aeiirii development; but one of the worst forms, as the Saiitii; like that "Grunting Man" case – you know.

'I finished the window, and hurried over to the great fireplace. This is a huge affair, and has a queer gallows-iron, I think they are called, projecting from the back of the arch. I sealed the opening with seven human hairs – the seventh crossing the six others.

'Then, just as I was making an end, a low, mocking whistle grew in the room. A cold, nervous pricking went up my spine, and 'round my forehead from the back. The hideous sound filled all the room with an extraordinary, grotesque parody of human whistling, too gigantic to be human – as if something gargantuan and monstrous made the sounds softly. As I stood there a last moment, pressing down the final seal, I had no doubt but that I had come across one of those rare and horrible cases of the *Inanimate* reproducing the functions of the *Animate*, I made a grab for my lamp, and went quickly to the door, looking over my shoulder, and listening for the thing that I expected. It came, just as I got my hand upon the handle – a squeal of incredible, malevolent anger, piercing through the low hooning of the whistling. I dashed out, slamming the door and locking it. I leant a little against the opposite wall of the corridor, feeling rather funny; for it had been a narrow squeak... "Theyr be noe sayfetie to be gained bye gayrds of holieness when the monyster hath pow'r to speak throe woode and stoene." So runs the passage in the Sigsand MS., and I proved it in that "Nodding Door" business. There is no protection against this particular form of monster, except, possibly, for a fractional period of time; for it can reproduce itself in, or take to its purpose, the very protective material which you may use, and has the power to "*forme* wythine the pentycle"; though not immediately. There is, of course, the possibility of the Unknown Last Line of the Saaamaaa Ritual being uttered; but it is too uncertain to count upon, and the danger is too hideous; and even then it has no power to protect for more than "maybee fyve beats of the harte," as the Sigsand has it.

'Inside of the room, there was now a constant, meditative, hooning whistling; but presently this ceased, and the silence seemed worse; for there is such a sense of hidden mischief in a silence.

'After a little, I sealed the door with crossed hairs, and then cleared off down the great passage, and so to bed.

'For a long time I lay awake; but managed eventually to get some sleep. Yet, about two o'clock I was waked by the hooning whistling of the room coming to me, even through the closed doors. The sound was tremendous, and seemed to beat through the whole house with a presiding sense of terror. As if (I remember thinking) some monstrous giant had been holding mad carnival with itself at the end of that great passage.

'I got up and sat on the edge of the bed, wondering whether to go along and have a look at the seal; and suddenly there came a thump on my door, and Tassoc walked in, with his dressing gown over his pajamas.

'"I thought it would have waked you, so I came along to have a talk," he said. "*I* can't sleep. Beautiful! Isn't it!"

'"Extraordinary!' I said, and tossed him my case.

'He lit a cigarette, and we sat and talked for about an hour; and all the time that noise went on, down at the end of the big corridor.

'Suddenly, Tassoc stood up: –

'"Let's take our guns, and go and examine the brute," he said, and turned toward the door.

'"No!" I said. "By Jove – *no!* I can't say anything definite, yet; but I believe that room is about as dangerous as it well can be."

'"Haunted – *really* haunted?" he asked, keenly and without any of his frequent banter.

'I told him, of course, that I could not say a definite *yes* or *no* to such a question; but that I hoped to be able to make a statement, soon. Then I gave him a little lecture on the False Re-Materialization of the Animate-Force through the Inanimate-Inert. He began then to see the particular way in the room might be dangerous, if it were really the subject of a manifestation.

'About an hour later, the whistling ceased quite suddenly, and Tassoc went off again to bed. I went back to mine, also, and eventually got another spell of sleep.

'In the morning, I went along to the room. I found the seals on the door intact. Then I went in. The window seals and the hair were all right; but the seventh hair across the great fireplace was broken. This set me thinking. I knew that it might, very possibly, have snapped, through my having tensioned it too highly; but then, again, it might have been broken by something else. Yet, it was scarcely possible that a man, for instance, could have passed between the six unbroken hairs; for no one would ever have noticed them, entering the room that way, you see; but just walked through them, ignorant of their very existence.

'I removed the other hairs, and the seals. Then I looked up the chimney. It went up straight, and I could see blue sky at the top. It was a big, open flue, and free from any suggestion of hiding places, or corners. Yet, of course, I did not trust to any such casual examination, and after breakfast, I put on my overalls, and climbed to the very top, sounding all the way; but I found nothing.

'Then I came down, and went over the whole of the room – floor, ceiling, and walls, mapping them out in six-inch squares, and sounding with both hammer and probe. But there was nothing abnormal.

'Afterward, I made a three-week search of the whole castle, in the same thorough way; but found nothing. I went even further, then; for at night, when the whistling commenced, I made a microphone test. You see, if the whistling were mechanically produced, this test would have made evident to me the working of the machinery, if there were any such concealed within the walls. It certainly was an up-to-date method of examination, as you must allow.

'Of course, I did not think that any of Tassoc's rivals had fixed up any mechanical contrivance; but I thought it just possible that there had been some such thing for producing the whistling, made away back in the years, perhaps with the intention of giving the room a reputation that would ensure its being free of inquisitive folk. You see what I mean? Well, of course, it was just possible, if this were the case, that someone knew the secret of the machinery, and was utilizing the knowledge to play this devil of a prank on Tassoc. The microphone test of the walls would certainly have made this known to me, as I have said; but there was nothing of the sort in the castle; so that I had practically no doubt at all now, but that it was a genuine case of what is popularly termed "haunting".

'All this time, every night, and sometimes most of each night, the hooning whistling of the Room was intolerable. It was as if an intelligence there knew that steps were being taken against it, and piped and hooned in a sort of mad, mocking contempt. I tell you, it was as extraordinary as it was horrible. Time after time, I went along – tiptoeing noiselessly on stockinged feet – to the sealed door (for I always kept the Room sealed). I went at all hours of the night, and often the whistling, inside, would seem to change to a brutally malignant note, as though the half-animate monster saw me plainly through the shut door. And all the time the shrieking, hooning whistling would fill the whole corridor, so that I used to feel a precious lonely chap, messing about there with one of Hell's mysteries.

'And every morning, I would enter the room, and examine the different hairs and seals. You see, after the first week, I had stretched parallel hairs all along the walls of the room, and along the ceiling; but over the floor, which was of polished stone, I had set out little, colorless wafers, tacky-side uppermost. Each wafer was numbered, and they were arranged after a definite plan, so that I should be able to trace the exact movements of any living thing that went across the floor.

'You will see that no material being or creature could possibly have entered that room, without leaving many signs to tell me about it. But nothing was ever disturbed, and I began to think that I should have to risk an attempt to stay the night in the room, in the Electric Pentacle. Yet, mind you, I knew that it would be a crazy thing to do; but I was getting stumped, and ready to do anything.

'Once, about midnight, I did break the seal on the door, and have a quick look in; but, I tell you, the whole Room gave one mad yell, and seemed to come toward me in a great belly of shadows, as if the walls had bellied in toward me. Of course, that must have been fancy. Anyway, the yell was sufficient, and I slammed the door, and locked it, feeling a bit weak down my spine. You know the feeling.

'And then, when I had got to that state of readiness for anything, I made something of a discovery. It was about one in the morning, and I was walking slowly 'round the castle, keeping in the soft grass. I had come under the shadow of the East Front, and far above me, I could hear the vile, hooning whistle of the Room, up in the darkness of the unlit wing. Then, suddenly, a little in front of me, I heard a man's voice, speaking low, but evidently in glee: –

''By George! You Chaps; but I wouldn't care to bring a wife home in that!' it said, in the tone of the cultured Irish.

'Someone started to reply; but there came a sharp exclamation, and then a rush, and I heard footsteps running in all directions. Evidently, the men had spotted me.

'For a few seconds, I stood there, feeling an awful ass. After all, *they* were at the bottom of the haunting! Do you see what a big fool it made me seem? I had no doubt but that they were some of Tassoc's rivals; and here I had been feeling in every bone that I had hit a real, bad, genuine Case! And then, you know, there came the memory of hundreds of details, that made me just as much in doubt again. Anyway, whether it was natural, or ab-natural, there was a great deal yet to be cleared up.

'I told Tassoc, next morning, what I had discovered, and through the whole of every night, for five nights, we kept a close watch 'round the East Wing; but there was never a sign of anyone prowling about; and all the time, almost from evening to dawn, that grotesque whistling would hoon incredibly, far above us in the darkness.

'On the morning after the fifth night, I received a wire from here, which brought me home by the next boat. I explained to Tassoc that I was simply bound to come away for a few days; but told him to keep up the watch 'round the castle. One thing I was very careful to do, and that was to make him absolutely promise never to go into the Room, between sunset and sunrise. I made it clear to him that we knew nothing definite yet, one way or the other; and if the room were what I had first thought it to be, it might be a lot better for him to die first, than enter it after dark.

'When I got here, and had finished my business, I thought you chaps would be interested; and also I wanted to get it all spread out clear in my mind; so I rung you up. I am going over again tomorrow, and when I get back, I ought to have something pretty extraordinary to tell you. By the way, there is a curious thing I forgot to tell you. I tried to get a phonographic record of the whistling; but it simply produced no impression on the wax at all. That is one of the things that has made me feel queer, I can tell you. Another extraordinary thing is that the microphone will not magnify the sound—will not even transmit it; seems to take no account of it, and acts as if it were nonexistent. I am absolutely and utterly stumped, up to the present. I am a wee bit curious to see whether any of your dear clever heads can make daylight of it. *I* cannot – not yet.'

He rose to his feet.

'Good night, all,' he said, and began to usher us out abruptly, but without offence, into the night.

A fortnight later, he dropped each of us a card, and you can imagine that I was not late this time. When we arrived, Carnacki took us straight into dinner, and when we had finished, and all made ourselves comfortable, he began again, where he had left off: –

'Now just listen quietly; for I have got something pretty queer to tell you. I got back late at night, and I had to walk up to the castle, as I had not warned them that I was coming. It was bright moonlight; so that the walk was rather a pleasure, than otherwise. When I got there, the whole place was in darkness, and I thought I would take a walk 'round outside, to see whether Tassoc or his brother was keeping watch. But I could not find them anywhere, and concluded that they had got tired of it, and gone off to bed.

'As I returned across the front of the East Wing, I caught the hooning whistling of the Room, coming down strangely through the stillness of the night. It had a queer note in it, I remember – low and constant, queerly meditative. I looked up at the window, bright in the moonlight, and got a sudden thought to bring a ladder from the stable yard, and try to get a look into the Room, through the window.

'With this notion, I hunted 'round at the back of the castle, among the straggle of offices, and presently found a long, fairly light ladder; though it was heavy enough for one, goodness knows! And I thought at first that I should never get it reared. I managed at last, and let the ends rest very quietly against the wall, a little below the sill of the larger window. Then, going silently, I went up the ladder. Presently, I had my face above the sill and was looking in alone with the moonlight.

'Of course, the queer whistling sounded louder up there; but it still conveyed that peculiar sense of something whistling quietly to itself – can you understand? Though, for all the meditative lowness of the note, the horrible, gargantuan quality was distinct – a mighty parody of the human, as if I stood there and listened to the whistling from the lips of a monster with a man's soul.

'And then, you know, I saw something. The floor in the middle of the huge, empty room, was puckered upward in the center into a strange soft-looking mound, parted at the top into an ever changing hole, that pulsated to that great, gentle hooning. At times, as I watched, I saw the heaving of the indented mound, gap across with a queer, inward suction, as with the drawing of an enormous breath; then the thing would dilate and pout once more to the incredible melody. And suddenly, as I stared, dumb, it came to me that the thing was living. I was looking at two enormous, blackened lips, blistered and brutal, there in the pale moonlight...

'Abruptly, they bulged out to a vast, pouting mound of force and sound, stiffened and swollen, and hugely massive and clean-cut in the moon-beams. And a great sweat lay heavy on the vast upper-lip. In the same moment of time, the whistling had burst into a mad screaming note, that seemed to stun me, even where I stood, outside of the window. And then, the following moment, I was staring blankly at the solid, undisturbed floor of the room – smooth, polished stone flooring, from wall to wall; and there was an absolute silence.

'You can picture me staring into the quiet Room, and knowing what I knew. I felt like a sick, frightened kid, and wanted to slide *quietly* down the ladder, and run away. But in that very instant, I heard Tassoc's voice calling to me from within the Room, for help, *help*. My God! but I got such an awful dazed feeling; and I had a vague, bewildered notion that, after all, it was the Irishmen who had got him in there, and were taking it out of him. And then the call came again, and I burst the window, and jumped in to help him. I had a confused idea that the call had come from within the shadow of the great fireplace, and I raced across to it; but there was no one there.

'"Tassoc!" I shouted, and my voice went empty-sounding 'round the great apartment; and then, in a flash, *I knew that Tassoc had never called*. I whirled 'round, sick with fear, toward the window, and as I did so, a frightful, exultant whistling scream burst through the Room. On my left, the end wall had bellied-in toward me, in a pair of gargantuan lips, black and utterly monstrous, to within a yard of my face. I fumbled for a mad instant at my revolver; not for *it*, but myself; for the danger was a thousand times worse than death. And then, suddenly, the Unknown Last Line of the Saaamaaa Ritual was whispered quite audibly in the room. Instantly, the thing happened that I have known once before. There came a sense as of dust falling continually and monotonously, and I knew that my life hung uncertain and suspended for a flash, in a brief, reeling vertigo of unseeable things. Then *that* ended, and I knew that I might live. My soul and body blended again, and life and power came to me. I dashed furiously at the window, and hurled myself out head-foremost; for I can tell you that I had stopped being afraid of death. I crashed down on to the ladder, and slithered, grabbing and grabbing; and so came some way or other alive to the bottom. And there I sat in the soft, wet grass, with the moonlight all about me; and far above, through the broken window of the Room, there was a low whistling.

'That is the chief of it. I was not hurt, and I went 'round to the front, and knocked Tasso – up. When they let me in, we had a long yarn, over some good whisky – for I was shaken to pieces – and I explained things as much as I could, I told Tassoc that the room would have to come down, and every fragment of it burned in a blast-furnace, erected within a pentacle. He nodded. There was nothing to say. Then I went to bed.

'We turned a small army on to the work, and within ten days, that lovely thing had gone up in smoke, and what was left was calcined, and clean.

'It was when the workmen were stripping the panelling, that I got hold of a sound notion of the beginnings of that beastly development. Over the great fireplace, after the great oak panels had been torn down, I found that there was let into the masonry a scrollwork of stone, with on it an old inscription, in ancient Celtic, that here in this room was burned Dian Tiansay, Jester of King Alzof, who made the Song of Foolishness upon King Ernore of the Seventh Castle.

'When I got the translation clear, I gave it to Tassoc. He was tremendously excited; for he knew the old tale, and took me down to the library to look at an old parchment that gave the story in detail. Afterward, I found that the incident was well-known about the countryside; but always regarded more as a legend than as history. And no one seemed ever to have dreamt that the old East Wing of Iastrae Castle was the remains of the ancient Seventh Castle.

'From the old parchment, I gathered that there had been a pretty dirty job done, away back in the years. It seems that King Alzof and King Ernore had been enemies by birthright, as you might say truly; but that nothing more than a little raiding had occurred on either side for years, until Dian Tiansay made the Song of Foolishness upon King Ernore, and sang it before King Alzof; and so greatly was it appreciated that King Alzof gave the jester one of his ladies, to wife.

'Presently, all the people of the land had come to know the song, and so it came at last to King Ernore, who was so angered that he made war upon his old enemy, and took and burned him and his castle; but Dian Tiansay, the jester, he brought with him to his own place, and having torn his tongue out because of the song which he had made and sung, he imprisoned him in the Room in the East Wing (which was evidently used for unpleasant purposes), and the jester's wife, he kept for himself, having a fancy for her prettiness.

'But one night, Dian Tiansay's wife was not to be found, and in the morning they discovered her lying dead in her husband's arms, and he sitting, whistling the Song of Foolishness, for he had no longer the power to sing it.

'Then they roasted Dian Tiansay, in the great fireplace – probably from that selfsame "galley-iron" which I have already mentioned. And until he died, Dian Tiansay ceased not to whistle the Song of Foolishness, which he could no longer sing. But afterward, "in that room" there was often heard at night the sound of something whistling; and there "grew a power in that room," so that none dared to sleep in it. And presently, it would seem, the King went to another castle; for the whistling troubled him.

'There you have it all. Of course, that is only a rough rendering of the translation of the parchment. But it sounds extraordinarily quaint. Don't you think so?'

'Yes,' I said, answering for the lot. 'But how did the thing grow to such a tremendous manifestation?'

'One of those cases of continuity of thought producing a positive action upon the immediate surrounding material,' replied Carnacki. 'The development must have been going forward through centuries, to have produced such a monstrosity. It was a true instance of Saiitii manifestation, which I can best explain by likening it to a living spiritual fungus, which involves the very structure of the aether-fiber itself, and, of course, in so doing, acquires an essential control over the "material substance" involved in it. It is impossible to make it plainer in a few words.'

'What broke the seventh hair?' asked Taylor.

But Carnacki did not know. He thought it was probably nothing but being too severely tensioned. He also explained that they found out that the men who had run away, had not been up to mischief; but had come over secretly, merely to hear the whistling, which, indeed, had suddenly become the talk of the whole countryside.

'One other thing,' said Arkright, 'have you any idea what governs the use of the Unknown Last Line of the Saaamaaa Ritual? I know, of course, that it was used by the Ab-human Priests in the Incantation of Raaaee; but what used it on your behalf, and what made it?'

'You had better read Harzan's Monograph, and my Addenda to it, on Astral and Astral Co-ordination and Interference,' said Carnacki. 'It is an extraordinary subject, and I can only say here that the human vibration may not be insulated from the astral (as is always believed to be the case, in interferences by the Ab-human), without immediate action being taken by those Forces which govern the spinning of the outer circle. In other words, it is being proved, time after time, that there is some inscrutable Protective Force constantly intervening between the human soul (not the body, mind you,) and the Outer Monstrosities. Am I clear?'

'Yes, I think so,' I replied. 'And you believe that the Room had become the material expression of the ancient Jester – that his soul, rotten with hatred, had bred into a monster – eh?' I asked.

'Yes,' said Carnacki, nodding, 'I think you've put my thought rather neatly. It is a queer coincidence that Miss Donnehue is supposed to be descended (so I have heard since) from the same King Ernore. It makes one think some curious thoughts, doesn't it? The marriage coming on, and the Room waking to fresh life. If she had gone into that room, ever… eh? *It* had waited a long time. Sins of the fathers. Yes, I've thought of that. They're to be married next week, and I am to be best man, which is a thing I hate.

And he won his bets, rather! Just think, *if* ever she had gone into that room. Pretty horrible, eh?'

He nodded his head, grimly, and we four nodded back. Then he rose and took us collectively to the door, and presently thrust us forth in friendly fashion on the Embankment and into the fresh night air.

'Good night,' we all called back, and went to our various homes. If she had, eh? If she had? That is what I kept thinking.

The Horse of the Invisible

William Hope Hodgson

I had that afternoon received an invitation from Carnacki. When I reached his place I found him sitting alone. As I came into the room he rose with a perceptibly stiff movement and extended his left hand. His face seemed to be badly scarred and bruised and his right hand was bandaged. He shook hands and offered me his paper, which I refused. Then he passed me a handful of photographs and returned to his reading.

Now, that is just Carnacki. Not a word had come from him and not a question from me. He would tell us all about it later. I spent about half an hour looking at the photographs which were chiefly 'snaps' (some by flash-light) of an extraordinarily pretty girl; though in some of the photographs it was wonderful that her prettiness was so evident for so frightened and startled was her expression that it was difficult not to believe that she had been photographed in the presence of some imminent and overwhelming danger.

The bulk of the photographs were of interiors of different rooms and passages and in every one the girl might be seen, either full length in the distance or closer, with perhaps little more than a hand or arm or portion of the head or dress included in the photograph. All of these had evidently been taken with some definite aim that did not have for its first purpose the picturing of the girl, but obviously of her surroundings and they made me very curious, as you can imagine.

Near the bottom of the pile, however, I came upon something *definitely* extraordinary. It was a photograph of the girl standing abrupt and clear in the great blaze of a flashlight, as was plain to be seen. Her face was turned a little upward as if she had been frightened suddenly by some noise. Directly above her, as though half-formed and coming down out of the shadows, was the shape of a single enormous hoof.

I examined this photograph for a long time without understanding it more than that it had probably to do with some queer case in which Carnacki was interested. When Jessop, Arkright and Taylor came in Carnacki quietly held out his hand for the photographs which I returned in the same spirit and afterward we all went in to dinner. When we had spent a quiet hour at the table we pulled our chairs 'round and made ourselves snug and Carnacki began:

'I've been North,' he said, speaking slowly and painfully between puffs at his pipe. 'Up to Hisgins of East Lancashire. It has been a pretty strange business all 'round, as I fancy you chaps will think, when I have finished. I knew before I went, something about the "horse story", as I have heard it called; but I never thought of it coming my way, somehow. Also I know *now* that I never considered it seriously – in spite of my rule always to keep an open mind. Funny creatures, we humans!

'Well, I got a wire asking for an appointment, which of course told me that there was some trouble. On the date I fixed old Captain Hisgins himself came up to see me. He told me a great many new details about the horse story; though naturally I had always known the main points and understood that if the first child were a girl, that girl would be haunted by the Horse during her courtship.

'It is, as you can see already, an extraordinary story and though I have always known about it, I have never thought it to be anything more than an old-time legend, as I have already hinted. You see, for seven generations the Hisgins family have had men children for their first-born and even the Hisginses themselves have long considered the tale to be little more than a myth.

'To come to the present, the eldest child of the reigning family is a girl and she has been often teased and warned in jest by her friends and relations that she is the first girl to be the eldest for seven generations and that she would have to keep her men friends at arm's length or go into a nunnery if she hoped to escape the haunting. And this, I think, shows us how thoroughly the tale had grown to be considered as nothing worthy of the least serious thought. Don't you think so?

'Two months ago Miss Hisgins became engaged to Beaumont, a young Naval Officer, and on the evening of the very day of the engagement, before it was even formally announced, a most extraordinary thing happened which resulted in Captain Hisgins making the appointment and my ultimately going down to their place to look into the thing.

'From the old family records and papers that were entrusted to me I found that there could be no possible doubt that prior to something like a hundred and fifty years ago there were some very extraordinary and disagreeable coincidences, to put the thing in the least emotional way. In the whole of the two centuries prior to that date there were five first-born girls out of a total of seven generations of the family. Each of these girls grew up to maidenhood and each became engaged, and each one died during the period of engagement, two by suicide, one by falling from a window, one from a "broken heart" (presumably heart failure, owing to sudden shock through fright). The fifth girl was killed one evening in the park 'round the house; but just how, there seemed to be no *exact* knowledge; only that there was an impression that she had been kicked by a horse. She was dead when found. Now, you see, all of these deaths might be attributed in a way – even the suicides – to natural causes, I mean as distinct from supernatural. You see? Yet, in every case the maidens had undoubtedly suffered some extraordinary and terrifying experiences during their various courtships for in all of the records there was mention either of the neighing of an unseen horse or of the sounds of an invisible horse galloping, as well as many other peculiar and quite inexplicable manifestations. You begin to understand now, I think, just how extraordinary a business it was that I was asked to look into.

'I gathered from one account that the haunting of the girls was so constant and horrible that two of the girls' lovers fairly ran away from their ladyloves. And I think it was this, more than anything else, that made me feel that there had been something more in it than a mere succession of uncomfortable coincidences.

'I got hold of these facts before I had been many hours in the house and after this I went pretty carefully into the details of the thing that happened on the night of Miss Hisgins's engagement to Beaumont. It seems that as the two of them were going through the big lower corridor, just after dusk and before the lamps had been lighted, there had been a sudden, horrible neighing in the corridor, close to them. Immediately afterward Beaumont received a tremendous blow or kick which broke his right forearm. Then the rest of the family and the servants came running to know what was wrong. Lights were brought and the corridor and, afterward, the whole house searched, but nothing unusual was found.

'You can imagine the excitement in the house and the half-incredulous, half-believing talk about the old legend. Then, later, in the middle of the night the old Captain was waked by the sound of a great horse galloping 'round and 'round the house.

'Several times after this both Beaumont and the girl said that they had heard the sounds of hoofs near to them after dusk, in several of the rooms and corridors.

'Three nights later Beaumont was waked by a strange neighing in the nighttime seeming to come from the direction of his sweetheart's bedroom. He ran hurriedly for her father and the two of them raced to her room. They found her awake and ill with sheer terror, having been awakened by the neighing, seemingly close to her bed.

'The night before I arrived, there had been a fresh happening and they were all in a frightfully nervy state, as you can imagine.

'I spent most of the first day, as I have hinted, in getting hold of details; but after dinner I slacked off and played billiards all the evening with Beaumont and Miss Hisgins. We stopped about ten o'clock and had coffee and I got Beaumont to give me full particulars about the thing that had happened the evening before.

'He and Miss Hisgins had been sitting quietly in her aunt's boudoir whilst the old lady chaperoned them, behind a book. It was growing dusk and the lamp was at her end of the table. The rest of the house was not yet lit as the evening had come earlier than usual.

'Well, it seems that the door into the hall was open and suddenly the girl said: "H'sh! what's that?"

'They both listened and then Beaumont heard it – the sound of a horse outside of the front door.

''Your father?' he suggested, but she reminded him that her father was not riding.

'Of course they were both ready to feel queer, as you can suppose, but Beaumont made an effort to shake this off and went into the hall to see whether anyone was at the entrance. It was pretty dark in the hall and he could see the glass panels of the inner draft door, clear-cut in the darkness of the hall. He walked over to the glass and looked through into the drive beyond, but there nothing in sight.

'He felt nervous and puzzled and opened the inner door and went out on to the carriage-circle. Almost directly afterward the great hall door swung to with a crash behind him. He told me that he had a sudden awful feeling of having been trapped in some way – that is how he put it. He whirled 'round and gripped the door handle, but something seemed to be holding it with a vast grip on the other side. Then, before he could be fixed in his mind that this was so, he was able to turn the handle and open the door.

'He paused a moment in the doorway and peered into the hall, for he had hardly steadied his mind sufficiently to know whether he was really frightened or not. Then he heard his sweetheart blow him a kiss out of the greyness of the big, unlit hall and he knew that she had followed him from the boudoir. He blew her a kiss back and stepped inside the doorway, meaning to go to her. And then, suddenly, in a flash of sickening knowledge he knew that it was not his sweetheart who had blown him that kiss. He knew that something was trying to tempt him alone into the darkness and that the girl had never left the boudoir. He jumped back and in the same instant of time he heard the kiss again, nearer to him. He called out at the top of his voice: "Mary, stay in the boudoir. Don't move out of the boudoir until I come to you." He heard her call something in reply from the boudoir and then he had struck a clump of a dozen or so matches and was holding them above his head and looking 'round the hall. There was no one in it, but even as the matches burned out there came the sounds of a great horse galloping down the empty drive.

'Now you see, both he and the girl had heard the sounds of the horse galloping; but when I questioned more closely I found that the aunt had heard nothing, though it is true she is a bit deaf, and she was further back in the room. Of course, both he and Miss Hisgins had been in an extremely nervous state and ready to hear anything. The door might have been slammed by a sudden puff of wind owing to some inner door being opened; and as for the grip on the handle, that may have been nothing more than the snick catching.

'With regard to the kisses and the sounds of the horse galloping, I pointed out that these might have seemed ordinary enough sounds, if they had been only cool enough to reason. As I told him, and as he knew, the sounds of a horse galloping carry a long way on the wind so that what he had heard might have been nothing more than a horse being ridden some distance away. And as for the kiss, plenty of quiet noises – the rustle of a paper or a leaf – have a somewhat similar sound, especially if one is in an overstrung condition and imagining things.

'I finished preaching this little sermon on commonsense versus hysteria as we put out the lights and left the billiard room. But neither Beaumont nor Miss Hisgins would agree that there had been any fancy on their parts.

'We had come out of the billiard room by this time and were going along the passage and I was still doing my best to make both of them see the ordinary, commonplace possibilities of the happening, when what killed my pig, as the saying goes, was the sound of a hoof in the dark billiard room we had just left.

'I felt the "creep" come on me in a flash, up my spine and over the back of my head. Miss Hisgins whooped like a child with the whooping cough and ran up the passage, giving little gasping screams. Beaumont, however, ripped 'round on his heels and jumped back a couple of yards. I gave back too, a bit, as you can understand.

'"There it is," he said in a low, breathless voice. "Perhaps you'll believe now."

'"There's certainly something," I whispered, never taking my gaze off the closed door of the billiard room.

'"H'sh!" he muttered. "There it is again."

'There was a sound like a great horse pacing 'round and 'round the billiard room with slow, deliberate steps. A horrible cold fright took me so that it seemed impossible to take a full breath, you know the feeling, and then I saw we must have been walking backward for we found ourselves suddenly at the opening of the long passage.

'We stopped there and listened. The sounds went on steadily with a horrible sort of deliberateness, as if the brute were taking a sort of malicious gusto in walking about all over the room which we had just occupied. Do you understand just what I mean?

'Then there was a pause and a long time of absolute quiet except for an excited whispering from some of the people down in the big hall. The sound came plainly up the wide stairway. I fancy they were gathered 'round Miss Hisgins, with some notion of protecting her.

'I should think Beaumont and I stood there, at the end of the passage for about five minutes, listening for any noise in the billiard room. Then I realized what a horrible funk I was in and I said to him: "I'm going to see what's there."

'"So'm I," he answered. He was pretty white, but he had heaps of pluck. I told him to wait one instant and I made a dash into my bedroom and got my camera and flashlight. I slipped my revolver into my right-hand pocket and a knuckle-duster over my left fist, where it was ready and yet would not stop me from being able to work my flashlight.

'Then I ran back to Beaumont. He held out his hand to show me that he had his pistol and I nodded, but whispered to him not to be too quick to shoot, as there might be some silly practical joking at work, after all. He had got a lamp from a bracket in the upper hall which he was holding in the crook of his damaged arm, so that we had a good light. Then we went down the passage toward the billiard room and you can imagine that we were a pretty nervous couple.

'All this time there had not been a sound, but abruptly when we were within perhaps a couple of yards of the door we heard the sudden clumping of a hoof on the solid *parquet* floor of the billiard room. In the instant afterward it seemed to me that the whole place shook beneath the ponderous hoof falls of some huge thing, *coming toward the door*. Both Beaumont and I gave back a pace or two, and then realized and hung on to our courage, as you might say, and waited. The great tread came right up to the door and then stopped and there was an instant of absolute silence, except that so far as I was concerned, the pulsing in my throat and temples almost deafened me.

'I dare say we waited quite half a minute and then came the further restless clumping of a great hoof. Immediately afterward the sounds came right on as if some invisible thing passed through the closed door and the ponderous tread was upon us. We jumped, each of us, to our side of the passage and I know that I spread myself stiff against the wall. The clungk clunck, clungk clunck, of the great hoof falls passed right between us and slowly and with deadly deliberateness, down the passage. I heard them through a haze of blood beats in my ears and temples and my body was extraordinarily rigid and pringling and I was horribly breathless. I stood for a little time like this, my head turned so that I could see up the passage. I was conscious only that there was a hideous danger abroad. Do you understand?

'And then, suddenly, my pluck came back to me. I was aware that the noise of the hoof beats sounded near the other end of the passage. I twisted quickly and got my camera to bear and snapped off the flashlight. Immediately afterward, Beaumont let fly a storm of shots down the passage and began to run, shouting: "It's after Mary. Run! Run!"

'He rushed down the passage and I after him. We came out on the main landing and heard the sound of a hoof on the stairs and after that, nothing. And from thence onward, nothing.

'Down below us in the big hall I could see a number of the household 'round Miss Hisgins, who seemed to have fainted and there were several of the servants clumped together a little way off, staring up at the main landing and no one saying a single word. And about some twenty steps up the stairs was the old Captain Hisgins with a drawn sword in his hand where he had halted, just below the last hoof sound. I think I never saw anything finer than the old man standing there between his daughter and that infernal thing.

'I daresay you can understand the queer feeling of horror I had at passing that place on the stairs where the sounds had ceased. It was as if the monster were still standing there, invisible. And the peculiar thing was that we never heard another sound of the hoof, either up or down the stairs.

'After they had taken Miss Hisgins to her room I sent word that I should follow, so soon as they were ready for me. And presently, when a message came to tell me that I could come any time, I asked her father to give me a hand with my instrument box and between us we carried it into the girl's bedroom. I had the bed pulled well out into the middle of the room, after which I erected the electric pentacle 'round the bed.

'Then I directed that lamps should be placed 'round the room, but that on no account must any light be made within the pentacle; neither must anyone pass in or out. The girl's mother I had placed within the pentacle and directed that her maid should sit without, ready to carry any message so as to make sure that Mrs Hisgins did not have to leave the pentacle. I suggested also that the girl's father should stay the night in the room and that he had better be armed.

'When I left the bedroom I found Beaumont waiting outside the door in a miserable state of anxiety. I told him what I had done and explained to him that Miss Hisgins was probably perfectly safe within the "protection"; but that in addition to her father remaining the night in the room, I intended to stand guard at the door. I told him that I should like him to keep me company, for I knew that he could never sleep, feeling as he did, and I should not be sorry to have a companion. Also, I wanted to have him under my own observation, for there was no doubt but that he was actually in greater danger in some ways than the girl. At least, that was my opinion and is still, as I think you will agree later.

'I asked him whether he would object to my drawing a pentacle 'round him for the night and got him to agree, but I saw that he did not know whether to be superstitious about it or to regard it more as a piece of foolish mumming; but he took it seriously enough when I gave him some particulars about the Black Veil case, when young Aster died. You remember, he said it was a piece of silly superstition and stayed outside. Poor devil!

'The night passed quietly enough until a little while before dawn when we both heard the sounds of a great horse galloping 'round and 'round the house just as old Captain Hisgins had described it. You can imagine how queer it made me feel and directly afterward, I heard someone stir within the bedroom. I knocked at the door, for I was uneasy, and the Captain came. I asked whether everything was right; to which he replied yes, and immediately asked me whether I had heard the galloping, so that I knew he had heard them also. I suggested that it might be well to leave the bedroom door open a little until the dawn came in, as there was certainly something abroad. This was done and he went back into the room, to be near his wife and daughter.

'I had better say here that I was doubtful whether there was any value in the "Defense" about Miss Hisgins, for what I term the "personal sounds" of the manifestation were so extraordinarily material that I was inclined to parallel the case with that one of Harford's where the hand of the child kept materializing within the pentacle and patting the floor. As you will remember, that was a hideous business.

'Yet, as it chanced, nothing further happened and so soon as daylight had fully come we all went off to bed.

'Beaumont knocked me up about midday and I went down and made breakfast into lunch. Miss Hisgins was there and seemed in very fair spirits, considering. She told me that I had made her feel almost safe for the first time for days. She told me also that her cousin, Harry Parsket, was coming down from London and she knew that he would do anything to help fight the ghost. And after that she and Beaumont went out into the grounds to have a little time together.

'I had a walk in the grounds myself and went 'round the house, but saw no traces of hoof marks and after that I spent the rest of the day making an examination of the house, but found nothing.

'I made an end of my search before dark and went to my room to dress for dinner. When I got down the cousin had just arrived and I found him one of the nicest men I have met for a long time. A chap with a tremendous amount of pluck, and the particular kind of man I like to have with me in a bad case like the one I was on. I could see that what puzzled him most was our belief in the genuineness of the haunting and I found myself almost wanting something to happen, just to show him how true it was. As it chanced, something did happen, with a vengeance.

'Beaumont and Miss Hisgins had gone out for a stroll just before the dusk and Captain Hisgins asked me to come into his study for a short chat whilst Parsket went upstairs with his traps, for he had no man with him.

'I had a long conversation with the old Captain in which I pointed out that the "haunting" had evidently no particular connection with the house, but only with the girl herself and that the sooner she was married, the better as it would give Beaumont a right to be with her at all times and further than this, it might be that the manifestations would cease if the marriage were actually performed.

'The old man nodded agreement to this, especially to the first part and reminded me that three of the girls who were said to have been "haunted" had been sent away from home and met their deaths whilst away. And then in the midst of our talk there came a pretty frightening interruption, for all at once the old butler rushed into the room, most extraordinarily pale:

'"Miss Mary, sir! Miss Mary, sir!" he gasped. "She's screaming ... out in the Park, sir! And they say they can hear the Horse—"

'The Captain made one dive for a rack of arms and snatched down his old sword and ran out, drawing it as he ran. I dashed out and up the stairs, snatched my camera-flashlight and a heavy revolver, gave one yell at Parsket's door: "The Horse!" and was down and into the grounds.

'Away in the darkness there was a confused shouting and I caught the sounds of shooting, out among the scattered trees. And then, from a patch of blackness to my left, there burst suddenly an infernal gobbling sort of neighing. Instantly I whipped 'round and snapped off the flashlight. The great light blazed out momentarily, showing me the leaves of a big tree close at hand, quivering in the night breeze, but I saw nothing else and then the ten-fold blackness came down upon me and I heard Parsket shouting a little way back to know whether I had seen anything.

'The next instant he was beside me and I felt safer for his company, for there was some incredible thing near to us and I was momentarily blind because of the brightness of the flashlight. "What was it? What was it?" he kept repeating in an excited voice. And all the time I was staring into the darkness and answering, mechanically, "I don't know. I don't know."

'There was a burst of shouting somewhere ahead and then a shot. We ran toward the sounds, yelling to the people not to shoot; for in the darkness and panic there was this danger also. Then there came two of the game-keepers racing hard up the drive with their lanterns and guns; and immediately afterward a row of lights dancing toward us from the house, carried by some of the men-servants.

'As the lights came up I saw we had come close to Beaumont. He was standing over Miss Hisgins and he had his revolver in his hand. Then I saw his face and there was a great wound across his forehead. By him was the Captain, turning his naked sword this way and that, and peering into the darkness; a little behind him stood the old butler, a battle-axe from one of the arm stands in the hall in his hands. Yet there was nothing strange to be seen anywhere.

'We got the girl into the house and left her with her mother and Beaumont, whilst a groom rode for a doctor. And then the rest of us, with four other keepers, all armed with guns and carrying lanterns, searched 'round the home park. But we found nothing.

'When we got back we found that the doctor had been. He had bound up Beaumont's wound, which luckily was not deep, and ordered Miss Hisgins straight to bed. I went upstairs with the Captain and found Beaumont on guard outside of the girl's door. I asked him how he felt and then, so soon as the girl and her mother were ready for us, Captain Hisgins and I went into the bedroom and fixed the pentacle again 'round the bed. They had already got lamps about the room and after I had set the same order of watching as on the previous night, I joined Beaumont outside of the door.

'Parsket had come up while I had been in the bedroom and between us we got some idea from Beaumont as to what had happened out in the Park. It seems that they were coming home after their stroll from the direction of the West Lodge. It had got quite dark and suddenly Miss Hisgins said: 'Hush!' and came to a standstill. He stopped and listened, but heard nothing for a little. Then he caught it – the sound of a horse, seemingly a long way off, galloping toward them over the grass. He told the girl that it was nothing and started to hurry her toward the house, but she was not deceived, of course. In less than a minute they heard it quite close to them in the darkness and they started running. Then Miss Hisgins caught her foot and fell. She began to scream and that is what the butler heard. As Beaumont lifted the girl he heard the hoofs come thudding right at him. He stood over her and fired all five chambers of his revolver right at the sounds. He told us that he was sure he saw something that looked like an enormous horse's head, right upon him in the light of the last flash of his pistol. Immediately afterward he was struck a tremendous blow which knocked him down and then the Captain and the butler came running up, shouting. The rest, of course, we knew.

'About ten o'clock the butler brought us up a tray, for which I was very glad, as the night before I had got rather hungry. I warned Beaumont, however, to be very particular not to drink any spirits and I also made him give me his pipe and matches. At midnight I drew a pentacle 'round him and Parsket and I sat one on each side of him, outside the pentacle, for I had no fear that there would be any manifestation made against anyone except Beaumont or Miss Hisgins.

'After that we kept pretty quiet. The passage was lit by a big lamp at each end so that we had plenty of light and we were all armed, Beaumont and I with revolvers and Parsket with a shotgun. In addition to my weapon I had my camera and flashlight.

'Now and again we talked in whispers and twice the Captain came out of the bedroom to have a word with us. About half-past one we had all grown very silent and suddenly, about twenty minutes later, I held up my hand, silently, for there seemed to be a sound of galloping out in the night. I knocked on the bedroom door for the Captain to open it and when he came I whispered to him that we thought we heard the Horse. For some time we stayed listening, and both Parsket and the Captain thought they heard it; but now I was not so sure, neither was Beaumont. Yet afterward, I thought I heard it again.

'I told Captain Hisgins I thought he had better go into the bedroom and leave the door a little open and this he did. But from that time onward we heard nothing and presently the dawn came in and we all went very thankfully to bed.

'When I was called at lunchtime I had a little surprise, for Captain Hisgins told me that they had held a family council and had decided to take my advice and have the marriage without a day's more delay than possible. Beaumont was already on his way to London to get a special License and they hoped to have the wedding next day.

'This pleased me, for it seemed the sanest thing to be done in the extraordinary circumstances and meanwhile I should continue my investigations; but until the marriage was accomplished, my chief thought was to keep Miss Hisgins near to me.

'After lunch I thought I would take a few experimental photographs of Miss Hisgins and her *surroundings*. Sometimes the camera sees things that would seem very strange to normal human eyesight.

'With this intention and partly to make an excuse to keep her in my company as much as possible, I asked Miss Hisgins to join me in my experiments. She seemed glad to do this and I spent several hours with her, wandering all over the house, from room to room and whenever the impulse came I took a flashlight of her and the room or corridor in which we chanced to be at the moment.

'After we had gone right through the house in this fashion, I asked her whether she felt sufficiently brave to repeat the experiments in the cellars. She said yes, and so I rooted out Captain Hisgins and Parsket, for I was not going to take her even into what you might call artificial darkness without help and companionship at hand.

'When we were ready we went down into the wine cellar, Captain Hisgins carrying a shotgun and Parsket a specially prepared background and a lantern. I got the girl to stand in the middle of the cellar whilst Parsket and the Captain held out the background behind her. Then I fired off the flash-light, and we went into the next cellar where we repeated the experiment.

'Then in the third cellar, a tremendous, pitch-dark place, something extraordinary and horrible manifested itself. I had stationed Miss Hisgins in the centre of the place, with her father and Parsket holding the background as before. When all was ready and just as I pressed the trigger of the "flash," there came in the cellar that dreadful, gobbling neighing that I had heard out in the Park. It seemed to come from somewhere above the girl and in the glare of the sudden light I saw that she was staring tensely upward, but at no visible thing. And then in the succeeding comparative darkness, I was shouting to the Captain and Parsket to run Miss Hisgins out into the daylight.

'This was done instantly and I shut and locked the door afterward making the First and Eighth signs of the Saaamaaa Ritual opposite to each post and connecting them across the threshold with a triple line.

'In the meanwhile Parsket and Captain Hisgins carried the girl to her mother and left her there, in a half fainting condition whilst I stayed on guard outside of the cellar door, feeling pretty horrible for I knew that there was some disgusting thing inside, and along with this feeling there was a sense of half ashamedness, rather miserable, you know, because I had exposed Miss Hisgins to the danger.

'I had got the Captain's shotgun and when he and Parsket came down again they were each carrying guns and lanterns. I could not possibly tell you the utter relief of spirit and body that came to me when I heard them coming, but just try to imagine what it was like, standing outside of that cellar. Can you?

'I remember noticing, just before I went to unlock the door, how white and ghastly Parsket looked and the old Captain was grey-looking and I wondered whether my face was like theirs. And this, you know, had its own distinct effect upon my nerves, for it seemed to bring the beastliness of the thing crashing down on to me in a fresh way. I know it was only sheer will power that carried me up to the door and made me turn the key.

'I paused one little moment and then with a nervy jerk sent the door wide open and held my lantern over my head. Parsket and the Captain came one on each side of me and held up their lanterns, but the place was absolutely empty. Of course, I did not trust to a casual look of this kind, but spent several hours with the help of the two others in sounding every square foot of the floor, ceiling and walls.

'Yet, in the end I had to admit that the place itself was absolutely normal and so we came away. But I sealed the door and outside, opposite each doorpost I made the First and Last signs of the Saaamaaa Ritual, joined them as before, with a triple line. Can you imagine what it was like, searching that cellar?

'When we got upstairs I inquired very anxiously how Miss Hisgins was and the girl came out herself to tell me that she was all right and that I was not to trouble about her, or blame myself, as I told her I had been doing.

'I felt happier then and went off to dress for dinner and after that was done, Parsket and I took one of the bathrooms to develop the negatives that I had been taking. Yet none of the plates had anything to tell us until we came to the one that was taken in the cellar. Parsket was developing and I had taken a batch of the fixed plates out into the lamplight to examine them.

'I had just gone carefully through the lot when I heard a shout from Parsket and when I ran to him he was looking at a partly-developed negative which he was holding up to the red lamp. It showed the girl plainly, looking upward as I had seen her, but the thing that astonished me was the shadow of an enormous hoof, right above her, as if it were coming down upon her out of the shadows. And you know, I had run her bang into that danger. That was the thought that was chief in my mind.

'As soon as the developing was complete I fixed the plate and examined it carefully in a good light. There was no doubt about it at all, the thing above Miss Hisgins was an enormous, shadowy hoof. Yet I was no nearer to coming to any definite knowledge and the only thing I could do was to warn Parsket to say nothing about it to the girl for it would only increase her fright, but I showed the thing to her father for I considered it right that he should know.

'That night we took the same precaution for Miss Hisgins's safety as on the two previous nights and Parsket kept me company; yet the dawn came in without anything unusual having happened and I went off to bed.

'When I got down to lunch I learnt that Beaumont had wired to say that he would be in soon after four; also that a message had been sent to the

Rector. And it was generally plain that the ladies of the house were in a tremendous fluster.

'Beaumont's train was late and he did not get home until five, but even then the Rector had not put in an appearance and the butler came in to say that the coachman had returned without him as he had been called away unexpectedly. Twice more during the evening the carriage was sent down, but the clergyman had not returned and we had to delay the marriage until the next day.

'That night I arranged the "Defense" 'round the girl's bed and the Captain and his wife sat up with her as before. Beaumont, as I expected, insisted on keeping watch with me and he seemed in a curiously frightened mood; not for himself, you know, but for Miss Hisgins. He had a horrible feeling he told me, that there would be a final, dreadful attempt on his sweetheart that night.

'This, of course, I told him was nothing but nerves; yet really, it made me feel very anxious; for I have seen too much not to know that under such circumstances a premonitory *conviction* of impending danger is not necessarily to be put down entirely to nerves. In fact, Beaumont was so simply and earnestly convinced that the night would bring some extraordinary manifestation that I got Parsket to rig up a long cord from the wire of the butler's bell, to come along the passage handy.

'To the butler himself I gave directions not to undress and to give the same order to two of the footmen. If I rang he was to come instantly, with the footmen, carrying lanterns and the lanterns were to be kept ready lit all night. If for any reason the bell did not ring and I blew my whistle, he was to take that as a signal in the place of the bell.

'After I had arranged all these minor details I drew a pentacle about Beaumont and warned him very particularly to stay within it, whatever happened. And when this was done, there was nothing to do but wait and pray that the night would go as quietly as the night before.

'We scarcely talked at all and by about one a.m. we were all very tense and nervous so that at last Parsket got up and began to walk up and down the corridor to steady himself a bit. Presently I slipped off my pumps and joined him and we walked up and down, whispering occasionally for something over an hour, until in turning I caught my foot in the bell cord and went down on my face; but without hurting myself or making a noise.

'When I got up Parsket nudged me.

'"Did you notice that the bell never rang?" he whispered.

'"Jove!" I said, "you're right."

'"Wait a minute," he answered. "I'll bet it's only a kink somewhere in the cord." He left his gun and slipped along the passage and taking the top lamp, tiptoed away into the house, carrying Beaumont's revolver ready in his right hand. He was a plucky chap, I remember thinking then, and again, later.

'Just then Beaumont motioned to me for absolute quiet. Directly afterward I heard the thing for which he listened – the sound of a horse galloping, out in the night. I think that I may say I fairly shivered. The sound died away and left a horrible, desolate, eerie feeling in the air, you know. I put my hand out to the bell cord, hoping Parsket had got it clear. Then I waited, glancing before and behind.

'Perhaps two minutes passed, full of what seemed like an almost unearthly quiet. And then, suddenly, down the corridor at the lighted end there sounded the clumping of a great hoof and instantly the lamp was thrown with a tremendous crash and we were in the dark. I tugged hard on the cord and blew the whistle; then I raised my snapshot and fired the flashlight. The corridor blazed into brilliant light, but there was nothing, and then the darkness fell like thunder. I heard the Captain at the bedroom door and shouted to him to bring out a lamp, *quick*; but instead something started to kick the door and I heard the Captain shouting within the bedroom and then the screaming of the women. I had a sudden horrible fear that the monster had got into the bedroom, but in the same instant from up the corridor there came abruptly the vile, gobbling neighing that we had heard in the park and the cellar. I blew the whistle again and groped blindly for the bell cord, shouting to Beaumont to stay in the Pentacle, whatever happened. I yelled again to the Captain to bring out a lamp and there came a smashing sound against the bedroom door. Then I had my matches in my hand, to get some light before that incredible, unseen Monster was upon us.

'The match scraped on the box and flared up dully and in the same instant I heard a faint sound behind me. I whipped 'round in a kind of mad terror and saw something in the light of the match – a monstrous horse-head close to Beaumont.

'"Look out, Beaumont!" I shouted in a sort of scream. "It's behind you!"

'The match went out abruptly and instantly there came the huge bang of Parsket's double-barrel (both barrels at once), fired evidently single-handed by Beaumont close to my ear, as it seemed. I caught a momentary glimpse of the great head in the flash and of an enormous hoof amid the belch of fire and smoke seeming to be descending upon Beaumont. In the same instant I fired three chambers of my revolver. There was the sound of a dull blow and then that horrible, gobbling neigh broke out close to me. I fired twice at the sound. Immediately afterward something struck me and I was knocked backward. I got on to my knees and shouted for help at the top of my voice. I heard the women screaming behind the closed door of the bedroom and was dully aware that the door was being smashed from the inside, and directly afterward I knew that Beaumont was struggling with some hideous thing near to me. For an instant I held back, stupidly, paralyzed with funk and then, blindly and in a sort of rigid chill of goose flesh I went to help him, shouting his name. I can tell you, I was nearly sick with the naked fear I had on me. There came a little, choking scream out of the darkness, and at that I jumped forward into the dark. I gripped a vast, furry ear. Then something struck me another great blow knocking me sick. I hit back, weak and blind and gripped with my other hand at the incredible thing. Abruptly I was dimly aware of a tremendous crash behind me and a great burst of light. There were other lights in the passage and a noise of feet and shouting. My hand-grips were torn from the thing they held; I shut my eyes stupidly and heard a loud yell above me and then a heavy blow, like a butcher chopping meat and then something fell upon me.

'I was helped to my knees by the Captain and the butler. On the floor lay an enormous horse-head out of which protruded a man's trunk and legs. On the wrists were fixed great hoofs. It was the monster. The Captain cut something with the sword that he held in his hand and stooped and lifted off the mask, for that is what it was. I saw the face then of the man who had worn it. It was Parsket. He had a bad wound across the forehead where the Captain's sword had bit through the mask. I looked bewilderedly from him to Beaumont, who was sitting up, leaning against the wall of the corridor. Then I stared at Parsket again.

'"By Jove!" I said at last, and then I was quiet for I was so ashamed for the man. You can understand, can't you? And he was opening his eyes. And you know, I had grown so to like him.

'And then, you know, just as Parsket was getting back his wits and looking from one to the other of us and beginning to remember, there happened a strange and incredible thing. For from the end of the corridor there sounded suddenly, the clumping of a great hoof. I looked that way and then instantly at Parsket and saw a horrible fear in his face and eyes. He wrenched himself 'round, weakly, and stared in mad terror up the corridor to where the sound had been, and the rest of us stared, in a frozen group. I remember vaguely half sobs and whispers from Miss Hisgins's bedroom, all the while that I stared frightenedly up the corridor.

'The silence lasted several seconds and then, abruptly there came again the clumping of the great hoof, away at the end of the corridor. And immediately afterward the clungk, clunk – clungk, clunk of mighty hoofs coming down the passage toward us.

'Even then, you know, most of us thought it was some mechanism of Parsket's still at work and we were in the queerest mixture of fright and doubt. I think everyone looked at Parsket. And suddenly the Captain shouted out:

'"Stop this damned fooling at once. Haven't you done enough?"

'For my part, I was now frightened for I had a *sense* that there was something horrible and wrong. And then Parsket managed to gasp out:

'"It's not me! My God! It's not me! My God! It's not me."

'And then, you know, it seemed to come home to everyone in an instant that there was really some dreadful thing coming down the passage. There was a mad rush to get away and even old Captain Hisgins gave back with the butler and the footmen. Beaumont fainted outright, as I found afterward, for he had been badly mauled. I just flattened back against the wall, kneeling as I was, too stupid and dazed even to run. And almost in the same instant the ponderous hoof falls sounded close to me and seeming to shake the solid floor as they passed. Abruptly the great sounds ceased and I knew in a sort of sick fashion that the thing had halted opposite to the door of the girl's bedroom. And then I was aware that Parsket was standing rocking in the doorway with his arms spread across, so as to fill the doorway with his body. Parsket was extraordinarily pale and the blood was running down his face from the wound in his forehead; and then I noticed that he seemed to be looking at something in the passage with a peculiar, desperate, fixed, incredibly masterful gaze. But there was really nothing to be seen. And suddenly the clungk, clunk – clungk, clunk recommenced and passed onward down the passage. In the same moment Parsket pitched forward out of the doorway on to his face.

'There were shouts from the huddle of men down the passage and the two footmen and the butler simply ran, carrying their lanterns, but the Captain went against the side-wall with his back and put the lamp he was carrying over his head. The dull tread of the Horse went past him, and left him unharmed and I heard the monstrous hoof falls going away and away through the quiet house and after that a dead silence.

'Then the Captain moved and came toward us, very slow and shaky and with an extraordinarily grey face.

'I crept toward Parsket and the Captain came to help me. We turned him over and, you know, I knew in a moment that he was dead; but you can imagine what a feeling it sent through me.

'I looked at the Captain and suddenly he said:

'"That – That – That—" and I know that he was trying to tell me that Parsket had stood between his daughter and whatever it was that had gone down the passage. I stood up and steadied him, though I was not very steady myself. And suddenly his face began to work and he went down on to his knees by Parsket and cried like some shaken child. Then the women came out of the doorway of the bedroom and I turned away and left him to them, whilst I over to Beaumont.

'That is practically the whole story and the only thing that is left to me is to try to explain some of the puzzling parts, here and there.

'Perhaps you have seen that Parsket was in love with Miss Hisgins and this fact is the key to a good deal that was extraordinary. He was doubtless responsible for some portions of the "haunting"; in fact I think for nearly everything, but, you know, I can prove nothing and what I have to tell you is chiefly the result of deduction.

'In the first place, it is obvious that Parsket's intention was to frighten Beaumont away and when he found that he could not do this, I think he grew so desperate that he really intended to kill him. I hate to say this, but the facts force me to think so.

'I am quite certain that it was Parsket who broke Beaumont's arm. He knew all the details of the so-called "Horse Legend", and got the idea to work upon the old story for his own end. He evidently had some method of slipping in and out of the house, probably through one of the many French windows, or possibly he had a key to one or two of the garden doors, and when he was supposed to be away, he was really coming down on the quiet and hiding somewhere in the neighborhood.

'The incident of the kiss in the dark hall I put down to sheer nervous imaginings on the part of Beaumont and Miss Hisgins, yet I must say that the sound of the horse outside of the front door is a little difficult to explain away. But I am still inclined to keep to my first idea on this point, that there was nothing really unnatural about it.

'The hoof sounds in the billiard room and down the passage were done by Parsket from the floor below by bumping up against the panelled ceiling with a block of wood tied to one of the window hooks. I proved this by an examination which showed the dents in the woodwork.

'The sounds of the horse galloping 'round the house were possibly made also by Parsket, who must have had a horse tied up in the plantation nearby, unless, indeed, he made the sounds himself, but I do not see how he could have gone fast enough to produce the illusion. In any case, I don't feel perfect certainty on this point. I failed to find any hoof marks, as you remember.

'The gobbling neighing in the park was a ventriloquial achievement on the part of Parsket and the attack out there on Beaumont was also by him, so that when I thought he was in his bedroom, he must have been outside all the time and joined me after I ran out of the front door. This is almost probable. I mean that Parsket was the cause, for if it had been something more serious he would certainly have given up his foolishness, knowing that there was no longer any need for it. I cannot imagine how he escaped being shot, both then and in the last mad action of which I have just told you. He was enormously without fear of any kind for himself as you can see.

'The time when Parsket was with us, when we thought we heard the Horse galloping 'round the house, we must have been deceived. No one was very sure, except, of course, Parsket, who would naturally encourage the belief.

'The neighing in the cellar is where I consider there came the first suspicion into Parsket's mind that there was something more at work than his sham haunting. The neighing was done by him in the same way that he did it in the park; but when I remember how ghastly he looked I feel sure that the sounds must have had some infernal quality added to them which frightened the man himself. Yet, later, he would persuade himself that he had been getting fanciful. Of course, I must not forget that the effect upon Miss Hisgins must have made him feel pretty miserable.

'Then, about the clergyman being called away, we found afterward that it was a bogus errand, or, rather, call and it is apparent that Parsket was at the bottom of this, so as to get a few more hours in which to achieve his end and what that was, a very little imagination will show you; for he had found that Beaumont would not be frightened away. I hate to think this, but I'm bound to. Anyway, it is obvious that the man was temporarily a bit off his normal balance. Love's a queer disease!

'Then, there is no doubt at all but that Parsket left the cord to the butler's bell hitched somewhere so as to give him an excuse to slip away naturally to clear it. This also gave him the opportunity to remove one of the passage lamps. Then he had only to smash the other and the passage was in utter darkness for him to make the attempt on Beaumont.

'In the same way, it was he who locked the door of the bedroom and took the key (it was in his pocket). This prevented the Captain from bringing a light and coming to the rescue. But Captain Hisgins broke down the door with the heavy fender curb and it was his smashing the door that sounded so confusing and frightening in the darkness of the passage.

'The photograph of the monstrous hoof above Miss Hisgins in the cellar is one of the things that I am less sure about. It might have been faked by Parsket, whilst I was out of the room, and this would have been easy enough, to anyone who knew how. But, you know, it does not look like a fake. Yet, there is as much evidence of probability that it was faked, as against; and the thing is too vague for an examination to help to a definite decision so that I will express no opinion, one way or the other. It is certainly a horrible photograph.

'And now I come to that last, dreadful thing. There has been no further manifestation of anything abnormal so that there is an extraordinary uncertainty in my conclusions. If we had not heard those last sounds and if

Parsket had not shown that enormous sense of fear the whole of this case could be explained in the way in which I have shown. And, in fact, as you have seen, I am of the opinion that almost all of it can be cleared up, but I see no way of going past the thing we heard at the last and the fear that Parsket showed.

'His death – no, that proves nothing. At the inquest it was described somewhat untechnically as due to heart spasm. That is normal enough and leaves us quite in the dark as to whether he died because he stood between the girl and some incredible thing of monstrosity.

'The look on Parsket's face and the thing he called out when he heard the great hoof sounds coming down the passage seem to show that he had the sudden realization of what before then may have been nothing more than a horrible suspicion. And his fear and appreciation of some tremendous danger approaching was probably more keenly real even than mine. And then he did the one fine, great thing!'

'And the cause?' I said. 'What caused it?'

Carnacki shook his head.

'God knows,' he answered, with a peculiar, sincere reverence. 'If that thing was what it seemed to be one might suggest an explanation which would not offend one's reason, but which may be utterly wrong. Yet I have thought, though it would take a long lecture on Thought Induction to get you to appreciate my reasons, that Parsket had produced what I might term a kind of "induced haunting," a kind of induced simulation of his mental conceptions to his desperate thoughts and broodings. It is impossible to make it clearer in a few words.'

'But the old story!' I said. 'Why may not there have been something in *that*?'

'There may have been something in it,' said Carnacki. 'But I do not think it had anything to do with this. I have not clearly thought out my reasons, yet; but later I may be able to tell you why I think so.'

'And the marriage? And the cellar – was there anything found there?' asked Taylor.

'Yes, the marriage was performed that day in spite of the tragedy,' Carnacki told us. 'It was the wisest thing to do considering the things that I cannot explain. Yes, I had the floor of that big cellar up, for I had a feeling I might find something there to give me some light. But there was nothing.

'You know, the whole thing is tremendous and extraordinary. I shall never forget the look on Parsket's face. And afterward the disgusting sounds of those great hoofs going away through the quiet house.'

Carnacki stood up.

'Out you go!' he said in friendly fashion, using the recognized formula.

And we went presently out into the quiet of the Embankment, and so to our homes.

The Searcher of the End House

William Hope Hodgson

It was still evening, as I remember, and the four of us, Jessop, Arkright, Taylor and I, looked disappointedly at Carnacki, where he sat silent in his great chair.

We had come in response to the usual card of invitation, which – as you know – we have come to consider as a sure prelude to a good story; and now, after telling us the short incident of the Three Straw Platters, he had lapsed into a contented silence, and the night not half gone, as I have hinted.

However, as it chanced, some pitying fate jogged Carnacki's elbow, or his memory, and he began again, in his queer level way: –

'The "Straw Platters" business reminds me of the "Searcher" Case, which I have sometimes thought might interest you. It was some time ago, in fact a deuce of a long time ago, that the thing happened; and my experience of what I might term "curious" things was very small at that time.

'I was living with my mother when it occurred, in a small house just outside of Appledorn, on the South Coast. The house was the last of a row of detached cottage villas, each house standing in its own garden; and very dainty little places they were, very old, and most of them smothered in roses; and all with those quaint old leaded windows, and doors of genuine oak. You must try to picture them for the sake of their complete niceness.

'Now I must remind you at the beginning that my mother and I had lived in that little house for two years; and in the whole of that time there had not been a single peculiar happening to worry us.

'And then, something happened.

'It was about two o'clock one morning, as I was finishing some letters, that I heard the door of my mother's bedroom open, and she came to the top of the stairs, and knocked on the banisters.

'"All right, dear," I called; for I suppose she was merely reminding me that I should have been in bed long ago; then I heard her go back to her room, and I hurried my work, for fear she should lie awake, until she heard me safe up to my room.

'When I was finished, I lit my candle, put out the lamp, and went upstairs. As I came opposite the door of my mother's room, I saw that it was open, called good night to her, very softly, and asked whether I should close the door. As there was no answer, I knew that she had dropped off to sleep again, and I closed the door very gently, and turned into my room, just across the passage. As I did so, I experienced a momentary, half-aware sense of a faint, peculiar, disagreeable odour in the passage; but it was not until the following night that I *realized* I had noticed a smell that offended me. You follow me? It is so often like that – one suddenly knows a thing that really recorded itself on one's consciousness, perhaps a year before.

'The next morning at breakfast, I mentioned casually to my mother that she had "dropped off", and I had shut the door for her. To my surprise, she assured me she had never been out of her room. I reminded her about the two raps she had given upon the banister; but she still was certain I must be mistaken; and in the end I teased her, saying she had grown so accustomed to my bad habit of sitting up late, that she had come to call me in her sleep. Of course, she denied this, and I let the matter drop; but I was more than a little puzzled, and did not know whether to believe my own explanation, or to take the mater's, which was to put the noises down to the mice, and the open door to the fact that she couldn't have properly latched it, when she went to bed. I suppose, away in the subconscious part of me, I had a stirring of less reasonable thoughts; but certainly, I had no real uneasiness at that time.

'The next night there came a further development. About two thirty a.m., I heard my mother's door open, just as on the previous night, and immediately afterward she rapped sharply, on the banister, as it seemed to me. I stopped my work and called up that I would not be long. As she made no reply, and I did not hear her go back to bed, I had a quick sense of wonder whether she might not be doing it in her sleep, after all, just as I had said.

'With the thought, I stood up, and taking the lamp from the table, began to go toward the door, which was open into the passage. It was then I got a sudden nasty sort of thrill; for it came to me, all at once, that my mother never knocked, when I sat up too late; she always called. You will understand I was not really frightened in any way; only vaguely uneasy, and pretty sure she must really be doing the thing in her sleep.

'I went quickly up the stairs, and when I came to the top, my mother was not there; but her door was open. I had a bewildered sense though believing she must have gone quietly back to bed, without my hearing her. I entered her room and found her sleeping quietly and naturally; for the vague sense of trouble in me was sufficiently strong to make me go over to look at her.

'When I was sure that she was perfectly right in every way, I was still a little bothered; but much more inclined to think my suspicion correct and that she had gone quietly back to bed in her sleep, without knowing what she had been doing. This was the most reasonable thing to think, as you must see.

'And then it came to me, suddenly, that vague, queer, mildewy smell in the room; and it was in that instant I became aware I had smelt the same strange, uncertain smell the night before in the passage.

'I was definitely uneasy now, and began to search my mother's room; though with no aim or clear thought of anything, except to assure myself that there was nothing in the room. All the time, you know, I never *expected really* to find anything; only my uneasiness had to be assured.

'In the middle of my search my mother woke up, and of course I had to explain. I told her about her door opening, and the knocks on the banister, and that I had come up and found her asleep. I said nothing about the smell, which was not very distinct; but told her that the thing happening twice had made me a bit nervous, and possibly fanciful, and I thought I would take a look 'round, just to feel satisfied.

'I have thought since that the reason I made no mention of the smell, was not only that I did not want to frighten my mother, for I was scarcely that myself; but because I had only a vague half-knowledge that I associated the smell with fancies too indefinite and peculiar to bear talking about. You will understand that I am able *now* to analyze and put the thing into words; but *then* I did not even know my chief reason for saying nothing; let alone appreciate its possible significance.

'It was my mother, after all, who put part of my vague sensations into words: –

'"What a disagreeable smell!" she exclaimed, and was silent a moment, looking at me. Then: – "You feel there's something wrong?" still looking at me, very quietly but with a little, nervous note of questioning expectancy.

'"I don't know," I said. "I can't understand it, unless you've really been walking about in your sleep."

'"The smell," she said.

'"Yes," I replied. "That's what puzzles me too. I'll take a walk through the house; but I don't suppose it's anything."

'I lit her candle, and taking the lamp, I went through the other bedrooms, and afterward all over the house, including the three underground cellars, which was a little trying to the nerves, seeing that I was more nervous than I would admit.

'Then I went back to my mother, and told her there was really nothing to bother about; and, you know, in the end, we talked ourselves into believing it was nothing. My mother would not agree that she might have been sleepwalking; but she was ready to put the door opening down to the fault of the latch, which certainly snicked very lightly. As for the knocks, they might be the old warped woodwork of the house cracking a bit, or a mouse rattling a piece of loose plaster. The smell was more difficult to explain; but finally we agreed that it might easily be the queer night smell of the moist earth, coming in through the open window of my mother's room, from the back garden, or – for that matter – from the little churchyard beyond the big wall at the bottom of the garden.

'And so we quietened down, and finally I went to bed, and to sleep.

'I think this is certainly a lesson on the way we humans can delude ourselves; for there was not one of these explanations that my reason could really accept. Try to imagine yourself in the same circumstances, and you will see how absurd our attempts to explain the happenings really were.

'In the morning, when I came down to breakfast, we talked it all over again, and whilst we agreed that it was strange, we also agreed that we had begun to imagine funny things in the backs of our minds, which now we felt half ashamed to admit. This is very strange when you come to look into it; but very human.

'And then that night again my mother's door was slammed once more just after midnight. I caught up the lamp, and when I reached her door, I found it shut. I opened it quickly, and went in, to find my mother lying with her eyes open, and rather nervous; having been waked by the bang of the door. But what upset me more than anything, was the fact that there was a disgusting smell in the passage and in her room.

'Whilst I was asking her whether she was all right, a door slammed twice downstairs; and you can imagine how it made me feel. My mother and I looked at one another; and then I lit her candle, and taking the poker from the fender, went downstairs with the lamp, beginning to feel really nervous. The cumulative effect of so many queer happenings was getting hold of me; and all the *apparently* reasonable explanations seemed futile.

'The horrible smell seemed to be very strong in the downstairs passage; also in the front room and the cellars; but chiefly in the passage. I made a very thorough search of the house, and when I had finished, I knew that all the lower windows and doors were properly shut and fastened, and that there was no living thing in the house, beyond our two selves. Then I went up to my mother's room again, and we talked the thing over for an hour or more, and in the end came to the conclusion that we might, after all, be reading too much into a number of little things; but, you know, inside of us, we did not believe this.

'Later, when we had talked ourselves into a more comfortable state of mind, I said good night, and went off to bed; and presently managed to get to sleep.

'In the early hours of the morning, whilst it was still dark, I was waked by a loud noise. I sat up in bed, and listened. And from downstairs, I heard: – bang, bang, bang, one door after another being slammed; at least, that is the impression the sounds gave to me.

'I jumped out of bed, with the tingle and shiver of sudden fright on me; and at the same moment, as I lit my candle, my door was pushed slowly open; I had left it unlatched, so as not to feel that my mother was quite shut off from me.

'"Who's there?" I shouted out, in a voice twice as deep as my natural one, and with a queer breathlessness, that sudden fright so often gives one. "Who's there?"

'Then I heard my mother saying: –

'"It's me, Thomas. Whatever is happening downstairs?"

'She was in the room by this, and I saw she had her bedroom poker in one hand, and her candle in the other. I could have smiled at her, had it not been for the extraordinary sounds downstairs.

'I got into my slippers, and reached down an old sword bayonet from the wall; then I picked up my candle, and begged my mother not to come; but I knew it would be little use, if she had made up her mind; and she had, with the result that she acted as a sort of rearguard for me, during our search. I know, in some ways, I was very glad to have her with me, as you will understand.

'By this time, the door slamming had ceased, and there seemed, probably because of the contrast, to be an appalling silence in the house. However, I led the way, holding my candle high, and keeping the sword bayonet very handy. Downstairs we found all the doors wide open; although the outer doors and the windows were closed all right. I began to wonder whether the noises had been made by the doors after all. Of one thing only were we sure, and that was, there was no living thing in the house, beside ourselves, while everywhere throughout the house, there was the taint of that disgusting odour.

'Of course it was absurd to try to make believe any longer. There was something strange about the house; and as soon as it was daylight, I set my mother to packing; and soon after breakfast, I saw her off by train.

'Then I set to work to try to clear up the mystery. I went first to the landlord, and told him all the circumstances. From him, I found that twelve or fifteen years back, the house had got rather a curious name from three or four tenants; with the result that it had remained empty a long while; in the end he had let it at a low rent to a Captain Tobias, on the one condition that he should hold his tongue, if he saw anything peculiar. The landlord's idea – as he told me frankly – was to free the house from these tales of "something queer," by keeping a tenant in it, and then to sell it for the best price he could get.

'However, when Captain Tobias left, after a ten years' tenancy, there was no longer any talk about the house; so when I offered to take it on a five years' lease, he had jumped at the offer. This was the whole story; so he gave me to understand. When I pressed him for details of the supposed peculiar happenings in the house, all those years back, he said the tenants had talked about a woman who always moved about the house at night. Some tenants never saw anything; but others would not stay out the first month's tenancy.

'One thing the landlord was particular to point out, that no tenant had ever complained about knockings, or door slamming. As for the smell, he seemed positively indignant about it; but why, I don't suppose he knew himself, except that he probably had some vague feeling that it was an indirect accusation on my part that the drains were not right.

'In the end, I suggested that he should come down and spend the night with me. He agreed at once, especially as I told him I intended to keep the whole business quiet, and try to get to the bottom of the curious affair; for he was anxious to keep the rumour of the haunting from getting about.

'About three o'clock that afternoon, he came down, and we made a thorough search of the house, which, however, revealed nothing unusual. Afterward, the landlord made one or two tests, which showed him the drainage was in perfect order; after that we made our preparations for sitting up all night.

'First, we borrowed two policemen's dark lanterns from the station nearby, and where the superintendent and I were friendly, and as soon as it was really dusk, the landlord went up to his house for his gun. I had the sword bayonet I have told you about; and when the landlord got back, we sat talking in my study until nearly midnight.

'Then we lit the lanterns and went upstairs. We placed the lanterns, gun and bayonet handy on the table; then I shut and sealed the bedroom doors; afterward we took our seats, and turned off the lights.

'From then until two o'clock, nothing happened; but a little after two, as I found by holding my watch near the faint glow of the closed lanterns, I had a time of extraordinary nervousness; and I bent toward the landlord, and whispered to him that I had a queer feeling something was about to happen, and to be ready with his lantern; at the same time I reached out toward mine. In the very instant I made this movement, the darkness which filled the passage seemed to become suddenly of a dull violet colour; not, as if a light had been shone; but as if the natural blackness of the night had changed colour. And then, coming through this violet night, through this violet-coloured gloom, came a little naked Child, running. In an extraordinary way, the Child seemed not to be distinct from the surrounding gloom; but almost as if it were a concentration of that extraordinary atmosphere; as if that gloomy colour which had changed the night, came from the Child. It seems impossible to make clear to you; but try to understand it.

'The Child went past me, running, with the natural movement of the legs of a chubby human child, but in an absolute and inconceivable silence. It was a very small Child, and must have passed under the table; but I saw the Child through the table, as if it had been only a slightly darker shadow than the coloured gloom. In the same instant, I saw that a fluctuating glimmer of violet light outlined the metal of the gun-barrels and the blade of the sword bayonet, making them seem like faint shapes of glimmering light, floating unsupported where the tabletop should have shown solid.

'Now, curiously, as I saw these things, I was subconsciously aware that I heard the anxious breathing of the landlord, quite clear and laboured, close to my elbow, where he waited nervously with his hands on the lantern. I realized in that moment that he saw nothing; but waited in the darkness, for my warning to come true.

'Even as I took heed of these minor things, I saw the Child jump to one side, and hide behind some half-seen object that was certainly nothing belonging to the passage. I stared, intently, with a most extraordinary thrill of expectant wonder, with fright making goose flesh of my back. And even as I stared, I solved for myself the less important problem of what the two black clouds were that hung over a part of the table. I think it very curious and interesting, the double working of the mind, often so much more apparent during times of stress. The two clouds came from two faintly shining shapes, which I knew must be the metal of the lanterns; and the things that looked black to the sight with which I was then seeing, could be nothing else but what to normal human sight is known as light. This phenomenon I have always remembered. I have twice seen a somewhat similar thing; in the Dark Light Case and in that trouble of Maetheson's, which you know about.

'Even as I understood this matter of the lights, I was looking to my left, to understand why the Child was hiding. And suddenly, I heard the landlord shout out: – "The Woman!" But I saw nothing. I had a disagreeable sense that something repugnant was near to me, and I was aware in the same moment that the landlord was gripping my arm in a hard, frightened grip. Then I was looking back to where the Child had hidden. I saw the Child peeping out from behind its hiding place, seeming to be looking up the passage; but whether in fear I could not tell. Then it came out, and ran headlong away, through the place where should have been the wall of my mother's bedroom; but the Sense with which I was seeing these things, showed me the wall only as a vague, upright shadow, unsubstantial. And immediately the child was lost to me, in the dull violet gloom. At the same time, I felt the landlord press back against me, as if something had passed close to him; and he called out again, a hoarse sort of cry: – "The Woman! The Woman!" and turned the shade clumsily from off his lantern. But I had seen no Woman; and the passage showed empty, as he shone the beam of his light jerkily to and fro; but chiefly in the direction of the doorway of my mother's room.

'He was still clutching my arm, and had risen to his feet; and now, mechanically and almost slowly, I picked up my lantern and turned on the light. I shone it, a little dazedly, at the seals upon the doors; but none were broken; then I sent the light to and fro, up and down the passage; but there was nothing; and I turned to the landlord, who was saying something in a rather incoherent fashion. As my light passed over his face, I noted, in a dull sort of way, that he was drenched with sweat.

'Then my wits became more handleable, and I began to catch the drift of his words: – "Did you see her? Did you see her?" he was saying, over and over again; and then I found myself telling him, in quite a level voice, that I had not seen any Woman. He became more coherent then, and I found that he had seen a Woman come from the end of the passage, and go past us; but he could not describe her, except that she kept stopping and looking about her, and had even peered at the wall, close beside him, as if looking for something. But what seemed to trouble him most, was that she had not seemed to see him at all. He repeated this so often, that in the end I told him, in an absurd sort of way, that he ought to be very glad she had not. What did it all mean? was the question; somehow I was not so frightened, as utterly bewildered. I had seen less then, than since; but what I had seen, had made me feel adrift from my anchorage of Reason.

'What did it mean? He had seen a Woman, searching for something. *I* had not seen this Woman. *I* had seen a Child, running away, and hiding from Something or Someone. *He* had not seen the Child, or the other things – only the Woman. And *I* had not seen her. What did it all mean?

'I had said nothing to the landlord about the Child. I had been too bewildered, and I realized that it would be futile to attempt an explanation. He was already stupid with the thing he had seen; and not the kind of man to understand. All this went through my mind as we stood there, shining the lanterns to and fro. All the time, intermingled with a streak of practical reasoning, I was questioning myself, what did it all mean? What was the Woman searching for; what was the Child running from?

'Suddenly, as I stood there, bewildered and nervous, making random answers to the landlord, a door below was violently slammed, and directly I caught the horrible reek of which I have told you.

'"There!" I said to the landlord, and caught his arm, in my turn. "The Smell! Do *you* smell it?"

'He looked at me so stupidly that in a sort of nervous anger, I shook him.

'"Yes," he said, in a queer voice, trying to shine the light from his shaking lantern at the stair head.

'"Come on!" I said, and picked up my bayonet; and he came, carrying his gun awkwardly. I think he came, more because he was afraid to be left alone, than because he had any pluck left, poor beggar. I never sneer at that kind of funk, at least very seldom; for when it takes hold of you, it makes rags of your courage.

'I led the way downstairs, shining my light into the lower passage, and afterward at the doors to see whether they were shut; for I had closed and latched them, placing a corner of a mat against each door, so I should know which had been opened.

'I saw at once that none of the doors had been opened; then I threw the beam of my light down alongside the stairway, in order to see the mat I had placed against the door at the top of the cellar stairs. I got a horrid thrill; for the mat was flat! I paused a couple of seconds, shining my light to and fro in the passage, and holding fast to my courage, I went down the stairs.

'As I came to the bottom step, I saw patches of wet all up and down the passage. I shone my lantern on them. It was the imprint of a wet foot on the oilcloth of the passage; not an ordinary footprint, but a queer, soft, flabby, spreading imprint, that gave me a feeling of extraordinary horror.

'Backward and forward I flashed the light over the impossible marks and saw them everywhere. Suddenly I noticed that they led to each of the closed doors. I felt something touch my back, and glanced 'round swiftly, to find the landlord had come close to me, almost pressing against me, in his fear.

'"It's all right," I said, but in a rather breathless whisper, meaning to put a little courage into him; for I could feel that he was shaking through all his body. Even then as I tried to get him steadied enough to be of some use, his gun went off with a tremendous bang. He jumped, and yelled with sheer terror; and I swore because of the shock.

'"Give it to me, for God's sake!" I said, and slipped the gun from his hand; and in the same instant there was a sound of running steps up the garden path, and immediately the flash of a bull's-eye lantern upon the fan light over the front door. Then the door was tried, and directly afterward there came a thunderous knocking, which told me a policeman had heard the shot.

'I went to the door, and opened it. Fortunately the constable knew me, and when I had beckoned him in, I was able to explain matters in a very short time. While doing this, Inspector Johnstone came up the path, having missed the officer, and seeing lights and the open door. I told him as briefly as possible what had occurred, and did not mention the Child or the Woman; for it would have seem too fantastic for him to notice. I showed him the queer, wet footprints and how they went toward the closed doors. I explained quickly about the mats, and how that the one against the cellar door was flat, which showed the door had been opened.

'The inspector nodded, and told the constable to guard the door at the top of the cellar stairs. He then asked the hall lamp to be lit, after which he took the policeman's lantern, and led the way into the front room. He paused with the door wide open, and threw the light all 'round; then he jumped into the room, and looked behind the door; there was no one there; but all over the polished oak floor, between the scattered rugs, went the marks of those horrible spreading footprints; and the room permeated with the horrible odour.

'The inspector searched the room carefully, and then went into the middle room, using the same precautions. There was nothing in the middle room, or in the kitchen or pantry; but everywhere went the wet footmarks through all the rooms, showing plainly wherever there were woodwork or oilcloth; and always there was the smell.

'The inspector ceased from his search of the rooms, and spent a minute in trying whether the mats would really fall flat when the doors were open, or merely ruckle up in a way as to appear they had been untouched; but in each case, the mats fell flat, and remained so.

'"Extraordinary!" I heard Johnstone mutter to himself. And then he went toward the cellar door. He had inquired at first whether there were windows to the cellar, and when he learned there was no way out, except by the door, he had left this part of the search to the last.

'As Johnstone came up to the door, the policeman made a motion of salute, and said something in a low voice; and something in the tone made me flick my light across him. I saw then that the man was very white, and he looked strange and bewildered.

'"What?" said Johnstone impatiently. "Speak up!"

'"A woman come along 'ere, sir, and went through this "ere door," said the constable, clearly, but with a curious monotonous intonation that is sometimes heard from an unintelligent man.

'"Speak up!" shouted the inspector.

'"A woman come along and went through this 'ere door," repeated the man, monotonously.

'The inspector caught the man by the shoulder, and deliberately sniffed his breath.

''"No!" he said. And then sarcastically: – "I hope you held the door open politely for the lady."

'"The door weren't opened, sir," said the man, simply.

'"Are you mad—" began Johnstone.

'"No," broke in the landlord's voice from the back. Speaking steadily enough. "I saw the Woman upstairs." It was evident that he had got back his control again.

'"I'm afraid, Inspector Johnstone," I said, "that there's more in this than you think. I certainly saw some very extraordinary things upstairs."

'The inspector seemed about to say something; but instead, he turned again to the door, and flashed his light down and 'round about the mat. I saw then that the strange, horrible footmarks came straight up to the cellar door; and the last print showed *under* the door; yet the policeman said the door had not been opened.

'And suddenly, without any intention, or realization of what I was saying, I asked the landlord: –

'"What were the feet like?"

'I received no answer; for the inspector was ordering the constable to open the cellar door, and the man was not obeying. Johnstone repeated the order, and at last, in a queer automatic way, the man obeyed, and pushed the door open. The loathsome smell beat up at us, in a great wave of horror, and the inspector came backward a step.

'"My God!" he said, and went forward again, and shone his light down the steps; but there was nothing visible, only that on each step showed the unnatural footprints.

'The inspector brought the beam of the light vividly on the top step; and there, clear in the light, there was something small, moving. The inspector bent to look, and the policeman and I with him. I don't want to disgust you; but the thing we looked at was a maggot. The policeman backed suddenly out of the doorway:

'"The churchyard," he said, "… at the back of the 'ouse."

'"Silence!" said Johnstone, with a queer break in the word, and I knew that at last he was frightened. He put his lantern into the doorway, and shone it from step to step, following the footprints down into the darkness; then he stepped back from the open doorway, and we all gave back with him. He looked 'round, and I had a feeling that he was looking for a weapon of some kind.

'"Your gun," I said to the landlord, and he brought it from the front hall, and passed it over to the inspector, who took it and ejected the empty shell from the right barrel. He held out his hand for a live cartridge, which the landlord brought from his pocket. He loaded the gun and snapped the breech. He turned to the constable: –

'"Come on," he said, and moved toward the cellar doorway.

'"I ain't comin', sir," said the policeman, very white in the face. With a sudden blaze of passion, the inspector took the man by the scruff and hove him bodily down into the darkness, and he went downward, screaming.

The inspector followed him instantly, with his lantern and the gun; and I after the inspector, with the bayonet ready. Behind me, I heard the landlord.

'At the bottom of the stairs, the inspector was helping the policeman to his feet, where he stood swaying a moment, in a bewildered fashion; then the inspector went into the front cellar, and his man followed him in stupid fashion; but evidently no longer with any thought of running away from the horror.

'We all crowded into the front cellar, flashing our lights to and fro. Inspector Johnstone was examining the floor, and I saw that the footmarks went all 'round the cellar, into all the corners, and across the floor. I thought suddenly of the Child that was running away from Something. Do you see the thing that I was seeing vaguely?

'We went out of the cellar in a body, for there was nothing to be found. In the next cellar, the footprints went everywhere in that queer erratic fashion, as of someone searching for something, or following some blind scent.

'In the third cellar the prints ended at the shallow well that had been the old water supply of the house. The well was full to the brim, and the water so clear that the pebbly bottom was plainly to be seen, as we shone the lights into the water. The search came to an abrupt end, and we stood about the well, looking at one another, in an absolute, horrible silence.

'Johnstone made another examination of the footprints; then he shone his light again into the clear shallow water, searching each inch of the plainly seen bottom; but there was nothing there. The cellar was full of the dreadful smell; and everyone stood silent, except for the constant turning of the lamps to and fro around the cellar.

'The inspector looked up from his search of the well, and nodded quietly across at me, with his sudden acknowledgment that our belief was now his belief, the smell in the cellar seemed to grow more dreadful, and to be, as it were, a menace – the material expression that some monstrous thing was there with us, invisible.

'"I think—" began the inspector, and shone his light toward the stairway; and at this the constable's restraint went utterly, and he ran for the stairs, making a queer sound in his throat.

'The landlord followed, at a quick walk, and then the inspector and I.

He waited a single instant for me, and we went up together, treading on the same steps, and with our lights held backward. At the top, I slammed and locked the stair door, and wiped my forehead, and my hands were shaking.

'The inspector asked me to give his man a glass of whisky, and then he sent him on his beat. He stayed a short while with the landlord and me, and it was arranged that he would join us again the following night and watch the Well with us from midnight until daylight. Then he left us, just as the dawn was coming in. The landlord and I locked up the house, and went over to his place for a sleep.

'In the afternoon, the landlord and I returned to the house, to make arrangements for the night. He was very quiet, and I felt he was to be relied on, now that he had been "salted", as it were, with his fright of the previous night.

'We opened all the doors and windows, and blew the house through very thoroughly; and in the meanwhile, we lit the lamps in the house, and took them into the cellars, where we set them all about, so as to have light everywhere. Then we carried down three chairs and a table, and set them in the cellar where the well was sunk. After that, we stretched thin piano wire across the cellar, about nine inches from the floor, at such a height that it should catch anything moving about in the dark.

'When this was done, I went through the house with the landlord, and sealed every window and door in the place, excepting only the front door and the door at the top of the cellar stairs.

'Meanwhile, a local wire-smith was making something to my order; and when the landlord and I had finished tea at his house, we went down to see how the smith was getting on. We found the thing complete. It looked rather like a huge parrot's cage, without any bottom, of very heavy gauge wire, and stood about seven feet high and was four feet in diameter. Fortunately, I remembered to have it made longitudinally in two halves, or else we should never have got it through the doorways and down the cellar stairs.

'I told the wire-smith to bring the cage up to the house so he could fit the two halves rigidly together. As we returned, I called in at an ironmonger's, where I bought some thin hemp rope and an iron rack pulley, like those used in Lancashire for hauling up the ceiling clothes racks, which you will find in every cottage. I bought also a couple of pitchforks.

'"We shan't want to touch it," I said to the landlord; and he nodded, rather white all at once.

'As soon as the cage arrived and had been fitted together in the cellar, I sent away the smith; and the landlord and I suspended it over the well, into which it fitted easily. After a lot of trouble, we managed to hang it so perfectly central from the rope over the iron pulley, that when hoisted to the ceiling and dropped, it went every time plunk into the well, like a candle-extinguisher. When we had it finally arranged, I hoisted it up once more, to the ready position, and made the rope fast to a heavy wooden pillar, which stood in the middle of the cellar.

'By ten o'clock, I had everything arranged, with the two pitchforks and the two police lanterns; also some whisky and sandwiches. Underneath the table I had several buckets full of disinfectant.

'A little after eleven o'clock, there was a knock at the front door, and when I went, I found Inspector Johnstone had arrived, and brought with him one of his plainclothes men. You will understand how pleased I was to see there would be this addition to our watch; for he looked a tough, nerveless man, brainy and collected; and one I should have picked to help us with the horrible job I felt pretty sure we should have to do that night.

'When the inspector and the detective had entered, I shut and locked the front door; then, while the inspector held the light, I sealed the door carefully, with tape and wax. At the head of the cellar stairs, I shut and locked that door also, and sealed it in the same way.

'As we entered the cellar, I warned Johnstone and his man to be careful not to fall over the wires; and then, as I saw his surprise at my arrangements, I began to explain my ideas and intentions, to all of which he listened with strong approval. I was pleased to see also that the detective was nodding his head, as I talked, in a way that showed he appreciated all my precautions.

'As he put his lantern down, the inspector picked up one of the pitchforks, and balanced it in his hand; he looked at me, and nodded.

'"The best thing," he said. "I only wish you'd got two more."

'Then we all took our seats, the detective getting a washing stool from the corner of the cellar. From then, until a quarter to twelve, we talked quietly, whilst we made a light supper of whisky and sandwiches; after which, we cleared everything off the table, excepting the lanterns and the pitchforks. One of the latter, I handed to the inspector; the other I took myself, and then, having set my chair so as to be handy to the rope which lowered the cage into the well, I went 'round the cellar and put out every lamp.

'I groped my way to my chair, and arranged the pitchfork and the dark lantern ready to my hand; after which I suggested that everyone should keep an absolute silence throughout the watch. I asked, also, that no lantern should be turned on, until I gave the word.

'I put my watch on the table, where a faint glow from my lantern made me able to see the time. For an hour nothing happened, and everyone kept an absolute silence, except for an occasional uneasy movement.

'About half-past one, however, I was conscious again of the same extraordinary and peculiar nervousness, which I had felt on the previous night. I put my hand out quickly, and eased the hitched rope from around the pillar. The inspector seemed aware of the movement; for I saw the faint light from his lantern, move a little, as if he had suddenly taken hold of it, in readiness.

'A minute later, I noticed there was a change in the colour of the night in the cellar, and it grew slowly violet tinted upon my eyes. I glanced to and fro, quickly, in the new darkness, and even as I looked, I was conscious that the violet colour deepened. In the direction of the well, but seeming to be at a great distance, there was, as it were, a nucleus to the change; and the nucleus came swiftly toward us, appearing to come from a great space, almost in a single moment. It came near, and I saw again that it was a little naked Child, running, and seeming to be of the violet night in which it ran.

'The Child came with a natural running movement, exactly as I described it before; but in a silence so peculiarly intense, that it was as if it brought the silence with it. About half-way between the well and the table, the Child turned swiftly, and looked back at something invisible to me; and suddenly it went down into a crouching attitude, and seemed to be hiding behind something that showed vaguely; but there was nothing there, except the bare floor of the cellar; nothing, I mean, of our world.

'I could hear the breathing of the three other men, with a wonderful distinctness; and also the tick of my watch upon the table seemed to sound as loud and as slow as the tick of an old grandfather's clock. Someway I knew that none of the others saw what I was seeing.

'Abruptly, the landlord, who was next to me, let out his breath with a little hissing sound; I knew then that something was visible to him. There came a creak from the table, and I had a feeling that the inspector was leaning forward, looking at something that I could not see. The landlord reached out his hand through the darkness, and fumbled a moment to catch my arm: –

'"The Woman!" he whispered, close to my ear. "Over by the well."

'I stared hard in that direction; but saw nothing, except that the violet colour of the cellar seemed a little duller just there.

'I looked back quickly to the vague place where the Child was hiding. I saw it was peering back from its hiding place. Suddenly it rose and ran straight for the middle of the table, which showed only as vague shadow half-way between my eyes and the unseen floor. As the Child ran under the table, the steel prongs of my pitchfork glimmered with a violet, fluctuating light. A little way off, there showed high up in the gloom, the vaguely shining outline of the other fork, so I knew the inspector had it raised in his hand, ready. There was no doubt but that he saw something. On the table, the metal of the five lanterns shone with the same strange glow; and about each lantern there was a little cloud of absolute blackness, where the phenomenon that is light to our natural eyes, came through the fittings; and in this complete darkness, the metal of each lantern showed plain, as might a cat's-eye in a nest of black cotton wool.

'Just beyond the table, the Child paused again, and stood, seeming to oscillate a little upon its feet, which gave the impression that it was lighter and vaguer than a thistle-down; and yet, in the same moment, another part of me seemed to know that it was to me, as something that might be beyond thick, invisible glass, and subject to conditions and forces that I was unable to comprehend.

'The Child was looking back again, and my gaze went the same way. I stared across the cellar, and saw the cage hanging clear in the violet light, every wire and tie outlined with its glimmering; above it there was a little space of gloom, and then the dull shining of the iron pulley which I had screwed into the ceiling.

'I stared in a bewildered way 'round the cellar; there were thin lines of vague fire crossing the floor in all directions; and suddenly I remembered the piano wire that the landlord and I had stretched. But there was nothing else to be seen, except that near the table there were indistinct glimmerings of light, and at the far end the outline of a dull glowing revolver, evidently in the detective's pocket. I remember a sort of subconscious satisfaction, as I settled the point in a queer automatic fashion. On the table, near to me, there was a little shapeless collection of the light; and this I knew, after an instant's consideration, to be the steel portions of my watch.

'I had looked several times at the Child, and 'round at the cellar, whilst I was decided these trifles; and had found it still in that attitude of hiding from something. But now, suddenly, it ran clear away into the distance, and was nothing more than a slightly deeper coloured nucleus far away in the strange coloured atmosphere.

'The landlord gave out a queer little cry, and twisted over against me, as if to avoid something. From the inspector there came a sharp breathing sound, as if he had been suddenly drenched with cold water. Then suddenly the violet colour went out of the night, and I was conscious of the nearness of something monstrous and repugnant.

'There was a tense silence, and the blackness of the cellar seemed absolute, with only the faint glow about each of the lanterns on the table. Then, in the darkness and the silence, there came a faint tinkle of water from the well, as if something were rising noiselessly out of it, and the water running back with a gentle tinkling. In the same instant, there came to me a sudden waft of the awful smell.

'I gave a sharp cry of warning to the inspector, and loosed the rope. There came instantly the sharp splash of the cage entering the water; and then, with a stiff, frightened movement, I opened the shutter of my lantern, and shone the light at the cage, shouting to the others to do the same.

'As my light struck the cage, I saw that about two feet of it projected from the top of the well, and there was something protruding up out of the water, into the cage. I stared, with a feeling that I recognized the thing; and then, as the other lanterns were opened, I saw that it was a leg of mutton. The thing was held by a brawny fist and arm, that rose out of the water. I stood utterly bewildered, watching to see what was coming. In a moment there rose into view a great bearded face, that I felt for one quick instant was the face of a drowned man, long dead. Then the face opened at the mouth part, and spluttered and coughed. Another big hand came into view, and wiped the water from the eyes, which blinked rapidly, and then fixed themselves into a stare at the lights.

'From the detective there came a sudden shout: –

'"Captain Tobias!" he shouted, and the inspector echoed him; and instantly burst into loud roars of laughter.

'The inspector and the detective ran across the cellar to the cage; and I followed, still bewildered. The man in the cage was holding the leg of mutton as far away from him, as possible, and holding his nose.

'"Lift thig dam trap, quig!" he shouted in a stifled voice; but the inspector and the detective simply doubled before him, and tried to hold their noses, whilst they laughed, and the light from their lanterns went dancing all over the place.

'"Quig! quig!" said the man in the cage, still holding his nose, and trying to speak plainly.

'Then Johnstone and the detective stopped laughing, and lifted the cage. The man in the well threw the leg across the cellar, and turned swiftly to go down into the well; but the officers were too quick for him, and had him out in a twinkling. Whilst they held him, dripping upon the floor, the inspector jerked his thumb in the direction of the offending leg, and the landlord, having harpooned it with one of the pitchforks, ran with it upstairs and so into the open air.

'Meanwhile, I had given the man from the well a stiff tot of whisky; for which he thanked me with a cheerful nod, and having emptied the glass at a draft, held his hand for the bottle, which he finished, as if it had been so much water.

'As you will remember, it was a Captain Tobias who had been the previous tenant; and this was the very man, who had appeared from the well. In the course of the talk that followed, I learned the reason for Captain Tobias leaving the house; he had been wanted by the police for smuggling. He had undergone imprisonment; and had been released only a couple of weeks earlier.

'He had returned to find new tenants in his old home. He had entered the house through the well, the walls of which were not continued to the bottom (this I will deal with later); and gone up by a little stairway in the cellar wall, which opened at the top through a panel beside my mother's bedroom. This panel was opened, by revolving the left doorpost of the bedroom door, with the result that the bedroom door always became unlatched, in the process of opening the panel.

'The captain complained, without any bitterness, that the panel had warped, and that each time he opened it, it made a cracking noise. This had been evidently what I mistook for raps. He would not give his reason for entering the house; but it was pretty obvious that he had hidden something, which he wanted to get. However, as he found it impossible to get into the house without the risk of being caught, he decided to try to drive us out, relying on the bad reputation of the house, and his own artistic efforts as a ghost. I must say he succeeded. He intended then to rent the house again, as before; and would then, of course have plenty of time to get whatever he had hidden. The house suited him admirably; for there was a passage – as he showed me afterward – connecting the dummy well with the crypt of the church beyond the garden wall; and these, in turn, were connected with certain caves in the cliffs, which went down to the beach beyond the church.

'In the course of his talk, Captain Tobias offered to take the house off my hands; and as this suited me perfectly, for I was about stalled with it, and the plan also suited the landlord, it was decided that no steps should be taken against him; and that the whole business should be hushed up.

'I asked the captain whether there was really anything queer about the house; whether he had ever seen anything. He said yes, that he had twice seen a Woman going about the house. We all looked at one another, when the captain said that. He told us she never bothered him, and that he had only seen her twice, and on each occasion it had followed a narrow escape from the Revenue people.

'Captain Tobias was an observant man; he had seen how I had placed the mats against the doors; and after entering the rooms, and walking all about them, so as to leave the foot-marks of an old pair of wet woollen slippers everywhere, he had deliberately put the mats back as he found them.

'The maggot which had dropped from his disgusting leg of mutton had been an accident, and beyond even his horrible planning. He was hugely delighted to learn how it had affected us.

'The mouldy smell I had noticed was from the little closed stairway, when the captain opened the panel. The door slamming was also another of his contributions.

'I come now to the end of the captain's ghost play; and to the difficulty of trying to explain the other peculiar things. In the first place, it was obvious there was something genuinely strange in the house; which made itself manifest as a Woman. Many different people had seen this Woman, under differing circumstances, so it is impossible to put the thing down to fancy; at the same time it must seem extraordinary that I should have lived two years in the house, and seen nothing; whilst the policeman saw the Woman, before he had been there twenty minutes; the landlord, the detective, and the inspector all saw her.

'I can only surmise that *fear* was in every case the key, as I might say, which opened the senses to the presence of the Woman. The policeman was a highly-strung man, and when he became frightened, was able to see the Woman. The same reasoning applies all 'round. *I* saw nothing, until I became really frightened; then I saw, not the Woman; but a Child, running away from Something or Someone. However, I will touch on that later. In short, until a very strong degree of fear was present, no one was affected by the Force which made Itself evident, as a Woman. My theory explains why some tenants were never aware of anything strange in the house, whilst others left immediately. The more sensitive they were, the less would be the degree of fear necessary to make them aware of the Force present in the house.

'The peculiar shining of all the metal objects in the cellar, had been visible only to me. The cause, naturally I do not know; neither do I know why I, alone, was able to see the shining.'

'The Child,' I asked. 'Can you explain that part at all? Why *you* didn't see the Woman, and why *they* didn't see the Child. Was it merely the same Force, appearing differently to different people?'

'No,' said Carnacki, 'I can't explain that. But I am quite sure that the Woman and the Child were not only two complete and different entities; but even they were each not in quite the same planes of existence.

'To give you a root idea, however, it is held in the Sigsand MS. that a child '*still*born' is 'Snatyched back bye thee Haggs.' This is crude; but may yet contain an elemental truth. Yet, before I make this clearer, let me tell you a thought that has often been made. It may be that physical birth is but a secondary process; and that prior to the possibility, the Mother Spirit searches for, until it finds, the small Element—the primal Ego or child's soul. It may be that a certain waywardness would cause such to strive to evade capture by the Mother Spirit. It may have been such a thing as this, that I saw. I have always tried to think so; but it is impossible to ignore the sense of repulsion that I felt when the unseen Woman went past me. This repulsion carries forward the idea suggested in the Sigsand MS., that a stillborn child is thus, because its ego or spirit has been snatched back by the 'Hags'. In other words, by certain of the Monstrosities of the Outer Circle. The thought is inconceivably terrible, and probably the more so because it is so fragmentary. It leaves us with the conception of a child's soul adrift half-way between two lives, and running through Eternity from Something incredible and inconceivable (because not understood) to our senses.

'The thing is beyond further discussion; for it is futile to attempt to discuss a thing, to any purpose, of which one has a knowledge so fragmentary as this. There is one thought, which is often mine. Perhaps there is a Mother Spirit—'

'And the well?' said Arkwright. 'How did the captain get in from the other side?'

'As I said before,' answered Carnacki. 'The side walls of the well did not reach to the bottom; so that you had only to dip down into the water, and come up again on the other side of the wall, under the cellar floor, and so climb into the passage. Of course, the water was the same height on both sides of the walls. Don't ask me who made the well entrance or the little stairway; for I don't know. The house was very old, as I have told you; and that sort of thing was useful in the old days.'

'And the Child,' I said, coming back to the thing which chiefly interested me. 'You would say that the birth must have occurred in that house; and in this way, one might suppose that the house to have become *en rapport,* if I can use the word in that way, with the Forces that produced the tragedy?'

'Yes,' replied Carnacki. 'This is, supposing we take the suggestion of the Sigsand MS., to account for the phenomenon.'

'There may be other houses—' I began.

'There are,' said Carnacki; and stood up.

'Out you go,' he said, genially, using the recognized formula. And in five minutes we were on the Embankment, going thoughtfully to our various homes.

The Real Right Thing

Henry James

I

When, after the death of Ashton Doyne—but three months after—George Withermore was approached, as the phrase is, on the subject of a "volume," the communication came straight from his publishers, who had been, and indeed much more, Doyne's own; but he was not surprised to learn, on the occurrence of the interview they next suggested, that a certain pressure as to the early issue of a Life had been brought to bear upon them by their late client's widow. Doyne's relations with his wife had been, to Withermore's knowledge, a very special chapter—which would present itself, by the way, as a delicate one for the biographer; but a sense of what she had lost, and even of what she had lacked, had betrayed itself, on the poor woman's part, from the first days of her bereavement, sufficiently to prepare an observer at all initiated for some attitude of reparation, some espousal even exaggerated of the interests of a distinguished name. George Withermore was, as he felt, initiated; yet what he had not expected was to hear that she had mentioned him as the person in whose hands she would most promptly place the materials for a book.

These materials—diaries, letters, memoranda, notes, documents of many sorts—were her property, and wholly in her control, no conditions at all attaching to any portion of her heritage; so that she was free at present to do as she liked—free, in particular, to do nothing. What Doyne would have arranged had he had time to arrange could be but supposition and guess.

Death had taken him too soon and too suddenly, and there was all the pity that the only wishes he was known to have expressed were wishes that put it positively out of account. He had broken short off—that was the way of it; and the end was ragged and needed trimming. Withermore was conscious, abundantly, how close he had stood to him, but he was not less aware of his comparative obscurity. He was young, a journalist, a critic, a hand-to-mouth character, with little, as yet, as was vulgarly said, to show. His writings were few and small, his relations scant and vague. Doyne, on the other hand, had lived long enough—above all had had talent enough—to become great, and among his many friends gilded also with greatness were several to whom his wife would have struck those who knew her as much more likely to appeal.

The preference she had, at all events, uttered—and uttered in a roundabout, considerate way that left him a measure of freedom—made our young man feel that he must at least see her and that there would be in any case a good deal to talk about. He immediately wrote to her, she as promptly named an hour, and they had it out. But he came away with his particular idea immensely strengthened. She was a strange woman, and he had never thought her an agreeable one; only there was something that touched him now in her bustling, blundering impatience. She wanted the book to make up, and the individual whom, of her husband's set, she probably believed she might most manipulate was in every way to help it to make up. She had not taken Doyne seriously enough in life, but the biography should be a solid reply to every imputation on herself. She had scantly known how such books were constructed, but she had been looking and had learned something. It alarmed Withermore a little from the first to see that she would wish to go in for quantity. She talked of "volumes"—but he had his notion of that.

"My thought went straight to *you*, as his own would have done," she had said almost as soon as she rose before him there in her large array of mourning—with her big black eyes, her big black wig, her big black fan and gloves, her general gaunt, ugly, tragic, but striking and, as might have been thought from a certain point of view, "elegant" presence. "You're the one he liked most; oh, *much!*"—and it had been quite enough to turn Withermore's head. It little mattered that he could afterward wonder if she had known Doyne enough, when it came to that, to be sure. He would have said for himself indeed that her testimony on such a point would scarcely have counted. Still, there was no smoke without fire; she knew at least what she meant, and he was not a person she could have an interest in flattering. They went up together, without delay, to the great man's vacant study, which was at the back of the house and looked over the large green garden—a beautiful and inspiring scene, to poor Withermore's view—common to the expensive row.

"You can perfectly work here, you know," said Mrs Doyne; "you shall have the place quite to yourself—I'll give it all up to you; so that in the evenings, in particular, don't you see? for quiet and privacy, it will be perfection."

Perfection indeed, the young man felt as he looked about—having explained that, as his actual occupation was an evening paper and his earlier hours, for a long time yet, regularly taken up, he would have to come always at night. The place was full of their lost friend; everything in it had belonged to him; everything they touched had been part of his life. It was for the moment too much for Withermore—too great an honour and even too great a care; memories still recent came back to him, and, while his heart beat faster and his eyes filled with tears, the pressure of his loyalty seemed almost more than he could carry. At the sight of his tears Mrs Doyne's own rose to her lids, and the two, for a minute, only looked at each other. He half expected her to break out: "Oh, help me to feel as I know you know I want to feel!" And after a little one of them said, with the other's deep assent—it didn't matter which: "It's here that we're *with* him." But it was definitely the young man who put it, before they left the room, that it was there he was with *them*.

The young man began to come as soon as he could arrange it, and then it was, on the spot, in the charmed stillness, between the lamp and the fire and with the curtains drawn, that a certain intenser consciousness crept over him. He turned in out of the black London November; he passed through the large, hushed house and up the red-carpeted staircase where he only found in his path the whisk of a soundless trained maid, or the reach, out of a doorway, of Mrs Doyne's queenly weeds and approving tragic face; and then, by a mere touch of the well-made door that gave so sharp and pleasant a click, shut himself in for three or four warm hours with the spirit—as he had always distinctly declared it—of his master. He was not a little frightened when, even the first night, it came over him that he had really been most affected, in the whole matter, by the prospect, the privilege, and the luxury, of this sensation. He had not, he could now reflect, definitely considered the question of the book—as to which there was here, even already, much to consider: he had simply let his affection and admiration—to say nothing of his gratified pride—meet, to the full, the temptation Mrs Doyne had offered them.

How did he know, without more thought, he might begin to ask himself, that the book was, on the whole, to be desired? What warrant had he ever received from Ashton Doyne himself for so direct and, as it were, so familiar an approach? Great was the art of biography, but there were lives and lives, there were subjects and subjects. He confusedly recalled, so far as that went, old words dropped by Doyne over contemporary compilations, suggestions of how he himself discriminated as to other heroes and other panoramas. He even remembered how his friend, at moments, would have seemed to show himself as holding that the "literary" career might—save in the case of a Johnson and a Scott, with a Boswell and a Lockhart to help—best content itself to be represented. The artist was what he *did*—he was nothing else. Yet how, on the other hand, was not *he*, George Withermore, poor devil, to have jumped at the chance of spending his winter in an intimacy so rich? It had been simply dazzling—that was the fact. It hadn't been the "terms," from the publishers—though these were, as they said at the office, all right; it had been Doyne himself, his company and contact and presence—it had been just what it was turning out, the possibility of an intercourse closer than that of life. Strange that death, of the two things, should have the fewer mysteries and secrets! The first night our young man was alone in the room it seemed to him that his master and he were really for the first time together.

II

Mrs Doyne had for the most part let him expressively alone, but she had on two or three occasions looked in to see if his needs had been met, and he had had the opportunity of thanking her on the spot for the judgment and zeal with which she had smoothed his way.

She had to some extent herself been looking things over and had been able already to muster several groups of letters; all the keys of drawers and cabinets she had, moreover, from the first placed in his hands, with helpful information as to the apparent whereabouts of different matters. She had put him, in a word, in the fullest possible possession, and whether or no her husband had trusted her, she at least, it was clear, trusted her husband's friend. There grew upon Withermore, nevertheless, the impression that, in spite of all these offices, she was not yet at peace, and that a certain unappeasable anxiety continued even to keep step with her confidence. Though she was full of consideration, she was at the same time perceptibly *there*: he felt her, through a supersubtle sixth sense that the whole connection had already brought into play, hover, in the still hours, at the top of landings and on the other side of doors, gathered from the soundless brush of her skirts the hint of her watchings and waitings. One evening when, at his friend's table, he had lost himself in the depths of correspondence, he was made to start and turn by the suggestion that someone was behind him. Mrs Doyne had come in without his hearing the door, and she gave a strained smile as he sprang to his feet. "I hope," she said, "I haven't frightened you."

"Just a little—I was so absorbed. It was as if, for the instant," the young man explained, "it had been himself."

The oddity of her face increased in her wonder. "Ashton?"

"He does seem so near," said Withermore.

"To you too?"

This naturally struck him. "He does then to you?"

She hesitated, not moving from the spot where she had first stood, but looking round the room as if to penetrate its duskier angles. She had a way of raising to the level of her nose the big black fan which she apparently never laid aside and with which she thus covered the lower half of her face, her rather hard eyes, above it, becoming the more ambiguous. "Sometimes."

"Here," Withermore went on, "it's as if he might at any moment come in. That's why I jumped just now. The time is so short since he really used to—it only *was* yesterday. I sit in his chair, I turn his books, I use his pens, I stir his fire, exactly as if, learning he would presently be back from a walk, I had come up here contentedly to wait. It's delightful—but it's strange."

Mrs Doyne, still with her fan up, listened with interest. "Does it worry you?"

"No—I like it."

She hesitated again. "Do you ever feel as if he were—a—quite—a—personally in the room?"

"Well, as I said just now," her companion laughed, "on hearing you behind me I seemed to take it so. What do we want, after all," he asked, "but that he shall be with us?"

"Yes, as you said he would be—that first time." She stared in full assent. "He *is* with us."

She was rather portentous, but Withermore took it smiling. "Then we must keep him. We must do only what he would like."

"Oh, only that, of course—only. But if he *is* here—?" And her sombre eyes seemed to throw it out, in vague distress, over her fan.

"It shows that he's pleased and wants only to help? Yes, surely; it must show that."

She gave a light gasp and looked again round the room. "Well," she said as she took leave of him, "remember that I too want only to help." On which, when she had gone, he felt sufficiently—that she had come in simply to see he was all right.

He was all right more and more, it struck him after this, for as he began to get into his work he moved, as it appeared to him, but the closer to the idea of Doyne's personal presence. When once this fancy had begun to hang about him he welcomed it, persuaded it, encouraged it, quite cherished it, looking forward all day to feeling it renew itself in the evening, and waiting for the evening very much as one of a pair of lovers might wait for the hour of their appointment. The smallest accidents humoured and confirmed it, and by the end of three or four weeks he had come quite to regard it as the consecration of his enterprise. Wasn't it what settled the question of what Doyne would have thought of what they were doing? What they were doing was what he wanted done, and they could go on, from step to step, without scruple or doubt. Withermore rejoiced indeed at moments to feel this certitude: there were times of dipping deep into some of Doyne's secrets when it was particularly pleasant to be able to hold that Doyne desired him, as it were, to know them. He was learning many things that he had not suspected, drawing many curtains, forcing many doors, reading many riddles, going, in general, as they said, behind almost everything. It was at an occasional sharp turn of some of the duskier of these wanderings "behind" that he really, of a sudden, most felt himself, in the intimate, sensible way, face to face with his friend; so that he could scarcely have told, for the instant, if their meeting occurred in the narrow passage and tight squeeze of the past, or at the hour and in the place that actually held him. Was it '67, or was it but the other side of the table?

Happily, at any rate, even in the vulgarest light publicity could ever shed, there would be the great fact of the way Doyne was "coming out." He was coming out too beautifully—better yet than such a partisan as Withermore could have supposed. Yet, all the while, as well, how would this partisan have represented to any one else the special state of his own consciousness? It wasn't a thing to talk about—it was only a thing to feel. There were moments, for instance, when, as he bent over his papers, the light breath of his dead host was as distinctly in his hair as his own elbows were on the table before him. There were moments when, had he been able to look up, the other side of the table would have shown him this companion as vividly as the shaded lamplight showed him his page. That he couldn't at such a juncture look up was his own affair, for the situation was ruled—that was but natural—by deep delicacies and fine timidities, the dread of too sudden or too rude an advance. What was intensely in the air was that if Doyne *was* there it was not nearly so much for himself as for the young priest of his altar. He hovered and lingered, he came and went, he might almost have been, among the books and the papers, a hushed, discreet librarian, doing the particular things, rendering the quiet aid, liked by men of letters.

Withermore himself, meanwhile, came and went, changed his place, wandered on quests either definite or vague; and more than once, when, taking a book down from a shelf and finding in it marks of Doyne's pencil, he got drawn on and lost, he had heard documents on the table behind him gently shifted and stirred, had literally, on his return, found some letter he had mislaid pushed again into view, some wilderness cleared by the opening of an old journal at the very date he wanted. How should he have gone so, on occasion, to the special box or drawer, out of fifty receptacles, that would help him, had not his mystic assistant happened, in fine prevision, to tilt its lid, or to pull it half open, in just the manner that would catch his eye?—in spite, after all, of the fact of lapses and intervals in which, *could* one have really looked, one would have seen somebody standing before the fire a trifle detached and over-erect—somebody fixing one the least bit harder than in life.

III

That this auspicious relation had in fact existed, had continued, for two or three weeks, was sufficiently proved by the dawn of the distress with which our young man found himself aware that he had, for some reason, from a certain evening, begun to miss it. The sign of that was an abrupt, surprised sense—on the occasion of his mislaying a marvellous unpublished page which, hunt where he would, remained stupidly, irrecoverably lost—that his protected state was, after all, exposed to some confusion and even to some depression. If, for the joy of the business, Doyne and he had, from the start, been together, the situation had, within a few days of his first new suspicion of it, suffered the odd change of their ceasing to be so. That was what was the matter, he said to himself, from the moment an impression of mere mass and quantity struck him as taking, in his happy outlook at his material, the place of his pleasant assumption of a clear course and a lively pace. For five nights he struggled; then, never at his table, wandering about the room, taking up his references only to lay them down, looking out of the window, poking the fire, thinking strange thoughts, and listening for signs and sounds not as he suspected or imagined, but as he vainly desired and invoked them, he made up his mind that he was, for the time at least, forsaken.

The extraordinary thing thus became that it made him not only sad not to feel Doyne's presence, but in a high degree uneasy. It was stranger, somehow, that he shouldn't be there than it had ever been that he *was*—so strange, indeed, at last that Withermore's nerves found themselves quite inconsequently affected. They had taken kindly enough to what was of an order impossible to explain, perversely reserving their sharpest state for the return to the normal, the supersession of the false. They were remarkably beyond control when, finally, one night, after resisting an hour or two, he simply edged out of the room. It had only now, for the first time, become impossible to him to remain there. Without design, but panting a little and positively as a man scared, he passed along his usual corridor and reached the top of the staircase. From this point he saw Mrs Doyne looking up at him from the bottom quite as if she had known he would come; and the most singular thing of all was that, though he had been conscious of no notion to resort to her, had only been prompted to relieve himself by escape, the sight of her position made him recognise it as just, quickly feel it as a part of some monstrous oppression that was closing over both of them. It was wonderful how, in the mere modern London hall, between the Tottenham Court Road rugs and the electric light, it came up to him from the tall black lady, and went again from him down to her, that he knew what she meant by looking as if he would know. He descended straight, she turned into her own little lower room, and there, the next thing, with the door shut, they were, still in silence and with queer faces, confronted over confessions that had taken sudden life from these two or three movements. Withermore gasped as it came to him why he had lost his friend. "He has been with *you?*"

With this it was all out—out so far that neither had to explain and that, when "What do you suppose is the matter?" quickly passed between them, one appeared to have said it as much as the other. Withermore looked about at the small, bright room in which, night after night, she had been living her life as he had been living his own upstairs. It was pretty, cosy, rosy; but she had by turns felt in it what he had felt and heard in it what he had heard. Her effect there—fantastic black, plumed and extravagant, upon deep pink—was that of some "decadent" coloured print, some poster of the newest school. "You understood he had left me?" he asked.

She markedly wished to make it clear. "This evening—yes. I've made things out."

"You knew—before—that he was with me?"

She hesitated again. "I felt he wasn't with *me*. But on the stairs—"

"Yes?"

"Well—he passed, more than once. He was in the house. And at your door—"

"Well?" he went on as she once more faltered.

"If I stopped I could sometimes tell. And from your face," she added, "tonight, at any rate, I knew your state."

"And that was why you came out?"

"I thought you'd come to me."

He put out to her, on this, his hand, and they thus, for a minute, in silence, held each other clasped. There was no peculiar presence for either, now—nothing more peculiar than that of each for the other. But the place had suddenly become as if consecrated, and Withermore turned over it again his anxiety. "What *is* then the matter?"

"I only want to do the real right thing," she replied after a moment.

"And are we not doing it?"

"I wonder. Are *you* not?"

He wondered too. "To the best of my belief. But we must think."

"We must think," she echoed. And they did think—thought, with intensity, the rest of that evening together, and thought, independently—Withermore at least could answer for himself—during many days that followed. He intermitted for a little his visits and his work, trying, in meditation, to catch himself in the act of some mistake that might have accounted for their disturbance. Had he taken, on some important point—or looked as if he might take—some wrong line or wrong view? had he somewhere benightedly falsified or inadequately insisted? He went back at last with the idea of having guessed two or three questions he might have been on the way to muddle; after which he had, above stairs, another period of agitation, presently followed by another interview, below, with Mrs Doyne, who was still troubled and flushed.

"He's there?"

"He's there."

"I knew it!" she returned in an odd gloom of triumph. Then as to make it clear: "He has not been again with *me*."

"Nor with me again to help," said Withermore.

She considered. "Not to help?"

"I can't make it out—I'm at sea. Do what I will, I feel I'm wrong."

She covered him a moment with her pompous pain. "How do you feel it?"

"Why, by things that happen. The strangest things. I can't describe them—and you wouldn't believe them."

"Oh yes, I would!" Mrs Doyne murmured.

"Well, he intervenes." Withermore tried to explain. "However I turn, I find him."

She earnestly followed. "'Find' him?"

"I meet him. He seems to rise there before me."

Mrs Doyne, staring, waited a little. "Do you mean you see him?"

"I feel as if at any moment I may. I'm baffled. I'm checked." Then he added: "I'm afraid."

"Of *him?*" asked Mrs Doyne.

He thought. "Well—of what I'm doing."

"Then what, that's so awful, *are* you doing?"

"What you proposed to me. Going into his life."

She showed, in her gravity, now, a new alarm. "And don't you *like* that?"

"Doesn't *he?* That's the question. We lay him bare. We serve him up. What is it called? We give him to the world."

Poor Mrs Doyne, as if on a menace to her hard atonement, glared at this for an instant in deeper gloom. "And why shouldn't we?"

"Because we don't know. There are natures, there are lives, that shrink. He mayn't wish it," said Withermore. "We never asked him."

"How *could* we?"

He was silent a little. "Well, we ask him now. That's, after all, what our start has, so far, represented. We've put it to him."

"Then—if he has been with us—we've had his answer."

Withermore spoke now as if he knew what to believe. "He hasn't been 'with' us—he has been against us."

"Then why did you think—"

"What I *did* think, at first—that what he wishes to make us feel is his sympathy? Because, in my original simplicity, I was mistaken. I was—I don't know what to call it—so excited and charmed that I didn't understand. But I understand at last. He only wanted to communicate. He strains forward out of his darkness; he reaches toward us out of his mystery; he makes us dim signs out of his horror."

"'Horror?'" Mrs Doyne gasped with her fan up to her mouth.

"At what we're doing." He could by this time piece it all together. "I see now that at first—"

"Well, what?"

"One had simply to feel he was there, and therefore not indifferent. And the beauty of that misled me. But he's there as a protest."

"Against *my* Life?" Mrs Doyne wailed.

"Against *any* Life. He's there to *save* his Life. He's there to be let alone."

"So you give up?" she almost shrieked.

He could only meet her. "He's there as a warning."

For a moment, on this, they looked at each other deep. "You *are* afraid!" she at last brought out.

It affected him, but he insisted. "He's there as a curse!"

With that they parted, but only for two or three days; her last word to him continuing to sound so in his ears that, between his need really to satisfy her and another need presently to be noted, he felt that he might not yet take up his stake. He finally went back at his usual hour and found her in her usual place. "Yes, I *am* afraid," he announced as if he had turned that well over and knew now all it meant. "But I gather that you're not."

She faltered, reserving her word. "What is it you fear?"

"Well, that if I go on I *shall* see him."

"And then—?"

"Oh, then," said George Withermore, "I *should* give up!"

She weighed it with her lofty but earnest air. "I think, you know, we must have a clear sign."

"You wish me to try again?"

She hesitated. "You see what it means—for me—to give up."

"Ah, but *you* needn't," Withermore said.

She seemed to wonder, but in a moment she went on. "It would mean that he won't take from me—" But she dropped for despair.

"Well, what?"

"Anything," said poor Mrs Doyne.

He faced her a moment more. "I've thought myself of the clear sign. I'll try again."

As he was leaving her, however, she remembered. "I'm only afraid that tonight there's nothing ready—no lamp and no fire."

"Never mind," he said from the foot of the stairs; "I'll find things."

To which she answered that the door of the room would probably, at any rate, be open; and retired again as if to wait for him. She had not long to wait; though, with her own door wide and her attention fixed, she may not have taken the time quite as it appeared to her visitor. She heard him, after an interval, on the stair, and he presently stood at her entrance, where, if he had not been precipitate, but rather, as to step and sound, backward and vague, he showed at least as livid and blank.

"I give up."

"Then you've seen him?"

"On the threshold—guarding it."

"Guarding it?" She glowed over her fan. "Distinct?"

"Immense. But dim. Dark. Dreadful," said poor George Withermore.

She continued to wonder. "You didn't go in?"

The young man turned away. "He forbids!"

"You say *I* needn't," she went on after a moment. "Well then, need I?"

"See him?" George Withermore asked.

She waited an instant. "Give up."

"You must decide." For himself he could at last but drop upon the sofa with his bent face in his hands. He was not quite to know afterwards how long he had sat so; it was enough that what he did next know was that he was alone among her favourite objects. Just as he gained his feet, however, with this sense and that of the door standing open to the hall, he found himself afresh confronted, in the light, the warmth, the rosy space, with her big black perfumed presence. He saw at a glance, as she offered him a huger, bleaker stare over the mask of her fan, that she had been above; and so it was that, for the last time, they faced together their strange question. "You've seen him?" Withermore asked.

He was to infer later on from the extraordinary way she closed her eyes, and, as if to steady herself, held them tight and long, in silence, that beside the unutterable vision of Ashton Doyne's wife his own might rank as an escape. He knew before she spoke that all was over. "I give up."

The Jolly Corner

Henry James

Chapter I

"Every one asks me what I 'think' of everything," said Spencer Brydon; "and I make answer as I can—begging or dodging the question, putting them off with any nonsense. It wouldn't matter to any of them really," he went on, "for, even were it possible to meet in that stand-and-deliver way so silly a demand on so big a subject, my 'thoughts' would still be almost altogether about something that concerns only myself." He was talking to Miss Staverton, with whom for a couple of months now he had availed himself of every possible occasion to talk; this disposition and this resource, this comfort and support, as the situation in fact presented itself, having promptly enough taken the first place in the considerable array of rather unattenuated surprises attending his so strangely belated return to America. Everything was somehow a surprise; and that might be natural when one had so long and so consistently neglected everything, taken pains to give surprises so much margin for play. He had given them more than thirty years—thirty-three, to be exact; and they now seemed to him to have organised their performance quite on the scale of that licence. He had been twenty-three on leaving New York—he was fifty-six today; unless indeed he were to reckon as he had sometimes, since his repatriation, found himself feeling; in which case he would have lived longer than is often allotted to man. It would have taken a century, he repeatedly said to himself, and said also to Alice Staverton, it would have taken a longer absence and a more averted mind than those even of which he had been guilty, to pile up the differences, the newnesses, the queernesses, above all the bignesses, for the better or the worse, that at present assaulted his vision wherever he looked.

The great fact all the while, however, had been the incalculability; since he *had* supposed himself, from decade to decade, to be allowing, and in the most liberal and intelligent manner, for brilliancy of change. He actually saw that he had allowed for nothing; he missed what he would have been sure of finding, he found what he would never have imagined. Proportions and values were upside-down; the ugly things he had expected, the ugly things of his far-away youth, when he had too promptly waked up to a sense of the ugly—these uncanny phenomena placed him rather, as it happened, under the charm; whereas the "swagger" things, the modern, the monstrous, the famous things, those he had more particularly, like thousands of ingenuous enquirers every year, come over to see, were exactly his sources of dismay. They were as so many set traps for displeasure, above all for reaction, of which his restless tread was constantly pressing the spring. It was interesting, doubtless, the whole show, but it would have been too disconcerting hadn't a certain finer truth saved the situation. He had distinctly not, in this steadier light, come over *all* for the monstrosities; he had come, not only in the last analysis but quite on the face of the act, under an impulse with which they had nothing to do. He had come—putting the thing pompously—to look at his "property," which he had thus for a third of a century not been within four thousand miles of; or, expressing it less sordidly, he had yielded to the humour of seeing again his house on the jolly corner, as he usually, and quite fondly, described it—the one in which he had first seen the light, in which various members of his family had lived and had died, in which the holidays of his overschooled boyhood had been passed and the few social flowers of his chilled adolescence gathered, and which, alienated then for so long a period, had, through the successive deaths of his two brothers and the termination of old arrangements, come wholly into his hands. He was the owner of another, not quite so "good"—the jolly corner having been, from far back, superlatively extended and consecrated; and the value of the pair represented his main capital, with an income consisting, in these later years, of their respective rents which (thanks precisely to their original excellent type) had never been depressingly low. He could live in "Europe," as he had been in the habit of living, on the product of these flourishing New York leases, and all the better since, that of the second structure, the mere number in its long row, having within a twelvemonth fallen in, renovation at a high advance had proved beautifully possible.

These were items of property indeed, but he had found himself since his arrival distinguishing more than ever between them. The house within the street, two bristling blocks westward, was already in course of reconstruction as a tall mass of flats; he had acceded, some time before, to overtures for this conversion—in which, now that it was going forward, it had been not the least of his astonishments to find himself able, on the spot, and though without a previous ounce of such experience, to participate with a certain intelligence, almost with a certain authority. He had lived his life with his back so turned to such concerns and his face addressed to those of so different an order that he scarce knew what to make of this lively stir, in a compartment of his mind never yet penetrated, of a capacity for business and a sense for construction. These virtues, so common all round him now, had been dormant in his own organism—where it might be said of them perhaps that they had slept the sleep of the just. At present, in the splendid autumn weather—the autumn at least was a pure boon in the terrible place—he loafed about his "work" undeterred, secretly agitated; not in the least "minding" that the whole proposition, as they said, was vulgar and sordid, and ready to climb ladders, to walk the plank, to handle materials and look wise about them, to ask questions, in fine, and challenge explanations and really "go into" figures.

It amused, it verily quite charmed him; and, by the same stroke, it amused, and even more, Alice Staverton, though perhaps charming her perceptibly less. She wasn't, however, going to be better-off for it, as *he* was—and so astonishingly much: nothing was now likely, he knew, ever to make her better-off than she found herself, in the afternoon of life, as the delicately frugal possessor and tenant of the small house in Irving Place to which she had subtly managed to cling through her almost unbroken New York career. If he knew the way to it now better than to any other address among the dreadful multiplied numberings which seemed to him to reduce the whole place to some vast ledger-page, overgrown, fantastic, of ruled and criss-crossed lines and figures—if he had formed, for his consolation, that habit, it was really not a little because of the charm of his having encountered and recognised, in the vast wilderness of the wholesale, breaking through the mere gross generalisation of wealth and force and success, a small still scene where items and shades, all delicate things, kept the sharpness of the notes of a high voice perfectly trained, and where economy hung about like the scent of a garden. His old friend lived with one maid and herself dusted her relics and trimmed her lamps and polished her silver; she stood oft, in the awful modern crush, when she could, but she sallied forth and did battle when the challenge was really to "spirit," the spirit she after all confessed to, proudly and a little shyly, as to that of the better time, that of *their* common, their quite far-away and antediluvian social period and order. She made use of the street-cars when need be, the terrible things that people scrambled for as the panic-stricken at sea scramble for the boats; she affronted, inscrutably, under stress, all the public concussions and ordeals; and yet, with that slim mystifying grace of her appearance, which defied you to say if she were a fair young woman who looked older through trouble, or a fine smooth older one who looked young through successful indifference with her precious reference, above all, to memories and histories into which he could enter, she was as exquisite for him as some pale pressed flower (a rarity to begin with), and, failing other sweetnesses, she was a sufficient reward of his effort. They had communities of knowledge, "their" knowledge (this discriminating possessive was always on her lips) of presences of the other age, presences all overlaid, in his case, by the experience of a man and the freedom of a wanderer, overlaid by pleasure, by infidelity, by passages of life that were strange and dim to her, just by "Europe" in short, but still unobscured, still exposed and cherished, under that pious visitation of the spirit from which she had never been diverted.

She had come with him one day to see how his "apartment-house" was rising; he had helped her over gaps and explained to her plans, and while they were there had happened to have, before her, a brief but lively discussion with the man in charge, the representative of the building firm that had undertaken his work. He had found himself quite "standing up" to this personage over a failure on the latter's part to observe some detail of one of their noted conditions, and had so lucidly argued his case that, besides ever so prettily flushing, at the time, for sympathy in his triumph, she had afterwards said to him (though to a slightly greater effect of irony) that he had clearly for too many years neglected a real gift. If he had but stayed at home he would have anticipated the inventor of the sky-scraper. If he had but stayed at home he would have discovered his genius in time really to start some new variety of awful architectural hare and run it till it burrowed in a gold mine. He was to remember these words, while the weeks elapsed, for the small silver ring they had sounded over the queerest and deepest of his own lately most disguised and most muffled vibrations. It had begun to be present to him after the first fortnight, it had broken out with the oddest abruptness, this particular wanton wonderment: it met him there—and this was the image under which he himself judged the matter, or at least, not a little, thrilled and flushed with it—very much as he might have been met by some strange figure, some unexpected occupant, at a turn of one of the dim passages of an empty house. The quaint analogy quite hauntingly remained with him, when he didn't indeed rather improve it by a still intenser form: that of his opening a door behind which he would have made sure of finding nothing, a door into a room shuttered and void, and yet so coming, with a great suppressed start, on some quite erect confronting presence, something planted in the middle of the place and facing him through the dusk. After that visit to the house in construction he walked with his companion to see the other and always so much the better one, which in the eastward direction formed one of the corners,—the "jolly" one precisely, of the street now so generally dishonoured and disfigured in its westward reaches, and of the comparatively conservative Avenue. The Avenue still had pretensions, as Miss Staverton said, to decency; the old people had mostly gone, the old names were unknown, and here and there an old association seemed to stray, all vaguely, like some very aged person, out too late, whom you might meet and feel the impulse to watch or follow, in kindness, for safe restoration to shelter.

They went in together, our friends; he admitted himself with his key, as he kept no one there, he explained, preferring, for his reasons, to leave the place empty, under a simple arrangement with a good woman living in the neighbourhood and who came for a daily hour to open windows and dust and sweep. Spencer Brydon had his reasons and was growingly aware of them; they seemed to him better each time he was there, though he didn't name them all to his companion, any more than he told her as yet how often, how quite absurdly often, he himself came. He only let her see for the present, while they walked through the great blank rooms, that absolute vacancy reigned and that, from top to bottom, there was nothing but Mrs Muldoon's broomstick, in a corner, to tempt the burglar. Mrs Muldoon was then on the premises, and she loquaciously attended the visitors, preceding them from room to room and pushing back shutters and throwing up sashes—all to show them, as she remarked, how little there was to see. There was little indeed to see in the great gaunt shell where the main dispositions and the general apportionment of space, the style of an age of ampler allowances, had nevertheless for its master their honest pleading message, affecting him as some good old servant's, some lifelong retainer's appeal for a character, or even for a retiring-pension; yet it was also a remark of Mrs Muldoon's that, glad as she was to oblige him by her noonday round, there was a request she greatly hoped he would never make of her. If he should wish her for any reason to come in after dark she would just tell him, if he "plased," that he must ask it of somebody else.

The fact that there was nothing to see didn't militate for the worthy woman against what one *might* see, and she put it frankly to Miss Staverton that no lady could be expected to like, could she? "craping up to thim top storeys in the ayvil hours." The gas and the electric light were off the house, and she fairly evoked a gruesome vision of her march through the great grey rooms—so many of them as there were too!—with her glimmering taper. Miss Staverton met her honest glare with a smile and the profession that she herself certainly would recoil from such an adventure. Spencer Brydon meanwhile held his peace—for the moment; the question of the "evil" hours in his old home had already become too grave for him. He had begun some time since to "crape," and he knew just why a packet of candles addressed to that pursuit had been stowed by his own hand, three weeks before, at the back of a drawer of the fine old sideboard that occupied, as a "fixture," the deep recess in the dining-room. Just now he laughed at his companions—quickly however changing the subject; for the reason that, in the first place, his laugh struck him even at that moment as starting the odd echo, the conscious human resonance (he scarce knew how to qualify it) that sounds made while he was there alone sent back to his ear or his fancy; and that, in the second, he imagined Alice Staverton for the instant on the point of asking him, with a divination, if he ever so prowled. There were divinations he was unprepared for, and he had at all events averted enquiry by the time Mrs Muldoon had left them, passing on to other parts.

There was happily enough to say, on so consecrated a spot, that could be said freely and fairly; so that a whole train of declarations was precipitated by his friend's having herself broken out, after a yearning look round: "But I hope you don't mean they want you to pull *this* to pieces!" His answer came, promptly, with his re-awakened wrath: it was of course exactly what they wanted, and what they were "at" him for, daily, with the iteration of people who couldn't for their life understand a man's liability to decent feelings. He had found the place, just as it stood and beyond what he could express, an interest and a joy. There were values other than the beastly rent-values, and in short, in short—! But it was thus Miss Staverton took him up. "In short you're to make so good a thing of your sky-scraper that, living in luxury on *those* ill-gotten gains, you can afford for a while to be sentimental here!" Her smile had for him, with the words, the particular mild irony with which he found half her talk suffused; an irony without bitterness and that came, exactly, from her having so much imagination—not, like the cheap sarcasms with which one heard most people, about the world of "society," bid for the reputation of cleverness, from nobody's really having any. It was agreeable to him at this very moment to be sure that when he had answered, after a brief demur, "Well, yes; so, precisely, you may put it!" her imagination would still do him justice. He explained that even if never a dollar were to come to him from the other house he would nevertheless cherish this one; and he dwelt, further, while they lingered and wandered, on the fact of the stupefaction he was already exciting, the positive mystification he felt himself create.

He spoke of the value of all he read into it, into the mere sight of the walls, mere shapes of the rooms, mere sound of the floors, mere feel, in his hand, of the old silver-plated knobs of the several mahogany doors, which suggested the pressure of the palms of the dead the seventy years of the past in fine that these things represented, the annals of nearly three generations, counting his grandfather's, the one that had ended there, and the impalpable ashes of his long-extinct youth, afloat in the very air like microscopic motes. She listened to everything; she was a woman who answered intimately but who utterly didn't chatter. She scattered abroad therefore no cloud of words; she could assent, she could agree, above all she could encourage, without doing that. Only at the last she went a little further than he had done himself. "And then how do you know? You may still, after all, want to live here." It rather indeed pulled him up, for it wasn't what he had been thinking, at least in her sense of the words, "You mean I may decide to stay on for the sake of it?"

"Well, *with* such a home—!" But, quite beautifully, she had too much tact to dot so monstrous an *i*, and it was precisely an illustration of the way she didn't rattle. How could any one—of any wit—insist on any one else's "wanting" to live in New York?

"Oh," he said, "I *might* have lived here (since I had my opportunity early in life); I might have put in here all these years. Then everything would have been different enough—and, I dare say, 'funny' enough. But that's another matter. And then the beauty of it—I mean of my perversity, of my refusal to agree to a 'deal'—is just in the total absence of a reason. Don't you see that if I had a reason about the matter at all it would *have* to be the other way, and would then be inevitably a reason of dollars? There are no reasons here *but* of dollars. Let us therefore have none whatever—not the ghost of one."

They were back in the hall then for departure, but from where they stood the vista was large, through an open door, into the great square main saloon, with its almost antique felicity of brave spaces between windows. Her eyes came back from that reach and met his own a moment. "Are you very sure the 'ghost' of one doesn't, much rather, serve—?"

He had a positive sense of turning pale. But it was as near as they were then to come. For he made answer, he believed, between a glare and a grin: "Oh ghosts—of course the place must swarm with them! I should be ashamed of it if it didn't. Poor Mrs Muldoon's right, and it's why I haven't asked her to do more than look in."

Miss Staverton's gaze again lost itself, and things she didn't utter, it was clear, came and went in her mind. She might even for the minute, off there in the fine room, have imagined some element dimly gathering. Simplified like the death-mask of a handsome face, it perhaps produced for her just then an effect akin to the stir of an expression in the "set" commemorative plaster. Yet whatever her impression may have been she produced instead a vague platitude. "Well, if it were only furnished and lived in—!"

She appeared to imply that in case of its being still furnished he might have been a little less opposed to the idea of a return. But she passed straight into the vestibule, as if to leave her words behind her, and the next moment he had opened the house-door and was standing with her on the steps. He closed the door and, while he re-pocketed his key, looking up and down, they took in the comparatively harsh actuality of the Avenue, which reminded him of the assault of the outer light of the Desert on the traveller emerging from an Egyptian tomb. But he risked before they stepped into the street his gathered answer to her speech. "For me it *is* lived in. For me it is furnished." At which it was easy for her to sigh "Ah yes!" all vaguely and discreetly; since his parents and his favourite sister, to say nothing of other kin, in numbers, had run their course and met their end there. That represented, within the walls, ineffaceable life.

It was a few days after this that, during an hour passed with her again, he had expressed his impatience of the too flattering curiosity—among the people he met—about his appreciation of New York. He had arrived at none at all that was socially producible, and as for that matter of his "thinking" (thinking the better or the worse of anything there) he was wholly taken up with one subject of thought. It was mere vain egoism, and it was moreover, if she liked, a morbid obsession. He found all things come back to the question of what he personally might have been, how he might have led his life and "turned out," if he had not so, at the outset, given it up. And confessing for the first time to the intensity within him of this absurd speculation—which but proved also, no doubt, the habit of too selfishly thinking—he affirmed the impotence there of any other source of interest, any other native appeal. "What would it have made of me, what would it have made of me? I keep for ever wondering, all idiotically; as if I could possibly know! I see what it has made of dozens of others, those I meet, and it positively aches within me, to the point of exasperation, that it would have made something of me as well. Only I can't make out what, and the worry of it, the small rage of curiosity never to be satisfied, brings back what I remember to have felt, once or twice, after judging best, for reasons, to burn some important letter unopened. I've been sorry, I've hated it—I've never known what was in the letter. You may, of course, say it's a trifle—!"

"I don't say it's a trifle," Miss Staverton gravely interrupted.

She was seated by her fire, and before her, on his feet and restless, he turned to and fro between this intensity of his idea and a fitful and unseeing inspection, through his single eye-glass, of the dear little old objects on her chimney-piece. Her interruption made him for an instant look at her harder. "I shouldn't care if you did!" he laughed, however; "and it's only a figure, at any rate, for the way I now feel. *Not* to have followed my perverse young course—and almost in the teeth of my father's curse, as I may say; not to have kept it up, so, 'over there,' from that day to this, without a doubt or a pang; not, above all, to have liked it, to have loved it, so much, loved it, no doubt, with such an abysmal conceit of my own preference; some variation from *that*, I say, must have produced some different effect for my life and for my 'form.' I should have stuck here—if it had been possible; and I was too young, at twenty-three, to judge, *pour deux sous*, whether it *were* possible. If I had waited I might have seen it was, and then I might have been, by staying here, something nearer to one of these types who have been hammered so hard and made so keen by their conditions. It isn't that I admire them so much—the question of any charm in them, or of any charm, beyond that of the rank money-passion, exerted by their conditions *for* them, has nothing to do with the matter: it's only a question of what fantastic, yet perfectly possible, development of my own nature I mayn't have missed. It comes over me that I had then a strange *alter ego* deep down somewhere within me, as the full-blown flower is in the small tight bud, and that I just took the course, I just transferred him to the climate, that blighted him for once and for ever."

"And you wonder about the flower," Miss Staverton said. "So do I, if you want to know; and so I've been wondering these several weeks. I believe in the flower," she continued, "I feel it would have been quite splendid, quite huge and monstrous."

"Monstrous above all!" her visitor echoed; "and I imagine, by the same stroke, quite hideous and offensive."

"You don't believe that," she returned; "if you did you wouldn't wonder. You'd know, and that would be enough for you. What you feel—and what I feel *for* you—is that you'd have had power."

"You'd have liked me that way?" he asked.

She barely hung fire. "How should I not have liked you?"

"I see. You'd have liked me, have preferred me, a billionaire!"

"How should I not have liked you?" she simply again asked.

He stood before her still—her question kept him motionless. He took it in, so much there was of it; and indeed his not otherwise meeting it testified to that. "I know at least what I am," he simply went on; "the other side of the medal's clear enough. I've not been edifying—I believe I'm thought in a hundred quarters to have been barely decent. I've followed strange paths and worshipped strange gods; it must have come to you again and again—in fact you've admitted to me as much—that I was leading, at any time these thirty years, a selfish frivolous scandalous life. And you see what it has made of me."

She just waited, smiling at him. "You see what it has made of *me*."

"Oh you're a person whom nothing can have altered. You were born to be what you are, anywhere, anyway: you've the perfection nothing else could have blighted. And don't you see how, without my exile, I shouldn't have been waiting till now—?" But he pulled up for the strange pang.

"The great thing to see," she presently said, "seems to me to be that it has spoiled nothing. It hasn't spoiled your being here at last. It hasn't spoiled this. It hasn't spoiled your speaking—" She also however faltered.

He wondered at everything her controlled emotion might mean. "Do you believe then—too dreadfully!—that I *am* as good as I might ever have been?"

"Oh no! Far from it!" With which she got up from her chair and was nearer to him. "But I don't care," she smiled.

"You mean I'm good enough?"

She considered a little. "Will you believe it if I say so? I mean will you let that settle your question for you?" And then as if making out in his face that he drew back from this, that he had some idea which, however absurd, he couldn't yet bargain away: "Oh you don't care either—but very differently: you don't care for anything but yourself."

Spencer Brydon recognised it—it was in fact what he had absolutely professed. Yet he importantly qualified. "*He* isn't myself. He's the just so totally other person. But I do want to see him," he added. "And I can. And I shall."

Their eyes met for a minute while he guessed from something in hers that she divined his strange sense. But neither of them otherwise expressed it, and her apparent understanding, with no protesting shock, no easy derision, touched him more deeply than anything yet, constituting for his stifled perversity, on the spot, an element that was like breatheable air. What she said however was unexpected. "Well, *I've* seen him."

"You—?"

"I've seen him in a dream."

"Oh a 'dream'—!" It let him down.

"But twice over," she continued. "I saw him as I see you now."

"You've dreamed the same dream—?"

"Twice over," she repeated. "The very same."

This did somehow a little speak to him, as it also gratified him. "You dream about me at that rate?"

"Ah about *him*!" she smiled.

His eyes again sounded her. "Then you know all about him." And as she said nothing more: "What's the wretch like?"

She hesitated, and it was as if he were pressing her so hard that, resisting for reasons of her own, she had to turn away. "I'll tell you some other time!"

Chapter II

It was after this that there was most of a virtue for him, most of a cultivated charm, most of a preposterous secret thrill, in the particular form of surrender to his obsession and of address to what he more and more believed to be his privilege. It was what in these weeks he was living for—since he really felt life to begin but after Mrs Muldoon had retired from the scene and, visiting the ample house from attic to cellar, making sure he was alone, he knew himself in safe possession and, as he tacitly expressed it, let himself go. He sometimes came twice in the twenty-four hours; the moments he liked best were those of gathering dusk, of the short autumn twilight; this was the time of which, again and again, he found himself hoping most. Then he could, as seemed to him, most intimately wander and wait, linger and listen, feel his fine attention, never in his life before so fine, on the pulse of the great vague place: he preferred the lampless hour and only wished he might have prolonged each day the deep crepuscular spell. Later—rarely much before midnight, but then for a considerable vigil—he watched with his glimmering light; moving slowly, holding it high, playing it far, rejoicing above all, as much as he might, in open vistas, reaches of communication between rooms and by passages; the long straight chance or show, as he would have called it, for the revelation he pretended to invite. It was a practice he found he could perfectly "work" without exciting remark; no one was in the least the wiser for it; even Alice Staverton, who was moreover a well of discretion, didn't quite fully imagine.

He let himself in and let himself out with the assurance of calm proprietorship; and accident so far favoured him that, if a fat Avenue "officer" had happened on occasion to see him entering at eleven-thirty, he had never yet, to the best of his belief, been noticed as emerging at two. He walked there on the crisp November nights, arrived regularly at the evening's end; it was as easy to do this after dining out as to take his way to a club or to his hotel. When he left his club, if he hadn't been dining out, it was ostensibly to go to his hotel; and when he left his hotel, if he had spent a part of the evening there, it was ostensibly to go to his club. Everything was easy in fine; everything conspired and promoted: there was truly even in the strain of his experience something that glossed over, something that salved and simplified, all the rest of consciousness. He circulated, talked, renewed, loosely and pleasantly, old relations—met indeed, so far as he could, new expectations and seemed to make out on the whole that in spite of the career, of such different contacts, which he had spoken of to Miss Staverton as ministering so little, for those who might have watched it, to edification, he was positively rather liked than not. He was a dim secondary social success—and all with people who had truly not an idea of him. It was all mere surface sound, this murmur of their welcome, this popping of their corks—just as his gestures of response were the extravagant shadows, emphatic in proportion as they meant little, of some game of *ombres chinoises*. He projected himself all day, in thought, straight over the bristling line of hard unconscious heads and into the other, the real, the waiting life; the life that, as soon as he had heard behind him the click of his great house-door, began for him, on the jolly corner, as beguilingly as the slow opening bars of some rich music follows the tap of the conductor's wand.

He always caught the first effect of the steel point of his stick on the old marble of the hall pavement, large black-and-white squares that he remembered as the admiration of his childhood and that had then made in him, as he now saw, for the growth of an early conception of style. This effect was the dim reverberating tinkle as of some far-off bell hung who should say where?—in the depths of the house, of the past, of that mystical other world that might have flourished for him had he not, for weal or woe, abandoned it. On this impression he did ever the same thing; he put his stick noiselessly away in a corner—feeling the place once more in the likeness of some great glass bowl, all precious concave crystal, set delicately humming by the play of a moist finger round its edge. The concave crystal held, as it were, this mystical other world, and the indescribably fine murmur of its rim was the sigh there, the scarce audible pathetic wail to his strained ear, of all the old baffled forsworn possibilities. What he did therefore by this appeal of his hushed presence was to wake them into such measure of ghostly life as they might still enjoy. They were shy, all but unappeasably shy, but they weren't really sinister; at least they weren't as he had hitherto felt them—before they had taken the Form he so yearned to make them take, the Form he at moments saw himself in the light of fairly hunting on tiptoe, the points of his evening shoes, from room to room and from storey to storey.

That was the essence of his vision—which was all rank folly, if one would, while he was out of the house and otherwise occupied, but which took on the last verisimilitude as soon as he was placed and posted. He knew what he meant and what he wanted; it was as clear as the figure on a cheque presented in demand for cash. His *alter ego* "walked"—that was the note of his image of him, while his image of his motive for his own odd pastime was the desire to waylay him and meet him. He roamed, slowly, warily, but all restlessly, he himself did—Mrs Muldoon had been right, absolutely, with her figure of their "craping"; and the presence he watched for would roam restlessly too. But it would be as cautious and as shifty; the conviction of its probable, in fact its already quite sensible, quite audible evasion of pursuit grew for him from night to night, laying on him finally a rigour to which nothing in his life had been comparable. It had been the theory of many superficially-judging persons, he knew, that he was wasting that life in a surrender to sensations, but he had tasted of no pleasure so fine as his actual tension, had been introduced to no sport that demanded at once the patience and the nerve of this stalking of a creature more subtle, yet at bay perhaps more formidable, than any beast of the forest. The terms, the comparisons, the very practices of the chase positively came again into play; there were even moments when passages of his occasional experience as a sportsman, stirred memories, from his younger time, of moor and mountain and desert, revived for him—and to the increase of his keenness—by the tremendous force of analogy. He found himself at moments—once he had placed his single light on some mantel-shelf or in some recess—stepping back into shelter or shade, effacing himself behind a door or in an embrasure, as he had sought of old the vantage of rock and tree; he found himself holding his breath and living in the joy of the instant, the supreme suspense created by big game alone.

He wasn't afraid (though putting himself the question as he believed gentlemen on Bengal tiger-shoots or in close quarters with the great bear of the Rockies had been known to confess to having put it); and this indeed—since here at least he might be frank!—because of the impression, so intimate and so strange, that he himself produced as yet a dread, produced certainly a strain, beyond the liveliest he was likely to feel. They fell for him into categories, they fairly became familiar, the signs, for his own perception, of the alarm his presence and his vigilance created; though leaving him always to remark, portentously, on his probably having formed a relation, his probably enjoying a consciousness, unique in the experience of man. People enough, first and last, had been in terror of apparitions, but who had ever before so turned the tables and become himself, in the apparitional world, an incalculable terror? He might have found this sublime had he quite dared to think of it; but he didn't too much insist, truly, on that side of his privilege. With habit and repetition he gained to an extraordinary degree the power to penetrate the dusk of distances and the darkness of corners, to resolve back into their innocence the treacheries of uncertain light, the evil-looking forms taken in the gloom by mere shadows, by accidents of the air, by shifting effects of perspective; putting down his dim luminary he could still wander on without it, pass into other rooms and, only knowing it was there behind him in case of need, see his way about, visually project for his purpose a comparative clearness. It made him feel, this acquired faculty, like some monstrous stealthy cat; he wondered if he would have glared at these moments with large shining yellow eyes, and what it mightn't verily be, for the poor hard-pressed *alter ego*, to be confronted with such a type.

He liked however the open shutters; he opened everywhere those Mrs Muldoon had closed, closing them as carefully afterwards, so that she shouldn't notice: he liked—oh this he did like, and above all in the upper rooms!—the sense of the hard silver of the autumn stars through the window-panes, and scarcely less the flare of the street-lamps below, the white electric lustre which it would have taken curtains to keep out. This was human actual social; this was of the world he had lived in, and he was more at his ease certainly for the countenance, coldly general and impersonal, that all the while and in spite of his detachment it seemed to give him. He had support of course mostly in the rooms at the wide front and the prolonged side; it failed him considerably in the central shades and the parts at the back. But if he sometimes, on his rounds, was glad of his optical reach, so none the less often the rear of the house affected him as the very jungle of his prey. The place was there more subdivided; a large "extension" in particular, where small rooms for servants had been multiplied, abounded in nooks and corners, in closets and passages, in the ramifications especially of an ample back staircase over which he leaned, many a time, to look far down—not deterred from his gravity even while aware that he might, for a spectator, have figured some solemn simpleton playing at hide-and-seek. Outside in fact he might himself make that ironic *rapprochement*; but within the walls, and in spite of the clear windows, his consistency was proof against the cynical light of New York.

It had belonged to that idea of the exasperated consciousness of his victim to become a real test for him; since he had quite put it to himself from the first that, oh distinctly! he could "cultivate" his whole perception. He had felt it as above all open to cultivation—which indeed was but another name for his manner of spending his time. He was bringing it on, bringing it to perfection, by practice; in consequence of which it had grown so fine that he was now aware of impressions, attestations of his general postulate, that couldn't have broken upon him at once. This was the case more specifically with a phenomenon at last quite frequent for him in the upper rooms, the recognition—absolutely unmistakeable, and by a turn dating from a particular hour, his resumption of his campaign after a diplomatic drop, a calculated absence of three nights—of his being definitely followed, tracked at a distance carefully taken and to the express end that he should the less confidently, less arrogantly, appear to himself merely to pursue. It worried, it finally quite broke him up, for it proved, of all the conceivable impressions, the one least suited to his book. He was kept in sight while remaining himself—as regards the essence of his position—sightless, and his only recourse then was in abrupt turns, rapid recoveries of ground. He wheeled about, retracing his steps, as if he might so catch in his face at least the stirred air of some other quick revolution. It was indeed true that his fully dislocalised thought of these manoeuvres recalled to him Pantaloon, at the Christmas farce, buffeted and tricked from behind by ubiquitous Harlequin; but it left intact the influence of the conditions themselves each time he was re-exposed to them, so that in fact this association, had he suffered it to become constant, would on a certain side have but ministered to his intenser gravity. He had made, as I have said, to create on the premises the baseless sense of a reprieve, his three absences; and the result of the third was to confirm the after-effect of the second.

On his return that night—the night succeeding his last intermission—he stood in the hall and looked up the staircase with a certainty more intimate than any he had yet known. "He's *there*, at the top, and waiting—not, as in general, falling back for disappearance. He's holding his ground, and it's the first time—which is a proof, isn't it? that something has happened for him." So Brydon argued with his hand on the banister and his foot on the lowest stair; in which position he felt as never before the air chilled by his logic. He himself turned cold in it, for he seemed of a sudden to know what now was involved. "Harder pressed?—yes, he takes it in, with its thus making clear to him that I've come, as they say, 'to stay.' He finally doesn't like and can't bear it, in the sense, I mean, that his wrath, his menaced interest, now balances with his dread. I've hunted him till he has 'turned'; that, up there, is what has happened—he's the fanged or the antlered animal brought at last to bay." There came to him, as I say—but determined by an influence beyond my notation!—the acuteness of this certainty; under which however the next moment he had broken into a sweat that he would as little have consented to attribute to fear as he would have dared immediately to act upon it for enterprise. It marked none the less a prodigious thrill, a thrill that represented sudden dismay, no doubt, but also represented, and with the selfsame throb, the strangest, the most joyous, possibly the next minute almost the proudest, duplication of consciousness.

"He has been dodging, retreating, hiding, but now, worked up to anger, he'll fight!"—this intense impression made a single mouthful, as it were, of terror and applause. But what was wondrous was that the applause, for the felt fact, was so eager, since, if it was his other self he was running to earth, this ineffable identity was thus in the last resort not unworthy of him. It bristled there—somewhere near at hand, however unseen still—as the hunted thing, even as the trodden worm of the adage must at last bristle; and Brydon at this instant tasted probably of a sensation more complex than had ever before found itself consistent with sanity. It was as if it would have shamed him that a character so associated with his own should triumphantly succeed in just skulking, should to the end not risk the open; so that the drop of this danger was, on the spot, a great lift of the whole situation. Yet with another rare shift of the same subtlety he was already trying to measure by how much more he himself might now be in peril of fear; so rejoicing that he could, in another form, actively inspire that fear, and simultaneously quaking for the form in which he might passively know it.

The apprehension of knowing it must after a little have grown in him, and the strangest moment of his adventure perhaps, the most memorable or really most interesting, afterwards, of his crisis, was the lapse of certain instants of concentrated conscious *combat*, the sense of a need to hold on to something, even after the manner of a man slipping and slipping on some awful incline; the vivid impulse, above all, to move, to act, to charge, somehow and upon something—to show himself, in a word, that he wasn't afraid. The state of "holding on" was thus the state to which he was momentarily reduced; if there had been anything, in the great vacancy, to seize, he would presently have been aware of having clutched it as he might under a shock at home have clutched the nearest chair-back. He had been surprised at any rate—of this he *was* aware—into something unprecedented since his original appropriation of the place; he had closed his eyes, held them tight, for a long minute, as with that instinct of dismay and that terror of vision. When he opened them the room, the other contiguous rooms, extraordinarily, seemed lighter—so light, almost, that at first he took the change for day. He stood firm, however that might be, just where he had paused; his resistance had helped him—it was as if there were something he had tided over. He knew after a little what this was—it had been in the imminent danger of flight. He had stiffened his will against going; without this he would have made for the stairs, and it seemed to him that, still with his eyes closed, he would have descended them, would have known how, straight and swiftly, to the bottom.

Well, as he had held out, here he was—still at the top, among the more intricate upper rooms and with the gauntlet of the others, of all the rest of the house, still to run when it should be his time to go. He would go at his time—only at his time: didn't he go every night very much at the same hour? He took out his watch—there was light for that: it was scarcely a quarter past one, and he had never withdrawn so soon. He reached his lodgings for the most part at two—with his walk of a quarter of an hour. He would wait for the last quarter—he wouldn't stir till then; and he kept his watch there with his eyes on it, reflecting while he held it that this deliberate wait, a wait with an effort, which he recognised, would serve perfectly for the attestation he desired to make. It would prove his courage—unless indeed the latter might most be proved by his budging at last from his place. What he mainly felt now was that, since he hadn't originally scuttled, he had his dignities—which had never in his life seemed so many—all to preserve and to carry aloft. This was before him in truth as a physical image, an image almost worthy of an age of greater romance. That remark indeed glimmered for him only to glow the next instant with a finer light; since what age of romance, after all, could have matched either the state of his mind or, "objectively," as they said, the wonder of his situation? The only difference would have been that, brandishing his dignities over his head as in a parchment scroll, he might then—that is in the heroic time—have proceeded downstairs with a drawn sword in his other grasp.

At present, really, the light he had set down on the mantel of the next room would have to figure his sword; which utensil, in the course of a minute, he had taken the requisite number of steps to possess himself of. The door between the rooms was open, and from the second another door opened to a third. These rooms, as he remembered, gave all three upon a common corridor as well, but there was a fourth, beyond them, without issue save through the preceding. To have moved, to have heard his step again, was appreciably a help; though even in recognising this he lingered once more a little by the chimney-piece on which his light had rested. When he next moved, just hesitating where to turn, he found himself considering a circumstance that, after his first and comparatively vague apprehension of it, produced in him the start that often attends some pang of recollection, the violent shock of having ceased happily to forget. He had come into sight of the door in which the brief chain of communication ended and which he now surveyed from the nearer threshold, the one not directly facing it. Placed at some distance to the left of this point, it would have admitted him to the last room of the four, the room without other approach or egress, had it not, to his intimate conviction, been closed *since* his former visitation, the matter probably of a quarter of an hour before. He stared with all his eyes at the wonder of the fact, arrested again where he stood and again holding his breath while he sounded his sense. Surely it had been *subsequently* closed—that is it had been on his previous passage indubitably open!

He took it full in the face that something had happened between—that he couldn't have noticed before (by which he meant on his original tour of all the rooms that evening) that such a barrier had exceptionally presented itself. He had indeed since that moment undergone an agitation so extraordinary that it might have muddled for him any earlier view; and he tried to convince himself that he might perhaps then have gone into the room and, inadvertently, automatically, on coming out, have drawn the door after him. The difficulty was that this exactly was what he never did; it was against his whole policy, as he might have said, the essence of which was to keep vistas clear. He had them from the first, as he was well aware, quite on the brain: the strange apparition, at the far end of one of them, of his baffled "prey" (which had become by so sharp an irony so little the term now to apply!) was the form of success his imagination had most cherished, projecting into it always a refinement of beauty. He had known fifty times the start of perception that had afterwards dropped; had fifty times gasped to himself. "There!" under some fond brief hallucination. The house, as the case stood, admirably lent itself; he might wonder at the taste, the native architecture of the particular time, which could rejoice so in the multiplication of doors—the opposite extreme to the modern, the actual almost complete proscription of them; but it had fairly contributed to provoke this obsession of the presence encountered telescopically, as he might say, focused and studied in diminishing perspective and as by a rest for the elbow.

It was with these considerations that his present attention was charged—they perfectly availed to make what he saw portentous. He *couldn't*, by any lapse, have blocked that aperture; and if he hadn't, if it was unthinkable, why what else was clear but that there had been another agent? Another agent?—he had been catching, as he felt, a moment back, the very breath of him; but when had he been so close as in this simple, this logical, this completely personal act? It was so logical, that is, that one might have *taken* it for personal; yet for what did Brydon take it, he asked himself, while, softly panting, he felt his eyes almost leave their sockets. Ah this time at last they *were*, the two, the opposed projections of him, in presence; and this time, as much as one would, the question of danger loomed. With it rose, as not before, the question of courage—for what he knew the blank face of the door to say to him was "Show us how much you have!" It stared, it glared back at him with that challenge; it put to him the two alternatives: should he just push it open or not? Oh to have this consciousness was to *think*—and to think, Brydon knew, as he stood there, was, with the lapsing moments, not to have acted! Not to have acted—that was the misery and the pang—was even still not to act; was in fact *all* to feel the thing in another, in a new and terrible way. How long did he pause and how long did he debate? There was presently nothing to measure it; for his vibration had already changed—as just by the effect of its intensity. Shut up there, at bay, defiant, and with the prodigy of the thing palpably proveably *done*, thus giving notice like some stark signboard—under that accession of accent the situation itself had turned; and Brydon at last remarkably made up his mind on what it had turned to.

It had turned altogether to a different admonition; to a supreme hint, for him, of the value of Discretion! This slowly dawned, no doubt—for it could take its time; so perfectly, on his threshold, had he been stayed, so little as yet had he either advanced or retreated. It was the strangest of all things that now when, by his taking ten steps and applying his hand to a latch, or even his shoulder and his knee, if necessary, to a panel, all the hunger of his prime need might have been met, his high curiosity crowned, his unrest assuaged—it was amazing, but it was also exquisite and rare, that insistence should have, at a touch, quite dropped from him. Discretion—he jumped at that; and yet not, verily, at such a pitch, because it saved his nerves or his skin, but because, much more valuably, it saved the situation. When I say he "jumped" at it I feel the consonance of this term with the fact that—at the end indeed of I know not how long—he did move again, he crossed straight to the door. He wouldn't touch it—it seemed now that he might if he would: he would only just wait there a little, to show, to prove, that he wouldn't. He had thus another station, close to the thin partition by which revelation was denied him; but with his eyes bent and his hands held off in a mere intensity of stillness. He listened as if there had been something to hear, but this attitude, while it lasted, was his own communication. "If you won't then—good: I spare you and I give up. You affect me as by the appeal positively for pity: you convince me that for reasons rigid and sublime—what do I know?—we both of us should have suffered. I respect them then, and, though moved and privileged as, I believe, it has never been given to man, I retire, I renounce—never, on my honour, to try again. So rest for ever—and let *me*!"

That, for Brydon, was the deep sense of this last demonstration—solemn, measured, directed, as he felt it to be. He brought it to a close, he turned away; and now verily he knew how deeply he had been stirred. He retraced his steps, taking up his candle, burnt, he observed, well-nigh to the socket, and marking again, lighten it as he would, the distinctness of his footfall; after which, in a moment, he knew himself at the other side of the house. He did here what he had not yet done at these hours—he opened half a casement, one of those in the front, and let in the air of the night; a thing he would have taken at any time previous for a sharp rupture of his spell. His spell was broken now, and it didn't matter—broken by his concession and his surrender, which made it idle henceforth that he should ever come back. The empty street—its other life so marked even by great lamp-lit vacancy—was within call, within touch; he stayed there as to be in it again, high above it though he was still perched; he watched as for some comforting common fact, some vulgar human note, the passage of a scavenger or a thief, some night-bird however base. He would have blessed that sign of life; he would have welcomed positively the slow approach of his friend the policeman, whom he had hitherto only sought to avoid, and was not sure that if the patrol had come into sight he mightn't have felt the impulse to get into relation with it, to hail it, on some pretext, from his fourth floor.

The pretext that wouldn't have been too silly or too compromising, the explanation that would have saved his dignity and kept his name, in such a case, out of the papers, was not definite to him: he was so occupied with the thought of recording his Discretion—as an effect of the vow he had just uttered to his intimate adversary—that the importance of this loomed large and something had overtaken all ironically his sense of proportion. If there had been a ladder applied to the front of the house, even one of the vertiginous perpendiculars employed by painters and roofers and sometimes left standing overnight, he would have managed somehow, astride of the window-sill, to compass by outstretched leg and arm that mode of descent. If there had been some such uncanny thing as he had found in his room at hotels, a workable fire-escape in the form of notched cable or a canvas shoot, he would have availed himself of it as a proof—well, of his present delicacy. He nursed that sentiment, as the question stood, a little in vain, and even—at the end of he scarce knew, once more, how long—found it, as by the action on his mind of the failure of response of the outer world, sinking back to vague anguish. It seemed to him he had waited an age for some stir of the great grim hush; the life of the town was itself under a spell—so unnaturally, up and down the whole prospect of known and rather ugly objects, the blankness and the silence lasted. Had they ever, he asked himself, the hard-faced houses, which had begun to look livid in the dim dawn, had they ever spoken so little to any need of his spirit? Great builded voids, great crowded stillnesses put on, often, in the heart of cities, for the small hours, a sort of sinister mask, and it was of this large collective negation that Brydon presently became conscious—all the more that the break of day was, almost incredibly, now at hand, proving to him what a night he had made of it.

He looked again at his watch, saw what had become of his time-values (he had taken hours for minutes—not, as in other tense situations, minutes for hours) and the strange air of the streets was but the weak, the sullen flush of a dawn in which everything was still locked up. His choked appeal from his own open window had been the sole note of life, and he could but break off at last as for a worse despair. Yet while so deeply demoralised he was capable again of an impulse denoting—at least by his present measure—extraordinary resolution; of retracing his steps to the spot where he had turned cold with the extinction of his last pulse of doubt as to there being in the place another presence than his own. This required an effort strong enough to sicken him; but he had his reason, which over-mastered for the moment everything else. There was the whole of the rest of the house to traverse, and how should he screw himself to that if the door he had seen closed were at present open? He could hold to the idea that the closing had practically been for him an act of mercy, a chance offered him to descend, depart, get off the ground and never again profane it. This conception held together, it worked; but what it meant for him depended now clearly on the amount of forbearance his recent action, or rather his recent inaction, had engendered. The image of the "presence" whatever it was, waiting there for him to go—this image had not yet been so concrete for his nerves as when he stopped short of the point at which certainty would have come to him. For, with all his resolution, or more exactly with all his dread, he did stop short—he hung back from really seeing. The risk was too great and his fear too definite: it took at this moment an awful specific form.

He knew—yes, as he had never known anything—that, *should* he see the door open, it would all too abjectly be the end of him. It would mean that the agent of his shame—for his shame was the deep abjection—was once more at large and in general possession; and what glared him thus in the face was the act that this would determine for him. It would send him straight about to the window he had left open, and by that window, be long ladder and dangling rope as absent as they would, he saw himself uncontrollably insanely fatally take his way to the street. The hideous chance of this he at least could avert; but he could only avert it by recoiling in time from assurance. He had the whole house to deal with, this fact was still there; only he now knew that uncertainty alone could start him. He stole back from where he had checked himself—merely to do so was suddenly like safety—and, making blindly for the greater staircase, left gaping rooms and sounding passages behind. Here was the top of the stairs, with a fine large dim descent and three spacious landings to mark off. His instinct was all for mildness, but his feet were harsh on the floors, and, strangely, when he had in a couple of minutes become aware of this, it counted somehow for help. He couldn't have spoken, the tone of his voice would have scared him, and the common conceit or resource of "whistling in the dark" (whether literally or figuratively) have appeared basely vulgar; yet he liked none the less to hear himself go, and when he had reached his first landing—taking it all with no rush, but quite steadily—that stage of success drew from him a gasp of relief.

The house, withal, seemed immense, the scale of space again inordinate; the open rooms, to no one of which his eyes deflected, gloomed in their shuttered state like mouths of caverns; only the high skylight that formed the crown of the deep well created for him a medium in which he could advance, but which might have been, for queerness of colour, some watery under-world. He tried to think of something noble, as that his property was really grand, a splendid possession; but this nobleness took the form too of the clear delight with which he was finally to sacrifice it. They might come in now, the builders, the destroyers—they might come as soon as they would. At the end of two flights he had dropped to another zone, and from the middle of the third, with only one more left, he recognised the influence of the lower windows, of half-drawn blinds, of the occasional gleam of street-lamps, of the glazed spaces of the vestibule. This was the bottom of the sea, which showed an illumination of its own and which he even saw paved—when at a given moment he drew up to sink a long look over the banisters—with the marble squares of his childhood. By that time indubitably he felt, as he might have said in a commoner cause, better; it had allowed him to stop and draw breath, and the case increased with the sight of the old black-and-white slabs. But what he most felt was that now surely, with the element of impunity pulling him as by hard firm hands, the case was settled for what he might have seen above had he dared that last look. The closed door, blessedly remote now, was still closed—and he had only in short to reach that of the house.

He came down further, he crossed the passage forming the access to the last flight and if here again he stopped an instant it was almost for the sharpness of the thrill of assured escape. It made him shut his eyes—which opened again to the straight slope of the remainder of the stairs. Here was impunity still, but impunity almost excessive; inasmuch as the side-lights and the high fantracery of the entrance were glimmering straight into the hall; an appearance produced, he the next instant saw, by the fact that the vestibule gaped wide, that the hinged halves of the inner door had been thrown far back. Out of that again the *question* sprang at him, making his eyes, as he felt, half-start from his head, as they had done, at the top of the house, before the sign of the other door. If he had left that one open, hadn't he left this one closed, and wasn't he now in *most* immediate presence of some inconceivable occult activity? It was as sharp, the question, as a knife in his side, but the answer hung fire still and seemed to lose itself in the vague darkness to which the thin admitted dawn, glimmering archwise over the whole outer door, made a semicircular margin, a cold silvery nimbus that seemed to play a little as he looked—to shift and expand and contract.

It was as if there had been something within it, protected by indistinctness and corresponding in extent with the opaque surface behind, the painted panels of the last barrier to his escape, of which the key was in his pocket. The indistinctness mocked him even while he stared, affected him as somehow shrouding or challenging certitude, so that after faltering an instant on his step he let himself go with the sense that here *was* at last something to meet, to touch, to take, to know—something all unnatural and dreadful, but to advance upon which was the condition for him either of liberation or of supreme defeat. The penumbra, dense and dark, was the virtual screen of a figure which stood in it as still as some image erect in a niche or as some black-vizored sentinel guarding a treasure. Brydon was to know afterwards, was to recall and make out, the particular thing he had believed during the rest of his descent. He saw, in its great grey glimmering margin, the central vagueness diminish, and he felt it to be taking the very form toward which, for so many days, the passion of his curiosity had yearned. It gloomed, it loomed, it was something, it was somebody, the prodigy of a personal presence.

Rigid and conscious, spectral yet human, a man of his own substance and stature waited there to measure himself with his power to dismay. This only could it be—this only till he recognised, with his advance, that what made the face dim was the pair of raised hands that covered it and in which, so far from being offered in defiance, it was buried, as for dark deprecation. So Brydon, before him, took him in; with every fact of him now, in the higher light, hard and acute—his planted stillness, his vivid truth, his grizzled bent head and white masking hands, his queer actuality of evening-dress, of dangling double eye-glass, of gleaming silk lappet and white linen, of pearl button and gold watch-guard and polished shoe. No portrait by a great modern master could have presented him with more intensity, thrust him out of his frame with more art, as if there had been "treatment," of the consummate sort, in his every shade and salience. The revulsion, for our friend, had become, before he knew it, immense—this drop, in the act of apprehension, to the sense of his adversary's inscrutable manoeuvre. That meaning at least, while he gaped, it offered him; for he could but gape at his other self in this other anguish, gape as a proof that *he*, standing there for the achieved, the enjoyed, the triumphant life, couldn't be faced in his triumph. Wasn't the proof in the splendid covering hands, strong and completely spread?—so spread and so intentional that, in spite of a special verity that surpassed every other, the fact that one of these hands had lost two fingers, which were reduced to stumps, as if accidentally shot away, the face was effectually guarded and saved.

"Saved," though, *would* it be?—Brydon breathed his wonder till the very impunity of his attitude and the very insistence of his eyes produced, as he felt, a sudden stir which showed the next instant as a deeper portent, while the head raised itself, the betrayal of a braver purpose. The hands, as he looked, began to move, to open; then, as if deciding in a flash, dropped from the face and left it uncovered and presented. Horror, with the sight, had leaped into Brydon's throat, gasping there in a sound he couldn't utter; for the bared identity was too hideous as *his*, and his glare was the passion of his protest. The face, *that* face, Spencer Brydon's?—he searched it still, but looking away from it in dismay and denial, falling straight from his height of sublimity. It was unknown, inconceivable, awful, disconnected from any possibility!—He had been "sold," he inwardly moaned, stalking such game as this: the presence before him was a presence, the horror within him a horror, but the waste of his nights had been only grotesque and the success of his adventure an irony. Such an identity fitted his at *no* point, made its alternative monstrous. A thousand times yes, as it came upon him nearer now, the face was the face of a stranger. It came upon him nearer now, quite as one of those expanding fantastic images projected by the magic lantern of childhood; for the stranger, whoever he might be, evil, odious, blatant, vulgar, had advanced as for aggression, and he knew himself give ground. Then harder pressed still, sick with the force of his shock, and falling back as under the hot breath and the roused passion of a life larger than his own, a rage of personality before which his own collapsed, he felt the whole vision turn to darkness and his very feet give way. His head went round; he was going; he had gone.

Chapter III

What had next brought him back, clearly—though after how long?—was Mrs Muldoon's voice, coming to him from quite near, from so near that he seemed presently to see her as kneeling on the ground before him while he lay looking up at her; himself not wholly on the ground, but half-raised and upheld—conscious, yes, of tenderness of support and, more particularly, of a head pillowed in extraordinary softness and faintly refreshing fragrance. He considered, he wondered, his wit but half at his service; then another face intervened, bending more directly over him, and he finally knew that Alice Staverton had made her lap an ample and perfect cushion to him, and that she had to this end seated herself on the lowest degree of the staircase, the rest of his long person remaining stretched on his old black-and-white slabs. They were cold, these marble squares of his youth; but *he* somehow was not, in this rich return of consciousness—the most wonderful hour, little by little, that he had ever known, leaving him, as it did, so gratefully, so abysmally passive, and yet as with a treasure of intelligence waiting all round him for quiet appropriation; dissolved, he might call it, in the air of the place and producing the golden glow of a late autumn afternoon. He had come back, yes—come back from further away than any man but himself had ever travelled; but it was strange how with this sense what he had come back *to* seemed really the great thing, and as if his prodigious journey had been all for the sake of it. Slowly but surely his consciousness grew, his vision of his state thus completing itself; he had been miraculously *carried* back—lifted and carefully borne as from where he had been picked up, the uttermost end of an interminable grey passage. Even with this he was suffered to rest, and what had now brought him to knowledge was the break in the long mild motion.

It had brought him to knowledge, to knowledge—yes, this was the beauty of his state; which came to resemble more and more that of a man who has gone to sleep on some news of a great inheritance, and then, after dreaming it away, after profaning it with matters strange to it, has waked up again to serenity of certitude and has only to lie and watch it grow. This was the drift of his patience—that he had only to let it shine on him. He must moreover, with intermissions, still have been lifted and borne; since why and how else should he have known himself, later on, with the afternoon glow intenser, no longer at the foot of his stairs—situated as these now seemed at that dark other end of his tunnel—but on a deep window-bench of his high saloon, over which had been spread, couch-fashion, a mantle of soft stuff lined with grey fur that was familiar to his eyes and that one of his hands kept fondly feeling as for its pledge of truth. Mrs Muldoon's face had gone, but the other, the second he had recognised, hung over him in a way that showed how he was still propped and pillowed. He took it all in, and the more he took it the more it seemed to suffice: he was as much at peace as if he had had food and drink. It was the two women who had found him, on Mrs Muldoon's having plied, at her usual hour, her latch-key—and on her having above all arrived while Miss Staverton still lingered near the house. She had been turning away, all anxiety, from worrying the vain bell-handle—her calculation having been of the hour of the good woman's visit; but the latter, blessedly, had come up while she was still there, and they had entered together. He had then lain, beyond the vestibule, very much as he was lying now—quite, that is, as he appeared to have fallen, but all so wondrously without bruise or gash; only in a depth of stupor. What he most took in, however, at present, with the steadier clearance, was that Alice Staverton had for a long unspeakable moment not doubted he was dead.

"It must have been that I *was*." He made it out as she held him. "Yes—I can only have died. You brought me literally to life. Only," he wondered, his eyes rising to her, "only, in the name of all the benedictions, how?"

It took her but an instant to bend her face and kiss him, and something in the manner of it, and in the way her hands clasped and locked his head while he felt the cool charity and virtue of her lips, something in all this beatitude somehow answered everything.

"And now I keep you," she said.

"Oh keep me, keep me!" he pleaded while her face still hung over him: in response to which it dropped again and stayed close, clingingly close. It was the seal of their situation—of which he tasted the impress for a long blissful moment in silence. But he came back. "Yet how did you know—?"

"I was uneasy. You were to have come, you remember—and you had sent no word."

"Yes, I remember—I was to have gone to you at one today." It caught on to their "old" life and relation—which were so near and so far. "I was still out there in my strange darkness—where was it, what was it? I must have stayed there so long." He could but wonder at the depth and the duration of his swoon.

"Since last night?" she asked with a shade of fear for her possible indiscretion.

"Since this morning—it must have been: the cold dim dawn of today. Where have I been," he vaguely wailed, "where have I been?" He felt her hold him close, and it was as if this helped him now to make in all security his mild moan. "What a long dark day!"

All in her tenderness she had waited a moment. "In the cold dim dawn?" she quavered.

But he had already gone on piecing together the parts of the whole prodigy. "As I didn't turn up you came straight—?"

She barely cast about. "I went first to your hotel—where they told me of your absence. You had dined out last evening and hadn't been back since. But they appeared to know you had been at your club."

"So you had the idea of *this*—?"

"Of what?" she asked in a moment.

"Well—of what has happened."

"I believed at least you'd have been here. I've known, all along," she said, "that you've been coming."

"'Known' it—?"

"Well, I've believed it. I said nothing to you after that talk we had a month ago—but I felt sure. I knew you *would*," she declared.

"That I'd persist, you mean?"

"That you'd see him."

"Ah but I didn't!" cried Brydon with his long wail. "There's somebody—an awful beast; whom I brought, too horribly, to bay. But it's not me."

At this she bent over him again, and her eyes were in his eyes. "No—it's not you." And it was as if, while her face hovered, he might have made out in it, hadn't it been so near, some particular meaning blurred by a smile. "No, thank heaven," she repeated, "it's not you! Of course it wasn't to have been."

"Ah but it *was*," he gently insisted. And he stared before him now as he had been staring for so many weeks. "I was to have known myself."

"You couldn't!" she returned consolingly. And then reverting, and as if to account further for what she had herself done, "But it wasn't only *that*, that you hadn't been at home," she went on. "I waited till the hour at which we had found Mrs Muldoon that day of my going with you; and she arrived, as I've told you, while, failing to bring any one to the door, I lingered in my despair on the steps. After a little, if she hadn't come, by such a mercy, I should have found means to hunt her up. But it wasn't," said Alice Staverton, as if once more with her fine intentions—"it wasn't only that."

His eyes, as he lay, turned back to her. "What more then?"

She met it, the wonder she had stirred. "In the cold dim dawn, you say? Well, in the cold dim dawn of this morning I too saw you."

"Saw *me*—?"

"Saw *him*," said Alice Staverton. "It must have been at the same moment."

He lay an instant taking it in—as if he wished to be quite reasonable. "At the same moment?"

"Yes—in my dream again, the same one I've named to you. He came back to me. Then I knew it for a sign. He had come to you."

At this Brydon raised himself; he had to see her better. She helped him when she understood his movement, and he sat up, steadying himself beside her there on the window-bench and with his right hand grasping her left. "*He* didn't come to me."

"You came to yourself," she beautifully smiled.

"Ah I've come to myself now—thanks to you, dearest. But this brute, with his awful face—this brute's a black stranger. He's none of *me*, even as I *might* have been," Brydon sturdily declared.

But she kept the clearness that was like the breath of infallibility. "Isn't the whole point that you'd have been different?"

He almost scowled for it. "As different as *that*—?"

Her look again was more beautiful to him than the things of this world. "Haven't you exactly wanted to know *how* different? So this morning," she said, "you appeared to me."

"Like *him*?"

"A black stranger!"

"Then how did you know it was I?"

"Because, as I told you weeks ago, my mind, my imagination, has worked so over what you might, what you mightn't have been—to show you, you see, how I've thought of you. In the midst of that you came to me—that my wonder might be answered. So I knew," she went on; "and believed that, since the question held you too so fast, as you told me that day, you too would see for yourself. And when this morning I again saw I knew it would be because you had—and also then, from the first moment, because you somehow wanted me. *He* seemed to tell me of that. So why," she strangely smiled, "shouldn't I like him?"

It brought Spencer Brydon to his feet. "You 'like' that horror—?"

"I *could* have liked him. And to me," she said, "he was no horror. I had accepted him."

"'Accepted'—?" Brydon oddly sounded.

"Before, for the interest of his difference—yes. And as *I* didn't disown him, as *I* knew him—which you at last, confronted with him in his difference, so cruelly didn't, my dear,—well, he must have been, you see, less dreadful to me. And it may have pleased him that I pitied him."

She was beside him on her feet, but still holding his hand—still with her arm supporting him. But though it all brought for him thus a dim light, "You 'pitied' him?" he grudgingly, resentfully asked.

"He has been unhappy, he has been ravaged," she said.

"And haven't I been unhappy? Am not I—you've only to look at me!—ravaged?"

"Ah I don't say I like him *better*," she granted after a thought. "But he's grim, he's worn—and things have happened to him. He doesn't make shift, for sight, with your charming monocle."

"No"—it struck Brydon; "I couldn't have sported mine 'down-town.' They'd have guyed me there."

"His great convex pince-nez—I saw it, I recognised the kind—is for his poor ruined sight. And his poor right hand—!"

"Ah!" Brydon winced—whether for his proved identity or for his lost fingers. Then, "He has a million a year," he lucidly added. "But he hasn't you."

"And he isn't—no, he isn't—*you*!" she murmured, as he drew her to his breast.

The Romance of Certain Old Clothes

Henry James

Towards the middle of the eighteenth century there lived in the Province of Massachusetts a widowed gentlewoman, the mother of three children, by name Mrs Veronica Wingrave. She had lost her husband early in life, and had devoted herself to the care of her progeny. These young persons grew up in a manner to reward her tenderness and to gratify her highest hopes. The first-born was a son, whom she had called Bernard, after his father. The others were daughters—born at an interval of three years apart. Good looks were traditional in the family, and this youthful trio were not likely to allow the tradition to perish. The boy was of that fair and ruddy complexion and that athletic structure which in those days (as in these) were the sign of good English descent—a frank, affectionate young fellow, a deferential son, a patronizing brother, a steadfast friend. Clever, however, he was not; the wit of the family had been apportioned chiefly to his sisters. The late Mr Wingrave had been a great reader of Shakespeare, at a time when this pursuit implied more freedom of thought than at the present day, and in a community where it required much courage to patronize the drama even in the closet: and he had wished to call attention to his admiration of the great poet by calling his daughters out of his favourite plays.

Upon the elder he had bestowed the romantic name of Rosalind, and the younger he had called Perdita, in memory of a little girl born between them, who had lived but a few weeks.

When Bernard Wingrave came to his sixteenth year his mother put a brave face upon it and prepared to execute her husband's last injunction.

This had been a formal command that, at the proper age, his son should be sent out to England, to complete his education at the university of Oxford, where he himself had acquired his taste for elegant literature. It was Mrs Wingrave's belief that the lad's equal was not to be found in the two hemispheres, but she had the old traditions of literal obedience. She swallowed her sobs, and made up her boy's trunk and his simple provincial outfit, and sent him on his way across the seas. Bernard presented himself at his father's college, and spent five years in England, without great honour, indeed, but with a vast deal of pleasure and no discredit. On leaving the university he made the journey to France.

In his twenty-fourth year he took ship for home, prepared to find poor little New England (New England was very small in those days) a very dull, unfashionable residence. But there had been changes at home, as well as in Mr Bernard's opinions. He found his mother's house quite habitable, and his sisters grown into two very charming young ladies, with all the accomplishments and graces of the young women of Britain, and a certain native-grown originality and wildness, which, if it was not an accomplishment, was certainly a grace the more.

Bernard privately assured his mother that his sisters were fully a match for the most genteel young women in the old country; whereupon poor Mrs Wingrave, you may be sure, bade them hold up their heads. Such was Bernard's opinion, and such, in a tenfold higher degree, was the opinion of Mr Arthur Lloyd. This gentleman was a college-mate of Mr Bernard, a young man of reputable family, of a good person and a handsome inheritance; which latter appurtenance he proposed to invest in trade in the flourishing colony. He and Bernard were sworn friends; they had crossed the ocean together, and the young American had lost no time in presenting him at his mother's house, where he had made quite as good an impression as that which he had received and of which I have just given a hint.

The two sisters were at this time in all the freshness of their youthful bloom; each wearing, of course, this natural brilliancy in the manner that became her best. They were equally dissimilar in appearance and character. Rosalind, the elder—now in her twenty-second year—was tall and white, with calm grey eyes and auburn tresses; a very faint likeness to the Rosalind of Shakespeare's comedy, whom I imagine a brunette (if you will), but a slender, airy creature, full of the softest, quickest impulses. Miss Wingrave, with her slightly lymphatic fairness, her fine arms, her majestic height, her slow utterance, was not cut out for adventures. She would never have put on a man's jacket and hose; and, indeed, being a very plump beauty, she may have had reasons apart from her natural dignity. Perdita, too, might very well have exchanged the sweet melancholy of her name against something more in consonance with her aspect and disposition.

She had the cheek of a gypsy and the eye of an eager child, as well as the smallest waist and lightest foot in all the country of the Puritans. When you spoke to her she never made you wait, as her handsome sister was wont to do (while she looked at you with a cold fine eye), but gave you your choke of a dozen answers before you had uttered half your thought.

The young girls were very glad to see their brother once more; but they found themselves quite able to spare part of their attention for their brother's friend. Among the young men their friends and neighbours, the belle jeunesse of the Colony, there were many excellent fellows, several devoted swains, and some two or three who enjoyed the reputation of universal charmers and conquerors. But the homebred arts and somewhat boisterous gallantry of these honest colonists were completely eclipsed by the good looks, the fine clothes, the punctilious courtesy, the perfect elegance, the immense information, of Mr Arthur Lloyd. He was in reality no paragon; he was a capable, honourable, civil youth, rich in pounds sterling, in his health and complacency and his little capital of uninvested affections. But he was a gentleman; he had a handsome person; he had studied and travelled; he spoke French, he played the flute, and he read verses aloud with very great taste. There were a dozen reasons why Miss Wingrave and her sister should have thought their other male acquaintance made but a poor figure before such a perfect man of the world. Mr Lloyd's anecdotes told our little New England maidens a great deal more of the ways and means of people of fashion in European capitals than he had any idea of doing. It was delightful to sit by and hear him and Bernard talk about the fine people and fine things they had seen. They would all gather round the fire after tea, in the little wainscoted parlour, and the two young men would remind each other, across the rug, of this, that and the other adventure. Rosalind and Perdita would often have given their ears to know exactly what adventure it was, and where it happened, and who was there, and what the ladies had on; but in those days a well-bred young woman was not expected to break into the conversation of her elders, or to ask too many questions; and the poor girls used therefore to sit fluttering behind the more languid—or more discreet—curiosity of their mother.

That they were both very fine girls Arthur Lloyd was not slow to discover; but it took him some time to make up his mind whether he liked the big sister or the little sister best. He had a strong presentiment—an emotion of a nature entirely too cheerful to be called a foreboding—that he was destined to stand up before the parson with one of them; yet he was unable to arrive at a preference, and for such a consummation a preference was certainly necessary, for Lloyd had too much young blood in his veins to make a choice by lot and be cheated of the satisfaction of falling in love. He resolved to take things as they came—to let his heart speak. Meanwhile he was on very pleasant footing. Mrs Wingrave showed a dignified indifference to his "intentions," equally remote from a carelessness of her daughter's honour and from that sharp alacrity to make him come to the point, which, in his quality of young man of property, he had too often encountered in the worldly matrons of his native islands. As for Bernard, all that he asked was that his friend should treat his sisters as his own; and as for the poor girls themselves, however each may have secretly longed that their visitor should do or say something "marked," they kept a very modest and contented demeanour.

Towards each other, however, they were somewhat more on the offensive. They were good friends enough, and accommodating bed-fellows (they shared the same four-poster), betwixt whom it would take more than a day for the seeds of jealousy to sprout and bear fruit; but they felt that the seeds had been sown on the day that Mr Lloyd came into the house. Each made up her mind that, if she should be slighted, she would bear her grief in silence, and that no one should be any the wiser; for if they had a great deal of ambition, they had also a large share of pride. But each prayed in secret, nevertheless, that upon her the selection, the distinction, might fall. They had need of a vast deal of patience, of self-control, of dissimulation. In those days a young girl of decent breeding could make no advances whatever, and barely respond, indeed, to those that were made. She was expected to sit still in her chair, with her eyes on the carpet, watching the spot where the mystic handkerchief should fall. Poor Arthur Lloyd was obliged to carry on his wooing in the little wainscoted parlour, before the eyes of Mrs Wingrave, her son, and his prospective sister-in-law. But youth and love are so cunning that a hundred signs and tokens might travel to and fro, and not one of these three pairs of eyes detect them in their passage. The two maidens were almost always together, and had plenty of chances to betray themselves. That each knew she was being watched, made not a grain of difference in the little offices they mutually rendered, or in the various household tasks they performed in common.

Neither flinched nor fluttered beneath the silent battery of her sister's eyes. The only apparent change in their habits was that they had less to say to each other. It was impossible to talk about Mr Lloyd, and it was ridiculous to talk about anything else. By tacit agreement they began to wear all their choice finery, and to devise such little implements of conquest, in the way of ribbons and top-knots and kerchiefs, as were sanctioned by indubitable modesty. They executed in the same inarticulate fashion a contract of fair play in this exciting game. "Is it better so?"

Rosalind would ask, tying a bunch of ribbons on her bosom, and turning about from her glass to her sister. Perdita would look up gravely from her work and examine the decoration. "I think you had better give it another loop," she would say, with great solemnity, looking hard at her sister with eyes that added, "upon my honour!" So they were for ever stitching and turning their petticoats, and pressing out their muslins, and contriving washes and ointments and cosmetics, like the ladies in the household of the vicar of Wakefield. Some three or four months went by; it grew to be midwinter, and as yet Rosalind knew that if Perdita had nothing more to boast of than she, there was not much to be feared from her rivalry. But Perdita by this time—the charming Perdita—felt that her secret had grown to be tenfold more precious than her sister's.

One afternoon Miss Wingrave sat alone—that was a rare accident—before her toilet-glass, combing out her long hair. It was getting too dark to see; she lit the two candles in their sockets, on the frame of her mirror, and then went to the window to draw her curtains. It was a grey December evening; the landscape was bare and bleak, and the sky heavy with snowclouds. At the end of the large garden into which her window looked was a wall with a little postern door, opening into a lane. The door stood ajar, as she could vaguely see in the gathering darkness, and moved slowly to and fro, as if someone were swaying it from the lane without. It was doubtless a servant-maid who had been having a tryst with her sweetheart. But as she was about to drop her curtain Rosalind saw her sister step into the garden and hum along the path which led to the house. She dropped the curtain, all save a little crevice for her eyes. As Perdita came up the path she seemed to be examining something in her hand, holding it close to her eyes. When she reached the house she stopped a moment, looked intently at the object, and pressed it to her lips.

Poor Rosalind slowly came back to her chair and sat down before her glass where, if she had looked at it less abstractly, she would have seen her handsome features sadly disfigured by jealousy. A moment afterwards the door opened behind her and her sister came into the room, out of breath, her cheeks aglow with the chilly air.

Perdita started. "Ah," said she, "I thought you were with our mother." The ladies were to go to a tea-party, and on such occasions it was the habit of one of the girls to help their mother to dress.

Instead of coming in, Perdita lingered at the door.

"Come in, come in," said Rosalind. "We have more than an hour yet. I should like you very much to give a few strokes to my hair." She knew that her sister wished to retreat, and that she could see in the glass all her movements in the room. "Nay, just help me with my hair," she said, "and I will go to mamma."

Perdita came reluctantly, and took the brush. She saw her sister's eyes, in the glass, fastened hard upon her hands. She had not made three passes when Rosalind clapped her own right hand upon her sister's left, and started out of her chair. "Whose ring is that?" she cried, passionately, drawing her towards the light.

On the young girl's third finger glistened a little gold ring, adorned with a very small sapphire.

Perdita felt that she need no longer keep her secret, yet that she must put a bold face on her avowal. "It's mine," she said proudly.

"Who gave it to you?" cried the other.

Perdita hesitated a moment. "Mr Lloyd."

"Mr Lloyd is generous, all of a sudden."

"Ah no," cried Perdita, with spirit, "not all of a sudden! He offered it to me a month ago."

"And you needed a month's begging to take it?" said Rosalind, looking at the little trinket, which indeed was not especially elegant, although it was the best that the jeweller of the Province could furnish. "I wouldn't have taken it in less than two."

"It isn't the ring," Perdita answered, "it's what it means!"

"It means that you are not a modest girl!" cried Rosalind. "Pray, does your mother know of your intrigue? does Bernard?"

"My mother has approved my 'intrigue,' as you call it. Mr Lloyd has asked for my hand, and mamma has given it. Would you have had him apply to you, dearest sister?"

Rosalind gave her companion a long look, full of passionate envy and sorrow. Then she dropped her lashes on her pale cheeks and turned away. Perdita felt that it had not been a pretty scene; but it was her sister's fault. However, the elder girl rapidly called back her pride, and turned herself about again. "You have my very best wishes," she said, with a low curtsey. "I wish you every happiness, and a very long life."

Perdita gave a bitter laugh. "Don't speak in that tone!" she cried. "I would rather you should curse me outright. Come, Rosy," she added, "he couldn't marry both of us."

"I wish you very great joy," Rosalind repeated, mechanically, sitting down to her glass again, "and a very long life, and plenty of children." There was something in the sound of these words not at all to Perdita's taste, "Will you give me a year to live at least?" she said. "In a year I can have one little boy—or one little girl at least.

If you will give me your brush again I will do your hair."

"Thank you," said Rosalind. "You had better go to mamma. It isn't becoming that a young lady with a promised husband should wait on a girl with none."

"Nay," said Perdita good-humouredly, "I have Arthur to wait upon me. You need my service more than I need yours."

But her sister motioned her away, and she left the room. When she had gone poor Rosalind fell on her knees before her dressing-table, buried her head in her arms, and poured out a flood of tears and sobs. She felt very much the better for this effusion of sorrow. When her sister came back she insisted on helping her to dress—on her wearing her prettiest things. She forced upon her acceptance a bit of lace of her own, and declared that now that she was to be married she should do her best to appear worthy of her lover's choice. She discharged these offices in stern silence; but, such as they were, they had to do duty as an apology and an atonement; she never made any other.

Now that Lloyd was received by the family as an accepted suitor nothing remained but to fix the wedding-day. It was appointed for the following April, and in the interval preparations were diligently made for the marriage. Lloyd, on his side, was busy with his commercial arrangements, and with establishing a correspondence with the great mercantile house to which he had attached himself in England. He was therefore not so frequent a visitor at Mrs Wingrave's as during the months of his diffidence and irresolution, and poor Rosalind had less to suffer than she had feared from the sight of the mutual endearments of the young lovers. Touching his future sister-in-law Lloyd had a perfectly clear conscience. There had not been a particle of love-making between them, and he had not the slightest suspicion that he had dealt her a terrible blow. He was quite at his ease; life promised so well, both domestically and financially. The great revolt of the Colonies Was not yet in the air, and that his connubial felicity should take a tragic turn it was absurd, it was blasphemous, to apprehend. Meanwhile, at Mrs Wingrave's, there was a greater rustling of silks, a more rapid clicking of scissors and flying of needles, than ever. The good lady had determined that her daughter should carry from home the genteelest outfit that her money could buy or that the country could furnish. All the sage women in the Province were convened, and their united taste was brought to bear on Perdita's wardrobe. Rosalind's situation, at this moment, was assuredly not to be envied. The poor girl had an inordinate love of dress, and the very best taste in the world, as her sister perfectly well knew. Rosalind was tall, she was stately and sweeping, she was made to earn stiff brocade and masses of heavy lace, such as belong to the toilet of a rich man's wife. But Rosalind sat aloof with her beautiful arms folded and her head averted, while her mother and sister and the venerable women aforesaid worried and wondered over their materials, oppressed by the multitude of their resources. One day there came in a beautiful piece of white silk, brocaded with heavenly blue and silver sent by the bridegroom himself—it not being thought amiss in those days that the husband-elect should contribute to the bride's trousseau. Perdita could think of no form or fashion which would do sufficient honour to the splendour of the material.

"Blue's your colour, sister, more than mine," she said, with appealing eyes. "It is a pity it's not for you. You would know what to do with it."

Rosalind got up from her place and looked at the great shining fabric, as it lay spread over the back of a chair. Then she took it up in her hands and felt it—lovingly, as Perdita could see—and turned about towards the mirror with it. She let it roll down to her feet, and flung the other end over her shoulder, gathering it in about her waist with her white arm, which was bare to the elbow. She threw back her head, and looked at her image, and a hanging tress of her auburn hair fell upon the gorgeous surface of the silk. It made a dazzling picture. The women standing about uttered a little "Look, look!" of admiration. "Yes, indeed," said Rosalind, quietly, "blue is my colour." But Perdita could see that her fancy had been stirred, and that she would now fall to work and solve all their silken riddles. And indeed she behaved very well, as Perdita, knowing her insatiable love of millinery, was quite ready to declare. Innumerable yards of lustrous silk and satin, of muslin, velvet and lace, passed through her cunning hands, without a jealous word coming from her lips. Thanks to her industry, when the wedding-day came Perdita was prepared to espouse more of the vanities of life than any fluttering young bride who had yet received the sacramental blessing of a New England divine.

It had been arranged that the young couple should go out and spend the first days of their wedded life at the country-house of an English gentleman—a man of rank and a very kind friend to Arthur Lloyd. He was a bachelor; he declared he should be delighted to give up the place to the influence of Hymen. After the ceremony at church—it had been performed by an English clergyman—young Mrs Lloyd hastened back to her mother's house to change her nuptial robes for a riding-dress. Rosalind helped her to effect the change, in the little homely room in which they had spent their undivided younger years. Perdita then hurried off to bid farewell to her mother, leaving Rosalind to follow. Then parting was short; the horses were at the door, and Arthur was impatient to start. But Rosalind had not followed, and Perdita hastened back to her room, opening the door abruptly. Rosalind, as usual, was before the glass, but in a position which caused the other to stand still, amazed. She had dressed herself in Perdita's cast-off wedding veil and wreath, and on her neck she had hung the full string of pearls which the young girl had received from her husband as a wedding-gift. These things had been hastily laid aside, to await their possessor's disposal on her return from the country. Bedizened by this unnatural garb Rosalind stood before the mirror, plunging a long look into its depths and reading heaven knows what audacious visions. Perdita was horrified. It was a hideous image of their old rivalry come to life again. She made a step towards her sister, as if to pull off the veil and the flowers. But catching her eyes in the glass, she stopped.

"Farewell, sweetheart," she said. "You might at least have waited till I had got out of the house!" And she hurried away from the room.

Mr Lloyd had purchased in Boston a house which to the taste of those days appeared as elegant as it was commodious; and here he very soon established himself with his young wife. He was thus separated by a distance of twenty miles from the residence of his mother-in-law. Twenty miles, in that primitive era of roads and conveyances, were as serious a matter as a hundred at the present day, and Mrs Wingrave saw but little of her daughter during the first twelvemonth of her marriage. She suffered in no small degree from Perdita's absence; and her affliction was not diminished by the fact that Rosalind had fallen into terribly low spirits and was not to be roused or cheered but by change of air and company. The real cause of the young lady's dejection the reader will not be slow to suspect. Mrs Wingrave and her gossips, however, deemed her complaint a mere bodily ill, and doubted not that she would obtain relief from the remedy just mentioned. Her mother accordingly proposed, on her behalf, a visit to certain relatives on the paternal side, established in New York, who had long complained that they were able to see so little of their New England cousins. Rosalind was despatched to these good people, under a suitable escort, and remained with them for several months. In the interval her brother Bernard, who had begun the practice of the law, made up his mind to take a wife. Rosalind came home to the wedding, apparently cured of her heartache, with bright roses and lilies in her face and a proud smile on her lips. Arthur Lloyd came over from Boston to see his brother-in-law married, but without his wife, who was expecting very soon to present him with an heir. It was nearly a year since Rosalind had seen him. She was glad—she hardly knew why—that Perdita had stayed at home. Arthur looked happy, but he was more grave and important than before his marriage.

She thought he looked "interesting"—for although the word, in its modern sense, was not then invented, we may be sure that the idea was. The truth is, he was simply anxious about his wife and her coming ordeal, Nevertheless, he by no means failed to observe Rosalind's beauty and splendour, and to note how she effaced the poor little bride. The allowance that Perdita had enjoyed for her dress had now been transferred to her sister, who turned it to wonderful account.

On the morning after the wedding he had a lady's saddle put on the horse of the servant who had come with him from town, and went out with the young girl for a ride. It was a keen, clear morning in January; the ground was bare and hard, and the horses in good condition—to say nothing of Rosalind, who was charming in her hat and plume, and her dark blue riding coat, trimmed with fur. They rode all the morning, lost their way and were obliged to stop for dinner at a farmhouse. The early winter dusk had fallen when they got home. Mrs Wingrave met them with a long face. A messenger had arrived at noon from Mrs Lloyd; she was beginning to be ill, she desired her husband's immediate return. The young man, at the thought that he had lost several hours, and that by hard riding he might already have been with his wife, uttered a passionate oath. He barely consented to stop for a mouthful of supper, but mounted the messenger's horse and started off at a gallop.

He reached home at midnight. His wife had been delivered of a little girl. "Ah, why weren't you with me?" she said, as he came to her bedside.

"I was out of the house when the man came. I was with Rosalind," said Lloyd, innocently.

Mrs Lloyd made a little moan, and turned away. But she continued to do very well, and for a week her improvement was uninterrupted. Finally, however, through some indiscretion in the way of diet or exposure, it was checked, and the poor lady grew rapidly worse. Lloyd was in despair. It very soon became evident that she was breathing her last. Mrs Lloyd came to a sense of her approaching end, and declared that she was reconciled with death. On the third evening after the change took place she told her husband that she felt she should not get through the night. She dismissed her servants, and also requested her mother to withdraw—Mrs Wingrave having arrived on the preceding day. She had had her infant placed on the bed beside her, and she lay on her side, with the child against her breast, holding her husband's hands. The night-lamp was hidden behind the heavy curtains of the bed, but the room was illuminated with a red glow from the immense fire of logs on the hearth.

"It seems strange not to be warmed into life by such a fire as that," the young woman said, feebly trying to smile. "If I had but a little of it in my veins! But I have given all my fire to this little spark of mortality." And she dropped her eyes on her child. Then raising them she looked at her husband with a long, penetrating gaze. The last feeling which lingered in her heart was one of suspicion. She had not recovered from the shock which Arthur had given her by telling her that in the hour of her agony he had been with Rosalind. She trusted her husband very nearly as well as she loved him; but now that she was called away forever she felt a cold horror of her sister. She felt in her soul that Rosalind had never ceased to be jealous of her good fortune; and a year of happy security had not effaced the young girl's image, dressed in her wedding-garments, and smiling with simulated triumph. Now that Arthur was to be alone, what might not Rosalind attempt? She was beautiful, she was engaging; what arts might she not use, what impression might she not make upon the young man's saddened heart? Mrs Lloyd looked at her husband in silence. It seemed hard, after all, to doubt of his constancy. His fine eyes were filled with tears; his face was convulsed with weeping; the clasp of his hands was warm and passionate. How noble he looked, how tender, how faithful and devoted! "Nay," thought Perdita, "he's not for such a one as Rosalind. He'll never forget me. Nor does Rosalind truly care for him; she cares only for vanities and finery and jewels." And she lowered her eyes on her white hands, which her husband's liberality had covered with rings, and on the lace ruffles which trimmed the edge of her nightdress. "She covets my rings and my laces more than she covets my husband."

At this moment the thought of her sister's rapacity seemed to cast a dark shadow between her and the helpless figure of her little girl. "Arthur," she said, "you must take off my rings. I shall not be buried in them. One of these days my daughter shall wear them—my rings and my laces and silks. I had them all brought out and shown me today. It's a great wardrobe—there's not such another in the Province; I can say it without vanity, now that I have done with it. It will be a great inheritance for my daughter when she grows into a young woman. There are things there that a man never buys twice, and if they are lost you will never again see the like. So you will watch them well. Some dozen things I have left to Rosalind: I have named them to my mother. I have given her that blue and silver; it was meant for her; I wore it only once, I looked ill in it.

But the rest are to be sacredly kept for this little innocent. It's such a providence that she should be my colour; she can wear my gowns; she has her mother's eyes. You know the same fashions come back even twenty years. She can wear my gowns as they are. They will lie there quietly waiting till she grows into them—wrapped in camphor and rose-leaves, and keeping their colours in the sweetscented darkness. She shall have black hair, she shall wear my carnation satin. Do you promise me, Arthur?"

"Promise you what, dearest?"

"Promise me to keep your poor little wife's old gowns."

"Are you afraid I shall sell them?"

"No, but that they may get scattered, My mother will have them properly wrapped up, and you shall lay them away under a double-lock. Do you know the great chest in the attic, with the iron bands? There is no end to what it will hold. You can put them all there. My mother and the housekeeper will do it, and give you the key. And you will keep the key in your secretary, and never give it to anyone but your child. Do you promise me?"

"Ah, yes, I promise you," said Lloyd, puzzled at the intensity with which his wife appeared to cling to this idea.

"Will you swear?" repeated Perdita.

"Yes, I swear."

"Well—I trust you—I trust you," said the poor lady, looking into his eyes with eyes in which, if he had suspected her vague apprehensions, he might have read an appeal quite as much as an assurance.

Lloyd bore his bereavement rationally and manfully. A month after his wife's death, in the course of business, circumstances arose which offered him an opportunity of going to England.

He took advantage of it, to change the current of his thoughts. He was absent nearly a year, during which his little girl was tenderly nursed and guarded by her grandmother. On his return he had his house again thrown open, and announced his intention of keeping the same state as during his wife's lifetime. It very soon came to be predicted that he would marry again, and there were at least a dozen young women of whom one may say that it was by no fault of theirs that, for six months after his return, the prediction did not come true. During this interval he still left his little daughter in Mrs Wingrave's hands, the latter assuring him that a change of residence at so tender an age would be full of danger for her health. Finally, however, he declared that his heart longed for his daughter's presence and that she must be brought up to town. He sent his coach and his housekeeper to fetch her home. Mrs Wingrave was in terror lest something should befall her on the road; and, in accordance with this feeling. Rosalind offered to accompany her.

She could return the next day. So she went up to town with her little niece, and Mr Lloyd met her on the threshold of his house, overcome with her kindness and with paternal joy. Instead of returning the next day Rosalind stayed out the week; and when at last she reappeared, she had only come for her clothes. Arthur would not hear of her coming home, nor would the baby. That little person cried and choked if Rosalind left her; and at the sight of her grief Arthur lost his wits, and swore that she was going to die. In fine, nothing would suit them but that the aunt should remain until the little niece had grown used to strange faces.

It took two months to bring this consummation about; for it was not until this period had elapsed that Rosalind took leave of her brother-in-law. Mrs Wingrave had shaken her head over her daughter's absence; she had declared that it was not becoming, that it was the talk of the whole country. She had reconciled herself to it only because, during the girl's visit, the household enjoyed an unwonted term of peace. Bernard Wingrave had brought his wife home to live, between whom and her sister-in-law there was as little love as you please. Rosalind was perhaps no angel; but in the daily practice of life she was a sufficiently good-natured girl, and if she quarrelled with Mrs Bernard, it was not without provocation. Quarrel, however, she did, to the great annoyance not only of her antagonist, but of the two spectators of these constant altercations. Her stay in the household of her brother-in-law, therefore, would have been delightful, if only because it removed her from contact with the object of her antipathy at home.

It was doubly—it was ten times—delightful, in that it kept her near the object of her early passion. Mrs Lloyd's sharp suspicions had fallen very far short of the truth. Rosalind's sentiment had been a passion at first, and a passion it remained—a passion of whose radiant heat, tempered to the delicate state of his feelings, Mr Lloyd very soon felt the influence. Lloyd, as I have hinted, was not a modern Petrarch; it was not in his nature to practise an ideal constancy. He had not been many days in the house with his sister-in-law before he began to assure himself that she was, in the language of that day, a devilish fine woman. Whether Rosalind really practised those insidious arts that her sister had been tempted to impute to her it is needless to enquire. It is enough to say that she found means to appear to the very best advantage. She used to seat herself every morning before the big fireplace in the dining-room, at work upon a piece of tapestry, with her little niece disporting herself on the carpet at her feet, or on the train of her dress, and playing with her woollen balls. Lloyd would have been a very stupid fellow if he had remained insensible to the rich suggestions of this charming picture. He was exceedingly fond of his little girl, and was never weary of taking her in his arms and tossing her up and down, and making her crow with delight. Very often, however, he would venture upon greater liberties than the young lady was yet prepared to allow, and then she would suddenly vociferate her displeasure.

Rosalind, at this, would drop her tapestry, and put out her handsome hands with the serious smile of the young girl whose virgin fancy has revealed to her all a mother's healing arts. Lloyd would give up the child, their eyes would meet, their hands would touch, and Rosalind would extinguish the little girl's sobs upon the snowy folds of the kerchief that crossed her bosom. Her dignity was perfect, and nothing could be more discreet than the manner in which she accepted her brother-in-law's hospitality. It may almost be said, perhaps, that there was something harsh in her reserve. Lloyd had a provoking feeling that she was in the house and yet was unapproachable. Half-an-hour after supper, at the very outset of the long winter evenings, she would light her candle, make the young man a most respectful curtsey, and march off to bed. If these were arts, Rosalind was a great artist. But their effect was so gentle, so gradual, they were calculated to work upon the young widower's fancy with a crescendo so finely shaded, that, as the reader has seen, several weeks elapsed before Rosalind began to feel sure that her returns would cover her outlay. When this became morally certain she packed up her trunk and returned to her mother's house. For three days she waited: on the fourth Mr Lloyd made his appearance—a respectful but pressing suitor, Rosalind heard him to the end, with great humility, and accepted him with infinite modesty. It is hard to imagine that Mrs Lloyd would have forgiven her husband; but if anything might have disarmed her resentment it would have been the ceremonious continence of this interview. Rosalind imposed upon her lover but a short probation. They were married, as was becoming, with great privacy—almost with secrecy—in the hope perhaps, as was waggishly remarked at the time, that the late Mrs Lloyd wouldn't hear of it.

The marriage was to all appearance a happy one, and each party obtained what each had desired—Lloyd "a devilish fine woman," and Rosalind—but Rosalind's desires, as the reader will have observed, had remained a good deal of a mystery. There were, indeed, two blots upon their felicity, but time would perhaps efface them. During the first three years of her marriage Mrs Lloyd failed to become a mother, and her husband on his side suffered heavy losses of money.

This latter circumstance compelled a material retrenchment in his expenditure, and Rosalind was perforce less of a fine lady than her sister had been. She contrived, however, to carry it like a woman of considerable fashion. She had long since ascertained that her sister's copious wardrobe had been sequestrated for the benefit of her daughter, and that it lay languishing in thankless gloom in the dusty attic. It was a revolting thought that these exquisite fabrics should await the good pleasure of a little girl who sat in a high chair and ate bread-and-milk with a wooden spoon. Rosalind had the good taste, however, to say nothing about the matter until several months had expired. Then, at last, she timidly broached it to her husband. Was it not a pity that so much finery should be lost?—for lost it would be, what with colours fading, and moths eating it up, and the change of fashions. But Lloyd gave her so abrupt and peremptory a refusal, that she saw, for the present, her attempt was vain. Six months went by, however, and brought with them new needs and new visions. Rosalind's thoughts hovered lovingly about her sister's relics. She went up and looked at the chest in which they lay imprisoned. There was a sullen defiance in its three great padlocks and its iron bands which only quickened her cupidity.

There was something exasperating in its incorruptible immobility. It was like a grim and grizzled old household servant, who locks his jaws over a family secret. And then there was a look of capacity in its vast extent, and a sound as of dense fullness, when Rosalind knocked its side with the toe of her little shoe, which caused her to flush with baffled longing. "It's absurd," she cried; "it's improper, it's wicked;" and she forthwith resolved upon another attack upon her husband.

On the following day, after dinner, when he had had his wine, she boldly began it. But he cut her short with great sternness.

"Once for all, Rosalind," said he, "it's out of the question. I shall be gravely displeased if you return to the matter."

"Very good," said Rosalind. "I am glad to learn the esteem in which I am held. Gracious heaven," she cried, "I am a very happy woman! It's an agreeable thing to feel one's self sacrificed to a caprice!" And her eyes filled with tears of anger and disappointment.

Lloyd had a good-natured man's horror of a woman's sobs, and he attempted—I may say he condescended—to explain. "It's not a caprice, dear, it's a promise," he said—"an oath."

"An oath? It's a pretty matter for oaths! and to whom, pray?"

"To Perdita," said the young man, raising his eyes for an instant, and immediately dropping them.

"Perdita—ah, Perdita!" and Rosalind's tears broke forth. Her bosom heaved with stormy sobs—sobs which were the long-deferred sequel of the violent fit of weeping in which she had indulged herself on the night when she discovered her sister's betrothal. She had hoped, in her better moments, that she had done with her jealousy; but her temper, on that occasion, had taken an ineffaceable hold, "And pray, what right had Perdita to dispose of my future?" she cried.

"What right had she to bind you to meanness and cruelty? Ah, I occupy a dignified place, and I make a very fine figure! I am welcome to what Perdita has left! And what has she left? I never knew till now how little! Nothing, nothing, nothing."

This was very poor logic, but it was very good as a "scene." Lloyd put his arm around his wife's waist and tried to kiss her, but she shook him off with magnificent scorn. Poor fellow! he had coveted a "devilish fine woman," and he had got one. Her scorn was intolerable. He walked away with his ears tingling—irresolute, distracted. Before him was his secretary, and in it the sacred key which with his own hand he had turned in the triple lock. He marched up and opened it, and took the key from a secret drawer, wrapped in a little packet which he had sealed with his own honest bit of glazonry. Je garde, said the motto—"I keep." But he was ashamed to put it back. He flung it upon the table beside his wife.

"Put it back!" she cried. "I want it not. I hate it!"

"I wash my hands of it," cried her husband. "God forgive me!"

Mrs Lloyd gave an indignant shrug of her shoulders, and swept out of the room, while the young man retreated by another door. Ten minutes later Mrs Lloyd returned, and found the room occupied by her little step-daughter and the nursery-maid. The key was not on the table. She glanced at the child. Her little niece was perched on a chair, with the packet in her hands. She had broken the seal with her own small fingers. Mrs Lloyd hastily took possession of the key.

At the habitual supper-hour Arthur Lloyd came back from his counting-room. It was the month of June, and supper was served by daylight. The meal was placed on the table, but Mrs Lloyd failed to make her appearance. The servant whom his master sent to call her came back with the assurance that her room was empty, and that the women informed him that she had not been seen since dinner. They had, in truth, observed her to have been in tears, and, supposing her to be shut up in her chamber, had not disturbed her. Her husband called her name in various parts of the house, but without response. At last it occurred to him that he might find her by taking the way to the attic. The thought gave him a strange feeling of discomfort, and he bade his servants remain behind, wishing no witness in his quest. He reached the foot of the staircase leading to the topmost flat, and stood with his hands on the banisters, pronouncing his wife's name. His voice trembled. He called again louder and more firmly. The only sound which disturbed the absolute silence was a faint echo of his own tones, repeating his question under the great eaves.

He nevertheless felt irresistibly moved to ascend the staircase. It opened upon a wide hall, lined with wooden closets, and terminating in a window which looked westward, and admitted the last rays of the sun. Before the window stood the great chest. Before the chest, on her knees, the young man saw with amazement and horror the figure of his wife. In an instant he crossed the interval between them, bereft of utterance. The lid of the chest stood open, exposing, amid their perfumed napkins, its treasure of stuffs and jewels. Rosalind had fallen backward from a kneeling posture, with one hand supporting her on the floor and the other pressed to her heart.

On her limbs was the stiffness of death, and on her face, in the fading light of the sun, the terror of something more than death. Her lips were parted in entreaty, in dismay, in agony; and on her blanched brow and cheeks there glowed the marks of ten hideous wounds from two vengeful ghostly hands.

Man-size in Marble

Edith Nesbit

Although every word of this story is as true as despair, I do not expect people to believe it. Nowadays a 'rational explanation' is required before belief is possible. Let me then, at once, offer the 'rational explanation' which finds most favour among those who have heard the tale of my life's tragedy. It is held that we were 'under a delusion,' Laura and I, on that 31st of October; and that this supposition places the whole matter on a satisfactory and believable basis. The reader can judge, when he, too, has heard my story, how far this is an 'explanation', and in what sense it is 'rational'. There were three who took part in this: Laura and I and another man. The other man still lives, and can speak to the truth of the least credible part of my story.

I never in my life knew what it was to have as much money as I required to supply the most ordinary needs – good colours, books, and cab-fares – and when we were married we knew quite well that we should only be able to live at all by 'strict punctuality and attention to business'. I used to paint in those days, and Laura used to write, and we felt sure we could keep the pot at least simmering. Living in town was out of the question, so we went to look for a cottage in the country, which should be at once sanitary and picturesque. So rarely do these two qualities meet in one cottage that our search was for some time quite fruitless. We tried advertisements, but most of the desirable rural residences which we did look at proved to be lacking in both essentials, and when a cottage chanced to have drains it always had stucco as well and was shaped like a tea-caddy.

And if we found a vine or rose-covered porch, corruption invariably lurked within. Our minds got so befogged by the eloquence of house-agents and the rival disadvantages of the fever-traps and outrages to beauty which we had seen and scorned, that I very much doubt whether either of us, on our wedding morning, knew the difference between a house and a haystack. But when we got away from friends and house-agents, on our honeymoon, our wits grew clear again, and we knew a pretty cottage when at last we saw one. It was at Brenzett – a little village set on a hill over against the southern marshes. We had gone there, from the seaside village where we were staying, to see the church, and two fields from the church we found this cottage. It stood quite by itself, about two miles from the village. It was a long, low building, with rooms sticking out in unexpected places. There was a bit of stone-work – ivy-covered and moss-grown, just two old rooms, all that was left of a big house that had once stood there – and round this stone-work the house had grown up. Stripped of its roses and jasmine it would have been hideous. As it stood it was charming, and after a brief examination we took it. It was absurdly cheap. The rest of our honeymoon we spent in grubbing about in second-hand shops in the county town, picking up bits of old oak and Chippendale chairs for our furnishing. We wound up with a run up to town and a visit to Liberty's, and soon the low oak-beamed lattice-windowed rooms began to be home. There was a jolly old-fashioned garden, with grass paths, and no end of hollyhocks and sunflowers, and big lilies. From the window you could see the marsh-pastures, and beyond them the blue, thin line of the sea. We were as happy as the summer was glorious, and settled down into work sooner than we ourselves expected. I was never tired of sketching the view and the wonderful cloud effects from the open lattice, and Laura would sit at the table and write verses about them, in which I mostly played the part of foreground.

We got a tall old peasant woman to do for us. Her face and figure were good, though her cooking was of the homeliest; but she understood all about gardening, and told us all the old names of the coppices and cornfields, and the stories of the smugglers and highwaymen, and, better still, of the 'things that walked', and of the 'sights' which met one in lonely glens of a starlight night. She was a great comfort to us, because Laura hated housekeeping as much as I loved folklore, and we soon came to leave all the domestic business to Mrs Dorman, and to use her legends in little magazine stories which brought in the jingling guinea.

We had three months of married happiness, and did not have a single quarrel. One October evening I had been down to smoke a pipe with the doctor – our only neighbour – a pleasant young Irishman. Laura had stayed at home to finish a comic sketch of a village episode for the *Monthly Marplot*. I left her laughing over her own jokes, and came in to find her a crumpled heap of pale muslin weeping on the window seat.

'Good heavens, my darling, what's the matter?' I cried, taking her in my arms. She leaned her little dark head against my shoulder and went on crying. I had never seen her cry before – we had always been so happy, you see – and I felt sure some frightful misfortune had happened.

'What *is* the matter? Do speak.'

'It's Mrs Dorman,' she sobbed.

'What has she done?' I inquired, immensely relieved.

'She says she must go before the end of the month, and she says her niece is ill; she's gone down to see her now, but I don't believe that's the reason, because her niece is always ill. I believe someone has been setting her against us. Her manner was so queer—'

'Never mind, Pussy,' I said; 'whatever you do, don't cry, or I shall have to cry too, to keep you in countenance, and then you'll never respect your man again!'

She dried her eyes obediently on my handkerchief, and even smiled faintly.

'But you see,' she went on, 'it is really serious, because these village people are so sheepy, and if one won't do a thing you may be quite sure none of the others will. And I shall have to cook the dinners, and wash up the hateful greasy plates; and you'll have to carry cans of water about, and clean the boots and knives – and we shall never have any time for work, or earn any money, or anything. We shall have to work all day, and only be able to rest when we are waiting for the kettle to boil!'

I represented to her that even if we had to perform these duties, the day would still present some margin for other toils and recreations. But she refused to see the matter in any but the greyest light. She was very unreasonable, my Laura, but I could not have loved her any more if she had been as reasonable as Whately.

'I'll speak to Mrs Dorman when she comes back, and see if I can't come to terms with her,' I said. 'Perhaps she wants a rise in her screw. It will be all right. Let's walk up to the church.'

The church was a large and lonely one, and we loved to go there, especially upon bright nights. The path skirted a wood, cut through it once, and ran along the crest of the hill through two meadows, and round the churchyard wall, over which the old yews loomed in black masses of shadow. This path, which was partly paved, was called 'the bier-balk', for it had long been the way by which the corpses had been carried to burial. The churchyard was richly treed, and was shaded by great elms which stood just outside and stretched their majestic arms in benediction over the happy dead. A large, low porch let one into the building by a Norman doorway and a heavy oak door studded with iron. Inside, the arches rose into darkness, and between them the reticulated windows, which stood out white in the moonlight. In the chancel, the windows were of rich glass, which showed in faint light their noble colouring, and made the black oak of the choir pews hardly more solid than the shadows. But on each side of the altar lay a grey marble figure of a knight in full plate armour lying upon a low slab, with hands held up in everlasting prayer, and these figures, oddly enough, were always to be seen if there was any glimmer of light in the church. Their names were lost, but the peasants told of them that they had been fierce and wicked men, marauders by land and sea, who had been the scourge of their time, and had been guilty of deeds so foul that the house they had lived in – the big house, by the way, that had stood on the site of our cottage – had been stricken by lightning and the vengeance of Heaven. But for all that, the gold of their heirs had bought them a place in the church. Looking at the bad hard faces reproduced in the marble, this story was easily believed.

The church looked at its best and weirdest on that night, for the shadows of the yew trees fell through the windows upon the floor of the nave and touched the pillars with tattered shade. We sat down together without speaking, and watched the solemn beauty of the old church, with some of that awe which inspired its early builders. We walked to the chancel and looked at the sleeping warriors. Then we rested some time on the stone seat in the porch, looking out over the stretch of quiet moonlit meadows, feeling in every fibre of our being the peace of the night and of our happy love; and came away at last with a sense that even scrubbing and black-leading were but small troubles at their worst.

Mrs Dorman had come back from the village, and I at once invited her to a *tête-à-tête*.

'Now, Mrs Dorman,' I said, when I had got her into my painting room, 'what's all this about your not staying with us?'

'I should be glad to get away, sir, before the end of the month,' she answered, with her usual placid dignity.

'Have you any fault to find, Mrs Dorman?'

'None at all, sir; you and your lady have always been most kind, I'm sure—'

'Well, what is it? Are your wages not high enough?'

'No, sir, I gets quite enough.'

'Then why not stay?'

'I'd rather not' – with some hesitation – 'my niece is ill.'

'But your niece has been ill ever since we came.'

No answer. There was a long and awkward silence. I broke it.

'Can't you stay for another month?' I asked.

'No, sir. I'm bound to go by Thursday.'

And this was Monday!

'Well, I must say, I think you might have let us know before. There's no time now to get any one else, and your mistress is not fit to do heavy housework. Can't you stay till next week?'

'I might be able to come back next week.'

I was now convinced that all she wanted was a brief holiday, which we should have been willing enough to let her have, as soon as we could get a substitute.

'But why must you go this week?' I persisted. 'Come, out with it.'

Mrs Dorman drew the little shawl, which she always wore, tightly across her bosom, as though she were cold. Then she said, with a sort of effort –

'They say, sir, as this was a big house in Catholic times, and there was a many deeds done here.'

The nature of the 'deeds' might be vaguely inferred from the inflection of Mrs Dorman's voice – which was enough to make one's blood run cold. I was glad that Laura was not in the room. She was always nervous, as highly-strung natures are, and I felt that these tales about our house, told by this old peasant woman, with her impressive manner and contagious credulity, might have made our home less dear to my wife.

'Tell me all about it, Mrs Dorman,' I said; 'you needn't mind about telling me. I'm not like the young people who make fun of such things.'

Which was partly true.

'Well, sir' – she sank her voice – 'you may have seen in the church, beside the altar, two shapes.'

'You mean the effigies of the knights in armour,' I said cheerfully.

'I mean them two bodies, drawed out man-size in marble,' she returned, and I had to admit that her description was a thousand times more graphic than mine, to say nothing of a certain weird force and uncanniness about the phrase 'drawed out man-size in marble'.

'They do say, as on All Saints' Eve them two bodies sits up on their slabs, and gets off of them, and then walks down the aisle, *in their marble'* – (another good phrase, Mrs Dorman) – 'and as the church clock strikes eleven they walks out of the church door, and over the graves, and along the bier-balk, and if it's a wet night there's the marks of their feet in the morning.'

'And where do they go?' I asked, rather fascinated.

'They comes back here to their home, sir, and if any one meets them—'

'Well, what then?' I asked.

But no – not another word could I get from her, save that her niece was ill and she must go. After what I had heard I scorned to discuss the niece, and tried to get from Mrs Dorman more details of the legend. I could get nothing but warnings.

'Whatever you do, sir, lock the door early on All Saints' Eve, and make the cross-sign over the doorstep and on the windows.'

'But has any one ever seen these things?' I persisted.

'That's not for me to say. I know what I know, sir.'

'Well, who was here last year?'

'No one, sir; the lady as owned the house only stayed here in summer, and she always went to London a full month afore *the* night. And I'm sorry to inconvenience you and your lady, but my niece is ill and I must go on Thursday.'

I could have shaken her for her absurd reiteration of that obvious fiction, after she had told me her real reasons.

She was determined to go, nor could our united entreaties move her in the least.

I did not tell Laura the legend of the shapes that 'walked in their marble', partly because a legend concerning our house might perhaps trouble my wife, and partly, I think, from some more occult reason. This was not quite the same to me as any other story, and I did not want to talk about it till the day was over. I had very soon ceased to think of the legend, however. I was painting a portrait of Laura, against the lattice window, and I could not think of much else. I had got a splendid background of yellow and grey sunset, and was working away with enthusiasm at her face. On Thursday Mrs Dorman went. She relented, at parting, so far as to say –

'Don't you put yourself about too much, ma'am, and if there's any little thing I can do next week, I'm sure I shan't mind.'

From which I inferred that she wished to come back to us after Halloween. Up to the last she adhered to the fiction of the niece with touching fidelity.

Thursday passed off pretty well. Laura showed marked ability in the matter of steak and potatoes, and I confess that my knives, and the plates, which I insisted upon washing, were better done than I had dared to expect.

Friday came. It is about what happened on that Friday that this is written. I wonder if I should have believed it, if any one had told it to me. I will write the story of it as quickly and plainly as I can. Everything that happened on that day is burnt into my brain. I shall not forget anything, nor leave anything out.

I got up early, I remember, and lighted the kitchen fire, and had just achieved a smoky success, when my little wife came running down, as sunny and sweet as the clear October morning itself. We prepared breakfast together, and found it very good fun. The housework was soon done, and when brushes and brooms and pails were quiet again, the house was still indeed. It is wonderful what a difference one makes in a house. We really missed Mrs Dorman, quite apart from considerations concerning pots and pans. We spent the day in dusting our books and putting them straight, and dined gaily on cold steak and coffee. Laura was, if possible, brighter and gayer and sweeter than usual, and I began to think that a little domestic toil was really good for her. We had never been so merry since we were married, and the walk we had that afternoon was, I think, the happiest time of all my life. When we had watched the deep scarlet clouds slowly pale into leaden grey against a pale-green sky, and saw the white mists curl up along the hedgerows in the distant marsh, we came back to the house, silently, hand in hand.

'You are sad, my darling,' I said, half-jestingly, as we sat down together in our little parlour. I expected a disclaimer, for my own silence had been the silence of complete happiness. To my surprise she said –

'Yes. I think I am sad, or rather I am uneasy. I don't think I'm very well. I have shivered three or four times since we came in, and it is not cold, is it?'

'No,' I said, and hoped it was not a chill caught from the treacherous mists that roll up from the marshes in the dying light. No – she said, she did not think so. Then, after a silence, she spoke suddenly –

'Do you ever have presentiments of evil?'

'No,' I said, smiling, 'and I shouldn't believe in them if I had.'

'I do,' she went on; 'the night my father died I knew it, though he was right away in the north of Scotland.' I did not answer in words.

She sat looking at the fire for some time in silence, gently stroking my hand. At last she sprang up, came behind me, and, drawing my head back, kissed me.

'There, it's over now,' she said. 'What a baby I am! Come, light the candles, and we'll have some of these new Rubinstein duets."

And we spent a happy hour or two at the piano.

At about half-past ten I began to long for the good-night pipe, but Laura looked so white that I felt it would be brutal of me to fill our sitting-room with the fumes of strong cavendish.

'I'll take my pipe outside,' I said.

'Let me come, too.'

'No, sweetheart, not tonight; you're much too tired. I shan't be long. Get to bed, or I shall have an invalid to nurse tomorrow as well as the boots to clean.'

I kissed her and was turning to go, when she flung her arms round my neck, and held me as if she would never let me go again. I stroked her hair.

'Come, Pussy, you're over-tired. The housework has been too much for you.'

She loosened her clasp a little and drew a deep breath.

'No. We've been very happy today, Jack, haven't we? Don't stay out too long.'

'I won't, my dearie.'

I strolled out of the front door, leaving it unlatched. What a night it was! The jagged masses of heavy dark cloud were rolling at intervals from horizon to horizon, and thin white wreaths covered the stars. Through all the rush of the cloud river, the moon swam, breasting the waves and disappearing again in the darkness. When now and again her light reached the woodlands they seemed to be slowly and noiselessly waving in time to the swing of the clouds above them. There was a strange grey light over all the earth; the fields had that shadowy bloom over them which only comes from the marriage of dew and moonshine, or frost and starlight.

I walked up and down, drinking in the beauty of the quiet earth and the changing sky. The night was absolutely silent. Nothing seemed to be abroad. There was no skurrying of rabbits, or twitter of the half-asleep birds. And though the clouds went sailing across the sky, the wind that drove them never came low enough to rustle the dead leaves in the woodland paths. Across the meadows I could see the church tower standing out black and grey against the sky. I walked there thinking over our three months of happiness – and of my wife, her dear eyes, her loving ways. Oh, my little girl! my own little girl; what a vision came then of a long, glad life for you and me together!

I heard a bell-beat from the church. Eleven already! I turned to go in, but the night held me. I could not go back into our little warm rooms yet. I would go up to the church. I felt vaguely that it would be good to carry my love and thankfulness to the sanctuary whither so many loads of sorrow and gladness had been borne by the men and women of the dead years.

I looked in at the low window as I went by. Laura was half lying on her chair in front of the fire. I could not see her face, only her little head showed dark against the pale blue wall. She was quite still. Asleep, no doubt. My heart reached out to her, as I went on. There must be a God, I thought, and a God who was good. How otherwise could anything so sweet and dear as she have ever been imagined?

I walked slowly along the edge of the wood. A sound broke the stillness of the night, it was a rustling in the wood. I stopped and listened. The sound stopped too. I went on, and now distinctly heard another step than mine answer mine like an echo. It was a poacher or a wood-stealer, most likely, for these were not unknown in our Arcadian neighbourhood. But whoever it was, he was a fool not to step more lightly. I turned into the wood, and now the footstep seemed to come from the path I had just left. It must be an echo, I thought. The wood looked perfect in the moonlight. The large dying ferns and the brushwood showed where through thinning foliage the pale light came down. The tree trunks stood up like Gothic columns all around me. They reminded me of the church, and I turned into the bier-balk, and passed through the corpse-gate between the graves to the low porch. I paused for a moment on the stone seat where Laura and I had watched the fading landscape. Then I noticed that the door of the church was open, and I blamed myself for having left it unlatched the other night. We were the only people who ever cared to come to the church except on Sundays, and I was vexed to think that through our carelessness the damp autumn airs had had a chance of getting in and injuring the old fabric. I went in. It will seem strange, perhaps, that I should have gone half-way up the aisle before I remembered – with a sudden chill, followed by as sudden a rush of self-contempt – that this was the very day and hour when, according to tradition, the 'shapes drawed out man-size in marble' began to walk.

Having thus remembered the legend, and remembered it with a shiver, of which I was ashamed, I could not do otherwise than walk up towards the altar, just to look at the figures – as I said to myself; really what I wanted was to assure myself, first, that I did not believe the legend, and, secondly, that it was not true. I was rather glad that I had come. I thought now I could tell Mrs Dorman how vain her fancies were, and how peacefully the marble figures slept on through the ghastly hour. With my hands in my pockets I passed up the aisle. In the grey dim light the eastern end of the church looked larger than usual, and the arches above the two tombs looked larger too. The moon came out and showed me the reason. I stopped short, my heart gave a leap that nearly choked me, and then sank sickeningly.

The 'bodies drawed out man-size' *were gone,* and their marble slabs lay wide and bare in the vague moonlight that slanted through the east window.

Were they really gone? or was I mad? Clenching my nerves, I stooped and passed my hand over the smooth slabs, and felt their flat unbroken surface. Had someone taken the things away? Was it some vile practical joke? I would make sure, anyway. In an instant I had made a torch of a newspaper, which happened to be in my pocket, and lighting it held it high above my head. Its yellow glare illumined the dark arches and those slabs. The figures *were* gone. And I was alone in the church; or was I alone?

And then a horror seized me, a horror indefinable and indescribable – an overwhelming certainty of supreme and accomplished calamity. I flung down the torch and tore along the aisle and out through the porch, biting my lips as I ran to keep myself from shrieking aloud. Oh, was I mad – or what was this that possessed me? I leaped the churchyard wall and took the straight cut across the fields, led by the light from our windows. Just as I got over the first stile, a dark figure seemed to spring out of the ground. Mad still with that certainty of misfortune, I made for the thing that stood in my path, shouting, 'Get out of the way, can't you!'

But my push met with a more vigorous resistance than I had expected. My arms were caught just above the elbow and held as in a vice, and the raw-boned Irish doctor actually shook me.

'Would ye?' he cried, in his own unmistakable accents – 'would ye, then?'

'Let me go, you fool,' I gasped. 'The marble figures have gone from the church; I tell you they've gone.'

He broke into a ringing laugh. 'I'll have to give ye a draught tomorrow, I see. Ye've bin smoking too much and listening to old wives' tales.'

'I tell you, I've seen the bare slabs.'

'Well, come back with me. I'm going up to old Palmer's – his daughter's ill; we'll look in at the church and let me see the bare slabs.'

'You go, if you like,' I said, a little less frantic for his laughter; 'I'm going home to my wife.'

'Rubbish, man,' said he; 'd'ye think I'll permit of that? Are ye to go saying all yer life that ye've seen solid marble endowed with vitality, and me to go all me life saying ye were a coward? No, sir – ye shan't do ut.'

The night air – a human voice – and I think also the physical contact with this six feet of solid common sense, brought me back a little to my ordinary self, and the word 'coward' was a mental shower-bath.

'Come on, then,' I said sullenly; 'perhaps you're right.'

He still held my arm tightly. We got over the stile and back to the church. All was still as death. The place smelt very damp and earthy. We walked up the aisle. I am not ashamed to confess that I shut my eyes: I knew the figures would not be there. I heard Kelly strike a match.

'Here they are, ye see, right enough; ye've been dreaming or drinking, asking yer pardon for the imputation.'

I opened my eyes. By Kelly's expiring vesta I saw two shapes lying 'in their marble' on their slabs. I drew a deep breath, and caught his hand.

'I'm awfully indebted to you,' I said. 'It must have been some trick of light, or I have been working rather hard, perhaps that's it. Do you know, I was quite convinced they were gone.'

'I'm aware of that,' he answered rather grimly; 'ye'll have to be careful of that brain of yours, my friend, I assure ye.'

He was leaning over and looking at the right-hand figure, whose stony face was the most villainous and deadly in expression.

'By Jove,' he said, 'something has been afoot here – this hand is broken.'

And so it was. I was certain that it had been perfect the last time Laura and I had been there.

'Perhaps someone has *tried* to remove them,' said the young doctor.

'That won't account for my impression,' I objected.

'Too much painting and tobacco will account for that, well enough.'

'Come along,' I said, 'or my wife will be getting anxious. You'll come in and have a drop of whisky and drink confusion to ghosts and better sense to me.'

'I ought to go up to Palmer's, but it's so late now I'd best leave it till the morning,' he replied. 'I was kept late at the Union, and I've had to see a lot of people since. All right, I'll come back with ye.'

I think he fancied I needed him more than did Palmer's girl, so, discussing how such an illusion could have been possible, and deducing from this experience large generalities concerning ghostly apparitions, we walked up to our cottage. We saw, as we walked up the garden-path, that bright light streamed out of the front door, and presently saw that the parlour door was open too. Had she gone out?

'Come in,' I said, and Dr Kelly followed me into the parlour. It was all ablaze with candles, not only the wax ones, but at least a dozen guttering, glaring tallow dips, stuck in vases and ornaments in unlikely places. Light, I knew, was Laura's remedy for nervousness. Poor child! Why had I left her? Brute that I was.

We glanced round the room, and at first we did not see her. The window was open, and the draught set all the candles flaring one way. Her chair was empty and her handkerchief and book lay on the floor. I turned to the window. There, in the recess of the window, I saw her. Oh, my child, my love, had she gone to that window to watch for me? And what had come into the room behind her? To what had she turned with that look of frantic fear and horror? Oh, my little one, had she thought that it was I whose step she heard, and turned to meet – what?

She had fallen back across a table in the window, and her body lay half on it and half on the window-seat, and her head hung down over the table, the brown hair loosened and fallen to the carpet. Her lips were drawn back, and her eyes wide, wide open. They saw nothing now. What had they seen last?

The doctor moved towards her, but I pushed him aside and sprang to her; caught her in my arms and cried—

'It's all right, Laura! I've got you safe, wifie.'

She fell into my arms in a heap. I clasped her and kissed her, and called her by all her pet names, but I think I knew all the time that she was dead. Her hands were tightly clenched. In one of them she held something fast. When I was quite sure that she was dead, and that nothing mattered at all any more, I let him open her hand to see what she held.

It was a grey marble finger.

John Charrington's Wedding

Edith Nesbit

No one ever thought that May Forster would marry John Charrington; but he thought differently, and things which John Charrington intended had a queer way of coming to pass. He asked her to marry him before he went up to Oxford. She laughed and refused him. He asked her again next time he came home. Again she laughed, tossed her dainty blonde head, and again refused. A third time he asked her; she said it was becoming a confirmed bad habit, and laughed at him more than ever.

John was not the only man who wanted to marry her: she was the belle of our village *coterie*, and we were all in love with her more or less; it was a sort of fashion, like heliotrope ties or Inverness capes. Therefore we were as much annoyed as surprised when John Charrington walked into our little local Club – we held it in a loft over the saddler's, I remember – and invited us all to his wedding.

'Your wedding?'

'You don't mean it?'

'Who's the happy fair? When's it to be?'

John Charrington filled his pipe and lighted it before he replied. Then he said—

'I'm sorry to deprive you fellows of your only joke – but Miss Forster and I are to be married in September.'

'You don't mean it?'

'He's got the mitten again, and it's turned his head.'

'No,' I said, rising, 'I see it's true. Lend me a pistol someone – or a first-class fare to the other end of Nowhere. Charrington has bewitched the only pretty girl in our twenty-mile radius. Was it mesmerism, or a love-potion, Jack?'

'Neither, sir, but a gift you'll never have – perseverance – and the best luck a man ever had in this world.'

There was something in his voice that silenced me, and all chaff of the other fellows failed to draw him further.

The queer thing about it was that when we congratulated Miss Forster, she blushed and smiled and dimpled, for all the world as though she were in love with him, and had been in love with him all the time. Upon my word, I think she had. Women are strange creatures.

We were all asked to the wedding. In Brixham every one who was anybody knew everybody else who was any one. My sisters were, I truly believe, more interested in the *trousseau* than the bride herself, and I was to be best man. The coming marriage was much canvassed at afternoon tea-tables, and at our little Club over the saddler's, and the question was always asked: 'Does she care for him?'

I used to ask that question myself in the early days of their engagement, but after a certain evening in August I never asked it again. I was coming home from the Club through the churchyard. Our church is on a thyme-grown hill, and the turf about it is so thick and soft that one's footsteps are noiseless.

I made no sound as I vaulted the low lichened wall, and threaded my way between the tombstones. It was at the same instant that I heard John Charrington's voice, and saw Her. May was sitting on a low flat gravestone, her face turned towards the full splendour of the western sun. Its expression ended, at once and for ever, any question of love for him; it was transfigured to a beauty I should not have believed possible, even to that beautiful little face.

John lay at her feet, and it was his voice that broke the stillness of the golden August evening.

'My dear, my dear, I believe I should come back from the dead if you wanted me!'

I coughed at once to indicate my presence, and passed on into the shadow fully enlightened.

The wedding was to be early in September. Two days before I had to run up to town on business. The train was late, of course, for we are on the South-Eastern, and as I stood grumbling with my watch in my hand, whom should I see but John Charrington and May Forster. They were walking up and down the unfrequented end of the platform, arm in arm, looking into each other's eyes, careless of the sympathetic interest of the porters.

Of course I knew better than to hesitate a moment before burying myself in the booking-office, and it was not till the train drew up at the platform, that I obtrusively passed the pair with my Gladstone, and took the corner in a first-class smoking-carriage. I did this with as good an air of not seeing them as I could assume. I pride myself on my discretion, but if John were travelling alone I wanted his company. I had it.

'Hullo, old man,' came his cheery voice as he swung his bag into my carriage; 'here's luck; I was expecting a dull journey!'

'Where are you off to?' I asked, discretion still bidding me turn my eyes away, though I saw, without looking, that hers were red-rimmed.

'To old Branbridge's,' he answered, shutting the door and leaning out for a last word with his sweetheart.

'Oh, I wish you wouldn't go, John,' she was saying in a low, earnest voice. 'I feel certain something will happen.'

'Do you think I should let anything happen to keep me, and the day after tomorrow our wedding-day?'

'Don't go,' she answered, with a pleading intensity which would have sent my Gladstone on to the platform and me after it. But she wasn't speaking to me. John Charrington was made differently; he rarely changed his opinions, never his resolutions.

He only stroked the little ungloved hands that lay on the carriage door.

'I must, May. The old boy's been awfully good to me, and now he's dying I must go and see him, but I shall come home in time for—' the rest of the parting was lost in a whisper and in the rattling lurch of the starting train.

'You're sure to come?' she spoke as the train moved.

'Nothing shall keep me,' he answered; and we steamed out. After he had seen the last of the little figure on the platform he leaned back in his corner and kept silence for a minute.

When he spoke it was to explain to me that his godfather, whose heir he was, lay dying at Peasmarsh Place, some fifty miles away, and had sent for John, and John had felt bound to go.

'I shall be surely back tomorrow,' he said, 'or, if not, the day after, in heaps of time. Thank Heaven, one hasn't to get up in the middle of the night to get married nowadays!'

'And suppose Mr Branbridge dies?'

'Alive or dead I mean to be married on Thursday!' John answered, lighting a cigar and unfolding the *Times*.

At Peasmarsh station we said 'goodbye,' and he got out, and I saw him ride off; I went on to London, where I stayed the night.

When I got home the next afternoon, a very wet one, by the way, my sister greeted me with –

'Where's Mr Charrington?'

'Goodness knows,' I answered testily. Every man, since Cain, has resented that kind of question.

'I thought you might have heard from him,' she went on, 'as you're to give him away to-morrow.'

'Isn't he back?' I asked, for I had confidently expected to find him at home.

'No, Geoffrey,' – my sister Fanny always had a way of jumping to conclusions, especially such conclusions as were least favourable to her fellow-creatures – 'he has not returned, and, what is more, you may depend upon it he won't. You mark my words, there'll be no wedding tomorrow.'

My sister Fanny has a power of annoying me which no other human being possesses.

'You mark my words,' I retorted with asperity, 'you had better give up making such a thundering idiot of yourself. There'll be more wedding tomorrow than ever you'll take the first part in.' A prophecy which, by the way, came true.

But though I could snarl confidently to my sister, I did not feel so comfortable when, late that night, I, standing on the doorstep of John's house, heard that he had not returned. I went home gloomily through the rain. Next morning brought a brilliant blue sky, gold sun, and all such softness of air and beauty of cloud as go to make up a perfect day. I woke with a vague feeling of having gone to bed anxious, and of being rather averse to facing that anxiety in the light of full wakefulness.

But with my shaving-water came a note from John which relieved my mind and sent me up to the Forsters' with a light heart.

May was in the garden. I saw her blue gown through the hollyhocks as the lodge gates swung to behind me. So I did not go up to the house, but turned aside down the turfed path.

'He's written to you too,' she said, without preliminary greeting, when I reached her side.

'Yes, I'm to meet him at the station at three, and come straight on to the church.'

Her face looked pale, but there was a brightness in her eyes, and a tender quiver about the mouth that spoke of renewed happiness.

'Mr Branbridge begged him so to stay another night that he had not the heart to refuse,' she went on. 'He is so kind, but I wish he hadn't stayed.'

I was at the station at half-past two. I felt rather annoyed with John. It seemed a sort of slight to the beautiful girl who loved him, that he should come as it were out of breath, and with the dust of travel upon him, to take her hand, which some of us would have given the best years of our lives to take.

But when the three o'clock train glided in, and glided out again having brought no passengers to our little station, I was more than annoyed. There was no other train for thirty-five minutes; I calculated that, with much hurry, we might just get to the church in time for the ceremony; but, oh, what a fool to miss that first train! What other man could have done it?

That thirty-five minutes seemed a year, as I wandered round the station reading the advertisements and the timetables, and the company's bye-laws, and getting more and more angry with John Charrington. This confidence in his own power of getting everything he wanted the minute he wanted it was leading him too far. I hate waiting. Every one does, but I believe I hate it more than any one else. The three thirty-five was late, of course.

I ground my pipe between my teeth and stamped with impatience as I watched the signals. Click. The signal went down. Five minutes later I flung myself into the carriage that I had brought for John.

'Drive to the church!' I said, as someone shut the door. 'Mr Charrington hasn't come by this train.'

Anxiety now replaced anger. What had become of the man? Could he have been taken suddenly ill? I had never known him have a day's illness in his life. And even so he might have telegraphed. Some awful accident must have happened to him. The thought that he had played her false never – no, not for a moment – entered my head. Yes, something terrible had happened to him, and on me lay the task of telling his bride. I almost wished the carriage would upset and break my head so that someone else might tell her, not I, who – but that's nothing to do with his story.

It was five minutes to four as we drew up at the churchyard gate. A double row of eager on-lookers lined the path from lychgate to porch. I sprang from the carriage and passed up between them. Our gardener had a good front place near the door. I stopped.

'Are they waiting still, Byles?' I asked, simply to gain time, for of course I knew they were by the waiting crowd's attentive attitude.

'Waiting, sir? No, no, sir; why, it must be over by now.'

'Over! Then Mr Charrington's come?'

'To the minute, sir; must have missed you somehow, and, I say, sir,' lowering his voice, 'I never see Mr John the least bit so afore, but my opinion is he's been drinking pretty free. His clothes was all dusty and his face like a sheet. I tell you I didn't like the looks of him at all, and the folks inside are saying all sorts of things. You'll see, something's gone very wrong with Mr John, and he's tried liquor. He looked like a ghost, and in he went with his eyes straight before him, with never a look or a word for none of us; him that was always such a gentleman!'

I had never heard Byles make so long a speech. The crowd in the churchyard were talking in whispers and getting ready rice and slippers to throw at the bride and bridegroom. The ringers were ready with their hands on the ropes to ring out the merry peal as the bride and bridegroom should come out.

A murmur from the church announced them; out they came. Byles was right. John Charrington did not look himself. There was dust on his coat, his hair was disarranged. He seemed to have been in some row, for there was a black mark above his eyebrow. He was deathly pale. But his pallor was not greater than that of the bride, who might have been carved in ivory – dress, veil, orange blossoms, face and all.

As they passed out the ringers stooped – there were six of them – and then, on the ears expecting the gay wedding peal, came the slow tolling of the passing bell.

A thrill of horror at so foolish a jest from the ringers passed through us all. But the ringers themselves dropped the ropes and fled like rabbits out into the sunlight. The bride shuddered, and grey shadows came about her mouth, but the bridegroom led her on down the path where the people stood with the handfuls of rice; but the handfuls were never thrown, and the wedding-bells never rang. In vain the ringers were urged to remedy their mistake: they protested with many whispered expletives that they would see themselves further first.

In a hush like the hush in the chamber of death the bridal pair passed into their carriage and its door slammed behind them.

Then the tongues were loosed. A babel of anger, wonder, conjecture from the guests and the spectators.

'If I'd seen his condition, sir,' said old Forster to me as we drove off, 'I would have stretched him on the floor of the church, sir, by Heaven I would, before I'd have let him marry my daughter!'

Then he put his head out of the window.

'Drive like hell,' he cried to the coachman; 'don't spare the horses.'

He was obeyed. We passed the bride's carriage. I forebore to look at it, and old Forster turned his head away and swore. We reached home before it.

We stood in the hall doorway, in the blazing afternoon sun, and in about half a minute we heard wheels crunching the gravel. When the carriage stopped in front of the steps old Forster and I ran down.

'Great Heaven, the carriage is empty! And yet—'

I had the door open in a minute, and this is what I saw –

No sign of John Charrington; and of May, his wife, only a huddled heap of white satin lying half on the floor of the carriage and half on the seat.

'I drove straight here, sir,' said the coachman, as the bride's father lifted her out; 'and I'll swear no one got out of the carriage.'

We carried her into the house in her bridal dress and drew back her veil. I saw her face. Shall I ever forget it? White, white and drawn with agony and horror, bearing such a look of terror as I have never seen since except in dreams. And her hair, her radiant blonde hair, I tell you it was white like snow.

As we stood, her father and I, half mad with the horror and mystery of it, a boy came up the avenue – a telegraph boy. They brought the orange envelope to me. I tore it open.

'Mr Charrington was thrown from the dogcart on his way to the station at half-past one. Killed on the spot!'

And he was married to May Forster in our parish church at *half-past three,* in presence of half the parish.

'I shall be married, dead or alive!'

What had passed in that carriage on the homeward drive? No one knows – no one will ever know. Oh, May! oh, my dear!

Before a week was over they laid her beside her husband in our little churchyard on the thyme-covered hill – the churchyard where they had kept their love-trysts.

Thus was accomplished John Charrington's wedding.

Uncle Abraham's Romance

Edith Nesbit

'No, my dear,' my Uncle Abraham answered me, 'no – nothing romantic ever happened to me – unless – but no: that wasn't romantic either—'

I was. To me, I being eighteen, romance was the world. My Uncle Abraham was old and lame. I followed the gaze of his faded eyes, and my own rested on a miniature that hung at his elbow-chair's right hand, a portrait of a woman, whose loveliness even the miniature-painter's art had been powerless to disguise – a woman with large lustrous eyes and perfect oval face.

I rose to look at it. I had looked at it a hundred times. Often enough in my baby days I had asked, 'Who's that, uncle?' always receiving the same answer: 'A lady who died long ago, my dear.'

As I looked again at the picture, I asked, 'Was she like this?'

'Who?'

'Your – your romance!'

Uncle Abraham looked hard at me. 'Yes,' he said at last. 'Very – very like.'

I sat down on the floor by him. 'Won't you tell me about her?'

'There's nothing to tell,' he said. 'I think it was fancy, mostly, and folly; but it's the realest thing in my long life, my dear.'

A long pause. I kept silence. 'Hurry no man's cattle' is a good motto, especially with old people.

'I remember,' he said in the dreamy tone always promising so well to the ear that a story delighteth – 'I remember, when I was a young man, I was very lonely indeed. I never had a sweetheart. I was always lame, my dear, from quite a boy; and the girls used to laugh at me.'

He sighed. Presently he went on –

'And so I got into the way of mooning off by myself in lonely places, and one of my favourite walks was up through our churchyard, which was set high on a hill in the middle of the marsh country. I liked that because I never met any one there. It's all over, years ago. I was a silly lad; but I couldn't bear of a summer evening to hear a rustle and a whisper from the other side of the hedge, or maybe a kiss as I went by.

'Well, I used to go and sit all by myself in the churchyard, which was always sweet with thyme, and quite light (on account of its being so high) long after the marshes were dark. I used to watch the bats flitting about in the red light, and wonder why God didn't make every one's legs straight and strong, and wicked follies like that. But by the time the light was gone I had always worked it off, so to speak, and could go home quietly and say my prayers without any bitterness.

'Well, one hot night in August, when I had watched the sunset fade and the crescent moon grow golden, I was just stepping over the low stone wall of the churchyard when I heard a rustle behind me. I turned round, expecting it to be a rabbit or a bird. It was a woman.'

He looked at the portrait. So did I.

'Yes,' he said, 'that was her very face. I was a bit scared and said something – I don't know what – and she laughed and said, 'Did I think she was a ghost?' and I answered back, and I stayed talking to her over the churchyard wall till 'twas quite dark, and the glowworms were out in the wet grass all along the way home.

'Next night I saw her again; and the next night and the next. Always at twilight time; and if I passed any lovers leaning on the stiles in the marshes it was nothing to me now.'

Again my uncle paused. 'It's very long ago,' he said slowly, 'and I'm an old man; but I know what youth means, and happiness, though I was always lame, and the girls used to laugh at me. I don't know how long it went on – you don't measure time in dreams – but at last your grandfather said I looked as if I had one foot in the grave, and he would be sending me to stay with our kin at Bath and take the waters. I had to go. I could not tell my father why I would rather had died than go.'

'What was her name, uncle?' I asked.

'She never would tell me her name, and why should she? I had names enough in my heart to call her by. Marriage? My dear, even then I knew marriage was not for me. But I met her night after night, always in our churchyard where the yew-trees were and the lichened gravestones. It was there we always met and always parted. The last time was the night before I went away. She was very sad, and dearer than life itself. And she said –

'"If you come back before the new moon I shall meet you here just as usual. But if the new moon shines on this grave and you are not here – you will never see me again any more."

'She laid her hand on the yellow lichened tomb against which we had been leaning. It was an old weather-worn stone, and bore on it the inscription—

'SUSANNAH KINGSNORTH,
Ob. 1713.'

'"I shall be here." I said.

'"I mean it," she said, with deep and sudden seriousness, "it is no fancy. You will be here when the new moon shines?"'

'I promised, and after a while we parted.

'I had been with my kinsfolk at Bath nearly a month. I was to go home on the next day, when, turning over a case in the parlour, I came upon that miniature. I could not speak for a minute. At last I said, with dry tongue, and heart beating to the tune of heaven and hell—

'"Who is this?"

'"That?" said my aunt. 'Oh! she was betrothed to one of our family many years ago, but she died before the wedding. They say she was a bit of a witch. A handsome one, wasn't she?'

'I looked again at the face, the lips, the eyes of my dear and lovely love, whom I was to meet tomorrow night when the new moon shone on that tomb in our churchyard.

'"Did you say she was dead?" I asked, and I hardly knew my own voice.

'"Years and years ago! Her name's on the back and her date—"

'I took the portrait from its faded red-velvet bed, and read on the back – 'SUSANNAH KINGSNORTH, *Ob.* 1713.'

'That was in 1813.' My uncle stopped short.

'What happened?' I asked breathlessly.

'I believe I had a fit,' my uncle answered slowly; 'at any rate, I was very ill.'

'And you missed the new moon on the grave?'

'I missed the new moon on the grave.'

'And you never saw her again?'

'I never saw her again—'

'But, uncle, do you really believe? – Can the dead? – was she – did you—'

My uncle took out his pipe and filled it.

'It's a long time ago,' he said, 'a many, many years. Old man's tales, my dear! Old man's tales! Don't you take any notice of them.'

He lighted the pipe, puffed silently a moment or two, and then added: 'But I know what youth means, and happiness, though I was lame, and the girls used to laugh at me.'

In the Dark

Edith Nesbit

It may have been a form of madness. Or it may be that he really was what is called haunted. Or it may – though I don't pretend to understand how – have been the development, through intense suffering, of a sixth sense in a very nervous, highly strung nature. Something certainly led him where They were. And to him They were all one.

He told me the first part of the story, and the last part of it I saw with my own eyes.

Chapter I

Haldane and I were friends even in our school-days. What first brought us together was our common hatred of Visger, who came from our part of the country. His people knew our people at home, so he was put on to us when he came. He was the most intolerable person, boy and man, that I have ever known. He would not tell a lie. And that was all right. But he didn't stop at that. If he were asked whether any other chap had done anything – been out of bounds, or up to any sort of lark – he would always say, 'I don't know, sir, but I believe so'. He never did know – we took care of that. But what he believed was always right. I remember Haldane twisting his arm to say how he knew about that cherry-tree business, and he only said, 'I don't know – I just feel sure. And I was right, you see.' What can you do with a boy like that?

We grew up to be men. At least Haldane and I did. Visger grew up to be a prig. He was a vegetarian and a teetotaller, and an all-wooler and Christian Scientist, and all the things that prigs are – but he wasn't a common prig. He knew all sorts of things that he oughtn't to have known, that he couldn't have known in any ordinary decent way. It wasn't that he found things out. He just knew them. Once, when I was very unhappy, he came into my rooms – we were all in our last year at Oxford – and talked about things I hardly knew myself. That was really why I went to India that winter. It was bad enough to be unhappy, without having that beast knowing all about it.

I was away over a year. Coming back, I thought a lot about how jolly it would be to see old Haldane again. If I thought about Visger at all, I wished he was dead. But I didn't think about him much.

I did want to see Haldane. He was always such a jolly chap – gay, and kindly, and simple, honourable, uptight, and full of practical sympathies. I longed to see him, to see the smile in his jolly blue eyes, looking out from the net of wrinkles that laughing had made round them, to hear his jolly laugh, and feel the good grip of his big hand. I went straight from the docks to his chambers in Gray's Inn, and I found him cold, pale, anaemic, with dull eyes and a limp hand, and pale lips that smiled without mirth, and uttered a welcome without gladness.

He was surrounded by a litter of disordered furniture and personal effects half packed. Some big boxes stood corded, and there were cases of books, filled and waiting for the enclosing boards to be nailed on.

'Yes, I'm moving,' he said. 'I can't stand these rooms. There's something rum about them – something devilish rum. I clear our tomorrow.'

The autumn dusk was filling the corners with shadows. 'You got the furs,' I said, just for something to say, for I saw the big case that held them lying corded among the others.

'Furs?' he said. 'Oh yes. Thanks awfully. Yes. I forgot about the furs.' He laughed, out of politeness, I suppose, for there was no joke about the furs. They were many and fine – the best I could get for money, and I had seen them packed and sent off when my heart was very sore. He stood looking at me, and saying nothing.

'Come out and have a bit of dinner,' I said as cheerfully as I could.

'Too busy,' he answered, after the slightest possible pause, and a glance round the room – 'look here – I'm awfully glad to see you – If you'd just slip over and order in dinner – I'd go myself-only – Well, you see how it is.'

I went. And when I came back, he had cleared a space near the fire, and moved his big gate-table into it. We dined there by candle light. I tried to be amusing. He, I am sure, tried to be amused. We did not succeed, either of us. And his haggard eyes watched me all the time, save in those fleeting moments when, without turning his head, he glanced back over his shoulder into the shadows that crowded round the little lighted place where we sat.

When we had dined and the man had come and taken away the dishes, I looked at Haldane very steadily, so that he stopped in a pointless anecdote, and looked interrogatively at me. 'Well?' I said.

'You're not listening,' he said petulantly. 'What's the matter?'

'That's what you'd better tell me,' I said.

He was silent, gave one of those furtive glances at the shadows, and stooped to stir the fire to – I knew it – a blaze that must light every corner of the room.

'You're all to pieces,' I said cheerfully. 'What have you been up to? Wine? Cards? Speculation? A woman? If you won't tell me, you'll have to tell your doctor. Why, my dear chap, you're a wreck.'

'You're a comfortable friend to have about the place,' he said, and smiled a mechanical smile not at all pleasant to see.

'I'm the friend you want, I think,' said I. 'Do you suppose I'm blind? Something's gone wrong and you've taken to something. Morphia, perhaps? And you've brooded over the thing till you've lost all sense of proportion. Out with it, old chap. I bet you a dollar it's not so bad as you think it.'

'If I could tell you – or tell anyone,' he said slowly, 'it wouldn't be so bad as it is. If I could tell anyone, I'd tell you. And even as it is, I've told you more than I've told anyone else.'

I could get nothing more out of him. But he pressed me to stay – would have given me his bed and made himself a shake-down, he said. But I had engaged my room at the Victoria, and I was expecting letters. So I left him, quite late – and he stood on the stairs, holding a candle over the bannisters to light me down.

When I went back next morning, he was gone. Men were moving his furniture into a big van with somebody's Pantechnicon painted on it in big letters.

He had left no address with the porter, and had driven off in a hansom with two portmanteaux – to Waterloo, the porter thought.

Well, a man has a right to the monopoly of his own troubles, if he chooses to have it. And I had troubles of my own that kept me busy.

Chapter II

It was more than a year later that I saw Haldane again. I had got rooms in the Albany by this time, and he turned up there one morning, very early indeed – before breakfast in fact. And if he looked ghastly before, he now looked almost ghostly. His face looked as though it had worn thin, like an oyster shell that has for years been cast up twice a day by the sea on a shore all pebbly. His hands were thin as bird's claws, and they trembled like caught butterflies.

I welcomed him with enthusiastic cordiality and pressed breakfast on him. This time, I decided, I would ask no questions. For I saw that none were needed. He would tell me. He intended to tell me. He had come here to tell me, and for nothing else.

I lit the spirit lamp – I made coffee and small talk for him, and I ate and drank, and waited for him to begin. And it was like this that he began:

'I am going,' he said, 'to kill myself – oh, don't be alarmed,' – I suppose I had said or looked something – 'I shan't do it here, or now. I shall do it when I have to – when I can't bear it any longer. And I want someone to know why. I don't want to feel that I'm the only living creature who does know. And I can trust you, can't I?'

I murmured something reassuring.

'I should like you, if you don't mind, to give me your word, that you won't tell a soul what I'm going to tell you, as long as I'm alive. Afterwards… you can tell whom you please.' I gave him my word.

He sat silent looking at the fire. Then he shrugged his shoulders.

'It's extraordinary how difficult it is to say it,' he said, and smiled. 'The fact is – you know that beast, George Visger.'

'Yes,' I said. 'I haven't seen him since I came back. Someone told me he'd gone to some island or other to preach vegetarianism to the cannibals. Anyhow, he's out of the way, bad luck to him.'

'Yes,' said Haldane, 'he's out of the way. But he's not preaching anything. In point of fact, he's dead.'

'Dead?' was all I could think of to say.

'Yes,' said he; 'it's not generally known, but he is.'

'What did he die of?' I asked, not that I cared. The bare fact was good enough for me.

'You know what an interfering chap he always was. Always knew everything. Heart to heart talks – and have everything open and above board. Well, he interfered between me and someone else – told her a pack of lies.'

'Lies?'

'Well, the things were true, but he made lies of them the way he told them-you know.' I did. I nodded. 'And she threw me over. And she died. And we weren't even friends. And I couldn't see her – before – I couldn't even… Oh, my God… But I went to the funeral. He was there. They'd asked him. And then I came back to my rooms. And I was sitting there, thinking. And he came up.

'He would do. It's just what he would do. The beast! I hope you kicked him out.'

'No, I didn't. I listened to what he'd got to say. He came to say, no doubt it was all for the best. And he hadn't known the things he told her. He'd only guessed. He'd guessed right, damn him. What right had he to guess right? And he said it was all for the best, because, besides that, there was madness in my family. He'd found that out too—'

'And is there?'

'If there is, I didn't know it. And that was why it was all for the best. So then I said, "There wasn't any madness in my family before, but there is now," and I got hold of his throat. I am not sure whether I meant to kill him; I ought to have meant to kill him. Anyhow, I did kill him. What did you say?'

I had said nothing. It is not easy to think at once of the tactful and suitable thing to say, when your oldest friend tells you that he is a murderer.

'When I could get my hands out of his throat – it was as difficult as it is to drop the handles of a galvanic battery – he fell in a lump on the hearthrug. And I saw what I'd done. How is it that murderers ever get found out?'

'They're careless, I suppose,' I found myself saying, 'they lose their nerve.'

'I didn't,' he said. 'I never was calmer, I sat down in the big chair and looked at him, and thought it all out. He was just off to that island – I knew that. He'd said goodbye to everyone. He'd told me that. There was no blood to get rid of – or only a touch at the corner of his slack mouth. He wasn't going to travel in his own name because of interviewers. Mr Somebody Something's luggage would be unclaimed and his cabin empty. No one would guess that Mr Somebody Something was Sir George Visger, FRS. It was all as plain as plain. There was nothing to get rid of, but the man. No weapon, no blood – and I got rid of him all right.'

'How?'

He smiled cunningly.

'No, no,' he said; 'that's where I draw the line. It's not that I doubt your word, but if you talked in your sleep, or had a fever or anything. No, no. As long as you don't know where the body is, don't you see, I'm all right. Even if you could prove that I've said all this – which you can't – it's only the wanderings of my poor unhinged brain. See?'

I saw. And I was sorry for him. And I did not believe that he had killed Visger. He was not the sort of man who kills people. So I said:

'Yes, old chap, I see. Now look here. Let's go away together, you and I – travel a bit and see the world, and forget all about that beastly chap.'

His eyes lighted up at that.

'Why,' he said, 'you understand. You don't hate me and shrink from me. I wish I'd told you before – you know – when you came and I was packing all my sticks. But it's too late now.

'Too late? Not a bit of it,' I said. 'Come, we'll pack our traps and be off tonight – out into the unknown, don't you know.

'That's where I'm going,' he said. 'You wait. When you've heard what's been happening to me, you won't be so keen to go travelling about with me.'

'But you've told me what's been happening to you,' I said, and the more I thought about what he had told me, the less I believed it.

'No,' he said, slowly, 'no – I've told you what happened to him. What happened to me is quite different. Did I tell you what his last words were? Just when I was coming at him. Before I'd got his throat, you know. He said, "Look out. You'll never to able to get rid of the body – besides, anger's sinful." You know that way he had, like a tract on its hind legs. So afterwards I got thinking of that. But I didn't think of it for a year. Because I did get rid of his body all right. And then I was sitting in that comfortable chair, and I thought, "Hullo, it must be about a year now, since that—" and I pulled out my pocket-book and went to the window to look at a little almanac I carry about – it was getting dusk-and sure enough it was a year, to the day. And then I remembered what he'd said. And I said to myself, "Not much trouble about getting rid of your body, you brute." And then I looked at the hearthrug and – Ah!' he screamed suddenly and very loud – 'I can't tell you – no, I can't.'

My man opened the door – he wore a smooth face over his wriggling curiosity. 'Did you call, sir?'

'Yes,' I lied. 'I want you to take a note to the bank, and wait for an answer.'

When he was got rid of, Haldane said: 'Where was I?'

'You were just telling me what happened after you looked at the almanac. What was it?'

'Nothing much,' he said, laughing softly, 'oh, nothing much – only that I glanced at the hearthrug – and there he was – the man I'd killed a year before. Don't try to explain, or I shall lose my temper. The door was shut. The windows were shut. He hadn't been there a minute before. And he was there then. That's all.'

Hallucination was one of the words I stumbled among.

'Exactly what I thought,' he said triumphantly, 'but – I touched it. It was quite real. Heavy, you know, and harder than live people are somehow, to the touch-more like a stone thing covered with kid the hands were, and the arms like a marble statue in a blue serge suit. Don't you hate men who wear blue serge suits?'

'There are halllucinations of touch too,' I found myself saying..

'Exactly what I thought,' said Haldane more triumphant than ever, 'but there are limits, you know – limits. So then I thought someone had got him out – the real him – and stuck him there to frighten me – while my back was turned, and I went to the place where I'd hidden him, and he was there-ah! – just as I'd left him. Only… it was a year ago. There are two of him there now.'

'My dear chap,' I said 'this is simply comic.'

'Yes,' he said, 'It is amusing. I find it so myself. Especially in the night when I wake up and think of it. I hope I shan't die in the dark, Winston. That's one of the reasons why I think I shall have to kill myself. I could be sure then of not dying in the dark.'

'Is that all?' I asked, feeling sure that it must be.

'No,' said Haldane at once. 'That's not all. He's come back to rue again. In a railway carriage it was. I'd been asleep. When I woke up, there he was lying on the seat opposite me. Looked just the same. I pitched him out on the line in Red Hill Tunnel. And if I see him again, I'm going out myself. I can't stand it. It's too much. I'd sooner go. Whatever the next world's like, there aren't things in it like that. We leave them here, in graves and boxes and… You think I'm mad. But I'm not. You can't help me – no one can help me. He knew, you see. He said I shouldn't be able to get rid of the body. And I can't get rid of it. I can't. I can't. He knew. He always did know things that he couldn't know. But I'll cut his game short. After all, I've got the ace of trumps, and I'll play it on his next trick. I give you my word of honour, Winston, that I'm not mad.'

'My dear old man,' I said, 'I don't think you're mad. But I do think your nerves are very much upset. Mine are a bit, too. Do you know why I went to India? It was because of you and her. I couldn't stay and see it, though I wished for your happiness and all that; you know I did. And when I came back, she . . . and you . . . Let's see it out together,' I said. 'You won't keep fancying things if you've got me to talk to. And I always said you weren't half a bad old duffer.'

'She liked you,' he said.

'Oh, yes,' I said, 'she liked me.'

Chapter III

That was how we came to go abroad together. I was full of hope for him. He'd always been such a splendid chap – so sane and strong. I couldn't believe that he was gone mad, gone for ever, I mean, so that he'd never come right again. Perhaps may own trouble made it easy for me to see things not quite straight. Anyway, I took him away to recover his mind's health, exactly as I should have taken him away to get strong after a fever. And the madness seemed to pass away, and in a month or two we were perfectly jolly, and I thought I had cured him. And I was very glad because of that old friendship of ours, and because she had loved him and liked me.

We never spoke of Visger. I thought he had forgotten all about him. I thought I understood how his mind, over-strained by sorrow and anger, had fixed on the man he hated, and woven a nightmare web of horror round that detestable personality. And I had got the whip hand of my own trouble. And we were as jolly as sandboys together all those months.

And we came to Bruges at last in our travels, and Bruges was very full, because of the Exhibition. We could only get one room and one bed. So we tossed for the bed, and the one who lost the toss was to make the best of the night in the armchair. And the bedclothes we were to share equitably.

We spent the evening at a café chantant and finished at a beer hall, and it was late and sleepy when we got back to the Grande Vigne. I took our key from its nail in the concierge's room, and we went up. We talked awhile, I remember, of the town, and the belfry, and the Venetian aspect of the canals by moonlight, and then Haldane got into bed, and I made a chrysalis of myself with my share of the blankets and fitted the tight roll into the armchair. I was not at all comfortable, but I was compensatingly tired, and I was nearly asleep when Haldane roused me up to tell me about his will.

'I've left everything to you, old man,' he said. 'I know I can trust you to see to everything.' 'Quite so,' said I, 'and if you don't mind, we'll talk about it in the morning.'

He tried to go on about it, and about what a friend I'd been, and all that, but I shut him up and told him to go to sleep. But no. He wasn't comfortable, he said. And he'd got a thirst like a lime kiln. And he'd noticed that there was no water-bottle in the room. 'And the water in the jug's like pale soup,' he said.

'Oh, all right,' said I. 'Light your candle and go and get some water, then, in Heaven's name, and let me get to sleep.'

But he said, 'No – you light it. I don't want to get out of bed in the dark. I might – I might step on something, mightn't I – or walk into something that wasn't there when I got into bed.'

'Rot,' I said, 'walk into your grandmother.' But I lit the candle all the same. He sat up in bed and looked at me-very pale-with his hair all tumbled from the pillow, and his eyes blinking and shining. 'That's better,' he said. And then, 'I say – look here. Oh – yes – I see. It's all right. Queer how they mark the sheets here. Blest if I didn't think it was blood, just for the minute.' The sheet was marked, not at the corner, as sheets are marked at home, but right in the middle where it turns down, with big, red, cross-stitching.

'Yes, I see,' I said, 'it is a queer place to mark it.'

'It's queer letters to have on it,' he said. 'G.V.'

'Grande Vigne,' I said. 'What letters do you expect them to mark things with? Hurry up.'

'You come too,' he said. 'Yes, it does stand for Grande Vigne, of course. I wish you'd come down too, Winston.'

'I'll go down,' I said and turned with the candle in my hand.

He was out of bed and close to me in a flash.

'No,' said he, 'I don't want to stay alone in the dark.'

He said it just as a frightened child might have done.

'All right then, come along,' I said. And we went. I tried to make some joke, I remember, about the length of his hair, and the cut of his pyjamas – but I was sick with disappointment. For it was almost quite plain to me, even then, that all my time and trouble had been thrown away, and that he wasn't cured after all. We went down as quietly as we could, and got a carafe of water from the long bare dining table in the salle à manger. He got hold of my arm at first, and then he got the candle away from me, and went very slowly, shading the light with his hand, and looking very carefully all about, as though he expected to see something that he wanted very desperately not to see. And of course, I knew what that something was. I didn't like the way he was going on. I can't at all express how deeply I didn't like it. And he looked over his shoulder every now and then, just as he did that first evening after I came back from India.

The thing got on my nerves so that I could hardly find the way back to our room. And when we got there, I give you my word, I more than half expected to see what he had expected to see – that, or something like that, on the hearthrug. But of course there was nothing.

I blew out the light and tightened my blankets round me – I'd been trailing them after me in our expedition. And I was settled in my chair when Haldane spoke.

'You've got all the blankets,' he said.

'No, I haven't,' said I, 'only what I've always had.' 'I can't find mine then,' he said and I could hear his teeth chattering. 'And I'm cold. I'm... For God's sake, light the candle. Light it. Light it. Something horrible...'

And I couldn't find the matches.

'Light the candle, light the candle,' he said, and his voice broke, as a boy's does sometimes in chapel. 'If you don't he'll come to me. It is so easy to come at any one in the dark. Oh Winston, light the candle, for the love of God! I can't die in the dark.'

'I am lighting it,' I said savagely, and I was feeling for the matches on the marble-topped chest of drawers, on the mantelpiece – everywhere but on the round centre table where I'd put them. 'You're not going to die. Don't be a fool,' I said. 'It's all right. I'll get a light in a second.'

He said, 'It's cold. It's cold. It's cold,' like that, three times. And then he screamed aloud, like a woman – like a child – like a hare when the dogs have got it. I had heard him scream like that once before.

'What is it?' I cried, hardly less loud. 'For God's sake, hold your noise. What is it?' There was an empty silence. Then, very slowly:

'It's Visger,' he said. And he spoke thickly, as through some stifling veil.

'Nonsense. Where?' I asked, and my hand closed on the matches as he spoke.

'Here,' he screamed sharply, as though he had torn the veil away, 'here, beside me. In the bed.' I got the candle alight. I got across to him.

He was crushed in a heap at the edge of the bed. Stretched on the bed beyond him was a dead man, white and very cold.

Haldane had died in the dark.

It was all so simple.

We had come to the wrong room. The man the room belonged to was there, on the bed he had engaged and paid for before he died of heart disease, earlier in the day. A French commis-voyageur representing soap and perfumery; his name, Felix Leblanc.

Later, in England, I made cautious enquiries. The body of a man had been found in the Red Hill tunnel – a haberdasher man named Simmons, who had drunk spirits of salts, owing to the depression of trade. The bottle was clutched in his dead hand.

For reasons that I had, I took care to have a police inspector with me when I opened the boxes that came to me by Haldane's will. One of them was the big box, metal lined, in which I had sent him the skins from India – for a wedding present, God help us all!

It was closely soldered.

Inside were the skins of beasts? No. The bodies of two men. One was identified, after some trouble, as that of a hawker of pens in city offices-subject to fits. He had died in one, it seemed. The other body was Visger's, right enough.

Explain it as you like. I offered you, if you remember, a choice of explanations before I began the story. I have not yet found the explanation that can satisfy me.

The Phantom Coach

Amelia Edwards

The circumstances I am about to relate to you have truth to recommend them. They happened to myself, and my recollection of them is as vivid as if they had taken place only yesterday. Twenty years, however, have gone by since that night. During those twenty years I have told the story to but one other person. I tell it now with a reluctance which I find it difficult to overcome. All I entreat, meanwhile, is that you will abstain from forcing your own conclusions upon me. I want nothing explained away. I desire no arguments. My mind on this subject is quite made up, and, having the testimony of my own senses to rely upon, I prefer to abide by it.

Well! It was just twenty years ago, and within a day or two of the end of the grouse season. I had been out all day with my gun, and had had no sport to speak of. The wind was due east; the month, December; the place, a bleak wide moor in the far north of England. And I had lost my way. It was not a pleasant place in which to lose one's way, with the first feathery flakes of a coming snowstorm just fluttering down upon the heather, and the leaden evening closing in all around. I shaded my eyes with my hand, and stared anxiously into the gathering darkness, where the purple moorland melted into a range of low hills, some ten or twelve miles distant. Not the faintest smoke-wreath, not the tiniest cultivated patch, or fence, or sheep-track, met my eyes in any direction. There was nothing for it but to walk on, and take my chance of finding what shelter I could, by the way. So I shouldered my gun again, and pushed wearily forward; for I had been on foot since an hour after daybreak, and had eaten nothing since breakfast.

Meanwhile, the snow began to come down with ominous steadiness, and the wind fell. After this, the cold became more intense, and the night came rapidly up. As for me, my prospects darkened with the darkening sky, and my heart grew heavy as I thought how my young wife was already watching for me through the window of our little inn parlour, and thought of all the suffering in store for her throughout this weary night. We had been married four months, and, having spent our autumn in the Highlands, were now lodging in a remote little village situated just on the verge of the great English moorlands. We were very much in love, and, of course, very happy. This morning, when we parted, she had implored me to return before dusk, and I had promised her that I would. What would I not have given to have kept my word!

Even now, weary as I was, I felt that with a supper, an hour's rest, and a guide, I might still get back to her before midnight, if only guide and shelter could be found.

And all this time, the snow fell and the night thickened. I stopped and shouted every now and then, but my shouts seemed only to make the silence deeper. Then a vague sense of uneasiness came upon me, and I began to remember stories of travellers who had walked on and on in the falling snow until, wearied out, they were fain to lie down and sleep their lives away. Would it be possible, I asked myself, to keep on thus through all the long dark night? Would there not come a time when my limbs must fail, and my resolution give way? When I, too, must sleep the sleep of death. Death! I shuddered. How hard to die just now, when life lay all so bright before me! How hard for my darling, whose whole loving heart but that thought was not to be borne! To banish it, I shouted again, louder and longer, and then listened eagerly. Was my shout answered, or did I only fancy that I heard a far-off cry? I halloed again, and again the echo followed. Then a wavering speck of light came suddenly out of the dark, shifting, disappearing, growing momentarily nearer and brighter. Running towards it at full speed, I found myself, to my great joy, face to face with an old man and a lantern.

'Thank God!' was the exclamation that burst involuntarily from my lips.

Blinking and frowning, he lifted his lantern and peered into my face.

'What for?' growled he, sulkily.

'Well – for you. I began to fear I should be lost in the snow.'

'Eh, then, folks do get cast away hereabouts fra' time to time, an' what's to hinder you from bein' cast away likewise, if the Lord's so minded?'

'If the Lord is so minded that you and I shall be lost together, friend, we must submit,' I replied; 'but I don't mean to be lost without you. How far am I now from Dwolding?'

'A gude twenty mile, more or less.'

'And the nearest village?'

'The nearest village is Wyke, an' that's twelve mile t'other side.'

'Where do you live, then?'

'Out yonder,' said he, with a vague jerk of the lantern.

'You're going home, I presume?'

'Maybe I am.'

'Then I'm going with you.'

The old man shook his head, and rubbed his nose reflectively with the handle of the lantern.

'It ain't o' no use,' growled he. 'He 'ont let you in – not he.'

'We'll see about that,' I replied, briskly. 'Who is He?'

'The master.'

'Who is the master?'

'That's nowt to you,' was the unceremonious reply.

'Well, well; you lead the way, and I'll engage that the master shall give me shelter and a supper tonight.'

'Eh, you can try him!' muttered my reluctant guide; and, still shaking his head, he hobbled, gnome-like, away through the falling snow. A large mass loomed up presently out of the darkness, and a huge dog rushed out, barking furiously.

'Is this the house?' I asked.

'Ay, it's the house. Down, Bey!' And he fumbled in his pocket for the key.

I drew up close behind him, prepared to lose no chance of entrance, and saw in the little circle of light shed by the lantern that the door was heavily studded with iron nails, like the door of a prison. In another minute he had turned the key and I had pushed past him into the house.

Once inside, I looked round with curiosity, and found myself in a great raftered hall, which served, apparently, a variety of uses. One end was piled to the roof with corn, like a barn. The other was stored with flour-sacks, agricultural implements, casks, and all kinds of miscellaneous lumber; while from the beams overhead hung rows of hams, flitches, and bunches of dried herbs for winter use. In the centre of the floor stood some huge object gauntly dressed in a dingy wrapping-cloth, and reaching half way to the rafters. Lifting a corner of this cloth, I saw, to my surprise, a telescope of very considerable size, mounted on a rude movable platform, with four small wheels. The tube was made of painted wood, bound round with bands of metal rudely fashioned; the speculum, so far as I could estimate its size in the dim light, measured at least fifteen inches in diameter. While I was yet examining the instrument, and asking myself whether it was not the work of some self-taught optician, a bell rang sharply.

'That's for you,' said my guide, with a malicious grin. 'Yonder's his room.'

He pointed to a low black door at the opposite side of the hall. I crossed over, rapped somewhat loudly, and went in, without waiting for an invitation. A huge, white-haired old man rose from a table covered with books and papers, and confronted me sternly.

'Who are you?' said he. 'How came you here? What do you want?'

'James Murray, barrister-at-law. On foot across the moor. Meat, drink, and sleep.'

He bent his bushy brows into a portentous frown.

'Mine is not a house of entertainment,' he said, haughtily. 'Jacob, how dared you admit this stranger?'

'I didn't admit him,' grumbled the old man. 'He followed me over the muir, and shouldered his way in before me. I'm no match for six foot two.'

'And pray, sir, by what right have you forced an entrance into my house?'

'The same by which I should have clung to your boat, if I were drowning. The right of self-preservation.'

'Self-preservation?'

'There's an inch of snow on the ground already,' I replied, briefly; 'and it would be deep enough to cover my body before daybreak.'

He strode to the window, pulled aside a heavy black curtain, and looked out.

'It is true,' he said. 'You can stay, if you choose, till morning. Jacob, serve the supper.'

With this he waved me to a seat, resumed his own, and became at once absorbed in the studies from which I had disturbed him.

I placed my gun in a corner, drew a chair to the hearth, and examined my quarters at leisure. Smaller and less incongruous in its arrangements than the hall, this room contained, nevertheless, much to awaken my curiosity. The floor was carpetless. The whitewashed walls were in parts scrawled over with strange diagrams, and in others covered with shelves crowded with philosophical instruments, the uses of many of which were unknown to me. On one side of the fireplace, stood a bookcase filled with dingy folios; on the other, a small organ, fantastically decorated with painted carvings of mediæval saints and devils. Through the half-opened door of a cupboard at the further end of the room, I saw a long array of geological specimens, surgical preparations, crucibles, retorts, and jars of chemicals; while on the mantelshelf beside me, amid a number of small objects, stood a model of the solar system, a small galvanic battery, and a microscope. Every chair had its burden. Every corner was heaped high with books. The very floor was littered over with maps, casts, papers, tracings, and learned lumber of all conceivable kinds.

I stared about me with an amazement increased by every fresh object upon which my eyes chanced to rest. So strange a room I had never seen; yet seemed it stranger still, to find such a room in a lone farmhouse amid those wild and solitary moors! Over and over again, I looked from my host to his surroundings, and from his surroundings back to my host, asking myself who and what he could be? His head was singularly fine; but it was more the head of a poet than of a philosopher. Broad in the temples, prominent over the eyes, and clothed with a rough profusion of perfectly white hair, it had all the ideality and much of the ruggedness that characterises the head of Louis van Beethoven. There were the same deep lines about the mouth, and the same stern furrows in the brow. There was the same concentration of expression. While I was yet observing him, the door opened, and Jacob brought in the supper. His master then closed his book, rose, and with more courtesy of manner than he had yet shown, invited me to the table.

A dish of ham and eggs, a loaf of brown bread, and a bottle of admirable sherry, were placed before me.

'I have but the homeliest farmhouse fare to offer you, sir,' said my entertainer. 'Your appetite, I trust, will make up for the deficiencies of our larder.'

I had already fallen upon the viands, and now protested, with the enthusiasm of a starving sportsman, that I had never eaten anything so delicious.

He bowed stiffly, and sat down to his own supper, which consisted, primitively, of a jug of milk and a basin of porridge. We ate in silence, and, when we had done, Jacob removed the tray. I then drew my chair back to the fireside. My host, somewhat to my surprise, did the same, and turning abruptly towards me, said:

'Sir, I have lived here in strict retirement for three-and-twenty years. During that time, I have not seen as many strange faces, and I have not read a single newspaper. You are the first stranger who has crossed my threshold for more than four years. Will you favour me with a few words of information respecting that outer world from which I have parted company so long?'

'Pray interrogate me,' I replied. 'I am heartily at your service.'

He bent his head in acknowledgment; leaned forward, with his elbows resting on his knees and his chin supported in the palms of his hands; stared fixedly into the fire; and proceeded to question me.

His inquiries related chiefly to scientific matters, with the later progress of which, as applied to the practical purposes of life, he was almost wholly unacquainted. No student of science myself, I replied as well as my slight information permitted; but the task was far from easy, and I was much relieved when, passing from interrogation to discussion, he began pouring forth his own conclusions upon the facts which I had been attempting to place before him. He talked, and I listened spellbound. He talked till I believe he almost forgot my presence, and only thought aloud. I had never heard anything like it then; I have never heard anything like it since. Familiar with all systems of all philosophies, subtle in analysis, bold in generalisation, he poured forth his thoughts in an uninterrupted stream, and, still leaning forward in the same moody attitude with his eyes fixed upon the fire, wandered from topic to topic, from speculation to speculation, like an inspired dreamer. From practical science to mental philosophy; from electricity in the wire to electricity in the nerve; from Watts to Mesmer, from Mesmer to Reichenbach, from Reichenbach to Swedenborg, Spinoza,

Condillac, Descartes, Berkeley, Aristotle, Plato, and the Magi and mystics of the East, were transitions which, however bewildering in their variety and scope, seemed easy and harmonious upon his lips as sequences in music. By-and-by – I forget now by what link of conjecture or illustration – he passed on to that field which lies beyond the boundary line of even conjectural philosophy, and reaches no man knows whither. He spoke of the soul and its aspirations; of the spirit and its powers; of second sight; of prophecy; of those phenomena which, under the names of ghosts, spectres, and supernatural appearances, have been denied by the sceptics and attested by the credulous, of all ages.

'The world,' he said, 'grows hourly more and more sceptical of all that lies beyond its own narrow radius; and our men of science foster the fatal tendency. They condemn as fable all that resists experiment. They reject as false all that cannot be brought to the test of the laboratory or the dissecting-room. Against what superstition have they waged so long and obstinate a war, as against the belief in apparitions? And yet what superstition has maintained its hold upon the minds of men so long and so firmly? Show me any fact in physics, in history, in archæology, which is supported by testimony so wide and so various. Attested by all races of men, in all ages, and in all climates, by the soberest sages of antiquity, by the rudest savage of today, by the Christian, the Pagan, the Pantheist, the Materialist, this phenomenon is treated as a nursery tale by the philosophers of our century. Circumstantial evidence weighs with them as a feather in the balance. The comparison of causes with effects, however valuable in physical science, is put aside as worthless and unreliable. The evidence of competent witnesses, however conclusive in a court of justice, counts for nothing. He who pauses before he pronounces, is condemned as a trifler. He who believes, is a dreamer or a fool.'

He spoke with bitterness, and, having said thus, relapsed for some minutes into silence. Presently he raised his head from his hands, and added, with an altered voice and manner, 'I, sir, paused, investigated, believed, and was not ashamed to state my convictions to the world. I, too, was branded as a visionary, held up to ridicule by my contemporaries, and hooted from that field of science in which I had laboured with honour during all the best years of my life. These things happened just three-and-twenty years ago. Since then, I have lived as you see me living now, and the world has forgotten me, as I have forgotten the world. You have my history.'

'It is a very sad one,' I murmured, scarcely knowing what to answer.

'It is a very common one,' he replied. 'I have only suffered for the truth, as many a better and wiser man has suffered before me.'

He rose, as if desirous of ending the conversation, and went over to the window.

'It has ceased snowing,' he observed, as he dropped the curtain, and came back to the fireside.

'Ceased!' I exclaimed, starting eagerly to my feet. 'Oh, if it were only possible – but no! it is hopeless. Even if I could find my way across the moor, I could not walk twenty miles tonight.'

'Walk twenty miles tonight!' repeated my host. 'What are you thinking of?'

'Of my wife,' I replied, impatiently. 'Of my young wife, who does not know that I have lost my way, and who is at this moment breaking her heart with suspense and terror.'

'Where is she?'

'At Dwolding, twenty miles away.'

'At Dwolding,' he echoed, thoughtfully. 'Yes, the distance, it is true, is twenty miles; but – are you so very anxious to save the next six or eight hours?'

'So very, very anxious, that I would give ten guineas at this moment for a guide and a horse.'

'Your wish can be gratified at a less costly rate,' said he, smiling. 'The night mail from the north, which changes horses at Dwolding, passes within five miles of this spot, and will be due at a certain cross-road in about an hour and a quarter. If Jacob were to go with you across the moor, and put you into the old coach-road, you could find your way, I suppose, to where it joins the new one?'

'Easily – gladly.'

He smiled again, rang the bell, gave the old servant his directions, and, taking a bottle of whisky and a wineglass from the cupboard in which he kept his chemicals, said:

'The snow lies deep, and it will be difficult walking tonight on the moor. A glass of usquebaugh before you start?'

I would have declined the spirit, but he pressed it on me, and I drank it. It went down my throat like liquid flame, and almost took my breath away.

'It is strong,' he said; 'but it will help to keep out the cold. And now you have no moments to spare. Good night!'

I thanked him for his hospitality, and would have shaken hands, but that he had turned away before I could finish my sentence. In another minute I had traversed the hall, Jacob had locked the outer door behind me, and we were out on the wide white moor.

Although the wind had fallen, it was still bitterly cold. Not a star glimmered in the black vault overhead. Not a sound, save the rapid crunching of the snow beneath our feet, disturbed the heavy stillness of the night. Jacob, not too well pleased with his mission, shambled on before in sullen silence, his lantern in his hand, and his shadow at his feet. I followed, with my gun over my shoulder, as little inclined for conversation as himself. My thoughts were full of my late host. His voice yet rang in my ears. His eloquence yet held my imagination captive. I remember to this day, with surprise, how my over-excited brain retained whole sentences and parts of sentences, troops of brilliant images, and fragments of splendid reasoning, in the very words in which he had uttered them. Musing thus over what I had heard, and striving to recall a lost link here and there, I strode on at the heels of my guide, absorbed and unobservant. Presently – at the end, as it seemed to me, of only a few minutes – he came to a sudden halt, and said:

'Yon's your road. Keep the stone fence to your right hand, and you can't fail of the way.'

'This, then, is the old coach-road?'

'Ay, 'tis the old coach-road.'

'And how far do I go, before I reach the cross-roads?'

'Nigh upon three mile.'

I pulled out my purse, and he became more communicative.

'The road's a fair road enough,' said he, 'for foot passengers; but 'twas over steep and narrow for the northern traffic. You'll mind where the parapet's broken away, close again the signpost. It's never been mended since the accident.'

'What accident?'

'Eh, the night mail pitched right over into the valley below – a gude fifty feet an' more – just at the worst bit o' road in the whole county.'

'Horrible! Were many lives lost?'

'All. Four were found dead, and t'other two died next morning.'

'How long is it since this happened?'

'Just nine year.'

'Near the signpost, you say? I will bear it in mind. Good night.'

'Gude night, sir, and thankee.' Jacob pocketed his half-crown, made a faint pretence of touching his hat, and trudged back by the way he had come.

I watched the light of his lantern till it quite disappeared, and then turned to pursue my way alone. This was no longer matter of the slightest difficulty, for, despite the dead darkness overhead, the line of stone fence showed distinctly enough against the pale gleam of the snow. How silent it seemed now, with only my footsteps to listen to; how silent and how solitary! A strange disagreeable sense of loneliness stole over me. I walked faster. I hummed a fragment of a tune. I cast up enormous sums in my head, and accumulated them at compound interest. I did my best, in short, to forget the startling speculations to which I had but just been listening, and, to some extent, I succeeded.

Meanwhile the night air seemed to become colder and colder, and though I walked fast I found it impossible to keep myself warm. My feet were like ice. I lost sensation in my hands, and grasped my gun mechanically. I even breathed with difficulty, as though, instead of traversing a quiet north country highway, I were scaling the uppermost heights of some gigantic Alp. This last symptom became presently so distressing, that I was forced to stop for a few minutes, and lean against the stone fence. As I did so, I chanced to look back up the road, and there, to my infinite relief, I saw a distant point of light, like the gleam of an approaching lantern. I at first concluded that Jacob had retraced his steps and followed me; but even as the conjecture presented itself, a second light flashed into sight – a light evidently parallel with the first, and approaching at the same rate of motion. It needed no second thought to show me that these must be the carriage-lamps of some private vehicle, though it seemed strange that any private vehicle should take a road professedly disused and dangerous.

There could be no doubt, however, of the fact, for the lamps grew larger and brighter every moment, and I even fancied I could already see the dark outline of the carriage between them. It was coming up very fast, and quite noiselessly, the snow being nearly a foot deep under the wheels.

And now the body of the vehicle became distinctly visible behind the lamps. It looked strangely lofty. A sudden suspicion flashed upon me. Was it possible that I had passed the cross-roads in the dark without observing the signpost, and could this be the very coach which I had come to meet?

No need to ask myself that question a second time, for here it came round the bend of the road, guard and driver, one outside passenger, and four steaming greys, all wrapped in a soft haze of light, through which the lamps blazed out, like a pair of fiery meteors.

I jumped forward, waved my hat, and shouted. The mail came down at full speed, and passed me. For a moment I feared that I had not been seen or heard, but it was only for a moment. The coachman pulled up; the guard, muffled to the eyes in capes and comforters, and apparently sound asleep in the rumble, neither answered my hail nor made the slightest effort to dismount; the outside passenger did not even turn his head. I opened the door for myself, and looked in. There were but three travellers inside, so I stepped in, shut the door, slipped into the vacant corner, and congratulated myself on my good fortune.

The atmosphere of the coach seemed, if possible, colder than that of the outer air, and was pervaded by a singularly damp and disagreeable smell. I looked round at my fellow-passengers. They were all three, men, and all silent. They did not seem to be asleep, but each leaned back in his corner of the vehicle, as if absorbed in his own reflections. I attempted to open a conversation.

'How intensely cold it is tonight,' I said, addressing my opposite neighbour.

He lifted his head, looked at me, but made no reply.

'The winter,' I added, 'seems to have begun in earnest.'

Although the corner in which he sat was so dim that I could distinguish none of his features very clearly, I saw that his eyes were still turned full upon me. And yet he answered never a word.

At any other time I should have felt, and perhaps expressed, some annoyance, but at the moment I felt too ill to do either. The icy coldness of the night air had struck a chill to my very marrow, and the strange smell inside the coach was affecting me with an intolerable nausea. I shivered from head to foot, and, turning to my left-hand neighbour, asked if he had any objection to an open window?

He neither spoke nor stirred.

I repeated the question somewhat more loudly, but with the same result. Then I lost patience, and let the sash down. As I did so, the leather strap broke in my hand, and I observed that the glass was covered with a thick coat of mildew, the accumulation, apparently, of years. My attention being thus drawn to the condition of the coach, I examined it more narrowly, and saw by the uncertain light of the outer lamps that it was in the last stage of dilapidation. Every part of it was not only out of repair, but in a condition of decay. The sashes splintered at a touch. The leather fittings were crusted over with mould, and literally rotting from the woodwork. The floor was almost breaking away beneath my feet. The whole machine, in short, was foul with damp, and had evidently been dragged from some outhouse in which it had been mouldering away for years, to do another day or two of duty on the road.

I turned to the third passenger, whom I had not yet addressed, and hazarded one more remark.

'This coach,' I said, 'is in a deplorable condition. The regular mail, I suppose, is under repair?'

He moved his head slowly, and looked me in the face, without speaking a word. I shall never forget that look while I live. I turned cold at heart under it. I turn cold at heart even now when I recall it. His eyes glowed with a fiery unnatural lustre. His face was livid as the face of a corpse. His bloodless lips were drawn back as if in the agony of death, and showed the gleaming teeth between.

The words that I was about to utter died upon my lips, and a strange horror – a dreadful horror – came upon me. My sight had by this time become used to the gloom of the coach, and I could see with tolerable distinctness. I turned to my opposite neighbour. He, too, was looking at me, with the same startling pallor in his face, and the same stony glitter in his eyes. I passed my hand across my brow. I turned to the passenger on the seat beside my own, and saw – oh Heaven! how shall I describe what I saw? I saw that he was no living man – that none of them were living men, like myself! A pale phosphorescent light – the light of putrefaction

– played upon their awful faces; upon their hair, dank with the dews of the grave; upon their clothes, earth-stained and dropping to pieces; upon their hands, which were as the hands of corpses long buried. Only their eyes, their terrible eyes, were living; and those eyes were all turned menacingly upon me!

A shriek of terror, a wild unintelligible cry for help and mercy, burst from my lips as I flung myself against the door, and strove in vain to open it.

In that single instant, brief and vivid as a landscape beheld in the flash of summer lightning, I saw the moon shining down through a rift of stormy cloud – the ghastly signpost rearing its warning finger by the wayside – the broken parapet – the plunging horses – the black gulf below. Then, the coach reeled like a ship at sea. Then, came a mighty crash – a sense of crushing pain – and then, darkness.

It seemed as if years had gone by when I awoke one morning from a deep sleep, and found my wife watching by my bedside. I will pass over the scene that ensued, and give you, in half a dozen words, the tale she told me with tears of thanksgiving. I had fallen over a precipice, close against the junction of the old coach-road and the new, and had only been saved from certain death by lighting upon a deep snowdrift that had accumulated at the foot of the rock beneath. In this snowdrift I was discovered at daybreak, by a couple of shepherds, who carried me to the nearest shelter, and brought a surgeon to my aid. The surgeon found me in a state of raving delirium, with a broken arm and a compound fracture of the skull. The letters in my pocket-book showed my name and address; my wife was summoned to nurse me; and, thanks to youth and a fine constitution, I came out of danger at last. The place of my fall, I need scarcely say, was precisely that at which a frightful accident had happened to the north mail nine years before.

I never told my wife the fearful events which I have just related to you. I told the surgeon who attended me; but he treated the whole adventure as a mere dream born of the fever in my brain. We discussed the question over and over again, until we found that we could discuss it with temper no longer, and then we dropped it. Others may form what conclusions they please – I know that twenty years ago I was the fourth inside passenger in that Phantom Coach.

The Red Room

H. G. Wells

'I can assure you,' said I, 'that it will take a very tangible ghost to frighten me.' And I stood up before the fire with my glass in my hand.

'It is your own choosing,' said the man with the withered arm, and glanced at me askance.

'Eight-and-twenty years,' said I, 'I have lived, and never a ghost have I seen as yet.'

The old woman sat staring hard into the fire, her pale ayes wide open. 'Ay,' she broke in; 'and eight-and-twenty years you have lived and never seen the likes of this house, I reckon. There's a many things to see, when one's still but eight-and-twenty.' She swayed her head slowly from side to side. 'A many things to see and sorrow for.'

I half suspected the old people were trying to enhance the spiritual terrors of their house by their droning insistence. I put down my empty glass on the table and looked about the room, and caught a glimpse of myself, abbreviated and broadened to an impossible sturdiness, in the queer old mirror at the end of the room. 'Well,' I said, 'if I see anything tonight, I shall be so much the wiser. For I come to the business with an open mind.'

'It's your own choosing,' said the man, with the withered arm, once more.

I heard the sound of a stick and a shambling step on the flags in the passage outside, and the door creaked on its hinges as a second old man entered, more bent, more wrinkled, more aged even than the first. He supported himself by a single crutch, his eyes were covered by a shade, and his lower lip, half averted, hung pale and pink from his decaying yellow teeth. He made straight for an armchair on the opposite side of the table, sat down clumsily, and began to cough. The man with the withered arm gave this newcomer a short glance of positive dislike; the old woman took no notice of his arrival, but remained with her eyes fixed steadily on the fire.

'I said – it's your own choosing,' said the man with the withered arm, when the coughing had ceased for a while.

'It's my own choosing,' I answered.

The man with the shade became aware of my presence for the first time, and threw his head back for a moment and sideways, to see me. I caught a momentary glimpse of his eyes, small and bright and inflamed. Then he began to cough and splutter again.

'Why don't you drink?' said the man with the withered arm, pushing the beer towards him. The man with the shade, poured out a glassful with a shaky arm that splashed half as much again on the deal table. A monstrous shadow of him crouched upon the wall and mocked his action as he poured and drank. I must confess I had scarce expected these grotesque custodians. There is to my mind something inhuman in senility, something crouching and atavistic; the human qualities seem to drop from old people insensibly day by day. The three of them made me feel uncomfortable, with their gaunt silences, their bent carriage, their evident unfriendliness to me and to one another.

'If,' said I, 'you will show me to this haunted room of yours, I will make myself comfortable there.'

The old man with the cough jerked his head back so suddenly that it startled me, and shot another glance of his red eyes at me from under the shade; but no one answered me. I waited a minute, glancing from one to the other.

'If,' I said a little louder, 'if you will show me to this haunted room of yours, I will relieve you from the task of entertaining me.'

'There's a candle on the slab outside the door,' said the man with the withered arm, looking at my feet as he addressed me. 'But if you go to the red room tonight—'

('This night of all nights!' said the old woman.)

'You go alone.'

'Very well,' I answered. 'And which way do I go?'

'You go along the passage for a bit,' said he, 'until you come to a door, and through that is a spiral staircase, and halfway up that is a landing and another door covered with baize. Go through that and down the long corridor to the end, and the red room is on your left up the steps.'

'Have I got that right?' I said, and repeated his directions. He corrected me in one particular.

'And are you really going?' said the man with the shade, looking at me again for the third time, with that queer, unnatural tilting of the face.

('This night of all nights!' said the old woman.)

'It is what I came for,' I said, and moved towards the door. As I did so, the old man with the shade rose and staggered round the table, so as to be closer to the others and to the fire. At the door I turned and looked at them, and saw they were all close together, dark against the firelight, staring at me over their shoulders, with an intent expression on their ancient faces.

'Good-night,' I said, setting the door open.

'It's your own choosing,' said the man with the withered arm.

I left the door wide open until the candle was well alight, and then I shut them in and walked down the chilly, echoing passage.

I must confess that the oddness of these three old pensioners in whose charge her ladyship had left the castle, and the deep-toned, old-fashioned furniture of the housekeeper's room in which they foregathered, affected me in spite of my efforts to keep myself at a matter-of-fact phase. They seemed to belong to another age, an older age, an age when things spiritual were different from this of ours, less certain; an age when omens and witches were credible, and ghosts beyond denying. Their very existence was spectral; the cut of their clothing, fashions born in dead brains. The ornaments and conveniences of the room about them were ghostly – the thoughts of vanished men, which still haunted, rather than participated in the world of today. But with an effort I sent such thoughts to the right-about. The long, draughty subterranean passage was chilly and dusty, and my candle flared and made the shadows cower and quiver. The echoes rang up and down the spiral staircase, and a shadow came sweeping up after me, and one fled before me into the darkness overhead. I came to the landing and stopped there for a moment, listening to a rustling that I fancied I heard;

then, satisfied of the absolute silence, I pushed open the baize-covered door and stood in the corridor.

The effect was scarcely what I expected, for the moonlight, coming in by the great window on the grand staircase, picked out everything in vivid black shadow or silvery illumination. Everything was in its place: the house might have been deserted on the yesterday instead of eighteen months ago. There were candles in the sockets of the sconces, and whatever dust had gathered on the carpets or upon the polished flooring was distributed so evenly as to be invisible in the moonlight. I was about to advance, and stopped abruptly. A bronze group stood upon the landing, hidden from me by the corner of the wall, but its shadow fell with marvellous distinctness upon the white panelling, and gave me the impression of someone crouching to waylay me. I stood rigid for half a minute perhaps. Then, with my hand in the pocket that held my revolver, I advanced, only to discover a Ganymede and Eagle glistening in the moonlight. That incident for at time restored my nerve, and a porcelain Chinaman on a buhl table, whose head rocked silently as I passed him, scarcely startled me.

The door to the red room and the steps up to it were in a shadowy corner. I moved my candle from side to side, in order to see clearly the nature of the recess in which I stood before opening the door. Here it was, thought I, that my predecessor was found, and the memory of that story gave me a sudden twinge of apprehension. I glanced over my shoulder at the Ganymede in the moonlight, and opened the door of the red room rather hastily, with my face half turned to the pallid silence of the landing.

I entered, closed the door behind me at once, turned the key I found in the lock within, and stood with the candle held aloft, surveying the scene of my vigil, the great red room of Lorraine Castle, in which the young duke had died. Or rather, in which he had begun his dying, for he had opened the door and fallen headlong down the steps I had just ascended. That had been the end of his vigil, of his gallant attempt to conquer the ghostly tradition of the place; and never, I thought, had apoplexy better served the ends of superstition. And there were other and older stories that clung to the room, back to the half-credible beginning of it all, the tale of a timid wife and the tragic end that came to her husband's jest of frightening her. And looking around that large shadowy room, with its shadowy window bays, its recesses and alcoves, one could well understand the legends that had sprouted in its black corners, its germinating darkness. My candle was a little tongue of flame in its vastness, that failed to pierce the opposite end of the room, and left an ocean of mystery and suggestion beyond its island of light.

I resolved to make a systematic examination of the place at once, and dispel the fanciful suggestions of its obscurity before they obtained a hold upon me. After satisfying myself of the fastening of the door, I began to walk about the room, peering round each article of furniture, tucking up the valances of the bed, and opening its curtains wide. I pulled up the blinds and examined the fastenings of the several windows before closing the shutters, leant forward and looked up the blackness of the wide chimney, and tapped the dark oak panelling for any secret opening. There were two big mirrors in the room, each with a pair of sconces bearing candles, and on the mantelshelf too, were more candles in china candlesticks. All these I lit one after the other. The fire was laid – an unexpected consideration from the old housekeeper – and I lit it, to keep down any disposition to shiver, and when it was burning well, I stood round with my back to it and regarded the room again. I had pulled up a chintz-covered armchair and a table, to form a kind of barricade before me, and on this lay my revolver ready to hand. My precise examination had done me good, but I still found the remoter darkness of the place, and its perfect stillness, too stimulating for the imagination. The echoing of the stir and crackling of the fire was no sort of comfort to me. The shadow in the alcove at the end in particular had that undefinable quality of a presence, that odd suggestion of a lurking, living thing, that comes so easily in silence and solitude. At last, to reassure myself, I walked with a candle into it, and satisfied myself that there was nothing tangible there. I stood that candle upon the floor of the alcove, and left it in that position.

By this time I was in a state of considerable nervous tension, although to my reason there was no adequate cause for the condition. My mind, however, was perfectly clear. I postulated quite unreservedly that nothing supernatural could happen, and to pass the time I began to string some rhymes together, Ingoldsby fashion, of the original legend of the place. A few I spoke aloud, but the echoes were not pleasant. For the same reason I also abandoned, after a time, a conversation with myself upon the impossibility of ghosts and haunting. My mind reverted to the three old and distorted people downstairs, and I tried to keep it upon that topic. The sombre reds and blacks of the room troubled me; even with seven candles the place was merely dim. The one in the alcove flared in a draught, and the fire-flickering kept the shadows and penumbra perpetually shifting and stirring. Casting about for a remedy, I recalled the candles I had seen in the passage, and, with a slight effort, walked out into the moonlight, carrying a candle and leaving the door open, and presently returned with as many as ten. These I put in various knick-knacks of china with which the room was sparsely adorned, lit and placed where the shadows had lain deepest, some on the floor, some in the window recesses, until at last my seventeen candles were so arranged that not an inch of the room darkened, but had the direct light of at least one of them. It occurred to me that when the ghost came, I could warn him not to trip over them. The room was now quite brightly illuminated. There was something very cheery and reassuring in these little streaming flames, and snuffing them gave me an occupation, and afforded a helpful sense of the passage of time. Even with that however, the brooding expectation of the vigil weighed heavily upon me. It was after midnight that the candle in the alcove suddenly went out, and the black shadow sprang back to its place. I did not see the candle go out; I simply turned and saw that the darkness was there, as one might start and see the unexpected presence of a stranger. 'By Jove!' said I aloud; 'That draught's a strong one!' and taking the matches from the table, I walked across the room in a leisurely manner to relight the corner again. My first match would not strike, and as I succeeded with the second, something seemed to blink on the wall before me. I turned my head involuntarily, and saw that the two candles on the little table by the fireplace were extinguished. I rose at once to my feet.

'Odd!' I said. 'Did I do that myself in a flash of absent-mindedness?'

I walked back, relit one, and as I did so, I saw the candle in the right sconce of one of the mirrors wink and go right out, and almost immediately its companion followed it. There was no mistake about it. The flame vanished, as if the wicks had been suddenly nipped between a finger and thumb, leaving the wick neither glowing nor smoking, but black. While I stood gaping, the candle at the foot of the bed went out, and the shadows seemed to take another step towards me.

'This won't do!' said I, and first one and then another candle on the mantelshelf followed. 'What's up?' I cried, with a queer high note getting into my voice somehow. At that the candle on the wardrobe went out, and the one I had relit in the alcove followed.

'Steady on!' I said. 'These candles are wanted,' speaking with a half-hysterical facetiousness, and scratching away at a match, all the while, for the mantel candlesticks. My hands trembled so much that twice I missed the rough paper of the matchbox. As the mantel emerged from darkness again, two candles in the remoter end of the window were eclipsed. But with the same match I also relit the larger mirror candles, and those on the floor near the doorway, so that for the moment I seemed to gain on the extinctions. But then in a volley there vanished four lights at once in different corners of the room, and I struck another match in quivering haste, and stood hesitating whither to take it.

As I stood undecided, an invisible hand seemed to sweep out the two candles on the table. With a cry of terror, I dashed at the alcove, then into the corner, and then into the window, relighting three, as two more vanished by the fireplace; then, perceiving a better way, I dropped the matches on the iron-bound deed-box in the corner, and caught up the bedroom candlestick. With this I avoided the delay of striking matches; but for all that the steady process of extinction went on, and the shadows I feared and fought against returned, and crept in upon me, first a step gained on this side of me and then on that. It was like a ragged storm-cloud sweeping out of the stars. Now and then one returned for a minute, and was lost again. I was now almost frantic with the horror of the coming darkness, and my self-possession deserted me. I leaped panting and dishevelled from candle to candle in a vain struggle against that remorseless advance.

I bruised myself on the thigh against the table, I sent a chair headlong, I stumbled and fell and whisked the cloth from the table in my fall. My candle rolled away from me, and I snatched another as I rose. Abruptly this was blown out, as I swung it off the table, by the wind of my sudden movement, and immediately the two remaining candles followed. But there was light still in the room, a red light that stayed off the shadows from me. The fire! Of course I could still thrust my candle between the bars and relight it!

I turned to where the flames were still dancing between the glowing coals, and splashing red reflections upon the furniture, made two steps towards the grate, and incontinently the flames dwindled and vanished, the glow vanished, the reflections rushed together and vanished, and as I thrust the candle between the bars darkness closed upon me like the shutting of an eye, wrapped about me in a stifling embrace, sealed my vision, and crushed the last vestiges of reason from my brain. The candle fell from my hand. I flung out my arms in a vain effort to thrust that ponderous blackness away from me, and, lifting up my voice, screamed with all my might – once, twice, thrice. Then I think I must have staggered to my feet. I know I thought suddenly of the moonlit corridor and, with my head bowed and my arms over my face, made a run for the door.

But I had forgotten the exact position of the door, and struck myself heavily against the corner of the bed. I staggered back, turned, and was either struck or struck myself against some other bulky furniture. I have a vague memory of battering myself thus, to and fro in the darkness, of a cramped struggle, and of my own wild crying as I darted to and fro, of a heavy blow at last upon my forehead, a horrible sensation of falling that lasted an age, of my last frantic effort to keep my footing, and then I remember no more.

I opened my eyes in daylight. My head was roughly bandaged, and the man with the withered arm was watching my face. I looked about me, trying to remember what had happened, and for a space I could not recollect. I turned to the corner, and saw the old woman, no longer abstracted, pouring out some drops of medicine from a little blue phial into a glass. 'Where am I?' I asked; 'I seem to remember you, and yet I cannot remember who you are.'

They told me then, and I heard of the haunted red room as one who hears a tale. 'We found you at dawn,' said he, 'and there was blood on your forehead and lips.'

It was very slowly I recovered my memory of my experience. 'You believe now,' said the old man, 'that the room is haunted?' He spoke no longer as one who greets an intruder, but as one who grieves for a broken friend.

'Yes,' said I, 'the room is haunted.'

'And you have seen it. And we, who have lived here all our lives, have never set eyes upon it. Because we have never dared… Tell us, is it truly the old earl who —'

'No,' said I, 'it is not.'

'I told you so,' said the old lady, with the glass in her hand. 'It is his poor young countess who was frightened—'

'It is not,' I said. 'There is neither ghost of earl nor ghost of countess in that room, there is no ghost there at all; but worse, far worse—'

'Well?' they said.

'The worst of all the things that haunt poor mortal man,' said I; 'and that is, in all its nakedness — Fear! Fear that will not have light nor sound, that will not bear with reason, that deafens and darkens and overwhelms. It followed me through the corridor, it fought against me in the room—'

I stopped abruptly. There was an interval of silence. My hand went up to my bandages.

Then the man with the shade sighed and spoke. 'That is it,' said he. 'I knew that was it. A power of darkness. To put such a curse upon a woman! It lurks there always. You can feel it even in the daytime, even of a bright summer's day, in the hangings, in the curtains, keeping behind you however you face about. In the dusk it creeps along the corridor and follows you, so that you dare not turn. There is Fear in that room of hers – black Fear, and there will be – so long as this house of sin endures.'

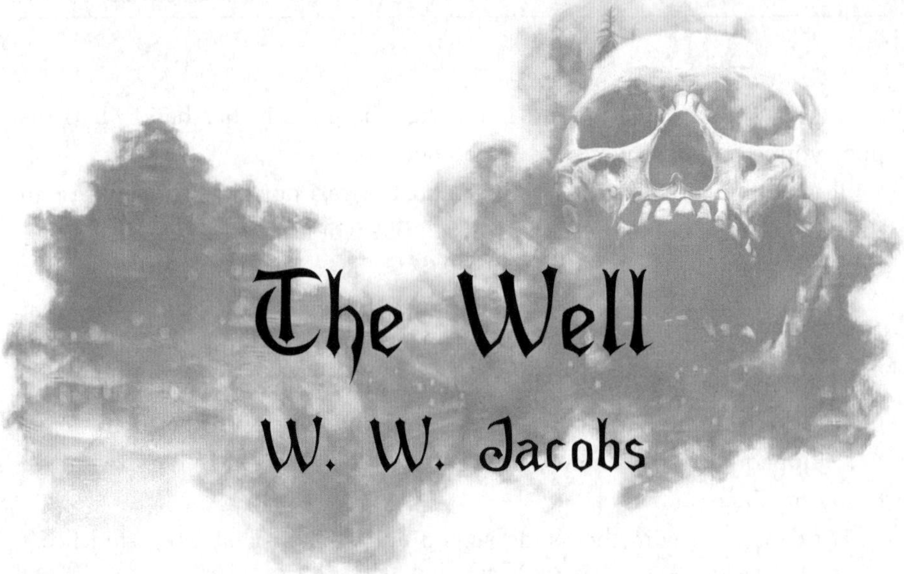

The Well

W. W. Jacobs

Two men stood in the billiard-room of an old country house, talking. Play, which had been of a half-hearted nature, was over, and they sat at the open window, looking out over the park stretching away beneath them, conversing idly.

'Your time's nearly up, Jem,' said one at length, 'this time six weeks you'll be yawning out the honeymoon and cursing the man – woman I mean – who invented them.'

Jem Benson stretched his long limbs in the chair and grunted in dissent.

'I've never understood it,' continued Wilfred Carr, yawning. 'It's not in my line at all; I never had enough money for my own wants, let alone for two. Perhaps if I were as rich as you or Croesus I might regard it differently.'

There was just sufficient meaning in the latter part of the remark for his cousin to forbear to reply to it. He continued to gaze out of the window and to smoke slowly.

'Not being as rich as Croesus – or you,' resumed Carr, regarding him from beneath lowered lids, 'I paddle my own canoe down the stream of Time, and, tying it to my friends' door-posts, go in to eat their dinners.'

'Quite Venetian,' said Jem Benson, still looking out of the window. 'It's not a bad thing for you, Wilfred, that you have the doorposts and dinners – and friends.'

Carr grunted in his turn. 'Seriously though, Jem,' he said, slowly, 'you're a lucky fellow, a very lucky fellow. If there is a better girl above ground than Olive, I should like to see her.'

'Yes,' said the other, quietly.

'She's such an exceptional girl,' continued Carr, staring out of the window. 'She's so good and gentle. She thinks you are a bundle of all the virtues.'

He laughed frankly and joyously, but the other man did not join him. 'Strong sense – of right and wrong, though,' continued Carr, musingly. 'Do you know, I believe that if she found out that you were not—'

'Not what?' demanded Benson, turning upon him fiercely, 'Not what?'

'Everything that you are,' returned his cousin, with a grin that belied his words, 'I believe she'd drop you.'

'Talk about something else,' said Benson, slowly; 'your pleasantries are not always in the best taste.'

Wilfred Carr rose and taking a cue from the rack, bent over the board and practiced one or two favourite shots. 'The only other subject I can talk about just at present is my own financial affairs,' he said slowly, as he walked round the table.

'Talk about something else,' said Benson again, bluntly.

'And the two things are connected,' said Carr, and dropping his cue he half sat on the table and eyed his cousin.

There was a long silence. Benson pitched the end of his cigar out of the window, and leaning back closed his eyes.

'Do you follow me?' inquired Carr at length.

Benson opened his eyes and nodded at the window.

'Do you want to follow my cigar?' he demanded.

'I should prefer to depart by the usual way for your sake,' returned the other, unabashed. 'If I left by the window all sorts of questions would be asked, and you know what a talkative chap I am.'

'So long as you don't talk about my affairs,' returned the other, restraining himself by an obvious effort, 'you can talk yourself hoarse.'

'I'm in a mess,' said Carr, slowly, 'a devil of a mess. If I don't raise fifteen hundred by this day fortnight, I may be getting my board and lodging free.'

'Would that be any change?' questioned Benson.

'The quality would,' retorted the other. 'The address also would not be good. Seriously, Jem, will you let me have the fifteen hundred?'

'No,' said the other, simply.

Carr went white. 'It's to save me from ruin,' he said, thickly.

'I've helped you till I'm tired,' said Benson, turning and regarding him, 'and it is all to no good. If you've got into a mess, get out of it. You should not be so fond of giving autographs away.'

'It's foolish, I admit,' said Carr, deliberately. 'I won't do so any more. By the way, I've got some to sell. You needn't sneer. They're not my own.'

'Whose are they?' inquired the other.

'Yours.'

Benson got up from his chair and crossed over to him. 'What is this?' he asked, quietly. 'Blackmail?'

'Call it what you like,' said Carr. 'I've got some letters for sale, price fifteen hundred. And I know a man who would buy them at that price for the mere chance of getting Olive from you. I'll give you first offer.'

'If you have got any letters bearing my signature, you will be good enough to give them to me,' said Benson, very slowly.

'They're mine,' said Carr, lightly; 'given to me by the lady you wrote them to. I must say that they are not all in the best possible taste.'

His cousin reached forward suddenly, and catching him by the collar of his coat pinned him down on the table.

'Give me those letters,' he breathed, sticking his face close to Carr's.

'They're not here,' said Carr, struggling. 'I'm not a fool. Let me go, or I'll raise the price.'

The other man raised him from the table in his powerful hands, apparently with the intention of dashing his head against it. Then suddenly his hold relaxed as an astonished-looking maid-servant entered the room with letters. Carr sat up hastily.

'That's how it was done,' said Benson, for the girl's benefit as he took the letters.

'I don't wonder at the other man making him pay for it, then,' said Carr, blandly.

'You will give me those letters?' said Benson, suggestively, as the girl left the room.

'At the price I mentioned, yes,' said Carr; 'but so sure as I am a living man, if you lay your clumsy hands on me again, I'll double it. Now, I'll leave you for a time while you think it over.'

He took a cigar from the box and lighting it carefully quitted the room. His cousin waited until the door had closed behind him, and then turning to the window sat there in a fit of fury as silent as it was terrible.

The air was fresh and sweet from the park, heavy with the scent of new-mown grass. The fragrance of a cigar was now added to it, and glancing out he saw his cousin pacing slowly by. He rose and went to the door, and then, apparently altering his mind, he returned to the window and watched the figure of his cousin as it moved slowly away into the moonlight. Then he rose again, and, for a long time, the room was empty.

†

It was empty when Mrs Benson came in some time later to say good-night to her son on her way to bed. She walked slowly round the table, and pausing at the window gazed from it in idle thought, until she saw the figure of her son advancing with rapid strides toward the house. He looked up at the window.

'Good-night,' said she.

'Good-night,' said Benson, in a deep voice.

'Where is Wilfred?'

'Oh, he has gone,' said Benson.

'Gone?'

'We had a few words; he was wanting money again, and I gave him a piece of my mind. I don't think we shall see him again.'

'Poor Wilfred!' sighed Mrs Benson. 'He is always in trouble of some sort. I hope that you were not too hard upon him.'

'No more than he deserved,' said her son, sternly. 'Good-night.'

II.

The well, which had long ago fallen into disuse, was almost hidden by the thick tangle of undergrowth which ran riot at that corner of the old park. It was partly covered by the shrunken half of a lid, above which a rusty windlass creaked in company with the music of the pines when the wind blew strongly. The full light of the sun never reached it, and the ground surrounding it was moist and green when other parts of the park were gaping with the heat.

Two people walking slowly round the park in the fragrant stillness of a summer evening strayed in the direction of the well.

'No use going through this wilderness, Olive,' said Benson, pausing on the outskirts of the pines and eyeing with some disfavour the gloom beyond.

'Best part of the park,' said the girl briskly; 'you know it's my favourite spot.'

'I know you're very fond of sitting on the coping,' said the man slowly, 'and I wish you wouldn't. One day you will lean back too far and fall in.'

'And make the acquaintance of Truth,' said Olive lightly. 'Come along.'

She ran from him and was lost in the shadow of the pines, the bracken crackling beneath her feet as she ran. Her companion followed slowly, and emerging from the gloom saw her poised daintily on the edge of the well with her feet hidden in the rank grass and nettles which surrounded it. She motioned her companion to take a seat by her side, and smiled softly as she felt a strong arm passed about her waist.

'I like this place,' said she, breaking a long silence, 'it is so dismal – so uncanny. Do you know I wouldn't dare to sit here alone, Jem. I should imagine that all sorts of dreadful things were hidden behind the bushes and trees, waiting to spring out on me. Ugh!'

'You'd better let me take you in,' said her companion tenderly; 'the well isn't always wholesome, especially in the hot weather.

'Let's make a move.'

The girl gave an obstinate little shake, and settled herself more securely on her seat.

'Smoke your cigar in peace,' she said quietly. 'I am settled here for a quiet talk. Has anything been heard of Wilfred yet?'

'Nothing.'

'Quite a dramatic disappearance, isn't it?' she continued. 'Another scrape, I suppose, and another letter for you in the same old strain; 'Dear Jem, help me out."

Jem Benson blew a cloud of fragrant smoke into the air, and holding his cigar between his teeth brushed away the ash from his coat sleeves.

'I wonder what he would have done without you,' said the girl, pressing his arm affectionately. 'Gone under long ago, I suppose. When we are married, Jem, I shall presume upon the relationship to lecture him. He is very wild, but he has his good points, poor fellow.'

'I never saw them,' said Benson, with startling bitterness. 'God knows I never saw them.'

'He is nobody's enemy but his own,' said the girl, startled by this outburst.

'You don't know much about him,' said the other, sharply. 'He was not above blackmail; not above ruining the life of a friend to do himself a benefit. A loafer, a cur, and a liar!'

The girl looked up at him soberly but timidly and took his arm without a word, and they both sat silent while evening deepened into night and the beams of the moon, filtering through the branches, surrounded them with a silver network. Her head sank upon his shoulder, till suddenly with a sharp cry she sprang to her feet.

'What was that?' she cried breathlessly.

'What was what?' demanded Benson, springing up and clutching her fast by the arm.

She caught her breath and tried to laugh.

'You're hurting me, Jem.'

His hold relaxed.

'What is the matter?' he asked gently. 'What was it startled you?'

'I was startled,' she said, slowly, putting her hands on his shoulder. 'I suppose the words I used just now are ringing in my ears, but I fancied that somebody behind us whispered 'Jem, help me out.''

'Fancy,' repeated Benson, and his voice shook; 'but these fancies are not good for you. You—are frightened—at the dark and the gloom of these trees. Let me take you back to the house.'

'No, I'm not frightened,' said the girl, reseating herself. 'I should never be really frightened of anything when you were with me, Jem. I'm surprised at myself for being so silly.'

The man made no reply but stood, a strong, dark figure, a yard or two from the well, as though waiting for her to join him.

'Come and sit down, sir,' cried Olive, patting the brickwork with her small, white hand, 'one would think that you did not like your company.'

He obeyed slowly and took a seat by her side, drawing so hard at his cigar that the light of it shone upon his fare at every breath. He passed his arm, firm and rigid as steel, behind her, with his hand resting on the brickwork beyond.

'Are you warm enough?' he asked tenderly, as she made a little movement. 'Pretty fair,' she shivered; 'one oughtn't to be cold at this time of the year, but there's a cold, damp air comes up from the well.'

As she spoke a faint splash sounded from the depths below, and for the second time that evening, she sprang from the well with a little cry of dismay.

'What is it now?' he asked in a fearful voice. He stood by her side and gazed at the well, as though half expecting to see the cause of her alarm emerge from it.

'Oh, my bracelet,' she cried in distress, 'my poor mother's bracelet. I've dropped it down the well.'

'Your bracelet!' repeated Benson, dully. 'Your bracelet? The diamond one?'

'The one that was my mother's,' said Olive. 'Oh, we can get it back surely. We must have the water drained off.'

'Your bracelet!' repeated Benson, stupidly.

'Jem,' said the girl in terrified tones, 'dear Jem, what is the matter?'

For the man she loved was standing regarding her with horror. The moon which touched it was not responsible for all the whiteness of the distorted face, and she shrank back in fear to the edge of the well. He saw her fear and by a mighty effort regained his composure and took her hand.

'Poor little girl,' he murmured, 'you frightened me. I was not looking when you cried, and I thought that you were slipping from my arms, down – down—'

His voice broke, and the girl throwing herself into his arms clung to him convulsively.

'There, there,' said Benson, fondly, 'don't cry, don't cry.'

'Tomorrow,' said Olive, half-laughing, half-crying, 'we will all come round the well with hook and line and fish for it. It will be quite a new sport.'

'No, we must try some other way,' said Benson. 'You shall have it back.'

'How?' asked the girl.

'You shall see,' said Benson. 'Tomorrow morning at latest you shall have it back. Till then promise me that you will not mention your loss to anyone. Promise.'

'I promise,' said Olive, wonderingly. 'But why not?'

'It is of great value, for one thing, and – but there – there are many reasons. For one thing it is my duty to get it for you.'

'Wouldn't you like to jump down for it?' she asked mischievously. 'Listen.'

She stooped for a stone and dropped it down.

'Fancy being where that is now,' she said, peering into the blackness; 'fancy going round and round like a mouse in a pail, clutching at the slimy sides, with the water filling your mouth, and looking up to the little patch of sky above.'

'You had better come in,' said Benson, very quietly. 'You are developing a taste for the morbid and horrible.'

The girl turned, and taking his arm walked slowly in the direction of the house; Mrs Benson, who was sitting in the porch, rose to receive them.

'You shouldn't have kept her out so long,' she said chidingly. 'Where have you been?'

'Sitting on the well,' said Olive, smiling, 'discussing our future.'

'I don't believe that place is healthy,' said Mrs Benson, emphatically. 'I really think it might be filled in, Jem.'

'All right,' said her son, slowly. 'Pity it wasn't filled in long ago.'

He took the chair vacated by his mother as she entered the house with Olive, and with his hands hanging limply over the sides sat in deep thought. After a time he rose, and going upstairs to a room which was set apart for sporting requisites selected a sea fishing line and some hooks and stole softly downstairs again. He walked swiftly across the park in the direction of the well, turning before he entered the shadow of the trees to look back at the lighted windows of the house. Then having arranged his line he sat on the edge of the well and cautiously lowered it.

He sat with his lips compressed, occasionally looking about him in a startled fashion, as though he half expected to see something peering at him from the belt of trees. Time after time he lowered his line until at length in pulling it up he heard a little metallic tinkle against the side of the well.

He held his breath then, and forgetting his fears drew the line in inch by inch, so as not to lose its precious burden. His pulse beat rapidly, and his eyes were bright. As the line came slowly in he saw the catch hanging to the hook, and with a steady hand drew the last few feet in. Then he saw that instead of the bracelet he had hooked a bunch of keys.

With a faint cry he shook them from the hook into the water below, and stood breathing heavily. Not a sound broke the stillness of the night. He walked up and down a bit and stretched his great muscles; then he came back to the well and resumed his task.

For an hour or more the line was lowered without result. In his eagerness he forgot his fears, and with eyes bent down the well fished slowly and carefully. Twice the hook became entangled in something, and was with difficulty released. It caught a third time, and all his efforts failed to free it. Then he dropped the line down the well, and with head bent walked toward the house.

He went first to the stables at the rear, and then retiring to his room for some time paced restlessly up and down. Then without removing his clothes he flung himself upon the bed and fell into a troubled sleep.

III.

Long before anybody else was astir he arose and stole softly downstairs. The sunlight was stealing in at every crevice, and flashing in long streaks across the darkened rooms. The dining-room into which he looked struck chill and cheerless in the dark yellow light which came through the lowered blinds. He remembered that it had the same appearance when his father lay dead in the house; now, as then, everything seemed ghastly and unreal; the very chairs standing as their occupants had left them the night before seemed to be indulging in some dark communication of ideas.

Slowly and noiselessly he opened the hall door and passed into the fragrant air beyond. The sun was shining on the drenched grass and trees, and a slowly vanishing white mist rolled like smoke about the grounds. For a moment he stood, breathing deeply the sweet air of the morning, and then walked slowly in the direction of the stables.

The rusty creaking of a pump-handle and a spatter of water upon the red-tiled courtyard showed that somebody else was astir, and a few steps farther he beheld a brawny, sandy-haired man gasping wildly under severe self-infliction at the pump.

'Everything ready, George?' he asked quietly.

'Yes, sir,' said the man, straightening up suddenly and touching his forehead. 'Bob's just finishing the arrangements inside. It's a lovely morning for a dip. The water in that well must be just icy.'

'Be as quick as you can,' said Benson, impatiently.

'Very good, sir,' said George, burnishing his face harshly with a very small towel which had been hanging over the top of the pump. 'Hurry up, Bob.'

In answer to his summons a man appeared at the door of the stable with a coil of stout rope over his arm and a large metal candlestick in his hand.

'Just to try the air, sir,' said George, following his master's glance, 'a well gets rather foul sometimes, but if a candle can live down it, a man can.'

His master nodded, and the man, hastily pulling up the neck of his shirt and thrusting his arms into his coat, followed him as he led the way slowly to the well.

'Beg pardon, sir,' said George, drawing up to his side, 'but you are not looking over and above well this morning. If you'll let me go down I'd enjoy the bath.'

'No, no,' said Benson, peremptorily.

'You ain't fit to go down, sir,' persisted his follower. 'I've never seen you look so before. Now if—'

'Mind your business,' said his master curtly.

George became silent and the three walked with swinging strides through the long wet grass to the well. Bob flung the rope on the ground and at a sign from his master handed him the candlestick.

'Here's the line for it, sir,' said Bob, fumbling in his pockets.

Benson took it from him and slowly tied it to the candlestick. Then he placed it on the edge of the well, and striking a match, lit the candle and began slowly to lower it.

'Hold hard, sir,' said George, quickly, laying his hand on his arm, 'you must tilt it or the string'll burn through.'

Even as he spoke the string parted and the candlestick fell into the water below.

Benson swore quietly.

'I'll soon get another,' said George, starting up.

'Never mind, the well's all right,' said Benson.

'It won't take a moment, sir,' said the other over his shoulder.

'Are you master here, or am I?' said Benson hoarsely.

George came back slowly, a glance at his master's face stopping the protest upon his tongue, and he stood by watching him sulkily as he sat on the well and removed his outer garments. Both men watched him curiously, as having completed his preparations he stood grim and silent with his hands by his sides.

'I wish you'd let me go, sir,' said George, plucking up courage to address him. 'You ain't fit to go, you've got a chill or something. I shouldn't wonder it's the typhoid. They've got it in the village bad.'

For a moment Benson looked at him angrily, then his gaze softened. 'Not this time, George,' he said, quietly. He took the looped end of the rope and placed it under his arms, and sitting down threw one leg over the side of the well.

'How are you going about it, sir?' queried George, laying hold of the rope and signing to Bob to do the same.

'I'll call out when I reach the water,' said Benson; 'then pay out three yards more quickly so that I can get to the bottom.'

'Very good, sir,' answered both.

Their master threw the other leg over the coping and sat motionless. His back was turned toward the men as he sat with head bent, looking down the shaft. He sat for so long that George became uneasy.

'All right, sir?' he inquired.

'Yes,' said Benson, slowly. 'If I tug at the rope, George, pull up at once. Lower away.'

The rope passed steadily through their hands until a hollow cry from the darkness below and a faint splashing warned them that he had reached the water. They gave him three yards more and stood with relaxed grasp and strained ears, waiting.

'He's gone under,' said Bob in a low voice.

The other nodded, and moistening his huge palms took a firmer grip of the rope.

Fully a minute passed, and the men began to exchange uneasy glances. Then a sudden tremendous jerk followed by a series of feebler ones nearly tore the rope from their grasp.

'Pull!' shouted George, placing one foot on the side and hauling desperately. 'Pull! pull! He's stuck fast; he's not coming; PULL!'

In response to their terrific exertions the rope came slowly in, inch by inch, until at length a violent splashing was heard, and at the same moment a scream of unutterable horror came echoing up the shaft.

'What a weight he is!' panted Bob. 'He's stuck fast or something. Keep still, sir; for heaven's sake, keep still.'

For the taut rope was being jerked violently by the struggles of the weight at the end of it. Both men with grunts and sighs hauled it in foot by foot.

'All right, sir,' cried George, cheerfully.

He had one foot against the well, and was pulling manfully; the burden was nearing the top. A long pull and a strong pull, and the face of a dead man with mud in the eyes and nostrils came peering over the edge. Behind it was the ghastly face of his master; but this he saw too late, for with a great cry he let go his hold of the rope and stepped back. The suddenness overthrew his assistant, and the rope tore through his hands. There was a frightful splash.

'You fool!' stammered Bob, and ran to the well helplessly.

'Run!' cried George. 'Run for another line.'

He bent over the coping and called eagerly down as his assistant sped back to the stables shouting wildly. His voice re-echoed down the shaft, but all else was silence.

Jerry Bundler

W. W. Jacobs

It wanted a few nights to Christmas, a festival for which the small market-town of Torchester was making extensive preparations. The narrow streets which had been thronged with people were now almost deserted; the cheap-jack from London, with the remnant of breath left him after his evening's exertions, was making feeble attempts to blow out his naphtha lamp, and the last shops open were rapidly closing for the night.

In the comfortable coffee-room of the old 'Boar's Head', half a dozen guests, principally commercial travellers, sat talking by the light of the fire. The talk had drifted from trade to politics, from politics to religion, and so by easy stages to the supernatural. Three ghost stories, never known to fail before, had fallen flat; there was too much noise outside, too much light within. The fourth story was told by an old hand with more success; the streets were quiet, and he had turned the gas out. In the flickering light of the fire, as it shone on the glasses and danced with shadows on the walls, the story proved so enthralling that George, the waiter, whose presence had been forgotten, created a very disagreeable sensation by suddenly starting up from a dark corner and gliding silently from the room.

'That's what I call a good story,' said one of the men, sipping his hot whisky. 'Of course it's an old idea that spirits like to get into the company of human beings. A man told me once that he travelled down the Great Western with a ghost and hadn't the slightest suspicion of it until the inspector came for tickets. My friend said the way that ghost tried to keep up appearances by feeling for it in all its pockets and looking on the floor was quite touching. Ultimately it gave it up and with a faint groan vanished through the ventilator.'

'That'll do, Hirst,' said another man.

'It's not a subject for jesting,' said a little old gentleman who had been an attentive listener. 'I've never seen an apparition myself, but I know people who have, and I consider that they form a very interesting link between us and the after-life. There's a ghost story connected with this house, you know.'

'Never heard of it,' said another speaker, 'and I've been here some years now.'

'It dates back a long time now,' said the old gentleman. 'You've heard about Jerry Bundler, George?'

'Well, I've just 'eard odds and ends, sir,' said the old waiter, 'but I never put much count to 'em. There was one chap 'ere what said 'e saw it, and the gov'ner sacked 'im prompt.'

'My father was a native of this town,' said the old gentleman, 'and knew the story well. He was a truthful man and a steady churchgoer, but I've heard him declare that once in his life he saw the appearance of Jerry Bundler in this house.'

'And who was this Bundler?' inquired a voice.

'A London thief, pickpocket, highwayman – anything he could turn his dishonest hand to,' replied the old gentleman; 'and he was run to earth in this house one Christmas week some eighty years ago. He took his last supper in this very room, and after he had gone up to bed a couple of Bow Street runners, who had followed him from London but lost the scent a bit, went up-stairs with the landlord and tried the door. It was stout oak, and fast, so one went into the yard, and by means of a short ladder got on to the window-sill, while the other stayed outside the door. Those below in the yard saw the man crouching on the sill, and then there was a sudden smash of glass, and with a cry he fell in a heap on the stones at their feet. Then in the moonlight they saw the white face of the pickpocket peeping over the sill, and while some stayed in the yard, others ran into the house and helped the other man to break the door in. It was difficult to obtain an entrance even then, for it was barred with heavy furniture, but they got in at last, and the first thing that met their eyes was the body of Jerry dangling from the top of the bed by his own handkerchief.'

'Which bedroom was it?' asked two or three voices together.

The narrator shook his head. 'That I can't tell you; but the story goes that Jerry still haunts this house, and my father used to declare positively that the last time he sleep here the ghost of Jerry Bundler lowered itself from the top of his bed and tried to strangle him.'

'That'll do,' said an uneasy voice. 'I wish you'd thought to ask your father which bedroom it was.'

'What for?' inquired the old gentleman.

'Well, I should take care not to sleep in it, that's all,' said the voice shortly.

'There's nothing to fear,' said the other. 'I don't believe for a moment that ghosts could really hurt one. In fact my father used to confess that it was only the unpleasantness of the thing that upset him, and that for all practical purposes Jerry's fingers might have been made of cotton-wool for all the harm they could do.'

'That's all very fine,' said the last speaker again; 'a ghost story is a ghost story, sir; but when a gentleman tells a tale of a ghost in the house in which one is going to sleep, I call it most ungentlemanly!'

'Pooh! nonsense!' said the old gentleman, rising; 'ghosts can't hurt you. For my own part; I should rather like to see one. Good night, gentlemen.'

'Good night,' said the others. 'And I only hope Jerry 'll pay you a visit,' added the nervous man as the door closed.

'Bring some more whisky, George,' said a stout commercial; 'I want keeping up when the talk turns this way.'

'Shall I light the gas, Mr Malcolm?' said George.

'No; the fire's very comfortable,' said the traveller. 'Now, gentlemen, any of you know any more?'

'I think we've had enough,' said another man; 'we shall be thinking we see spirits next, and we're not all like the old gentleman who's just gone.'

'Old humbug!' said Hirst. 'I should like to put him to the test. Suppose I dress up as Jerry Bundler and go and give him a chance of displaying his courage?'

'Bravo!' said Malcolm huskily, drowning one or two faint 'Noes.' 'Just for the joke, gentlemen.'

'No, no! Drop it, Hirst,' said another man.

'Only for the joke,' said Hirst, somewhat eagerly. 'I've got some things up-stairs in which I am going to play in the 'Rivals' – knee-breeches, buckles, and all that sort of thing. It's a rare chance. If you'll wait a bit I'll give you a full dress rehearsal, entitled, "Jerry Bundler; or The Nocturnal Strangler."'

'You won't frighten us,' said the commercial, with a husky laugh.

'I don't know that,' said Hirst sharply; 'it's a question of acting, that's all. I'm pretty good, ain't I, Somers?'

'Oh, you're all right – for an amateur,' said his friend, with a laugh.

'I'll bet you a level sov. you don't frighten me,' said the stout traveller.

'Done!' said Hirst. 'I'll take the bet to frighten you first and the old gentleman afterwards. These gentlemen shall be the judges.'

'You won't frighten us, sir,' said another man, 'because we're prepared for you; but you'd better leave the old man alone. It's dangerous play.'

'Well, I'll try you first,' said Hirst, springing up. 'No gas, mind.'

He ran lightly upstairs to his room, leaving the others, most of whom had been drinking somewhat freely, to wrangle about his proceedings. It ended in two of them going to bed.

'He's crazy on acting,' said Somers, lighting his pipe. 'Thinks he's the equal of anybody almost. It doesn't matter with us, but I wou't let him go to the old man. And he won't mind so long as he gets an opportunity of acting to us.'

'Well, I hope he'll hurry up,' said Malcolm, yawning; 'it's after twelve now.'

Nearly half an hour passed. Malcolm drew his watch from his pocket and was busy winding it, when George, the waiter, who had been sent on an errand to the bar, burst suddenly into the room and rushed towards them.

' 'E's comin', gentlemen,' he said breathlessly.

'Why, you're frightened, George,' said the stout commercial, with a chuckle.

'It was the suddenness of it,' said George sheepishly; 'and besides, I didn't look for seein' 'im in the bar. There's only a glimmer of light there, and 'e was sitting on the floor behind the bar. I nearly trod on 'im.'

'Oh, you'll never make a man, George,' said Malcolm.

'Well, it took me unawares,' said the waiter. 'Not that I'd have gone to the bar by myself if I'd known 'e was there, and I don't believe you would either, sir.'

'Nonsense!' said Malcolm. 'I'll go and fetch him in.'

'You don't know what it's like, sir,' said George, catching him by the sleeve. 'It ain't fit to look at by yourself, it ain't, indeed. It's got the – *What's that?'*

They all started at the sound of a smothered cry from the staircase and the sound of somebody running hurriedly along the passage. Before anybody could speak, the door flew open and a figure bursting into the room flung itself gasping and shivering upon them.

'What is it? What's the matter?' demanded Malcolm. 'Why, it's Mr Hirst.' He shook him roughly and then held some spirit to his lips. Hirst drank it greedily and with a sharp intake of his breath gripped him by the arm.

'Light the gas, George,' said Malcolm.

The waiter obeyed hastily. Hirst, a ludicrous but pitiable figure in knee-breeches and coat, a large wig all awry, and his face a mess of grease paint, clung to him, trembling.

'Now what's the matter?' asked Malcolm.

'I've seen it,' said Hirst, with a hysterical sob. 'Lord, I'll never play the fool again, never!'

'Seen what?' said the others.

'Him – it – the ghost – anything!' said Hirst wildly.

'Rot!' said Malcolm uneasily.

'I was coming down the stairs,' said Hirst. 'Just capering down – as I thought – it ought to do. I felt a tap—'

He broke off suddenly and peered nervously through the open door into the passage.

'I thought I saw it again,' he whispered. 'Look – at the foot of the stairs. Can you see anything?'

'No, there's nothing there,' said Malcolm, whose own voice shook a little. 'Go on. You felt a tap on your shoulder—'

'I turned round and saw it – a little wicked head and a white dead face. Pah!'

'That's what I saw in the bar,' said George. ''Orrid it was – devilish!'

Hirst shuddered, and, still retaining his nervous grip of Malcolm's sleeve, dropped into a chair.

'Well, it's a most unaccountable thing,' said the dumbfounded Malcolm, turning round to the others. 'It's the last time I come to this house.'

'I leave tomorrow,' said George. 'I wouldn't go down to that bar again by myself, no, not for fifty pounds!'

'It's talking about the thing that's caused it, I expect,' said one of the men; 'we've all been talking about this and having it in our minds. Practically we've been forming a spiritualistic circle without knowing it.'

'Hang the old gentleman!' said Malcolm heartily. 'Upon my soul, I'm half afraid to go to bed. It's odd they should both think they saw something.'

'I saw it as plain as I see you, sir,' said George solemnly. 'P'raps if you keep your eyes turned up the passage you'll see it for yourself.'

They followed the direction of his finger, but saw nothing, although one of them fancied that a head peeped round the corner of the wall.

'Who'll come down to the bar?' said Malcolm, looking round.

'You can go, if you like,' said one of the others, with a faint laugh; 'we'll wait here for you.'

The stout traveller walked towards the door and took a few steps up the passage. Then he stopped. All was quite silent, and he walked slowly to the end and looked down fearfully towards the glass partition which shut off the bar. Three times he made as though to go to it; then he turned back, and, glancing over his shoulder, came hurriedly back to the room.

'Did you see it, sir?' whispered George. 'Don't know,' said Malcolm shortly. 'I fancied I saw something, but it might have been fancy. I'm in the mood to see anything just now. How are you feeling now, sir?'

'Oh, I feel a bit better now,' said Hirst, somewhat brusquely, as all eyes were turned upon him. 'I daresay you think I'm easily scared, but you didn't see it.'

'Not at all,' said Malcolm, smiling faintly despite himself.

'I'm going to bed,' said Hirst, noticing the smile and resenting it. 'Will you share my room with me, Somers?'

'I will with pleasure,' said his friend, 'provided you don't mind sleeping with the gas on full all night.'

He rose from his seat, and bidding the company a friendly good night, left the room with his crestfallen friend. The others saw them to the foot of the stairs, and having heard their door close, returned to the coffee-room.

'Well, I suppose the bet's off?' said the stout commercial, poking the fire and then standing with his legs apart on the hearthrug; 'though, as far as

I can see, I won it. I never saw a man so scared in all my life. Sort of poetic justice about it, isn't there?'

'Never mind about poetry or justice,' said one of his listeners; 'who's going to sleep with me?'

'I will,' said Malcolm affably.

'And I suppose we share a room together, Mr Leek?' said the third man, turning to the fourth.

'No, thank you,' said the other briskly; 'I don't believe in ghosts. If anything comes into my room I shall shoot it.'

'That won't hurt a spirit, Leek,' said Malcolm decisively.

'Well the noise'll be like company to me,' said Leek, 'and it'll wake the house too. But if you're nervous, sir,' he added with a grin to the man who had suggested sharing his room, 'George'll be only too pleased to sleep on the door-mat inside your room, I know.'

'That I will, sir,' said George fervently; 'and if you gentlemen would only come down with me to the bar to put the gas out, I could never be sufficiently grateful.'

They went out in a body, with the exception of Leek, peering carefully before them as they went. George turned the light out in the bar and they returned unmolested to the coffee-room, and, avoiding the sardonic smile of Leek, prepared to separate for the night.

'Give me the candle while you put the gas out, George,' said the traveller.

The waiter handed it to him and extinguished the gas, and at the same moment all distinctly heard a step in the passage outside. It stopped at the door, and as they watched with bated breath, the door creaked and slowly opened. Malcolm fell back open-mouthed, as a white, leering face, with sunken eyeballs and close-cropped bullet head, appeared at the opening.

For a few seconds the creature stood regarding them, blinking in a strange fashion at the candle. Then, with a sidling movement, it came a little way into the room and stood there as if bewildered.

Not a man spoke or moved, but all watched with a horrible fascination as the creature removed its dirty neckcloth and its head rolled on its shoulder. For a minute it paused, and then holding the rag before it, moved towards Malcolm.

The candle went out suddenly with a flash and a bang. There was a smell of powder, and something writhing in the darkness on the floor. A faint, choking cough, and then silence. Malcolm was the first to speak. 'Matches,' he said in a strange voice. George struck one. Then he leapt at the gas and a burner flamed from the match. Malcolm touched the thing on the floor with his foot and found it soft. He looked at his companions. They mouthed inquiries at him, but he shook his head. He lit the candle, and, kneeling down, examined the silent thing on the floor. Then he rose swiftly, and dipping his handkerchief in the water jug, bent down again and grimly wiped the white face. Then he sprang back with a cry of incredulous horror, pointing at it. Leek's pistol fell to the floor and he shut out the sight with his hands, but the others, crowding forward, gazed spell-bound at the dead face of Hirst.

Before a word was spoken the door opened and Somers hastily entered the room. His eyes fell on the floor. 'Good God!' he cried. 'You didn't—'

Nobody spoke.

'I told him not to,' he said in a suffocating voice. 'I told him not to. I told him—'

He leaned against the wall, deathly sick, put his arms out feebly, and fell fainting into the traveller's arms.

The Shadowy Third

Ellen Glasgow

When the call came I remember that I turned from the telephone in a romantic flutter. Though I had spoken only once to the great surgeon, Roland Maradick, I felt on that December afternoon that to speak to him only once—to watch him in the operating-room for a single hour—was an adventure which drained the colour and the excitement from the rest of life. After all these years of work on typhoid and pneumonia cases, I can still feel the delicious tremor of my young pulses; I can still see the winter sunshine slanting through the hospital windows over the white uniforms of the nurses.

"He didn't mention me by name. Can there be a mistake?" I stood, incredulous yet ecstatic, before the superintendent of the hospital.

"No, there isn't a mistake. I was talking to him before you came down." Miss Hemphill's strong face softened while she looked at me. She was a big, resolute woman, a distant Canadian relative of my mother's, and the kind of nurse I had discovered in the month since I had come up from Richmond, that Northern hospital boards, if not Northern patients, appear instinctively to select. From the first, in spite of her hardness, she had taken a liking—I hesitate to use the word "fancy" for a preference so impersonal—to her Virginia cousin. After all, it isn't every Southern nurse, just out of training, who can boast a kinswoman in the superintendent of a New York hospital.

"And he made you understand positively that he meant me?" The thing was so wonderful that I simply couldn't believe it.

"He asked particularly for the nurse who was with Miss Hudson last week when he operated. I think he didn't even remember that you had a name. When I asked if he meant Miss Randolph, he repeated that he wanted the nurse who had been with Miss Hudson. She was small, he said, and cheerful-looking. This, of course, might apply to one or two of the others, but none of these was with Miss Hudson."

"Then I suppose it is really true?" My pulses were tingling. "And I am to be there at six o'clock?"

"Not a minute later. The day nurse goes off duty at that hour, and Mrs Maradick is never left by herself for an instant."

"It is her mind, isn't it? And that makes it all the stranger that he should select me, for I have had so few mental cases."

"So few cases of any kind," Miss Hemphill was smiling, and when she smiled I wondered if the other nurses would know her. "By the time you have gone through the treadmill in New York, Margaret, you will have lost a good many things besides your inexperience. I wonder how long you will keep your sympathy and your imagination? After all, wouldn't you have made a better novelist than a nurse?"

"I can't help putting myself into my cases. I suppose one ought not to?"

"It isn't a question of what one ought to do, but of what one must. When you are drained of every bit of sympathy and enthusiasm, and have got nothing in return for it, not even thanks, you will understand why I try to keep you from wasting yourself."

"But surely in a case like this—for Doctor Maradick?"

"Oh, well, of course—for Doctor Maradick." She must have seen that I implored her confidence, for, after a minute, she let fall carelessly a gleam of light on the situation: "It is a very sad case when you think what a charming man and a great surgeon Doctor Maradick is."

Above the starched collar of my uniform I felt the blood leap in bounds to my cheeks. "I have spoken to him only once," I murmured, "but he is charming, and so kind and handsome, isn't he?"

"His patients adore him."

"Oh, yes, I've seen that. Everyone hangs on his visits." Like the patients and the other nurses, I also had come by delightful, if imperceptible, degrees to hang on the daily visits of Doctor Maradick. He was, I suppose, born to be a hero to women. From my first day in his hospital, from the moment when I watched, through closed shutters, while he stepped out of his car, I have never doubted that he was assigned to the great part in the play. If I had been ignorant of his spell—of the charm he exercised over his hospital—I should have felt it in the waiting hush, like a drawn breath, which followed his ring at the door and preceded his imperious footstep on the stairs. My first impression of him, even after the terrible events of the next year, records a memory that is both careless and splendid. At that moment, when, gazing through the chinks in the shutters, I watched him, in his coat of dark fur, cross the pavement over the pale streaks of sunshine, I knew beyond any doubt—I knew with a sort of infallible prescience—that my fate was irretrievably bound up with his in the future. I knew this, I repeat, though Miss Hemphill would still insist that my foreknowledge was merely a sentimental gleaning from indiscriminate novels. But it wasn't only first love, impressionable as my kinswoman believed me to be. It wasn't only the way he looked. Even more than his appearance—more than the shining dark of his eyes, the silvery brown of his hair, the dusky glow in his face—even more than his charm and his magnificence, I think, the beauty and sympathy in his voice won my heart. It was a voice, I heard someone say afterwards, that ought always to speak poetry.

So you will see why—if you do not understand at the beginning, I can never hope to make you believe impossible things!—so you will see why I accepted the call when it came as an imperative summons. I couldn't have stayed away after he sent for me. However much I may have tried not to go, I know that in the end I must have gone. In those days, while I was still hoping to write novels, I used to talk a great deal about "destiny" (I have learned since then how silly all such talk is), and I suppose it was my "destiny" to be caught in the web of Roland Maradick's personality. But I am not the first nurse to grow love-sick about a doctor who never gave her a thought.

"I am glad you got the call, Margaret. It may mean a great deal to you. Only try not to be too emotional." I remember that Miss Hemphill was holding a bit of rose-geranium in her hand while she spoke—one of the patients had given it to her from a pot she kept in her room, and the scent of the flower is still in my nostrils—or my memory. Since then—oh, long since then—I have wondered if she also had been caught in the web.

"I wish I knew more about the case." I was pressing for light. "Have you ever seen Mrs Maradick?"

"Oh, dear, yes. They have been married only a little over a year, and in the beginning she used to come sometimes to the hospital and wait outside while the doctor made his visits. She was a very sweet-looking woman then—not exactly pretty, but fair and slight, with the loveliest smile, I think, I have ever seen. In those first months she was so much in love that we used to laugh about it among ourselves. To see her face light up when the doctor came out of the hospital and crossed the pavement to his car, was as good as a play. We never tired of watching her—I wasn't superintendent then, so I had more time to look out of the window while I was on day duty. Once or twice she brought her little girl in to see one of the patients. The child was so much like her that you would have known them anywhere for mother and daughter."

I had heard that Mrs Maradick was a widow, with one child, when she first met the doctor, and I asked now, still seeking an illumination I had not found, "There was a great deal of money, wasn't there?"

"A great fortune. If she hadn't been so attractive, people would have said, I suppose, that Doctor Maradick married her for her money. Only," she appeared to make an effort of memory, "I believe I've heard somehow that it was all left in trust away from Mrs Maradick if she married again. I can't, to save my life, remember just how it was; but it was a queer will, I know, and Mrs Maradick wasn't to come into the money unless the child didn't live to grow up. The pity of it—"

A young nurse came into the office to ask for something—the keys, I think, of the operating-room, and Miss Hemphill broke off inconclusively as she hurried out of the door. I was sorry that she left off just when she did. Poor Mrs Maradick! Perhaps I was too emotional, but even before I saw her I had begun to feel her pathos and her strangeness.

My preparations took only a few minutes. In those days I always kept a suitcase packed and ready for sudden calls; and it was not yet six o'clock when I turned from Tenth Street into Fifth Avenue, and stopped for a minute, before ascending the steps, to look at the house in which Doctor Maradick lived. A fine rain was falling, and I remember thinking, as I turned the corner, how depressing the weather must be for Mrs Maradick. It was an old house, with damp-looking walls (though that may have been because of the rain) and a spindle-shaped iron railing which ran up the stone steps to the black door, where I noticed a dim flicker through the old-fashioned fanlight. Afterwards I discovered that Mrs Maradick had been born in the house—her maiden name was Calloran—and that she had never wanted to live anywhere else. She was a woman—this I found out when I knew her better—of strong attachments to both persons and places; and though Doctor Maradick had tried to persuade her to move uptown after her marriage, she had clung, against his wishes, to the old house in lower Fifth Avenue. I dare say she was obstinate about it in spite of her gentleness and her passion for the doctor. Those sweet, soft women, especially when they have always been rich, are sometimes amazingly obstinate. I have nursed so many of them since—women with strong affections and weak intellects—that I have come to recognize the type as soon as I set eyes upon it.

My ring at the bell was answered after a little delay, and when I entered the house I saw that the hall was quite dark except for the waning glow from an open fire which burned in the library. When I gave my name, and added that I was the night nurse, the servant appeared to think my humble presence unworthy of illumination. He was an old negro butler, inherited perhaps from Mrs Maradick's mother, who, I learned afterwards, was from South Carolina; and while he passed me on his way up the staircase, I heard him vaguely muttering that he "wa'n't gwinter tu'n on dem lights twel de chile had done playin'."

To the right of the hall, the soft glow drew me into the library, and crossing the threshold timidly, I stooped to dry my wet coat by the fire. As I bent there, meaning to start up at the first sound of a footstep, I thought how cosy the room was after the damp walls outside to which some bared creepers were clinging; and I was watching the strange shapes and patterns the firelight made on the old Persian rug, when the lamps of a slowly turning motor flashed on me through the white shades at the window. Still dazzled by the glare, I looked round in the dimness and saw a child's ball of red and blue rubber roll towards me out of the gloom of the adjoining room. A moment later, while I made a vain attempt to capture the toy as it spun past me, a little girl darted airily, with peculiar lightness and grace, through the doorway, and stopped quickly, as if in surprise at the sight of a stranger. She was a small child—so small and slight that her footsteps made no sound on the polished floor of the threshold; and I remember thinking while I looked at her that she had the gravest and sweetest face I had ever seen. She couldn't—I decided this afterwards—have been more than six or seven years old, yet she stood there with a curious prim dignity, like the dignity of an elderly person, and gazed up at me with enigmatical eyes. She was dressed in Scotch plaid, with a bit of red ribbon in her hair, which was cut in a fringe over her forehead and hung very straight to her shoulders. Charming as she was, from her uncurled brown hair to the white socks and black slippers on her little feet, I recall most vividly the singular look in her eyes, which appeared in the shifting light to be of an indeterminate colour. For the odd thing about this look was that it was not the look of childhood at all. It was the look of profound experience, of bitter knowledge.

"Have you come for your ball?" I asked; but while the friendly question was still on my lips, I heard the servant returning. In my confusion I made a second ineffectual grasp at the plaything, which had rolled away from me into the dusk of the drawing-room. Then, as I raised my head, I saw that the child also had slipped from the room; and without looking after her I followed the old negro into the pleasant study above, where the great surgeon awaited me.

Ten years ago, before hard nursing had taken so much out of me, I blushed very easily, and I was aware at the moment when I crossed Doctor Maradick's study that my cheeks were the colour of peonies. Of course, I was a fool—no one knows this better than I do—but I had never been alone, even for an instant, with him before, and the man was more than a hero to me, he was—there isn't any reason now why I should blush over the confession—almost a god. At that age I was mad about the wonders of surgery, and Roland Maradick in the operating-room was magician enough to have turned an older and more sensible head than mine. Added to his great reputation and his marvelous skill, he was, I am sure of this, the most splendid-looking man, even at forty-five, that one could imagine. Had he been ungracious—had he been positively rude to me, I should still have adored him; but when he held out his hand, and greeted me in the charming way he had with women, I felt that I would have died for him. It is no wonder that a saying went about the hospital that every woman he operated on fell in love with him. As for the nurses—well, there wasn't a single one of them who had escaped his spell—not even Miss Hemphill, who could have been scarcely a day under fifty.

"I am glad you could come, Miss Randolph. You were with Miss Hudson last week when I operated?"

I bowed. To save my life I couldn't have spoken without blushing the redder.

"I noticed your bright face at the time. Brightness, I think, is what Mrs Maradick needs. She finds her day nurse depressing." His eyes rested so kindly upon me that I have suspected since that he was not entirely unaware of my worship. It was a small thing, heaven knows, to flatter his vanity—a nurse just out of a training-school—but to some men no tribute is too insignificant to give pleasure.

"You will do your best, I am sure." He hesitated an instant—just long enough for me to perceive the anxiety beneath the genial smile on his face—and then added gravely, "We wish to avoid, if possible, having to send her away."

I could only murmur in response, and after a few carefully chosen words about his wife's illness, he rang the bell and directed the maid to take me upstairs to my room. Not until I was ascending the stairs to the third storey did it occur to me that he had really told me nothing. I was as perplexed about the nature of Mrs Maradick's malady as I had been when I entered the house.

I found my room pleasant enough. It had been arranged—at Doctor Maradick's request, I think—that I was to sleep in the house, and after my austere little bed at the hospital, I was agreeably surprised by the cheerful look of the apartment into which the maid led me. The walls were papered in roses, and there were curtains of flowered chintz at the window, which looked down on a small formal garden at the rear of the house. This the maid told me, for it was too dark for me to distinguish more than a marble fountain and a fir-tree, which looked old, though I afterwards learned that it was replanted almost every season.

In ten minutes I had slipped into my uniform and was ready to go to my patient; but for some reason—to this day I have never found out what it was that turned her against me at the start—Mrs Maradick refused to receive me. While I stood outside her door I heard the day nurse trying to persuade her to let me come in. It wasn't any use, however, and in the end

I was obliged to go back to my room and wait until the poor lady got over her whim and consented to see me. That was long after dinner—it must have been nearer eleven than ten o'clock—and Miss Peterson was quite worn out by the time she came for me.

"I'm afraid you'll have a bad night," she said as we went downstairs together. That was her way, I soon saw, to expect the worst of everything and everybody.

"Does she often keep you up like this?"

"Oh, no, she is usually very considerate. I never knew a sweeter character. But she still has this hallucination—"

Here again, as in the scene with Doctor Maradick, I felt that the explanation had only deepened the mystery. Mrs Maradick's hallucination, whatever form it assumed, was evidently a subject for evasion and subterfuge in the household. It was on the tip of my tongue to ask, "What is her hallucination?"—but before I could get the words past my lips we had reached Mrs Maradick's door, and Miss Peterson motioned me to be silent. As the door opened a little way to admit me, I saw that Mrs Maradick was already in bed, and that the lights were out except for a night-lamp burning on a candle-stand beside a book and a carafe of water.

"I won't go in with you," said Miss Peterson in a whisper; and I was on the point of stepping over the threshold when I saw the little girl, in the dress of Scotch plaid, slip by me from the dusk of the room into the electric light of the hall. She held a doll in her arms, and as she went by she dropped a doll's work-basket in the doorway. Miss Peterson must have picked up the toy, for when I turned in a minute to look for it I found that it was gone. I remember thinking that it was late for a child to be up—she looked delicate, too—but, after all, it was no business of mine, and four years in a hospital had taught me never to meddle in things that do not concern me. There is nothing a nurse learns quicker than not to try to put the world to rights in a day.

When I crossed the floor to the chair by Mrs Maradick's bed, she turned over on her side and looked at me with the sweetest and saddest smile.

"You are the night nurse," she said in a gentle voice; and from the moment she spoke I knew that there was nothing hysterical or violent about her mania—or hallucination, as they called it. "They told me your name, but I have forgotten it."

"Randolph—Margaret Randolph." I liked her from the start, and I think she must have seen it.

"You look very young, Miss Randolph."

"I am twenty-two, but I suppose I don't look quite my age. People usually think I am younger."

For a minute she was silent, and while I settled myself in the chair by the bed, I thought how strikingly she resembled the little girl I had seen first in the afternoon, and then leaving her room a few moments before. They had the same small, heart-shaped faces, coloured ever so faintly; the same straight, soft hair, between brown and flaxen; and the same large, grave eyes, set very far apart under arched eyebrows. What surprised me most, however, was that they both looked at me with that enigmatical and vaguely wondering expression—only in Mrs Maradick's face the vagueness seemed to change now and then to a definite fear—a flash, I had almost said, of startled horror.

I sat quite still in my chair, and until the time came for Mrs Maradick to take her medicine not a word passed between us. Then, when I bent over her with the glass in my hand, she raised her head from the pillow and said in a whisper of suppressed intensity:

"You look kind. I wonder if you could have seen my little girl?"

As I slipped my arm under the pillow I tried to smile cheerfully down on her. "Yes, I've seen her twice. I'd know her anywhere by her likeness to you."

A glow shone in her eyes, and I thought how pretty she must have been before illness took the life and animation out of her features. "Then I know you're good." Her voice was so strained and low that I could barely hear it. "If you weren't good you couldn't have seen her."

I thought this queer enough, but all I answered was, "She looked delicate to be sitting up so late." A quiver passed over her thin features, and for a minute I thought she was going to burst into tears. As she had taken the medicine, I put the glass back on the candle-stand, and bending over the bed, smoothed the straight brown hair, which was as fine and soft as spun silk, back from her forehead. There was something about her—I don't know what it was—that made you love her as soon as she looked at you.

"She always had that light and airy way, though she was never sick a day in her life," she answered calmly after a pause. Then, groping for my hand, she whispered passionately, "You must not tell him—you must not tell any one that you have seen her!"

"I must not tell any one?" Again I had the impression that had come to me first in Doctor Maradick's study, and afterwards with Miss Peterson on the staircase, that I was seeking a gleam of light in the midst of obscurity.

"Are you sure there isn't any one listening—that there isn't any one at the door?" she asked, pushing aside my arm and raising herself on the pillows.

"Quite, quite sure. They have put out the lights in the hall."

"And you will not tell him? Promise me that you will not tell him." The startled horror flashed from the vague wonder of her expression. "He doesn't like her to come back, because he killed her."

"Because he killed her!" Then it was that light burst on me in a blaze. So this was Mrs Maradick's hallucination! She believed that her child was dead—the little girl I had seen with my own eyes leaving her room; and she believed that her husband—the great surgeon we worshipped in the hospital—had murdered her. No wonder they veiled the dreadful obsession in mystery! No wonder that even Miss Peterson had not dared to drag the horrid thing out into the light! It was the kind of hallucination one simply couldn't stand having to face.

"There is no use telling people things that nobody believes," she resumed slowly, still holding my hand in a grasp that would have hurt me if her fingers had not been so fragile. "Nobody believes that he killed her. Nobody believes that she comes back every day to the house. Nobody believes—and yet you saw her—"

"Yes, I saw her—but why should your husband have killed her?" I spoke soothingly, as one would speak to a person who was quite mad. Yet she was not mad, I could have sworn this while I looked at her.

For a moment she moaned inarticulately, as if the horror of her thoughts were too great to pass into speech. Then she flung out her thin, bare arm with a wild gesture.

"Because he never loved me!" she said. "He never loved me!"

"But he married you," I urged gently while I stroked her hair. "If he hadn't loved you, why should he have married you?"

"He wanted the money—my little girl's money. It all goes to him when I die."

"But he is rich himself. He must make a fortune from his profession."

"It isn't enough. He wanted millions." She had grown stern and tragic. "No, he never loved me. He loved someone else from the beginning—before I knew him."

It was quite useless, I saw, to reason with her. If she wasn't mad, she was in a state of terror and despondency so black that it had almost crossed the border-line into madness. I thought once that I would go upstairs and bring the child down from her nursery; but, after a moment's hesitation, I realized that Miss Peterson and Doctor Maradick must have long ago tried all these measures. Clearly, there was nothing to do except soothe and quiet her as much as I could; and this I did until she dropped into a light sleep which lasted well into the morning.

By seven o'clock I was worn out—not from work but from the strain on my sympathy—and I was glad, indeed, when one of the maids came in to bring me an early cup of coffee. Mrs Maradick was still sleeping—it was a mixture of bromide and chloral I had given her—and she did not wake until Miss Peterson came on duty an hour or two later. Then, when I went downstairs, I found the dining-room deserted except for the old housekeeper, who was looking over the silver. Doctor Maradick, she explained to me presently, had his breakfast served in the morning-room on the other side of the house.

"And the little girl? Does she take her meals in the nursery?"

She threw me a startled glance. Was it, I questioned afterwards, one of distrust or apprehension?

"There isn't any little girl. Haven't you heard?"

"Heard? No. Why, I saw her only yesterday." The look she gave me—I was sure of it now—was full of alarm.

"The little girl—she was the sweetest child I ever saw—died just two months ago of pneumonia."

"But she couldn't have died." I was a fool to let this out, but the shock had completely unnerved me. "I tell you I saw her yesterday."

The alarm in her face deepened. "That is Mrs Maradick's trouble. She believes that she still sees her."

"But don't you see her?" I drove the question home bluntly.

"No." She set her lips tightly. "I never see anything."

So I had been wrong, after all, and the explanation, when it came, only accentuated the terror. The child was dead—she had died of pneumonia two months ago—and yet I had seen her, with my own eyes, playing ball in the library; I had seen her slipping out of her mother's room, with her doll in her arms.

"Is there another child in the house? Could there be a child belonging to one of the servants?" A gleam had shot through the fog in which I was groping.

"No, there isn't any other. The doctors tried bringing one once, but it threw the poor lady into such a state she almost died of it. Besides, there wouldn't be any other child as quiet and sweet-looking as Dorothea. To see her skipping along in her dress of Scotch plaid used to make me think of a fairy, though they say that fairies wear nothing but white or green."

"Has any one else seen her—the child, I mean—any of the servants?"

"Only old Gabriel, the coloured butler, who came with Mrs Maradick's mother from South Carolina. I've heard that negroes often have a kind of second sight—though I don't know that that is just what you would call it. But they seem to believe in the supernatural by instinct, and Gabriel is so old and dotty—he does no work except answer the door-bell and clean the silver—that nobody pays much attention to anything that he sees—"

"Is the child's nursery kept as it used to be?"

"Oh, no. The doctor had all the toys sent to the children's hospital. That was a great grief to Mrs Maradick; but Doctor Brandon thought, and all the nurses agreed with him, that it was best for her not to be allowed to keep the room as it was when Dorothea was living."

"Dorothea? Was that the child's name?"

"Yes, it means the gift of God, doesn't it? She was named after the mother of Mrs Maradick's first husband, Mr Ballard. He was the grave, quiet kind—not the least like the doctor."

I wondered if the other dreadful obsession of Mrs Maradick's had drifted down through the nurses or the servants to the housekeeper; but she said nothing about it, and since she was, I suspected, a garrulous person, I thought it wiser to assume that the gossip had not reached her.

A little later, when breakfast was over and I had not yet gone upstairs to my room, I had my first interview with Doctor Brandon, the famous alienist who was in charge of the case. I had never seen him before, but from the first moment that I looked at him I took his measure almost by intuition. He was, I suppose, honest enough—I have always granted him that, bitterly as I have felt towards him. It wasn't his fault that he lacked red blood in his brain, or that he had formed the habit, from long association with abnormal phenomena, of regarding all life as a disease. He was the sort of physician—every nurse will understand what I mean—who deals instinctively with groups instead of with individuals. He was long and solemn and very round in the face; and I hadn't talked to him ten minutes before I knew he had been educated in Germany, and that he had learned over there to treat every emotion as a pathological manifestation. I used to wonder what he got out of life—what anyone got out of life who had analyzed away everything except the bare structure.

When I reached my room at last, I was so tired that I could barely remember either the questions Doctor Brandon had asked or the directions he had given me. I fell asleep, I know, almost as soon as my head touched the pillow; and the maid who came to inquire if I wanted luncheon decided to let me finish my nap. In the afternoon, when she returned with a cup of tea, she found me still heavy and drowsy. Though I was used to night nursing, I felt as if I had danced from sunset to daybreak. It was fortunate, I reflected, while I drank my tea, that every case didn't wear on one's sympathies as acutely as Mrs Maradick's hallucination had worn on mine.

Through the day I did not see Doctor Maradick; but at seven o'clock when I came up from my early dinner on my way to take the place of Miss Peterson, who had kept on duty an hour later than usual, he met me in the hall and asked me to come into his study. I thought him handsomer than ever in his evening clothes, with a white flower in his buttonhole. He was going to some public dinner, the housekeeper told me, but, then, he was always going somewhere. I believe he didn't dine at home a single evening that winter.

"Did Mrs Maradick have a good night?" He had closed the door after us, and turning now with the question, he smiled kindly, as if he wished to put me at ease in the beginning.

"She slept very well after she took the medicine. I gave her that at eleven o'clock."

For a minute he regarded me silently, and I was aware that his personality—his charm—was focussed upon me. It was almost as if I stood in the centre of converging rays of light, so vivid was my impression of him.

"Did she allude in any way to her—to her hallucination?" he asked.

How the warning reached me—what invisible waves of sense-perception transmitted the message—I have never known; but while I stood there, facing the splendour of the doctor's presence, every intuition cautioned me that the time had come when I must take sides in the household. While I stayed there I must stand either with Mrs Maradick or against her.

"She talked quite rationally," I replied after a moment.

"What did she say?"

"She told me how she was feeling, that she missed her child, and that she walked a little every day about her room."

His face changed—how I could not at first determine.

"Have you seen Doctor Brandon?"

"He came this morning to give me his directions."

"He thought her less well today. He has advised me to send her to Rosedale."

I have never, even in secret, tried to account for Doctor Maradick. He may have been sincere. I tell only what I know—not what I believe or imagine—and the human is sometimes as inscrutable, as inexplicable, as the supernatural.

While he watched me I was conscious of an inner struggle, as if opposing angels warred somewhere in the depths of my being. When at last I made my decision, I was acting less from reason, I knew, than in obedience to the pressure of some secret current of thought. Heaven knows, even then, the man held me captive while I defied him.

"Doctor Maradick," I lifted my eyes for the first time frankly to his, "I believe that your wife is as sane as I am—or as you are."

He started. "Then she did not talk freely to you?"

"She may be mistaken, unstrung, piteously distressed in mind"—I brought this out with emphasis—"but she is not—I am willing to stake my future on it—a fit subject for an asylum. It would be foolish—it would be cruel to send her to Rosedale."

"Cruel, you say?" A troubled look crossed his face, and his voice grew very gentle. "You do not imagine that I could be cruel to her?"

"No, I do not think that." My voice also had softened.

"We will let things go on as they are. Perhaps Doctor Brandon may have some other suggestion to make." He drew out his watch and compared it with the clock—nervously, I observed, as if his action were a screen for his discomfiture or perplexity. "I must be going now. We will speak of this again in the morning."

But in the morning we did not speak of it, and during the month that I nursed Mrs Maradick I was not called again into her husband's study. When I met him in the hall or on the staircase, which was seldom, he was as charming as ever; yet, in spite of his courtesy, I had a persistent feeling that he had taken my measure on that evening, and that he had no further use for me.

As the days went by Mrs Maradick seemed to grow stronger. Never, after our first night together, had she mentioned the child to me; never had she alluded by so much as a word to her dreadful charge against her husband. She was like any woman recovering from a great sorrow, except that she was sweeter and gentler. It is no wonder that everyone who came near her loved her; for there was a mysterious loveliness about her like the mystery of light, not of darkness. She was, I have always thought, as much of an angel as it is possible for a woman to be on this earth. And yet, angelic as she was, there were times when it seemed to me that she both hated and feared her husband. Though he never entered her room while I was there, and I never heard his name on her lips until an hour before the end, still I could tell by the look of terror in her face whenever his step passed down the hall that her very soul shivered at his approach.

During the whole month I did not see the child again, though one night, when I came suddenly into Mrs Maradick's room, I found a little garden, such as children make out of pebbles and bits of box, on the window-sill. I did not mention it to Mrs Maradick, and a little later, as the maid lowered the shades, I noticed that the garden had vanished. Since then I have often wondered if the child were invisible only to the rest of us, and if her mother still saw her. But there was no way of finding out except by questioning, and Mrs Maradick was so well and patient that I hadn't the heart to question. Things couldn't have been better with her than they were, and I was beginning to tell myself that she might soon go out for an airing, when the end came so suddenly.

It was a mild January day—the kind of day that brings the foretaste of spring in the middle of winter, and when I came downstairs in the afternoon, I stopped a minute by the window at the end of the hall to look down on the box maze in the garden. There was an old fountain, bearing two laughing boys in marble, in the centre of the gravelled walk, and the water, which had been turned on that morning for Mrs Maradick's pleasure, sparkled now like silver as the sunlight splashed over it. I had never before felt the air quite so soft and springlike in January; and I thought, as I gazed down on the garden, that it would be a good idea for Mrs Maradick to go out and bask for an hour or so in the sunshine. It seemed strange to me that she was never allowed to get any fresh air except the air that came through her windows.

When I went into her room, however, I found that she had no wish to go out. She was sitting, wrapped in shawls, by the open window, which looked down on the fountain; and as I entered she glanced up from a little book she was reading. A pot of daffodils stood on the window-sill—she was very fond of flowers and we tried always to keep some growing in her room.

"Do you know what I am reading, Miss Randolph?" she asked in her soft voice; and she read aloud a verse while I went over to the candle-stand to measure out a dose of medicine.

"'If thou hast two loaves of bread, sell one and buy daffodils, for bread nourisheth the body, but daffodils delight the soul.' That is very beautiful, don't you think so?"

I said "Yes," that it was beautiful; and then I asked her if she wouldn't go downstairs and walk about in the garden.

"He wouldn't like it," she answered; and it was the first time she had mentioned her husband to me since the night I came to her. "He doesn't want me to go out."

I tried to laugh her out of the idea; but it was no use, and after a few minutes I gave up and began talking of other things. Even then it did not occur to me that her fear of Doctor Maradick was anything but a fancy. I could see, of course, that she wasn't out of her head; but sane persons, I knew, sometimes have unaccountable prejudices, and I accepted her dislike as a mere whim or aversion. I did not understand then and—I may as well confess this before the end comes—I do not understand any better today. I am writing down the things I actually saw, and I repeat that I have never had the slightest twist in the direction of the miraculous.

The afternoon slipped away while we talked—she talked brightly when any subject came up that interested her—and it was the last hour of day—that grave, still hour when the movement of life seems to droop and falter for a few precious minutes—that brought us the thing I had dreaded silently since my first night in the house. I remember that I had risen to close the window, and was leaning out for a breath of the mild air, when there was the sound of steps, consciously softened, in the hall outside, and Doctor Brandon's usual knock fell on my ears. Then, before I could cross the room, the door opened, and the doctor entered with Miss Peterson. The day nurse, I knew, was a stupid woman; but she had never appeared to me so stupid, so armoured and encased in her professional manner, as she did at that moment.

"I am glad to see that you are taking the air." As Doctor Brandon came over to the window, I wondered maliciously what devil of contradictions had made him a distinguished specialist in nervous diseases.

"Who was the other doctor you brought this morning?" asked Mrs Maradick gravely; and that was all I ever heard about the visit of the second alienist.

"Someone who is anxious to cure you." He dropped into a chair beside her and patted her hand with his long, pale fingers. "We are so anxious to cure you that we want to send you away to the country for a fortnight or so. Miss Peterson has come to help you to get ready, and I've kept my car waiting for you. There couldn't be a nicer day for a trip, could there?"

The moment had come at last. I knew at once what he meant, and so did Mrs Maradick. A wave of colour flowed and ebbed in her thin cheeks, and I felt her body quiver when I moved from the window and put my arms on her shoulders. I was aware again, as I had been aware that evening in Doctor Maradick's study, of a current of thought that beat from the air around into my brain. Though it cost me my career as a nurse and my reputation for sanity, I knew that I must obey that invisible warning.

"You are going to take me to an asylum," said Mrs Maradick.

He made some foolish denial or evasion; but before he had finished I turned from Mrs Maradick and faced him impulsively. In a nurse this was flagrant rebellion, and I realized that the act wrecked my professional future. Yet I did not care—I did not hesitate. Something stronger than I was driving me on.

"Doctor Brandon," I said, "I beg you—I implore you to wait until tomorrow. There are things I must tell you."

A queer look came into his face, and I understood, even in my excitement, that he was mentally deciding in which group he should place me—to which class of morbid manifestations I must belong.

"Very well, very well, we will hear everything," he replied soothingly; but I saw him glance at Miss Peterson, and she went over to the wardrobe for Mrs Maradick's fur coat and hat.

Suddenly, without warning, Mrs Maradick threw the shawls away from her, and stood up. "If you send me away," she said, "I shall never come back. I shall never live to come back."

The grey of twilight was just beginning, and while she stood there, in the dusk of the room, her face shone out as pale and flower-like as the daffodils on the window-sill. "I cannot go away!" she cried in a sharper voice. "I cannot, go away from my child!"

I saw her face clearly; I heard her voice; and then—the horror of the scene sweeps back over me!—I saw the door open slowly and the little girl run across the room to her mother. I saw the child lift her little arms, and I saw the mother stoop and gather her to her bosom. So closely locked were they in that passionate embrace that their forms seemed to mingle in the gloom that enveloped them.

"After this can you doubt?" I threw out the words almost savagely—and then, when I turned from the mother and child to Doctor Brandon and Miss Peterson, I knew breathlessly—oh, there was a shock in the discovery!—that they were blind to the child. Their blank faces revealed the consternation of ignorance, not of conviction. They had seen nothing except the vacant arms of the mother and the swift, erratic gesture with which she stooped to embrace some invisible presence. Only my vision—and I have asked myself since if the power of sympathy enabled me to penetrate the web of material fact and see the spiritual form of the child—only my vision was not blinded by the clay through which I looked.

"After this can you doubt?" Doctor Brandon had flung my words back to me. Was it his fault, poor man, if life had granted him only the eyes of flesh? Was it his fault if he could see only half of the thing there before him?

But they couldn't see, and since they couldn't see I realized that it was useless to tell them. Within an hour they took Mrs Maradick to the asylum;

and she went quietly, though when the time came for parting from me she showed some faint trace of feeling. I remember that at the last, while we stood on the pavement, she lifted her black veil, which she wore for the child, and said: "Stay with her, Miss Randolph, as long as you can. I shall never come back."

Then she got into the car and was driven off, while I stood looking after her with a sob in my throat. Dreadful as I felt it to be, I didn't, of course, realize the full horror of it, or I couldn't have stood there quietly on the pavement. I didn't realize it, indeed, until several months afterwards when word came that she had died in the asylum. I never knew what her illness was, though I vaguely recall that something was said about "heart failure"—a loose enough term. My own belief is that she died simply of the terror of life.

To my surprise Doctor Maradick asked me to stay on as his office nurse after his wife went to Rosedale; and when the news of her death came there was no suggestion of my leaving. I don't know to this day why he wanted me in the house. Perhaps he thought I should have less opportunity to gossip if I stayed under his roof; perhaps he still wished to test the power of his charm over me. His vanity was incredible in so great a man. I have seen him flush with pleasure when people turned to look at him in the street, and I know that he was not above playing on the sentimental weakness of his patients. But he was magnificent, heaven knows! Few men, I imagine, have been the objects of so many foolish infatuations.

The next summer Doctor Maradick went abroad for two months, and while he was away I took my vacation in Virginia. When we came back the work was heavier than ever—his reputation by this time was tremendous—and my days were so crowded with appointments, and hurried flittings to emergency cases, that I had scarcely a minute left in which to remember poor Mrs Maradick. Since the afternoon when she went to the asylum the child had not been in the house; and at last I was beginning to persuade myself that the little figure had been an optical illusion—the effect of shifting lights in the gloom of the old rooms—not the apparition I had once believed it to be. It does not take long for a phantom to fade from the memory—especially when one leads the active and methodical life I was forced into that winter. Perhaps—who knows?—(I remember telling myself) the doctors may have been right, after all, and the poor lady may have actually been out of her mind. With this view of the past, my judgment of Doctor Maradick insensibly altered. It ended, I think, in my acquitting him altogether. And then, just as he stood clear and splendid in my verdict of him, the reversal came so precipitately that I grow breathless now whenever I try to live it over again. The violence of the next turn in affairs left me, I often fancy, with a perpetual dizziness of the imagination.

It was in May that we heard of Mrs Maradick's death, and exactly a year later, on a mild and fragrant afternoon, when the daffodils were blooming in patches around the old fountain in the garden, the housekeeper came into the office, where I lingered over some accounts, to bring me news of the doctor's approaching marriage.

"It is no more than we might have expected," she concluded rationally. "The house must be lonely for him—he is such a sociable man. But I can't help feeling," she brought out slowly after a pause in which I felt a shiver pass over me, "I can't help feeling that it is hard for that other woman to have all the money poor Mrs Maradick's first husband left her."

"There is a great deal of money, then?" I asked curiously.

"A great deal." She waved her hand, as if words were futile to express the sum. "Millions and millions!"

"They will give up this house, of course?"

"That's done already, my dear. There won't be a brick left of it by this time next year. It's to be pulled down and an apartment-house built on the ground."

Again the shiver passed over me. I couldn't bear to think of Mrs Maradick's old home falling to pieces.

"You didn't tell me the name of the bride," I said. "Is she someone he met while he was in Europe?"

"Dear me, no! She is the very lady he was engaged to before he married Mrs Maradick, only she threw him over, so people said, because he wasn't rich enough. Then she married some lord or prince from over the water; but there was a divorce, and now she has turned again to her old lover. He is rich enough now, I guess, even for her!"

It was all perfectly true, I suppose; it sounded as plausible as a story out of a newspaper; and yet while she told me I felt, or dreamed that I felt, a sinister, an impalpable hush in the air. I was nervous, no doubt; I was shaken by the suddenness with which the housekeeper had sprung her news on me; but as I sat there I had quite vividly an impression that the old house was listening—that there was a real, if invisible, presence somewhere in the room or the garden. Yet, when an instant afterwards I glanced through the long window which opened down to the brick terrace, I saw only the faint sunshine over the deserted garden, with its maze of box, its marble fountain, and its patches of daffodils.

The housekeeper had gone—one of the servants, I think, came for her—and I was sitting at my desk when the words of Mrs Maradick on that last evening floated into my mind. The daffodils brought her back to me; for I thought, as I watched them growing, so still and golden in the sunshine, how she would have enjoyed them. Almost unconsciously I repeated the verse she had read to me:

"If thou hast two loaves of bread, sell one and buy daffodils"—and it was at this very instant, while the words were still on my lips, that I turned my eyes to the box maze, and saw the child skipping rope along the gravelled path to the fountain.

Quite distinctly, as clear as day, I saw her come, with what children call the dancing step, between the low box borders to the place where the daffodils bloomed by the fountain. From her straight brown hair to her frock of Scotch plaid and her little feet, which twinkled in white socks and black slippers over the turning rope, she was as real to me as the ground on which she trod or the laughing marble boys under the splashing water. Starting up from my chair, I made a single step to the terrace. If I could only reach her—only speak to her—I felt that I might at last solve the mystery. But with the first flutter of my dress on the terrace, the airy little form melted into the quiet dusk of the maze. Not a breath stirred the daffodils, not a shadow passed over the sparkling flow of the water; yet, weak and shaken in every nerve, I sat down on the brick step of the terrace and burst into tears. I must have known that something terrible would happen before they pulled down Mrs Maradick's home.

The doctor dined out that night. He was with the lady he was going to marry, the housekeeper told me; and it must have been almost midnight when I heard him come in and go upstairs to his room. I was downstairs because I had been unable to sleep, and the book I wanted to finish I had left that afternoon in the office. The book—I can't remember what it was—had seemed to me very exciting when I began it in the morning; but after the visit of the child I found the romantic novel as dull as a treatise on nursing. It was impossible for me to follow the lines, and I was on the point of giving up and going to bed, when Doctor Maradick opened the front door with his latch-key and went up the staircase. "There can't be a bit of truth in it." I thought over and over again as I listened to his even step ascending the stairs. "There can't be a bit of truth in it." And yet, though I assured myself that "there couldn't be a bit of truth in it," I shrank, with a creepy sensation, from going through the house to my room in the third storey. I was tired out after a hard day, and my nerves must have reacted morbidly to the silence and the darkness. For the first time in my life I knew what it was to be afraid of the unknown, of the unseen; and while I bent over my book, in the glare of the electric light, I became conscious presently that I was straining my senses for some sound in the spacious emptiness of the rooms overhead. The noise of a passing motor-car in the street jerked me back from the intense hush of expectancy; and I can recall the wave of relief that swept over me as I turned to my book again and tried to fix my distracted mind on its pages.

I was still sitting there when the telephone on my desk rang, with what seemed to my overwrought nerves a startling abruptness, and the voice of the superintendent told me hurriedly that Doctor Maradick was needed at the hospital. I had become so accustomed to these emergency calls in the night that I felt reassured when I had rung up the doctor in his room and had heard the hearty sound of his response. He had not yet undressed, he said, and would come down immediately while I ordered back his car, which must just have reached the garage.

"I'll be with you in five minutes!" he called as cheerfully as if I had summoned him to his wedding.

I heard him cross the floor of his room; and before he could reach the head of the staircase, I opened the door and went out into the hall in order that I might turn on the light and have his hat and coat waiting. The electric button was at the end of the hall, and as I moved towards it, guided by the glimmer that fell from the landing above, I lifted my eyes to the staircase, which climbed dimly, with its slender mahogany balustrade, as far as the third storey. Then it was, at the very moment when the doctor, humming gaily, began his quick descent of the steps, that I distinctly saw—I will swear to this on my deathbed—a child's skipping-rope lying loosely coiled, as if it had dropped from a careless little hand, in the bend of the staircase. With a spring I had reached the electric button, flooding the hall with light; but as I did so, while my arm was still outstretched behind me, I heard the humming voice change to a cry of surprise or terror, and the figure on the staircase tripped heavily and stumbled with groping hands into emptiness. The scream of warning died in my throat while I watched him pitch forward down the long flight of stairs to the floor at my feet. Even before I bent over him, before I wiped the blood from his brow and felt for his silent heart, I knew that he was dead.

Something—it may have been, as the world believes, a misstep in the dimness, or it may have been, as I am ready to bear witness, an invisible judgment—something had killed him at the very moment when he most wanted to live.

No. 252 Rue M. le Prince

Ralph Adams Cram

WHEN in May, 1886, I found myself at last in Paris, I naturally determined to throw myself on the charity of an old chum of mine, Eugene Marie d'Ardeche, who had forsaken Boston a year or more ago on receiving word of the death of an aunt who had left him such property as she possessed. I fancy this windfall surprised him not a little, for the relations between the aunt and nephew had never been cordial, judging from Eugene's remarks touching the lady, who was, it seems, a more or less wicked and witch-like old person, with a penchant for black magic, at least such was the common report.

Why she should leave all her property to d'Ardeche, no one could tell, unless it was that she felt his rather hobbledehoy tendencies towards Buddhism and occultism might some day lead him to her own unhallowed height of questionable illumination. To be sure d'Ardeche reviled her as a bad old woman, being himself in that state of enthusiastic exaltation which sometimes accompanies a boyish fancy for occultism; but in spite of his distant and repellent attitude, Mlle. Blaye de Tartas made him her sole heir, to the violent wrath of a questionable old party known to infamy as the Sar Torrevieja, the "King of the Sorcerers." This malevolent old portent, whose gray and crafty face was often seen in the Rue M. le Prince during the life of Mlle. de Tartas had, it seems, fully expected to enjoy her small wealth after her death; and when it appeared that she had left him only the contents of the gloomy old house in the Quartier Latin, giving the house itself and all else of which she died possessed to her nephew in America, the Sar proceeded to remove everything from the place, and then to curse it elaborately and comprehensively, together with all those who should ever dwell therein.

Whereupon he disappeared.

This final episode was the last word I received from Eugene, but I knew the number of the house, 252 Rue M. le Prince. So, after a day or two given to a first cursory survey of Paris, I started across the Seine to find Eugene and compel him to do the honors of the city.

Everyone who knows the Latin Quarter knows the Rue M. le Prince, running up the hill towards the Garden of the Luxembourg. It is full of queer houses and odd corners,—or was in '86,—and certainly No. 252 was, when I found it, quite as queer as any. It was nothing but a doorway, a black arch of old stone between and under two new houses painted yellow. The effect of this bit of seventeenth-century masonry, with its dirty old doors, and rusty broken lantern sticking gaunt and grim out over the narrow sidewalk, was, in its frame of fresh plaster, sinister in the extreme.

I wondered if I had made a mistake in the number; it was quite evident that no one lived behind those cobwebs. I went into the doorway of one of the new hôtels and interviewed the concierge.

No, M. d'Ardeche did not live there, though to be sure he owned the mansion; he himself resided in Meudon, in the country house of the late Mlle. de Tartas. Would Monsieur like the number and the street?

Monsieur would like them extremely, so I took the card that the concierge wrote for me, and forthwith started for the river, in order that I might take a steamboat for Meudon. By one of those coincidences which happen so often, being quite inexplicable, I had not gone twenty paces down the street before I ran directly into the arms of Eugene d'Ardeche. In three minutes we were sitting in the queer little garden of the Chien Bleu, drinking vermouth and absinthe, and talking it all over.

"You do not live in your aunt's house?" I said at last, interrogatively.

"No, but if this sort of thing keeps on I shall have to. I like Meudon much better, and the house is perfect, all furnished, and nothing in it newer than the last century. You must come out with me tonight and see it. I have got a jolly room fixed up for my Buddha. But there is something wrong with this house opposite. I can't keep a tenant in it,—not four days. I have had three, all within six months, but the stories have gone around and a man would as soon think of hiring the Cour des Comptes to live in as No. 252. It is notorious. The fact is, it is haunted the worst way."

I laughed and ordered more vermouth.

"That is all right. It is haunted all the same, or enough to keep it empty, and the funny part is that no one knows *how* it is haunted. Nothing is ever seen, nothing heard. As far as I can find out, people just have the horrors there, and have them so bad they have to go to the hospital afterwards. I have one ex-tenant in the Bicêtre now. So the house stands empty, and as it covers considerable ground and is taxed for a lot, I don't know what to do about it. I think I'll either give it to that child of sin, Torrevieja, or else go and live in it myself. I shouldn't mind the ghosts, I am sure."

"Did you ever stay there?"

"No, but I have always intended to, and in fact I came up here today to see a couple of rake-hell fellows I know, Fargeau and Duchesne, doctors in the Clinical Hospital beyond here, up by the Parc Mont Souris. They promised that they would spend the night with me some time in my aunt's house,—which is called around here, you must know, 'la Bouche d'Enfer,'—and I thought perhaps they would make it this week, if they can get off duty. Come up with me while I see them, and then we can go across the river to Véfour's and have some luncheon, you can get your things at the Chatham, and we will go out to Meudon, where of course you will spend the night with me."

The plan suited me perfectly, so we went up to the hospital, found Fargeau, who declared that he and Duchesne were ready for anything, the nearer the real "bouche d'enfer" the better; that the following Thursday they would both be off duty for the night, and that on that day they would join in an attempt to outwit the devil and clear up the mystery of No. 252.

"Does M. l'Américain go with us?" asked Fargeau.

"Why of course," I replied, "I intend to go, and you must not refuse me, d'Ardeche; I decline to be put off. Here is a chance for you to do the honors of your city in a manner which is faultless. Show me a real live ghost, and I will forgive Paris for having lost the Jardin Mabille."

So it was settled.

Later we went down to Meudon and ate dinner in the terrace room of the villa, which was all that d'Ardeche had said, and more, so utterly was its atmosphere that of the seventeenth century. At dinner Eugene told me more about his late aunt, and the queer goings on in the old house.

Mlle. Blaye lived, it seems, all alone, except for one female servant of her own age; a severe, taciturn creature, with massive Breton features and a Breton tongue, whenever she vouchsafed to use it. No one ever was seen to enter the door of No. 252 except Jeanne the servant and the Sar Torrevieja, the latter coming constantly from none knew whither, and always entering, *never leaving*. Indeed, the neighbors, who for eleven years had watched the old sorcerer sidle crab-wise up to the bell almost every day, declared vociferously that *never* had he been seen to leave the house. Once, when they decided to keep absolute guard, the watcher, none other than Maître Garceau of the Chien Bleu, after keeping his eyes fixed on the door from ten o'clock one morning when the Sar arrived until four in the afternoon, during which time the door was unopened (he knew this, for had he not gummed a ten-centime stamp over the joint and was not the stamp unbroken) nearly fell down when the sinister figure of Torrevieja slid wickedly by him with a dry "Pardon, Monsieur!" and disappeared again through the black doorway.

This was curious, for No. 252 was entirely surrounded by houses, its only windows opening on a courtyard into which no eye could look from the hôtels of the Rue M. le Prince and the Rue de l'Ecole, and the mystery was one of the choice possessions of the Latin Quarter.

Once a year the austerity of the place was broken, and the denizens of the whole quarter stood open-mouthed watching many carriages drive up to No. 252, many of them private, not a few with crests on the door panels, from all of them descending veiled female figures and men with coat collars turned up. Then followed curious sounds of music from within, and those whose houses joined the blank walls of No. 252 became for the moment popular, for by placing the ear against the wall strange music could distinctly be heard, and the sound of monotonous chanting voices now and then. By dawn the last guest would have departed, and for another year the hôtel of Mlle. de Tartas was ominously silent.

Eugene declared that he believed it was a celebration of "Walpurgisnacht," and certainly appearances favored such a fancy.

"A queer thing about the whole affair is," he said, "the fact that every one in the street swears that about a month ago, while I was out in

Concarneau for a visit, the music and voices were heard again, just as when my revered aunt was in the flesh. The house was perfectly empty, as I tell you, so it is quite possible that the good people were enjoying an hallucination."

I must acknowledge that these stories did not reassure me; in fact, as Thursday came near, I began to regret a little my determination to spend the night in the house. I was too vain to back down, however, and the perfect coolness of the two doctors, who ran down Tuesday to Meudon to make a few arrangements, caused me to swear that I would die of fright before I would flinch. I suppose I believed more or less in ghosts, I am sure now that I am older I believe in them, there are in fact few things I can *not* believe. Two or three inexplicable things had happened to me, and, although this was before my adventure with Rendel in Pæstum, I had a strong predisposition to believe some things that I could not explain, wherein I was out of sympathy with the age.

Well, to come to the memorable night of the twelfth of June, we had made our preparations, and after depositing a big bag inside the doors of No. 252, went across to the Chien Bleu, where Fargeau and Duchesne turned up promptly, and we sat down to the best dinner Père Garceau could create.

I remember I hardly felt that the conversation was in good taste. It began with various stories of Indian fakirs and Oriental jugglery, matters in which Eugene was curiously well read, swerved to the horrors of the great Sepoy mutiny, and thus to reminiscences of the dissecting-room. By this time we had drunk more or less, and Duchesne launched into a photographic and Zolaesque account of the only time (as he said) when he was possessed of the panic of fear; namely, one night many years ago, when he was locked by accident into the dissecting-room of the Loucine, together with several cadavers of a rather unpleasant nature. I ventured to protest mildly against the choice of subjects, the result being a perfect carnival of horrors, so that when we finally drank our last *crème de cacao* and started for "la Bouche d'Enfer," my nerves were in a somewhat rocky condition.

It was just ten o'clock when we came into the street. A hot dead wind drifted in great puffs through the city, and ragged masses of vapor swept the purple sky; an unsavory night altogether, one of those nights of hopeless lassitude when one feels, if one is at home, like doing nothing but drink mint juleps and smoke cigarettes.

Eugene opened the creaking door, and tried to light one of the lanterns; but the gusty wind blew out every match, and we finally had to close the outer doors before we could get a light. At last we had all the lanterns going, and I began to look around curiously. We were in a long, vaulted passage, partly carriageway, partly footpath, perfectly bare but for the street refuse which had drifted in with eddying winds. Beyond lay the courtyard, a curious place rendered more curious still by the fitful moonlight and the flashing of four dark lanterns. The place had evidently been once a most noble palace. Opposite rose the oldest portion, a three-story wall of the time of Francis I, with a great wisteria vine covering half. The wings on either side were more modern, seventeenth century, and ugly, while towards the street was nothing but a flat unbroken wall.

The great bare court, littered with bits of paper blown in by the wind, fragments of packing cases, and straw, mysterious with flashing lights and flaunting shadows, while low masses of torn vapor drifted overhead, hiding, then revealing the stars, and all in absolute silence, not even the sounds of the streets entering this prison-like place, was weird and uncanny in the extreme. I must confess that already I began to feel a slight disposition towards the horrors, but with that curious inconsequence which so often happens in the case of those who are deliberately growing scared, I could think of nothing more reassuring than those delicious verses of Lewis Carroll's:—

"Just the place for a Snark! I have said it twice,
That alone should encourage the crew.
Just the place for a Snark! I have said it thrice,
What I tell you three times is true,"

—which kept repeating themselves over and over in my brain with feverish insistence.

Even the medical students had stopped their chaffing, and were studying the surroundings gravely.

"There is one thing certain," said Fargeau, "*anything* might have happened here without the slightest chance of discovery. Did ever you see such a perfect place for lawlessness?"

"And *anything* might happen here now, with the same certainty of impunity," continued Duchesne, lighting his pipe, the snap of the match making us all start. "D'Ardeche, your lamented relative was certainly well fixed; she had full scope here for her traditional experiments in demonology."

"Curse me if I don't believe that those same traditions were more or less founded on fact," said Eugene. "I never saw this court under these conditions before, but I could believe anything now. What's that!"

"Nothing but a door slamming," said Duchesne, loudly.

"Well, I wish doors wouldn't slam in houses that have been empty eleven months."

"It is irritating," and Duchesne slipped his arm through mine; "but we must take things as they come. Remember we have to deal not only with the spectral lumber left here by your scarlet aunt, but as well with the supererogatory curse of that hell-cat Torrevieja. Come on! let's get inside before the hour arrives for the sheeted dead to squeak and gibber in these lonely halls. Light your pipes, your tobacco is a sure protection against 'your whoreson dead bodies'; light up and move on."

We opened the hall door and entered a vaulted stone vestibule, full of dust, and cobwebby.

"There is nothing on this floor," said Eugene, "except servants' rooms and offices, and I don't believe there is anything wrong with them. I never heard that there was, any way. Let's go up stairs."

So far as we could see, the house was apparently perfectly uninteresting inside, all eighteenth-century work, the façade of the main building being, with the vestibule, the only portion of the Francis I work.

"The place was burned during the Terror," said Eugene, "for my great-uncle, from whom Mlle. de Tartas inherited it, was a good and true Royalist; he went to Spain after the Revolution, and did not come back until the accession of Charles X, when he restored the house, and then died, enormously old. This explains why it is all so new."

The old Spanish sorcerer to whom Mlle. de Tartas had left her personal property had done his work thoroughly. The house was absolutely empty, even the wardrobes and bookcases built in had been carried away; we went through room after room, finding all absolutely dismantled, only the windows and doors with their casings, the parquet floors, and the florid Renaissance mantels remaining.

"I feel better," remarked Fargeau. "The house may be haunted, but it don't look it, certainly; it is the most respectable place imaginable."

"Just you wait," replied Eugene. "These are only the state apartments, which my aunt seldom used, except, perhaps, on her annual 'Walpurgisnacht.' Come up stairs and I will show you a better *mise en scène.*"

On this floor, the rooms fronting the court, the sleeping-rooms, were quite small,—("They are the bad rooms all the same," said Eugene,)—four of them, all just as ordinary in appearance as those below. A corridor ran behind them connecting with the wing corridor, and from this opened a door, unlike any of the other doors in that it was covered with green baize, somewhat moth-eaten. Eugene selected a key from the bunch he carried, unlocked the door, and with some difficulty forced it to swing inward; it was as heavy as the door of a safe.

"We are now," he said, "on the very threshold of hell itself; these rooms in here were my scarlet aunt's unholy of unholies. I never let them with the rest of the house, but keep them as a curiosity. I only wish Torrevieja had kept out; as it was, he looted them, as he did the rest of the house, and nothing is left but the walls and ceiling and floor. They are something, however, and may suggest what the former condition must have been. Tremble and enter."

The first apartment was a kind of anteroom, a cube of perhaps twenty feet each way, without windows, and with no doors except that by which we entered and another to the right. Walls, floor, and ceiling were covered with a black lacquer, brilliantly polished, that flashed the light of our lanterns in a thousand intricate reflections. It was like the inside of an enormous Japanese box, and about as empty. From this we passed to another room, and here we nearly dropped our lanterns. The room was circular, thirty feet or so in diameter, covered by a hemispherical dome; walls and ceiling were dark blue, spotted with gold stars; and reaching from floor to floor across the dome stretched a colossal figure in red lacquer of a nude woman kneeling, her legs reaching out along the floor on either side, her head touching the lintel of the door through which we had entered, her arms forming its sides, with the forearms extended and stretching along the walls until they met the long feet. The most astounding, misshapen, absolutely terrifying thing, I think, I ever saw. From the navel hung a great white object, like the traditional roe's egg of the Arabian Nights. The floor was of red lacquer, and in it was inlaid a pentagram the size of the room, made of wide strips of brass. In the centre of this pentagram was a circular disk of black stone, slightly saucer-shaped, with a small outlet in the middle.

The effect of the room was simply crushing, with this gigantic red figure crouched over it all, the staring eyes fixed on one, no matter what his position. None of us spoke, so oppressive was the whole thing.

The third room was like the first in dimensions, but instead of being black it was entirely sheathed with plates of brass, walls, ceiling, and floor,—tarnished now, and turning green, but still brilliant under the lantern light. In the middle stood an oblong altar of porphyry, its longer dimensions on the axis of the suite of rooms, and at one end, opposite the range of doors, a pedestal of black basalt.

This was all. Three rooms, stranger than these, even in their emptiness, it would be hard to imagine. In Egypt, in India, they would not be entirely out of place, but here in Paris, in a commonplace *hôtel,* in the Rue M. le Prince, they were incredible.

We retraced our steps, Eugene closed the iron door with its baize covering, and we went into one of the front chambers and sat down, looking at each other.

"Nice party, your aunt," said Fargeau. "Nice old party, with amiable tastes; I am glad we are not to spend the night in *those* rooms."

"What do you suppose she did there?" inquired Duchesne. "I know more or less about black art, but that series of rooms is too much for me."

"My impression is," said d'Ardeche, "that the brazen room was a kind of sanctuary containing some image or other on the basalt base, while the stone in front was really an altar,—what the nature of the sacrifice might be I don't even guess. The round room may have been used for invocations and incantations. The pentagram looks like it. Any way it is all just about as queer and *fin de siècle* as I can well imagine. Look here, it is nearly twelve, let's dispose of ourselves, if we are going to hunt this thing down."

The four chambers on this floor of the old house were those said to be haunted, the wings being quite innocent, and, so far as we knew, the floors below. It was arranged that we should each occupy a room, leaving the doors open with the lights burning, and at the slightest cry or knock we were all to rush at once to the room from which the warning sound might come. There was no communication between the rooms to be sure, but, as the doors all opened into the corridor, every sound was plainly audible.

The last room fell to me, and I looked it over carefully.

It seemed innocent enough, a commonplace, square, rather lofty Parisian sleeping-room, finished in wood painted white, with a small marble mantel, a dusty floor of inlaid maple and cherry, walls hung with an ordinary French paper, apparently quite new, and two deeply embrasured windows looking out on the court.

I opened the swinging sash with some trouble, and sat down in the window seat with my lantern beside me trained on the only door, which gave on the corridor.

The wind had gone down, and it was very still without,—still and hot. The masses of luminous vapor were gathering thickly overhead, no longer urged by the gusty wind. The great masses of rank wisteria leaves, with here and there a second blossoming of purple flowers, hung dead over the window in the sluggish air. Across the roofs I could hear the sound of a belated *fiacre* in the streets below. I filled my pipe again and waited.

For a time the voices of the men in the other rooms were a companionship, and at first I shouted to them now and then, but my voice echoed rather unpleasantly through the long corridors, and had a suggestive way of reverberating around the left wing beside me, and coming out at a broken window at its extremity like the voice of another man. I soon gave up my attempts at conversation, and devoted myself to the task of keeping awake.

It was not easy; why did I eat that lettuce salad at Père Garceau's? I should have known better. It was making me irresistibly sleepy, and wakefulness was absolutely necessary. It was certainly gratifying to know that I could sleep, that my courage was by me to that extent, but in the interests of science I must keep awake. But almost never, it seemed, had sleep looked so desirable. Half a hundred times, nearly, I would doze for an instant, only to awake with a start, and find my pipe gone out. Nor did the exertion of relighting it pull me together. I struck my match mechanically, and with the first puff dropped off again. It was most vexing. I got up and walked around the room. It was most annoying. My cramped position had almost put both my legs to sleep. I could hardly stand. I felt numb, as though with cold. There was no longer any sound from the other rooms, nor from without. I sank down in my window seat. How dark it was growing! I turned up the lantern. That pipe again, how obstinately it kept going out! and my last match was gone. The lantern, too, was *that* going out? I lifted my hand to turn it up again. It felt like lead, and fell beside me.

Then I awoke,—absolutely. I remembered the story of "The Haunters and the Haunted." *This* was the Horror. I tried to rise, to cry out. My body was like lead, my tongue was paralyzed. I could hardly move my eyes. And the light was going out. There was no question about that. Darker and darker yet; little by little the pattern of the paper was swallowed up in the advancing night. A prickling numbness gathered in every nerve, my right arm slipped without feeling from my lap to my side, and I could not raise it,—it swung helpless. A thin, keen humming began in my head, like the cicadas on a hillside in September. The darkness was coming fast.

Yes, this was it. Something was subjecting me, body and mind, to slow paralysis. Physically I was already dead. If I could only hold my mind, my consciousness, I might still be safe, but could I? Could I resist the mad horror of this silence, the deepening dark, the creeping numbness? I knew that, like the man in the ghost story, my only safety lay here.

It had come at last. My body was dead, I could no longer move my eyes. They were fixed in that last look on the place where the door had been, now only a deepening of the dark.

Utter night: the last flicker of the lantern was gone. I sat and waited; my mind was still keen, but how long would it last? There was a limit even to the endurance of the utter panic of fear.

Then the end began. In the velvet blackness came two white eyes, milky, opalescent, small, far away,—awful eyes, like a dead dream. More beautiful than I can describe, the flakes of white flame moving from the perimeter inward, disappearing in the centre, like a never ending flow of opal water into a circular tunnel. I could not have moved my eyes had I possessed the power: they devoured the fearful, beautiful things that grew slowly, slowly larger, fixed on me, advancing, growing more beautiful, the white flakes of light sweeping more swiftly into the blazing vortices, the awful fascination deepening in its insane intensity as the white, vibrating eyes grew nearer, larger.

Like a hideous and implacable engine of death the eyes of the unknown Horror swelled and expanded until they were close before me, enormous, terrible, and I felt a slow, cold, wet breath propelled with mechanical regularity against my face, enveloping me in its fetid mist, in its charnel-house deadliness.

With ordinary fear goes always a physical terror, but with me in the presence of this unspeakable Thing was only the utter and awful terror of the mind, the mad fear of a prolonged and ghostly nightmare. Again and again I tried to shriek, to make some noise, but physically I was utterly dead. I could only feel myself go mad with the terror of hideous death. The eyes were close on me,—their movement so swift that they seemed to be but palpitating flames, the dead breath was around me like the depths of the deepest sea.

Suddenly a wet, icy mouth, like that of a dead cuttle-fish, shapeless, jelly-like, fell over mine. The horror began slowly to draw my life from me, but, as enormous and shuddering folds of palpitating jelly swept sinuously around me, my will came back, my body awoke with the reaction of final fear, and I closed with the nameless death that enfolded me.

What was it that I was fighting? My arms sunk through the unresisting mass that was turning me to ice. Moment by moment new folds of cold jelly swept round me, crushing me with the force of Titans. I fought to wrest my mouth from this awful Thing that sealed it, but, if ever I succeeded and caught a single breath, the wet, sucking mass closed over my face again before I could cry out. I think I fought for hours, desperately, insanely, in a silence that was more hideous than any sound,—fought until I felt final death at hand, until the memory of all my life rushed over me like a flood, until I no longer had strength to wrench my face from that hellish succubus, until with a last mechanical struggle I fell and yielded to death.

†

Then I heard a voice say, "If he is dead, I can never forgive myself; I was to blame."

Another replied, "He is not dead, I know we can save him if only we reach the hospital in time. Drive like hell, *cocher*! twenty francs for you, if you get there in three minutes."

Then there was night again, and nothingness, until I suddenly awoke and stared around. I lay in a hospital ward, very white and sunny, some yellow *fleurs-de-lis* stood beside the head of the pallet, and a tall sister of mercy sat by my side.

To tell the story in a few words, I was in the Hôtel Dieu, where the men had taken me that fearful night of the twelfth of June. I asked for Fargeau or Duchesne, and by and by the latter came, and sitting beside the bed told me all that I did not know.

It seems that they had sat, each in his room, hour after hour, hearing nothing, very much bored, and disappointed. Soon after two o'clock Fargeau, who was in the next room, called to me to ask if I was awake. I gave no reply, and, after shouting once or twice, he took his lantern and came to investigate. The door was locked on the inside! He instantly called d'Ardeche and Duchesne, and together they hurled themselves against the door. It resisted. Within they could hear irregular footsteps dashing here and there, with heavy breathing. Although frozen with terror, they fought to destroy the door and finally succeeded by using a great slab of marble that formed the shelf of the mantel in Fargeau's room. As the door crashed in, they were suddenly hurled back against the walls of the corridor, as though by an explosion, the lanterns were extinguished, and they found themselves in utter silence and darkness.

As soon as they recovered from the shock, they leaped into the room and fell over my body in the middle of the floor. They lighted one of the lanterns, and saw the strangest sight that can be imagined. The floor and walls to the height of about six feet were running with something that seemed like stagnant water, thick, glutinous, sickening. As for me, I was drenched with the same cursed liquid. The odor of musk was nauseating. They dragged me away, stripped off my clothing, wrapped me in their coats, and hurried to the hospital, thinking me perhaps dead. Soon after sunrise d'Ardeche left the hospital, being assured that I was in a fair way to recovery, with time, and with Fargeau went up to examine by daylight the traces of the adventure that was so nearly fatal. They were too late. Fire engines were coming down the street as they passed the Académie. A neighbor rushed up to d'Ardeche: "O Monsieur! what misfortune, yet what fortune! It is true *la Bouche d'Enfer*—I beg pardon, the residence of the lamented Mlle. de Tartas,—was burned, but not wholly, only the ancient building. The wings were saved, and for that great credit is due the brave firemen. Monsieur will remember them, no doubt."

It was quite true. Whether a forgotten lantern, overturned in the excitement, had done the work, or whether the origin of the fire was more supernatural, it was certain that "the Mouth of Hell" was no more. A last engine was pumping slowly as d'Ardeche came up; half a dozen limp, and one distended, hose stretched through the *porte cochère*, and within only the façade of Francis I remained, draped still with the black stems of the wisteria. Beyond lay a great vacancy, where thin smoke was rising slowly. Every floor was gone, and the strange halls of Mlle. Blaye de Tartas were only a memory.

With d'Ardeche I visited the place last year, but in the stead of the ancient walls was then only a new and ordinary building, fresh and respectable; yet the wonderful stories of the old *Bouche d'Enfer* still lingered in the quarter, and will hold there, I do not doubt, until the Day of Judgment.

The Dead Valley

Ralph Adams Cram

I have a friend, Olof Ehrensvärd, a Swede by birth, who yet, by reason of a strange and melancholy mischance of his early boyhood, has thrown his lot with that of the New World. It is a curious story of a headstrong boy and a proud and relentless family: the details do not matter here, but they are sufficient to weave a web of romance around the tall yellow-bearded man with the sad eyes and the voice that gives itself perfectly to plaintive little Swedish songs remembered out of childhood. In the winter evenings we play chess together, he and I, and after some close, fierce battle has been fought to a finish—usually with my own defeat—we fill our pipes again, and Ehrensvärd tells me stories of the far, half-remembered days in the fatherland, before he went to sea: stories that grow very strange and incredible as the night deepens and the fire falls together, but stories that, nevertheless, I fully believe.

One of them made a strong impression on me, so I set it down here, only regretting that I cannot reproduce the curiously perfect English and the delicate accent which to me increased the fascination of the tale. Yet, as best I can remember it, here it is.

"I never told you how Nils and I went over the hills to Hallsberg, and how we found the Dead Valley, did I? Well, this is the way it happened. I must have been about twelve years old, and Nils Sjöberg, whose father's estate joined ours, was a few months younger. We were inseparable just at that time, and whatever we did, we did together.

"Once a week it was market day in Engelholm, and Nils and I went always there to see the strange sights that the market gathered from all the surrounding country. One day we quite lost our hearts, for an old man from across the Elfborg had brought a little dog to sell, that seemed to us the most beautiful dog in all the world. He was a round, woolly puppy, so funny that Nils and I sat down on the ground and laughed at him, until he came and played with us in so jolly a way that we felt that there was only one really desirable thing in life, and that was the little dog of the old man from across the hills. But alas! we had not half money enough wherewith to buy him, so we were forced to beg the old man not to sell him before the next market day, promising that we would bring the money for him then. He gave us his word, and we ran home very fast and implored our mothers to give us money for the little dog.

"We got the money, but we could not wait for the next market day. Suppose the puppy should be sold! The thought frightened us so that we begged and implored that we might be allowed to go over the hills to Hallsberg where the old man lived, and get the little dog ourselves, and at last they told us we might go. By starting early in the morning we should reach Hallsberg by three o'clock, and it was arranged that we should stay there that night with Nils's aunt, and, leaving by noon the next day, be home again by sunset.

"Soon after sunrise we were on our way, after having received minute instructions as to just what we should do in all possible and impossible circumstances, and finally a repeated injunction that we should start for home at the same hour the next day, so that we might get safely back before nightfall.

"For us, it was magnificent sport, and we started off with our rifles, full of the sense of our very great importance: yet the journey was simple enough, along a good road, across the big hills we knew so well, for Nils and I had shot over half the territory this side of the dividing ridge of the Elfborg. Back of Engelholm lay a long valley, from which rose the low mountains, and we had to cross this, and then follow the road along the side of the hills for three or four miles, before a narrow path branched off to the left, leading up through the pass.

"Nothing occurred of interest on the way over, and we reached Hallsberg in due season, found to our inexpressible joy that the little dog was not sold, secured him, and so went to the house of Nils's aunt to spend the night.

"Why we did not leave early on the following day, I can't quite remember; at all events, I know we stopped at a shooting range just outside of the town, where most attractive pasteboard pigs were sliding slowly through painted foliage, serving so as beautiful marks. The result was that we did not get fairly started for home until afternoon, and as we found ourselves at last pushing up the side of the mountain with the sun dangerously near their summits, I think we were a little scared at the prospect of the examination and possible punishment that awaited us when we got home at midnight.

"Therefore we hurried as fast as possible up the mountain side, while the blue dusk closed in about us, and the light died in the purple sky. At first we had talked hilariously, and the little dog had leaped ahead of us with the utmost joy. Latterly, however, a curious oppression came on us; we did not speak or even whistle, while the dog fell behind, following us with hesitation in every muscle.

"We had passed through the foothills and the low spurs of the mountains, and were almost at the top of the main range, when life seemed to go out of everything, leaving the world dead, so suddenly silent the forest became, so stagnant the air. Instinctively we halted to listen.

"Perfect silence,—the crushing silence of deep forests at night; and more, for always, even in the most impenetrable fastnesses of the wooded mountains, is the multitudinous murmur of little lives, awakened by the darkness, exaggerated and intensified by the stillness of the air and the great dark: but here and now the silence seemed unbroken even by the turn of a leaf, the movement of a twig, the note of night bird or insect. I could hear the blood beat through my veins; and the crushing of the grass under our feet as we advanced with hesitating steps sounded like the falling of trees.

"And the air was stagnant,—dead. The atmosphere seemed to lie upon the body like the weight of sea on a diver who has ventured too far into its awful depths. What we usually call silence seems so only in relation to the din of ordinary experience. This was silence in the absolute, and it crushed the mind while it intensified the senses, bringing down the awful weight of inextinguishable fear.

"I know that Nils and I stared towards each other in abject terror, listening to our quick, heavy breathing, that sounded to our acute senses like the fitful rush of waters. And the poor little dog we were leading justified our terror. The black oppression seemed to crush him even as it did us. He lay close on the ground, moaning feebly, and dragging himself painfully and slowly closer to Nils's feet. I think this exhibition of utter animal fear was the last touch, and must inevitably have blasted our reason—mine anyway; but just then, as we stood quaking on the bounds of madness, came a sound, so awful, so ghastly, so horrible, that it seemed to rouse us from the dead spell that was on us.

"In the depth of the silence came a cry, beginning as a low, sorrowful moan, rising to a tremulous shriek, culminating in a yell that seemed to tear the night in sunder and rend the world as by a cataclysm. So fearful was it that I could not believe it had actual existence: it passed previous experience, the powers of belief, and for a moment I thought it the result of my own animal terror, an hallucination born of tottering reason.

"A glance at Nils dispelled this thought in a flash. In the pale light of the high stars he was the embodiment of all possible human fear, quaking with an ague, his jaw fallen, his tongue out, his eyes protruding like those of a hanged man. Without a word we fled, the panic of fear giving us strength, and together, the little dog caught close in Nils's arms, we sped down the side of the cursed mountains,—anywhere, goal was of no account: we had but one impulse—to get away from that place.

"So under the black trees and the far white stars that flashed through the still leaves overhead, we leaped down the mountain side, regardless of path or landmark, straight through the tangled underbrush, across mountain streams, through fens and copses, anywhere, so only that our course was downward.

"How long we ran thus, I have no idea, but by and by the forest fell behind, and we found ourselves among the foothills, and fell exhausted on the dry short grass, panting like tired dogs.

"It was lighter here in the open, and presently we looked around to see where we were, and how we were to strike out in order to find the path that would lead us home. We looked in vain for a familiar sign. Behind us rose the great wall of black forest on the flank of the mountain: before us lay the undulating mounds of low foothills, unbroken by trees or rocks, and beyond, only the fall of black sky bright with multitudinous stars that turned its velvet depth to a luminous gray.

"As I remember, we did not speak to each other once: the terror was too heavy on us for that, but by and by we rose simultaneously and started out across the hills.

"Still the same silence, the same dead, motionless air—air that was at once sultry and chilling: a heavy heat struck through with an icy chill that felt almost like the burning of frozen steel. Still carrying the helpless dog, Nils pressed on through the hills, and I followed close behind. At last, in front of us, rose a slope of moor touching the white stars. We climbed it wearily, reached the top, and found ourselves gazing down into a great, smooth valley, filled half way to the brim with—what?

"As far as the eye could see stretched a level plain of ashy white, faintly phosphorescent, a sea of velvet fog that lay like motionless water, or rather like a floor of alabaster, so dense did it appear, so seemingly capable of sustaining weight. If it were possible, I think that sea of dead white mist struck even greater terror into my soul than the heavy silence or the deadly cry—so ominous was it, so utterly unreal, so phantasmal, so impossible, as it lay there like a dead ocean under the steady stars. Yet through that mist *we must go*! there seemed no other way home, and, shattered with abject fear, mad with the one desire to get back, we started down the slope to where the sea of milky mist ceased, sharp and distinct around the stems of the rough grass.

"I put one foot into the ghostly fog. A chill as of death struck through me, stopping my heart, and I threw myself backward on the slope. At that instant came again the shriek, close, close, right in our ears, in ourselves, and far out across that damnable sea I saw the cold fog lift like a waterspout and toss itself high in writhing convolutions towards the sky. The stars began to grow dim as thick vapor swept across them, and in the growing dark I saw a great, watery moon lift itself slowly above the palpitating sea, vast and vague in the gathering mist.

"This was enough: we turned and fled along the margin of the white sea that throbbed now with fitful motion below us, rising, rising, slowly and steadily, driving us higher and higher up the side of the foothills.

"It was a race for life; that we knew. How we kept it up I cannot understand, but we did, and at last we saw the white sea fall behind us as we staggered up the end of the valley, and then down into a region that we knew, and so into the old path. The last thing I remember was hearing a strange voice, that of Nils, but horribly changed, stammer brokenly, 'The dog is dead!' and then the whole world turned around twice, slowly and resistlessly, and consciousness went out with a crash.

"It was some three weeks later, as I remember, that I awoke in my own room, and found my mother sitting beside the bed. I could not think very well at first, but as I slowly grew strong again, vague flashes of recollection began to come to me, and little by little the whole sequence of events of that awful night in the Dead Valley came back. All that I could gain from what was told me was that three weeks before I had been found in my own bed, raging sick, and that my illness grew fast into brain fever. I tried to speak of the dread things that had happened to me, but I saw at once that no one looked on them save as the hauntings of a dying frenzy, and so I closed my mouth and kept my own counsel.

"I must see Nils, however, and so I asked for him. My mother told me that he also had been ill with a strange fever, but that he was now quite well again. Presently they brought him in, and when we were alone I began to speak to him of the night on the mountain. I shall never forget the shock that struck me down on my pillow when the boy denied everything: denied having gone with me, ever having heard the cry, having seen the valley, or feeling the deadly chill of the ghostly fog. Nothing would shake his determined ignorance, and in spite of myself I was forced to admit that his denials came from no policy of concealment, but from blank oblivion.

"My weakened brain was in a turmoil. Was it all but the floating phantasm of delirium? Or had the horror of the real thing blotted Nils's mind into blankness so far as the events of the night in the Dead Valley were concerned? The latter explanation seemed the only one, else how explain the sudden illness which in a night had struck us both down? I said nothing more, either to Nils or to my own people, but waited, with a growing determination that, once well again, I would find that valley if it really existed.

"It was some weeks before I was really well enough to go, but finally, late in September, I chose a bright, warm, still day, the last smile of the dying summer, and started early in the morning along the path that led to Hallsberg. I was sure I knew where the trail struck off to the right, down which we had come from the valley of dead water, for a great tree grew by the Hallsberg path at the point where, with a sense of salvation, we had found the home road. Presently I saw it to the right, a little distance ahead.

"I think the bright sunlight and the clear air had worked as a tonic to me, for by the time I came to the foot of the great pine, I had quite lost faith in the verity of the vision that haunted me, believing at last that it was indeed but the nightmare of madness. Nevertheless, I turned sharply to the right, at the base of the tree, into a narrow path that led through a dense thicket. As I did so I tripped over something. A swarm of flies sung into the air around me, and looking down I saw the matted fleece, with the poor little bones thrusting through, of the dog we had bought in Hallsberg.

"Then my courage went out with a puff, and I knew that it all was true, and that now I was frightened. Pride and the desire for adventure urged me on, however, and I pressed into the close thicket that barred my way. The path was hardly visible: merely the worn road of some small beasts, for, though it showed in the crisp grass, the bushes above grew thick and hardly penetrable. The land rose slowly, and rising grew clearer, until at last I came out on a great slope of hill, unbroken by trees or shrubs, very like my memory of that rise of land we had topped in order that we might find the dead valley and the icy fog. I looked at the sun; it was bright and clear, and all around insects were humming in the autumn air, and birds were darting to and fro. Surely there was no danger, not until nightfall at least; so I began to whistle, and with a rush mounted the last crest of brown hill.

"There lay the Dead Valley! A great oval basin, almost as smooth and regular as though made by man. On all sides the grass crept over the brink of the encircling hills, dusty green on the crests, then fading into ashy brown, and so to a deadly white, this last color forming a thin ring, running in a long line around the slope. And then? Nothing. Bare, brown, hard earth, glittering with grains of alkali, but otherwise dead and barren. Not a tuft of grass, not a stick of brushwood, not even a stone, but only the vast expanse of beaten clay.

"In the midst of the basin, perhaps a mile and a half away, the level expanse was broken by a great dead tree, rising leafless and gaunt into the air. Without a moment's hesitation I started down into the valley and made for this goal. Every particle of fear seemed to have left me, and even the valley itself did not look so very terrifying. At all events, I was driven by an overwhelming curiosity, and there seemed to be but one thing in the world to do,—to get to that Tree! As I trudged along over the hard earth,

I noticed that the multitudinous voices of birds and insects had died away. No bee or butterfly hovered through the air, no insects leaped or crept over the dull earth. The very air itself was stagnant.

"As I drew near the skeleton tree, I noticed the glint of sunlight on a kind of white mound around its roots, and I wondered curiously. It was not until I had come close that I saw its nature.

"All around the roots and barkless trunk was heaped a wilderness of little bones. Tiny skulls of rodents and of birds, thousands of them, rising about the dead tree and streaming off for several yards in all directions, until the dreadful pile ended in isolated skulls and scattered skeletons. Here and there a larger bone appeared,—the thigh of a sheep, the hoofs of a horse, and to one side, grinning slowly, a human skull.

"I stood quite still, staring with all my eyes, when suddenly the dense silence was broken by a faint, forlorn cry high over my head. I looked up and saw a great falcon turning and sailing downward just over the tree. In a moment more she fell motionless on the bleaching bones.

"Horror struck me, and I rushed for home, my brain whirling, a strange numbness growing in me. I ran steadily, on and on. At last I glanced up. Where was the rise of hill? I looked around wildly. Close before me was the dead tree with its pile of bones. I had circled it round and round, and the valley wall was still a mile and a half away.

"I stood dazed and frozen. The sun was sinking, red and dull, towards the line of hills. In the east the dark was growing fast. Was there still time? *Time!* It was not *that* I wanted, it was *will*! My feet seemed clogged as in a nightmare. I could hardly drag them over the barren earth. And then I felt the slow chill creeping through me. I looked down. Out of the earth a thin mist was rising, collecting in little pools that grew ever larger until they joined here and there, their currents swirling slowly like thin blue smoke. The western hills halved the copper sun. When it was dark I should hear that shriek again, and then I should die. I knew that, and with every remaining atom of will I staggered towards the red west through the writhing mist that crept clammily around my ankles, retarding my steps.

"And as I fought my way off from the Tree, the horror grew, until at last I thought I was going to die. The silence pursued me like dumb ghosts, the still air held my breath, the hellish fog caught at my feet like cold hands.

"But I won! though not a moment too soon. As I crawled on my hands and knees up the brown slope, I heard, far away and high in the air, the cry that already had almost bereft me of reason. It was faint and vague, but unmistakable in its horrible intensity. I glanced behind. The fog was dense and pallid, heaving undulously up the brown slope. The sky was gold under the setting sun, but below was the ashy gray of death. I stood for a moment on the brink of this sea of hell, and then leaped down the slope. The sunset opened before me, the night closed behind, and as I crawled home weak and tired, darkness shut down on the Dead Valley."

Postscript

There seem to be certain well-defined roots existing in all countries, from which spring the current legends of the supernatural; and therefore for the germs of the stories in this book the Author claims no originality. These legends differ one from the other only in local color and in individual treatment. If the Author has succeeded in clothing one or two of these norms in some slightly new vesture, he is more than content.

BOSTON, *July 3, 1895.*

The Night Wire

H. F. Arnold

"New York, September 30 CP FLASH

"Ambassador Holliwell died here today. The end came suddenly as the ambassador was alone in his study..."

There is something ungodly about these night wire jobs. You sit up here on the top floor of a skyscraper and listen in to the whispers of a civilization. New York, London, Calcutta, Bombay, Singapore — they're your next-door neighbors after the streetlights go dim and the world has gone to sleep.

Alone in the quiet hours between two and four, the receiving operators doze over their sounders and the news comes in. Fires and disasters and suicides. Murders, crowds, catastrophes. Sometimes an earthquake with a casualty list as long as your arm. The night wire man takes it down almost in his sleep, picking it off on his typewriter with one finger.

Once in a long time you prick up your ears and listen. You've heard of someone you knew in Singapore, Halifax or Paris, long ago. Maybe they've been promoted, but more probably they've been murdered or drowned. Perhaps they just decided to quit and took some bizarre way out. Made it interesting enough to get in the news.

But that doesn't happen often. Most of the time you sit and doze and tap, tap on your typewriter and wish you were home in bed.

Sometimes, though, queer things happen. One did the other night, and I haven't got over it yet. I wish I could.

You see, I handle the night manager's desk in a western seaport town; what the name is, doesn't matter.

There is, or rather was, only one night operator on my staff, a fellow named John Morgan, about forty years of age, I should say, and a sober, hard-working sort.

He was one of the best operators I ever knew, what is known as a "double" man. That means he could handle two instruments at once and type the stories on different typewriters at the same time. He was one of the three men I ever knew who could do it consistently, hour after hour, and never make a mistake.

Generally, we used only one wire at night, but sometimes, when it was late and the news was coming fast, the Chicago and Denver stations would open a second wire, and then Morgan would do his stuff. He was a wizard, a mechanical automatic wizard which functioned marvelously but was without imagination.

On the night of the sixteenth he complained of feeling tired. It was the first and last time I had ever heard him say a word about himself, and I had known him for three years.

It was just three o'clock and we were running only one wire. I was nodding over the reports at my desk and not paying much attention to him, when he spoke.

"Jim," he said, "does it feel close in here to you?"

"Why, no, John," I answered, "but I'll open a window if you like."

"Never mind," he said. "I reckon I'm just a little tired."

That was all that was said, and I went on working. Every ten minutes or so I would walk over and take a pile of copy that had stacked up neatly beside the typewriter as the messages were printed out in triplicate.

It must have been twenty minutes after he spoke that I noticed he had opened up the other wire and was using both typewriters. I thought it was a little unusual, as there was nothing very "hot" coming in. On my next trip I picked up the copy from both machines and took it back to my desk to sort out the duplicates.

The first wire was running out the usual sort of stuff and I just looked over it hurriedly. Then I turned to the second pile of copy. I remembered it particularly because the story was from a town I had never heard of: "Xebico." Here is the dispatch. I saved a duplicate of it from our files:

"Xebico, Sept 16 CP BULLETIN

"The heaviest mist in the history of the city settled over the town at 4 o'clock yesterday afternoon. All traffic has stopped and the mist hangs like a pall over everything. Lights of ordinary intensity fail to pierce the fog, which is constantly growing heavier.

"Scientists here are unable to agree as to the cause, and the local weather bureau states that the like has never occurred before in the history of the city.

"At 7 P.M. last night the municipal authorities...

(more)

That was all there was. Nothing out of the ordinary at a bureau headquarters, but, as I say, I noticed the story because of the name of the town.

†

It must have been fifteen minutes later that I went over for another batch of copy. Morgan was slumped down in his chair and had switched his green electric light shade so that the gleam missed his eyes and hit only the top of the two typewriters.

Only the usual stuff was in the righthand pile, but the lefthand batch carried another story from Xebico. All press dispatches come in "takes," meaning that parts of many different stories are strung along together, perhaps with but a few paragraphs of each coming through at a time. This second story was marked "add fog." Here is the copy:

"At 7 P.M. the fog had increased noticeably. All lights were now invisible and the town was shrouded in pitch darkness.

"As a peculiarity of the phenomenon, the fog is accompanied by a sickly odor, comparable to nothing yet experienced here."

Below that in customary press fashion was the hour, 3:27, and the initials of the operator, JM.

There was only one other story in the pile from the second wire. Here it is:

"2nd add Xebico Fog.

"Accounts as to the origin of the mist differ greatly. Among the most unusual is that of the sexton of the local church, who groped his way to headquarters in a hysterical condition and declared that the fog originated in the village churchyard.

"'It was first visible as a soft gray blanket clinging to the earth above the graves,' he stated. 'Then it began to rise, higher and higher. A subterranean breeze seemed to blow it in billows, which split up and then joined together again.

"'Fog phantoms, writhing in anguish, twisted the mist into queer forms and figures. And then, in the very thick midst of the mass, something moved.

"'I turned and ran from the accursed spot. Behind me I heard screams coming from the houses bordering on the graveyard.'

"Although the sexton's story is generally discredited, a party has left to investigate. Immediately after telling his story, the sexton collapsed and is now in a local hospital, unconscious."

Queer story, wasn't it. Not that we aren't used to it, for a lot of unusual stories come in over the wire. But for some reason or other, perhaps because it was so quiet that night, the report of the fog made a great impression on me.

It was almost with dread that I went over to the waiting piles of copy. Morgan did not move, and the only sound in the room was the tap-tap of the sounders. It was ominous, nerve-racking.

There was another story from Xebico in the pile of copy. I seized on it anxiously.

"New Lead Xebico Fog CP

"The rescue party which went out at 11 P.M. to investigate a weird story of the origin of a fog which, since late yesterday, has shrouded the city in darkness has failed to return. Another and larger party has been dispatched.

"Meanwhile, the fog has, if possible, grown heavier. It seeps through the cracks in the doors and fills the atmosphere with a depressing odor of decay. It is oppressive, terrifying, bearing with it a subtle impression of things long dead.

"Residents of the city have left their homes and gathered in the local church, where the priests are holding services of prayer. The scene is beyond description. Grown folk and children are alike terrified and many are almost beside themselves with fear.

"Amid the whisps of vapor which partly veil the church auditorium, an old priest is praying for the welfare of his flock. They alternately wail and cross themselves.

"From the outskirts of the city may be heard cries of unknown voices. They echo through the fog in queer uncadenced minor keys. The sounds resemble nothing so much as wind whistling through a gigantic tunnel. But the night is calm and there is no wind. The second rescue party… (more)"

I am a calm man and never in a dozen years spent with the wires, have I been known to become excited, but despite myself I rose from my chair and walked to the window.

Could I be mistaken, or far down in the canyons of the city beneath me did I see a faint trace of fog? Pshaw! It was all imagination.

In the pressroom the click of the sounders seemed to have raised the tempo of their tune. Morgan alone had not stirred from his chair. His head sunk between his shoulders, he tapped the dispatches out on the typewriters with one finger of each hand.

He looked asleep, but no; endlessly, efficiently, the two machines rattled off line after line, as relentlessly and effortlessly as death itself. There was something about the monotonous movement of the typewriter keys that fascinated me. I walked over and stood behind his chair, reading over his shoulder the type as it came into being, word by word.

Ah, here was another:

"Flash Xebico CP

"There will be no more bulletins from this office. The impossible has happened. No messages have come into this room for twenty minutes. We are cut off from the outside and even the streets below us.

"I will stay with the wire until the end.

"It is the end, indeed. Since 4 P.M. yesterday the fog has hung over the city. Following reports from the sexton of the local church, two rescue parties were sent out to investigate conditions on the outskirts of the city. Neither party has ever returned nor was any word received from them. It is quite certain now that they will never return.

"From my instrument I can gaze down on the city beneath me. From the position of this room on the thirteenth floor, nearly the entire city can be seen. Now I can see only a thick blanket of blackness where customarily are lights and life.

"I fear greatly that the wailing cries heard constantly from the outskirts of the city are the death cries of the inhabitants. They are constantly increasing in volume and are approaching the center of the city.

"The fog yet hangs over everything. If possible, it is even heavier than before, but the conditions have changed. Instead of an opaque, impenetrable wall of odorous vapor, there now swirls and writhes a shapeless mass in contortions of almost human agony. Now and again the mass parts and I catch a brief glimpse of the streets below.

"People are running to and fro, screaming in despair. A vast bedlam of sound flies up to my window, and above all is the immense whistling of unseen and unfelt winds.

"The fog has again swept over the city and the whistling is coming closer and closer.

"It is now directly beneath me.

"God! An instant ago the mist opened and I caught a glimpse of the streets below.

"The fog is not simply vapor—it lives! By the side of each moaning and weeping human is a companion figure, an aura of strange and vari-colored hues. How the shapes cling! Each to a living thing!

"The men and women are down. Flat on their faces. The fog figures caress them lovingly. They are kneeling beside them. They are—but I dare not tell it.

"The prone and writhing bodies have been stripped of their clothing. They are being consumed—piecemeal.

"A merciful wall of hot, steaming vapor has swept over the whole scene. I can see no more.

"Beneath me the wall of vapor is changing colors. It seems to be lighted by internal fires. No, it isn't. I have made a mistake. The colors are from above, reflections from the sky.

"Look up! Look up! The whole sky is in flames. Colors as yet unseen by man or demon. The flames are moving; they have started to intermix; the colors are rearranging themselves. They are so brilliant that my eyes burn, they are a long way off.

"Now they have begun to swirl, to circle in and out, twisting in intricate designs and patterns. The lights are racing each with each, a kaleidoscope of unearthly brilliance.

"I have made a discovery. There is nothing harmful in the lights. They radiate force and friendliness, almost cheeriness. But by their very strength, they hurt.

"As I look, they are swinging closer and closer, a million miles at each jump. Millions of miles with the speed of light. Aye, it is light of quintessence of all light. Beneath it the fog melts into a jeweled mist radiant, rainbow-colored of a thousand varied spectra.

"I can see the streets. Why, they are filled with people! The lights are coming closer. They are all around me. I am enveloped. I..."

†

The message stopped abruptly. The wire to Xebico was dead. Beneath my eyes in the narrow circle of light from under the green lamp-shade, the black printing no longer spun itself, letter by letter, across the page.

The room seemed filled with a solemn quiet, a silence vaguely impressive, powerful.

I looked down at Morgan. His hands had dropped nervelessly at his sides, while his body had hunched over peculiarly. I turned the lamp-shade back, throwing light squarely in his face. His eyes were staring, fixed.

†

Filled with a sudden foreboding, I stepped beside him and called Chicago on the wire. After a second the sounder clicked its answer.

Why? But there was something wrong. Chicago was reporting that Wire Two had not been used throughout the evening.

"Morgan!" I shouted. "Morgan! Wake up, it isn't true. Someone has been hoaxing us. Why..." In my eagerness I grasped him by the shoulder.

His body was quite cold. Morgan had been dead for hours. Could it be that his sensitized brain and automatic fingers had continued to record impressions even after the end?

I shall never know, for I shall never again handle the night shift. Search in a world atlas discloses no town of Xebico. Whatever it was that killed John Morgan will forever remain a mystery.

Wolverden Tower

Grant Allen

I

Maisie Llewelyn had never been asked to Wolverden before; therefore, she was not a little elated at Mrs West's invitation. For Wolverden Hall, one of the loveliest Elizabethan manor-houses in the Weald of Kent, had been bought and fitted up in appropriate style (the phrase is the upholsterer's) by Colonel West, the famous millionaire from South Australia. The Colonel had lavished upon it untold wealth, fleeced from the backs of ten thousand sheep and an equal number of his fellow-countrymen; and Wolverden was now, if not the most beautiful, at least the most opulent country-house within easy reach of London.

Mrs West was waiting at the station to meet Maisie. The house was full of Christmas guests already, it is true; but Mrs West was a model of stately, old-fashioned courtesy: she would not have omitted meeting one among the number on any less excuse than a royal command to appear at Windsor. She kissed Maisie on both cheeks – she had always been fond of Maisie – and, leaving two haughty young aristocrats (in powdered hair and blue-and-gold livery) to hunt up her luggage by the light of nature, sailed forth with her through the door to the obsequious carriage.

The drive up the avenue to Wolverden Hall Maisie found quite delicious. Even in their leafless winter condition the great limes looked so noble; and the ivy-covered hall at the end, with its mullioned windows, its Inigo Jones porch, and its creeper-clad gables, was as picturesque a building as the ideals one sees in Mr Abbey's sketches. If only Arthur Hume had been one of the party now, Maisie's joy would have been complete. But what was the use of thinking so much about Arthur Hume, when she didn't even know whether Arthur Hume cared for her?

A tall, slim girl, Maisie Llewelyn, with rich black hair, and ethereal features, as became a descendant of Llewelyn ap Iorwerth. The sort of girl we none of us would have called anything more than 'interesting' till Rossetti and Burne-Jones found eyes for us to see that the type is beautiful with a deeper beauty than that of your obvious pink-and-white prettiness. Her eyes, in particular, had a lustrous depth that was almost superhuman, and her fingers and nails were strangely transparent in their waxen softness.

'You won't mind my having put you in a ground-floor room in the new wing, my dear, will you?' Mrs West inquired, as she led Maisie personally to the quarters chosen for her. 'You see, we 're so unusually full, because of these tableaux!'

Maisie gazed round the ground-floor room in the new wing with eyes of mute wonder. If this was the kind of lodging for which Mrs West thought it necessary to apologise, Maisie wondered of what sort were those better rooms which she gave to the guests she delighted to honour. It was a large and exquisitely decorated chamber, with the softest and deepest Oriental carpet Maisie's feet had ever felt, and the daintiest curtains her eyes had ever lighted upon. True, it opened by French windows on to what was nominally the ground in front; but as the Italian terrace, with its formal balustrade and its great stone balls, was raised several feet above the level of the sloping garden below, the room was really on the first floor for all practical purposes. Indeed, Maisie rather liked the unwonted sense of space and freedom which was given by this easy access to the world without; and, as the windows were secured by great shutters and fasteners, she had no counterbalancing fear lest a nightly burglar should attempt to carry off her little pearl necklet or her amethyst brooch, instead of directing his whole attention to Mrs West's famous diamond tiara.

She moved naturally to the window. She was fond of nature. The view it disclosed over the Weald at her feet was wide and varied. Misty range lay behind misty range, in a faint December haze, receding and receding, till away to the south, half hidden by vapour, the Sussex downs loomed vague in the distance. The village church, as happens so often in the case of old lordly manors, stood within the grounds of the Hall, and close by the house. It had been built, her hostess said, in the days of the Edwards, but had portions of an older Saxon edifice still enclosed in the chancel. The one eyesore in the view was its new white tower, recently restored (or rather, rebuilt), which contrasted most painfully with the mellow grey stone and mouldering corbels of the nave and transept.

'What a pity it's been so spoiled!' Maisie exclaimed, looking across at the tower. Coming straight as she did from a Merioneth rectory, she took an ancestral interest in all that concerned churches.

'Oh, my dear!' Mrs West cried, 'please don't say that, I beg of you, to the Colonel. If you were to murmur "spoiled" to him you'd wreck his digestion. He's spent ever so much money over securing the foundations and reproducing the sculpture on the old tower we took down, and it breaks his dear heart when anybody disapproves of it. For some people, you know, are so absurdly opposed to reasonable restoration.'

'Oh, but this isn't even restoration, you know,' Maisie said, with the frankness of twenty, and the specialist interest of an antiquary's daughter. 'This is pure reconstruction.'

'Perhaps so,' Mrs West answered. 'But if you think so, my dear, don't breathe it at Wolverden.'

A fire, of ostentatiously wealthy dimensions, and of the best glowing coal burned bright on the hearth, but the day was mild, and hardly more than autumnal. Maisie found the room quite unpleasantly hot. She opened the windows and stepped out on the terrace. Mrs West followed her. They paced up and down the broad gravelled platform for a while – Maisie had not yet taken off her travelling-cloak and hat? and then strolled half unconsciously towards the gate of the church. The churchyard, to hide the tombstones of which the parapet had been erected, was full of quaint old monuments, with broken-nosed cherubs, some of them dating from a comparatively early period. The porch, with its sculptured niches deprived of their saints by puritan hands, was still rich and beautiful in its carved detail. On the seat inside an old woman was sitting. She did not rise as the lady of the manor approached, but went on mumbling and muttering inarticulately to herself in a sulky undertone. Still, Maisie was aware, none the less, that the moment she came near a strange light gleamed suddenly in the old woman's eyes, and that her glance was fixed upon her. A faint thrill of recognition seemed to pass like a flash through her palsied body. Maisie knew not why, but she was dimly afraid of the old woman's gaze upon her.

'It's a lovely old church!' Maisie said, looking up at the trefoil finials on the porch – 'all, except the tower.'

'We had to reconstruct it,' Mrs West answered apologetically. Mrs West's general attitude in life was apologetic, as though she felt she had no right to so much more money than her fellow-creatures. 'It would have fallen if we hadn't done something to buttress it up. It was really in a most dangerous and critical condition.'

'Lies! lies! lies!' the old woman burst out suddenly, though in a strange, low tone, as if speaking to herself. 'It would not have fallen – they knew it would not. It could not have fallen. It would never have fallen if they had not destroyed it. And even then – I was there when they pulled it down – each stone clung to each, with arms and legs and hands and claws, till they burst them asunder by main force with their new-fangled stuff – I don't know what they call it – dynamite, or something. It was all of it done for one man's vainglory!'

'Come away, dear,' Mrs West whispered. But Maisie loitered.

'Wolverden Tower was fasted thrice,' the old woman continued, in a sing-song quaver. 'It was fasted thrice with souls of maids against every assault of man or devil. It was fasted at the foundation against earthquake and ruin. It was fasted at the top against thunder and lightning. It was fasted in the middle against storm and battle. And there it would have stood for a thousand years if a wicked man had not raised a vainglorious hand against it. For that's what the rhyme says?

'Fasted thrice with souls of men.
Stands the tower of Wolverden;
Fasted thrice with maidens' blood.
A thousand years of fire and flood
Shall see it stand as erst it stood.'

She paused a moment, then, raising one skinny hand towards the brand new stone, she went on in the same voice, but with malignant fervour?

'A thousand years the tower shall stand
Till ill assailed by evil hand;
By evil hand in evil hour.
Fasted thrice with warlock's power.
Shall fall the stanes of Wulfhere's tower.'

She tottered off as she ended, and took her seat on the edge of a depressed vault in the churchyard close by, still eyeing Maisie Llewellyn with a weird and curious glance, almost like the look which a famishing man casts upon the food in a shop-window.

'Who is she?' Maisie asked, shrinking away in undefined terror.

'Oh, old Bessie,' Mrs West answered, looking more apologetic (for the parish) than ever. 'She's always hanging about here. She has nothing else to do, and she's an outdoor pauper. You see, that's the worst of having the church in one's grounds, which is otherwise picturesque and romantic and baronial; the road to it's public; you must admit all the world; and old Bessie will come here. The servants are afraid of her. They say she's a witch. She has the evil eye, and she drives girls to suicide. But they cross her hand with silver all the same, and she tells them their fortunes – gives them each a butler. She's full of dreadful stories about Wolverden Church? stories to make your blood run cold, my dear, compact with old superstitions and murders, and so forth. And they're true, too, that's the worst of them. She's quite a character. Mr Blaydes, the antiquary, is really attached to her; he says she's now the sole living repository of the traditional folklore and history of the parish. But I don't care for it myself. It 'gars one greet', as we say in Scotland. Too much burying alive in it, don't you know, my dear, to quite suit my fancy.'

They turned back as she spoke towards the carved wooden lych-gate, one of the oldest and most exquisite of its class in England. When they reached the vault by whose doors old Bessie was seated, Maisie turned once more to gaze at the pointed lancet windows of the Early English choir, and the still more ancient dog-tooth ornament of the ruined Norman Lady Chapel.

'How solidly it's built!' she exclaimed, looking up at the arches which alone survived the fury of the Puritan. 'It really looks as if it would last for ever.'

Old Bessie had bent her head, and seemed to be whispering something at the door of the vault. But at the sound she raised her eyes, and, turning her wizened face towards the lady of the manor, mumbled through her few remaining fang-like teeth an old local saying, 'Bradbury for length, Wolverden for strength, and Church Hatton for beauty!'

'Three brothers builded churches three;
And fasted thrice each church shall be:
Fasted thrice with maidens' blood.
To make them safe from fire and flood;
Fasted thrice with souls of men.
Hatton, Bradbury, Wolverden!'

'Come away,' Maisie said, shuddering. 'I'm afraid of that woman. Why was she whispering at the doors of the vault down there? I don't like the look of her.'

'My dear,' Mrs West answered, in no less terrified a tone, 'I will confess I don't like the look of her myself. I wish she'd leave the place. I've tried to make her. The Colonel offered her fifty pounds down and a nice cottage in Surrey if only she'd go – she frightens me so much; but she wouldn't hear of it. She said she must stop by the bodies of her dead – that's her style, don't you see: a sort of modern ghoul, a degenerate vampire – and from the bodies of her dead in Wolverden Church no living soul should ever move her.'

II

For dinner Maisie wore her white satin Empire dress, high-waisted, low-necked, and cut in the bodice with a certain baby-like simplicity of style which exactly suited her strange and uncanny type of beauty. She was very much admired. She felt it, and it pleased her. The young man who took her in, a subaltern of engineers, had no eyes for any one else; while old Admiral Wade, who sat opposite her with a plain and skinny dowager, made her positively uncomfortable by the persistent way in which he stared at her simple pearl necklet.

After dinner, the tableaux. They had been designed and managed by a famous Royal Academician, and were mostly got up by the members of the house-party. But two or three actresses from London had been specially invited to help in a few of the more mythological scenes; for, indeed, Mrs West had prepared the entire entertainment with that topsy-turvy conscientiousness and scrupulous sense of responsibility to society which pervaded her view of millionaire morality. Having once decided to offer the county a set of tableaux, she felt that millionaire morality absolutely demanded of her the sacrifice of three weeks' time and several hundred pounds' money in order to discharge her obligations to the county with becoming magnificence.

The first tableau, Maisie learned from the gorgeous programme, was 'Jephthah's Daughter'. The subject was represented at the pathetic moment when the doomed virgin goes forth from her father's house with her attendant maidens to bewail her virginity for two months upon the mountains, before the fulfilment of the awful vow which bound her father to offer her up for a burnt offering. Maisie thought it too solemn and tragic a scene for a festive occasion. But the famous R.A. had a taste for such themes, and his grouping was certainly most effectively dramatic.

'A perfect symphony in white and grey,' said Mr Wills, the art critic.

'How awfully affecting!' said most of the young girls.

'Reminds me a little too much, my dear, of old Bessie's stories,' Mrs West whispered low, leaning from her seat across two rows to Maisie.

A piano stood a little on one side of the platform, just in front of the curtain. The intervals between the pieces were filled up with songs, which, however, had been evidently arranged in keeping with the solemn and half-mystical tone of the tableaux. It is the habit of amateurs to take a long time in getting their scenes in order, so the interposition of the music was a happy thought as far as its prime intention went. But Maisie wondered they could not have chosen some livelier song for Christmas Eve than 'Oh, Mary, go and call the cattle home, and call the cattle home, and call the cattle home, across the sands of Dee.' Her own name was Mary when she signed it officially, and the sad lilt of the last line, 'But never home came she,' rang unpleasantly in her ear through the rest of the evening.

The second tableau was the 'Sacrifice of Iphigenia'. It was admirably rendered. The cold and dignified father, standing, apparently unmoved, by the pyre; the cruel faces of the attendant priests; the shrinking form of the immolated princess; the mere blank curiosity and inquiring interest of the helmeted heroes looking on, to whom this slaughter of a virgin victim was but an ordinary incident of the Achean religion. All these had been arranged by the Academical director with consummate skill and pictorial cleverness. But the group that attracted Maisie most among the components of the scene was that of the attendant maidens, more conspicuous here in their flowing white chitons than even they had been when posed as companions of the beautiful and ill-fated Hebrew victim. Two in particular excited her close attention – two very graceful and spiritual-looking girls, in long white robes of no particular age or country, who stood at the very end near the right edge of the picture. 'How lovely they are, the two last on the right!' Maisie whispered to her neighbour – an Oxford undergraduate with a budding moustache. 'I do so admire them!'

'Do you?' he answered, fondling the moustache with one dubious finger. 'Well, now, do you know, I don't think I do. They're rather coarse-looking. And besides, I don't quite like the way they've got their hair done up in bunches; too fashionable, isn't it? – too much of the present day – I don't care to see a girl in a Greek costume, with her coiffure so evidently turned out by Truefitt's!'

'Oh, I don't mean those two,' Maisie answered, a little shocked he should think she had picked out such meretricious faces; 'I mean the two beyond them again—the two with their hair so simply and sweetly done – the ethereal-looking dark girls.'

The undergraduate opened his mouth, and stared at her in blank amazement for a moment. 'Well, I don't see??' he began, and broke off suddenly. Something in Maisie's eye seemed to give him pause. He fondled his moustache, hesitated and was silent.

'How nice to have read the Greek and know what it all means!' Maisie went on, after a minute. 'It's a human sacrifice, of course; but, please, what is the story?'

The undergraduate hummed and hawed. 'Well, it's in Euripides, you know,' he said, trying to look impressive, 'and – er – and I haven't taken up Euripides for my next examination. But I think it's like this. Iphigenia was a daughter of Agamemnon's, don't you know, and he had offended Artemis or somebody – some other Goddess; and he vowed to offer up to her the most beautiful thing that should be born that year, by way of reparation – just like Jephthah. Well, Iphigenia was considered the most beautiful product of the particular twelvemonth? don't look at me like that, please! you – you make me nervous – and so, when the young woman grew up – well, I don't quite recollect the ins and outs of the details, but it's a human sacrifice business, don't you see; and they're just going to kill her, though I believe a hind was finally substituted for the girl, like the ram for Isaac; but I must confess I've a very vague recollection of it.' He rose from his seat uneasily. 'I'm afraid,' he went on, shuffling about for an excuse to move, 'these chairs are too close. I seem to be incommoding you.'

He moved away with a furtive air. At the end of the tableau one or two of the characters who were not needed in succeeding pieces came down from the stage and joined the body of spectators, as they often do, in their character-dresses – a good opportunity, in point of fact, for retaining through the evening the advantages conferred by theatrical costume, rouge, and pearl-powder. Among them the two girls Maisie had admired so much glided quietly toward her and took the two vacant seats on either side, one of which had just been quitted by the awkward undergraduate. They were not only beautiful in face and figure, on a closer view, but Maisie found them from the first extremely sympathetic. They burst into talk with her, frankly and at once, with charming ease and grace of manner. They were ladies in the grain, in instinct and breeding. The taller of the two, whom the other addressed as Yolande, seemed particularly pleasing. The very name charmed Maisie. She was friends with them at once. They both possessed a certain nameless attraction that constitutes in itself the best possible introduction. Maisie hesitated to ask them whence they came, but it was clear from their talk they knew Wolverden intimately.

After a minute the piano struck up once more. A famous Scotch vocalist, in a diamond necklet and a dress to match, took her place on the stage, just in front of the footlights. As chance would have it, she began singing the song Maisie most of all hated. It was Scott's ballad of 'Proud Maisie', set to music by Carlo Ludovici?

'Proud Maisie is in the wood.
Walking so early;
Sweet Robin sits on the bush.

Singing so rarely.
'Tell me, thou bonny bird.
When shall I marry me?'
'When six braw gentlemen
Kirkward shall carry ye.'
'Who makes the bridal bed.
Birdie, say truly?'
'The grey-headed sexton
That delves the grave duly.
'The glow-worm o'er grave and stone
Shall light thee steady;
'The owl from the steeple sing.
Welcome, Proud lady.'

Maisie listened to the song with grave discomfort. She had never liked it, and tonight it appalled her. She did not know that just at that moment Mrs West was whispering in a perfect fever of apology to a lady by her side, 'Oh dear! oh dear! what a dreadful thing of me ever to have permitted that song to be sung here tonight! It was horribly thoughtless! Why, now I remember, Miss Llewelyn's name, you know, is Maisie! And there she is listening to it with a face like a sheet! I shall never forgive myself!'

The tall, dark girl by Maisie's side, whom the other called Yolande, leaned across to her sympathetically. 'You don't like that song?' she said, with just a tinge of reproach in her voice as she said it.

'I hate it!' Maisie answered, trying hard to compose herself.

'Why so?' the tall, dark girl asked, in a tone of calm and singular sweetness. 'It is sad, perhaps; but it's lovely – and natural!'

'My own name is Maisie,' her new friend replied, with an ill-repressed shudder. 'And somehow that song pursues me through life I seem always to hear the horrid ring of the words, "When six braw gentlemen kirkward shall carry ye." I wish to Heaven my people had never called me Maisie!'

'And yet why?' the tall, dark girl asked again, with a sad, mysterious air. 'Why this clinging to life – this terror of death? this inexplicable attachment to a world of misery? And with such eyes as yours, too! Your eyes are like mine!' which was a compliment, certainly, for the dark girl's own pair were strangely deep and lustrous. 'People with eyes such as those, that can look into futurity, ought not surely to shrink from a mere gate like death! For death is but a gate – the gate of life in its fullest beauty. It is written over the door, "Mors janua vit".'

'What door?' Maisie asked, for she remembered having read those self-same words, and tried in vain to translate them, that very day, though the meaning was now clear to her.

The answer electrified her: 'The gate of the vault in Wolverden church-yard.'

She said it very low, but with pregnant expression.

'Oh, how dreadful!' Maisie exclaimed, drawing back. The tall, dark girl half frightened her.

'Not at all,' the girl answered. 'This life is so short, so vain, so transitory! And beyond it is peace – eternal peace – the calm of rest – the joy of the spirit.'

'You come to anchor at last,' her companion added.

'But if – one has somebody one would not wish to leave behind?' Maisie suggested timidly.

'He will follow before long,' the dark girl replied with quiet decision, interpreting rightly the sex of the indefinite substantive. 'Time passes so quickly. And if time passes quickly in time, how much more, then, in eternity!'

'Hush, Yolande,' the other dark girl put in, with a warning glance; 'there's a new tableau coming. Let me see, is this "The Death of Ophelia"? No, that's number four; this is number three, "The Martyrdom of St Agnes".'

III

'My dear,' Mrs West said, positively oozing apology, when she met Maisie in the supper-room, 'I'm afraid you've been left in a corner by yourself almost all the evening!'

'Oh dear, no,' Maisie answered with a quiet smile. 'I had that Oxford undergraduate at my elbow at first; and afterwards those two nice girls, with the flowing white dresses and the beautiful eyes, came and sat beside me. What's their name, I wonder?'

'Which girls?' Mrs West asked, with a little surprise in her tone, for her impression was rather that Maisie had been sitting between two empty chairs for the greater part of the evening, muttering at times to herself in the most uncanny way, but not talking to anybody.

Maisie glanced round the room in search of her new friends, and for some time could not see them. At last, she observed them in a remote alcove, drinking red wine by themselves out of Venetian-glass beakers. 'Those two,' she said, pointing towards them. 'They're such charming girls! Can you tell me who they are? I've quite taken a fancy to them.'

Mrs West gazed at them for a second – or rather, at the recess towards which Maisie pointed – and then turned to Maisie with much the same oddly embarrassed look and manner as the undergraduate's. 'Oh, those!' she said slowly, peering through and through her, Maisie thought. 'Those – must be some of the professionals from London. At any rate? – I'm not sure which you mean – over there by the curtain, in the Moorish nook, you say – well, I can't tell you their names! So they must be professionals.'

She went off with a singularly frightened manner. Maisie noticed it and wondered at it. But it made no great or lasting impression.

When the party broke up, about midnight or a little later, Maisie went along the corridor to her own bedroom. At the end, by the door, the two other girls happened to be standing, apparently gossiping.

'Oh, you've not gone home yet?' Maisie said, as she passed, to Yolande.

'No, we're stopping here,' the dark girl with the speaking eyes answered.

Maisie paused for a second. Then an impulse burst over her. 'Will you come and see my room?' she asked, a little timidly.

'Shall we go, Hedda?' Yolande said, with an inquiring glance at her companion.

Her friend nodded assent. Maisie opened the door, and ushered them into her bedroom.

The ostentatiously opulent fire was still burning brightly, the electric light flooded the room with its brilliancy, the curtains were drawn, and the shutters fastened. For a while the three girls sat together by the hearth and gossiped quietly. Maisie liked her new friends – their voices were so gentle, soft, and sympathetic, while for face and figure they might have sat as models to Burne-Jones or Botticelli. Their dresses, too, took her delicate Welsh fancy; they were so dainty, yet so simple. The soft silk fell in natural folds and dimples. The only ornaments they wore were two curious brooches of very antique workmanship – as Maisie supposed – somewhat Celtic in design, and enamelled in blood-red on a gold background. Each carried a flower laid loosely in her bosom. Yolande's was an orchid with long, floating streamers, in colour and shape recalling some Southern lizard; dark purple spots dappled its lip and petals. Hedda's was a flower of a sort Maisie had never before seen – the stem spotted like a viper's skin, green flecked with russet-brown, and uncanny to look upon; on either side, great twisted spirals of red-and-blue blossoms, each curled after the fashion of a scorpion's tail, very strange and lurid. Something weird and witch-like about flowers and dresses rather attracted Maisie; they affected her with the half-repellent fascination of a snake for a bird; she felt such blossoms were fit for incantations and sorceries. But a lily-of-the-valley in Yolande's dark hair gave a sense of purity which assorted better with the girl's exquisitely calm and nun-like beauty.

After a while Hedda rose. 'This air is close,' she said. 'It ought to be warm outside tonight, if one may judge by the sunset. May I open the window?'

'Oh, certainly, if you like,' Maisie answered, a vague foreboding now struggling within her against innate politeness.

Hedda drew back the curtains and unfastened the shutters. It was a moonlit evening. The breeze hardly stirred the bare boughs of the silver birches. A sprinkling of soft snow on the terrace and the hills just whitened the ground. The moon lighted it up, falling full upon the Hall; the church and tower below stood silhouetted in dark against a cloudless expanse of starry sky in the background. Hedda opened the window. Cool, fresh air blew in, very soft and genial, in spite of the snow and the lateness of the season. 'What a glorious night!' she said, looking up at Orion overhead. 'Shall we stroll out for a while in it?'

If the suggestion had not thus been thrust upon her from outside, it would never have occurred to Maisie to walk abroad in a strange place, in evening dress, on a winter's night, with snow whitening the ground; but Hedda's voice sounded so sweetly persuasive, and the idea itself seemed so natural now she had once proposed it, that Maisie followed her two new friends on to the moonlit terrace without a moment's hesitation.

They paced once or twice up and down the gravelled walks. Strange to say, though a sprinkling of dry snow powdered the ground under foot, the air itself was soft and balmy. Stranger still, Maisie noticed, almost without noticing it, that though they walked three abreast, only one pair of footprints – her own – lay impressed on the snow in a long trail when they turned at either end and re-paced the platform. Yolande and Hedda must step lightly indeed; or perhaps her own feet might be warmer or thinner shod, so as to melt the light layer of snow more readily.

The girls slipped their arms through hers. A little thrill coursed through her. Then, after three or four turns up and down the terrace, Yolande led the way quietly down the broad flight of steps in the direction of the church on the lower level. In that bright, broad moonlight Maisie went with them undeterred; the Hall was still alive with the glare of electric lights in bedroom windows; and the presence of the other girls, both wholly free from any signs of fear, took off all sense of terror or loneliness. They strolled on into the churchyard. Maisie's eyes were now fixed on the new white tower, which merged in the silhouette against the starry sky into much the same grey and indefinite hue as the older parts of the building. Before she quite knew where she was, she found herself at the head of the worn stone steps which led into the vault by whose doors she had seen old Bessie sitting. In the pallid moonlight, with the aid of the greenish reflection from the snow, she could just read the words inscribed over the portal, the words that Yolande had repeated in the drawing-room, 'Mors janua vit'.

Yolande moved down one step. Maisie drew back for the first time with a faint access of alarm. 'You're – you're not going down there!' she exclaimed, catching her breath for a second.

'Yes, I am,' her new friend answered in a calmly quiet voice. 'Why not? We live here.'

'You live here?' Maisie echoed, freeing her arms by a sudden movement and standing away from her mysterious friends with a tremulous shudder.

'Yes, we live here,' Hedda broke in, without the slightest emotion. She said it in a voice of perfect calm, as one might say it of any house in a street in London.

Maisie was far less terrified than she might have imagined beforehand would be the case under such unexpected conditions. The two girls were so simple, so natural, so strangely like herself, that she could not say she was really afraid of them. She shrank, it is true, from the nature of the door at which they stood, but she received the unearthly announcement that they lived there with scarcely more than a slight tremor of surprise and astonishment.

'You will come in with us?' Hedda said in a gently enticing tone. 'We went into your bedroom.'

Maisie hardly liked to say no. They seemed so anxious to show her their home. With trembling feet she moved down the first step, and then the second. Yolande kept ever one pace in front of her. As Maisie reached the third step, the two girls, as if moved by one design, took her wrists in their hands, not unkindly, but coaxingly. They reached the actual doors of the vault itself – two heavy bronze valves, meeting in the centre. Each bore a ring for a handle, pierced through a Gorgon's head embossed upon the surface. Yolande pushed them with her hand. They yielded instantly to her light touch, and opened inward. Yolande, still in front, passed from the glow of the moon to the gloom of the vault, which a ray of moonlight just descended obliquely. As she passed, for a second, a weird sight met Maisie's eyes. Her face and hands and dress became momentarily self-luminous – but through them, as they glowed, she could descry within every bone and joint of her living skeleton, dimly shadowed in dark through the luminous haze that marked her body.

Maisie drew back once more, terrified. Yet her terror was not quite what one could describe as fear: it was rather a vague sense of the profoundly mystical. 'I can't! I can't!' she cried, with an appealing glance. 'Hedda! Yolande! I cannot go with you.'

Hedda held her hand tight, and almost seemed to force her. But Yolande, in front, like a mother with her child, turned round with a grave smile. 'No, no,' she said reprovingly. 'Let her come if she will, Hedda, of her own accord, not otherwise. The tower demands a willing victim.'

Her hand on Maisie's wrist was strong but persuasive. It drew her without exercising the faintest compulsion. 'Will you come with us, dear?' she said, in that winning silvery tone which had captivated Maisie's fancy from the very first moment they spoke together. Maisie gazed into her eyes. They were deep and tender. A strange resolution seemed to nerve her for the effort. 'Yes, yes – I – will – come – with you,' she answered slowly.

Hedda on one side, Yolande on the other, now went before her, holding her wrists in their grasp, but rather enticing than drawing her. As each reached the gloom, the same luminous appearance which Maisie had noticed before spread over their bodies, and the same weird skeleton shape showed faintly through their limbs in darker shadow. Maisie crossed the threshold with a convulsive gasp. As she crossed it she looked down at her own dress and body. They were semi-transparent, like the others', though not quite so self-luminous; the framework of her limbs appeared within in less certain outline, yet quite dark and distinguishable.

The doors swung to of themselves behind her. Those three stood alone in the vault of Wolverden.

Alone, for a minute or two; and then, as her eyes grew accustomed to the grey dusk of the interior, Maisie began to perceive that the vault opened out into a large and beautiful hall or crypt, dimly lighted at first, but becoming each moment more vaguely clear and more dreamily definite. Gradually she could make out great rock-hewn pillars, Romanesque in their outline or dimly Oriental, like the sculptured columns in the caves of Ellora, supporting a roof of vague and uncertain dimensions, more or less strangely dome-shaped. The effect on the whole was like that of the second impression produced by some dim cathedral, such as Chartres or Milan, after the eyes have grown accustomed to the mellow light from the stained-glass windows, and have recovered from the blinding glare of the outer sunlight. But the architecture, if one may call it so, was more mosque-like and magical. She turned to her companions. Yolande and Hedda stood still by her side; their bodies were now self-luminous to a greater degree than even at the threshold; but the terrible transparency had disappeared altogether; they were once more but beautiful though strangely transfigured and more than mortal women.

Then Maisie understood in her own soul, dimly, the meaning of those mystic words written over the portal. 'Mors janua vit'. Death is the gate of life; and also the interpretation of that awful vision of death dwelling within them as they crossed the threshold; for through that gate they had passed to this underground palace.

Her two guides still held her hands, one on either side. But they seemed rather to lead her on now, seductively and resistlessly, than to draw or compel her. As she moved in through the hall, with its endless vistas of shadowy pillars, seen now behind, now in dim perspective, she was gradually aware that many other people crowded its aisles and corridors. Slowly they took shape as forms more or less clad, mysterious, varied, and of many ages. Some of them wore flowing robes, half mediaeval in shape, like the two friends who had brought her there. They looked like the saints on a stained-glass window. Others were girt merely with a light and floating Coan sash; while some stood dimly nude in the darker recesses of the temple or palace. All leaned eagerly forward with one mind as she approached, and regarded her with deep and sympathetic interest. A few of them murmured words – mere cabalistic sounds which at first she could not understand; but as she moved further into the hall, and saw at each step more clearly into the gloom, they began to have a meaning for her. Before long, she was aware that she understood the mute tumult of voices at once by some internal instinct. The Shades addressed her; she answered them. She knew by intuition what tongue they spoke; it was the Language of the Dead; and, by passing that portal with her two companions, she had herself become enabled both to speak and understand it.

A soft and flowing tongue, this speech of the Nether World – all vowels it seemed, without distinguishable consonants; yet dimly recalling every other tongue, and compounded, as it were, of what was common to all of them. It flowed from those shadowy lips as clouds issue inchoate from a mountain valley; it was formless, uncertain, vague, but yet beautiful. She hardly knew, indeed, as it fell upon her senses, if it were sound or perfume.

Through this tenuous world Maisie moved as in a dream, her two companions still cheering and guiding her. When they reached an inner shrine or chantry of the temple she was dimly conscious of more terrible forms pervading the background than any of those that had yet appeared to her. This was a more austere and antique apartment than the rest; a shadowy cloister, prehistoric in its severity; it recalled to her mind something indefinitely inter'ate between the huge unwrought trilithons of Stonehenge and the massive granite pillars of Philaend Luxor. At the further end of the sanctuary a sort of Sphinx looked down on her, smiling mysteriously. At its base, on a rude megalithic throne, in solitary state, a High Priest was seated. He bore in his hand a wand or sceptre. All round, a strange court of half-unseen acolytes and shadowy hierophants stood attentive. They were girt, as she fancied, in what looked like leopards' skins, or in the fells of some earlier prehistoric lion. These wore sabre-shaped teeth suspended by a string round their dusky necks; others had ornaments of uncut amber, or hatchets of jade threaded as collars on a cord of sinew.

A few, more barbaric than savage in type, flaunted torques of gold as armlets and necklets.

The High Priest rose slowly and held out his two hands, just level with his head, the palms turned outward. 'You have brought a willing victim as Guardian of the Tower?' he asked, in that mystic tongue, of Yolande and Hedda.

'We have brought a willing victim,' the two girls answered.

The High Priest gazed at her. His glance was piercing. Maisie trembled less with fear than with a sense of strangeness, such as a neophyte might feel on being first presented at some courtly pageant. 'You come of your own accord?' the Priest inquired of her in solemn accents.

'I come of my own accord,' Maisie answered, with an inner consciousness that she was bearing her part in some immemorial ritual. Ancestral memories seemed to stir within her.

'It is well,' the Priest murmured. Then he turned to her guides. 'She is of royal lineage?' he inquired, taking his wand in his hand again.

'She is a Llewelyn,' Yolande answered, 'of royal lineage, and of the race that, after your own, earliest bore sway in this land of Britain. She has in her veins the blood of Arthur, of Ambrosius, and of Vortigern.'

'It is well,' the Priest said again. 'I know these princes.' Then he turned to Maisie. 'This is the ritual of those who build,' he said, in a very deep voice. 'It has been the ritual of those who build from the days of the builders of Lokmariaker and Avebury. Every building man makes shall have its human soul, the soul of a virgin to guard and protect it. Three souls it requires as a living talisman against chance and change. One soul is the soul of the human victim slain beneath the foundation-stone; she is the guardian spirit against earthquake and ruin. One soul is the soul of the human victim slain when the building is half built up; she is the guardian spirit against battle and tempest. One soul is the soul of the human victim who flings herself of her own free will off tower or gable when the building is complete; she is the guardian spirit against thunder and lightning. Unless a building be duly fasted with these three, how can it hope to stand against the hostile powers of fire and flood and storm and earthquake?'

An assessor at his side, unnoticed till then, took up the parable. He had a stern Roman face, and bore a shadowy suit of Roman armour. 'In times of old,' he said, with iron austerity, 'all men knew well these rules of building. They built in solid stone to endure for ever: the works they erected have lasted to this day, in this land and others. So built we the amphitheatres of Rome and Verona; so built we the walls of Lincoln, York, and London. In the blood of a king's son laid we the foundation-stone: in the blood of a king's son laid we the coping-stone: in the blood of a maiden of royal line fasted we the bastions against fire and lightning. But in these latter days, since faith grows dim, men build with burnt brick and rubble of plaster; no foundation spirit or guardian soul do they give to their bridges, their walls, or their towers: so bridges break, and walls fall in, and towers crumble, and the art and mystery of building aright have perished from among you.'

He ceased. The High Priest held out his wand and spoke again. 'We are the Assembly of Dead Builders and Dead Victims,' he said, 'for this mark of Wolverden; all of whom have built or been built upon in this holy site of immemorial sanctity. We are the stones of a living fabric. Before this place was a Christian church, it was a temple of Woden. And before it was a temple of Woden, it was a shrine of Hercules. And before it was a shrine of Hercules, it was a grove of Nodens. And before it was a grove of Nodens, it was a Stone Circle of the Host of Heaven. And before it was a Stone Circle of the Host of Heaven, it was the grave and tumulus and underground palace of Me, who am the earliest builder of all in this place; and my name in my ancient tongue is Wolf, and I laid and hallowed it. And after me, Wolf, and my namesake Wulfhere, was this barrow called Ad Lupum and Wolverden. And all these that are here with me have built and been built upon in this holy site for all generations. And you are the last who come to join us.'

Maisie felt a cold thrill course down her spine as he spoke these words; but courage did not fail her. She was dimly aware that those who offer themselves as victims for service must offer themselves willingly; for the gods demand a voluntary victim; no beast can be slain unless it nod assent; and none can be made a guardian spirit who takes not the post upon him of his own free will. She turned meekly to Hedda. 'Who are you?' she asked, trembling.

'I am Hedda,' the girl answered, in the same soft sweet voice and winning tone as before; 'Hedda, the daughter of Gorm, the chief of the Northmen who settled in East Anglia. And I was a worshipper of Thor and Odin. And when my father, Gorm, fought against Alfred, King of Wessex, was I taken prisoner. And Wulfhere, the Kenting, was then building the first church and tower of Wolverden. And they baptized me, and shrived me, and I consented of my own free will to be built under the foundation-stone. And there my body lies built up to this day; and I am the guardian spirit against earthquake and ruin.'

'And who are you?' Maisie asked, turning again to Yolande.

'I am Yolande Fitz-Aylwin,' the tall dark girl answered; 'a royal maiden too, sprung from the blood of Henry Plantagenet. And when Roland Fitz-Stephen was building anew the choir and chancel of Wulfhere's minster, I chose to be immured in the fabric of the wall, for love of the Church and all holy saints; and there my body lies built up to this day; and I am the guardian against battle and tempest.'

Maisie held her friend's hand tight. Her voice hardly trembled. 'And I?' she asked once more. 'What fate for me? Tell me!'

'Your task is easier far,' Yolande answered gently. 'For you shall be the guardian of the new tower against thunder and lightning. Now, those who guard against earthquake and battle are buried alive under the foundation-stone or in the wall of the building; there they die a slow death of starvation and choking. But those who guard against thunder and lightning cast themselves alive of their own free will from the battlements of the tower, and die in the air before they reach the ground; so their fate is the easiest and the lightest of all who would serve mankind; and thenceforth they live with us here in our palace.'

Maisie clung to her hand still tighter. 'Must I do it?' she asked, pleading.

'It is not must,' Yolande replied in the same caressing tone, yet with a calmness as of one in whom earthly desires and earthly passions are quenched for ever. 'It is as you choose yourself. None but a willing victim may be a guardian spirit. This glorious privilege comes but to the purest and best amongst us. Yet what better end can you ask for your soul than to dwell here in our midst as our comrade for ever, where all is peace, and to preserve the tower whose guardian you are from evil assaults of lightning and thunderbolt?'

Maisie flung her arms round her friend's neck. 'But – I am afraid,' she murmured. Why she should even wish to consent she knew not, yet the strange serene peace in these strange girls' eyes made her mysteriously in love with them and with the fate they offered her. They seemed to move like the stars in their orbits. 'How shall I leap from the top?' she cried. 'How shall I have courage to mount the stairs alone, and fling myself off from the lonely battlement?'

Yolande unwound her arms with a gentle forbearance. She coaxed her as one coaxes an unwilling child. 'You will not be alone,' she said, with a tender pressure. 'We will all go with you. We will help you and encourage you. We will sing our sweet songs of life-in-death to you. Why should you draw back? All we have faced it in ten thousand ages, and we tell you with one voice, you need not fear it. 'Tis life you should fear – life, with its dangers, its toils, its heartbreakings. Here we dwell for ever in unbroken peace. Come, come, and join us!'

She held out her arms with an enticing gesture. Maisie sprang into them, sobbing. 'Yes, I will come,' she cried in an access of hysterical fervour. 'These are the arms of Death – I embrace them. These are the lips of Death – I kiss them. Yolande, Yolande, I will do as you ask me!'

The tall dark girl in the luminous white robe stooped down and kissed her twice on the forehead in return. Then she looked at the High Priest. 'We are ready,' she murmured in a low, grave voice. 'The Victim consents. The Virgin will die. Lead on to the tower. We are ready! We are ready!'

IV

From the recesses of the temple – if temple it were – from the inmost shrines of the shrouded cavern, unearthly music began to sound of itself; with wild modulation, on strange reeds and tabors. It swept through the aisles like a rushing wind on an aeolian harp; at times it wailed with a voice like a woman's; at times it rose loud in an organ-note of triumph; at times it sank low into a pensive and melancholy flute-like symphony. It waxed and waned; it swelled and died away again; but no man saw how or whence it proceeded. Wizard echoes issued from the crannies and vents in the invisible walls; they sighed from the ghostly interspaces of the pillars; they keened and moaned from the vast over-hanging dome of the palace. Gradually the song shaped itself by weird stages into a processional measure. At its sound the High Priest rose slowly from his immemorial seat on the mighty cromlech which formed his throne.

The Shades in leopards' skins ranged themselves in bodiless rows on either hand; the ghostly wearers of the sabre-toothed lions' fangs followed like ministrants in the footsteps of their hierarch.

Hedda and Yolande took their places in the procession. Maisie stood between the two, with hair floating on the air; she looked like a novice who goes up to take the veil, accompanied and cheered by two elder sisters.

The ghostly pageant began to move. Unseen music followed it with fitful gusts of melody. They passed down the main corridor, between shadowy Doric or Ionic pillars which grew dimmer and ever dimmer again in the distance as they approached, with slow steps, the earthward portal.

At the gate, the High Priest pushed against the valves with his hand. They opened outward.

He passed into the moonlight. The attendants thronged after him. As each wild figure crossed the threshold the same strange sight as before met Maisie's eyes. For a second of time each ghostly body became self-luminous, as with some curious phosphorescence; and through each, at the moment of passing the portal, the dim outline of a skeleton loomed briefly visible. Next instant it had clothed itself as with earthly members.

Maisie reached the outer air. As she did so, she gasped. For a second, its chilliness and freshness almost choked her. She was conscious now that the atmosphere of the vault, though pleasant in its way, and warm and dry, had been loaded with fumes as of burning incense, and with somnolent vapours of poppy and mandragora. Its drowsy ether had cast her into a lethargy. But after the first minute in the outer world, the keen night air revived her. Snow lay still on the ground a little deeper than when she first came out, and the moon rode lower; otherwise, all was as before, save that only one or two lights still burned here and there in the great house on the terrace. Among them she could recognise her own room, on the ground floor in the new wing, by its open window.

The procession made its way across the churchyard towards the tower. As it wound among the graves an owl hooted. All at once Maisie remembered the lines that had so chilled her a few short hours before in the drawing-room?

'The glow-worm o'er grave and stone
Shall light thee steady;

The owl from the steeple sing.
'Welcome, proud lady!"

But, marvellous to relate, they no longer alarmed her. She felt rather that a friend was welcoming her home; she clung to Yolande's hand with a gentle pressure.

As they passed in front of the porch, with its ancient yew-tree, a stealthy figure glided out like a ghost from the darkling shadow. It was a woman, bent and bowed, with quivering limbs that shook half palsied. Maisie recognised old Bessie. 'I knew she would come!' the old hag muttered between her toothless jaws. 'I knew Wolverden Tower would yet be duly fasted!'

She put herself, as of right, at the head of the procession. They moved on to the tower, rather gliding than walking. Old Bessie drew a rusty key from her pocket, and fitted it with a twist into the brand new lock. 'What turned the old will turn the new,' she murmured, looking round and grinning. Maisie shrank from her as she shrank from not one of the Dead; but she followed on still into the ringers' room at the base of the tower.

Thence a staircase in the corner led up to the summit. The High Priest mounted the stair, chanting a mystic refrain, whose runic sounds were no longer intelligible to Maisie. As she reached the outer air, the Tongue of the Dead seemed to have become a mere blank of mingled odours and murmurs to her. It was like a summer breeze, sighing through warm and resinous pinewoods. But Yolande and Hedda spoke to her yet, to cheer her, in the language of the living. She recognised that as revenants they were still in touch with the upper air and the world of the embodied.

They tempted her up the stair with encouraging fingers. Maisie followed them like a child, in implicit confidence. The steps wound round and round, spirally, and the staircase was dim; but a supernatural light seemed to fill the tower, diffused from the bodies or souls of its occupants. At the head of all, the High Priest still chanted as he went his unearthly litany; magic sounds of chimes seemed to swim in unison with his tune as they mounted. Were those floating notes material or spiritual? They passed the belfry; no tongue of metal wagged; but the rims of the great bells resounded and reverberated to the ghostly symphony with sympathetic music. Still they passed on and on, upward and upward. They reached the ladder that alone gave access to the final story. Dust and cobwebs already clung to it. Once more Maisie drew back. It was dark overhead and the luminous haze began to fail them. Her friends held her hands with the same kindly persuasive touch as ever. 'I cannot!' she cried, shrinking away from the tall, steep ladder. 'Oh, Yolande, I cannot!'

'Yes, dear,' Yolande whispered in a soothing voice. 'You can. It is but ten steps, and I will hold your hand tight. Be brave and mount them!'

The sweet voice encouraged her. It was like heavenly music. She knew not why she should submit, or, rather, consent; but none the less she consented. Some spell seemed cast over her. With tremulous feet, scarcely realising what she did, she mounted the ladder and went up four steps of it.

Then she turned and looked down again. Old Bessie's wrinkled face met her frightened eyes. It was smiling horribly. She shrank back once more, terrified. 'I can't do it,' she cried, 'if that woman comes up! 'I'm not afraid of you, dear,' she pressed Yolande's hand, 'but she, she is too terrible!'

Hedda looked back and raised a warning finger. 'Let the woman stop below,' she said; 'she savours too much of the evil world. We must do nothing to frighten the willing victim.'

The High Priest by this time, with his ghostly fingers, had opened the trap-door that gave access to the summit. A ray of moonlight slanted through the aperture. The breeze blew down with it. Once more Maisie felt the stimulating and reviving effect of the open air. Vivified by its freshness, she struggled up to the top, passed out through the trap, and found herself standing on the open platform at the summit of the tower.

The moon had not yet quite set. The light on the snow shone pale green and mysterious. For miles and miles around she could just make out, by its aid, the dim contour of the downs, with their thin white mantle, in the solemn silence. Range behind range rose faintly shimmering. The chant had now ceased; the High Priest and his acolytes were mingling strange herbs in a mazar-bowl or chalice. Stray perfumes of myrrh and of cardamoms were wafted towards her. The men in leopards' skins burnt smouldering sticks of spikenard. Then Yolande led the postulant forward again, and placed her close up to the new white parapet. Stone heads of virgins smiled on her from the angles. 'She must front the east,' Hedda said in a tone of authority: and Yolande turned her face towards the rising sun accordingly.

Then she opened her lips and spoke in a very solemn voice. 'From this new-built tower you fling yourself,' she said, or rather intoned, 'that you may serve mankind, and all the powers that be, as its guardian spirit against thunder and lightning. Judged a virgin, pure and unsullied in deed and word and thought, of royal race and ancient lineage – a Cymry of the Cymry – you are found worthy to be intrusted with this charge and this honour. Take care that never shall dart or thunderbolt assault this tower, as She that is below you takes care to preserve it from earthquake and ruin, and She that is midway takes care to preserve it from battle and tempest. This is your charge. See well that you keep it.'

She took her by both hands. 'Mary Llewelyn,' she said, 'you willing victim, step on to the battlement.'

Maisie knew not why, but with very little shrinking she stepped as she was told, by the aid of a wooden footstool, on to the eastward-looking parapet. There, in her loose white robe, with her arms spread abroad, and her hair flying free, she poised herself for a second, as if about to shake out some unseen wings and throw herself on the air like a swift or a swallow.

'Mary Llewelyn,' Yolande said once more, in a still deeper tone, with ineffable earnestness, 'cast yourself down, a willing sacrifice, for the service of man, and the security of this tower against thunderbolt and lightning.'

Maisie stretched her arms wider, and leaned forward in act to leap, from the edge of the parapet, on to the snow-clad churchyard.

V

One second more and the sacrifice would have been complete. But before she could launch herself from the tower, she felt suddenly a hand laid upon her shoulder from behind to restrain her. Even in her existing state of nervous exaltation she was aware at once that it was the hand of a living and solid mortal, not that of a soul or guardian spirit. It lay heavier upon her than Hedda's or Yolande's. It seemed to clog and burden her. With a violent effort she strove to shake herself free, and carry out her now fixed intention of self-immolation, for the safety of the tower. But the hand was too strong for her. She could not shake it off. It gripped and held her.

She yielded, and, reeling, fell back with a gasp on to the platform of the tower. At the selfsame moment a strange terror and commotion seemed to seize all at once on the assembled spirits. A weird cry rang voiceless through the shadowy company. Maisie heard it as in a dream, very dim and distant. It was thin as a bat's note; almost inaudible to the ear, yet perceived by the brain or at least by the spirit. It was a cry of alarm, of fright, of warning. With one accord, all the host of phantoms rushed hurriedly forward to the battlements and pinnacles. The ghostly High Priest went first, with his wand held downward; the men in leopards' skins and other assistants followed in confusion. Theirs was a reckless rout. They flung themselves from the top, like fugitives from a cliff, and floated fast through the air on invisible pinions. Hedda and Yolande, ambassadresses and intermediaries with the upper air, were the last to fly from the living presence. They clasped her hand silently, and looked deep into her eyes. There was something in that calm yet regretful look that seemed to say, 'Farewell! We have tried in vain to save you, sister, from the terrors of living.'

The horde of spirits floated away on the air, as in a witches' Sabbath, to the vault whence it issued. The doors swung on their rusty hinges, and closed behind them. Maisie stood alone with the hand that grasped her on the tower.

The shock of the grasp, and the sudden departure of the ghostly band in such wild dismay, threw Maisie for a while into a state of semi-unconsciousness. Her head reeled round; her brain swam faintly. She clutched for support at the parapet of the tower. But the hand that held her sustained her still. She felt herself gently drawn down with quiet mastery, and laid on the stone floor close by the trap-door that led to the ladder.

The next thing of which she could feel sure was the voice of the Oxford undergraduate. He was distinctly frightened and not a little tremulous. 'I think,' he said very softly, laying her head on his lap, 'you had better rest a while, Miss Llewelyn, before you try to get down again. I hope I didn't catch you and disturb you too hastily. But one step more, and you would have been over the edge. I really couldn't help it.'

'Let me go,' Maisie moaned, trying to raise herself again, but feeling too faint and ill to make the necessary effort to recover the power of motion. 'I want to go with them! I want to join them!'

'Some of the others will be up before long,' the undergraduate said, supporting her head in his hands; 'and they'll help me to get you down again. Mr Yates is in the belfry. Meanwhile, if I were you, I'd lie quite still, and take a drop or two of this brandy.'

He held it to her lips. Maisie drank a mouthful, hardly knowing what she did. Then she lay quiet where he placed her for some minutes. How they lifted her down and conveyed her to her bed she scarcely knew. She was dazed and terrified. She could only remember afterward that three or four gentlemen in roughly huddled clothes had carried or handed her down the ladder between them. The spiral stair and all the rest were a blank to her.

VI

When she next awoke she was lying in her bed in the same room at the Hall, with Mrs West by her side, leaning over her tenderly. Maisie looked up through her closed eyes and just saw the motherly face and grey hair bending above her. Then voices came to her from the mist, vaguely: 'Yesterday was so hot for the time of year, you see!' 'Very unusual weather, of course, for Christmas.' 'But a thunderstorm! So strange! I put it down to that. The electrical disturbance must have affected the poor child's head.' Then it dawned upon her that the conversation she heard was passing between Mrs West and a doctor.

She raised herself suddenly and wildly on her arms. The bed faced the windows. She looked out and beheld – the tower of Wolverden church, rent from top to bottom with a mighty rent, while half its height lay tossed in fragments on the ground in the churchyard.

'What is it?' she cried wildly, with a flush as of shame.

'Hush, hush!' the doctor said. 'Don't trouble! Don't look at it!'

'Was it? after I came down?' Maisie moaned in vague terror.

The doctor nodded. 'An hour after you were brought down,' he said, 'a thunderstorm broke over it. The lightning struck and shattered the tower. They had not yet put up the lightning-conductor. It was to have been done on Boxing Day.'

A weird remorse possessed Maisie's soul. 'My fault!' she cried, starting up. 'My fault, my fault! I have neglected my duty!'

'Don't talk,' the doctor answered, looking hard at her. 'It is always dangerous to be too suddenly aroused from these curious overwrought sleeps and trances.'

'And old Bessie?' Maisie exclaimed, trembling with an eerie presentiment.

The doctor glanced at Mrs West. 'How did she know?' he whispered. Then he turned to Maisie. 'You may as well be told the truth as suspect it,' he said slowly. 'Old Bessie must have been watching there. She was crushed and half buried beneath the falling tower.'

'One more question, Mrs West,' Maisie murmured, growing faint with an access of supernatural fear. 'Those two nice girls who sat on the chairs at each side of me through the tableaux, are they hurt? Were they in it?'

Mrs West soothed her hand. 'My dear child,' she said gravely, with quiet emphasis, 'there were no other girls. This is mere hallucination. You sat alone by yourself through the whole of the evening.'

Brickett Bottom

Amyas Northcote

The Reverend Arthur Maydew was the hard-working incumbent of a large parish in one of our manufacturing towns. He was also a student and a man of no strong physique, so that when an opportunity was presented to him to take an annual holiday by exchanging parsonages with an elderly clergyman, Mr Roberts, the Squarson of the Parish of Overbury, and an acquaintance of his own, he was glad to avail himself of it.

Overbury is a small and very remote village in one of our most lovely and rural counties, and Mr Roberts had long held the living of it.

Without further delay we can transport Mr Maydew and his family, which consisted only of two daughters, to their temporary home. The two young ladies, Alice and Maggie, the heroines of this narrative, were at that time aged twenty-six and twenty-four years respectively. Both of them were attractive girls, fond of such society as they could find in their own parish and, the former especially, always pleased to extend the circle of their acquaintance. Although the elder in years, Alice in many ways yielded place to her sister, who was the more energetic and practical and upon whose shoulders the bulk of the family cares and responsibilities rested. Alice was inclined to be absent-minded and emotional and to devote more of her thoughts and time to speculations of an abstract nature than her sister.

Both of the girls, however, rejoiced at the prospect of a period of quiet and rest in a pleasant country neighbourhood, and both were gratified at knowing that their father would find in Mr Roberts' library much that would entertain his mind, and in Mr Roberts' garden an opportunity to indulge freely in his favourite game of croquet. They would have, no doubt, preferred some cheerful neighbours, but Mr Roberts was positive in his assurances that there was no one in the neighbourhood whose acquaintance would be of interest to them.

The first few weeks of their new life passed pleasantly for the Maydew family. Mr Maydew quickly gained renewed vigour in his quiet and congenial surroundings, and in the delightful air, while his daughters spent much of their time in long walks about the country and in exploring its beauties.

One evening late in August the two girls were returning from a long walk along one of their favourite paths, which led along the side of the Downs. On their right, as they walked, the ground fell away sharply to a narrow glen, named Brickett Bottom, about three-quarters of a mile in length, along the bottom of which ran a little-used country road leading to a farm, known as Blaise's Farm, and then onward and upward to lose itself as a sheep track on the higher Downs.

On their side of the slope some scattered trees and bushes grew, but beyond the lane and running up over the farther slope of the glen was a thick wood, which extended away to Carew Court, the seat of a neighbouring magnate, Lord Carew. On their left the open Down rose above them and beyond its crest lay Overbury.

The girls were walking hastily, as they were later than they had intended to be and were anxious to reach home. At a certain point at which they had now arrived the path forked, the right-hand branch leading down into Brickett Bottom and the left-hand turning up over the Down to Overbury.

Just as they were about to turn into the left-hand path Alice suddenly stopped and pointing downwards exclaimed: 'How very curious, Maggie! Look, there is a house down there in the Bottom, which we have, or at least I have, never noticed before, often as we have walked up the Bottom.'

Maggie followed with her eyes her sister's pointing finger.

'I don't see any house,' she said.

'Why, Maggie,' said her sister, 'can't you see it! A quaint-looking, old-fashioned red brick house, there just where the road bends to the right. It seems to be standing in a nice, well-kept garden too.'

Maggie looked again, but the light was beginning to fade in the glen and she was short-sighted to boot.

'I certainly don't see anything,' she said, 'but then I am so blind and the light is getting bad; yes, perhaps I do see a house,' she added, straining her eyes.

'Well, it is there,' replied her sister, 'and tomorrow we will come and explore it.'

Maggie agreed readily enough, and the sisters went home, still speculating on how they had happened not to notice the house before and resolving firmly on an expedition thither the next day. However, the expedition did not come off as planned, for that evening Maggie slipped on the stairs and fell, spraining her ankle in such a fashion as to preclude walking for some time.

Notwithstanding the accident to her sister, Alice remained possessed by the idea of making further investigations into the house she had looked down upon from the hill the evening before; and the next day, having seen Maggie carefully settled for the afternoon, she started off for Brickett Bottom. She returned in triumph and much intrigued over her discoveries, which she eagerly narrated to her sister.

Yes. There was a nice, old-fashioned red brick house, not very large and set in a charming, old-world garden in the Bottom. It stood on a tongue of land jutting out from the woods, just at the point where the lane, after a fairly straight course from its junction with the main road half a mile away, turned sharply to the right in the direction of Blaise's Farm. More than that, Alice had seen the people of the house, whom she described as an old gentleman and a lady, presumably his wife. She had not clearly made out the gentleman, who was sitting in the porch, but the old lady, who had been in the garden busy with her flowers, had looked up and smiled pleasantly at her as she passed. She was sure, she said, that they were nice people and that it would be pleasant to make their acquaintance.

Maggie was not quite satisfied with Alice's story. She was of a more prudent and retiring nature than her sister; she had an uneasy feeling that, if the old couple had been desirable or attractive neighbours, Mr Roberts would have mentioned them, and knowing Alice's nature she said what she could to discourage her vague idea of endeavouring to make acquaintance with the owners of the red brick house.

On the following morning, when Alice came to her sister's room to inquire how she did, Maggie noticed that she looked pale and rather absent-minded, and, after a few commonplace remarks had passed, she asked:

'What is the matter, Alice? You don't look yourself this morning.'

Her sister gave a slightly embarrassed laugh.

'Oh, I am all right,' she replied, 'only I did not sleep very well. I kept on dreaming about the house. It was such an odd dream too the house seemed to be home, and yet to be different.'

'What, that house in Brickett Bottom?' said Maggie. 'Why, what is the matter with you, you seem to be quite crazy about the place?'

'Well, it is curious, isn't it, Maggie, that we should have only just discovered it, and that it looks to be lived in by nice people? I wish we could get to know them.'

Maggie did not care to resume the argument of the night before and the subject dropped, nor did Alice again refer to the house or its inhabitants for some little time. In fact, for some days the weather was wet and Alice was forced to abandon her walks, but when the weather once more became fine she resumed them, and Maggie suspected that Brickett Bottom formed one of her sister's favourite expeditions. Maggie became anxious over her sister, who seemed to grow daily more absent-minded and silent, but she refused to be drawn into any confidential talk, and Maggie was nonplussed.

One day, however, Alice returned from her afternoon walk in an unusually excited state of mind, of which Maggie sought an explanation. It came with a rush. Alice said that, that afternoon, as she approached the house in Brickett Bottom, the old lady, who as usual was busy in her garden, had walked down to the gate as she passed and had wished her good day.

Alice had replied and, pausing, a short conversation had followed. Alice could not remember the exact tenor of it, but, after she had paid a compliment to the old lady's flowers, the latter had rather diffidently asked her to enter the garden for a closer view. Alice had hesitated, and the old lady had said 'Don't be afraid of me, my dear, I like to see young ladies about me and my husband finds their society quite necessary to him.' After a pause she went on: 'Of course nobody has told you about us. My husband is Colonel Paxton, late of the Indian Army, and we have been here for many,

many years. It's rather lonely, for so few people ever see us. Do come in and meet the Colonel.'

'I hope you didn't go in,' said Maggie rather sharply.

'Why not?' replied Alice.

'Well, I don't like Mrs Paxton asking you in that way,' answered Maggie.

'I don't see what harm there was in the invitation,' said Alice.

'I didn't go in because it was getting late and I was anxious to get home; but—'

'But what?' asked Maggie.

Alice shrugged her shoulders.

'Well,' she said, 'I have accepted Mrs Paxton's invitation to pay her a little visit tomorrow.'

And she gazed defiantly at Maggie.

Maggie became distinctly uneasy on hearing of this resolution. She did not like the idea of her impulsive sister visiting people on such slight acquaintance, especially as they had never heard them mentioned before. She endeavoured by all means, short of appealing to Mr Maydew, to dissuade her sister from going, at any rate until there had been time to make some inquiries as to the Paxtons. Alice, however, was obdurate.

What harm could happen to her? she asked. Mrs Paxton was a charming old lady. She was going early in the afternoon for a short visit. She would be back for tea and croquet with her father and, anyway, now that Maggie was laid up, long solitary walks were unendurable and she was not going to let slip the chance of following up what promised to be a pleasant acquaintance.

Maggie could do nothing more. Her ankle was better and she was able to get down to the garden and sit in a long chair near her father, but walking was still quite out of the question, and it was with some misgivings that on the following day she watched Alice depart gaily for her visit, promising to be back by half-past four at the very latest.

The afternoon passed quietly till nearly five, when Mr Maydew, looking up from his book, noticed Maggie's uneasy expression and asked:

'Where is Alice?'

'Out for a walk,' replied Maggie; and then after a short pause she went on: 'And she has also gone to pay a call on some neighbours whom she has recently discovered.'

'Neighbours,' ejaculated Mr Maydew, 'what neighbours? Mr Roberts never spoke of any neighbours to me.'

'Well, I don't know much about them,' answered Maggie. 'Only Alice and I were out walking the day of my accident and saw, or at least she saw, for I am so blind I could not quite make it out, a house in Brickett Bottom. The next day she went to look at it closer, and yesterday she told me that she had made the acquaintance of the people living in it. She says that they are a retired Indian officer and his wife, a Colonel and Mrs Paxton, and Alice describes Mrs Paxton as a charming old lady, who pressed her to come and see them. So she has gone this afternoon, but she promised me she would be back long before this.'

Mr Maydew was silent for a moment and then said:

'I am not well pleased about this. Alice should not be so impulsive and scrape acquaintance with absolutely unknown people. Had there been nice neighbours in Brickett Bottom, I am certain Mr Roberts would have told us.'

The conversation dropped; but both father and daughter were disturbed and uneasy and, tea having been finished and the clock striking half-past five, Mr Maydew asked Maggie:

'When did you say Alice would be back?'

'Before half-past four at the latest, father.'

'Well, what can she be doing? What can have delayed her? You say you did not see the house,' he went on.

'No,' said Maggie, 'I cannot say I did. It was getting dark and you know how short-sighted I am.'

'But surely you must have seen it at some other time,' said her father.

'That is the strangest part of the whole affair,' answered Maggie. 'We have often walked up the Bottom, but I never noticed the house, nor had Alice till that evening. I wonder,' she went on after a short pause, 'if it would not be well to ask Smith to harness the pony and drive over to bring her back. I am not happy about her – I am afraid—'

'Afraid of what?' said her father in the irritated voice of a man who is growing frightened.

'What can have gone wrong in this quiet place? Still, I'll send Smith over for her.'

So saying he rose from his chair and sought out Smith, the rather dull-witted gardener-groom attached to Mr Roberts' service.

'Smith,' he said, 'I want you to harness the pony at once and go over to Colonel Paxton's in Brickett Bottom and bring Miss Maydew home.'

The man stared at him.

'Go where, sir?' he said.

Mr Maydew repeated the order and the man, still staring stupidly, answered:

'I never heard of Colonel Paxton, sir. I don't know what house you mean.'

Mr Maydew was now growing really anxious.

'Well, harness the pony at once,' he said; and going back to Maggie he told her of what he called Smith's stupidity, and asked her if she felt that her ankle would be strong enough to permit her to go with him and Smith to the Bottom to point out the house.

Maggie agreed readily and in a few minutes the party started off. Brickett Bottom, although not more than three-quarters of a mile away over the Downs, was at least three miles by road; and as it was nearly six o'clock before Mr Maydew left the Vicarage, and the pony was old and slow, it was getting late before the entrance to Brickett Bottom was reached. Turning into the lane the cart proceeded slowly up the Bottom, Mr Maydew and Maggie looking anxiously from side to side, whilst Smith drove stolidly on looking neither to time right nor left.

'Where is the house?' said Mr Maydew presently.

'At the bend of the road,' answered Maggie, her heart sickening as she looked out through the failing light to see the trees stretching their ranks in unbroken formation along it. The cart reached the bend. 'It should be here,' whispered Maggie.

They pulled up. Just in front of them the road bent to the right round a tongue of land, which, unlike the rest of the right-hand side of the road, was free from trees and was covered only by rough grass and stray bushes. A closer inspection disclosed evident signs of terraces having once been formed on it, but of a house there was no trace.

'Is this the place?' said Mr Maydew in a low voice.

Maggie nodded.

'But there is no house here,' said her father. 'What does it all mean? Are you sure of yourself, Maggie? Where is Alice?'

Before Maggie could answer a voice was heard calling 'Father! Maggie!' The sound of the voice was thin and high and, paradoxically, it sounded both very near and yet as if it came from some infinite distance. The cry was thrice repeated and then silence fell. Mr Maydew and Maggie stared at each other.

'That was Alice's voice,' said Mr Maydew huskily, 'she is near and in trouble, and is calling us. Which way did you think it came from, Smith?' he added, turning to the gardener.

'I didn't hear anybody calling,' said the man.

'Nonsense!' answered Mr Maydew.

And then he and Maggie both began to call 'Alice. Alice. Where are you?' There was no reply and Mr Maydew sprang from the cart, at the same time bidding Smith to hand the reins to Maggie and come and search for the missing girl. Smith obeyed him and both men, scrambling up the turfy bit of ground, began to search and call through the neighbouring wood. They heard and saw nothing, however, and after an agonised search Mr Maydew ran down to the cart and begged Maggie to drive on to Blaise's Farm for help leaving himself and Smith to continue the search. Maggie followed her father's instructions and was fortunate enough to find Mr Rumbold, the farmer, his two sons and a couple of labourers just returning from the harvest field.

She explained what had happened, and the farmer and his men promptly volunteered to form a search party, though Maggie, in spite of her anxiety, noticed a queer expression on Mr Rumbold's face as she told him her tale.

The party, provided with lanterns, now went down the Bottom, joined Mr Maydew and Smith and made an exhaustive but absolutely fruitless search of the woods near the bend of the road.

No trace of the missing girl was to be found, and after a long and anxious time the search was abandoned, one of the young Rumbolds volunteering to ride into the nearest town and notify the police.

Maggie, though with little hope in her own heart, endeavoured to cheer her father on their homeward way with the idea that Alice might have returned to Overbury over the Downs whilst they were going by road to the Bottom, and that she had seen them and called to them in jest when they were opposite the tongue of land.

However, when they reached home there was no Alice and, though the next day the search was resumed and full inquiries were instituted by the police, all was to no purpose. No trace of Alice was ever found, the last human being that saw her having been an old woman, who had met her going down the path into the Bottom on the afternoon of her disappearance, and who described her as smiling but looking 'queerlike'.

This is the end of the story, but the following may throw some light upon it.

The history of Alice's mysterious disappearance became widely known through the medium of the Press and Mr Roberts, distressed beyond measure at what had taken place, returned in all haste to Overbury to offer what comfort and help he could give to his afflicted friend and tenant.

He called upon the Maydews and, having heard their tale, sat for a short time in silence. Then he said:

'Have you ever heard any local gossip concerning this Colonel and Mrs Paxton?'

'No,' replied Mr Maydew, 'I never heard their names until the day of my poor daughter's fatal visit.'

'Well,' said Mr Roberts, 'I will tell you all I can about them, which is not very much, I fear.'

He paused and then went on: 'I am now nearly seventy-five years old, and for nearly seventy years no house has stood in Brickett Bottom. But when I was a child of about five there was an old-fashioned, red brick house standing in a garden at the bend of the road, such as you have described. It was owned and lived in by a retired Indian soldier and his wife, a Colonel and Mrs Paxton. At the time I speak of, certain events having taken place at the house and the old couple having died, it was sold by their heirs to Lord Carew, who shortly after pulled it down on the ground that it interfered with his shooting. Colonel and Mrs Paxton were well known to my father, who was the clergyman here before me, and to the neighbourhood in general. They lived quietly and were not unpopular, but the Colonel was supposed to possess a violent and vindictive temper. Their family consisted only of themselves, their daughter and a couple of servants, the Colonel's old Army servant and his Eurasian wife. Well, I cannot tell you details of what happened, I was only a child; my father never liked gossip and in later years, when he talked to me on the subject, he always avoided any appearance of exaggeration or sensationalism.'

'However, it is known that Miss Paxton fell in love with and became engaged to a young man to whom her parents took a strong dislike. They used every possible means to break off the match, and many rumours were set on foot as to their conduct – undue influence, even cruelty were charged against them. I do not know the truth, all I can say is that Miss Paxton died and a very bitter feeling against her parents sprang up. My father, however, continued to call, but was rarely admitted. In fact, he never saw Colonel Paxton after his daughter's death and only saw Mrs Paxton once or twice. He described her as an utterly broken woman, and was not surprised at her following her daughter to the grave in about three months' time. Colonel Paxton became, if possible, more of a recluse than ever after his wife's death and himself died not more than a month after her under circumstances which pointed to suicide. Again a crop of rumours sprang up, but there was no one in particular to take action, the doctor certified Death from Natural Causes, and Colonel Paxton, like his wife and daughter, was buried in this churchyard. The property passed to a distant relative, who came down to it for one night shortly afterwards; he never came again, having apparently conceived a violent dislike to the place, but arranged to pension off the servants and then sold the house to Lord Carew, who was glad to purchase this little island in the middle of his property. He pulled it down soon after he had bought it, and the garden was left to relapse into a wilderness.'

Mr Roberts paused.

'Those are all the facts,' he added.

'But there is something more,' said Maggie.

Mr Roberts hesitated for a while.

'You have a right to know all,' he said almost to himself; then louder he continued: 'What I am now going to tell you is really rumour, vague and uncertain; I cannot fathom its truth or its meaning. About five years after the house had been pulled down a young maidservant at Carew Court was out walking one afternoon. She was a stranger to the village and a new-coiner to the Court. On returning home to tea she told her fellow-servants that as she walked down Brickett Bottom, which place she described clearly, she passed a red brick house at the bend of the road and that a kind-faced old lady had asked her to step in for a while. She did not go in, not because she had any suspicions of there being anything uncanny, but simply because she feared to be late for tea.

'I do not think she ever visited the Bottom again and she had no other similar experience, so far as I am aware.

'Two or three years later, shortly after my father's death, a travelling tinker with his wife and daughter camped for the night at the foot of the Bottom. The girl strolled away up the glen to gather blackberries and was never seen or heard of again. She was searched for in vain – of course, one does not know the truth – and she may have run away voluntarily from her parents, although there was no known cause for her doing so.

'That,' concluded Mr Roberts, 'is all I can tell you of either facts or rumours; all that I can now do is to pray for you and for her.'

The Lost Ghost

Mary Eleanor Wilkins Freeman

Mrs John Emerson, sitting with her needlework beside the window, looked out and saw Mrs Rhoda Meserve coming down the street, and knew at once by the trend of her steps and the cant of her head that she meditated turning in at her gate. She also knew by a certain something about her general carriage—a thrusting forward of the neck, a bustling hitch of the shoulders—that she had important news. Rhoda Meserve always had the news as soon as the news was in being, and generally Mrs John Emerson was the first to whom she imparted it. The two women had been friends ever since Mrs Meserve had married Simon Meserve and come to the village to live.

Mrs Meserve was a pretty woman, moving with graceful flirts of ruffling skirts; her clear-cut, nervous face, as delicately tinted as a shell, looked brightly from the plumy brim of a black hat at Mrs Emerson in the window. Mrs Emerson was glad to see her coming. She returned the greeting with enthusiasm, then rose hurriedly, ran into the cold parlour and brought out one of the best rocking-chairs. She was just in time, after drawing it up beside the opposite window, to greet her friend at the door.

"Good-afternoon," said she. "I declare, I'm real glad to see you. I've been alone all day. John went to the city this morning. I thought of coming over to your house this afternoon, but I couldn't bring my sewing very well. I am putting the ruffles on my new black dress skirt."

"Well, I didn't have a thing on hand except my crochet work," responded Mrs Meserve, "and I thought I'd just run over a few minutes."

"I'm real glad you did," repeated Mrs Emerson. "Take your things right off. Here, I'll put them on my bed in the bedroom. Take the rocking-chair."

Mrs Meserve settled herself in the parlour rocking-chair, while Mrs Emerson carried her shawl and hat into the little adjoining bedroom. When she returned Mrs Meserve was rocking peacefully and was already at work hooking blue wool in and out.

"That's real pretty," said Mrs Emerson.

"Yes, I think it's pretty," replied Mrs Meserve.

"I suppose it's for the church fair?"

"Yes. I don't suppose it'll bring enough to pay for the worsted, let alone the work, but I suppose I've got to make something."

"How much did that one you made for the fair last year bring?"

"Twenty-five cents."

"It's wicked, ain't it?"

"I rather guess it is. It takes me a week every minute I can get to make one. I wish those that bought such things for twenty-five cents had to make them. Guess they'd sing another song. Well, I suppose I oughtn't to complain as long as it is for the Lord, but sometimes it does seem as if the Lord didn't get much out of it."

"Well, it's pretty work," said Mrs Emerson, sitting down at the opposite window and taking up her dress skirt.

"Yes, it is real pretty work. I just LOVE to crochet."

The two women rocked and sewed and crocheted in silence for two or three minutes. They were both waiting. Mrs Meserve waited for the other's curiosity to develop in order that her news might have, as it were, a befitting stage entrance. Mrs Emerson waited for the news. Finally she could wait no longer.

"Well, what's the news?" said she.

"Well, I don't know as there's anything very particular," hedged the other woman, prolonging the situation.

"Yes, there is; you can't cheat me," replied Mrs Emerson.

"Now, how do you know?"

"By the way you look."

Mrs Meserve laughed consciously and rather vainly.

"Well, Simon says my face is so expressive I can't hide anything more than five minutes no matter how hard I try," said she. "Well, there is some news. Simon came home with it this noon. He heard it in South Dayton. He had some business over there this morning. The old Sargent place is let."

Mrs Emerson dropped her sewing and stared.

"You don't say so!"

"Yes, it is."

"Who to?"

"Why, some folks from Boston that moved to South Dayton last year. They haven't been satisfied with the house they had there—it wasn't large enough. The man has got considerable property and can afford to live pretty well. He's got a wife and his unmarried sister in the family. The sister's got money, too. He does business in Boston and it's just as easy to get to Boston from here as from South Dayton, and so they're coming here. You know the old Sargent house is a splendid place."

"Yes, it's the handsomest house in town, but—"

"Oh, Simon said they told him about that and he just laughed. Said he wasn't afraid and neither was his wife and sister. Said he'd risk ghosts rather than little tucked-up sleeping-rooms without any sun, like they've had in the Dayton house. Said he'd rather risk SEEING ghosts, than risk being ghosts themselves. Simon said they said he was a great hand to joke."

"Oh, well," said Mrs Emerson, "it is a beautiful house, and maybe there isn't anything in those stories. It never seemed to me they came very straight anyway. I never took much stock in them. All I thought was—if his wife was nervous."

"Nothing in creation would hire me to go into a house that I'd ever heard a word against of that kind," declared Mrs Meserve with emphasis. "I wouldn't go into that house if they would give me the rent. I've seen enough of haunted houses to last me as long as I live."

Mrs Emerson's face acquired the expression of a hunting hound.

"Have you?" she asked in an intense whisper.

"Yes, I have. I don't want any more of it."

"Before you came here?"

"Yes; before I was married—when I was quite a girl."

Mrs Meserve had not married young. Mrs Emerson had mental calculations when she heard that.

"Did you really live in a house that was—" she whispered fearfully.

Mrs Meserve nodded solemnly.

"Did you really ever—see—anything—"

Mrs Meserve nodded.

"You didn't see anything that did you any harm?"

"No, I didn't see anything that did me harm looking at it in one way, but it don't do anybody in this world any good to see things that haven't any business to be seen in it. You never get over it."

There was a moment's silence. Mrs Emerson's features seemed to sharpen.

"Well, of course I don't want to urge you," said she, "if you don't feel like talking about it; but maybe it might do you good to tell it out, if it's on your mind, worrying you."

"I try to put it out of my mind," said Mrs Meserve.

"Well, it's just as you feel."

"I never told anybody but Simon," said Mrs Meserve. "I never felt as if it was wise perhaps. I didn't know what folks might think. So many don't believe in anything they can't understand, that they might think my mind wasn't right. Simon advised me not to talk about it. He said he didn't believe it was anything supernatural, but he had to own up that he couldn't give any explanation for it to save his life. He had to own up that he didn't believe anybody could. Then he said he wouldn't talk about it. He said lots of folks would sooner tell folks my head wasn't right than to own up they couldn't see through it."

"I'm sure I wouldn't say so," returned Mrs Emerson reproachfully. "You know better than that, I hope."

"Yes, I do," replied Mrs Meserve. "I know you wouldn't say so."

"And I wouldn't tell it to a soul if you didn't want me to."

"Well, I'd rather you wouldn't."

"I won't speak of it even to Mr Emerson."

"I'd rather you wouldn't even to him."

"I won't."

Mrs Emerson took up her dress skirt again; Mrs Meserve hooked up another loop of blue wool. Then she begun:

"Of course," said she, "I ain't going to say positively that I believe or disbelieve in ghosts, but all I tell you is what I saw. I can't explain it. I don't pretend I can, for I can't. If you can, well and good; I shall be glad, for it will stop tormenting me as it has done and always will otherwise. There hasn't been a day nor a night since it happened that I haven't thought of it, and always I have felt the shivers go down my back when I did."

"That's an awful feeling," Mrs Emerson said.

"Ain't it? Well, it happened before I was married, when I was a girl and lived in East Wilmington. It was the first year I lived there. You know my family all died five years before that. I told you."

Mrs Emerson nodded.

"Well, I went there to teach school, and I went to board with a Mrs Amelia Dennison and her sister, Mrs Bird. Abby, her name was—Abby Bird. She was a widow; she had never had any children. She had a little money—Mrs Dennison didn't have any—and she had come to East Wilmington and bought the house they lived in. It was a real pretty house, though it was very old and run down. It had cost Mrs Bird a good deal to put it in order. I guess that was the reason they took me to board. I guess they thought it would help along a little. I guess what I paid for my board about kept us all in victuals. Mrs Bird had enough to live on if they were careful, but she had spent so much fixing up the old house that they must have been a little pinched for awhile.

"Anyhow, they took me to board, and I thought I was pretty lucky to get in there. I had a nice room, big and sunny and furnished pretty, the paper and paint all new, and everything as neat as wax. Mrs Dennison was one of the best cooks I ever saw, and I had a little stove in my room, and there was always a nice fire there when I got home from school. I thought I hadn't been in such a nice place since I lost my own home, until I had been there about three weeks.

"I had been there about three weeks before I found it out, though I guess it had been going on ever since they had been in the house, and that was most four months. They hadn't said anything about it, and I didn't wonder, for there they had just bought the house and been to so much expense and trouble fixing it up.

"Well, I went there in September. I begun my school the first Monday. I remember it was a real cold fall, there was a frost the middle of September, and I had to put on my winter coat. I remember when I came home that night (let me see, I began school on a Monday, and that was two weeks from the next Thursday), I took off my coat downstairs and laid it on the table in the front entry. It was a real nice coat—heavy black broadcloth trimmed with fur; I had had it the winter before. Mrs Bird called after me as I went upstairs that I ought not to leave it in the front entry for fear somebody might come in and take it, but I only laughed and called back to her that I wasn't afraid. I never was much afraid of burglars.

"Well, though it was hardly the middle of September, it was a real cold night. I remember my room faced west, and the sun was getting low, and the sky was a pale yellow and purple, just as you see it sometimes in the winter when there is going to be a cold snap. I rather think that was the night the frost came the first time. I know Mrs Dennison covered up some flowers she had in the front yard, anyhow. I remember looking out and seeing an old green plaid shawl of hers over the verbena bed. There was a fire in my little wood-stove. Mrs Bird made it, I know. She was a real motherly sort of woman; she always seemed to be the happiest when she was doing something to make other folks happy and comfortable. Mrs Dennison told me she had always been so. She said she had coddled her husband within an inch of his life. 'It's lucky Abby never had any children,' she said, 'for she would have spoilt them.'

"Well, that night I sat down beside my nice little fire and ate an apple. There was a plate of nice apples on my table. Mrs Bird put them there. I was always very fond of apples. Well, I sat down and ate an apple, and was having a beautiful time, and thinking how lucky I was to have got board in such a place with such nice folks, when I heard a queer little sound at my door. It was such a little hesitating sort of sound that it sounded more like a fumble than a knock, as if someone very timid, with very little hands, was feeling along the door, not quite daring to knock. For a minute I thought it was a mouse. But I waited and it came again, and then I made up my mind it was a knock, but a very little scared one, so I said, 'Come in.'

"But nobody came in, and then presently I heard the knock again. Then I got up and opened the door, thinking it was very queer, and I had a frightened feeling without knowing why.

"Well, I opened the door, and the first thing I noticed was a draught of cold air, as if the front door downstairs was open, but there was a strange close smell about the cold draught. It smelled more like a cellar that had been shut up for years, than out-of-doors. Then I saw something. I saw my coat first. The thing that held it was so small that I couldn't see much of anything else. Then I saw a little white face with eyes so scared and wishful that they seemed as if they might eat a hole in anybody's heart. It was a dreadful little face, with something about it which made it different from any other face on earth, but it was so pitiful that somehow it did away a good deal with the dreadfulness. And there were two little hands spotted purple with the cold, holding up my winter coat, and a strange little far-away voice said: 'I can't find my mother.'

"'For Heaven's sake,' I said, 'who are you?'

"Then the little voice said again: 'I can't find my mother.'

"All the time I could smell the cold and I saw that it was about the child; that cold was clinging to her as if she had come out of some deadly cold place. Well, I took my coat, I did not know what else to do, and the cold was clinging to that. It was as cold as if it had come off ice. When I had the coat I could see the child more plainly. She was dressed in one little white garment made very simply. It was a nightgown, only very long, quite covering her feet, and I could see dimly through it her little thin body mottled purple with the cold. Her face did not look so cold; that was a clear waxen white. Her hair was dark, but it looked as if it might be dark only because it was so damp, almost wet, and might really be light hair. It clung very close to her forehead, which was round and white. She would have been very beautiful if she had not been so dreadful.

"'Who are you?' says I again, looking at her.

"She looked at me with her terrible pleading eyes and did not say anything.

"'What are you?' says I. Then she went away. She did not seem to run or walk like other children. She flitted, like one of those little filmy white butterflies, that don't seem like real ones they are so light, and move as if they had no weight. But she looked back from the head of the stairs. 'I can't find my mother,' said she, and I never heard such a voice.

"'Who is your mother?' says I, but she was gone.

"Well, I thought for a moment I should faint away. The room got dark and I heard a singing in my ears. Then I flung my coat onto the bed. My hands were as cold as ice from holding it, and I stood in my door, and called first Mrs Bird and then Mrs Dennison. I didn't dare go down over the stairs where that had gone. It seemed to me I should go mad if I didn't see somebody or something like other folks on the face of the earth. I thought

I should never make anybody hear, but I could hear them stepping about downstairs, and I could smell biscuits baking for supper. Somehow the smell of those biscuits seemed the only natural thing left to keep me in my right mind. I didn't dare go over those stairs. I just stood there and called, and finally I heard the entry door open and Mrs Bird called back:

"'What is it? Did you call, Miss Arms?'

"'Come up here; come up here as quick as you can, both of you,' I screamed out; 'quick, quick, quick!'

"I heard Mrs Bird tell Mrs Dennison: 'Come quick, Amelia, something is the matter in Miss Arms' room.' It struck me even then that she expressed herself rather queerly, and it struck me as very queer, indeed, when they both got upstairs and I saw that they knew what had happened, or that they knew of what nature the happening was.

"'What is it, dear?' asked Mrs Bird, and her pretty, loving voice had a strained sound. I saw her look at Mrs Dennison and I saw Mrs Dennison look back at her.

"'For God's sake,' says I, and I never spoke so before—'for God's sake, what was it brought my coat upstairs?'

"'What was it like?' asked Mrs Dennison in a sort of failing voice, and she looked at her sister again and her sister looked back at her.

"'It was a child I have never seen here before. It looked like a child,' says I, 'but I never saw a child so dreadful, and it had on a nightgown, and said she couldn't find her mother. Who was it? What was it?'

"I thought for a minute Mrs Dennison was going to faint, but Mrs Bird hung onto her and rubbed her hands, and whispered in her ear (she had the cooingest kind of voice), and I ran and got her a glass of cold water. I tell you it took considerable courage to go downstairs alone, but they had set a lamp on the entry table so I could see. I don't believe I could have spunked up enough to have gone downstairs in the dark, thinking every second that child might be close to me. The lamp and the smell of the biscuits baking seemed to sort of keep my courage up, but I tell you I didn't waste much time going down those stairs and out into the kitchen for a glass of water. I pumped as if the house was afire, and I grabbed the first thing I came across in the shape of a tumbler: it was a painted one that Mrs Dennison's Sunday school class gave her, and it was meant for a flower vase.

"Well, I filled it and then ran upstairs. I felt every minute as if something would catch my feet, and I held the glass to Mrs Dennison's lips, while Mrs Bird held her head up, and she took a good long swallow, then she looked hard at the tumbler.

"'Yes,' says I, 'I know I got this one, but I took the first I came across, and it isn't hurt a mite.'

"'Don't get the painted flowers wet,' says Mrs Dennison very feebly, 'they'll wash off if you do.'

"'I'll be real careful,' says I. I knew she set a sight by that painted tumbler.

"The water seemed to do Mrs Dennison good, for presently she pushed Mrs Bird away and sat up. She had been laying down on my bed.

"'I'm all over it now,' says she, but she was terribly white, and her eyes looked as if they saw something outside things. Mrs Bird wasn't much better, but she always had a sort of settled sweet, good look that nothing could disturb to any great extent. I knew I looked dreadful, for I caught a glimpse of myself in the glass, and I would hardly have known who it was.

"Mrs Dennison, she slid off the bed and walked sort of tottery to a chair. 'I was silly to give way so,' says she.

"'No, you wasn't silly, sister,' says Mrs Bird. 'I don't know what this means any more than you do, but whatever it is, no one ought to be called silly for being overcome by anything so different from other things which we have known all our lives.'

"Mrs Dennison looked at her sister, then she looked at me, then back at her sister again, and Mrs Bird spoke as if she had been asked a question.

"'Yes,' says she, 'I do think Miss Arms ought to be told—that is, I think she ought to be told all we know ourselves.'

"'That isn't much,' said Mrs Dennison with a dying-away sort of sigh. She looked as if she might faint away again any minute. She was a real delicate-looking woman, but it turned out she was a good deal stronger than poor Mrs Bird.

"'No, there isn't much we do know,' says Mrs Bird, 'but what little there is she ought to know. I felt as if she ought to when she first came here.'

"'Well, I didn't feel quite right about it,' said Mrs Dennison, 'but I kept hoping it might stop, and any way, that it might never trouble her, and you had put so much in the house, and we needed the money, and I didn't know but she might be nervous and think she couldn't come, and I didn't want to take a man boarder.'

"'And aside from the money, we were very anxious to have you come, my dear,' says Mrs Bird.

"'Yes,' says Mrs Dennison, 'we wanted the young company in the house; we were lonesome, and we both of us took a great liking to you the minute we set eyes on you.'

"And I guess they meant what they said, both of them. They were beautiful women, and nobody could be any kinder to me than they were, and I never blamed them for not telling me before, and, as they said, there wasn't really much to tell.

"They hadn't any sooner fairly bought the house, and moved into it, than they began to see and hear things. Mrs Bird said they were sitting together in the sitting-room one evening when they heard it the first time. She said her sister was knitting lace (Mrs Dennison made beautiful knitted lace) and she was reading the Missionary Herald (Mrs Bird was very much interested in mission work), when all of a sudden they heard something. She heard it first and she laid down her Missionary Herald and listened, and then Mrs Dennison she saw her listening and she drops her lace. 'What is it you are listening to, Abby?' says she. Then it came again and they both heard, and the cold shivers went down their backs to hear it, though they didn't know why. 'It's the cat, isn't it?' says Mrs Bird.

"'It isn't any cat,' says Mrs Dennison.

"'Oh, I guess it MUST be the cat; maybe she's got a mouse,' says Mrs Bird, real cheerful, to calm down Mrs Dennison, for she saw she was 'most scared to death, and she was always afraid of her fainting away. Then she opens the door and calls, 'Kitty, kitty, kitty!' They had brought their cat with them in a basket when they came to East Wilmington to live. It was a real handsome tiger cat, a tommy, and he knew a lot.

"Well, she called 'Kitty, kitty, kitty!' and sure enough the kitty came, and when he came in the door he gave a big yawl that didn't sound unlike what they had heard.

"'There, sister, here he is; you see it was the cat,' says Mrs Bird. 'Poor kitty!'

"But Mrs Dennison she eyed the cat, and she give a great screech.

"'What's that? What's that?' says she.

"'What's what?' says Mrs Bird, pretending to herself that she didn't see what her sister meant.

"'Somethin's got hold of that cat's tail,' says Mrs Dennison. 'Somethin's got hold of his tail. It's pulled straight out, an' he can't get away. Just hear him yawl!'

"'It isn't anything,' says Mrs Bird, but even as she said that she could see a little hand holding fast to that cat's tail, and then the child seemed to sort of clear out of the dimness behind the hand, and the child was sort of laughing then, instead of looking sad, and she said that was a great deal worse. She said that laugh was the most awful and the saddest thing she ever heard.

"Well, she was so dumfounded that she didn't know what to do, and she couldn't sense at first that it was anything supernatural. She thought it must be one of the neighbour's children who had run away and was making free of their house, and was teasing their cat, and that they must be just nervous to feel so upset by it. So she speaks up sort of sharp.

"'Don't you know that you mustn't pull the kitty's tail?' says she. 'Don't you know you hurt the poor kitty, and she'll scratch you if you don't take care. Poor kitty, you mustn't hurt her.'

"And with that she said the child stopped pulling that cat's tail and went to stroking her just as soft and pitiful, and the cat put his back up and rubbed and purred as if he liked it. The cat never seemed a mite afraid, and that seemed queer, for I had always heard that animals were dreadfully afraid of ghosts; but then, that was a pretty harmless little sort of ghost.

"Well, Mrs Bird said the child stroked that cat, while she and Mrs Dennison stood watching it, and holding onto each other, for, no matter how hard they tried to think it was all right, it didn't look right. Finally Mrs Dennison she spoke.

"'What's your name, little girl?' says she.

"Then the child looks up and stops stroking the cat, and says she can't find her mother, just the way she said it to me. Then Mrs Dennison she gave such a gasp that Mrs Bird thought she was going to faint away, but she didn't. 'Well, who is your mother?' says she. But the child just says again 'I can't find my mother—I can't find my mother.'

"'Where do you live, dear?' says Mrs Bird.

"'I can't find my mother,' says the child.

"Well, that was the way it was. Nothing happened. Those two women stood there hanging onto each other, and the child stood in front of them, and they asked her questions, and everything she would say was: 'I can't find my mother.'

"Then Mrs Bird tried to catch hold of the child, for she thought in spite of what she saw that perhaps she was nervous and it was a real child, only perhaps not quite right in its head, that had run away in her little nightgown after she had been put to bed.

"She tried to catch the child. She had an idea of putting a shawl around it and going out—she was such a little thing she could have carried her easy enough—and trying to find out to which of the neighbours she belonged. But the minute she moved toward the child there wasn't any child there; there was only that little voice seeming to come from nothing, saying 'I can't find my mother,' and presently that died away.

"Well, that same thing kept happening, or something very much the same. Once in awhile Mrs Bird would be washing dishes, and all at once the child would be standing beside her with the dish-towel, wiping them. Of course, that was terrible. Mrs Bird would wash the dishes all over. Sometimes she didn't tell Mrs Dennison, it made her so nervous. Sometimes when they were making cake they would find the raisins all picked over, and sometimes little sticks of kindling-wood would be found laying beside the kitchen stove. They never knew when they would come across that child, and always she kept saying over and over that she couldn't find her mother. They never tried talking to her, except once in awhile Mrs Bird would get desperate and ask her something, but the child never seemed to hear it; she always kept right on saying that she couldn't find her mother.

"After they had told me all they had to tell about their experience with the child, they told me about the house and the people that had lived there before they did. It seemed something dreadful had happened in that house. And the land agent had never let on to them. I don't think they would have bought it if he had, no matter how cheap it was, for even if folks aren't really afraid of anything, they don't want to live in houses where such dreadful things have happened that you keep thinking about them. I know after they told me I should never have stayed there another night, if I hadn't thought so much of them, no matter how comfortable I was made; and I never was nervous, either. But I stayed. Of course, it didn't happen in my room. If it had I could not have stayed."

"What was it?" asked Mrs Emerson in an awed voice.

"It was an awful thing. That child had lived in the house with her father and mother two years before. They had come—or the father had—from a real good family. He had a good situation: he was a drummer for a big leather house in the city, and they lived real pretty, with plenty to do with. But the mother was a real wicked woman. She was as handsome as a picture, and they said she came from good sort of people enough in Boston, but she was bad clean through, though she was real pretty spoken and most everybody liked her. She used to dress out and make a great show, and she never seemed to take much interest in the child, and folks began to say she wasn't treated right.

"The woman had a hard time keeping a girl. For some reason one wouldn't stay. They would leave and then talk about her awfully, telling all kinds of things. People didn't believe it at first; then they began to. They said that the woman made that little thing, though she wasn't much over five years old, and small and babyish for her age, do most of the work, what there was done; they said the house used to look like a pig-sty when she didn't have help. They said the little thing used to stand on a chair and wash dishes, and they'd seen her carrying in sticks of wood most as big as she was many a time, and they'd heard her mother scolding her. The woman was a fine singer, and had a voice like a screech-owl when she scolded.

"The father was away most of the time, and when that happened he had been away out West for some weeks. There had been a married man hanging about the mother for some time, and folks had talked some; but they weren't sure there was anything wrong, and he was a man very high up, with money, so they kept pretty still for fear he would hear of it and make trouble for them, and of course nobody was sure, though folks did say afterward that the father of the child had ought to have been told.

"But that was very easy to say; it wouldn't have been so easy to find anybody who would have been willing to tell him such a thing as that, especially when they weren't any too sure. He set his eyes by his wife, too. They said all he seemed to think of was to earn money to buy things to deck her out in. And he about worshiped the child, too. They said he was a real nice man. The men that are treated so bad mostly are real nice men. I've always noticed that.

"Well, one morning that man that there had been whispers about was missing. He had been gone quite a while, though, before they really knew that he was missing, because he had gone away and told his wife that he had to go to New York on business and might be gone a week, and not to worry if he didn't get home, and not to worry if he didn't write, because he should be thinking from day to day that he might take the next train home and there would be no use in writing. So the wife waited, and she tried not to worry until it was two days over the week, then she run into a neighbour's and fainted dead away on the floor; and then they made inquiries and found out that he had skipped—with some money that didn't belong to him, too.

"Then folks began to ask where was that woman, and they found out by comparing notes that nobody had seen her since the man went away; but three or four women remembered that she had told them that she thought of taking the child and going to Boston to visit her folks, so when they hadn't seen her around, and the house shut, they jumped to the conclusion that was where she was. They were the neighbours that lived right around her, but they didn't have much to do with her, and she'd gone out of her way to tell them about her Boston plan, and they didn't make much reply when she did.

"Well, there was this house shut up, and the man and woman missing and the child. Then all of a sudden one of the women that lived the nearest remembered something. She remembered that she had waked up three nights running, thinking she heard a child crying somewhere, and once she waked up her husband, but he said it must be the Bisbees' little girl, and she thought it must be. The child wasn't well and was always crying. It used to have colic spells, especially at night. So she didn't think any more about it until this came up, then all of a sudden she did think of it. She told what she had heard, and finally folks began to think they had better enter that house and see if there was anything wrong.

"Well, they did enter it, and they found that child dead, locked in one of the rooms. (Mrs Dennison and Mrs Bird never used that room; it was a back bedroom on the second floor.)

"Yes, they found that poor child there, starved to death, and frozen, though they weren't sure she had frozen to death, for she was in bed with clothes enough to keep her pretty warm when she was alive. But she had been there a week, and she was nothing but skin and bone. It looked as if the mother had locked her into the house when she went away, and told her not to make any noise for fear the neighbours would hear her and find out that she herself had gone.

"Mrs Dennison said she couldn't really believe that the woman had meant to have her own child starved to death. Probably she thought the little thing would raise somebody, or folks would try to get in the house and find her. Well, whatever she thought, there the child was, dead.

"But that wasn't all. The father came home, right in the midst of it; the child was just buried, and he was beside himself. And—he went on the track of his wife, and he found her, and he shot her dead; it was in all the papers at the time; then he disappeared. Nothing had been seen of him since. Mrs Dennison said that she thought he had either made way with himself or got out of the country, nobody knew, but they did know there was something wrong with the house.

"'I knew folks acted queer when they asked me how I liked it when we first came here,' says Mrs Dennison, 'but I never dreamed why till we saw the child that night.'

"I never heard anything like it in my life," said Mrs Emerson, staring at the other woman with awestruck eyes.

"I thought you'd say so," said Mrs Meserve. "You don't wonder that I ain't disposed to speak light when I hear there is anything queer about a house, do you?"

"No, I don't, after that," Mrs Emerson said.

"But that ain't all," said Mrs Meserve.

"Did you see it again?" Mrs Emerson asked.

"Yes, I saw it a number of times before the last time. It was lucky I wasn't nervous, or I never could have stayed there, much as I liked the place and much as I thought of those two women; they were beautiful women, and no mistake. I loved those women. I hope Mrs Dennison will come and see me sometime.

"Well, I stayed, and I never knew when I'd see that child. I got so I was very careful to bring everything of mine upstairs, and not leave any little thing in my room that needed doing, for fear she would come lugging up my coat or hat or gloves or I'd find things done when there'd been no live being in the room to do them. I can't tell you how I dreaded seeing her; and worse than the seeing her was the hearing her say, 'I can't find my mother.' It was enough to make your blood run cold. I never heard a living child cry for its mother that was anything so pitiful as that dead one. It was enough to break your heart.

"She used to come and say that to Mrs Bird oftener than to any one else. Once I heard Mrs Bird say she wondered if it was possible that the poor little thing couldn't really find her mother in the other world, she had been such a wicked woman.

"But Mrs Dennison told her she didn't think she ought to speak so nor even think so, and Mrs Bird said she shouldn't wonder if she was right. Mrs Bird was always very easy to put in the wrong. She was a good woman, and one that couldn't do things enough for other folks. It seemed as if that was what she lived on. I don't think she was ever so scared by that poor little ghost, as much as she pitied it, and she was 'most heartbroken because she couldn't do anything for it, as she could have done for a live child.

"'It seems to me sometimes as if I should die if I can't get that awful little white robe off that child and get her in some clothes and feed her and stop her looking for her mother,' I heard her say once, and she was in earnest. She cried when she said it. That wasn't long before she died.

"Now I am coming to the strangest part of it all. Mrs Bird died very sudden. One morning—it was Saturday, and there wasn't any school—I went downstairs to breakfast, and Mrs Bird wasn't there; there was nobody but Mrs Dennison. She was pouring out the coffee when I came in. 'Why, where's Mrs Bird?' says I.

"'Abby ain't feeling very well this morning,' says she; 'there isn't much the matter, I guess, but she didn't sleep very well, and her head aches, and she's sort of chilly, and I told her I thought she'd better stay in bed till the house gets warm.' It was a very cold morning.

"'Maybe she's got cold,' says I.

"'Yes, I guess she has,' says Mrs Dennison. 'I guess she's got cold. She'll be up before long. Abby ain't one to stay in bed a minute longer than she can help.'

"Well, we went on eating our breakfast, and all at once a shadow flickered across one wall of the room and over the ceiling the way a shadow will sometimes when somebody passes the window outside. Mrs Dennison and I both looked up, then out of the window; then Mrs Dennison she gives a scream.

"'Why, Abby's crazy!' says she. 'There she is out this bitter cold morning, and—and—' She didn't finish, but she meant the child. For we were both looking out, and we saw, as plain as we ever saw anything in our lives, Mrs Abby Bird walking off over the white snow-path with that child holding fast to her hand, nestling close to her as if she had found her own mother.

"'She's dead,' says Mrs Dennison, clutching hold of me hard. 'She's dead; my sister is dead!'

"She was. We hurried upstairs as fast as we could go, and she was dead in her bed, and smiling as if she was dreaming, and one arm and hand was stretched out as if something had hold of it; and it couldn't be straightened even at the last—it lay out over her casket at the funeral."

"Was the child ever seen again?" asked Mrs Emerson in a shaking voice.

"No," replied Mrs Meserve; "that child was never seen again after she went out of the yard with Mrs Bird."

The Burned House

Vincent O'Sullivan

One night at the end of dinner, the last time I crossed the Atlantic, somebody in our group remarked that we were just passing over the spot where the Lusitania had gone down. Whether this was the case or not, the thought of it was enough to make us rather grave, and we dropped into some more or less serious discussion about the emotions of men and women who see all hope gone, and realize that they are going to sink with the vessel. From that the talk wandered to the fate of the drowned: was not theirs, after all, a fortunate end? Somebody related details from the narratives of those who had been all but drowned in the accidents of the war. A Scotch lady inquired fancifully if the ghosts of those who are lost at sea ever appear above the waters and come aboard ships. Would there be danger of seeing one when the light was turned out in her cabin? This put an end to all seriousness, and most of us laughed. But a little tight-faced man from Fall River, bleak and iron-gray, who had been listening attentively, did not laugh. The lady noticed his decorum and appealed to him for support.

"You are like me—you believe in ghosts?" she asked lightly.

He hesitated, thinking it over.

"In ghosts?" he repeated slowly. "N-no; I don't know as I do. I've never had any personal experience that way. I've never seen the ghost of any one I knew. Has anybody here?"

No one replied. Instead, most of us laughed again, a little uneasily, perhaps.

"Well, I guess not," resumed the man from Fall River. "All the same, strange-enough things happen in life, even if you cut out ghosts, that you can't clear up by laughing. You laugh till you've had some experience big enough to shock you, and then you don't laugh any more. It's like being thrown out of a car—"

At this moment there was a blast on the whistle, and everybody rushed up on deck. As it turned out, we had only entered into a belt of fog. On the upper deck I fell in again with the New-Englander, smoking a cigar and walking up and down. We took a few turns together, and he referred to the conversation at dinner. Our laughter evidently rankled in his mind.

"So many damn' strange things happen in life that you can't account for," he protested. "You go on laughing at faith-healing and at dreams and this and that, and then something comes along that you just can't explain. You have got to throw up your hands and allow that it doesn't answer to any tests our experience has provided us with. Now, I guess I'm as matter of fact a man as any of those folks down there. I'm in the outfitting business. My favorite author is Ingersoll; whenever I go on a journey like this I carry one of his books. If you read Ingersoll and think Ingersoll year in, year out, you don't have much use for wool-gathering. But once I had an experience which I had to conclude was out of the ordinary. Whether other people believe it or not, or whether they think they can explain it, don't matter; it happened to me, and I could no more doubt it than I could doubt having had a tooth pulled after the dentist had done it. I only wish Ingersoll was still alive; I'd like to put it up to him. If you will sit down here with me in this corner out of the wind, I'll tell you how it was.

"Some years ago I had to be for several months in New York. I was before the courts; it doss not signify now what for, and it is all forgotten by this time. But it was a long and worrying case, and it aged me by twenty years. Well, sir, all through the trial, in that grimy court-room, I kept thinking and thinking of a fresh little place I knew in the Vermont hills; and I helped to get through the hours by thinking that if things went well with me I'd go there at once. And so it was that on the very next morning after I was acquitted I stepped on the cars at the Grand Central station.

"It was the early fall; the days were closing in, and it was night and cold when I arrived. The village was very dark and deserted; they don't go out much after dark in those parts, anyhow, and the keen mountain wind was enough to quell any lingering desire. The hotel was not one of those modern places called inns from sentiment in America, which are equipped and upholstered like the great city hotels; it was one of the real old-fashioned New England taverns, about as uncomfortable places as there are on earth, where the idea is to show the traveler that traveling is a penitential state, and that morally and physically the best place for him is home. The landlord brought me a kind of supper, with his hat on and a pipe in his mouth. The room was chilly; but when I asked for a fire, he said he guessed he couldn't go out to the wood-pile till morning. There was nothing else to do when I had eaten my supper but to go outside, both to get the smell of the lamp out of my nose and to warm myself by a short walk.

"As I did not know the country well, I did not mean to go far. But although it was an overcast night, with a high north-east wind and an occasional flurry of rain, the moon was up, and even concealed by clouds as it was, it yet lit the night with a kind of twilight gray, not vivid, like the open moonlight, but good enough to see some distance. On account of this I prolonged my stroll, and kept walking on and on till I was a considerable way from the village, and in a region as lonely as anywhere in the State. Great trees and shrubs bordered the road, and many feet below was a mountain stream. What with the passion of the wind pouring through the high trees and the shout of the water racing among the boulders, it seemed to me sometimes like the noise of a crowd of people, and two or three times I turned to see if a crowd might be out after me, well as I knew that no crowd could be there. Sometimes the branches of the trees became so thick that I was walking as if in a black pit, unable to see my hand close to my face. Then, coming out from the tunnel of branches, I would step once more into a gray clearness which opened the road and surrounding country a good way on all sides.

"I suppose it might be some three quarters of an hour I had been walking when I came to a fork of the road. One branch ran downward, getting almost on a level with the bed of the torrent. The other mounted in a steep hill, and this, after a little idle debating, I decided to follow. After I had climbed for more than half a mile, thinking that if I should happen to lose track of one of the landmarks I should be very badly lost, the path—for it was now no more than that—curved, and I came out on a broad plateau. There, to my astonishment, I saw a house. It was a good-sized wooden house, three stories high, with a piazza round two sides of it, and from the elevation on which it stood it commanded a far stretch of country. There were a few great trees at a little distance from the house, and behind it, a stone's-throw away, was a clump of bushes. Still, it looked lonely and stark, offering its four sides unprotected to the winds. For all that, I was very glad to see it. 'It does not matter now,' I thought, 'whether I have lost my way or not. The house people will set me right.'

"But when I came up to it, I found that it was, to all appearance, uninhabited. The shutters were closed on all the windows; there was not a spark of light anywhere. There was something about it, something sinister and barren, that gave me the kind of shiver you have at the door of a room where you know that a dead man lies inside, or if you get thinking hard about dropping over the rail into that black waste of waters out there. This feeling, you know, isn't altogether unpleasant; you relish all the better your present security. It was the same with me standing before that house. I was not really scared. I was alone up here, miles from any kind of help, at the mercy of whoever might be lurking behind the shutters of that sullen house; but I felt that by all the chances I was perfectly alone and safe. My sensation of the uncanny was due to the effect on the nerves produced by wild scenery and the unexpected sight of a house in such a very lonely situation. Thus I reasoned, and instead of following the road farther, I walked over the grass till I came to a stone wall perhaps two hundred and fifty yards in front of the house, and rested my arms on it, looking forth at the scene.

"On the crests of the hills far away a strange light lingered, like the first touch of dawn in the sky on a rainy morning or the last glimpse of twilight before night comes. Between me and the hills was a wide stretch of open country. On my right hand was an apple-orchard, and I observed that a stile had been made in the wall of piled stones to enable the house people to go back and forth.

"Now, after I had been there leaning on the wall some considerable time, I saw a man coming toward me through the orchard. He was walking with a good, free stride, and as he drew nearer I could see that he was a tall, sinewy fellow between twenty-five and thirty, with a shaven face, wearing the slouch-hat of that country, a dark woolen shirt, and high boots. When he reached the stile and began climbing over it, I bade him good night in neighborly fashion. He made no reply, but he looked me straight in the face, and the look gave me a qualm. Not that it was an evil face, mind you,—it was a handsome, serious face,—but it was ravaged by some terrible passion: stealth was on it, ruthlessness, and a deadly resolution, and at the same time such a look as a man driven by some uncontrollable power might throw on surrounding things, asking for comprehension and mercy. It was impossible for me to resent his churlishness, his thoughts were so certainly elsewhere. I doubt if he even saw me.

"He could not have gone by more than a quarter of a minute when I turned to look after him. He had disappeared. The plateau lay bare before me, and it seemed impossible that even if he had sprinted like an athlete he could have got inside the house in so little time. But I have always made it a rule to attribute what I cannot understand to natural causes that I have failed to observe. I said to myself that no doubt the man had gone back into the orchard by some other opening in the wall lower down, or there might be some flaw in my vision owing to the uncertain and distorting light.

"But even as I continued to look toward the house, leaning my back now against the wall, I noticed that there were lights springing up in the windows behind the shutters. They were flickering lights, now bright, now dim, and had a ruddy glow like firelight. Before I had looked long, I became convinced that it was indeed firelight: the house was on fire. Black smoke began to pour from the roof; the red sparks flew in the wind. Then at a window above the roof of the piazza the shutters were thrown open, and I heard a woman shriek. I ran toward the house as hard as I could, and when I drew near I could see her plainly.

"She was a young woman; her hair fell in disorder over her white night-gown. She stretched out her bare arms, screaming. I saw a man come behind and seize her. But they were caught in a trap. The flames were licking round the windows, and the smoke was killing them. Even now the part of the house where they stood was caving in.

"Appalled by this horrible tragedy, which had thus suddenly risen before me, I made my way still nearer the house, thinking that if the two could struggle to the side of the house not bounded by the piazza they might jump, and I might break the fall. I was shouting this at them; I was right up close to the fire; and then I was struck by—I noticed for the first time an astonishing thing—the flames had no heat in them!

"I was standing near enough to the fire to be singed by it, and yet I felt no heat. The sparks were flying about my head; some fell on my hands, and they did not burn. And now I perceived that although the smoke was rolling in columns, I was not choked by the smoke, and that there had been no smell of smoke since the fire broke out. Neither was there any glare against the sky.

"As I stood there stupefied, wondering how these things could be, the whole house was swept by a very tornado of flame, and crashed down in a red ruin.

"Stricken to the heart by this abominable catastrophe, I made my way uncertainly down the hill, shouting for help. As I came to a little wooden bridge spanning the torrent, just beyond where the roads forked, I saw what appeared to be a rope in loose coils lying there. I saw that part of it was fastened to the railing of the bridge and hung outside, and I looked over. There was a man's body swinging by the neck between the road and the stream. I leaned over still farther, and then I recognized him as the man I had seen coming out of the orchard. His hat had fallen off, and the toes of his boots just touched the water.

"It seemed hardly possible, and yet it was certain. That was the man, and he was hanging there. I scrambled down at the side of the bridge, and put out my hand to seize the body, so that I might lift it up and relieve the weight on the rope. I succeeded in clutching hold of his loose shirt, and for a second I thought that it had come away in my hand. Then I found that my hand had closed on nothing; I had clutched nothing but air. And yet the figure swung by the neck before my eyes!

"I was suffocated with such horror that I feared for a moment I must lose consciousness. The next minute I was running and stumbling along that dark road in mortal anxiety, my one idea being to rouse the town and bring men to the bridge. That, I say, was my intention; but the fact is that when I came at last in sight of the village, I slowed down instinctively and began to reflect. After all, I was unknown there; I had just gone through a disagreeable trial in New York, and rural people were notoriously given to groundless suspicion. I had had enough of the law and of arrests without sufficient evidence. The wisest thing would be to drop a hint or two before the landlord and judge by his demeanor whether to proceed.

"I found him sitting where I had left him, smoking, in his shirt-sleeves, with his hat on.

"'Well,' he said slowly, 'I didn't know where the gosh-blamed blazes you had got to. Been to see the folks?'

"I told him I had been taking a walk. I went on to mention casually the fork in the road, the hill, and the plateau.

"'And who lives in that house,' I asked with a good show of indifference, 'on top of the hill?'

"He stared.

"'House? There ain't no house up there,' he said positively. 'Old Joe Snedeker, who owns the land, says he's going to build a house up there for his son to live in when he gets married; but he ain't begun yet, and some folks reckon he never will.'

"'I feel sure I saw a house,' I protested feebly. But I was thinking—no heat in the fire, no substance in the body. I had not the courage to dispute.

"The landlord looked at me not unkindly. 'You seem sort of sick,' he remarked. 'Guess you been doin' too much down in the city. What you want is to go to bed.'"

The man from Fall River paused, and for a moment we sat silent, listening to the pant of the machinery, the thrumming of the wind in the wire stays, and the lash of the sea. Some voices were singing on the deck below. I considered him with the shade of contemptuous superiority we feel, as a rule, toward those who tell us their dreams or what some fortune-teller has predicted.

"Hallucinations," I said at last, with reassuring indulgence. "Trick of the vision, toxic ophthalmia. After the long strain of your trial your nerves were shattered."

"That's what I thought myself," he replied shortly, "especially after I had been out to the plateau the next morning and saw no sign that a house had ever stood there."

"And no corpse at the bridge?" I said, and laughed.

"And no corpse at the bridge."

He tried to get a light for another cigar. This took him some little time, and when at last he managed it, he got out of his chair and stood looking down at me.

"Now listen here. I told you that the thing happened several years ago. I'd got almost to forget it; if you can only persuade yourself that a thing is a freak of imagination, it pretty soon gets dim inside your head. Delusions have no staying power once it is realized that they are delusions. Whenever it did come back to me I used to think how near I had once been to going out of my mind. That was all.

"Well, last year I went up to that village again from Boston. I went to the same hotel and found the same landlord. He remembered me at once as 'The feller who come up from the city and thought he see a house. I believe you had the jim-jams,' he said.

"We laughed, and the landlord spat.

"'There's been a house there since; though.'

"'Has there?'

"'Why, yes; an' it ha' been as well if there never had been. Old man Snedeker built it for his son, a fine big house with a piazza on two sides. The son, young Joe, got courting Mamie Elting from here around. She'd gone down to work in a store somewhere in Connecticut — darned if I can remember where. New Haven or Danbury, maybe. Well, sir, she used to get carrying on with another young feller 'bout here, Jim Travers, and Jim was sure wild about her; used to save up his quarters to go down State to see her. But she turned him down in the end, and married Joe; I guess because Joe had the house, and the old man's money to expect. Well, poor Jim must ha' gone plumb crazy. What do you think he did? The very first night the new-wed pair spent in that house he burned it down. Burned the two of them in their bed, and he was as nice and quiet a feller as you want to see. He may ha' been full of whisky at the time.'

"'No, he wasn't,' I said.

"The landlord looked surprised.

"'I guess you've heard some about it?'

"'No; go on.'

"'Yes, sir, he burned them in their bed. And then what do you think he did? He hung himself at the little bridge half a mile below. Do you remember where the road divides? Well, it was there. I saw his body hanging there myself the next morning. The toes of his boots were just touching the water.'"

When I Was Dead

Vincent O'Sullivan

"And yet my heart
Will not confess he owes the malady
That doth my life besiege."
—*All's Well That Ends Well*

That was the worst of Ravenel Hall. The passages were long and gloomy, the rooms were musty and dull, even the pictures were sombre and their subjects dire. On an autumn evening, when the wind soughed and ailed through the trees in the park, and the dead leaves whistled and chattered, while the rain clamoured at the windows, small wonder that folks with gentle nerves went a-straying in their wits! An acute nervous system is a grievous burthen on the deck of a yacht under sunlit skies: at Ravenel the chain of nerves was prone to clash and jangle a funeral march. Nerves must be pampered in a tea-drinking community; and the ghost that your grandfather, with a skinful of port, could face and never tremble, sets you, in your sobriety, sweating and shivering; or, becoming scared (poor ghost!) of your bulged eyes and dropping jaw, he quenches expectation by not appearing at all. So I am left to conclude that it was tea which made my acquaintance afraid to stay at Ravenel. Even Wilvern gave over; and as he is in the Guards, and a polo player his nerves ought to be strong enough. On the night before he went I was explaining to him my theory, that if you place some drops of human blood near you, and then concentrate your thoughts, you will after a while see before you a man or a woman who will stay with you during long hours of the night, and even meet you at unexpected places during the day. I was explaining this theory, I repeat, when he interrupted me with words, senseless enough, which sent me fencing and parrying strangers,—on my guard.

"I say, Alistair, my dear chap!" he began, "you ought to get out of this place and go up to Town and knock about a bit—you really ought, you know."

"Yes," I replied, "and get poisoned at the hotels by bad food and at the clubs by bad talk, I suppose. No, thank you: and let me say that your care for my health enervates me."

"Well, you can do as you like," says he, rapping with his feet on the floor. "I'm hanged if I stay here after tomorrow I'll be staring mad if I do!"

He was my last visitor. Some weeks after his departure I was sitting in the library with my drops of blood by me. I had got my theory nearly perfect by this time; but there was one difficulty. The figure which I had ever before me was the figure of an old woman with her hair divided in the middle, and her hair fell to her shoulders, white on one side and black on the other. She as a very complete old woman; but, alas! she was eyeless, and when I tried to construct the eyes she would shrivel and rot in my sight. But tonight I was thinking, thinking, as I had never thought before, and the eyes were just creeping into the head when I heard terrible crash outside as if some heavy substance had fallen. Of a sudden the door was flung open and two maid-servants entered they glanced at the rug under my chair, and at that they turned a sick white, cried on God, and huddled out.

"How dare you enter the library in this manner?" I demanded sternly. No answer came back from them, so I started in pursuit. I found all the servants in the house gathered in a knot at the end of the passage.

"Mrs Pebble," I said smartly, to the housekeeper, "I want those two women discharged tomorrow. It's an outrage! You ought to be more careful." But she was not attending to me. Her face was distorted with terror.

"Ah dear, ah dear!" she went. "We had better all go to the library together," says she to the others.

"Am I master of my own house, Mrs Pebble?" I inquired, bringing my knuckles down with a bang on the table.

None of them seemed to see me or hear me: I might as well have been shrieking in a desert. I followed them down the passage, and forbade them to enter the library.

But they trooped past me, and stood with a clutter round the hearth-rug. Then three or four of them began dragging and lifting, as if they were lifting a helpless body, and stumbled with their imaginary burthen over to a sofa. Old Soames, the butler, stood near.

"Poor young gentleman!" he said with a sob. "I've knowed him since he was a baby. And to think of him being dead like this and so young, too!"

I crossed the room. "What's all this, Soames!" I cried, shaking him roughly by the shoulders. "I'm not dead. I'm here—here!" As he did not stir I got a little scared. "Soames, old friend!" I called, "don't you know me! Don't you know the little boy you used to play with? Say I'm not dead, Soames, please, Soames!"

He stooped down and kissed the sofa. "I think one of the men ought to ride over to the village for the doctor, Mr Soames," says Mrs Pebble; and he shuffled out to give the order.

Now, this doctor was an ignorant dog, whom I had been forced to exclude from the house because he went about proclaiming his belief in a saving God, at the same time that he proclaimed himself a man of science. He, I was resolved, should never cross my threshold, and I followed Mrs Pebble through the house, screaming out prohibition. But I did not catch even a groan from her, not a nod of the head, nor a cast of the eye, to show that she had heard.

I met the doctor at the door of the library. "Well," I sneered, throwing my hand in his face, "have you come to teach me some new prayers?"

He brushed by me as if he had not felt the blow, and knelt down by the sofa.

"Rupture of a vessel on the brain, I think," he says to Soames and Mrs Pebble after a short moment. "He has been dead some hours. Poor fellow! You had better telegraph for his sister, and I will send up the undertaker to arrange the body."

"You liar!" I yelled. "You whining liar! How have you the insolence to tell my servants that I am dead, when you see me here face to face?"

He was far in the passage, with Soames and Mrs Pebble at his heels, ere I had ended, and not one of the three turned round.

All that night I sat in the library. Strangely enough, I had no wish to sleep nor during the time that followed, had I any craving to eat. In the morning the men came, and although I ordered them out, they proceeded to minister about something I could not see. So all day I stayed in the library or wandered about the house, and at night the men came again bringing with them a coffin. Then, in my humour, thinking it shame that so fine a coffin should be empty I lay the night in it and slept a soft dreamless sleep—the softest sleep I have ever slept. And when the men came the next day I rested still, and the undertaker shaved me. A strange valet!

On the evening after that, I was coming downstairs, when I noted some luggage in the hall, and so learned that my sister had arrived. I had not seen this woman since her marriage, and I loathed her more than I loathed any creature in this ill-organised world. She was very beautiful, I think—tall, and dark, and straight as a ram-rod—and she had an unruly passion for scandal and dress. I suppose the reason I disliked her so intensely was, that she had a habit of making one aware of her presence when she was several yards off. At half-past nine o'clock my sister came down to the library in a very charming wrap, and I soon found that she was as insensible to my presence as the others. I trembled with rage to see her kneel down by the coffin—my coffin; but when she bent over to kiss the pillow I threw away control.

A knife which had been used to cut string was lying upon a table: I seized it and drove it into her neck. She fled from the room screaming.

"Come! come!" she cried, her voice quivering with anguish. "The corpse is bleeding from the nose."

Then I cursed her.

On the evening of the third day there was a heavy fall of snow. About eleven o'clock I observed that the house was filled with blacks and mutes and folk of the county, who came for the obsequies. I went into the library and sat still, and waited. Soon came the men, and they closed the lid of the coffin and bore it out on their shoulders. And yet I sat, feeling rather sadly that something of mine had been taken away: I could not quite think what. For half-an-hour perhaps—dreaming, dreaming: and then I glided to the hall door. There was no trace left of the funeral; but after a while I sighted a black thread winding slowly across the white plain.

"I'm not dead!" I moaned, and rubbed my face in the pure snow, and tossed it on my neck and hair. "Sweet God, I am not dead."

My Enemy and Myself

Vincent O'Sullivan

In the garden, when I was a child, I used to stare for hours at the white roses. In these there was for me a certain strangeness, which was yet quite human; for I know that I was full of sorrow if I found the petals strewn over the hushed grass. I had a terror of great waters, wild and lonely; I saw an austere dignity in the moon shining on a flat sea; things, cordage and broken spars, cast ashore by the ocean, told me wonderful, sad tales. And because my head was thick with thoughts, I had little speech; and for this I was laughed at and called stupid: "He was always a dull child," murmured my mother, bending over me, when I, in the crisis of a fever, was on the point of embarking for a vague land. As I grew older, I still dwelt within my soul, a satisfied prisoner: the complaint of huge trees in a storm; the lash and surge of breakers on an iron coast; the sound of certain words; the sight of dim colours which blend sometimes in gray sunsets; the heavy scent of some exquisite poisonous flower; a contemplation of youthful forms engaged in an unruly game;—ah! in these things also I found perfect sensation and ecstacy. Still, my tongue held to its old stubbornness: I was ever delayed by a habit of commonplace speech, a shame at exposing my thoughts. In time I won a cloud of easy acquaintance; but my awkwardness in conversation, my tendency to be maladroit,—call it what you like! always stepped between when I was about to make a friend. Then, at last, came Jacquette.

I remember that she was playing a composition by Chopin, a curious black-coloured thing, when I first came into her company; and now, even as I write, when our love is over, I hear that sombre music again. But the important matter is, that here was the person I had been seeking so long; here was the mind to meet with my mind; with her I could, at length, get out of myself (as we now say); become free. All the dear thoughts which had for years dwelt with me in close privateness, I gave to her all my desires, all my mean hopes. Ah! the merry airs we had then: her bright laughter which, as wind, drove glumness, as foam, before it! I think I tired her of my enthusiasms and decisions; but it was so sweet to have someone to listen and understand, and she never would admit that she was tired. Nay! one morning in the apple-orchard, when the wind was turning her hair to the sunshine, she kissed me very prettily on the mouth.

After that, I forget how long it was till I came in one night and found my enemy sitting with her at the fireside. He was not my enemy then, mind you: indeed, I thought him a nice, pleasant creature, with a mighty handsome face. We became familiar: he seemed to like me, and I was sure I had gained another friend. The months glided by, and we three came to sitting together late of nights: he and Jacquette, the wise people, silent, gazing at each other; I, the fool, in the middle, talking in a youthful, impassioned way. Once I paused suddenly, and looked up, and caught a somewhat contemptuous smile peeping from the corners of Jacquette's mouth and dancing in her eyes; while he, for an answer, fell a-laughing into her face. Of course, I must have wearied them both, bored them (as we say) to desperation; but I was a very young man, with all the warmth and admiration of the young; and in the time of youth, a woman is always older than a man. Besides, I loved her so much, and I had such strange pleasure in loving her, that I think it was rather cruel of her to laugh.

"Why did you laugh at me?" I asked, when I was twisting a garland of wild roses for her hair.

"Oh, I didn't laugh! "she exclaimed. "Or if I did,"she added, looking down with a tooth on her lip, "it must have been because I was so pleased to hear you saying beautiful words to us—poor ignorant things!"

The next day I had an affair of great importance in the town where I lived, so I told Jacquette that on account of this affair I could not go down, as my custom was, to her cottage by the sea, that night. But as the day waned, and the night closed in, I became the thrall of a longing to hear her singing voice, to play fantastic music with her delightfully. Thus it came about that it was nearly eleven o'clock when I reached the shore, and hearkened to the calling sea. There was a note of melancholy, almost a sob, in the noise of it tonight: and that, taken with a monstrous depression, filled me strangely with a desire to die—to give up life at this point! I saw a light in Jacquette's bedroom, but the rest of the little house was dark; and I was turning away, when my hand chanced to strike the door-handle, which I pushed, and found the door not locked. Let me go in! (thinks I): I shall sit awhile and dream of Jacquette, and a few chords touched softly on the piano will tell my love I am dreaming of her. Here (perhaps you will say!) I was wrong: but I was ready to welcome a servant's company, or, in spite of his growing offensiveness, my enemy's, should I find him there, rather than be alone with my saddening thoughts. The room I chose to sit in, because there was a dying fire in it, was just under Jacquette's bedroom; and ere I had sat a minute, I became conscious of voices in the room above. As soon as I made out the man's voice, a thousand serpents seemed literally to eat their way into my brain, turning my vision red; and I lay for an hour, maybe, on the carpet, fainting, and stricken, and dazed. Now, at last, after an hour I was myself, or rather more than myself, with every nerve tight as a fiddle-string, still seeing red, as I unclasped the long jack-knife, which the Greek sailor had given me, and laid it in the hollow of my hand.

I knew that it would dawn by three o'clock, so I stood quite still, only moving my tongue over my dry lips, and shaking my head to keep a sweat from running into my eyes. A cat cried in the road, and the breakers thundered against the rocks.

A little before dawn, while it was yet dark, I heard a murmur of low voices—her voice and my enemy's; and then the man came down the stairs.

"Good night, my sweet love!" said Jacquette.

"O my darling, good night!" came from my enemy, and so he banged the door behind him.

One moment I paused to peer through the window, and make sure of my man. Then I fetched a run, and was on him like a panther, holding him close, with his hot breath scorching my face. Coming on him from behind, as I did, the middle finger of my left hand struck his eye, and now, as I pressed, the eye bulged out.

"My friend," he groaned, "for Christ's sake, have pity!"

"To hell with your friendship!" I said. "Much pity you had for my honour!" says I, and with that I let him have the knife in his throat, and the blood spurted over my hands hot and sticky. As soon as I could get free of his clutch, I looked up at Jacquette's bedroom window, and there she was, sure enough! in her nightdress, with the blind in her hand, gazing out. Straight up to her room I went, and flung open the door. She turned to me gray and whingeing.

"My little love,"she began.

I put my hands on my hips and spat hard into her face. Then I tramped down stairs and out of the lonely cottage.

I had not the least fear of detection: the servants slept in an out-house, and the place was too desolate for any chance passenger.

I stood triumphing by the corpse of my enemy; but even as I looked the moon shewed from a rift of cloud, lighting the blood, and the hue left by violent death in the features, and I ran for my life from that hideous one-eyed thing.

I came to the town, and to a house where I lay constantly, about four o'clock, in a curious trembling fit. I bathed my head and hands, however, in a heavy perfume, and then became strangely calm, and fell to thinking of the Tightness of the deed. Just there was the consoling thought: certainly I had done a murder, but in doing it I had delivered punishment to a traitress and her paramour. Now that the thing was over, it was clearly my duty to forget all about it as soon as possible; and this I set myself to do, aided by a cigarette and a novel of the ingenious Miss Jane Austen. I had succeeded in my aim, I was clear-minded and very serene, when of a sudden something heavy fell against the door of my room.

"At this hour?" I murmured in surprise, and went to the door.

A body that nearly knocked me down, the dead body of a man, fell into the room, and lay, face downward, on the carpet. Then I did the one act I shall never cease to regret:

From a movement of kindness, pity, curiosity, what you will! I bent down and turned over the corpse. Slowly the thing got to its feet; and my enemy, with a dry gaping wound in his throat, and his eye hanging from its socket by a bit of skin, stood before me, face to face.

"O God, have mercy!" I screamed, and beat on the wall with my hands; and again and again:—"God, have mercy!"

"You do well to ask God for mercy," says my enemy; "for you will not get much from men." He stood by the fire-place.

"I beg of you" I said, in a low, passionate voice, "I beg of you, by all you find dear, for the sake of our old friendship, to leave this place, to let me go free."

He shook his head. "For Jacquette's sake?" He laughed harshly.

"My friend," I said to my enemy, "for Christ's sake, have pity!"

"Pity you?" says he, in a jeer. "You!"

As I looked at him, I was stung into strong fury. My eyes clung to the wound in his throat, and my fingers ached to close in it—to misuse it, to maul it.

But as I sprang at him, he gave a shriek that woke the town; a shriek of fear too, let me think it at this last, like to that of a lost soul when the gates of hell have closed behind for ever: and when the people of the house rushed in, they found me kneeling by his dead body, with my knife in my enemy's throat, and his new blood, bright and wet, on my hands.

The Lady of Rosemount

Thomas Graham Jackson

'And so, Charlton, you're going to spend part of the Long at Rosemount Abbey. I envy you. It's an awfully jolly old place, and you'll have a really good time.'

'Yes,' said Charlton, 'I am looking forward to it immensely. I have never seen it; you know it has only lately come to my uncle and they only moved into it last Christmas, I forgot that you knew it and had been there.'

'Oh! I don't know it very well,' said Edwards: 'I spent a few days there a year or two ago with the last owner. It will suit you down to the ground, for you are mad about old abbeys and ruins, and you'll find enough there to satisfy the whole Society of Antiquaries as well as yourself. When do you go?'

'Very soon. I must be at home for a week or so after we go down, and then I think my uncle will expect me at Rosemount. What are you going to do?'

'Well! I hardly know. Nothing very exciting. Perhaps take a short run abroad a little later. But I shall have to read part of the Long, for I am in for Greats next term. By the way, it is just possible I may be somewhere in your direction, for I have friends near Rosemount who want me to spend part of the vac. down there.'

'All right,' said Charlton, 'don't forget to come over and see me. I hope I may still be there. Meanwhile, au revoir, old man, and good luck to you.'

Charlton remained some time at his window looking on the quad of his college. Term at Oxford was just over and the men were rapidly going down. Hansoms were waiting at the gate, scouts and messengers were clattering down the staircases with portmanteaux and other paraphernalia proper to youth, and piling them on the cabs, friends were shaking hands, and bidding goodbye. In a few hours the college would be empty, and solitude would descend upon it for four months, broken only by occasional visitors, native or transatlantic. The flight of the men would be followed by that of the Dons to all parts of Europe or beyond, the hive would be deserted, and the porter would reign supreme over a vast solitude, monarch of all he surveyed.

Charlton was not due to go down till the next morning. He dined in the junior common-room with three or four other men, the sole survivors of the crowd, and then retired to his rooms to finish his packing. That done, he sat on the window-seat looking into the quad. It was a brilliant night; the moonshine slept on the grass, and silvered the grey walls and mullioned windows opposite, while the chapel and hall were plunged in impenetrable shadow. Everything was as still as death; no sound from the outer world penetrated the enclosure, and for the busy hive of men within, there was now the silence of a desert. There is perhaps no place where silence and solitude can be more sensibly felt than the interior of an Oxford college in vacation time, and there was something in the scene that appealed to the temperament of the young man who regarded it.

Henry Charlton was an only child. His father had died when he was a lad, and his mother, broken down by grief, had foresworn society and lived a very retired life in the country. At Winchester and Oxford he naturally mixed with others and made acquaintances, but his home life was somewhat sombre and his society restricted. He grew up a self-contained, reserved lad, with few friendships, though those he formed were sincere and his attachments were strong. His temperament – poetical, and tinged with melancholy – naturally inclined to romance, and from his early youth he delighted in antiquarian pursuits, heraldic lore, and legend. At school and college he revelled in the ancient architecture by which he was surrounded. His tastes even carried him further, into the region of psychical research, and the dubious revelations of spiritualism; though a certain wholesome vein of scepticism saved him from plunging deeply into those mazes, whether of truth or imposture. As he sat at his window, the familiar scene put on an air of romance. The silence sank into his soul; the windows where a friendly light was wont to shine through red curtains, inviting a visit, were now blind and dark; mystery enveloped the well-known walls; they seemed a place for the dead, no longer a habitation for living men, of whom he might be the last survivor. At last, rising from his seat, and half laughing at his own romantic fancies, Henry Charlton went to bed.

A few weeks later he descended from the train at the little country station of Brickhill, in Northamptonshire, and while the porter was collecting his traps on a hand-barrow, he looked out for the carriage that was to meet him. 'Hallo! Harry, here you are,' said a voice behind him, and turning round he was warmly greeted by his cousin, Charley Wilmot. A car was waiting, into which he and his belongings were packed, and in five minutes they were off, bowling along one of the wide Northamptonshire roads, with a generous expanse of green-sward on each side between the hedges, and the hedgerow timber. The country was new to Henry Charlton, and he looked about him with interest. The estate of Rosemount had lately come unexpectedly by the death of a distant relation of his uncle, Sir Thomas Wilmot, and the family had hardly had time yet to settle down in their new home. His cousin Charley was full of the novelty of the situation, and the charms of the Abbey.

'I can tell you, it's a rattling old place,' said he, 'full of odd holes and corners, and there are the ruins of the church with all sorts of old things to be seen; but you'll have lots of time to look about and see it all, and here we are, and there's my dad waiting to welcome you at the hall-door.'

They had turned in at a lodge-gate, and passed up an avenue at the end of which Henry could see a hoary pile of stone gables, mullioned windows, massive chimneys, and a wide-arched portal, hospitably open, where Sir Thomas stood to welcome his nephew.

Some years had passed since Henry had seen his relatives, and he was glad to be with them again. A houseful of lively cousins rather younger than himself, had in former days afforded a welcome change from his own rather melancholy home, and he looked forward with pleasure to renewing the intimacy. His young cousin Charley was just at the end of his time at Eton, and was to go to university in October. The girls, Kate and Cissy, had shot up since he used to play with them in the nursery, and were now too old to be kissed. His uncle and aunt were as kind as ever, and after he had answered their inquiries about his mother, and given an account of his uneventful journey down, the whole party adjourned to the garden where tea awaited them under the trees, and then Henry for the first time saw something of the Abbey of Rosemount.

This ancient foundation, of Sanctus Egidius in Monte Rosarum, had been a Benedictine house, dating from the twelfth century, which at the Dissolution was granted to a royal favourite, who partly dismantled and partly converted it into a residence for himself. His descendants in the time of James I had pulled down a great part of the conventual buildings and substituted for the inconvenient cells of the monks a more comfortable structure in the style of that day. Many fragments of the Abbey, however, were incorporated into the later house. The refectory of the monks was kept, and formed the great hall of the mansion with its vaulted roof and traceried windows, in which there even remained some of the old storied glass. The Abbot's kitchen still furnished Sir Thomas's hospitable board, and among the offices and elsewhere were embedded parts of the domestic buildings. North of the refectory, according to the usual Benedictine plan, had been the cloister and beyond that the church, which lay at a slightly lower level, the lie of the ground inclining that way from the summit of the Mount of Roses on which the habitable part of the convent had been built. Of the cloister enough remained, though much broken and dilapidated, to show what it had been, but the greater part of the church was destroyed for the sake of its materials when the Jacobean house was built. A considerable part of the nave, however, was still standing, part of it even with its vaulted roof intact, and of the rest, enough of the lower part of the walls was left to show that the church had been of a fair size, though not on the scale of the larger establishments.

Henry Charlton, with the greedy eye of the born antiquary, took in the general scheme of the Abbey with his tea and buttered toast under the shade of the elms that bounded the lawn on that side of the house. But he had to control his impatience to visit the ruins, for after tea his cousins insisted on a game of tennis, which lasted till it was time to dress for dinner, and after dinner it was too late and too dark for exploration.

They dined in the great hall, once the monks' refectory, but not too large for modem comfort, the Abbey having been one of the smaller houses of the Order, and the number of the brotherhood limited. Henry was enchanted and could not restrain the expression of his enthusiasm.

'Ah!' said his aunt, 'I remember your mother told me you were crazy about architecture and antiquities. Well, you'll have your fill of them here. For my part, I often sigh for a little more modern convenience.'

'But my dear aunt,' said Henry, 'there is so much to make up for little inconveniences in living in this lovely old place that they might be forgotten.'

'Why, what do you know about house-keeping?' said his aunt, 'I should like you to hear Mrs Baldwin, the housekeeper, on the subject. How she toils up one staircase only to have to go down another. The house, she says, is made up of stairs that are not wanted, and crooked passages that might have been straight, and it took the maids a fortnight to learn their way to the food-store.'

'It's of no use, mother,' said Charley, 'you'll never convince him. He would like to have those old monks back again, and to be one of them himself with a greasy cowl on his head and sandals on his naked feet, and nothing to eat but herbs washed down with water.'

'No, no!' said Henry, laughing, 'I don't want them back, for I like my present company too well. But I confess I like to call up in imagination the men who built and lived in these old walls, I believe I shall dream of them tonight.'

'Well, Harry,' said his uncle, 'you may dream of them as much as you please, so long as you don't bring them back to turn us out. And you shall have every opportunity, for you are to sleep in a bit of the old convent that the abbey builders of the modem house spared; and who knows but that the ghost of its former occupant may not take you at your word and come back to revisit his old quarters.'

Harry laughed as they rose from table, and said he trusted his visitor would not treat him as an intruder.

The long summer day had enabled them to finish dinner by daylight, and there was still light enough for the old painted glass to be seen. It was very fragmentary, and not one of the pictures was perfect. In one of the lights they could make out part of a female figure richly dressed; she had been holding something that was broken away, and beside her was the lower half of an unmistakable demon, with hairy legs and cloven hoof. The legend below ran thus, the last word being imperfect:

QVALITER DIABOLVS TENTAVIT COMITISSAM ALI...

The next light was still more imperfect, but there was part of the same female figure in violent action, with the fragment of a legend:

HIC COMITISSA TENTATA A DI…

Other parts evidently of the same story remained in the next window, but they were too fragmentary to be understood. In one light was a piece of a monk's figure and part of a legend:

HIC FRATER PAVLVS DAT COMI…

The last of all was tolerably perfect. It represented a female robed in black, and holding in her hand a little model of a church. She was on her knees prostrate before the Pope, who was seated and extended his hand in the act of benediction. The legend below said:

HIC COMITISSA A PAPA ABSOLVTA EST.

Henry was much interested and wanted to know the story of the sinful Countess; but none of the party could tell him, and indeed, none of them had till then paid much attention to the glass. Sir Thomas had once made a slight attempt to trace the identity of the Countess, but with little success, and had soon given up the search.

'There is an antiquarian problem for you to solve, Harry,' said he, 'but I don't know where you should look for the solution. The annals of Rosemount are very imperfect. In those within my reach I could find nothing bearing on the subject.'

'I am afraid, sir,' said Harry, 'if you failed I am not likely to succeed, for I am only a very humble antiquary, and should not know where to begin. It seems to me, however, that the story must have had something to do with the history of the Abbey, and that its fortunes were connected with the wicked Countess, or the monks would not have put her story in their windows.'

'Well, then, there you have a clue to follow up,' said his uncle, 'and now let us join the ladies.' The room where Henry Charlton was to sleep was on the ground floor in one corner of the house, and looked out upon the cloister and the ruined abbey-church. It was, as his uncle had said, a relic of the domestic part of the Abbey, and when he had parted with his cousin Charley, who guided him thither, he looked round the apartment with the keenest interest. It was a fair-sized room, low-pitched, with a ceiling of massive black timbers, plastered between the joists. The wall was so thick that there was room for a little seat in the window recess on each side, which was reached by a step, for the window sill was rather high above the floor. Opposite the window yawned a wide fireplace with dogs for wood-logs, and a heap of wood ashes lying on the hearth. The walls were panelled with oak up to the ceiling, and the floor, where not covered with rugs, was of the same material polished brightly. But for the toilet appliances of modern civilisation the room was unaltered from the time when the last brother of the convent left it, never to return. Henry tried to picture to himself his predecessor in the apartment; he imagined him sitting at the table, reading or writing, or on his knees in prayer; on his simple shelf would have been his few books and manuscripts, borrowed from the convent library, to which he had to return them when they met in chapter once a year, under severe penalty in case of loss or damage. As he lay on his bed Henry tried to imagine what his own thoughts would have been had he himself been that ghostly personage five centuries ago; he fancied himself in the choir of the great church; he heard the sonorous Gregorian chanting by a score of deep manly voices, ringing in the vaulted roof, and echoing through the aisles; he saw the embroidered vestments, the lights that shone clearer and brighter as the shades of evening wrapped arcade and triforium in gloom and mystery, and turned to blackness the storied windows that lately gleamed with the hues of the sapphire, the ruby and the emerald. Pleased with these fancies he lay awake till the clock struck twelve and then insensibly the vision faded and he fell asleep.

His sleep was not untroubled. Several times he half awoke, only to drop off again and resume the thread of a tiresome dream that puzzled and worried him but led to no conclusion. When morning came, he awoke in earnest, and tried to piece together the fragments he could remember, but made little of them. He seemed to have seen the monk sitting at the table as he had pictured him in imagination the evening before. The monk was not reading but turning over some little bottles which he took from a leathern case, and he seemed to be waiting for someone or something. Then Henry in his dream fancied that someone did come and something did happen, but what it was he could not remember, and of the visitor he could recall nothing, except that he felt there was a personality present, but not so as to be seen and recognised; more an impression than a fact. He could remember, however, a hand stretched out towards the seated figure and the objects he was handling. More than this he could not distinctly recall, but the same figures recurred each time he fell asleep with slightly varied attitude, though with no greater distinctness. For the monk he could account by the thoughts that had been in his mind the night before, but for the incident in his dream, if so vague a matter could be called an incident, he could trace no suggestion in his own mind.

The bright summer morning and the merry party at breakfast soon drove the memory of the dream out of his head. After breakfast there were the horses and dogs to be seen, and the garden to be visited, and it was not till the afternoon that his cousins let him satisfy his longing to visit the ruins of the church and cloister. There they all went in a body. The cloister lawn was mown smoothly and well tended, and here and there barely rising above the green sward were the stones that marked the resting places of the brotherhood. Part of the cloister retained its traceried windows and vaulted roof, and on the walls were inscribed the names of abbots and monks whose bones lay beneath the pavement. At the end of the western walk a finely sculptured door led into the nave of the church, the oldest part of the building, built when the ruder Norman work was just melting into greater refinement. Henry was in raptures, and vowed that neither Fountains nor Rievaulx could show anything more perfect. The girls were delighted to find their favourite parts of the building appreciated, and led him from point to point, determined that he should miss nothing.

'And now,' said Cissy, 'you have to see the best bit of all, hasn't he, Kate? We don't show it to everybody for fear strangers might do mischief.'

So saying she pushed open a door in the side wall and led them into a chantry chapel built out between two of the great buttresses of the nave aisle. It was indeed a gem of architecture of the purest fourteenth-century Gothic and Henry stood entranced before its loveliness. The delicate traceries on wall and roof were carved with the finish of ivory, and though somewhat stained by weather, for the windows had lost their glass, had kept all their sharp precision. Part of the outer wall had given way, weeds and ivy had invaded and partly covered the floor, and a thick mass of vegetation was piled up under the windows against the masonry.

'What a pity to let this lovely place get into such a mess,' said Henry. 'I have never seen anything more beautiful.'

'Well,' said Charley, 'it wouldn't take long to clear all this rubbish away. Suppose we set to work and do it?'

So while the girls sat and looked on, the two men fetched some garden tools, and cut, hacked and pulled up the weeds and ivy and brambles, which they threw out by the breach in the wall, and soon made a partial clearance. Henry had begun on the mass that stood breast-high next the window, when a sudden exclamation made the others look at him. He was peering down into the mass of vegetation, of which he had removed the top layer, with an expression of amazement that drew the others to his side. Looking up at them out of the mass of ivy was a face, the face of a beautiful woman, her hair disposed in graceful masses, and bound by a slender coronet. It was evident that under the pile of vegetation was a tomb with an effigy that had long been hidden, and the very existence of which had been forgotten. When the rest of the vegetation had been cleared away there appeared an altar tomb on the top of which lay the alabaster figure of a woman. The sides bore escutcheons of heraldry and had evidently once been coloured. The figure was exquisitely modelled, the work of no mean sculptor; the hands were crossed on the breast, and the drapery magnificently composed. But with the head of the figure the artist had surpassed himself. It was a triumph of sculpture. The features were of perfect beauty, regular and classical, but there was something about it that went beyond beauty, something akin to life, something that seemed to respond to the gaze of the observer, and to attract him unconsciously whether he would or not. The group of discoverers hung over it in a sort of fascination for some minutes saying nothing. At last Kate, the elder girl, drew back with a slight shiver, and said 'Oh! What is it, what is the matter with me, I feel as if there was something wrong; it is too beautiful; I don't like it; come away, Cissy,' and she drew her sister out of the chapel, in a sort of tremor. Charley followed them, and Henry was left alone with his gaze still fixed on the lovely face. As he looked he seemed to read fresh meaning in the cold alabaster features. The mouth, though perfectly composed in rest, appeared to express a certain covert satire. The eyes were represented as open, and they seemed to regard him with a sort of amused curiosity. There was a kind of diablerie about the whole figure. It was a long time before he could remove his eyes from the face that seemed to understand and return his gaze, and it was not without a wrench that at last he turned away. The features of the image seemed to be burned into his brain, and to remain fixed there indelibly, whether pleasurably or not he could not decide, for mixed with a strange attraction and even fascination he was conscious of an undercurrent of terror, and even of aversion, as from something unclean. As he moved away, his eye caught an inscription in Gothic lettering round the edge of the slab on which the figure lay.

HIC JACET ALIANORA COMITISSA PECCATRIX QVÆ OBIIT
ANO DNI MCCCL CVIVS ANIMÆ MISEREATVR DEVS.

He copied the epitaph in his notebook, remarking that it differed from the usual formula, and then closing the door of the chantry he followed his cousins back to the house.

'Well, here you are at last,' said Lady Wilmot, as Charley and his sisters emerged on the lawn. 'What a time you have been in the ruins, and the tea is getting cold. And what have you done with Harry?'

'Oh, mother,' cried Cissy, 'we have had such an adventure. You know that little chantry chapel we are so fond of; well, we thought it wanted tidying up, and so we cleared away the weeds and rubbish, and what do you think we found? Why, the most lovely statue you ever saw, and we left Harry looking at it as if he had fallen in love with it and could not tear himself away.'

'By Jove!' said Charley, 'just like old Pygmalion, who fell in love with a statue and got Venus to bring it to life for him.'

'Don't talk so, Charley,' said Kate, 'I am sure I don't want this stone lady to come to life. There is something uncanny about her, I can't describe what, but was very glad to get away from her.'

'Yes, mother,' said Cissy, 'Kate was quite frightened of the stone lady and dragged me away, just as I was longing to look at her, for you never saw anything so lovely in your life.'

'But there is one thing I noticed, father,' said Charley, 'that I think wants looking to. I noticed a bad crack in that fine vault over the chantry which looks dangerous, and I think Parsons should be sent to have a look at it.'

'Thank you, Charley,' said Sir Thomas, 'I should be sorry if anything happened to that part of the building, for archeologists tell me it's the most perfect thing of its kind in England. Parsons is busy on other matters for the next few days, but I will have it seen to next week. By the way, we shall have another visitor tonight. You remember Harry's college friend, Mr Edwards; I heard he was staying at the Johnstons and so I asked him to come here for a few days while Harry is with us, and here I think he comes across the lawn.'

Edwards had some previous acquaintance with the Wilmots, and was soon set down to tea with the rest, and engaged for lawn tennis afterwards, a game in which he had earned a great reputation.

Harry Charlton did not appear till the party were assembled in the drawing-room before dinner. On leaving the Abbey he was possessed by a disinclination for the lively society on the lawn. His nerves were in a strange flutter; he felt as if something unusual was impending, as if he had passed a barrier and shut the gate behind him, and had entered on a new life where strange experiences awaited him. He could not account for it. He tried to dismiss the finding of the statue as a mere antiquarian discovery, interesting both in history and in art; but it would not do. That face, with its enigmatical expression, haunted him, and would not be dismissed. He felt that this was not the end of the adventure; that in some mysterious way the dead woman of five centuries back had touched his life, and that more would come of it. To that something more he looked forward with the same indefinable mixture of attraction and repulsion which he had felt in the chapel while gazing at those pure alabaster features. He must be alone. He could not at present come back to the converse of ordinary life, and he set off on a swinging walk through field and woodland to try and steady his nerves, so as to meet his friends in the evening with composure. A good ten-mile stretch did something to restore him to his usual spirits. He was pleased to find his friend Edwards, of whose coming he had not been told, and when he took his place at the dinner table next to his aunt there was nothing unusual in his manner.

The conversation during dinner naturally turned on the discovery that had been made in the Abbey that afternoon. It was singular that so remarkable a work of art should have been forgotten, and been overlooked by the Northamptonshire Archæological Society, which had so many enthusiastic antiquaries in its ranks. There had been meetings of the society in the ruins, papers about them had been read and published, plans had been made and illustrations drawn of various parts of the building, including the chantry itself, but there was no mention or indication given of the monument either in the text or in the plates. Strange that no one should ever have thought of looking into that tangle of brambles by which it was concealed, till that very day.

'I must go first thing tomorrow,' said Sir Thomas, 'to see your wonderful discovery. The next thing will be to find out who this pretty lady was.'

'That I think I can tell you, sir,' said Henry, who now spoke for almost the first time, 'and I think it helps to solve the mystery of the sinful Countess in the painted windows opposite, which puzzled us last night.'

All eyes were turned to the fragments of painted glass in the hall windows, as Henry continued. 'You see in the first window the devil is tempting the Countess ALI—, the rest of her name being lost. Well, on the tomb is an epitaph, which gives the missing part. She is the Countess Alianora; no further title is given. But whoever she was, the lady whose tomb we found is the same no doubt as the lady whose adventures were depicted in the windows.'

'Now I know,' broke in Kate, 'why I was frightened in the chapel. She was a wicked woman, and something told me so, and made me want to go away from her.'

'Well,' said Lady Wilmot, 'let us hope she mended her ways and ended her life well. You see, she went to Rome and was absolved by the Pope.'

'Yes, but I bet she did not get absolution for nothing,' said Charley. 'Just look at her in the last picture and you will see she has a church in her hand. Depend on it, she got her wicked deeds pardoned in return for her gifts to Rosemount Abbey; and I daresay she rebuilt a great part of it and among the rest her own chantry.'

'Charley,' said Edwards, 'you ought to be a lawyer; you make out such a good case for the prosecution.'

'At all events,' said Sir Thomas, 'Charley gives us a good lead for our research. I will look out the old deeds and try to find what connection, if any, there was between Rosemount Abbey and a Countess Alianora of some place unknown.'

The rest of the evening passed in the usual way. A few friends from neighbouring houses joined the party; there was a little impromptu dancing, and it was near midnight by the time they retired to rest. Henry had enjoyed himself like the rest, and forgot the adventure of the afternoon till he found himself once more alone in the monastic cell, looking out on the ruined Abbey. The recollection of his dream of the night before then for the first time recurred to him; he wondered whether it had any connection with his later experience in the chantry, but he could trace none whatever. The dream seemed merely one of those fanciful imaginings with which we are all familiar, devoid of any further meaning.

He was not, however, destined to repose quietly. This time his dream showed him the same monk, he recognised him by his coarse features and shaggy brows, but he was in the nave of a church, and in the massive round pillars and severe architecture of the arches and triforium, Henry knew the nave of Rosemount Abbey, not as now, in ruins, but vaulted and entire. It was nearly dark, and the choir behind the pulpitum was wrapped in gloom, in the midst of which twinkled a few lights before the high altar and the various saintly shrines. The monk held something small in his hand, and was evidently, as on the night before, waiting for somebody or something. At last Henry was aware that somebody had indeed come. A shadowy figure draped in black moved swiftly out from behind a pillar and approached the monk. What the figure was he tried in vain to discover. All he could see was that just as had happened on the night before, a hand was stretched out and took something from the monk, which it promptly hid in the drapery with which the figure was covered. The hand, however, was more clearly seen this time. It was a woman's hand, white and delicate, and a jewel sparkled on her finger. The scene caused Henry a dull terror, as of some unknown calamity, or as of some crime that he had witnessed, and he woke with a start and found himself in a cold sweat.

He got up and paced his apartment to and fro, and then looked out of the window. It was brilliant moonlight, throwing strong shadows of the broken walls across the quiet cloister garth where the monks of old lay quietly sleeping till the last dread summons should awake them. The light fell full on the ancient nave walls

'Where buttress and buttress alternately
Seemed framed of ebon and ivory'

and the light touched with the magic of mystery the delicate traceries of the chantry where lay the Countess Alianora. Her face flashed upon his memory, with its enigmatical expression, half attracting, half repelling, and an irresistible desire impelled him to see her again. His window was open and the ground only a few feet below. He dressed himself hastily, and clambered out. Everything was still; all nature seemed asleep, not a breath of wind moved the trees or stirred the grass as he slowly passed along the cloister: his mind was in a strange state of nervous excitement; he was almost in a trance as he advanced into the nave where the shadows of column and arch fell black on the broken pavement. He paused a moment at the gate which led into the chantry, and then entered as if in a dream, for everything seemed to him unreal, and he himself a mere phantom. At last he stood beside the tomb and looked down on the lovely countenance which had bewitched him in the afternoon. The moonlight fell upon it, investing it with an unearthly mystery and charm. Its beauty was indescribable: never had he conceived anything so lovely. The strange semi-satirical expression of which he had been conscious in the afternoon had disappeared; nothing could be read in the features but sweetness and allurement. A passionate impulse seized him, and he bent down and kissed her on the lips. Was it fancy or was it real, that soft lips of warm life seemed to meet his own? He knew not: a delirious ecstasy transported him, the scene faded before his eyes and he sank on the floor in a swoon.

How long he lay he never knew. When he came to himself the moon had set, and he was in darkness. An indefinable terror seized him. He struggled to his feet, burst out of the Abbey, fled to his rooms, scrambling in through the window, and threw himself panting on his bed.

Henry Charlton was the last to appear next morning at the breakfast-table. He was pale and out of spirits, and roused himself with difficulty to take part in the discussion as to what was to be done that day. After breakfast he pleaded a headache, and retired with a book to the library, while the others betook themselves to various amusements or employments. The girls were in the garden where they found old Donald the gardener, whose life had been spent at Rosemount, and in whose eyes the garden was as much his as his master's, and perhaps more so.

'Yes, missy,' he was saying, 'the weeds do grow terrible this fine weather, and as you was saying it is time we cleaned up a bit in the old

Abbey. But I see the young gentlemen has been doing a bit theirselves, chucking all them briars and rubbish out on the grass just as I had mown and tidied it.'

'Why Donald,' said Cissy, 'you ought to have thanked them, for that chapel was in an awful mess, and they have saved you some trouble.'

'Well, miss, I suppose they pleased theirselves, but that's not where I should have meddled, no, no!' and so saying he moved away.

'But why not there,' said Kate, 'why not there of all places?'

'Oh! I say nothing about it,' said Donald. 'Only folk do say that there's them there as don't like to be disturbed.'

'Indeed; what do they say in the village about it?'

'Oh! ay! I say nothing. I don't meddle with things above me. And I shan't tell ye any more, miss, it's not good for young women to know.'

'But do you know, Donald,' said Cissy, 'what we found there?'

'What did you find, miss? Not her? Oh, Lord! She was found once before, and no good come of it. There, don't ask me any more about it. It's not good for young women to know.' So saying Donald wheeled his barrow away into another part of the garden.

'Father,' said Kate, to Sir Thomas who now came up. 'Donald knows all about the tomb and the statue, and he won't tell us anything, except that the people think it unlucky to meddle with it. Have you ever heard of any superstition about it.'

'Nothing at all,' said he. 'I have just been down to look at your discovery. The statue is a wonderful piece of work. I have never seen anything finer either here or in Italy. But the chapel is in a bad way and part of the roof threatens to fall. I have just sent word to Parsons to come tomorrow morning and attend to it.'

They were joined presently by Edwards and Charley, and the day passed pleasantly enough, with the usual amusements of a country house in holiday time. Henry did not take much part with them. He was abstracted and inattentive, and altogether out of spirits. He had but a confused idea of what had happened the previous night, but there seemed still to linger on his lips that mystic, perhaps unhallowed kiss, and there still floated before his eyes the mocking enigma of that lovely countenance. He dreaded the approach of night, not knowing what it might bring, and did his best to divert his mind to other things, but without much success.

His friend Edwards was much concerned at the change in his behaviour, and asked Charley whether Henry had been upset in any way during his visit. He was assured that till yesterday afternoon Henry had been as happy and companionable as possible, and that it was only that morning that the change had come over him.

'But I can tell you one thing,' said Charley, 'I believe he was out of his room last night, for the flowerbeds show footmarks, and the creepers are torn outside his window, showing someone had been getting in and out, and there certainly has been no burglary in the house. Do you know whether he walks in his sleep?'

'I have never heard that he does,' said Edwards. 'We can't very well ask him whether anything is wrong, for he does not seem to invite inquiry, and has rather avoided us all day. But if it is a case of sleep-walking we might perhaps keep a look-out tonight to prevent his coming to mischief.'

'All right,' said Charley. 'My room is over his and looks out the same way. I'll try and keep awake till midnight, and will call you if I see anything of him.'

'That's well,' said Edwards, 'but we must be careful and not be seen, for it is dangerous to wake a somnambulist I believe.'

And so they departed to their several chambers.

The first part of the night passed peacefully enough with Henry. He had no dreams to trouble him, but towards midnight he began to turn uneasily in his bed, and to be oppressed by an uneasy feeling that he was not alone. He awoke to find the moon shining as brilliantly as on the previous night, and bringing into view every detail of the ancient buildings opposite. A dull sense of some sinister influence weighed upon him: someone was with him whom he could not see, whispering in his ear, 'You are mine; you are mine.' He could see no form, but to his mental vision was clearly visible the countenance of the figure in the chapel, now with the satirical, mocking expression more fully shown, and he felt himself drawn on he knew not whither. Again the mocking lips seemed to say, 'You are mine, you are mine.' Half unconsciously he rose from his bed, and advanced towards the window. A faintly visible form seemed to move before him, he saw the features of the countess more plainly, and without knowing how he got there he found himself outside the room in the cloister garth, and entering the shade of the cloister. Something impalpable glided on before him, turning on him the face that attracted him though it mocked him, and which he could not but follow, though with an increasing feeling of terror and dislike. Still on his ear fell the words, 'You are mine, you are mine,' and he was helpless to resist the spell that drew him on and on farther into the gloom of the ruined nave. And now the shape gathered consistency and he seemed to see the Countess Alianora standing facing him. On her features the same mocking smile, on her finger the jewel of his dream. 'You are mine,' she seemed to say, 'mine, mine, you sealed it with a kiss,' and she outstretched her arms; but as she stood before him in her marvellous and unearthly beauty, a change came over her; her face sank into ghastly furrows, her limbs shrivelled, and as she advanced upon him, a mass of loathly corruption, and stretched out her horrible arms to embrace him he uttered a dreadful scream as of a soul in torture, and sank fainting on the ground.

'Edwards, Edwards, come quick,' cried Charley, beating at his door. 'Harry is out of his room, and there is something with him, I don't know what it is, but hurry up or some mischief may happen.'

His friend was ready in a moment, and the two crept cautiously downstairs, and as the readiest way, not to disturb the household, got out into the cloister through the window of Harry's room. They noticed on the way that his bed had been slept in, and was tossed about in disorder. They took the way of the cloister by which Charley had seen Harry go, and had just reached the door that led into the nave when his unearthly scream of terror fell on their ears. They rushed into the church, crying, 'Harry, Harry, here we are what is it, where are you?' and having no reply they searched as well as they could in the moonlight. They found him at last, stretched on the ground at the entrance to the fatal chantry chapel. At first they thought he was dead, but his pulse beat faintly, and they carried him out, still insensible, into the outer air. He showed some signs of life before long, but remained unconscious. The house was aroused and he was put to bed, and messengers were sent for the doctor. As they watched by his bedside, a thundering crash startled them; looking out of the window they saw a cloud of dust where the chantry had been, and next morning it was seen that the roof had fallen in, and destroyed it.

Harry Charlton lay many weeks with a brain fever. From his cries and ravings something was gathered of the horrors of that fatal night, but he would never be induced to tell the whole story after he recovered.

The fallen ruin was removed, and Sir Thomas hoped that the beautiful statue might have escaped. But strange to say, though every fragment of masonry was carefully examined and accounted for, no trace could be found of any alabaster figure nor of the tomb of the Comitissa Alianora.